GI *Brides*

GI Brides

GRACE
LIVINGSTON HILL

BARBOUR BOOKS
An Imprint of Barbour Publishing, Inc.

© 2015 by Grace Livingston Hill

Print ISBN 978-1-60260-434-6

eBook Editions:
Adobe Digital Edition (.epub) 978-1-63409-260-9
Kindle and MobiPocket Edition (.prc) 978-1-63409-261-6

All scripture quotations are taken from the King James Version of the Bible.

This book is a work of fiction. Names, characters, places, and incidents are ei-ther products of the author's imagination or used fictitiously. Any similarity to actual people, organizations, and/or events is purely coincidental.

Cover Photo: © Susan Fox / Trevillion Images

Published by Barbour Books, an imprint of Barbour Publishing, Inc., P.O. Box 719, Uhrichsville, Ohio 44683, www.barbourbooks.com

Our mission is to publish and distribute inspirational products offering exceptional value and biblical encouragement to the masses.

ecpa Member of the
Evangelical Christian
Publishers Association

Printed in the United States of America.

Contents

Through These Fires

Chapter 1

The sunset was startling that night, bursting angrily through ominous clouds that had seemed impenetrable all day, and fairly tearing them to inky tatters, letting the fire of evening blaze into a terror-stricken world sodden with grief and bewilderment. Like an indomitable flag of mingled vengeance and hope, it pierced the dome of heaven and waved courageously, a call, a summons across the thunderous sky and above a drab, discouraged world. It broke the leaden bars and threw down a challenge to disheartened, straggling fighters who had been brave that morning when the battle began, and who had gone on through a day of horror, seeing their comrades fall about them, facing a cruel foe, fighting on with failing strength, and in the face of what seemed hopeless odds.

And then that fire of glory burst through and flung its

challenge, and the leaders seemed to gather courage from the flaming banner in the sky. Herding their scattered comrades together, they took new heart of hope, and turning, renewed the warfare more fiercely than before.

Benedict Barron was one of those discouraged fainting soldiers who had fought all day on very little food, and who more and more was feeling the hopelessness of what he was doing. What useless wasting of life and blood for a mere bare strip of land that didn't seem worth fighting for. And yet he had fought, and would continue to fight, he knew, as long as there was any strength left in him.

Mackenzie, their haggard-faced captain, drew them into a brief huddle and spoke a few low, desperate words, pointing toward that gray distance before them that looked so barren and worthless, so unworthy of struggle.

"Do you see that land ahead?" he asked his men, a fierce huskiness in his vibrant voice. "It looks gray and empty to us now, but it is the way to a great wealth of oil wells! It is the way to victory, for one side or the other. Which shall it be? Victory for us, or for our enemies? If the Germans get those oil wells they undoubtedly will win! We are trying to head them off. Are you game?"

There was a moment of dead silence while his words sank into the tired hearts of the exhausted men, as they looked at their captain's grim, determined face, and thrilled with the words he had spoken. Then those tired soldiers took a deep breath and brought forth a cheer, in which Victory echoed down the gray slopes toward the enemy, Victory for freedom! Not for the enemy! And it was Benedict Barron whose voice led the cheer, and beside him his comrade Sam Newlin took it up.

Oil wells down there in the gray darkness, banner of fire in the sky, lighting the way to victory. Yes, they would go, every one of those tired soldiers, even if it meant giving their lives in the effort. It was worth it. Never would they let the enemy have free access to all that oil. This was what they had left their homes and their dear ones to do, and they would do it, even unto death. Victory! On to Victory!

They plunged down toward the dim gray twilight ahead, Ben Barron's face alight from the brightness above him, his lips set, his gaze ahead, new strength pouring through his veins. The weariness of the day was forgotten. A new impetus had come, a reason for winning the victory. Something to be greatly desired, symbolized by that bright, arrogant banner of fire above them.

Into the dusk Ben Barron plunged with the flaming banner above, looking toward the land they must take and hold at all costs. The dying sun in its downward course shot vividly out with its great red eye, bloodshot, daring the men not to falter. Then suddenly it dropped into its deep blue shroud leaving only shreds of ragged gold as a hint of the glory that might be won. Afterward darkness! For even the edges of glory-gold were blotted out in the darkest night those men had ever known.

A great droning arose in the sky behind, and it seemed to Ben Barron that he was alone with all the responsibility resting on him. There were oncoming planes, an ominous, determined sound, their twinkling lights starring the heavens as if they had a right to be there, reminding one of satanic entrances: *"I will be like the most High"*—the arrogance of Lucifer.

The men groaned in spirit, and thrust forward. But

suddenly came a sound of menace, and like bright, wicked stars, fire dropped from the skies, blazing up in wide fierce waves of flame sweeping before them, filling all the place through which they were supposed to pass.

Bewildered, they looked to their captain, hesitated an instant, until they heard his determined, husky voice ring out definitely:

"Press on!"

"Fire!" they breathed in a united voice of anguish.

"*Press on!*" came Captain Mackenzie's answer swiftly. "You *must* go through these fires! This land must be held at all *costs!*"

Afterward it came to Ben to wonder why. Oh, he knew the answer, the oil wells must be held. The enemy must not take them. But why did fires have to come and obstruct the way? It was hard enough before the fires came. How were they to go through fire? Where was God? Had He forgotten them? Why did He allow this fire to come? It seemed a strange thought to come to Ben Barron as he crept stealthily through the shadows into the realm of light where the enemies' guns could so easily be trained upon them. But at the time he was occupied with accomplishing this journey toward the fire, with the firm intention of going through it. There was a job to be done on the other side of this wall of fire, and he must do it!

And then there was the wall of fire, just ahead!

"Here she comes!" yelled Sam. "Let's go!"

Great tongues of flame, roaring and hissing and overhead falling flames! It seemed like the end. And yet Ben knew he must go through. Even if he died doing it, he must go. Those oil wells must be held. The Germans must not get them. Perhaps just his effort was needed for the victory. Perhaps if he failed others would fail also. The circle of defenders must not be broken! The strength of a chain was in its weakest link. He must not be that weakest link. His place in the formation must be steady, held to the end!

How hot the flames! How far that heat reached! He had to turn his face away from the scorch to rest his eyes, or they would not be able to see to go on. And the flaming fields ahead would soon burn over. He must creep through as soon as they were bearable. He must not be turned back nor halted by mere hot earth. It was night, and the wind was cold. They would soon cool off enough for him to go on.

These thoughts raced through his fevered brain, as he crept forward seeing ahead now beyond those dancing fires, the dark forms of other enemies, their guns surely aimed! He could hear the reverberations of their shots as they whistled past him. He had to creep along close to the ground to dodge those bullets.

It seemed an eternity that he was creeping on in the firelit darkness, pausing when more fire came down from above, to hide behind a chance rock, or a group of stark trees that had not been consumed, gasping in the interval to catch a breath that seemed to escape from his control.

At times there came the captain's voice, in odd places, at tense intervals, almost like the voice of God, and Ben's over-weary mind sometimes confused the two, so that they became convinced that it was God who was leading them on, speaking to them out of the fire.

Perhaps it was hunger that made his head feel so light, but he had not thought of food. There were pellets in his wallet that he could take for this, but he was too tired to make the effort to reach them. If only he might close his eyes and sleep for a moment! But there was the fire, and the order was heard again, "Forward!"

They must all pass through. There was no time to wait for the blistering ground to cool. They must pass through quickly. They had been taught their manner of procedure. Through this fire—and then the enemy beyond! There would be bullets. He could hear one singing close now! There would be another close behind that. Their spacing was easy to judge.

There! There it came. A stinging pain pierced his shoulder, and burned down his left arm like liquid fire. But he must not notice it. He was one of a unit. If any in their battalion failed, then others might fail. They *must not* fail! That rich oil country must be held at any cost. The captain's words seemed to still be on the air, close to his ear, though it was a long time since they had been spoken. But they rang in his heart clearly as at first. "Forward! *Through these fires.*"

There came a moment with clear, ringing words of command when they struggled up to their feet and actually plunged through. The scorching heat! The roaring of the flames! The noise of planes overhead! The falling of more fire! All was confusion! Could they pass through?

Afterward there was fierce fighting. No time to think of wounds and the pain stinging down his arm. It was only a part of his job. He had to hold those oil wells!

The night was long, and there were more fires to cross. More fighting, the ground strewn with wounded and dying, nothing that one would want to remember if one ever got home. Home! Peace! Was there still such a place as home? Was there any peace *any*where?

A strange fleeting vision of a quiet morning, he on his way

somewhere importantly, a young schoolboy in a world that still held joy. A little girl in a blue calico dress that matched her eyes, swinging on a gate as he passed. Just a little, *little* girl, swinging on a gate and giving him a shy smile as he passed. He didn't know the little girl. The family were newcomers in the neighborhood, but he smiled back and said, "Hello! Who are you?" And she had answered sweetly, "I'm Lexie." And he had laughed and said, "That's a cute name! Is it short for Lexicon?" But she had shaken her head and answered, "No. It's Alexia. Alexia Kendall," she replied in quite a reproving tone.

Strange that he should think of this now, so many years later, a brief detached picture of a child on a gate smiling, a cool morning with sunshine and birds, and a syringa bush near the little house that belonged to the midst of this scene of carnage, with the scorching smell of fire on his garments, and in his hair and eyebrows. Just a sweet little stranger in a quiet, bright morning with dew on the grass by the roadside, peace on the hills, and no walls of fire to cross! Strange! Ah! If he might just pause to think of that morning so long ago, it would rest him! But there were those wells, and more fire ahead, and the enemy, and overhead more planes! There came a flock of shells! The enemy again! Was he out of his head? This didn't seem real. Oh, why did these fires have to come? It was bad enough without them!

But now he was in the thick of the fight again, and his vision cleared. Strange how you could always go on when there was a need and you realized what it meant if you lost the fight! He must go on! Could he weather this awful heat again, with the pain in his shoulder to bear? Back there on that dewy morning going from his home to school, what would he have said if anyone had told him that this was what he had to do to prove his part in the righteousness of the world? Would he have dared to grow up and go on toward this?

But yes! He *had* to. A boy had to grow into a man. Did everyone have to go through a fire of some kind?

That little girl in the blue dress? Where was she? He had never seen her again since that morning. His parents had moved away from that town, and he had never gone back. Strange that he should remember her, a child. Even remember her name. Alexia Kendall! Would he ever see her again? And if he did, would he know her? Probably not. But if he ever came through this inferno and went back to his own land he would try to find her, and thank her for having come with that cool, happy memory of a little girl swinging on a gate, carefree and smiling. No wall of fire engulfing her! Oh no! God wouldn't ever let that happen to a pretty little thing like that. Little Alexia! She must be safe and happy. Why, that was why he had to win this war, to make the world safe for such little happy girls as that one! Of course! The very thought of it cooled and steadied his brain, kept his mind sane.

There! There came another shower of fire! Fire and dew side by side in his mind. Oh, these were fantastic thoughts! Was he going out of his head again? Oh, for a drop of that dew on the grass, that morning so long ago!

"If I ever get through I'll thank her, if I can find her!" he promised himself. "I'll pay tribute to her for helping me think this thing through."

Halfway round the earth, Alexia stood in a doorway, holding a telegram in her trembling hand, a cold tremor running over her as she read.

In the house, the same little house with the white fence where she had swung on the gate so many years ago, her bags were all packed to go back to college for her final term, with a delightful, important defense job promised her as soon as she was graduated.

And now here came this telegram right out of the blue, as it were, to hinder all her plans and tie her down to an intolerable existence with no outlook of relief ahead! This message might be laying the burden of a lifetime job on her slender shoulders. It was unthinkable! This couldn't be happening to her after she had worked so hard to get to the place she had reached.

Alexia's father had died a year after she had swung joyously on the gate that spring morning when Benedict Barron had passed by and seen her. But Alexia's mother had worked hard, a little sewing, a little catering, an occasional story or article written in the small hours of the night when her body was weary, but which brought in a small wage, and she had kept her little family together.

The family consisted of the two little girls. One a young stepdaughter a couple of years older than Lexie, and very badly spoiled by an old aunt who had had charge of her since her own mother had died and until her father married again.

It would have been easier for the mother after her husband's death, if this stepdaughter could have gone back to the aunt who had spoiled her and set her young feet in the wrong, selfish way. But the old aunt had died before the father, and there was no one else to care or to come to the rescue, so Alexia's mother did her brave best to teach the other girl to love her, to love her little sister, and to be less self-centered. She worked on, keeping a happy home behind the white gate, and putting away a little here, a little there, for the education she meant for both girls to have. Elaine was as well as her own little girl.

But Elaine was not bent on studies. She skimmed through three years of high school carrying on a lively flirtation with every boy in the grade, and cutting the rules of the institution right and left. Mrs. Kendall often had to go up to the school to meet with the principal and promise to do her best to make Elaine see the world as it was, and not as she wished it to be. And so with many a heartbreak and sigh, with tears of discouragement and prayers for patience, she dragged Elaine through high school by force, as it were, and landed her in a respectable college for young women where the mother hoped she would do better. But Elaine, during the latter half of her first year in college, ran away with a handsome boy from a boys' college not many miles away, and got married. So for a time the mother had only one girl to look after, and the way seemed a little easier. The boy who had married Elaine was the son of wealthy parents, and Mrs. Kendall hoped that at last Elaine would settle down and be happy under ideal circumstances where she could have all the luxury that her lazy little soul desired, and the way would be open for herself to have a little peace.

But they soon found out that they were by no means rid of Elaine. Again and again there would be trouble, and Elaine would come back plaintively to her long-suffering stepmother for help to settle her difficulties. The wealthy parents had not taken a liking to Elaine, in spite of her beauty and grace, and they soon discovered her tricky ways of procuring money from them that they would not have chosen to give. Again and again the stepmother would have to sacrifice something she needed, or something she had hoped to get Alexia, in order to cover some of the other girl's indiscretions. It ended finally in a sharp quarrel and a quick divorce, which not only failed to teach the selfish girl a lesson but also left her bitter and exceedingly hard to live with.

She had come back to her stepmother, of course, utterly refusing to return to her studies. She spent her time bewailing her fate and sulking in bitterness, unable to see that it was all her own fault.

All this had made a great part of Alexia's school days most unhappy. Elaine would sulk and weep and blame them all, and there would be periods of deep gloom in the little house behind the white gate where Lexie used to swing so cheerfully. So, amid battle after battle life went on until Lexie was in high school. Then, wonder of wonders, Elaine fell in love with a poor young man, and in spite of all the worldly wisdom they offered her to show her how this time she would not have money to ease the burdens of life, she married him. She wouldn't believe that they would be poor. She said Richard Carnell was brilliant and would soon be making money enough, and anyway she loved him, and off she went to the far west.

So Lexie went on in high school in peace, with sometimes a really new dress all her own and not one made over from one of Elaine's. Mrs. Kendall settled down to work harder than ever to save to put her girl through college.

It was about the time that Elaine's first baby arrived, when Lexie was still in her second year at high school, that she took to writing her stepmother again in high, scrawling letters asking to borrow money. There was always a plausible tale of ill luck and a plea of ill health on her part that made it necessary for her to hire a servant, sometimes two, and she didn't like to ask Dick for the extra money. He was so sweet and generous to her. "And, Mother," she added naively, "wasn't there some money my father left that rightly belongs to me anyway?"

There wasn't, but the stepmother sent her a small amount of money to help out a little, realizing that it would not be the last time this request would be made. She also told her plainly that her father had left no money at all. His business had failed just before his last illness, and she herself had had to get a job and work hard to make both ends meet ever since.

The next time Elaine wrote she said that she distinctly remembered her father telling her own mother before she died that their child would never be in need, that he had taken care of that and put away a sufficient sum to keep her in comfort for years.

As Elaine was between two and a half and three years old when her own mother died, that seemed a rather fantastic story, but Mrs. Kendall had learned long ago not to expect sane logic nor absolute accuracy from Elaine in her statements, and she had patiently let it go.

Lexie, as she grew older and came to know the state of things fully, was very indignant at the stepsister who had darkened the sunshine in her young life time after time, and one day when she was in her second year of college, she brought the subject out in the open, telling her mother that she thought the time had come to let Elaine understand all that she had done for her through the years and how she had actually gone without necessities to please the girl's whims. Elaine had a husband now and a home of her own. Perhaps it was only a rented house, but her husband was making enough money to enable her to live comfortably, and Elaine had no right to try and get money from them any longer. Suppose Elaine did have three children, she had two servants to help her now, didn't she? Elaine would complain of course, she had always done that, and say she was sick and miserable. But she went out a great deal, belonged to bridge clubs and things that cost money and took time and strength. Why should her stepmother have to sacrifice to help out every time Elaine wanted to give a party or buy a new dress? Oh, Lexie was beginning to see things very straight then, and though she was born with a sweet, generous nature, she couldn't bear to see her dear mother taken advantage of by a selfish girl who was never grateful for anything that was done for her.

But Mrs. Kendall, though she acknowledged that there was a great deal of truth in what her daughter said, told Lexie that she felt an obligation toward Elaine because of a promise she had made Elaine's father before he died. He had been greatly troubled about Elaine, convinced that he had been to blame for leaving her so long with the old aunt who had spoiled her. He implored his wife to look after her as if she were her own, and she had promised she would. Furthermore she had begged Lexie to try to feel toward Elaine as if she were her own sister, and to be kind and considerate of her needs, even if she, the mother, should be taken away. So with tears Lexie had kissed her mother, and promised, "Of course, Mother dear. I'll do everything I can for her. If she would only let you alone, though, and not be continually implying that you were using or hiding money of hers."

Lexie's mother died during Lexie's third year of college. Elaine sent a telegram of condolence, and regretted that she could not come East for the funeral because of ill health and lack of funds for the journey.

This ended the pleas for money for the time being, and poor Lexie had to bear her sorrow and the heavy burdens that fell upon her young shoulders alone. Though there was no heartbreak for her in the fact of Elaine's absence. Elaine had never been a comfortable member of the family to have around.

Elaine sent brief, scant letters that harped continually on her own ill health as well as the amount of work there was connected with a family of children, especially for a sick mother, and one whose social duties were essential for her husband's business success.

Lexie had been more than usually busy of course, since her mother's death, and she had taken very little time to reply at length to these scattered letters. Her attention was more than full with her examinations and arranging for a war job after graduation. If she thought of Elaine at all, it was to be thankful that she seemed to have a good husband and was fully occupied in a far corner of the country where she was not likely to appear on the scene.

Lexie had come back during vacation to attend to some business connected with the little home that her mother had left free from debt. She had felt it should be rented, or perhaps sold, though she shrank from giving it up. But she had put away a great many of her small treasures, and arranged everything so that the house could be rented if a tenant appeared. Now she was about to return to her college for the final term. Her train would leave that evening, and her bags were packed and ready. She was about to eat the simple lunch of scrambled eggs, bread and butter, and milk that she had but just prepared and set on the corner of the kitchen table when the doorbell rang and the telegram arrived. The telegram was from Elaine!

Lexie stood in the open doorway shivering in the cold and read it, taking in the full import of each typewritten word and letting them beat in upon her heart like giant blows. Strangely it came to her as she read what her mother before her must have felt whenever Elaine had launched one of her drives for help. Only her mother had never let it be known how she felt. For the sake of the love she bore her husband and the promise she had made at his deathbed, she had borne it all sweetly. And now it was her turn, and her mother had expected her to do the same. But this was appalling! This was more than even Mother would have anticipated.

Then she read the telegram again.

DICK IN THE ARMY FIGHTING OVERSEAS. RE-
PORTED MISSING IN ACTION. PROBABLY DEAD.
I AM COMING HOME WITH THE CHILDREN.
HAVE BEEN QUITE ILL. HAVE ROOMS READY.
AM BRINGING A NURSE. WILL REACH THE
CITY FIVE THIRTY P.M. MEET TRAIN WITH
COMFORTABLE CAR.
ELAINE

Lexie grew weak all over and, turning, tottered into the house closing the door behind her. She went into the dining room and dropped down into a chair beside that lunch she had not eaten, laying her head down on her folded arms on the corner of the table, her heart crying out in discouragement. Now what was she to do? How like Elaine to spring a thing like this on her without warning. Giving orders as if she were a rich woman! Sending her word at the last minute so that it would be impossible to stop her.

Lexie felt her head and looked at her watch. Could she possibly send a telegram to the train and stop her? Turn her back? Tell her she was about to leave for college? Her own train left at two thirty. There was no other train that night. What if she were to pay no attention to the telegram? Just let Elaine come on with her nurse and her three children and see what she had done! It was time she had a good lesson of course. She simply couldn't expect her sister to take over the burden of her life this way.

On the other hand, there was her promise to her mother, and in fact, what would Elaine do if she arrived and found no car waiting, no house open, no key to open it?

Well, she had a nurse with her, let them go to a hotel!

But suppose she had no money? Still, she must have some money or she could not have bought her tickets and started. She couldn't have afforded a nurse. But then, of course, Elaine never bothered about affording anything. She always got what she wanted first and let somebody else worry about paying for it.

But how did Elaine happen to telegraph to her here? Ah! She had not told her sister that she was expecting to go back to college during the midyear vacation and do a little studying while things were quiet. Elaine expected her to be here in the home of course, during holidays, as she invariably had been previously. If she had carried out her plans and that telegram had been a couple of hours later in arriving, she would have been gone and the telegram would not have found her. What then would have happened to Elaine? Well, why not *go* and let happen what would happen? Surely Elaine would find some way of taking care of her children. She couldn't exactly come down upon her at college. She wouldn't know where she had gone either. Why not *go*?

❧❦❧

It must have been five minutes that Lexie sat with her forehead down upon her folded hands trying to think this thing through. The same old fight that had shadowed all her life thus far! Was it going on to the end for her as it had gone on for her mother? Or should she make a stand now and stop it?

And then would come the thought that Elaine seemed to be in real trouble now, her husband probably dead, herself sick—and very likely she really was! It didn't take much to make Elaine sick when things didn't happen her way. And those three children! She *couldn't* let them suffer because they happened to have an insufferable mother! She had never seen those three children, but children were always pathetic if they were in trouble! Oh, what should she do?

Here she was ready to leave, just time to eat those cold scrambled eggs that had been so nice and hot when that telegram arrived. Her house was all ready either to close for the present or to rent if a tenant came, her things packed away under lock and key in the attic, and all her arrangements for the rest of the college year made. There was still time to take a taxi to the North Station and get her train before that western train arrived with the onslaught of the enemy, and yet she wasn't going to have the nerve to do it! She felt it in her heart behind all her indignation and bitter disappointment that she wasn't going to leave Elaine in a tight spot. She had been brought up a lady, and she couldn't do it. She had been taught to give even a little more than was asked, and she was going to go on doing it the rest of her life. . .maybe.

But no! She *wouldn't*! She *mustn't*! She would just stay long enough to have a showdown with her sister. She would make her understand that there was no money anywhere and the job she had secured was on condition that she had finished her college course. She must do that or her whole life would suffer. She would let Elaine understand that she could not shoulder the burden of her family. She would stay long enough for that. It was what her mother probably should have done, and now it was *her* duty. She would try to be kind and sympathetic with Elaine in her sorrow, and she would try to help her back to a degree of health, but then she would make her understand that it was only right *she* should get a job herself and support her children. Yes, she would do that! She would not weaken. She had a right and a responsibility to think of herself and her own career, too. Of course even if she had to help Elaine financially, it was essential that she finish her course and get ready to earn as much as possible for them all. Yes, that was what she would do!

And now, just how should she go about all this? Shouldn't she begin at once to be firm with Elaine? To let her understand that she couldn't afford taxis and cars? What ought she to do? Wire the train that Elaine must get a taxi, or just not make any reply at all? And how should she prepare for this unexpected invasion? For, indeed, it seemed to her as she lifted tear-filled eyes and looked about the room, like an invasion of an enemy.

She felt condemned as the thought framed itself into words in her mind, but she had to accept the way she felt about it. And thinking back over the years and her mother's words from time to time, she knew this was something her mother would have told her she must do as far as was possible. Perhaps it would not turn out to be as bad as it promised. Perhaps it was only for a brief space while Elaine adjusted herself to her circumstances, but whatever it was, it was something that her mother would have expected her to do, something that perhaps God expected her to do.

Not that Lexie had ever thought much about God except in a faraway, general way, but somewhere there was a Power that was commanding her. It was as if there was an ordeal ahead that challenged her. Why? Was it right she should go? It was like a wall of fire before her, through which she must pass, and there was now no longer a question whether she would go. She knew she would. The only thing was to work out just what was the wisest way to do it.

With her eyes shut tight to force back the two tears that persisted in coming into them, Lexie kept her face down and pressed her temples to try and think. Whatever she was going to do for the winter, it was *now*, *today*, that she had to settle. She wasn't going to run away from the message that had come at this last minute. If this was an emergency, and a time of grief—and obviously it was—just common decency required that she do something about it. Therefore she *must* stay here in the house until Elaine came, and they could talk it out. She must see if her sister was really sick, sicker than she used to be sometimes when she just didn't want to go places and do things that seemed to be her duty. If she was really sick, of course, Lexie must stay and do something about it until some other arrangement could be made, sometime, somewhere. That could be held in abeyance until Elaine was here.

Next, the house must be put in order to accommodate the oncoming guests, or else there must be some room or rooms hired somewhere to accommodate them. Undoubtedly the home would be the cheapest arrangement, unless it might open the way for Elaine to take too much for granted. But there again she must wait until she knew the exact situation. And last, but by no means the least important, was the matter of transportation from the city for an invalid, or a supposed invalid. But that, too, would have to be accepted as a fact until the contrary was proven. And now she began to see how hard her mother's way must have been. Must she go to the expense of going down to the city after them? There was much to be done in the house to make it habitable if they were coming here. She would have no time to do it if she went to the city.

What she finally did was to run out to a public telephone and call up the Traveler's Aid at the city station, asking the representative to meet the train and arrange for whatever way of conveyance she felt was necessary, giving a message that she was unable to meet the train herself. She made it plain that none of them had much money to spend for anything that was not a necessity, and unless the invalid felt she could afford taxis, and was utterly unable to travel otherwise, please make some other arrangement.

The woman who answered her call was a sensible person with a voice of understanding and seemed to take in the situation thoroughly. When Lexie came out of the telephone booth there was a relieved feeling in her mind and less trouble in her eyes. At least she had provided a way of transportation, and that matter was disposed of without her having to go into the city. Now she would be able to get a bed ready for Elaine. Even if she wasn't going to stay in the house all night, there would have to be a suitable bed for her to lie down on as soon as she arrived—if she *really* was sick. Somehow Lexie was more and more uncertain about that. She had known Elaine so long and so well. But she climbed to the well-ordered attic, where everything was put away carefully, and searched out blankets, pillows, sheets and pillowcases, a few towels, and some soap. These would be necessities at once of course.

As she worked, her mind was busy thinking about a most uncertain future. Trying to plan for a way ahead in which her most unwilling feet must go. Some urge within her soul forbade that she shrink back and shirk the necessity.

Yet she was not the only one in the world who had trouble.

Chapter 2

They were fighting a war, out across the ocean. Well, she was fighting a war with herself at home. With herself? No, maybe it wasn't with herself. Maybe it was something that affected the world—that is, a little piece of it. It might even be important to the world how she took this added burden that had come upon her. Could that be possible? From God's standpoint, perhaps.

So Lexie thought to herself as she went about swiftly putting Elaine's old room to rights, enough to rights to make a place for her to lie down when she arrived. Of course she would do her best to make her see how impossible it would be for her to stay, but there had to be a place for her to lie down.

Hastily she made up the bed with such things as she had been able to find in the attic without unpacking too many boxes. She wanted Elaine to realize how inconvenient her coming in this sudden way had been for her. And yet all the time as she thought it she knew Elaine *wouldn't* realize. Elaine would just take it for granted that it was her due to be served and would probably growl at the service, too, considering it inadequate.

She drew a deep sigh and wished with all her heart that the telegram had not arrived until she had left for college. Perhaps Elaine would have been discouraged then and gone back west. Still, of course she wouldn't. Elaine wasn't made that way. Elaine demanded service, and if it wasn't on hand where she chose to be, she turned heaven and earth until it came. Oh, why did this have to come to her after all the other hard things she had been through? Other girls had normal lives with pleasant families and nobody much to torment them. And here she was saddled not only with her unpleasant sister but also her three unknown children who would probably be as unpleasant as their parent, poor little things! And she couldn't stand it! No, she *couldn't*! How could a young girl only twenty, with her own way to make and her college finals just at hand, be expected to take over and bring up a family of three children, to say nothing of their mother, who probably by this time was posing as a hopeless invalid and doing it so prettily that everybody else would pity her?

But there was no use thinking such bitter thoughts. Whatever else her sister was not, she certainly was in trouble enough now with her husband as good as dead, for that was what "missing in action" usually meant. And if she really loved him, as she *said* she did, it was hard of course. Although it was hard for Lexie to believe that Elaine really loved anybody but herself.

It was perhaps fortunate for Lexie's firm resolves to be frank with Elaine and make her understand how hard she was making things, that there was very little time to relent. For Lexie's sweet temper and natural generosity were apt to make her softhearted, and if there had been a great deal of time to prepare for her unwelcome guest, she might in spite of herself have done much to make the house look homelike and livable again. But there was not much time, and there were limitations due to the fact that most of the pleasant furnishings and treasured things of the family were securely packed and locked away. It would take time to unpack, air, and put them about in their places again. That would hardly be worthwhile if Elaine was only to be there a few hours, or at most a few days. Perhaps if she was really sick she ought to go to a hospital. Although Elaine always hated the very name of hospital and refused to be sent to one, she had been there when her children were born, and perhaps had got over her foolish ideas of prejudice against it. But if she went to the hospital, what would become of the three children? Because, of course, no hospital would allow them to come when they were not sick. And there was no one, no relative, who could be called in to look after them. It would just mean that she, Lexie, would have to stay with them, and she *couldn't* do that. She *must* go back to college! For economy's sake if for nothing else, she must finish her course and get her job!

And there she would pause and sit down in despair. Oh, why, *why* did this thing have to come to her just at this time when she was putting every bit of nerve and energy into an attempt to finish her course with honor and at least a degree of excellence?

This question was still beating itself back and forth in Lexie's heart when at last she realized that it was time for the travelers to arrive, and there was nothing she could do about it but wait.

But as time went on and nothing happened, Lexie was frantic. She decided to run down to the drugstore and telephone to that Traveler's Aid again. If she didn't get her now she would be gone, relieved by the night operator, and they might not be able to tell her anything. So closing the door and slipping the key under the old cocoa mat where they used to hide it when they were children, she hurried down the street and telephoned.

It was some time before she succeeded in getting the Traveler's Aid and discovered that the shift had already changed and another woman was on duty. The other woman, however, could give her a little information from their record. Yes, the train had been met, the family was on board, and their representative had put them in a very good taxi. The lady had insisted on a comfortable one. It cost a little more, but she said she didn't care, and they were started off soon after arriving. "The nurse who was with them," added the woman, "seemed unwilling to remain with the case. She said she felt she had made a mistake coming, was homesick, and wanted to return west on the next train. We finally persuaded her to stay with the lady until she reached her destination, but she said she wanted you notified to get another nurse at once, as she was returning to the city with the taxi. She never expected to have to look after three children as well as a helpless patient. If we had known how to reach you we would have phoned, but they said you had no telephone. We thought you ought to know. Somebody will have to look after the lady. She seemed quite helpless."

Lexie's heart sank as she thanked the woman and hung

up the receiver. So! The atmosphere was growing blacker and blacker. Now what was she to do? Would she have to look after Elaine herself? She groaned in spirit and hurried back to the house, but as she opened the white gate she sighted a taxi coming down the road. They had *come*, and the fight was on! It was going to be bad, but she had to go through it somehow.

And then the taxi stopped before the door, and three children descended in a body and stared at her and the house.

"Is that the house?" asked a supercilious girl of seven, with a sneer on her lips and a frown on her brow. "Good night! That's not a house, that's a dump! What did you bring us here for, Elaine? We can't live in a tiny little place like that!"

Then a boy of five blared out hatefully: "It's not a house, it's a dump! I ain't a-gonta live in a dump like that! Jeepers! You can't do that to me!"

And a little girl of three began to cry and bawl out, "I wantta go home! I *won't* stay here! You're mean to bring us here!"

"Shut up!" said the woman Lexie supposed was the nurse. "Don't you know your mother's sick?"

"I don't care 'f she is," roared the boy. "She hadn't ought to uv brought us here, an' I ain't a-gonta stay, *so there*!"

Two of the neighbors who lived in houses across the street came curiously out to their doors and looked at the arrivals in amazement. Then seeing Lexie coming out to the gate hurriedly, they decided that these must be her new tenants and beat a hasty retreat indoors again, probably with sinking hearts at the prospect of such loudmouthed children for neighbors.

But Lexie went quickly to the side of the taxi where her sister still lay back among pillows, wanly, and tried to manage a welcoming smile for her.

"*My dear!*" she said, hoping her voice sounded cordial, at least to the nurse. "I was so sorry that I couldn't manage to meet you in the city—"

"Yes?" said Elaine in her coldest, haughtiest tone. "I was, too. Such a jaunt as I've had coming out! I should think you might at least have managed to send some neighbor. Mr. Brotherton I'm sure would have been glad to come after me if you had asked him, but I know you never did like him. I couldn't understand why—" complained the sweet, drawling voice.

"Sorry, Elaine, but Mr. Brotherton has moved away. Gone to Washington, doing something in a war job."

"The very idea!" said Elaine, as if this was somehow her sister's fault. "Well, then, why didn't you ask Mr. Wilson, or Mr. Jackson? Their cars are old and shabby I suppose, but they would have done in a pinch."

"Mr. Wilson's car has been sold," said Lexie coldly. "They couldn't afford to run it any longer in the present state of gas and tires, and Mr. Jackson works in a defense plant in the city and takes a lot of other workers with him to the plant in his car every morning. He doesn't return till six o'clock. And there isn't any other available car in the neighborhood. I'm sorry you had an uncomfortable ride, but now, I guess we should make some arrangements before you get out. You know, your telegram just caught me as I was about to leave for college, and I have the house all ready for renting, in case a tenant comes while I am gone. Things aren't very livable here, and I thought you might not care to stay. A great deal of the furniture is stored in the attic. I didn't know if you would want to go to a hotel in the city till you could make further arrangements."

Lexie was talking fast, trying to get her ideas across before

Elaine could interrupt. There was a shadow in her troubled eyes as she studied Elaine's face. Elaine did look white and drawn. There were dark circles under her eyes, too, and the old petulant pout to her lips grew into a decided sneer as she looked her sister down.

"But you can't do that!" she said in her high, angry voice. "*Rent* the house! Want an *idea*! It's *my* home as well as yours, isn't it? You didn't ask my permission to rent it. Of course you couldn't get enough rent for this little dump away out here in the country anyway, to make it pay. Not enough for me to consent. After it was divided between us it would be nothing. And it will shelter us anyway. No, certainly not! I won't consent to renting! I'm going to stay right here and look into my father's affairs. I'm quite sure there was some money left to me, if your mother didn't use it up sending you in luxury to an expensive college! It's high time I looked after things!"

Lexie's lips set firmly in a thin line, and two spots of angry color flew into her pale cheeks. But she couldn't stand here and fight, with this strange nurse and the taxi driver looking on. Besides the neighbors were coming back to their front doors to see what it was all about. Lexie took a deep breath and summoned her courage.

"Very well," she said quietly. "Suppose we get you into the house then. I fixed a bed for you to lie down on in your old room. Can we get you upstairs?"

"No," said Elaine crossly, "I'm not able to walk upstairs. Not unless the driver would carry me up."

"No *ma'am*," spoke up the driver sharply. "I'm not allowed to stop long enough to do anything like that. Not unless you wantta pay me five dollars extra."

"Oh dear! The idea! Well, what's the matter with the downstairs sitting room, Lexie? That was always a pleasant room anyway, and handier for carrying my meals, too."

"Oh," gasped Lexie. "Why, there isn't anything in it. No bed. No furniture at all! It would take some time to get a bed downstairs and set it up. I don't believe I would be able to do that by myself either."

"No furniture! How ridiculous! What have you done with the furniture? I hope you didn't have the temerity to sell any of it. I intend to pick out what I want of it first before that happens. You know it was *all my* father's anyway."

"Oh no," said Lexie. "Some of it was Mother's. She used to tell me about the old rocking chair and bureau that were her grandmother's, and there were several things that I bought myself with the first money I earned. But I guess we won't fight over that." Lexie ended with a fleeting smile. "We must get you in and comfortable first, and then perhaps you would like me to send for a doctor, would you?"

"Certainly not! I don't want any little one-horse doctor from this dinky town. I'm under a noted specialist, you know, and I'll have to contact someone in the city whom my doctor recommends. But I suppose if you have let things get into this barren state I'll have to do the best I can for tonight. I suppose I'll have to try to get up the stairs with the help of the driver and the nurse. Nurse, you carry my wraps and pillows up first and make it comfortable for me, and then when you come down we'll go up slowly. Perhaps it won't be so impossible."

"Well, if you hurry I'll help you up," said the nurse grimly, "but then I'm done. And I'll thank you to pay me what you promised for bringing you over."

"Oh, dear me! How tiresome! What kind of a nurse are you anyway, talking that way to an invalid? Of course you'll get paid. My sister will look after all that. I've spent every cent I had when I started. Lexie, will you attend to this, and get enough for the driver, too? How much was it, driver? Five dollars, did you say?"

"No, lady, it was seven dollars and a half."

"But I'm sure you said five. I distinctly remember you said five."

"Look here, lady. My car registers the miles, see? And I havta go by the meter. I gave you the slip. It's seven dollars and a half. I told ya before we started I couldn't say just how much it would be till I saw how many miles it was, and you, lady, you didn't know! You just said it wasn't far."

"Oh dear! How tiresome you are! Lexie, get five dollars for him. He'll have to be satisfied with that or nothing. And Lexie, get about twenty more. I'll have to pay the nurse for some things she bought for me on the way, and the meals we had on the train. How much was it in all? I have the memorandum here somewhere. Hurry, Lexie, and let's get this thing over and get me to bed as quickly as possible. I feel as if I might be going to faint again. All this discussion is bad for me. Won't you get the money quickly?"

Lexie was looking aghast.

"I'm sorry, Elaine. I just haven't got that much money. I had only about three or four dollars left when I got my ticket paid for."

"Oh, that's all right, Lexie, run in the house and make out a check. Make two, one for the driver and one for the nurse.

Here! Here's the nurse's bill. Add ten to it for her trouble on the way."

Great trouble descended upon Lexie.

"I'm sorry, Elaine, but I haven't got my checkbook here. I left it at college. You know, I only came up for a couple of days to get the house in order to rent. The agent wrote me that he thought he had a tenant, and I knew this was the only time I could get away from my classes to do this work, so I came in a great rush and brought very little baggage. Just an overnight bag. So I have no checkbook."

"Well, but surely you can find an old checkbook around the house somewhere. Go look in your old desk. Or go borrow a blank check from the neighbors."

"No," said Lexie positively. "I have no money in our local bank here. My account is in the bank at college town. I'm sorry, but remember I didn't know you were even coming. In fact, Elaine, I haven't very much money left, not even in the bank. It has cost a good deal for the last days of college."

"Oh yes?" said the sister with a hateful inflection in her tone. "Of course you'll say that. Well, what has become of the money? I know there was a whole lot saved up for *our* college courses, and *half* of that was *mine*, you know. Suppose you hand that over. That ought to be plenty to pay these two, and get rid of them."

"I'm sorry, Elaine, but the money that was for our college courses was only what my mother had saved from her own salary in the job where she worked as long as her health allowed, and there was only enough left to bury her."

"Oh *really*! You must have had *some funeral*! I suppose you bought a plot in the most expensive part of the cemetery, and ordered the handsomest casket on the list!"

Sudden tears sprang into Lexie's eyes as she remember the plain simple casket, the cheapest thing that could be had, that had been her mother's choice in the few words of direction she had left behind her.

"No!" she said, choking down a sob and shaking her head with a quick, gasping motion. "It wasn't like that! Oh, please *don't*, Elaine! She loved you and did her best for you. She had no show nor expense at her going. If you had chosen to come, you would have seen. You would have been ashamed to say what you have just said."

"There! I thought you would find fault with me for not coming to her funeral! But I tell you I was too sick to travel, and it happened that I had no one to leave my children with. My husband was gone to war, and I was alone. You don't seem to care what my situation was."

"Don't, Elaine, please. I'm not finding fault with you, and of course I know you were sick. Now let's end this useless talk and get you into the house and try to make you as comfortable as possible. Remember, you hired these people, and if a check will satisfy them it's you who will have to give it."

Lexie turned and ran up the walk into the house, thankful to have her sudden rush of tears hidden for the moment. But she found to her dismay that she was not alone in the house. The children, unobserved for the time, had taken full possession. The oldest girl was ransacking the bookcase, pulling out armful after armful of Lexie's cherished books and casting them hit-or-miss about the floor, some halfway open, some tumbled in a heap with their pages turned in messily, some piled crookedly.

The little boy had placed a stool before a table that he had shoved against the fireplace. Then he had climbed to the top of the table to investigate the clock that stood on the mantel. As Lexie arrived in the room he was about to pull off the hands of the clock, and crowing as he did it.

The youngest girl was seated in the dining room calmly eating up the cold scrambled eggs and bread and butter that Lexie had arranged for her own hurried lunch. She could see her through the doorway, and was only thankful that she was harmlessly occupied for the moment. She made a dash for the boy on the table, put firm hands about his tough young wrists, holding them so tightly that he was forced to let go of the frail clock hands, and then she swept him from the table and swung him around to plant his feet on the floor. He set up the most unearthly howl she had ever heard from the lips of a child, and promptly started his stubby young toes to kicking her shins most unmercifully.

For answer she reached down and enfolded him in a grip such as he had seldom encountered. Lexie was indignant enough to hold even that fierce young animal quiet for the moment.

"You lemme alone!" he shrieked, and his voice rang out to the mother and nurse and driver in the taxi—and beyond to the whole neighborhood.

"*Stop!*" said Lexie in a low, tense voice. "Stop, do you hear me! If you don't stop this instant I shall spank you."

"You shan't spank me. You ain't my mother. She never spanks me! You *couldn't* spank me. I dare y' to!"

Lexie bore down upon him again, taking him by surprise, turned him firmly around and laid several smart spanks on the

42

young bare legs below the abbreviated trousers. Sharp, stinging slaps they were, cutting into the soft young flesh and bringing quick color to the surface.

The older girl suddenly rose from her literary pursuits and went over to her brother. She lifted her skinny little fists and struck at Lexie's face, an ineffectual blow.

"You stop that! You just let my brother alone!" she shrieked. "Don't you dare touch my brother. My mother'll kill you if you lay a hand on my brother. My mother don't believe in spankings. You stop, or I'll *bite* you!" and she sprang at Lexie's wrist. But Lexie drew back just in time and administered a sharp slap on the little girl's open mouth, which sent the child roaring out to her mother, with great, angry tears rolling heavily down her thin little face.

This was a bad beginning, but Lexie knew that she must take her stand, right at the start, if she had to live with children like this, and she couldn't have them wrecking everything in the house just in the first few minutes, whether they stayed or not.

"Now," she said as she drew a deep breath and tried to stop trembling, and to talk gently but firmly. "You can sit there and think about what you have done. You're not going to be allowed to break things here! You've got to act like a little gentleman if you want to be treated like one. Otherwise I shall spank you. I won't have this kind of thing going on. If you behave yourself we can have a pleasant time together, and there will be things you will enjoy, but if you act like a naughty boy you'll have to be treated like one."

She turned and swept the table back into its place, took the clock from the mantel, and locked it inside the bookcase out of reach. Then catching up her purse she hurried out to the group at the gate.

The little girl was engaged in giving an account of the altercation in the house: "That lady in the house is spanking Gerald. She took him up in her arms and held him tight and slapped him awful hard on his bare legs! She's a hateful old thing! Don't let's stay here in this dump, Elaine. Let's go back to our home! She's a wicked old woman!"

And from the house there issued such young masculine roars of rage as made the whole neighborhood ring and echo, and brought every householder to the doors and windows to see what had happened to their usually peaceful community.

To this accompaniment Lexie hurried out, counting out her money as she came.

"I have five seventy-five," she said as she handed out the money, distress in her face.

"Shut up, Angelica!" said the mother fretfully. "Why bring that up now? Wait until I get into the house and I'll settle with your aunt. And you, Lexie, go on back to the house with your stingy pocketbook. I've settled with these two. They are getting me to bed and then they're going. I found I had a little change left in my purse, and I was tired of waiting on you. Now, Nurse, lift me up and help me get on my feet. Then I can manage to walk between you and the driver. Lexie, suppose you go into the house and get me a cup of coffee. I'll need it after walking so far. Perhaps you can make yourself that useful. And for heaven's sake, keep your hands off my children. If you can't control your temper, I don't see how we are going to stand having you around."

Lexie wanted to tell her sister that she wouldn't have to

stand having her there, that she was going back to college, but she shut her gentle lips firmly and hurried into the house.

A moment later she met her sister at the door with a good, cold glass of water.

"I'm sorry, Elaine, there isn't a bit of coffee in the house. I thought perhaps this glass of water would help."

Elaine looked at the water with disdain.

"*Water!*" she said with contempt. "How does it happen there is no coffee in the house?"

"I found a little box of tea in the pantry," said Lexie. "Would you like a cup of tea? I put the kettle on. It will be ready very soon."

"*Tea!*" said Elaine contemptuously. "You know I never could abide tea. You certainly are about as little help as anybody I ever saw. Get out of my way. I can't stand here forever!" And she edged her way slowly and ostentatiously into the house. Then with many sighs and groanings she was helped up the stairs to the bed Lexie had prepared for her. Even then it was some minutes before the unhappy invalid was settled on the bed, her hat off, her shoes unfastened, and the two assistants departed, thanking their stars that they did not have to stay around that unpleasant woman any longer.

Lexie came hastily up the stairs after watching them depart, and felt that her war had begun.

"You'll simply *have* to help me get into bed!" said her sister sharply. "I'm not able to sit up here another minute."

"Of course," said Lexie gently, bringing skillful hands to the task. "I'm sorry you're feeling so miserable. Would you like me to go out and try to find a doctor?"

"Mercy no, not out here. You'll have to telephone to the

city for a doctor. I don't let every Tom, Dick, and Harry doctor me. I've been under a specialist, you know. Can't you find me a nurse before dark? I've simply *got* to have a nurse. I'm scarcely able to lift my hand to my head. The journey has been so hard on me—and the anxiety about Dick. It's been awful! I'm sure I thought my own sister would be sympathetic enough to provide a nurse for me and have a heartening meal ready."

"I'm sorry, Elaine," said Lexie sadly. "I did all I could in the time you gave me. But you said you were bringing a nurse. I didn't know you would need one, you know. But wait until we get you comfortable in bed and then we can talk over what to do."

"Talk over!" said Elaine with a rising voice. "What is there to talk over, I'd like to know? I should think you'd have all you could do to get us some supper and fix beds for the children, and find a nurse for me. You'll have to call up and get a servant, too, I should think. With three children we can't get on without at least one servant."

"Elaine, we'll have to consider how we can do all that," said Lexie firmly but sorrowfully. "As I told you I have only enough money to barely exist until I get my job, and even that isn't here. I'll have to go back to college and graduate first. Have you money to hire a nurse and a servant and let me go to my work?"

"Well, I should say not," said Elaine. "I'm down very nearly to the last cent as I told you. I expected you to finance that nurse and driver, but since you shirked out of that you'll certainly have to get the nurse and servant."

"That I can't do," said Lexie. "I simply haven't got the money!"

"Oh, very well," said the older sister coldly. "Have it your own way. We'll send for my lawyer in the morning and get hold of the money that belongs to me that your mother hoarded away, or I'll know the reasons why. Just suppose you go out and get some supper ready."

Elaine dropped down with a sigh on the pillows and closed her eyes, and Lexie, with a hopeless look at her sister, turned and went downstairs wondering how she was going to work out this problem in a good and righteous way. How could she ever go through all this future that had suddenly spread itself out before her shrinking feet? This torture! Why did it have to come to her? Wasn't it hard enough without all this?

Chapter 3

Lexie cast a helpless look around the neat little kitchen and began rummaging in the pantry. Obviously the first need of the invalid was something to eat. Could she find anything?

There was half a loaf of bread left, and a little butter. She could make some toast. If she could only find some coffee! Then suddenly she remembered a canister up on the top shelf where her mother used to keep coffee. Maybe there would be a little in it. She climbed up and took it down, and rejoiced to find two or three teaspoonfuls of coffee left. It must have been there some time, and probably wouldn't be as good as fresh-ly ground coffee, but at least it was something. Hurriedly she went about making it, and soon had a little tray ready. Toast and coffee and a bit of jam from a jar in the preserve closet. There was not much of anything left since her mother was gone, but she was glad to find even a little that was edible.

As she started up the stairs she sent a glance out-of-doors. The three children were out on the sidewalk watching the neighbors' children who had come home from school and were playing hopscotch. Thankful that for the time being they were occupied, she hurried up with the tray.

"I found a little coffee in Mother's old canister," she announced cheerfully as she came into Elaine's room. "I made you a cup, a little toast, too. There isn't much butter, but it's better than nothing."

Elaine turned over and scanned the tray scornfully.

"That the best you can do?" she said hatefully. But she reached for the cup and drank the coffee thirstily.

"I despise coffee without cream," she announced when she put down the cup.

"Well, there wasn't any cream." Lexie smiled. "Of course there was nothing to do but bring what I had. And now, Elaine, if you're going to stay here for the night I'll have to go down to the store and get a few things. There isn't even an egg in the house, and there are only three slices of bread left."

"Well, for mercy sake! Why don't you telephone for supplies? You can't be spared to go down to the store. Somebody needs to look after those children! And they'll be howling for food pretty soon. Be sure you get a lot of sweet things or Gerald won't eat a thing. Get cookies. And that butter wasn't so good. Get a better quality, even if you have to pay more. I can't eat strong butter."

"Well, I'm sorry, Elaine, but that butter was some Mrs. Spicer gave me when I came yesterday, and I'm not sure I can get butter. You know we haven't any ration cards here, and you can't eat butter without points. The war is upsetting a good many old habits, but I suppose we have to be patient till things right themselves."

"The perfect idea!" said Elaine. "Of course I brought my ration books along, but they are in the trunks. They won't come till tomorrow. It's outrageous! Can't you tell the storekeeper we have just arrived and I am sick?"

"I can *tell* him, yes," laughed Lexie, "but I'm sure from what Mrs. Wilson told me the other day that it won't do any good. He is not *allowed* to sell butter without coupons. However, I'll find something somehow. Now lie still and take a little nap. Will the children be all right playing by themselves?"

"Well, I'm sure I don't know. I certainly can't look after them," said the indifferent mother. "For pity's sake, don't stay long! And Lexie, while you're out, telephone my lawyer and ask him to come over right away, this evening if possible; if not, early in the morning. You'll find his address in my bag. I think I dropped it on the table in the living room as I came by. His name is Bettinger Thomas."

"Elaine! You don't mean Bett Thomas! The boy you used to go to high school with!"

"Why certainly!" said Elaine getting into her high, shrieking tone, prepared for an argument. "What's the matter with that?"

"But, Elaine! My dear, perhaps you didn't know, but he's scarcely considered respectable. He's been connected with several shady cases the last few years. I don't suppose you'd heard."

"Oh fiddlesticks! What difference does that make? He's a *friend*, and he's promised to see me through. I wrote to him. He was recommended to me out where I lived as being one who would carry his case no matter what, and that is what I want."

"But, Elaine, he's unspeakable! You wouldn't want to talk to him. You can't ask him to come here!"

"Can't I? Watch me! If you won't telephone him, I'll find somebody who can. Go hunt that nurse for me. She'll do what I ask her, and get her mighty quick, too!"

Lexie stood at the foot of the stairs for a moment speechless, too angry to dare to utter a sound. Then she turned silently and went out of the house and down the street. Wild thoughts were rushing through her mind. How was she going to endure this? How could she go on? Was there any reason why she should?

By the time she had reached the corner, and passed several smiling neighbors who greeted her cheerily, she had so far recovered her normal temper as to be able to smile, at least faintly. After all, why should she be so angry? Just because Elaine was determined to secure an unscrupulous lawyer to try to hunt out a flaw in her dear mother's dealings? Well, why should she be so upset? They certainly couldn't find any evidence. But a lawyer like Bett Thomas could *make* evidence even if there wasn't any; he could get low-down people to swear to things that counted for evidence. She had heard of some of his dealings. Oh, what *should* she do? She couldn't have her dear dead mother's honorable name blackened by being dragged through a court trial. And yet—well, there was a God! Her mother believed that. And deep in her heart she did, too, although she had never paid much heed to Him, except that she had always tried to order her life in a good and right way as her mother had taught her. *God, oh God, why did You let all this come to me?*

Didn't You want me to succeed, and graduate, and get that job, and take care of myself in a good, respectable way? So why did I have to go through this fire?

Lexie arrived at the store just before it closed for the evening. She hurried in and began to look around. What could she get without ration stamps? Of course Elaine had said her ration books were in her trunk and would be there in the morning. Of course there were cereals, but Elaine never had liked them, and would her pestiferous children scorn them, too? If she had the opportunity she would like to teach them to like them, but that really wasn't her present duty. She had hard problems to settle at once, and her immediate necessity was to get something they would all eat happily, and it wasn't going to be easy, either. Of course there were eggs, and she purchased a supply of those. They kept milk at the store, and she got a couple of bottles. No butter or meat because they were both rationed. No sugar either. How would Elaine stand that? Well, she would have to settle that difficulty with the government, although she would probably act as if it were all her sister's fault. Well, cookies and cakes! They would supply sweetness for the children. There were apples and pears and a few bananas, but there was no telling what the spoiled youngsters would condescend to eat.

She bought a few potatoes, some spinach and celery. There were oranges, too. At the end, Lexie struggled home with a towering paper bundle in her arms, and a heavy paper bag with a handle in one hand, all full to overflowing. It was surprising how much she had been able to get with the little money she had. On her way home she was thinking how profoundly thankful she was that the nurse and the driver had not had to take *her* money. She wondered how much more Elaine had hidden in her purse. Well, there was no use thinking about that. They must have a talk that evening, or perhaps it would have to wait until morning if Elaine was not disposed to talk tonight.

When she got back to the little white house she found she was very tired, and would have liked nothing better than just to sit down and cry. But that wouldn't get anybody anywhere. There had to be some supper made right away. It was after half past six. And she heard Elaine calling her fretfully.

She hurried upstairs and found Elaine sitting up angrily in bed, arguing with a trio of naughty children.

"I know you are hungry," she was saying angrily, as if the children were to blame for being hungry, "but your aunt didn't have any supper ready for us, and what can we do?"

"She's *bad*! I *hate* her!" roared Gerald, glaring at her from the foot of the bed.

"You certainly have been gone long enough to buy out the store," Elaine snarled at her sister. "I hope you got us a good, hearty meal."

"I'm afraid not," said Lexie. "The store was just about to close, and I had very little money, but I got all I could without ration books."

"Fiddlesticks. Couldn't they trust you for the coupons? Didn't you tell them we would give them the coupons tomorrow?"

"They are not allowed to sell things without the coupons."

"That's absurd when they've known you for years. They *know* you wouldn't cheat them."

"Well, they can't do that for anybody. Now, I'll go down and get something for the children to eat, and then you can tell me what you would like."

"Well, I can tell you now. I want a cup of decent coffee and a good, tender, juicy beefsteak."

"But, my dear, we can't get beefsteak or coffee without coupons, or any more butter!"

The little boy began to howl.

"I want some butter!" he protested. "I want some bread and a lot of butter!"

"There isn't any tonight, Gerald. But maybe I can find some jam down in the cellar. Won't that do?" asked Lexie brightly.

"No, it *won't*," he roared. "I won't eat your old jam! I want *butter*! A lot of it! You're a bad old aunt, you are, and I don't like you."

In despair Lexie went downstairs and concocted the nicest supper she could out of the supply she had bought.

The children came down presently, one at a time. Angelica first. Lexie, hurrying to get everything on the table, heard the child calling, "*Hi*, Elaine! There's hard-boiled egg-wheels on the spinach, and the potatoes have their overcoats on."

And then she heard a howl from Gerald: "I don't like old spinach! I won't eat it, even if it has got old egg-wheels on it. I hate spinach. I want *beef*steak!"

Lexie took a deep breath. This was going to be an endurance test, it seemed. Oh why, why, *why*?

"Run up and call the other children, Angel," she said with a forced smile. "I'm just going to take the omelet up, and it needs to be eaten while it's piping hot."

The little girl gave one eager, hungry look at her aunt's bright face and hurried upstairs, calling the news about the omelet as she went.

But she came down again soon with a haughty imitation of her mother's tone.

"Elaine says it's no use for you to try to stuff spinach down us. We won't eat it. We *never* do! And she thinks that's pretty poor fare for the first meal when your relatives come home. She says we don't eat spinach nor omelet, and *you can't make us!*"

"Oh," said Lexie cheerfully, "that's too bad, isn't it, when we can't get anything else but what I've got here. But of course you don't *have* to eat it unless you like. I'm not going to try to stuff it down you. I only thought maybe you were hungry, and since these were the only things I could get for us tonight, you might be glad to have them. But if you don't want them, that's all right with me. As soon as I get the dishes washed and everything put away I'll try and fix a place for you to sleep. If you get to sleep soon I don't suppose you'll mind being hungry for tonight."

Angelica looked at her aunt aghast as she set the puffy brown omelet on the table, put the open dish of bright green spinach with its wheels of yellow and white egg beside it, and then sat down as if she were going to eat it all by herself. Deliberately she helped herself to some of each dish on the table and began to eat with slow, small bites, smiling at the little girl pleasantly. Suddenly Angelica set up a howl: "Come down here quick, Gerry! She's eating it all up! She's got a nice dinner all ready and she's *eating it up herself*! Hurry up and bring Bluebell down with you. Hurry, or it will all be gone!"

Lexie smiled to herself as she realized that she had conquered for once. Perhaps that was the way to manage them. Let them think you didn't care whether they ate or not. So she went steadily on eating slow mouthfuls while Angelica fairly danced up and down in a fury.

"Gerald! *Ger-a-l-d!* Come *quick!* She's eating it all up from us, and I'm *h-o-n-g-ry!*"

"Oh," said Lexie pleasantly. "Would you like to have some dinner? Suppose you sit down here beside me. What would you like to have?"

"I want some of that puffy om-let!" announced Angelica, slamming herself into the chair indicated. "And I want some of that nice green stuff with yellow wheels on it."

Lexie put a small amount of spinach on the child's plate, with a slice of lovely hard-boiled egg on the top, and beside it a helping of beautifully browned omelet. The little girl lost no time in sampling the food.

"It's *good!*" she screamed. Gerald, who suddenly had appeared in the doorway with Bluebell by the hand, looked on jealously.

Lexie paid no attention to him until he came closer to the table.

"I *want* some!" he announced.

"Oh, do you?" said Lexie calmly. "Well, sit down on this other side, and I'll put a big book on a chair for the baby."

Amazingly, they were finally seated, eating with zest.

"I want some *more,*" said Angelica, handing out her plate. "I want some milk, too. You've got milk."

"Why, of course. You can all have milk!" said Lexie, filling a glass for each one.

At last without any coaxing they ate, heartily, eagerly, and asked for more.

When the spinach and potatoes were all gone, except for the small portion she had kept in the warming oven for Elaine in case she would deign to eat it, Lexie brought out a generous plate of cookies and a pear apiece, and the children by this time were almost appreciative.

"Say, these cookies are good," said Angelica, setting the pace for the others. "They've got good raisins in them."

"I don't like cookies," said Gerald. "I'druther have chocolate cake."

"Well, that's too bad," said Lexie sympathetically. "Sorry we haven't any chocolate cake. You don't need to eat cookies if you don't like them," and she drew the plate back and did not pass it to him.

Gerald's reply was to rise up on his chair and reach out for the plate, knocking over Bluebell's glass of milk and sending a stream of milk over the table.

"I will so have some cookies! You can't keep me from having some!" declared the obstreperous child. "You just want to keep them all for yourself, but you shan't."

Lexie, rescuing the glass of milk before the entire contents were broadcast, said gently: "Oh, I'm sorry. Did you want some? I understood you to say you didn't like them." She lifted the cookie plate before Gerald succeeded in plunging a willful hand into its midst. "Sit down, Gerald, and I'll pass them to you."

Gerald settled back astonished, about to howl but thought better of it, and soon had his mouth stuffed full of so much cookie he couldn't speak.

When that meal was concluded Lexie felt as if she had fought a battle, but she felt reasonably satisfied with the result. The children were still munching cookies and demanding more pears, and Bluebell was nodding with sleep in her chair. Lexie hadn't eaten much except those first few decoy mouthfuls, but she drank a little milk and hurried upstairs with the tray for Elaine. She was greeted as she entered the room by sounds of heartrending sobs, and Elaine turned a woebegone face to meet her.

"So you did decide to bring me something at last, did you? Of course I am only an uninteresting invalid, and it doesn't matter if I starve, but you certainly might have brought me a crust of bread."

"Well, I'm sorry, Elaine," said Lexie with a sudden, quick sigh. "I thought you would want the children fed first. And I'm not altogether sure you'll like what I've brought, but it was all I could get tonight. Toast and jam, a glass of milk. It isn't bad if you'd try it. I made a little new omelet for you, too, so it would come to you hot. Of course, it isn't the beefsteak you wanted, but I'm afraid from all I hear, that you won't get much of that these days."

Elaine surveyed the tray with dissatisfaction and was about to discount everything on it, but Lexie spoke first.

"Now I'll go and see if I can find some blankets and things to make up beds for the children. They are dropping over with weariness. If you need anything, send Angelica up to the attic after me," and she quickly retired from the room before her sister had time to say anything more. But when she came down, every crumb and drop was gone from the tray, and Elaine had retired to her pillow to prepare for another weeping spell.

"Did you contact my lawyer?" she asked sharply.

"Oh no, of course not. I hadn't time. I knew you all would have to have some supper. Now, do you want Bluebell to sleep with you?"

"Heavens no! Do you think I could be bothered that way,

me, in my condition? She'll sleep all right by herself. She's not used to being petted, not since I've been sick, anyway. Not since the nurse left."

Lexie gazed in compassion at the poor baby, now asleep on the floor in the dining room, tears on her cheeks and an intermittent hectic sob shaking her baby shoulders. Poor little mite, with nobody taking care of her, and already a hard, belligerent set to her little lips! What could she do for her? Obviously she was the first one to be made comfortable. The rest could wait.

In quick thought, she reviewed the possibilities of the house. There were two folding cots in the attic. She could easily bring those down for the two older children. There were plenty of blankets, now that she had opened the big old chest in which they were packed. But there was no crib for Bluebell. The last one in the family must have been her own, and only a very valuable piece of unneeded furniture would have survived so many years. But there was a wide couch in the room that used to be her mother's. She could make a bed for the baby up there, and herself sleep in her mother's bed, if she got any chance to sleep at all in this disorganized household.

Swiftly she went to work and soon had a comfortable place for Bluebell with chairs to guard the side so she couldn't roll off. Then she brought down the cots, an armful of sheets and blankets, and made up two beds for Angelica and Gerald.

"What in the world are you doing there in the next room?" called Elaine. "It seems to me you might keep a little still and give me a chance to sleep. And what is the mater with those two children? They've done nothing but wrangle since you brought the baby upstairs. I should think you might amuse them a few minutes and let me get a little rest before that lawyer comes. What time did he say he would be here?"

"There'll be no lawyer here tonight," said Lexie firmly. "And the best amusement these children can have is a little sleep. I've made up two cots here, and they'll soon be in bed. You better tell them what to do about nighties. I've got some things to attend to in the kitchen, and it's time we were all asleep. We're very tired. Angelica, go ask your mother where you can find your night things."

Lexie hurried away to find more blankets and left her petulant sister to deal with the two sleepy children. Returning a few minutes later she found all three in tears. Elaine crying heartbrokenly into her pillow like a well-bred invalid, Angelica struggling with a resistant button in the back of her dress, which wasn't really a sewed-on button at all, but was only pinned on with a safety pin. Gerald was howling as usual.

"I won't sleep in that old cot. I just *won't, so there*! I want a real bed, not an old cot!"

Lexie, tired as she was, breezed into the room and spoke cheerfully.

"Well, come now, we're going to play the game of go-to-bed. Who wants to be *It*?"

The two young wailers stopped instantly, surveyed her for a moment, and then changed face and put on eagerness.

"I would like to be *It*," said Angelica sedately, with a speculative attention that showed she was interested.

Then Gerald sounded his trumpet.

"That's not fair! *I* choose to be *It*! I'm the youngest, and you ought to let me be It. Isn't that so, Elaine? Mustn't they let me be It? I won't play if I can't be It!"

Then came Elaine's sharp voice: "Certainly, Lexie. You must

let Gerald have what he wants or he won't go to sleep tonight, and I shan't get any rest." But Lexie chimed right over Elaine's voice, just as if she hadn't heard her at all. Lexie said cheerfully: "Why yes, of course, you can be It *next*. You can't be first because you didn't choose to be as soon as I spoke. However, you can be It *second*, and that gives you a chance to watch the game and see if you can improve on the way Angel did it. That gives you quite an advantage, you see. Besides, there's a prize! That is, there are two prizes, and one is just as good as the other, because the winner of the second prize gets to choose whether he'll have one just like the first, or a new one. But there's one rule that makes them both alike. There positively won't be any prize at all if there is a *single squeal* or *yell* or *howl*. It's got to be all very quiet and gentle, because your mother is sick and needs taken care of. Now, are you ready to hear the rules?"

"I am!" said Angelica. "I'm *very* quiet."

"Me, too!" said the little boy in a subdued tone.

"Very well, then," said Lexie. "Rule number one is that everything must proceed very quietly, no running nor pushing nor shoving. Rule number two—no dropping shoes noisily, nor fighting for hairbrushes. Rule number three—you must not leave your clothes on the floor. Lay them nicely on the chairs at the foot of the beds. You will find your nightclothes each lying on your cots. Put them on smoothly and get quietly into bed. I will watch the clock and see which gets in first, and afterward if you are still quite quiet I will award the two prizes. Angelica gets the first chance to wash while Gerry takes off his shoes and stockings and puts them nicely by the chair. Then Gerry takes his turn washing, and the hands and faces must be clean, and I mean *clean*, you know. Now, are you ready? If you are, go stand on the edge of that board in the floor and watch my raised hands. When I drop them, you may start. Ready?"

The two children scuttled across the room and toed the crack in the floor, watching her eagerly, silently. Lexie thrilled as she saw their interested faces. Then she dropped her hands.

"Go!" she said quietly.

Gerald dropped silently to the floor and went at the knot in his shoestring, while Angelica scurried to the bathroom. Silently, swiftly, earnestly they worked. Lexie was astonished that her game had interested them. From what she had seen of the children so far, she had not dared to hope that it would.

Angelica was back in a trice, and Gerald gave a last yank to his shoestring and dashed to take his place at the washbowl.

In five minutes those two children were snuggled in their cots under the blankets awaiting the prizes with eagerness, and there hadn't been a single argument about which cot should be occupied by which child!

Lexie brought a large chocolate drop to Angelica, and gave the little boy his choice between another and a date. He chose the chocolate, and both lay happily licking their chocolates while their tired young eyes blinked into quick sleepiness, and it wasn't many minutes before both were sound asleep.

"Well," said Elaine jealously, "what in the world did you do to them? I never saw them succumb so quickly. Did you give them a box of candy apiece, or administer a sleeping tablet?"

"Neither," whispered Lexie, laughing. "We played a game of going to bed. I'll teach you how tomorrow. Now, do you want anything yourself before you go to sleep? Do you want something more to eat or drink, or are you going right to sleep?"

"No, I don't want anything more to eat. I want you to go

out somewhere and telephone to that lawyer. That's the first thing on the docket. And next I want you to go wherever you keep such things, and bring me all of Mamma's private papers. I want to look them over before the lawyer gets here."

Lexie stood still a moment and faced her sister quietly. Then she said: "Sorry! That's impossible! I will not ever telephone that man! I can't stop *your* trusting him, but I can refuse to have anything to do with the matter. And if you persist in it, I shall simply have to go away and leave you. I cannot have anything to do with Bettinger Thomas."

"Oh, how silly and unkind and prejudiced you are! I didn't think you'd be unkind when I'm so ill! I can't see why you couldn't call him up and just say I wanted to see him. He'll understand. He knew I was going to call him. I sent him a telegram and told him I would call. You needn't let him know who you are. *Please*, Lex, do it *for me!*"

"No, Elaine, it's for your sake that I can't do it. I know him to be a bad, unprincipled man, and I'll save you from him if I can."

"You mean you'll do everything to save the money for yourself," sneered Elaine. "Well, if you won't do that, please go somewhere and telephone for a nurse. I've got to have one *tonight*."

"No, Elaine, I can't do that either. The only place near here where they have a telephone is down at Mrs. Hadley's, and she has gone to stay a week with her daughter in New York."

"Well, surely you can go down to the drugstore and phone."

"Elaine, if you were dying and the only thing that would save you was a nurse, I'd go at the risk of my life. But you're not dying, and what you need is some sleep. No nurse could get out here anyway tonight. You know we are a long way out, and—really, Elaine—I'm just about all in. I feel as if I couldn't drag another step."

"Oh really?" I don't see what you've done to make you tired. You've simply been loafing here all day, haven't you? I didn't think you were so selfish! Well, anyway, if you'll go wherever you keep such things and find Mamma's papers right now, I'll be satisfied. I couldn't sleep until I have a chance to look them over."

Lexie looked at her sister sadly.

"I've told you twice that there are no papers. The only paper I know anything about is the deed of this house, and that is in a safe-deposit box in the bank out where my college is. It is absolutely the only paper I have that has anything to do with any financial matters. If you don't believe me you'll have to do what you want to, but I'm going to bed! I'm just done out!"

Lexie walked out of the room to her own, and wrapping the only unused blanket about her she dropped wearily down on her bed, a few steps from the sleeping Bluebell.

Chapter 4

Although the relaxation was grateful to Lexie's weary body, she did not fall asleep at once. She realized that her hard day was not yet over. There were things she must decide, many questions that she must settle now in the silent night while all her tormentors were asleep. In the morning she would have to have a settlement with her sister, and she must make up her mind beforehand just what attitude she was going to take and stick to it. That was the only way to manage Elaine. She knew that from her girlhood days.

First, there was the question of finances. Elaine must have some money—perhaps not much—or she would never have come all this way home. But she must have a *little* or she would not have produced some for that nurse and driver. If she had none at all, what were they to do? They had the house, of course, but could they even afford to keep the house going if there was no money to run it and nothing to buy food with? Elaine would have to consider that. She wasn't altogether devoid of common sense when she could be gotten down to facts, but at present her mind seemed to be filled with the idea that there was a large sum of money that her father had left and to which she had a right. Until she got over that obsession, there wasn't much she could hope to do with her. But must she go on this way from day to day and wait until Elaine came to her senses? Definitely the question of money was first. She must settle with Elaine the first thing in the morning. But above all, she must *not* give up her college and her job unless it became absolutely necessary.

Before dawn began to creep into the window and lay rosy fingers on the old wallpaper above the bed, Lexie had fallen into an uneasy sleep. In the near future, there was still a relentless sister and three terrible infants who were determined to bend the earth to their wishes. But a new day was coming that undoubtedly would be tempestuous, with decisions to be made that would be difficult, yet in spite of them all she *must* go on, through whatever was in store for her reluctant feet. She must go on and *conquer*, doing what was in the Almighty's plan for her life. She must not be blinded by darkness, nor fire, nor opposition of any sort. It was a war perhaps between her sister and herself, but she must remember that Elaine was the daughter of her own father, and there was a certain obligation upon her as the daughter of a beloved father to treat his other daughter with all kindness and unselfishness, even if Elaine persisted in being selfish toward her. It was what was *right*, not what she *wanted*. It was—it *had* to be—what God, if He cared about such things at all, must expect of her! Just why she felt that way, she didn't know. But she did, and so she must go on. Even if it meant eventually that she would have to come back and nurse Elaine, and try to get along with those terrific children! Of course it wouldn't be so hard to get along with the children if she had a right to order their lives and make them behave, but Elaine would never stand for that.

When Lexie at last awoke and adjusted her mind to the present day with its problems, she got up hurriedly and tiptoed out of the room. Bluebell was still asleep and looked very sweet without the petulance of the new day upon her yet. But Lexie couldn't afford to stop and admire her young niece. She went downstairs, started some cereal, fixed a tray for Elaine, and set the table with as little ceremony as she possibly could. Whatever this new day turned out to be, it was certain it would be very full, and she must not be lavish with dishes that would have to be washed.

The family was tired and had not been used to arising early, so Lexie had a chance to get a real breakfast herself. Toast and scrambled eggs, the lunch she had prepared for herself the day before and hadn't eaten. It would taste good now, and give her a new heart of hope for the day's worries. Besides, she would have opportunity to go over quietly her resolves of the night before and check up on them. See if they were really wise in the light of day.

Lexie had washed her own cup and plate and written a list of a few things she ought to get at the grocery when she heard the children waking up. She hurried upstairs and endeavored to greet them and enthuse them with the game-spirit that had worked so well the night before, but they were cross and utterly alien again. So with a mere bright word for them to get quickly dressed and come down to breakfast, she hurried back to the kitchen and prepared a generous dish of cereal and another of scrambled eggs, got out the bottle of milk she had saved for morning, squeezed orange juice enough for four glasses, finished the tray for Elaine, and took it upstairs, setting it beside Elaine's bed. She seemed to still be sleeping; so she summoned the half-dressed children in a whisper, and they all went down to breakfast.

While they were eating she talked to them.

"Your mother is sick," she said gently.

"Naw, she ain't sick," announced Gerald. "She's just kidding you. She gets up and walks around whenever you go downstairs."

"I wouldn't say that, Gerry. She's probably trying to help all she can. Now listen. There is a great deal to do today. I wonder if you three couldn't help a bit? Will you try?"

"What are we to do?" inquired Angelica coldly.

"Well, first, trying to be as quiet about everything as possible so you won't make your mother worse. She doesn't feel at all well, you know."

"Will there be a prize?" asked the little girl.

"Well, there might be," said Lexie thoughtfully. "I hadn't thought of that. I felt you would like to do this for your mother's sake."

"*Why?*" asked the child with a hard look in her eyes.

Lexie was startled. Did any children feel such an utter lack of care for their mother that the thought of doing anything for her sake made no appeal? What should she say? But Angelica was waiting with hard impish eyes for an answer.

"Why, just because she's your mother, you know."

"Oh! *That!*" said the Angel-child. "That's no reason at all."

But suddenly the conversation was interrupted by a sharp call from Elaine.

"Here are some apples and pears you can have when you finish your scrambled eggs and toast," said Lexie. "Now, sit quietly while I'm gone, and we'll see what will come next. I've got to go to your mother."

She hurried upstairs.

"Have you sent for a nurse, Lexie? Or have you changed your mind and called my lawyer? I want to get him before he goes out. And you better give an order to have a phone put in right way, then we won't have to bother you to go downtown every time we turn around."

For answer, Lexie quietly closed the door and sat down.

"Elaine, there are a few things we have got to talk about before I do anything more."

"Oh *indeed*! Well, make it snappy! I've got my mind on important matters."

"*This* is important. It's about money, Elaine. Have *you* got any? You know we can't do anything without money. Not even telephone. I told you last night how much money I had, and I spent nearly all of it to get those things for supper and break-fast. Now I think we ought to have an understanding. How much money have you got?"

Elaine stared at her disagreeably.

"That's none of your business!" she said angrily. "We'll have money enough when you fork over what your mother salted down. And until then you can *charge* things."

"I'm afraid not," said Lexie. "People are not giving charge

accounts much anywhere, not new ones anyway, and if you have had them a long time you have to pay your bills every month *on time* or the government steps in and closes your account for you."

"Oh *really*? I doubt it. I think we can get by!" said Elaine in a superior tone. "You just charge whatever I ask you to get, and I'll take the consequences."

"Does that mean you haven't any money, Elaine? Because *I* really haven't. My ticket is bought back to college. I got a round-trip. And my board is paid at college. That is, I have a job working so many hours in the dining room that covers my board and room till commencement is over. And I have a job, a good one, as I told you, after I graduate, but it is dependent upon my graduation. So, you see, it is important that I get back to college as soon as possible. That is why I am asking about money. Have you enough to take care of yourself and the children and look out for your nurse and everything if go back right away? I could of course wait till I could get somebody to stay with you and act as nurse."

Elaine looked at her in amazed disgust.

"Do you mean that you would actually *desert* your poor sick sister and her poor little orphaned children and go running back to your old school, just so you can *graduate*? I never heard of such an unnatural girl as you have developed into!"

"Elaine, how would you think I would live if I don't go? And how could I help you any? I have not been able to save anything, but I knew I had this good job coming if I finished my course."

"That's ridiculous! You could get a job *here*."

"I'm afraid not, Elaine, at least not as good as the one I

have. You see, I was especially recommended by the college for the one I have, and the government sets the scale of wages, so it is really worthwhile. And of course I couldn't be of much help to you, even for a little while, without some money. What would we live on?"

"Oh, how absurd!" said Elaine. "There are always jobs to be had. As if there were any better ones out where your college is! And certainly my father's daughter could easily be recommended anywhere. No mere college would have to do it. And what's three months more of college, and a mere trifle of a diploma? You'll never need a diploma anyway. You'll likely be my housekeeper all your life, and I don't care whether you have three months more education or not. Now just put all such notions out of your head and get ready to go on my errands. I've written out a list of them and given you a few telephone numbers I happened to have. You better take the two younger children with you. Angelica can amuse herself with some books out of the bookcase, and run errands for me if I need her, and I can rest better with the younger ones out of the way."

Lexie looked at her sister astonished. Then she shook her head.

"No, I couldn't take the children. It's a long walk I have to go, and they would get very tired. It would take me too long with the children. You see, I have some errands of my own, too. Let me see your list."

"Well, I must say, you are not very accommodating. I supposed when I came home I would have the care that the word *home* generally implies, but it seems not. What do you suppose I'll do alone with the children? I'm not able to get up and look after them."

Lexie's eyes and voice were very grave.

"I don't know, Elaine. But they are your children, and you ought to have enough authority over them to keep them in order for the short time I shall be gone."

"It won't be such a short time, my dear sister, after you have done all the things I want you to do. Just cast your eye over that list."

Lexie looked at the list, and her expression grew firm.

"You will notice the order in which I have written my wishes," said Elaine. "I had a distinct purpose in that, and I want you to observe it carefully. First, call my lawyer. I've given you his phone number. Tell him to come at once! He must, to get here before you do, and it is for that reason I want you to take the children. I don't want to be bothered with them while I am talking to him. Then of course you must order the telephone put in. And next, I want you to contact the nurse. I've given you several addresses where you'll be likely to find one. Of course the best hospitals will know of one. And Lexie, make it plain that I won't take her at all if she can't come *right away*! I need her *at once*. Tell her I'll talk with her about her wages when she gets here. Tell her to take a taxi and that I'm rather helpless and need her at once! And next I want you to stop at Arnold's and get me a box of those lovely caramels he used to sell. Be sure you get the same kind. You know what they are. And bring them with you if you can't get him to send them. If he would send them at once I would have something to offer the lawyer. Or you might get a couple of packs of cigarettes. I'm practically out of them. Any good brand. I don't suppose this dinky town has every kind. And then I wish you would call up Carroll Dayton and ask her the address of that dressmaker she wrote me about, and if she thinks I could get her to alter some dresses for me at once. I've been too ill to look after my wardrobe, and I need some things at once. And *next*—"

Suddenly Lexie handed back the list to her sister.

"I'm sorry, Elaine, but I'll not have time for all that. I'll try to get someone to stay with you, but I can't do all those other things now. And anyway, unless you have a lot of money, those things will have to wait indefinitely, I'm afraid. *I* certainly haven't the money. Now, I'm going, and you'll have to take over with the children. I'll send them to you. I *ought* to get through and get the noon train if possible, but failing in that I *must* get the night train, if I can find you a nurse. You see I'm already twenty-four hours late, and you must remember that I have a job and obligations. But of course I'll find somebody first to be with you. I won't leave you alone. Good-bye, I'll get back as soon as I can."

Lexie flashed a nervous, chilly little smile at her sister and, turning, ran out the door with Elaine calling wildly after her: "Lexie, Lexie! You can't leave me that way! You can't! You *can't!*"

But Lexie went on down the stairs uncompromisingly. She sent the three children back to their mother with a smile and a promise that she would bring them each something nice if they were good and did what their mother told them all the time she was gone. Then catching up her hat and coat from the chair where she had deposited them five minutes before, she hurried out of the house, resolved not to listen to Elaine's frantic calling. It was the only way! She was sure she was right. They could not go on without money, and the only way she could make sure of that was to keep this job that she had been so happy over only yesterday. Maybe it did seem heartless to her sister, but if Elaine had no money, *somebody* must provide it, and she knew by experience that there was little hope of her getting a job in this vicinity.

And Elaine, convinced at last that it was useless to scream for her sister, rose from her bed of illness, dressed her hair in the most approved style, made up her face with just enough blue shadows under her eyes to look like an interesting invalid, put on a ravishing negligee from her suitcase and a pair of charming slippers, manicured her nails carefully, and went downstairs. She placed herself becomingly on the old couch in the living room that had seen so many years of hard service in the family. Then she called Angelica to her and instructed her to go across the street to Mrs. Wilson's house and ask if she would kindly call up the number written on the slip of paper she carried when she went to do her marketing and ask Mr. Thomas if he would come out and see her at once about important business. Elaine was not one who ever allowed the grass to grown under her feet, and would not be stopped in her endeavors by a mere illness, no matter how dramatically it had been built up.

Angelica was like her mother. She entered into the importance of being trusted with such a message and went on the errand with avidity. But she soon returned with the news that Mrs. Wilson wasn't at home. The neighbors had said she had taken a defense job, so Miss Angelica had tried other neighbors, who each in turn examined the bit of paper with its unknown numbers, and asked several curious questions. Just one finally volunteered to send the message, but came back to the child after she had done so in high dudgeon.

"Say, little girl, was that lawyer you wanted me to phone

Bettinger Thomas, do you happen to know?"

"Why yes," said Angelica importantly. "I guess it was. I heard my aunt and my mother talking about him and they called him 'Bett' Thomas. They said they used to go to school with him." Angelica always enjoyed repeating important information.

"Well," said the helpful neighbor, "if I had known that I wouldn't have stirred a step to send that message. You can go back to your mother, little girl, and tell her that man isn't fit for her to speak to. Tell her her mother wouldn't have allowed her to send for him if she had been alive. Mrs. Kendall was a good woman, and she would be horrified to have that man allowed to come to her house. Your mother has been away so long she probably doesn't remember how her mother felt about him. Or maybe she never knew how her mother felt."

"She wasn't her *mother*," said the Angel pertly, "she was only her *step*mother, and stepmothers don't count!" said the child, tossing her dark curls saucily and flouncing away from the neighbor. She hotfooted it back to her mother to report.

"You mean they had the impertinence to say that to *you*?" asked Elaine furiously. "My word! What are we coming to when the neighbors around here would dare to send *me* a message like that! Well, you can just go straight back and tell those old busybodies that they don't know what they are talking about. You can tell them that I've known Bettinger Thomas for years, and I trust him thoroughly, and they better look out saying things like that about him. He is a smart lawyer, and when he hears that he'll certainly get it back on them in some way that they won't like. Being a lawyer, of course, he knows how."

So being a smart child and obedient when it suited her

purposes, Angelica went on her way with her retort, and gave it forth with embellishments according to her own sharp little tongue. As the hour of Lexie's absence lengthened into two, there drew up at the little white house a costly car, shining in chromium, polished to the last degree, and the hovering neighbors, from furtive hiding places, identified the fat, pompous man who got out as none other than Bettinger Thomas himself. They shook their heads and murmured sorrowful comments to one another on what "poor, dear Mrs. Kendall" would say if she could only know.

"And it's a mercy they can't know such things in heaven," exclaimed the neighbor who knew the least about it, "because she certainly couldn't be happy knowing it. She was *such* a good woman!"

Lexie, on her way, would have hurried even faster than she did if she had known what was going on back in the little white house. For though she had known her sister well for years, it never entered her head that Elaine would go to the length of getting up from her sickbed and taking things in her own hands to get that reprobate of a lawyer. Trouble, trouble, there seemed to be trouble on every side, and somehow she must go through it and work out a sane and wise solution to all these difficulties. If only God was here to tell her what to do!

Then it came to her suddenly that of course God was here, and He knew all about her troubles. He would know the wise way to work it out. He would know whether she ought to insist on going back to college to finish her course and get her good job, or whether she ought to stay here and look after this unreasonable, unpleasant sister and her three naughty children.

Oh, God, won't You please show me what to do? her discouraged young heart cried out as she walked down the pleasant street and wondered that it could seem so pleasant when she was having so much trouble. "God, please help me!"

Her mother had taught her to believe in God. She did, of course, but she had never really done much about it—only said her prayers religiously every night, and gone to church when it was convenient. But she knew in her heart that that wasn't really being even just polite to God. If He were a neighbor, or a mere acquaintance, she would feel that she had to have more of a pleasant contact than just that in order to be really polite. These thoughts condemned her as she walked along. *Please, God, forgive me! I didn't realize that I was being rude and indifferent to You. But now, I've nobody else to go to. Won't You forgive, and help me, please? Should I give up everything and let my selfish sister manage my life? Oh, but I can't do that! We wouldn't have any money if I have no job. I'm almost sure Elaine hasn't any money. And anyway, I wouldn't want to live on her money. Not even if I worked for her. I couldn't. I just couldn't, dear God! And what shall I do about a nurse? They cost a great deal of money, I'm sure. And it isn't likely Elaine has enough money for that. Even if she gets a little from her husband's pay in the army, she wouldn't have enough for that, and to run the house. If she had had enough money for all her needs, I'm sure she never would have come to me, back to the little house that she always despised. Oh, dear God, what shall I do?*

Softly this prayer was going over and over in her heart with a longing and a kind of wonder that had never come to her before when she was trying to pray. This was just something that breathed from her inner being, from a newborn trust that had come from her great need—a kind of a desperate feeling that she was appealing to the only possible source of help. And if He wouldn't help her, she was done.

These thoughts filled her mind as she went swiftly on her way. She was not thinking of the immediate mission before her, for in the hard watches of the night she had settled definitely, step by step, just what that would be.

First, although she felt it was useless on account of expense, she must call up the hospitals and nurses' agencies, and make careful inquiry about what could be done. That had to be done for Elaine's satisfaction. For she would never give up the idea of having a really important nurse from some established hospital unless she found it was impossible for her to pay such a nurse. So this was the first matter to be got out of the way.

Lexie went to the telephone and called up the various places she had on her list. And of course it turned out to be not only out of the question for financial reasons to get such a nurse, but she found that any nurse was almost impossible to get. So many had gone into war work that the hospitals themselves were hopelessly understaffed, and they could not suggest any agency or nurse that would be at all a possibility in the immediate future. They added that conditions were getting more and more strenuous, and nurses were almost impossible to get anywhere.

Lexie tried all the possibilities that Elaine had suggested, and got nowhere so far as a nurse to come out to the little house was concerned. But she carefully wrote down opposite each name on her list every bit of information she had gleaned.

Then, because her watch warned her that this was the hour when she would likely find the dean of her college in his office, she put in a long-distance call for him, and had a five-minute talk with him, telling him in brief phrases what had befallen her and asking his advice. This talk greatly heartened her, for the dean gave her his promise to do all that was possible to help her that she might graduate with her class. He suggested certain preparations she might make in her home, and a possibility of a delayed examination in case her sister was too ill for her to leave at once or she could find no one suitable to stay with her. He promised also to hold her job for her for a few days until she could let him know just what she could arrange to do, and to use his influence to get her job that was to come after her graduation, transferred to the city near her home in case she had to stay there. He told her to write him more definitely in a day or two, or better still to come on for a short time, or anyway telephone him again. His words and tone were so kind and considerate that they brought tears of relief to her tired eyes. At least she had one friend who was sorry for her distress and would do all in his power to help her. Though more and more she became certain that she had to remain for a while at least, and see Elaine and her children safely settled somewhere, somehow.

Then with firmly set lips and determined eyes she started out on her final quest, in search of an old acquaintance who used to live not far from them in the days when her mother was alive. One Lucinda Forbes, a practical nurse, a staid, elderly woman with a homely face and somewhat crude ways, but with a heart of kindness, who would perhaps be willing to undertake even a thankless job as one attending Elaine would be sure to find it. Lucinda Forbes had loved her mother because of numerous little kindnesses that she had done for the lonely woman, and just because she had loved Mrs. Kendall, Lexie hoped she might be willing to look out for Elaine and her family, at least for a little time until she could finish her course and come back.

Of course Elaine wouldn't like it. She had always despised the woman, who was much too plainspoken for her ease of mind. And neither would Lucinda like it, because she knew Elaine of old, and had little patience with her selfish ways. But at least she might help out in this emergency for a time.

There was, too, the possibility that she might be sick, or moved away, or gone into war work, or even dead. Lucinda might be rather old for such a job, too, but at least she would try for her because she knew of no other one she could get at present. So she took a bus to the place where she remembered Lucinda had moved the last time she heard of her.

It was rather a long bus ride, and Lexie was tired and discouraged before she got there, but when she reached the house she found Lucinda was no longer there. She had gone to a single room in a dreary little house in a back street, and when Lexie finally reached her she was just about to leave that and go out to hunt still another abiding place.

"I can't afford this room any longer," she told Lexie with a tired look and a stray tear wandering down her cheek. "You know, I'm not able to do so much nursing now. They want younger women, and I can't seem to get in anywhere."

Lexie's hope rose.

"Oh Lucinda! I'm so sorry for you! But—are you free now? That would be wonderful for us. Would you be willing to come to us for a little while anyway, until you get something better?"

"*You!* Oh Miss Lexie! Would I be *willing*? But I thought you were away at college! You're not married, are you?"

"No," laughed Lexie, "not married, nor likely to be. And I *am* in college. Or, that is, I *was*, until yesterday afternoon, and still am if I can manage it. You see, I've only till spring till I graduate. But yesterday I got a telegram from Elaine. You know, she's married, but her husband has gone off to war, and she's sick. She has come home with her three children! I just didn't know what to do. I can't bear to give up my college when I'm so nearly done, and a splendid job waiting for me when and if I graduate. But Elaine is sick! And I don't know what I ought to do. I was wondering if it would be possible for you to come and stay with us—at least with Elaine and the children—while I go back to college and try to finish up?"

"*Oh Elaine!*" said Lucinda with a dismal look settling on her grim old countenance. "I'd come for *you* of course, but— *Elaine*—she's another proposition. She and I never did get on, you know. She was always too snooty and treated me like the dust of the earth."

"Yes, I know," said Lexie sadly. "I remembered that of course, and I wasn't sure you would be willing. I know you two never did agree. Of course Elaine is rather hard to please. But—she's my sister! I *have* to do something about it. And you were the only one I could think of who might possibly help me out until I can get through this hard place."

"Well, of course," said Lucinda relenting, "when you put it that way—and your mommy was always so good to me!"

"But there's another thing I should tell you, Cinda," said Lexie. "We couldn't pay you much. Not now, anyway. After I'm through college I hope to be able to earn enough to pay something, but for the present it wouldn't be much but your board and room."

"Oh, I wouldn't stop for the money, Miss Lexie," said Lucinda airily. "Of course a room and a few bites to eat is all I need for a while now, anyway, seein' I've got to move out of this room, poor as it is. And I oughtta be thankful to get a place to lay me head, and a crust now and then. The only thing—that Elaine. I never did favor her. But of course, as you say, she's your sister, and you can't help that! Well, when do you want me to come?"

"Oh Cinda, I'm so glad you will consider it! You don't know what it means to me. And I'd like you to come as soon as you can. Now, right away, today. Can you come back with me?"

"Well, no, not just to say *back*, for I've got to wait till me man comes to get me trunk. But he said he'd be here in about an hour or so, and I'll tell you what I'll do. I'll get him to let me ride along with him and bring me trunk and all, and start in living."

"That will be wonderful, Lucinda! It's like a great burden rolled away. I know there are going to be hard things about it, Cinda, but I hope they won't be too hard. If you find things getting unbearable, please try to remember that we are having a war, and things are all mixed up anyway, and we've got to win this war. And the way to do it is for everybody to win in their own hearts, and try to keep calm, and not mind when other people are unpleasant."

"I know, Miss Lexie, and I guess I can stand as much as the next one. But when it comes to Miss Elaine, I just know I'll speak me mind too often, and she won't like it!"

"Well, try not to, Cinda, and perhaps it won't be as bad as you fear."

"Well, maybe not. But I'll not bank on that much. I'll

just think it's something I've got to weather, for your sake, and your sweet mommy's. Good-bye and thank ye kindly for remembering me. So long. I'll be seein' you within the day." Greatly relieved, Lexie went on her way back to the house, stopping only to buy a few necessities at the store, and when she came in sight of the little white house, there was that great shining limousine parked before the door. Inside the house, awaiting her return, its obnoxious owner, ready with his little pig-eyes to look her over, and attempt to startle her into admissions that would help him to win this case he was so eager to undertake.

Chapter 5

With quickened heartbeats Lexie hurried on, wondering whose car that could be and what had happened since she left the house. Was something wrong, some accident perhaps to one of the children, and some of the neighbors had sent for a doctor? But that car did not look like one belonging to any local doctor. Surely Elaine hadn't gone to the length of sending for some city doctor!

She hurried in and there sat Bettinger Thomas, and there on the couch reclined Elaine, laughing and talking with the man Lexie felt was nothing short of a moral leper.

Lexie paused in the doorway for an instant, looking from her sister to the caller in amazement, and suddenly became aware that the obnoxious visitor was studying herself with open, fulsome admiration in his little pig-eyes.

"Why, it's little Lexie, isn't it?" he said in honeyed tones. "And how you've grown! You're really pretty, aren't you? And I used to think you were awfully plain beside your lovely sister. But you certainly have blossomed out. You're a very handsome girl, Lexie."

Lexie flashed a fiery glance at him, utter contempt in her expression, and turned toward the kitchen with her bundles, vouchsafing no reply. But Elaine stormed out at her.

"You're being rude, Lexie. This is Mr. Thomas. You used to know him in your school days. He has come to talk over our finances with us, and help us to get to a better understanding. Sit down, won't you? Mr. Thomas is in rather a hurry, and we mustn't hinder him."

"You'll have to excuse me, Elaine," said Lexie coolly. "I have some things to do, and there is nothing I care to discuss with Mr. Thomas."

Lexie turned and went into the kitchen, shutting the door firmly. She walked into the pantry, shutting that door to keep out the sound of her sister's angry voice calling her.

"Lexie! Lexie! You ridiculous child! How rude you are! Lexie, come here this minute. I've *got* to explain this to you!"

Lexie stood for a moment with her back to the pantry door, her bundles still in her arms, one hand on her heart, struggling to keep her tears back. The kitchen was very still, and Elaine's complaint was plainly heard, but she did not intend to answer it. She could not go into the living room and hear Elaine making complaints of her own dear mother. If Elaine wanted to do that she would have to do it without her as an audience. It was dreadful that Elaine would do a thing like that! Actually charge her mother with being dishonest! And before that great lump of iniquity, *Bett Thomas*!

Then she heard steps coming toward the kitchen. She heard the door open, and heard a man's voice calling her. "Lexie! Oh Lexie! Where are you, you little rascal?"

Well, she certainly wouldn't answer him. She stood perfectly still, suddenly aware that her bundle-laden arms were aching. But she would not move to reveal her presence. Not until she heard the man coming toward the pantry, heard his prying hand on the knob of the pantry door. The impudent fellow! But Elaine had probably told him where to find her.

Quietly she swayed forward to the shelf and deposited her groceries. Then she turned and faced the man who had dared to come after her.

"Here, you little monkey you, come out of hiding!" he said jocosely. "We haven't any time to waste being coy! I came up here in the midst of a busy morning to discuss business matters, and you'll *have* to come in here and answer some questions. I can't be played with, even if you are a pretty girl!"

"I beg your pardon," said Lexie coldly, tip-tilting her chin haughtily. "I really have nothing to discuss, and you'll please take your hand off my arm. I don't like it! Let me pass, please. I'm busy in the kitchen."

Lexie made a sudden, unexpected dash, slipping by him into the kitchen. She went over to the sink, where she turned on the water and began noisily to wash some potatoes, and to fill the kettle with water.

"But you don't understand," said the very much annoyed and determined man, "this is an important matter, and I haven't time to waste waiting for you any longer. You'll understand when you are brought up in court how important it is that you should attend to the matter now and perhaps save yourself from an extended trial, where I warn you you will have no friends to save you from trouble."

"Really?" said Lexie. "Just why should I be brought to trial? I'm not aware of having done anything that the law would be interested in."

"Very well, then, you better come into the other room and let me tell you why you will surely be brought to trial unless you can answer my questions in a satisfactory way."

"Questions?" said Lexie airily, although she was inwardly quaking. "What questions are there that you could possibly have a right to ask?"

"Well, you see, I am your sister's lawyer, and she is suing you for the money her father left in trust with your mother for his elder daughter."

"Oh," said Lexie, suddenly thoughtful, "is that what she is doing? And just why should she think I know anything about it?"

"Of course you would know, and were probably in collusion with your mother in secreting the money, and diverting it all to your own uses. And now, if you will come into the other room and sit down where we can talk, I will explain to you how you can make the whole matter very simple by just being willing to cooperate with us. It will be a great deal easier and better if you will put aside your animosity and cooperate with us. It will be cheaper and better for you in the end if you will come at once and tell all you know about this."

Lexie studied her pompous antagonist for a minute, and though she was boiling inside she realized that she would get nowhere by angry resistance.

"Very well," she said suddenly, in a quiet tone, as she began to roll down her sleeves and preceded the man into the living room, infuriated by his fulsome flattery.

"That's the good girl!" he commended loudly. "I knew you were too pretty a girl to put up a fight. Now, we shall see how quickly we can get this matter under way. Suppose you sit here," and he indicated a chair close to the one where he had been sitting.

Lexie sat down in a straight chair across the room from the one suggested.

"Now, just what did you want to ask me?" she said in a cold haughty tone, a tone that made her appear so much older and wiser than she really was that Elaine stared at her young sister in amazement.

"That's better!" said the big man with a kind of rumbling satisfaction in his voice. "Now we can get somewhere. First, Lexie, let me ask you to think back to your childhood and tell me carefully what you remember of financial discussions between your father and mother. Way back as far as you can remember. You can remember a time, can't you, perhaps when you were playing about in the room and you heard your father tell your mother that he had left quite a large sum of money in trust for his elder daughter, Elaine, money that had been her own mother's, and that someday he hoped it all went well to leave something for you his younger daughter? You remember that, do you not?"

"No," said Lexie calmly, "I do not remember any such thing."

"Well, suppose you repeat what you do remember on that subject."

"I do not remember my father and mother discussing

money in any way," said Lexie quietly.

"Think back. Think hard. Tell us what you do recall."

Lexie did not reply, and the lawyer was annoyed.

"Let us put it in another way," said Thomas. "You may not remember such a conversation, but you knew, did you not, that there was such a sum of money put away in trust for your sister?"

"No," said Lexie promptly. "I did not. Because there was not any such sum put away. My father may have intended to do something like that, but I am sure it was never done."

"And what makes you so sure, Miss Positive?" asked the fat man impudently.

"I am sure because my mother worked hard after my father's death to pay his funeral expenses, and afterward to get money enough to send us both to college. She often came home too weary to eat her supper, but she wouldn't give up her work. She said she had promised my father that we should both have a good education, and she was saving every cent from her own needs to make it possible. I was a witness to all this, and so was my sister."

A cunning look came over the fat face of the man.

"Yes? And what became of that money? Did your sister get her share of it? Did she get her education?"

"No, she got married instead of going to college. But Mother gave her her half of the money as a wedding gift. I saw her do it. And then when she got her divorce and was in terrible straits, she gave her my share, too. I suggested it, and was glad to give it to help her out. But Mother got evening work in addition to her day job, and started in to try and save money for my college course. That was what killed her. She only lived another year, and when her funeral expenses were paid, I had fifty dollars in the bank because mother earned it for me. But if Elaine wants that, she can have it. It's all I have. And that's all I have to tell you. Now, I'll be excused, if you please. I have a train to catch and a lot to do before I go."

Lexie rose quickly and flashed out of the room before the two astonished listeners could stop her, but before she had closed the door behind her she heard the lawyer say: "Well, that's a very unlikely story! We'll have to put the screws on that girl and tighten them till she opens up and gives us the truth. You could see she knows where all your money is all righty, or she never would have offered to give up that fifty. You better get at her in earnest and find out just what she knows. Of course I can't do a thing without evidence. And when she finds she has to produce *evidence* for all that pretty story she told, she may come across."

Lexie hurried upstairs to her own room and locked her door. She would not be haled into another questioning.

With swift fingers she put the room to rights, packed her few belongings that she had used during the night, and then came softly out and went upstairs to the one attic room, where Lucinda would have to sleep, for Lucinda would soon be here and there must be a place to receive her or she would vanish into thin air.

Lexie worked rapidly, pulling out bedding, making up the single bed that had stood sheathed in an old bedspread, unused, for four long years. A bright tear or two fell on the sheets as she smoothed them over the old mattress, thinking of her dear mother, who was gone away from her forever. What would her mother do if she were here and knew all that she was going through?

But she must not cry like this. Lucinda would be coming, and if she saw her crying it would in all probability bring on a tirade that would wreck all her plans for hoping to keep Lucinda with Elaine, even for a short time.

With firm resolve she wiped her eyes and hurried through the bed making, brought a pitcher of water to the little oak washstand, found fresh towels, a piece of soap. She remembered the tears with which she had laid away these things after her dear mother was gone, thinking that perhaps she would never unpack them again, not wanting to recall the precious days of which they reminded her.

She wiped the dust from a little old rocker, plumped up its patchwork cushion, straightened the small mirror, set the window shade straight, and then turned away. The room was as ready as she could make it.

As she went softly down the stairs she had a fleeting wish that she had dared to give Lucinda a room on the second floor. It was surely her due if she was willing to undertake the job of nursing this strange household while she was away. But she knew if she did, it would bring on a torrent of abuse and scorn from Elaine, and probably break up the whole affair even before it was begun. And perhaps Lucinda herself would have chosen the attic room, as a refuge from all that she would surely have to bear even for a little while under Elaine's domination.

So she went quietly down to the kitchen and began to get some lunch on the table. As she did so she heard the children trooping back to the house. They had been across the street playing with some children when she returned, probably sent by their mother to get rid of them while she transacted her business with her lawyer. Well, she would give the children some lunch. That would keep them still for a few minutes, and occupy her troubled, trembling hands.

But suddenly she had a feeling that she was not alone, and looking up she saw Bettinger Thomas standing in the open doorway with a fiendish grin on his face.

"Oh, so you thought you'd get by with a tale like that, did you? Well, you've got another guess coming. You can walk right in here, young lady, and come clean. Walk! Your sister wants you."

Chapter 6

The way had been long and hard, day after day under fire, night after night creeping furtively from bush to bush, from shadow to shadow, sometimes alone, and now and again in contact with others of the same group. It seemed endless, and Benedict Barron felt that he was scarcely human anymore. When there was food, coarse and poor for the most part, he wolfed it, and when there was no food he drew in his belt tighter and crept forward. He had to go on! It was an order! Just why he who had never been prepared for an existence of this sort had been selected for this special service, he couldn't tell. It was all a part of the bewildering medley of war; he was only a cog in a wheel that turned on and on relentlessly. He was nothing but an automaton whose business it was to move on and through, no matter how the fires burned, no matter how hot the ground was where he crawled, thankful only that he still had ammunition for a few more shots at the spitfires that peppered him so constantly, thankful that there was still enough blood left in his body to keep going.

And from time to time there would come a lull in the starlit nights when the fires for the moment had ceased to fall, and a cool breeze would blow. Not for long, but always it would remind him of that cool mountain town back in his homeland, and the little girl in blue swinging on the gate. Then he would remember his intention to write someday and tell her about how the thought of her had helped him through the horror of these days and nights. Someday he would surely write to her, if he lived to find quiet and a pen and paper, or even just a pencil and an old envelope.

Now there was a river in the way, a deep, wide river, and he was so tired. If he could only rest before trying to swim. Would he ever get across?

Then as he plunged into the dark, cold waters, his senses sharpened, and he seemed to be hearing words from long ago. His mother's voice, or was that his grandmother's, reading from the Bible? Ah! It was his grandfather, reading at family worship, a favorite chapter. The words seemed graven in his heart. He had heard them so many times when he was a little boy—strange that after so many years they should come back to him just now when he was going through this experience!

"When thou passest through the waters, I will be with thee; and through the rivers, they shall not overflow thee." Was He here? *"When thou walkest through the fire,"* ah, there was fire ahead, on the other side of that river, great walls of fire that he was expected to pass through— Was that God's voice speaking these

old familiar words, or just his old grandfather? He couldn't stop to reason now. It took all his energy to get across this wide dark water and keep his ammunition dry. But maybe God had let his grandfather ring out those words from heaven where he went long years ago, words that he knew God Himself uttered centuries ago. Could they perhaps have been meant for him down in this present modern-century stress, and his great need? These deep, dark waters were a terrible barrier. He could not get on, yet if God was here perhaps he would get through to his duty, and the fire on the opposite shore. The words went ringing on in his heart, in that strangely familiar voice: *"When thou walkest through the fire, thou shalt not be burned; neither shall the flame kindle upon thee."*

Were these words really being spoken to him, or was this just a trick of his imagination? His *sick* imagination?

And then the shore, and the fire raging close at hand! Ah! Now the *fire* again!

All through that awful night, the fiercest of them all, those words kept ringing when each man of them felt that the final test had come, the end had arrived. It was a fight to the death, and they expected death—in fact, almost welcomed the relief it would bring to have it over, just the end and the peace that death could bring. But as they fought through that night and the day that followed, and then as another night came down, grim determination, and courage that seemed to be born from above, had kept them going. Dropping down with pain and exhaustion, then rousing and in that vital energy that does not die in desperate need, going on—even when it had seemed to the enemy that they were conquered. "We must not lose," each said in his heart, "we must win! We're dying, yes, all right, but our death must win this war!"

So it was when the fire came over Ben Barron again, and that burning flame fell and went through his very being in one great, overwhelming stab. He dropped to the blackened hot sand in the deep night, as the fire burned itself out. There he lay through the darkness and pain and sickness that seemed but a lingering death.

But before his senses went out and left him in the blank darkness, he saw those mountains of home rise about him, felt the cooling breezes blow over this throbbing temples, and saw again the little girl in a blue dress swinging on the white gate, with a song on his lips and a light in her eyes. He found himself wondering in his pain: Was this heaven, and was he going in without any more preparation than this? Just a transfer from a battlefield to the Presence of God? Strange that he had never thought of that possibility before. Death? Yes. He had counted *that* cost, had been willing to go, but the thought of what would come after, going into God's presence, hadn't been presented to his mind, either by himself or by any sermon he had heard. And he didn't somehow feel ready for the Presence of God.

In his delirium he looked around—the little white gate— it was there yet, and the little girl in the blue dress. Could she perhaps be an angel? Would she remember him? The little girl on the gate, and the jaunty schoolboy? Would she perhaps remember him? She had helped him once as he passed on through these fires, could she help him again, now, in case this happened to be heaven he had reached? He hadn't written that letter to thank her for the help she had given in that wild, hot fire, by sending cool mountain breezes. He had surely meant to write that letter. Where was he now? *Was* this heaven? And how had he dared drift in here, if it was?

Dozing off into delirium, it came to him to wonder about the Presence of God, into which he was probably going. How would he be received there? Had he done a creditable job of fighting? Could he pass on his merits as a soldier or not?

But God didn't care about his courage as a soldier, did He? He was too big and too powerful Himself to care about a little thing a soldier could do, all in the way of his job, wasn't He? It wasn't as if he had done something outstanding, like bringing down his plane in the midst of a lot of Japanese soldiers and getting away with it. He was only a plain soldier, a fighter, going through fire. Was the fire all done, or would it come again and devour him before he was ushered into the Presence of God? Would God listen if he tried to tell Him how hot those fires had been? How hard it was to keep on with that bullet in his shoulder and the blood seeping away all the time making him weaker? Or did God know already? Perhaps He did. Those words from the Bible that his grandfather used to read seemed to ring that way. His mother used to think God knew and cared about everything and everybody. "His own," she used to say. "God cares for His own." But that meant people who had done something about it, "accepted Him" they used to call it in Sunday school many years ago. And he had never really done anything about it, not even joined the church when the other kids did. He didn't see standing up before the world and nodding assent to things he wasn't sure of, and then likely going out and acting just the same. The world wouldn't seem any difference in him, and would wonder why he did it anyway. But now, perhaps about to approach into the Presence of God, he wished he had. If he could say, "I'm a member of the old First Presbyterian Church in Nassau in good little old New York state where my grandmother lived, and where Grandfather was an elder and respected," would that make any difference when he was introduced to the Presence? But somehow he didn't seem to feel that even that would make him acceptable. He would be just one of many dead men, and what would God want of a dead church member anyway, since he had never thought about God, nor had Him in mind at all when alive?

If he only knew somebody who knew God well, perhaps that would make a difference. Of course his mother, and his grandmother, but they were already gone. He couldn't likely find them "up there" before he had to make his entrance into the Presence. That little girl in the blue dress? She was here somewhere. He had seen her in his vision. Child or angel? Would she help him? She had brought a memory of dew and cool mountain air down there on the hot battlefield. She had cooled his forehead—little Lexie. Had that been her cool little child-sized hand on his fevered brow? Would she introduce him to God? He was almost certain she knew God. If he could just see her again, he would ask her. Where had she gone?

In his delirium he tried to rise, but the pain in his shoulder made him faint and fall back. And then the world went out and he was a long time in the darkness. But it couldn't have been heaven, could it? Dark like that? He seemed to remember a verse he had learned in Sunday school, *"And there shall be no night there."* What would a place be like with no night? No falling fires? No bombs?

It was sometime during that night that the Lord came and

stood beside him, looking deep into his eyes, speaking gently: *"Ben Barron, I came with you, as I promised, through the water, and through the fire. I am the Lord your God. . .your Savior. If you want me I will go with you all the rest of the way. For I have loved you. You need not be afraid when I am with you."*

The wonder and the awe of it made him forget his pain. Could this be heaven, here on this scorched battlefield? If not, how was it that he was already in the Presence of God? Perhaps heaven was anywhere where God was? Or was he already dead of his wounds, and this was the heaven above?

Then even the thought of heaven vanished and he sank into oblivion. If there were more fires, he did not know it. Bombs bursting about him made no impression. If he thought at all, he thought he was dead.

He never knew when comrades came to him, touched his forehead, felt for his pulse, shook their heads.

"Take him up carefully, he's got a bad wound. He may not be last to get there."

"Do you think it's worthwhile to take him in? It seems to me only a matter of a few minutes. He many not live to get there. The room is limited you know, and there are so many who stand a better chance of getting well."

"Take him in," said the sergeant. "Give him his chance. He's a good guy. He'd do as much for you."

A murmur of assent, gentle handling, lifted and borne. He never knew any of it. If he had, he would have been grateful.

To the swarming semi-privacy of an overcrowded ward he was taken, in a foreign hospital, understaffed, undersupplied, and the weary rushing doctors and nurses with too many patients to attend did their best for him in the intervals between what they considered duty toward more important patients. There was so little hope for Barron. He had lain too long on the battlefield, too long in suffering and loss of blood.

Yet because God had come to him out there on that battlefield and given him a vision of Himself, and spoken a quiet word to his soul, he lived on unexpectedly; slowly, very slowly, he began to recover. It seemed incredible to the nurses, even to the skillful doctors who had done their poor best for him with the small equipment given them. All were astonished at the vitality that kept him alive. Until at last one day they began to understand that he was really coming back to life again.

"Well, Barron, you're going to get well!" the head doctor said to him one morning as he made his hurried rounds. "That's swell. You'll be begging us to let you go back to your outfit again pretty soon, I suppose."

Benedict Barron turned dreamy eyes to the doctor and studied his face, examined his smile, responded with a comprehending glint in his own eyes.

"Is the fire still there?" he asked after a minute. "Isn't it all over yet?"

The nurse murmured something about where he had been picked up, and the doctor frowned.

"Oh, I understand!" he said. "No, Barron, the fire in that particular spot you manned is out. Definitely out. They couldn't take what you gave 'em. The battle has moved farther on, up over the last mountain stronghold. It won't be long now till we have 'em completely licked!" He gave Ben Barron an affable grin, as well as he could control the poor tired muscles of his face, and Ben tried to smile back.

"Good boy!" said the doctor. "You're definitely on the mend

now, and I guess you're glad they don't need you to go through any more fires at present. It was a pretty tough job you had, man! I'm sure you'll do your best the rest of your life to forget all about it."

Ben Barron looked at him startled for a moment, with eyes that had so recently been seeing into another world. Then he slowly shook his head.

"No," he said softly, "I shall never forget. I don't think I want to forget."

"You don't *want* to forget?" said the doctor, astonished. "Why, that's strange. I'm sure if I had been there I would want to forget it. Why don't you?"

Ben Barron gave a slow smile that lit up his whole face.

"Because, you see, I met God out there. I had never met Him before. But I met Him, and He talked with me, and now I know Him. I shall never mind dying anymore because now I know the Lord."

The doctor studied him, startled, with a strange, unaccustomed tenderness about his mouth and moisture in his eyes, and then he said in a grave, husky tone: "Oh, I see!" and he turned away and cleared his throat. "Well, you wouldn't of course if you had that experience! Well, so long. I'm glad you're better. And I'll be seeing you."

Then he went out in the corridor where the nurses were talking together in low tones, and approached one.

"Say, have you noticed, is that guy in the last bed a bit touched in the head?"

"Why no, Doctor," said the nurse who had been attending Barron. "I hadn't noticed it. Why, did he seem wrong to you? He's a very quiet fellow."

"Yes, quiet enough perhaps, but he seems to have been seeing visions, or else he hasn't quite got back to normal yet. Keep a watch on him, will you, and let me know if there are any abnormal developments." And then he looked into the room once more furtively and gazed at Ben Barron as he lay there on his cot with his eyes closed and a look of real peace on his face. The doctor went on to other patients, wondering to himself, would having a vision of God bring peace to everyone who was wounded? *Was* there a God? He had always thought he didn't believe there was, but perhaps there was Something. Some Force or Power that worked on weary spirits through nerves that were worn to a frazzle. But that soldier really acted as if he was ready to go out again and fight. As if he really *wanted* to go if there was more fighting to be done. Pity they couldn't have more soldiers seeing visions if it worked like that on them. This Barron must be a regular guy.

From that day on Benedict Barron grew steadily better, and one morning he asked his nurse for writing materials.

"I want to write a letter," he said with an apologetic smile.

"Oh! Do you feel able?"

"Sure! I guess I can manage."

"Going to write to your mother?" she asked as she handed him a tablet and pencil, and arranged his pillows so he could write with the least exertion.

He gave her a sad little smile.

"One can't write letters to heaven," he said. "That's where my mother is now. She doesn't have to worry about me not getting home."

"Oh!" said the nurse with gentleness in her voice. "I'm sorry! I didn't know."

"Don't be sorry," he said. "I'm glad she's there. She hasn't had to worry about this war at all."

"You've got something there!" said the nurse gravely. But she asked no more questions about the letter. And when it was finished she took it to mail, and studied the address carefully. Miss Alexia Kendall, Nassau Park, N.Y., U.S.A. An oddly lovely name. Some girl he knew back in the United States. How interesting! She held the letter with respect in her face, and started it out on its long journey.

Ben Barron lay there on his hard narrow cot thinking over the words he had written, and wondering if they would ever reach the person to whom they were addressed.

He knew the words by heart because he had been framing them over and over, reframing them in his mind for days and days before he started to write. And so now he went over them again, questioning each word to be sure it was just the right one.

Miss Alexia Kendall,
Nassau Park, N.Y., U.S.A.

My dear Miss Kendall:

Do you remember one day when you were a little girl out swinging on the gate in front of your house and a high school boy came by and asked your name? You said it was Lexie, and I've been remembering it all these years, for I was that schoolboy.

I never saw you anymore because my mother and I went away in a few days, and I've never been back there, for my grandmother, whom we were visiting, died that summer. But I've never forgotten the picture of you swinging on the gate in the sunshine with a smile on your happy, little face. You wore a blue dress the color of your eyes, and there was dew on the grass at the side of the road, and sunshine on your curls, mountains in the distance.

I'm a soldier now, fighting to keep our world clean and good for little girls such as you were, and I've been through fire. One night when I lay wounded on the dark hot sand where the fire had raged, that picture of the mountains, and the dew, and you swinging on the gate with your happy face came to me, and it was like a breath of comfort from my home long ago. And then it seemed to me you came and laid your little cool hand on my hot forehead, and your hand was like my mother's touch. She's been gone five years now. Your touch helped me a lot, and I thought I'd like to tell you, and thank you for it. Do you mind?

Of course I know you're grown up now, and may have forgotten the laughing boy I was, whom you never saw but once. You may have moved away, or changed your name, and this may never reach you. You may have even left the earth. But if you are alive and get this, you'll forgive me for writing just to thank you, won't you? Because you really gave me comfort.

Gratefully yours,
Benedict Barron

Ben Barron fell asleep thinking over that letter with a great relief in his mind that he had accomplished it, for it represented to him a debt that he owed the little girl. And now, if there were still more fires for him to pass through, he was ready when they sent him out once more.

Chapter 7

Lexie looked at Bettinger Thomas with astonishment mixed with a deep anger. She was not a girl who was quickly angered, but she knew who this man was, what decent people thought of him, and felt herself insulted by his very tone. Should she go into the other room with him and put herself into his power for even another few minutes? Let Elaine see that she had had to give in? No, she couldn't do that. She could see that just polite dignity wasn't going to make this man understand that he couldn't bully her around this way. She had got to get out of his way, or get hold of somebody who could help and protect her. But who could that possibly be? She wasn't sure of any of the neighbors being at home. Most of them were doing defense work. Besides, Lucinda was due there at any time now, and she must be here to meet her, or all her morning's work would be wasted.

Lucinda would be no help in this matter. True, she had a sharp tongue and well knew how to use it, but that wouldn't get anywhere with Bett Thomas nor with Elaine either. It would simply turn Elaine hopelessly against Lucinda, and then where would she be? She didn't know of another person she could get to stay with Elaine.

All this was going through her mind like a flash while she stood and faced her hateful antagonist, and suddenly her mind was made up. She wasn't going into the living room with this man, and she wasn't going to talk finances over with Elaine in his presence. She didn't know just what she was going to do afterward, but she knew she was going to get out of the house for the moment.

The children were just outside the dining room door now, and arguing with all their might, making a great clatter. Lexie gave a quick glance at the table. Everything was on it they would need except some scrambled eggs she had intended making for them. They could come in and eat without the eggs.

She lifted her chin independently.

"Excuse me," she said almost haughtily, although there was nothing really haughty in Lexie's makeup except on an occasion when she felt desperate. "I couldn't come immediately. There is something I must do first."

Then she quickly opened the door on the clamoring children whose noise drowned any protest the lawyer was trying to make.

"Angelica, stop talking and bring the children in to their lunch. It is all here on the table. Now be a good girl and take care of Bluebell," and as they trooped in Lexie stepped out and shut the door sharply behind her, flying frantically down the walk and out into the street.

She turned sharply into a side street, running as if she were intending to hurry back in a moment, and when she heard the front door open and a man's voice calling her, she was out of sight. He couldn't know just which way to look. But she did not pause to watch if he would follow her. Of course he had his car there and his chauffeur. They could follow her. What should she do?

She knew that Mrs. Turnbull in the next street just back went early to her job in a riveting plant. No one would be at home there and she could slide through that yard and make her escape to the main highway that led down to the drugstore. If she got there she might be able to hide, or—oh, if there was only someone to whom she could telephone for help! And yet who was there, and what could she say when she found them? The man in the drugstore was no help. He was an old man, a stranger to her, a newcomer since Lexie went to college. But she dashed into the store, and was thankful there were two or three patrons in there talking with the proprietor. She went into the telephone booth and sat down, shutting the door and opening the telephone book, wildly searching her memory for some name she could call where she might at least ask advice—some of her father's or her mother's old friends, who for their sake would be kind enough to advise her what to do. But suddenly her eye fell on a name. Foster. That was a familiar name. Judge Foster was her father's old friend. Was he still alive, and would she dare call on him for advice?

Her hands were trembling as she turned the pages, and tears blurred into her eyes as she tried to think what to do. She simply could not go back and face that obnoxious man, and listen to his slanderous words about her dear mother!

Then there was the name Judge James Foster, and the old address where she had often gone as a little girl with her father to see his friend, and perhaps on business. Dared she call him? There were two addresses. His residence and his office. She would try the office first. Perhaps this wasn't the right thing to do, but what else was there for her?

Her fingers were trembling as she dialed the number, and her voice was shy and frightened as she asked the severe lady secretary at the other end of the wire for Judge Foster.

"Who is it, please?" came the response.

"Oh," said Lexie, "I—tell him it is the daughter of his old friend George Kendall. Tell him it is important, and I won't take but a minute of his time."

"Hold the wire, please," the severe voice said.

A moment more and she heard the man's kindly voice, an old, kind, dependable voice, and her frightened heart leaped thankfully.

"Oh, Judge Foster, is that you? Really *you*? This is Lexie. You wouldn't remember the little girl who used to come with her father, George Kendall, to your house sometimes, but surely you would remember my father?"

"Why certainly, I remember my dear old friend George Kendall, and *of course* I remember you, little Lexie! I remember you well. You used to have such a happy, little smiling face and sunny curls. Yes, I remember you, and have often wondered where you were. What can I do for you, Lexie? I'd like to see you again. Where are you?"

"I'm out at our little house. That is, I'm at a public telephone now, not far from the cottage. But I'm in awful perplexity, and I thought perhaps you would let me ask you a question or two, and tell me what you think my father would want me to do."

"Why, of course, little girl. What is the matter?"

"Well, you see, I've been working my way through college and am ready to graduate in June, but my half sister—you remember my father had another daughter—Elaine?"

"Yes, I remember Elaine. She was older, was she not? And she did not have a very happy face, though she was quite pretty."

"Yes," gasped Lexie, and felt that her counselor understood the situation fully. "Well, I came back here to put the house in shape to rent, and while I was here got a telegram from Elaine. Her husband was in the army, and word had come he was missing in action. She said she was sick and she was coming home with her three children. And before I could do anything about it she arrived with a trained nurse, who left as soon as they got here. Elaine seems to have no money and says she is too sick to do anything, and I am due back at my college where I have a job and important examinations to take, finals, you know. But the worst of it is that Elaine claims that our father told her when she was a little girl that there was a large sum of money left by her own mother for her and that when she was of age she would get it. And now she is obsessed with the idea that the money must have been left in my mother's trust and that Mother has spent it on me and herself."

"Impossible! Outrageous! Absurd! Of course there was nothing of the sort!" shouted the judge.

Lexie caught her breath.

"And now," she said, her voice trembling full of tears, "she says she is going to sue me for it. This morning she sent her oldest child to a neighbor and got her to telephone for an awful lawyer she has been corresponding with. He is a bad man, a man we knew in school when he was a boy. Bettinger Thomas. Perhaps you have heard of him."

"I should say I have!" said the judge, indignation in his voice. "He is a villain if there ever was one."

"Oh, I am so glad you understand!" gasped Lexie gratefully. "I was afraid you wouldn't. Well, he is at the house now. He has been asking me all sorts of insulting questions about what Mother did with that money, and putting words into my mouth to which he wants me to assent. I told him I knew nothing about any such thing, never heard my father speak of any such money. I said I knew he was in financial trouble when he died, and that Mother worked very hard to pay the funeral expenses and then to put aside money for us both to go to college. When Elaine married instead of going to college, she gave her share to her as a wedding gift, and started in to do extra evening work to get money for my college. But she died from overwork. I told him that, and then I went out of the room. But the lawyer chased me into the kitchen and insisted I come back to answer more questions. I made an excuse and slipped out of the house to this telephone. I'm very much ashamed to bother you, but I knew that you understood my father's ways and wishes, and that you would know if there was ever any money left to Elaine that we did not know about. I do so need someone to advise me what to do, how to answer that awful lawyer. He is very crude and tries to bully me into saying what he tells me to. Please, do you think I should answer him? And what should I say?"

"Say nothing, my dear! Just refuse to answer his questions. You say you have already told him you never heard of any such money, and so, if you cannot get away from him, then simply tell him: 'I have nothing further to say.'"

"Oh, thank you! I am so relieved," said Lexie with almost tears in her voice. "I had hoped to get away, but I can't go till the woman comes whom I hope I've secured to stay with Elaine. Do you think I ought to go at all when she is sick? You see, I have a job out there when I have finished my course."

"I certainly think you should finish your college course if possible," said the judge, "but I'd have to know more about this to rightly advise you. When and where can I see you? Should I come out there? Or can you come to my office?"

"Perhaps I could get away to come there," said Lexie. "I can't be sure whether we could talk at home without Elaine hearing everything. Of course she ought to hear everything, but how she would act when she heard it is another thing. Can I call you this afternoon and let you know if I am free to come?"

"You certainly can. I'll be here at four o'clock. And until then, if I were you I would keep away from that lawyer if you can. If that's impossible just sit quietly, calmly, and do not answer his questions, beyond saying once or twice, 'I'm sorry, that's all I have to say,' or, if necessary again, 'I do not know.' Don't lose your temper, or try to make smart answers. He has a way of nagging people into that. Just be calm. Even a vacant smile is better than getting excited or frightened, or making unwise answers. Wait until we can talk together. Keep your answers for a trial, if it has to come to a trial. But personally I don't think it will. Certainly I know all about your father's affairs. He told me everything when he was first taken sick, and asked me to look out for you. I'm so glad you came to me. I had rather lost sight of you."

"Oh, thank you, Judge. This is a great relief to me to know there is someone who will help if I get into trouble."

"You won't get into trouble, my dear. Not from that man. I'll look out for him. But your sister. Remember, she will be likely to do some goading of you also."

"Oh yes, she has already!" sighed Lexie.

"Well, don't be goaded. Just take it smiling as far as you can, and keep sweet. There is no point in getting angry, though I grant you there will probably be plenty to make you angry."

"Yes," said Lexie, "there will! But I'll just keep quiet and act dumb."

"That's the idea, child! And now, will you be all right till four o'clock? Well, call me up if anything unforeseen happens, and meantime don't worry."

Lexie went quietly back to the house and entered through the kitchen to the dining room where the children were squabbling over which should have the biggest cookie, and suddenly there came upon her a new strength to deal with the situation. She went over to Gerald and putting a firm hand about this wrist, folded her other hand over the cookie he had just taken from the wailing Bluebell.

"Oh no, we don't do that!" she said in a low voice. "Gentlemen don't snatch cookies from babies. And you are the only gentleman of the party, so you must act like one."

Bluebell had ceased to howl and was listening, and suddenly broke into a joyful smile.

"Oh, is this a party?" she inquired happily.

"Why yes, I suppose you might call it a little party," said Lexie. "Suppose you try to act as if you were at a party, and that will make it a party, you know."

"*She* don't act nice at parties," said Gerald, pointing his crummy finger at Bluebell.

"Oh, but gentlemen don't try to bring out other people's faults," said Lexie. "Suppose you pass the plate to Bluebell and say 'Bluebell, will you have another cookie?'"

Gerald was intrigued by this suggestion and took the plate with zest, imitating Lexie's little speech with an effective tone until Angelica giggled.

"Oh, but you mustn't laugh when a gentleman is being polite," said Lexie. "Gerry did that very nicely. Now, Gerry pass the plate to Angel."

Gerald entered into the game eagerly, and Angelica went one better and reached gracefully for her cookie, with a slight bow, and said: "Thank you very kindly, brother!"

They were just in the midst of this little game when the door opened and there stood the lawyer, pompously glaring at Lexie.

"So!" he said irately. "You keep your sister waiting while you play a game with the children. Is that your important duty that hindered you from responding to your sister's urgent call for you?"

Lexie looked up coldly.

"I'll be there in a moment," she said, in a tone of decided dismissal.

"I'll say you will!" said the man, striding over to where she stood and laying hold of her arm to draw her along.

But just as he did so Bluebell reached out her short, fat arm to snatch Gerald's cookie and unheeding, knocked against and swept her brimming glass of milk across the edge of the table and straight on to the immaculate suit of the lawyer, deluging the front of his coat and pouring milk down his perfectly creased trousers.

The fat lawyer's hand dropped suddenly from Lexie's rigid arm, and with an angry cry he stood back and looked down at himself in dismay and fury.

Then he lifted his eyes to the staring baby, who was giggling delightedly at the catastrophe she had wrought, and a look like a thundercloud passed over his fat, flabby face.

"You little *brat*!" he said furiously. "You little *devil you*!" and he lifted his heavy hand and administered a sound slap on the round pink cheek of the baby. The sound reached into the next room to the excitable mother, who was languishing on the couch, waiting for her annoying sister to appear. But when she heard the resounding slap she sprang furiously to her feet and dashed quite agilely over to the door, which she opened with a snap.

"What are you doing, Lexie? Slapping my baby? You outrageous girl! To think you would vent your fury on a baby! A poor little innocent. What can she have done to deserve a cruel slap like that?"

Her indignant tones were drowned by Bluebell's first heartrending shriek of horror at the chastisement she had suffered at the hand of a stranger. It was the "stranger" part that was to her the most terrible, added to the fact that she hadn't at all intended to douse the gentleman's elegant suit. There were plenty of times when she *had* intended to do terrible things, when she *should* have been chastised, but this was not one of them.

In fact, it hadn't entirely dawned upon her that she was in the least to blame for this catastrophe. She had only been trying to snatch Gerald's cookie, and the deluge had been a mere incidental consequence. So why the slap? Besides, it hurt! And as this fact became more and more evident to her stinging facial nerves, Bluebell howled the louder. In fact, one might call the noise she made a roar, drowning everything else completely out.

Lexie opened her mouth to deny any part in that slap, but saw there was no use. It would not even get across while the child was crying. It was maddening. Elaine stood acting the plaintive mother part, flashing her eyes at her sister, casting apologetic glances at the lawyer who was wholly engrossed in mopping up his new suit with a pair of expensive, imported handkerchiefs, and ignoring everything else. Nobody was doing a thing to comfort the distressed baby.

Then suddenly Lexie caught a glimpse of Bluebell's puckered lip, and came over with a soft old napkin snatched quickly from the sideboard linen drawer, dipped it in a glass of water from the table, and gently wiped the bruised cheek that distinctly bore the red imprint of heavy fingers, with a wide bleeding scratch where a sharply manicured fingernail had ripped the delicate skin.

Elaine watched with jealous eyes.

"Oh yes," she sneered mockingly, "you're making a great show of trying to be kind and gentle, now that you've slapped her! Even brought the blood! That's you all over, Lexie! Slap an innocent little baby till the blood comes and then pretend to be so sorry for her! *Slap* a *baby*! How *could* you? For what, I'd like to know? And then pet her up in the presence of others!

I'll teach you to slap my child! How *dare* you!"

Suddenly Angelica spoke up shrilly.

"Aunt Lexie *didn't* slap Bluebell! It was that man who slapped her." She pointed an accusing finger at Bettinger Thomas. "Aunt Lexie was standing over on the other side of the table, and that man was trying to make her go in the other room. Bluebell reached over to snatch Gerry's cookie and knocked her glass of milk over on his pants, and it made him mad. He slapped her hard, and *scratched* her. I *saw* him! He's a bad old man! That neighbor-lady told me he was. She said you oughtn't to have him come here, he was a bad man! She said your muvver wouldn't like it!"

"Be still, Angelica! You're a naughty girl to say things like that! I've told you not to repeat things the neighbors say. The neighbors are bad people to talk that way! And of course it was your aunt Lexie that slapped Bluebell. You mustn't contradict me!"

"No, it wasn't Aunt Lexie that slapped her. I saw it. It was that bad old man. He was mad because his pants got all milky."

Bettinger Thomas lifted a very red face and angry eyes. There was no apology in his glance, only annoyance.

"This is a new and very expensive suit!" he declared in furious explanation. "I am attending an important luncheon at the country club this morning, and now my suit is ruined! It is all that girl's fault, too. If she had come into the other room when I told her you wanted her, this never would have happened. I am sorry. I shall have to put the price of this suit on your account. It was quite expensive!"

"Well, if it was Lexie's fault she will of course want to pay for it."

"Yes, and it won't be the only thing she has to pay for if she

122

keeps on in the way she has started. It may be that we shall have to resort to having her arrested and put under charge if she continues to refuse to tell what she knows."

Lexie caught her breath softly and closed her trembling lips. Then she remembered what her friend the judge had said. She must not talk. And certainly she must not cry.

She closed her lips tight in a think line. She put her mind on the effort not to look angry. Anger at present, and in this company, could not help. Neither must she look frightened. She wasn't frightened now that Judge Foster was her friend and was going to help her through this trouble.

The trembling that was in her fingers came from her frightened heart. It was crying out to God to help her, to show her what to do, to save the situation for her, since she did not know what to do herself. Crying out to God as she would have cried to Judge Foster if he had been there. She was glad that God was always present. She could call to Him when she had not time to reach her father's friend the judge.

And then, most unexpectedly, Lawyer Thomas stopped mopping his elegant clothes and gave a quick glance at his watch.

"I shall have to ask you to excuse me," he said looking at Elaine. "I must go home at once and change to another suit. I shall have to hurry, as it is most important that I should be on time. You will excuse me, won't you? I'll try to return tomorrow morning, or at the latest the next day. Meantime get all the evidence together that you can find, and put the pressure on your sister. She is the key to it all, you know. But I'll have to say good-bye now."

"Oh, but I can't possibly wait till tomorrow!" wailed Elaine in distress.

"Sorry, my dear lady, but tomorrow will be the very first moment I can spare, if indeed I can come then. I'll bear you in mind, however, and come as soon as possible. And now brace up and get your evidence. I can't do anything without that, you know. Good morning!" And hastily the obnoxious lawyer went out the door and down to his car.

Chapter 8

Elaine stood appalled and angry as he vanished, and then she turned her fury on Lexie: "Well, now I suppose you think you've done it! You hateful, cruel thing, you! Torment a poor, sick sister this way! Come up with little trifling, silly devices to have your own way and get rid of my nice, kind lawyer. Spoil his wonderful new suit for him, and send him off before we were done with our business! I hadn't told him half the things I wanted him to know. And you *intended* this to happen, of course. I *know you*! You always did work against me whenever you could. I remember that since you were a mere baby! You and your mother before you! Oh, why did my poor mistaken father ever marry that scheming, determined woman?"

Lexie stood there for a moment and listened aghast while Elaine rattled on. Long ago she had formed the habit of letting

Elaine finish entirely whatever she had to say on a subject, for she had found by bitter experience it was the only way ever to get done a matter. If you interrupted her she would only go back and say it all over again. So, remembering, she stood quite still and waited until Elaine had talked herself out. And then suddenly Elaine, troubled by Bluebell's low wail that kept on bleating from her cookie-crumbed lips, turned toward her baby.

"You poor child! Poor little baby! Her own auntie slapped her when she hadn't done anything at all! Naughty auntie! Aunt Lexie doesn't love you. She doesn't care how much she hurts you."

Lexie winced at that, telling the baby lies about her, but she knew if she tried to speak, her indignation would come to the front and take control of her, and that must not be. So she kept still, until finally Elaine turned toward her again with a direct question.

"Tell me, Lexie, just *why* did you slap the child so unmercifully? I can't understand it. I thought you were always kind to children. That was the reason I felt perfectly safe in coming to you while I was so sick. I couldn't look after the children myself. Why did you do it?"

"But I didn't slap her," said Lexie quietly. "I wasn't even near her. I was trying to get away from that man. He had hold of my arm and was dragging me across the room. What made you think I slapped her, Elaine?"

"Of course you slapped her, Lexie. There is no use in lying about it, even if you are angry. Have a little sense."

"No, Aunt Lexie *didn't* slap Bluebell, Elaine," Gerald said. "That old man slapped her. I saw him! He was mad 'cause his pants got all milky."

"Yes, I see you have bribed those children to side with you. I call that pretty rank for you not only to slap the baby but bribe my children to lie for you!"

"Stop!" said Lexie. "Elaine, you must be crazy to say such things. Now, I'm not going to talk any more about this. I have told you the truth. I *didn't* slap her, and if you won't believe it, I can't help it. Suppose we just forget it all and try to get this family straightened out. Would you like some lunch, Elaine? Why don't you go and lie down again and I'll bring you a tray?"

"No, *thanks*! I don't want you to bring me a tray. I'm sure I couldn't eat anything you brought. Where is that nurse you were going to get?"

"She will be here in a little while, as soon as she can get packed. Do you feel able to sit down here at the table and take just a bite? How about a glass of milk?"

"No!" said Elaine sharply. "I detest milk. You know it always disagrees with me. I want some coffee. Where *is* that nurse? *Where* did you locate her? At one of the hospitals or an agency?"

"No," said Lexie quietly, "there wasn't one to be had at any hospital or agency. The hospitals are suffering for lack of nurses themselves. But I finally found a woman who was about to take another job. She is an elderly woman and doesn't mind being where there are children. I think perhaps she'll be willing to stay if you are all very pleasant to her."

"*Pleasant* to her! The *idea*! *Really*, I don't care to have a nurse like that! I want a regular trained nurse, a graduate nurse! A young, strong woman! I can't endure an elderly woman with set ways that has to be coddled."

"Well, I'm sorry, Elaine, I tried every place on your list, and there wasn't one. They all gave me the same story. The young, strong nurses have all gone to war, and the hospitals are suffering for lack of them. I think for the present everybody will have to put up with what they can get, or get on without help."

"Oh fiddlesticks!" said Elaine angrily. "I'm quite sure I can find a regular nurse if I try myself. And as for this woman, if I don't like her, I shan't stand her for a minute, do you hear?"

Lexie turned hopelessly away from her sister and went toward the kitchen.

"Suit yourself," she said with a sigh. "I've done the best I could. Now I'll go and make you another cup of coffee. There is just a little left in the canister. We'll have to use it carefully, for we can't get any more till someone goes to the ration board."

"Oh, how utterly silly!" said Elaine, walking languidly into the living room and flinging herself on the couch. "I certainly wish I had stayed in the West. I never had any trouble like this there. My housekeeper looked after all such annoying questions. I wish I had stayed there!"

And Lexie, in the kitchen, could not fail to hear, and echoed in her heart with a sigh: *I certainly wish you had!* But she faithfully shut her lips tight and did not let the words out.

By the time Lexie had the coffee ready and took it in to her sister, Elaine was settled on her couch again with a handkerchief in her hand and great tears rolling down her cheeks. She paused in her grief long enough to announce again to her sister that if she didn't like the new nurse, she didn't intend to keep her, and Lexie needn't think she would.

"Well, that's all right, Elaine," said Lexie, "but, you see, I have to go away at least for a few days, and wouldn't it be well for you to have somebody who could at least get you something to eat while I am gone?"

"You have to go *away*! How can you? You wouldn't leave me in this helpless condition, would you?"

"That's it, Elaine," said Lexie trying to be patient. "I shall probably *have* to go. If there was any way to avoid it for the present, or to put it off a few days, I certainly would. I'm not sure I can. But while I'm gone, there ought to be somebody here with you—that is, if you intend staying."

"Staying?" yelled Elaine. "What else can I do? I'm here, and I've spent practically all the money I have to get here. Of course I'm staying. I never thought you would dare go away and leave me alone."

"I'm not leaving you alone, Elaine. I've got a woman who is entirely able to make you comfortable if you will let her, and I'm just suggesting that you'll have to put up with her, even if she doesn't happen to take your fancy, at least for a little while."

"Well, I like that! Talking to your poor sick sister that way! What would your precious mother think of that kind of talk, I'd like to know."

"I'm sorry, Elaine, but this seems to be necessary. Even if I don't finish college I've got to go back and get my things, settle up my bank account, report about the job I have, and the job I'm supposed to get after I'm through."

"Oh, that's all nonsense!" said Elaine petulantly. "That's just an excuse. That could all be done by mail or telephone."

"Elaine, I have no money to telephone until I go back and get it. There are people for whom I have been doing things who owe me, and I would likely never get it at all until I went. It may be that I won't have to stay long, but while I am gone there must be somebody here with you. So please don't antagonize her."

"Oh *indeed*! Well, I'll just let you know that I don't intend to toady to anybody if I don't like them. And as for your jobs, you can send them postcards that you can't come back. I can lend you money enough for that myself."

Lexie gave her sister a steady look, but said no more, and began to tremble for the meeting of Lucinda with Elaine. Would Elaine remember her? If she only wouldn't, perhaps they could get by for a little while, but probably there was no such luck as that.

Lexie made short work of her own lunch, and putting the kitchen to rights after it. Meanwhile, she tried to think her way through the rest of the day, though she ought not to make any definite plans until she had talked with Judge Foster.

It was just as she was putting away the last dishes that a little boy came to the back door and peered in.

"That you, Miss Lexie?" he said in a low tone. "Say, Mr. Maitland sent me over from the drugstore to tell you there's someone on the telephone wants to speak to you. Name's Foster."

"Oh!" said Lexie softly. "All right, I'll come right away."

She wiped her hands on the roller towel and dashed softly out the door, running her hands through her soft brown, curly hair as she ran, for she knew it was awry. She wasn't vain, but she knew the neighbors would probably be looking out their windows, and she hated to look disheveled.

It was Judge Foster.

"Lexie, I find I have to drive out your way at three o'clock to see a business friend who is very ill. It is important that I talk with him before tomorrow's court session. Could I pick you up somewhere near your home and take you along? Then we could talk. It isn't a long drive, but it's about the only time I can possibly spare today. Will that be all right with you?"

"Wonderful!" said Lexie. "I could meet you at the drugstore. Then Elaine needn't know where I have gone. I'll tell her later, but I don't want to be questioned till I have talked with you."

"That's the best thing to do. Yes, I remember where that store is, corner of Main and Cooper Streets, isn't it? Be there sharp at half past four, and I think I can promise to get you back in an hour."

"All right. I'll be there!" said Lexie with a ring of relief in her voice, and then she hurried back to the house again, wondering what she should do when she had to leave if Lucinda hadn't come yet. But of course that would have to settle itself somehow. Perhaps it would be just as well for Lucinda to come while she was gone, although Elaine *might* send her off. There was no telling. But perhaps she would come before.

Back at the house she found Elaine had cried herself to sleep, which relieved the situation for the time being so that she could finish putting the kitchen in order. Then she sat down at the kitchen table and wrote a list of things she must attend to before she went away to college, if indeed she found she could get away at all.

It was just as she finished her list that she heard a truck drive up to the door, and hurrying out found that Lucinda had arrived. She could dimly hear the children's voices across the street arguing with the neighbor's children, and was thankful that for the moment they were absent.

The truck driver, who was an old friend of Lucinda's,

accommodatingly carried Lucinda's trunk to the attic, and Lexie took Lucinda up and was glad that she was pleased with her simple little room.

"It isn't much of a place to put you, Lucinda," she apologized, "but I thought you would rather be up here by yourself. You would have more privacy. There's nothing else up there but the big storeroom, and no chance for you to be interrupted when you want to rest."

"Oh, it suits me fine!" said Lucinda. "I'm real pleased to have this much of a room over me so soon. It's just Providence, I can't help thinking. Somehow He always did look out for me when I got in a jam. At least it must be Providence, for there isn't anybody else bothering about what becomes of me. So it must be Providence. And now, Miss Lexie, I'll be changing my dress, and then ya can show me the ways about, and I'll take over. You just tell what you want of me and go on about your business. You'll want supper got, and anything else you have in mind just write me a line on a paper. I can read real good, and then I needn't trust to me forgettery."

So Lexie told her briefly about the location of rooms and that there wasn't very much in the house to eat until she could go to the ration board.

"Oh, we'll make out," said Lucinda. "I know more ways to get meals out o' nothin' than you can shake a stick at, and good enough for that Elaine one, too. Get me a lemon, an' a mushroom, an' a pimento an' I'll make out. Me hand's right in it when the pocketbook and the pantry is low."

"Oh Cinda! That sounds good!" said Lexie with relief. "I've been so worried. You see, I came down from college for just a day, and we haven't any ration cards yet. I haven't had time to find out where to go for them even, and I've got so many things to do. This afternoon I've got to see an old friend of Father's and find out about some business matters, and I'm not sure whether I can get in touch with that ration board yet or not."

"Don't worry, little girl," said Cinda. "Trust me! I'll scare up some kind of a meal, and if she don't like it, she can lump it. But I'll risk but what I can make something she'll like. What have you got on hand? Any canned goods?"

"There's some fruit of Mother's canning, a few cans of soup and vegetables, I guess, too. I haven't looked them over very carefully. There's been so much else to do. But there are eggs and potatoes, and a loaf of bread."

"Well, I'll make out with those for a time or two, and if worse comes to worst, there's me own ration card. I been savin' up a point or two, and a bit coupon fer coffee and sugar. You can take *them* down and cash 'em in. Being out on a case, and then having to move, I didn't have any chance to cook. Get half a pound of butter and a bit of meat, even a quarter of a pound ground will go a good ways. I guess I could find me way to the stores if I got stuck whiles you are gone. But anyhow, where are the children you was telling about? Can't they go on errands?"

"Why, they're mere babies, all but Angelica, and they don't know the way anywhere yet. You better not count on that. They are across the road playing with a neighbor's children, but I hear them fighting. I suppose I ought to go and get them, and introduce them to you, but I'm afraid they'll bother you a lot while you're trying to work."

"That don't make any matter. I'm here to work, and to stand what's to stand. You run along and I'll make out. Don't bother about the children. They'll turn up. If they don't, I'll go hunt 'em. And you needn't bother to wake up that Elaine. Leave her lay an' sleep. I'll interjuice meself, and mebbe it'll be that much better fer results. Got any lemons here? I'll make her a nice cold drink. Too bad you haven't got any ice. But we'll manage. You run along. Here! I'll get those coupons for you before I go down."

Very quietly they went downstairs, and Elaine was either still asleep or simulating it very well.

Lucinda stood for an instant in the doorway looking keenly toward the invalid, and then with nodding head and set lips went her way, following Lexie to the kitchen. Lexie showed her all the meagre stores, whispered a moment with her, and then caught up her hat and coat left on a chair in a convenient shadowed corner and went out.

She did not go out the front gate nor take their street, but crossed the back fence into the fields and got herself down to the drugstore without the danger of Elaine's discovering she was going out. She certainly didn't want Elaine to know about this interview with Judge Foster. It would bring on a tirade she was certain.

Lexie thought she was far ahead of the time named, but she had scarcely reached the corner next to the drugstore when she saw the judge's car coming from the opposite direction and drawing up to the curb.

She hadn't been at all sure she would know him, for it had been a number of years since she had seen him. But when he swung out of the car and glanced around him and toward the store, she knew him at once. She ran toward him just as she used to do when she was a little girl downtown with her father, running to greet her father's friend.

Oh, the judge's hair was a little whiter, and the fine lines around his eyes were graved a little deeper, but there was the same keen twinkle in the wise blue eyes, the same kindly look about the strong, smiling lips.

He whirled to look at her, and the smile beamed out.

"Little Lexie!" he exclaimed, reaching out a hearty hand to grasp hers. "You haven't changed a mite, only grown a little taller! Hop in, little girl, and let's get on our way. This is a beautiful day, and I'm anticipating a pleasant ride. I'm sorry it had to be your troubles that brought us together, but I'm mighty glad to be in touch with you again. And now, suppose we get the business out of the way first, and then we can really enjoy our ride. Suppose you begin at the beginning and tell me the whole story. Begin when your mother died, and tell me what you have been doing since."

So Lexie told her simple story, and the wise old man watched her, studying her lovely expression as she talked.

When she came to her college life, he asked a few questions that put her whole present situation before him. Working her way through by doing little menial tasks here and there, and now and then tutoring some other student. She told it all most briefly, answering the judge's questions in a few words, and hastened on to the main issue, the story of Elaine's arrival with her three children just as she herself was about to leave to go back to college, and then the amazing claim of her sister, and her demand for money.

Very carefully now she answered every question the judge put to her and then settled back in the car.

"That's all," she said with a troubled sigh. "Now, what shall I do? I meant to go back to college today at the latest, but I had to stay till Lucinda came. She wouldn't have known where things were nor what to do. I knew I could trust Lucinda, but she had to understand."

"I see! That was wise. And now, you say she has come?"

"Yes, she came just a few minutes ago."

"And how did Elaine take it?"

"She's still asleep, or seems to be. She doesn't know I've gone away. I slipped out the back door and across the fields."

"Good girl! And now, let's see about this money business. You're right, my dear. Your father didn't leave any money at all, not that I know of. Your mother finished paying for the little house you own. That's right, isn't it? I thought so. I have all the papers that showed what your mother spent since your father died. She took great care to send me everything, as it came on the calendar, and I have kept them all together in a safe-deposit box, so they are safe and can be used in court if they should ever be required. But really, my dear, I don't believe it will ever come to that. I think if it seems to be getting that far I will have a little talk with that rascal of a lawyer your sister has secured, and show him just where he can get off. I know he is a rascal, and I know too many things about what he has done to trust him for one minute. Of course he is very tricky, but he probably has been made to feel that there is some large sum of money involved, or he never would have wasted his precious time monkeying with it. Has your sister by any means told him how much she thinks is involved in this case?"

"I'm afraid she has," said Lexie with trouble in her eyes. "But I don't know how much she is claiming. She seems to think I have it hidden away somewhere and am using it for myself. They are going to sue me for it, and he has done his best to make me own up to whatever he says. He even told Elaine that if I kept on refusing to talk, the quickest way to make me tell the truth would be to have me arrested and regularly charge me with being a party to the theft. He said that would bring me to terms quicker than anything he knew."

"Yes," said the judge gravely, "that sounds like his tactics. But, my dear, there is a great deal of boasting about that. I scarcely think he would try a thing like that with you. However, we'll take steps to make that thing impossible. And now, my dear, if I were you I would go to college right away. Tonight, if there is a train, or certainly tomorrow morning, and see what arrangements you can make there, in case your sister is really as ill as she makes out and you find you have to be at home for a time. But anyhow I would go at once and get what matters you have to attend to out there in shape, so you will be ready for any emergency. Perhaps that, too, will avert a clash about this maid you think she won't like. If she is sick she'll have to accept whatever services she has till she can get in touch with you again. And meantime you can put your business in order so you can return if necessary."

"Oh," said Lexie with relief. "You think I have a right to go? You think my father and mother wouldn't blame me for running off and leaving Elaine sick? And all her naughty little children to be looked out for by a woman who couldn't possibly love them enough to make it really pleasant for them?"

"Yes, I think you are right to go and get your affairs arranged. I think Elaine needs to understand you have to. I certainly think your mother and father would want you to do this. Maybe you can't stay there, of course, but if not, there may be some way for you to go on studying and run back a few days for examinations. That can probably be arranged. And about your job, well, I don't know. I might be able to get that work transferred to this vicinity. And again, I might be able to offer you something even better in my office. It depends on the movements of the woman who is now my secretary. I might let you take over later. However, we will look into this and see how things come out. Certainly I won't let you down, my dear."

"Oh, that would be wonderful!" said Lexie wistfully. "But I never have had experience as a secretary. I'm afraid I wouldn't be worth much to you."

The judge looked at her with a kindly smile.

"Don't worry! I fancy you could learn, and I often have more than one secretary. Now, here we are at the house where I have to stop. I'll let you sit in the car and wait if you don't mind. There are a few magazines in the backseat. Help yourself. And I won't be any longer than I can help."

But Lexie did not spend any time reading magazines. She had too much to think about, too much to be thankful for in that she had found her father's old friend and he was so inclined to be helpful. She sat still and thought her way ahead.

She decided not to tell Elaine anything about Judge Foster. She was sure she would immediately tell Bett Thomas, and there was no telling how he might involve Judge Foster. She must move as cautiously as possible.

But anyway she would have to see what had happened during her absence before she decided definitely what she would do. It was rather late for her to get the night train of course. But if she could slip off in the morning before Elaine was awake, it certainly would be easier. That would have to depend largely on whether there had been a terrible eruption between Lucinda and Elaine. If there had, and Cinda refused to stay, she would have to wait and make some other arrangement, but she hoped she had made the woman understand how necessary she was to her plans, at least for a few days.

But as she neared the house she began to have an uneasy fear of what might have happened while she was away. Oh, what should she do if Elaine had sent Cinda away? There wasn't anybody, not *any*body that Lexie knew of who would be willing to come as Cinda had, without pay, and who would stand Elaine's imperiousness even temporarily, like Cinda.

So as she bade Judge Foster good-bye, and promised to let him know at once how things came out, a shadow was beginning to creep into her eyes and a worry into her heart.

Chapter 9

Lucinda was in the kitchen beating up biscuits with some prepared flour she found among Lexie's purchases. That didn't take shortening, of which there was as yet none in the house, and it would provide something more interesting than the continual diet of dry toast without butter. She was trying to think what she could make that would be tasty and take the place of meat, which of course had not been purchased yet. Then suddenly she discovered a package of spaghetti and cheese preparation that ought to make an attractive dish. If Elaine didn't happen to like it, why, that was just too bad. It was the best she could do. But she hastened to make a pitcher of good strong lemonade. It didn't take much sugar, and would be heartening for an invalid perhaps—if she really was an invalid, Cinda had her doubts. She knew Elaine of old.

She wished, as she finished stirring the concoction, that she had some ice, considered going to the neighbor's to beg a tiny piece and decided against it. Instead she wet an old napkin and folded it about the pitcher setting it in the open window where there was a good breeze. Give it a little time in that breeze and the evaporation from the wet cloth would make the lemonade almost as cold as if it were iced.

Then she set about preparing the table as if she were expecting a real dinner with all the fixings. There was lettuce. There were apples and nuts, a little jar of mayonnaise dressing, and some cottage cheese, too. She could make a fine salad with those. Even a raisin or two might be added to give it character. Cinda tramped quietly about that little kitchen quite pleased with herself, thankful that the children had not yet appeared. Although she was not unmindful of them, and prepared three little jelly tarts for them when they should arrive.

The tarts were in the oven baking when Cinda heard a sharp call:

"Lexie! What on earth are you doing out there in the kitchen so long? Aren't you *ever* coming in to *see* me? Do you realize that I haven't had a mouthful to eat since breakfast? *Lexie!* Where *are* you! *Why* don't you answer me?"

"Coming!" sang out Cinda in as good an imitation of Lexie's voice as she could manage. She stepped to the window, flung off the napkin from around the pitcher, placed it on the tray already prepared, with a couple of vanilla wafers on the thin old china plate beside the pretty crystal glass. Then she tramped into the living room bearing her offering.

Elaine looked up startled.

"Oh! Who are you?" she said coldly. "And where is my sister? Didn't she hear me call her?"

Cinda drew up a little table to the couch and laid her tray upon it quite within reach of the invalid. Then she poured a nice glass of lemonade into the glass from the frosty pitcher before she answered.

"Why, I'm the new nurse," she said pleasantly—more pleasantly than she felt. "Your sister had to go on some errands. She'll be back in a little while. You can tell me anything you want done."

"Oh! Indeed!" said Elaine. "You're the nurse, are you? Where's your uniform? I like my nurses to wear their uniforms. I'm very particular about that. Which hospital do you come from?"

Cinda looked the younger woman down, contempt beginning to dawn in her eyes until suddenly she remembered her promise to Lexie, and what she said in her heart, too! She lifted her belligerent chin proudly and spoke in honeyed tones.

"I'm not from no hospital. I'm just a private nurse. And very *special*! I been on duty too long to be dependent on hospitals and agencies and the like. And I don't hold with wearing uniforms fer everyday work, especially in small houses. I think they're out of place and too pretentious. A uniform's all right if you don't do nothin' but nurse, but if ya havta cook some, and look after the family, it makes too much work to be washing uniforms all the time. Me, I didn't bring me uniforms with me. I didn't think they'd fit the job. Not unless there's two or three servants to help with the work. Is that drink cold enough? Sorry I didn't have ice, but ya see, we haven't got—that is to say, organized yet—and I understand the ice men don't come around every day during these wartimes. It's awful, ain't it, what we havta put up with, but then it's war, and we gotta be patriotic. Is there sugar enough in the glass? I didn't dast use too much because I wasn't sure just when yer ration card would come through, an' I wouldn't want ya to be without sugar in yer tea. Could I be gettin' anything else fer ya?"

Elaine turned and looked at the woman.

"Haven't I seen you before?" she said. "What's your name?"

It was just at that moment that Lexie arrived at the back door, and Cinda turned and hurried away.

"Excuse me," she said. "I think I hear somebody at the kitchen door," and she vanished from the room, leaving Elaine's question hanging in midair.

Then Lexie breezed in quietly and pleasantly, bearing in her countenance enough of the cheer from her hour with the judge to give her an appearance of authority.

"Oh Elaine," she said in an interested tone, "you've had a nice long sleep, haven't you? Do you feel better? I hope you do, and that you're going to be able to eat a little supper. You've scarcely eaten a thing since you came."

"There hasn't been anything fit to eat!" said Elaine grumpily. "It does seem to me that you had time enough after my telegram arrived to get some decent food in the house, when I took all that trouble to let you know I was coming."

Lexie drew a deep breath and tried to smile.

"Sorry, Elaine, but I didn't dare do anything about it until I was sure you were going to stay more than an hour or two. I didn't think you would be satisfied with a closed-up house and everything packed away, and I thought it best to wait till I could talk to you about it. You see, I didn't understand that you would feel you had to stay here when you found that I was not living here."

"No," said Elaine. "I didn't figure on anything like that, but I knew you would *have* to stop college when I got here and you found what you were up against."

"I see," said Lexie, refusing to argue the matter. "Well, now suppose we put the matter aside and try to see what we can make out of things as they are. It really isn't worthwhile to argue about it. Are you ready for something to eat yet, or do you want me to go and get the children? It seems they must be tired and hungry by this time, and I think the new nurse has dinner almost ready, if I may judge by the nice pleasant odors that are filling the house. I think I'd better go out and see if she found everything, or maybe needs my help in anything. I'll look for the children, too, and bring them back with me. I'll be back in a minute!" And Lexie vanished, not heeding her sister's fretful, insistent call.

She soon came back with the three children trooping after her and escorted them to the dining room, where their mother heard them clamoring happily that they wanted "some o' that, an' that, an' a *lot* of real honey." Real honey in a honeycomb, Lexie had bought the last time she went to the store, and it went well with the hot biscuits Cinda had made and the milk that filled their glasses.

So Elaine called in vain for her sister, and finally started to rise and find out why Lexie didn't answer her call, but came face-to-face with Cinda and such a tempting-looking tray that she suffered herself to be arranged with a table by her side and a napkin tucked in at her neck and a plate put within her reach. There was a cup of real coffee filling the room with its delicate aroma. For Cinda had some precious coffee from her own rationing, which she had brought with her, and had used a tiny bit of it to "work her lady" as she told herself grimly. She wanted with all her might to help Lexie, brave little Lexie, and she determined if good food and giving up her own cup of coffee now and then would help, she would do it. Lexie wasn't going to be the only one to sacrifice.

So Elaine ate her supper quiet, interestedly, and Lexie and the children ate theirs in comparative peace, save for the gossip that Angelica and Gerald retailed from time to time, concerning the misdeeds of "that bad old lawyer" who had come to see their mother that morning and of whom they had that afternoon overheard not a little that was not intended for their ears.

But Lexie managed those children into bed very soon, for they were really tired from hard play, climbing trees and digging in gardens where they shouldn't have been, and piling wood by other people's back doors where it wasn't intended to be. They were tired and dirty. So Lexie, tired as she was, managed a bath apiece and got them into bed, one at a time, and they were very soon all three sound asleep. The mother none the wiser. Perhaps that was one secret of their subjection, for they and their mother did not seem to get on at all well together.

Very tired, at last Lexie responded to an angry call from Elaine and went in to sink in a chair and let Elaine complain.

"Lexie, did you know that maid out in the kitchen isn't a trained nurse at all? She says she is something special, but I know better. She hasn't even a uniform. At least she says she left them all packed up at home, but I'm inclined to think she never had any. She hasn't the least sign of real training, and I told you I wouldn't have any other."

"I know, Elaine," said Lexie wearily, "but there really wasn't anybody else to be had."

"Fiddlesticks! I'll wager *I* can find somebody when I get well enough to take over the matter. However, she brought me a very creditable supper when you consider what she had to make it with. But Lexie, did you know she was the old woman who used to live down the lane behind the mulberry bushes? She says her name is Lucinda, and I began to remember about her. I should have thought you would have known she never would do. She was half-crazy or something, wasn't she?"

"No, she wasn't crazy. She's a very wise old woman, and very kindly if you don't antagonize her. But Elaine, she was the only one I knew to go after. You know I've been away from this region for almost four years, and it isn't easy now to pick up anybody to do anything. Besides, she was just about moving, and it meant something to her to have a room at once; that was the only reason she was willing to come. That and because she knew us. And besides, I had to tell her we hadn't anything to pay her with at present, and most people wouldn't come to a place like that anyway. And by the way, Elaine, we've simply got to talk about money. Have you enough to pay the grocery bill while I'm gone away to see how I can get my affairs straightened out? Because I have hardly anything left, and I'm not sure there is enough food in the house to last more than a couple of days. But if you say your ration books are in your trunk, why, we ought to be able to get things as soon as they come, but they will have to be paid for at once. They have no charge accounts at any of our stores out here anymore, and even the larger stores in the city insist on having charge accounts paid up every month or you have to give up the account."

"How perfectly horrid!" said Elaine. "I'll speak to my lawyer and see what can be done about that. I simply won't buy where I can't have things charged."

"But you don't understand. *All* the stores are that way now. *Everybody* is obliged to pay, no matter how wealthy they are."

"Well, we'll see. Bettinger will be out in the morning. He telegraphed a little while ago and said he would, and if he can't make some arrangement with a store near here, I'll just borrow some money from him, that's all."

"Borrow of *him*! Oh Elaine!" cried Lexie in despair. Please, *please*, don't do that! You just don't understand. It is all wrong."

"Nonsense! It's you that does not understand, my prissy little sister. I've always known how to get what I wanted from any man, and I shall get it this time, too! I'd thank you not to say any more such things about my lawyer, and not to poison the minds of my innocent little children about him either. I mean that! And what's more, if you don't stop this nonsense, I'll tell him what you are saying about him, and I'll tell him *right before you*, too! It's time you stopped passing on such slanderous gossip. Do you understand?"

Lexie caught her breath and closed her eyes for an instant.

"I understand that I'm very tired, and I've simply *got* to go to bed or I won't be fit to get up in the morning," she answered desperately. "Can I help you any before I go, Elaine, or can you manage alone?"

"No, you needn't help me. I don't care for such unwilling assistance as I get from you anyway. You can send that so-called nurse in to help me to bed. If she's a nurse she ought to be able to do that at least."

Lexie looked at her sister aghast for a minute. Would

Cinda be willing to perform menial services for Elaine, or not? Then she turned and went softly out to consult with Lucinda.

But before she could say anything to Lucinda, that dignitary spoke first in an indignant whisper: "Sure I'll do it. This once, anyhow. Yes, I heard every blessed word she said, and it's no more'n I expected. If I was you I'd go your journey the first thing in the morning and not let her know you're going till you're gone. That way you'll be out of the house when that dratted lawyer comes, and you won't have to bother with him. And you leave the rest to me. Them childer'll be all right. I can get on with 'em, an' ef I can't I know how to spank good and proper, and keep their mammy from finding out about it, too. So you don't need to fret. I'll carry on till you come back, anyway, and if it gets so bad I have to quit after that, why I'll just quit. That is, if you say so. You're my real boss, you know. Not *her*."

Lexie smiled a tired little smile.

"All right! Thank you, Cinda. I'll go as you suggest. Early. You'll know how to order and save points, won't you? And if I find I can't return at once, at least I can send you a check for five dollars right away when I get my checkbook, and perhaps that'll go till I can send you more. Though *perhaps* my sister will have *some* money to pay for things. I don't know. You might ask her, if you need anything very badly. I do hope she won't borrow of that terrible man, but I'm afraid I can't do anything about it, not till I can get some money that some people owe me, anyway."

"Now, Miss Lexie, you go right along, and I'll manage somehow. There's canned goods in this house enough to keep from starving for a long time, and if your sister wants something

better, let her get it! Doesn't she get something off the government of her husband being in the army? Or doesn't she? She
oughtta, I should think."

"I don't know, Cinda. She doesn't tell me things like that.
Even if I ask her she doesn't tell me. She's got an idea in her
head that our father left some money for her and that my
mother and I used it up, and she's trying to get it out of me
somehow. I don't know how she ever got that notion. But she
has it, and unless she can find out the truth about it and know
there never was any, I'm sure I don't see how I'm ever going to
get along with her."

"Well, Miss Lexie, you just run along to your college and
get your matters straightened out, and then if you want you
can telegraph me what you want I should do, and I'll do it. You
trust me. I can hannell things all right. Now go right to bed, an'
I'll wake you up in plenty o' time in the mornin'."

So Lexie finally went to bed, creeping in softly beside the
sleeping Bluebell and praying that God would somehow bring
her affairs out right, thinking with great gratitude of Judge
Foster as she fell asleep.

But Judge Foster was lying at that very moment in a hospital bed, unconscious, as a result of an automobile accident.

Lexie, happily ignorant of this, went on her cautious way
the next morning, rejoicing that she had so strong and wise a
friend as Judge Foster, who had made her see so plainly that she
need not be frightened but might go safely on in the right way.

Chapter 10

*L*ater in the day, after Lexie had had a long talk with the dean of her college, and he had given her two propositions to choose from, she went to her old room and sat down in perplexity. Should she try to stay here in college now for three months more, and get through with her examinations before she went home, trusting that she could get another job at home afterward? Or should she accept the dean's offer to make arrangements with the university in the city near home to let her finish her course and take examinations with them? Or what would be best? At last she went to the telephone and called up Judge Foster's office to ask his advice. He had told her to do so if she felt at all worried about anything. But when she finally succeeded in getting the judge's office, what was her dismay to be told by that cold-voiced secretary of his that Judge Foster was unable to talk with her as he was lying unconscious in the hospital and they were not even sure he would recover.

She hung up the receiver and sat limply down in a chair in the quiet office room where she was phoning. Not only was she filled with sorrow because this dear old friend of the years was in danger of his life, but she was also overcome with a great dismay. This newly found old friend was gone again, taken away from her need, and she had to go on *without* his help, at least until he got well. Perhaps he might *never* get well and she would have to go on through her sea of perplexities alone! Suddenly Lexie put her head down on her folded arms on the desk and wept.

"Oh God! You'll have to take over for me! I haven't any other friend to guide me, and I don't know what to do. Should I stay here and finish and let Elaine see what a mess she's made of things, or should I go home and try to help and see this thing through? Is this something You are expecting—wanting me to do for You? For righteousness? Won't You please show me right away?"

It was just then that the telephone girl from the dean's office opened the door and said: "Oh, you're still here, aren't you, Miss Kendall? I was afraid you had gone. There is someone calling you from your hometown. They want to speak with you right away. They say it's very important. Will you take it on this phone?"

Lexie sat up and looked at the girl in amazement. It seemed so much like an answer to her prayer, that call from home. For of course no one would have called her unless something had happened. Or would they? She tried to summon up reasons, but her tired brain could think of nothing but that this message would decide one way or the other what she must do.

Yes, it was Lucinda's unmistakable voice.

"Miss Lexie, that you? Now ain't that somethin', to think I could get you right away! Miss Lexie, I'm that sorry, but things has been happenin' thick an' fast ever since you left this mornin', an' I'm sorry, but I guess you gotta come back right away. First, Elaine she took on somethin' terrible when she found you'd left without tellin' her, an' she cried herself sick. An' then her lawyer, he sent a message he couldn't come out today, 'count of a court case he hadta try, an' that angered her. An' then Miss Angelica had a fistfight with that boy that's visitin' acrost the road, an' got herself a black eye, an' Miss Elaine went out an' give that boy a regular jawin' an' finally hit him with a broom when he was sassy. Then his aunt come out an' give back words an' threatened to send fer the p'loice. An' then while that was goin' on, Gerry, he went out an' monkeyed with the neighbor's lawn mower an' cut his foot bad, an' I hadta send for the doctor. An' whiles he was comin', Bluebell, she went out, an' got stung by a big bumblebee in the clover, an' she was crying fit ta raise the dead, an' her mamma all in hystericks when the doctor come. An' meself that near crazy I wasn't knowin' which ta do first. An' then ta crown all, that Elaine went up ta the attic and pulled out every blessed thing from the boxes an' trunks and bureaus an' left 'em all strewed around the floor. She told me she was looking among your mother's things for some very important papers she needed for evidence, an' she claimed to have found what she wanted in your mother's diary book. So I guess you better come back an' set things goin' straight. I'm awful sorry ta havta call you, but it's me that don't know what to do first."

So! Her orders had come. This was her duty, obviously, to go back home and take over. One couldn't expect Cinda to do everything. She must go at once.

So, God had undertaken, and this was His order! But He would go with her! He would be there to show her step by step what to do. Was that it?

She closed her eyes for one breath of a second, and then drawing a deep breath and glancing up at the clock, she said: "All right, Cinda! I'm taking the first train in the morning. I'll be there a little after two o'clock. You carry on till I get there, please, Cinda."

"I sure will, Miss Lexie. An' don't you worry none. I'll do just as I would be, an' no mistake. Me heart is all right, even if me brain don't always work the way Miss Elaine thinks it should. Goo'-bye. I'll look out for everything." And she hung up.

Lexie turned from the telephone and went swiftly back to the dean's office.

"I've got to go back," she said breathlessly. I've just had a phone call. I must leave on the morning train. Will I have to come back here again to get my credentials for that examination, in case I find opportunity to take the examinations in my own city?"

The dean shook his head and smiled with his characteristic kindness.

"No," he said kindly, "I'll fill out the paper for you right away, and I'll write my friend in the university in your city tonight. I'm sure it can be arranged. I'm sorry you can't finish with us, however, for I had counted on using you later in our college. I felt you would fit right in here. Nevertheless, if the way opens later for that, you will let us know, please."

Much relieved, Lexie came away with her papers, and hurried to her room to pack, trying not to think about what she might be returning to, doing her best to keep her anger from rising when she thought of Elaine mauling over her mother's precious papers, and reading her own intimate words not written for others' eyes.

It was a sad, confused time, hustling the simple belongings into her trunk, stopping to say good-bye to the friends she had made in the college, trying to explain breathlessly about a sick sister with her children. And then behind it all, in her heart there was an ache of worry about the kind old friend of her father's who was lying unconscious and in danger in a hospital. Oh, if she could only ask his advice about this. But that was out—nobody to go to now but God. Would God care, and go with her and guide her? she wondered fearsomely. She hurried with her packing, praying that all would be well. This was something she *had* to go through. It was going to be hard, and maybe long and disappointing, but it was right she should do it, and she *must* do it even if everything else she had wanted had to be given up. It was sort of like the boys who went to war. They *had* to go, even though it wasn't a pleasant prospect. They had to stay and fight it out, even though it might end in death for themselves. And in a way, this was like that. This was death to herself, of her own life and plans. Giving up for righteousness' sake. She must go, but perhaps God would go with her. Surely it was He who had answered her prayer by letting her know that she was needed at home at once. Only, what was she going to be able to do when she got there? Oh, if Judge Foster would only get well so she could talk to him for a little while. But perhaps if she talked to God in the same way she would have talked to Judge Foster, He would somehow make her know what she ought to do.

So all the way of the journey she sat with closed eyes, her head back on the seat, trying to talk the situation over with God, and to realize that His Presence must be there with her, ready to help, if she would only put herself into His hands and be willing to hand over her own wishes.

When Lexie reached the street in which the little white house was located, she sighted the shining limousine again parked before the white gate, pompous, liveried chauffeur and all, and with quick resolve she turned and skirted that end of the street and slipped into the field behind the house. She did not intend to encounter that lawyer again, not if she could help herself.

But now she had the advantage of coming in quietly by the back door when they thought she was far away and had no idea she was returning. Yet she wished she knew what was going on, and just what line Elaine was taking. There was no telling how she might have twisted words of her mother's diary to serve her own purposes.

Very quietly she entered the kitchen and put her suitcase down in the laundry entirely out of sight from even a casual observer passing through either the dining room or kitchen. Then cautiously she went over to the side wall close to the dining room door.

The door into the living room was wide open. She could even see the large flat foot of the lawyer as he lounged in the big chair by the table, but she kept well back so she could not be seen herself. It was obvious that she could not go upstairs without being seen by him. She would have to stay here until he was gone. Softly she swayed back again, entirely out of sight, and suddenly she became aware of another figure across in the dining room, unobtrusively planted just inside the partly open china closet door. This china closet was next to the living room door, but its doorway opened in such a way that one could stand inside and reach dishes without being seen from the living room. And that was where Cinda was standing. She was absolutely motionless, and in such an attitude that upon the appearance of anyone from the living room she could in an instant appear to be exceedingly busy picking out the right dishes and selecting the linen from the linen drawer for the meal she was preparing. But in the meantime, she was motionless, listening with all her might! It was all too apparent that Cinda had no scruples against listening in on any conversation that went on in that household, of which she was for the time the custodian.

And while Lexie would not have justified a listener under ordinary circumstances, nor have felt justified in arranging to listen herself, somehow she couldn't help being glad that Cinda was there, ready to be a witness, should there be need of a witness to anything that went on. Anyhow, there was nothing she could do about it, unless she should walk right in and reveal to her sister and Mr. Thomas that she had arrived home and was in a position to hear what they were saying. And after all, hadn't she a right to hear if there was a conspiracy going on against her, and that involved using evidence Elaine imagined she had found among her mother's papers? Certainly she must understand this thing fully.

So Lexie kept very still and listened through the long silences while papers rattled and the lawyer cleared his throat and coughed a little now and then. At last she heard a final page turned in whatever papers he was reading, and the whole bunch was laid down on the table. Lexie wished she dared step over nearer the door to see if that was really her mother's diary he had been perusing, but she knew if she should be discovered now it would only precipitate trouble, so she remained as still as stone and listened.

"Yes, well, Elaine," said the lawyer with his offensively intimate tone, "that is valuable, of course, especially that reference to yourself, and the distress you seem to have caused her by asking for money. But there is no definite evidence. Nothing decisive enough. I will say, however, that there are three or four distinct sentences there that if elaborated upon somewhat, might prove to be just what we want. How good are you at imitating handwriting?"

"Well," said Elaine, "I used to be good at that sort of thing at school. They said I would make a great counterfeiter," and she laughed excitedly. "What is it you want me to write? I used to try and imitate Mamma's handwriting. I remember several times when I wrote excuses for absence from school and signed her name, and the teacher never knew the difference."

"Well, I should think you would be quite clever at this, then. Just the changing of a word here and there and the evidence is perfect. See here! There is plenty of room right there to make this read, 'Her father wanted her to have this money.' And where it says 'it was her father's wish,' make it read 'it was her mother's wish.' And then if you can insert on this line below, '*It was her mother's money left to her*, my husband said before he died.' Then down on this next vacant line, 'My conscience will be clear if I give her *some* of it, and give the rest to my own child.'"

The hot blood rolled over Lexie's cheeks and receded, leaving her white and stricken as she listened to this perfidy, and she waited for her sister to reply, hoping against hope that Elaine would demur. But Elaine's only answer to all this was a light laugh.

"Is that all, Mr. Thomas? Why, that's easy. And it doesn't seem at all wrong. It just makes the meaning of what is written clearer, doesn't it? But would just those little changes give you the evidence you want?"

"Well, they certainly would make a great difference. But you must be careful to make the writing so like the rest that there will be no questioning it. Would it be possible, do you think, to use the same kind of ink? Would there be an old bottle of ink about that might have been used to write the rest of this little book?"

"Why, yes, I wouldn't be at all surprised if I could find some. In fact, I think I saw a bottle of ink standing on Mamma's desk when I was looking through it for this book."

"That would be very good," asserted the lawyer importantly. "But now, Elaine, you know, there is one very important matter still unsettled. You do not know definitely how much money is involved in this matter, nor where that money is located. I shall have to know that, of course, before I can be sure that it is worth my while to go deeply into this at all. You know there are expenses involved. This matter alone of hiring witnesses to prove these things. That takes plenty of money. And you haven't given me any but the vaguest idea of how much money there will be when we get track of it."

"Oh, but I told you I was willing to give you ten percent of all that I get, regardless of how much it is," said Elaine sweetly.

"And I have always supposed that my mother's estate that she left in trust for me was from thirty thousand dollars to perhaps seventy-five or a hundred thousand! That of course is what I have hired you to find out for me.

"Well, but suppose the money cannot be found, or suppose it has been spent, you can sue my sister for it, can't you?"

"Well, yes, I suppose we can, provided we can prove beyond any doubt that the money was there when your father died, that it was in his wife's trust and left entirely to you."

"Oh, but I'm sure it was," said Elaine in her sweetest, most confident tone. "Of course I wouldn't have sent for you if I hadn't been entirely sure."

"But, my dear, why didn't you look up these claims several years ago? I should have supposed you would have done so as soon as you were married, and while you had a husband to help in looking up your evidence."

"Oh, but you see I didn't think of such things then. I had a husband to support me, and it didn't occur to me that I would be left alone with three little children to support on simply nothing! But I'm sure you'll be able to work this out, won't you? You wrote me that you were sure you could."

"Why, yes of course, but again, Elaine, as I told you, it will cost you something to get witnesses to substantiate your claims. Well, now I think that is all for today, and I'm very glad you found this diary. If you will work these changes out as I suggested, and as quickly as possible, we will get right to work on the case. Of course, in case you find that your sister has spent all this money that ought to have been yours, has she any money or property that we can levy on?"

"Oh yes, she has a part ownership in this house, or, that

is, I believe she claims it is all hers, since she says her mother paid for it. Of course we know she didn't. But if worse came to worst, we could claim on this house, couldn't we?"

"This house?" said the lawyer. "Why yes, I suppose so. But my dear, surely you know that this house would be a mere drop in the bucket when we are talking in terms of fifty or a hundred thousand dollars. You couldn't possibly expect to get more than five or six thousand dollars out of this plain little house in this locality, you know. Seven thousand at the most."

"Oh, *really*? Is that all? But I always supposed this was a very valuable property indeed. My father used to say it was."

"Well, that a number of years ago, and property depreciates. But of course there would be other ways to get money out of your sister. If she had a job we could arrange that a certain percentage of her wages would be paid directly to you. There are ways to make such arrangements. However, that we can talk over later. And now I really must go. I am late for an appointment already. And you, my dear, will get right to work on that diary and make the changes, please. Bye-bye, and take care of yourself, darling!"

Heavy footsteps went out the door and down the path to the street. At once the expensive engine began to turn and was soon on its way. The obnoxious lawyer was sped away out of sight.

Lexie had waited during the talk, silent but boiling with rage, appalled at the lengths Elaine was willing to go to accomplish her ends, and wondering what she ought to do.

Of course if Judge Foster was well, she would have carried the story at once to him. But since he was in the hospital, even if he was better, she must not worry him with her affairs now.

But God! God was there! She could send a quick SOS for help from Him fully, and go each step as He seemed to direct.

But now suddenly this interview had come to an end, and something must be done. She must decide just what she was going to do. She must be wary and careful. She must not let Elaine know just yet that she was at home nor that she had heard the interview between the lawyer and her sister. And yet she must contrive some way to get hold of that precious diary before Elaine could mutilate it in any way. However, that was something that would take time and thought to work out, and the first thing she must do was to see Cinda somewhere—out in the yard perhaps where Elaine could not hear them talking. And it wouldn't be impossible for her to slip out the back door now without making a bit of noise, but she must attract Cinda's attention before she left, for she must find out if anything more had happened. She also needed to find out if Cinda had heard this shameful talk between the lawyer and her sister.

But before Lexie could make a move, she heard Cinda stamping out into the kitchen, making her footsteps sound as if they came from the cellar door and had not been near the dining room. Cinda was clever. She had come across that room so silently that not even a fly could have heard her. And when she saw Lexie, she lifted one eyebrow and winked one eye as if she had known all the time that Lexie was there. Had she? Dear old Cinda!

So with a quick motion, Lexie covered the space between herself and the back door and crooked her finger at Cinda to follow. Cinda, without a sound beyond a slight nod of her head, rattled some pans on the stove and then slid out of the door into the backyard.

They went out behind the old chicken house far enough from the house so that their voices could not be heard.

"Aw, but I'm glad to see you home!" said Cinda. "Such goin's on as there has been! Did you hear all that stuff they was gettin' off just now? How *much* did you hear? I didn't hear you come in, but I was hopin' you'd get in on some of it. And I was that glad when I got out here an' saw you."

"I got in while the lawyer was reading the diary. Was there much before that?"

"Not so much. Only he come in and told her she was havin' ta pay somethin' down or he couldn't do anythin'. An' then she cried an' said she didn't have much. She said she'd give him twenty-five dollars, but she had ta keep somethin' ta live on till she got her fortune. Then he give in an' said okay, he'd do it if she'd pay ten down, an' the rest as she got it from the government. She cried a lot, but she give him the ten. I hid behind the portiere an' seen her. An' then she told him about the diary. It seems he put her up to lookin' in the attic whilst you was gone, an' he ast her a lot of questions about didn't she find any deeds of property, ur any receipts of your ma havin' paid any large sums to anybody, an' she cried a lot more an' sobbed out no, she hadn't, an' then he took the book an' began to read. That musta been about the time you come in. I thought I heard a little click of the kitchen latch, but I didn't dast move enough to look. I figure it was better I should hear the rest. But I'm mighty glad you came."

"Oh, so am I, Cinda! But if I only knew what I am to do now! I thought I had a friend to help me when I went away, a judge, a friend of my own daddy's. He promised to help me, but when I tried to reach him after you telephoned, they said he was unconscious in the hospital from an automobile accident, and they weren't even sure he was going to live."

"Now, ain't that a shame, Miss Lexie! But don't you worry none. I'll stick by you, and something'll turn up."

"Thank you, Cinda. I knew I could count on you. And now, there is one thing I've got to do, and that is to get that diary of Mother's away from Elaine. I can't have that tampered with!"

"Of course not, Miss Lexie. And you can count on me for that. I can snoop around and find out what she does with it, and snitch it away somehow and hide it for you."

"Well, be careful, Cinda. You don't want to get mixed up in this. That lawyer of hers can make trouble for *any*body, and if he *wants* to he is capable of putting us all in jail."

"Don't you worry about me, Miss Lexie. I didn't cut me eyeteeth just yesterday. I can take care of meself. Now, go your ways, whatever that is, and I'll keep a watch out. Where you going? To the store? Because you don't need to today. She give me some ration cards an' money an' I went an' bought her a steak. That was what she said she wanted. An' I got plenty other things, butter and coffee and sugar, and some canned stuff and more vegetables. I figured it would be better to have some things on hand than to be continually having to run down to the store and leave them three babies to wander around alone without anybody to look after 'em. You might, however, get me a bit of cinnamon and ginger. There's a can of pumpkin in the closet and I thought a pumpkin pie might come in handy, seein's there's some molasses that needs eatin', so the ants won't be prancin' all over the shelf."

"All right, Cinda. I'll get anything else you need. I've a little more money now, if Elaine didn't give you enough. But I shan't be gone long. I just want to telephone and find out about Judge Foster."

"Yes, you do that," said Cinda understandingly. "If there's anybody needs a good friend, I'd say it was you, and I guess the good Lord understands that, too. You might ask Him to see to that!"

"Oh, I have, Cinda—all the way home! Oh Cinda, I'm glad you know Him, too."

"Well, I ain't sayin' how well I know Him, but I've always felt when it come to the last pinch that the Lord wouldn't let me down. Now you run along, and I won't let her know you've come back yet."

So Lexie hurried down to the drugstore to telephone to the judge's office, hoping it wasn't closing time yet. She wouldn't feel free to telephone his house.

She was greatly relieved to hear the cold-voiced secretary.

"Oh, is this Judge Foster's secretary?" she asked eagerly.

"It *is*!" said the cold voice.

"Well, I'm just the daughter of an old friend of his, and I'm calling to know how he is. Has he recovered consciousness yet? I've been so worried."

"Oh!" said the cold secretary, giving her voice a space in which to warm up a little. "Why yes, Judge Foster has recovered consciousness somewhat. That is, the doctor thinks he is a trifle better, and he has a chance to recover. Of course that is not certain yet, but it is more hopeful than yesterday."

"Oh, that is so good!" said Lexie, with tears in her voice. "I was so worried."

"Of course he won't be able to talk with anyone, not now,

nor probably for a long time."

"Of course," said Lexie sadly. "But if you should have a chance when he is better, will you tell him Lexie Kendall sent him her love, and tell him—I've been praying for him."

The secretary evidently was embarrassed by the message.

"Why yes, surely," she said formally. "I'm sure he'll be much pleased when he hears that. Suppose you give me your name and address. It's my business to keep a record of all calls."

So Lexie gave her name and address, and turned sadly away from the telephone. Of course she hadn't really expected that she would get even as good news as that he was a little better, but it saddened her to feel so utterly cut off from her only earthly friend, now in this new perplexity.

Chapter 11

Meanwhile, Cinda felt that this was her time to act. Great interests were at stake and she seemed to be the only one who could do anything about it. She resolved that she and she only would be responsible for securing that little diary book that seemed to be playing such an important part in these affairs.

So Cinda prepared a delicious drink, a combination of grape juice and ginger ale and one or two other small spicy ingredients known only to herself. By this time she had arranged to have plenty of ice on hand, and the drink was cold and sparkling.

Elaine was just about to settle down at the desk to experiment with the writing she was supposed to do in the little blue diary that lay closed before her on the desk, when Cinda entered bearing the drink.

Cinda was all honey and smiles, with oily words.

"Miss Elaine, my lady," she said obsequiously, "I brought you a nice pleasant drink. I'm sure you'll like it. It was always a favorite of my best patients, an' this mornin' when I went to the store I made out to get the ingredients so that you could try it. And now I thought, she's tired, with all that discussion with her lawyer, an' she oughtta lie right down an' take a rest, so I'll take her drink in to her and get her to drink it an' then lie down on the bed in her quiet room an' have a little sleep, an' then she'll feel real better. Now you go into your room, and I'll draw the shades for ya and keep the childer real still when they come home an' not let 'em bother. An' when you wake up you'll feel like a new woman."

This was Elaine's language. She simply thrived on such talk.

Graciously she accepted the glass, for she was thirsty and the frosty crystal tempted her after her hectic discussion with Bettinger Thomas.

"Why, yes, this is really delicious, Cinda. I'll have to get you to make some of this for me when I have callers," she said.

Oh, if Cinda could just keep up this line of talk, Elaine would be as putty in her hands, but Cinda was so raring mad inside that it was a question how long she could endure in honeyed tones. Still, Cinda realized the necessity for strategy, and she was ready to endure as long as the time required her services. Amazingly she was able to coax Elaine into her bedroom, making her lean on her arm as she led her there. She lowered her gently to the bed, threw a light blanket across her shoulders, adjusted the shades, opened a window where there was a pleasant breeze, and tiptoed out, closing the door after her gently.

As she passed the desk she noted the little book that had figured so largely in the afternoon's affairs. She moved with extraordinary stealth across the room. Her large, capable hand enveloped the small leather-bound book and swept it up under her apron, conveying it in safety into the outer kitchen. She secreted it, wrapped in a clean dish towel, down in the capacious pocket of Lexie's coat that was bulked above her suitcase in the little laundry down on the far side of the laundry tub where Elaine would never in the world bother to go.

With some satisfaction she turned to the kitchen and prepared an unusually fine supper for the silly dupe, who by this time must be sound asleep, as there came no sound at all from the bedroom where she had stowed her. Fortunately the children were making a victory garden with the children across the street, a neighboring daughter of the house having decided that something ought to be done with those children if the whole neighborhood was not to suffer. So she had set them all at something really worthwhile, and the children were greatly intrigued. It was probably the first time in their young lives that anyone had ever set them at something that was worth doing, and they liked it.

But Cinda was thinking hard and fast. Something must be done with that book to make it impossible for Elaine to find it again. She didn't understand just what all this trouble was about, but she was keen enough to know that something very crooked was about to be put over upon Lexie, and the book was a part of it all. So, having purloined the book, she didn't intend to have her efforts fail.

She planned her work at the sink under the window looking toward that back way across the fields where Lexie had disappeared, and when she caught a glimpse of the slender figure in the dark blue dress that she knew was Lexie, she took opportunity to slip out the back door and meet her down by the fence, the book still wrapped in its dish towel and further hidden in a paper bag.

"Here it is," she said in a low, eager whisper, "and you'd best take it and put it in the bank out of harm's way before you get home and she knows you're here. Can't you put it in one of these little boxes they keep jewelry and valuables in at the bank? I should think that would be the only way. Then they would never know you had it. I didn't tell her you had come home. She's asleep, and she won't know what's become of it. Maybe she'll think the lawyer took it."

Lexie peered into the paper bag, turned back the dish towel, and then with a mist of sudden tears in her eyes said: "Oh Cinda! You're wonderful!"

"That's okay with me, Miss Lexie, but don't waste precious time now. You've just about enough time to get to the bank before it closes. I looked at the clock before I come out, an' you can't tell what minute herself will wake up an' come yellin' out the back door, an' see you standin' here with the book. Then the fat's in the fire! *So go!* An' don't you dare bring that book back with you! You leave it in the bank, even if they're closed an' you havta pound on the door to make 'em let you in. Hurry, *quick!* An' if you can think of something to do to stay away awhile longer, that would be all right, too, an' let her get over the excitement of not finding the book when she wakes up, before *you* are home, so she can't connect it with you. Now, go! Leave the rest to me!"

Lexie turned with quick, thankful comprehension and

sped across the field back toward the village, laying plans as she went. Why, Cinda was really a wonder! She had planned the whole thing out cleverly, for Lexie really couldn't have hidden that book in the house where Elaine could not have found it. Just what Elaine would say, whom she would blame, when she discovered it was gone, Lexie hadn't stopped to think. At least *she* had the book, and she needn't tell her sister where it was. Elaine needn't suspect that she even knew about it. Trust Cinda for that.

Lexie arrived breathless at the bank almost ten minutes before closing time, having done some very rapid running. She paused inside the door to get her breath. Then she walked up to the cashier, whom she had known for years, and said she wanted to put her small account in the bank, and she wanted a safe-deposit box to keep some valuable papers in.

It didn't take long to arrange the whole thing, get a new checkbook, make out a check from her college bank to put in her new account, take over the safe-deposit box, and lock the book safely inside. Then Lexie went out into the street again and tried to decide just what she would do next.

She had her handbag with her, for she had taken that when she first went to telephone about Judge Foster. And in her bag were the letters written by the dean of her college. Why shouldn't she go down to the university in the city, and see what arrangements they were willing to make for her examinations? It was just as well to get it settled now as any time, and it really would be well of course to keep away until Elaine had gotten over her first excitement about the loss of the book.

So she took a bus down to the university and spent an interesting two hours meeting different college dignitaries and explaining her situation. She was greatly relieved to find that her credentials would be accepted and arrangements would be made for her necessary work if she would come down next week.

Lexie went home quite relieved about her examinations. It looked as if everything was going to be all right for her getting through without going back to college, although she was going to miss sorely the friends and associations she had made there. But still it was a relief to know that the people in the university were going to be cooperative and kindly. She was so elated about it that she almost forgot that she was going home to face Elaine and a trying situation.

As she turned the corner into her own street she began to wonder what Cinda had had to meet. Would she have had sense enough to evade Elaine's questioning, or had she let a small tempest arise that would make the night intolerable? Well, as she was just arriving Elaine would not likely blame her with the loss of the book—at least not tonight. Not unless Cinda had been tricked into admitting too much. But she felt pretty sure Cinda could be counted on to keep a secret what she knew.

Lexie entered breezily, and found the three children noisily eating a very pleasant-looking meal of corn meal, glasses of rich milk, and big dishes of applesauce peppered with cinnamon. It looked very nice, and the children were going into it with zest. The little group at the table seemed very calm, and not as if there had been any kind of an emotional upheaval in the house lately. Lexie wondered if Elaine could still be asleep, or what had happened.

But a twinkle in Cinda's eye assured her that everything

was all right so far, and a slight wave of Cinda's hand with a little grin sent her into the other room.

Elaine had wakened late in the afternoon after a refreshing sleep, probably made possible by the talk she had had that morning with her lawyer, and his assurance that a little writing in a good imitation of the rest of the diary would work wonders. But when she awoke and found herself rested, and came around in due course to the train of thought that had put her to sleep, she rose. She spent a few minutes in beautifying herself just in case her lawyer changed his mind and decided to return that afternoon, and then sauntered into the living room. She went over to the desk, intending to practice writing the lines the lawyer had suggested and then finish them off so they would be ready for him when he came tomorrow. But when she sat down there was no book on the desk where she thought she had left it, and after pulling out the desk drawers and poking around in the cubbyholes to find it, thinking she herself had put it away out of sight, she grew a bit frantic. She rose and went to the door, her hand on the knob, thinking to ask Cinda if she had seen it, but her natural caution warned her. Perhaps she had carried it into the bedroom with her and slipped it under her pillow. But why should she do that? There was nobody in the house who would be interested, or know what significance that special book could have. But she went into the bedroom and searched the bed and surroundings most thoroughly without result. Then Elaine went back to the desk and searched the whole room more thoroughly than she had ever looked for anything in her life before. At last, utterly exhausted, she dropped herself down on the couch and wondered just what she should do about it. Was it at all possible that

Mr. Thomas could have taken it with him, put it in his pocket absentmindedly? She tried to visualize him doing it, and yet wasn't sure at all. If they only had a telephone! If she could only call him up and ask if he had taken the book without knowing it! Would she dare go across the street herself and try to telephone? Of course if that should get to Lexie's ears, she would not be able to carry out this idea of being an invalid and needing not only care and nursing but also money. Finally, after due thought, she called Cinda.

Cinda appeared promptly and cheerfully with the most innocent expression on her face.

"Cinda, were any of the children in the living room while I was asleep?"

"Oh no, ma'am. I didn't see none of them in there."

"Has my sister been home?"

"No ma'am, she's not been in the house."

"Well, I don't understand it, Cinda. There's an important little book of mine gone. I had it there on the desk. I'm positive I left it there, and I can't find it anywhere. It's just the kind of thing Gerry or even Bluebell might take a fancy to and carry off. I wish you'd call them and we'll ask them."

So Cinda marshaled the children over from across the street, and their mother conducted an almost thorough examination, but they all declared they hadn't seen any little book at all.

"Didn't *you* see it here, Cinda? You didn't put it away or anything, did you? It's very important that I find it at once!"

"No ma'am, I never monkey with *your* papers. I never took notice of anything at all of *yours*, my lady! Too bad you lost something important. But mebbe it'll turn up in good time.

Aren't you getin' hungry, Miss 'Laine? I got a nice supper planned. Go an' read awhile, an' I'll be bringing in your tray after a bit."

If Lexie could have heard her she would have stood in awe of Cinda's histrionic ability, for she certainly was playing her part well and really getting away with it. Her innocent air and her willingness to please threw Elaine entirely off her guard. Elaine loved to be served in this spirit. Perhaps Lexie was too honest-hearted to try to gain her end by subtlety, although she had had years of suffering under Elaine's selfishness and greed. She watched her own dear mother suffer also. When she had thought it over honestly she knew that one should not always yield to such greedy demands.

Well, Lexie wasn't there to see it all but was greatly relieved when she reached home to find a comparative calm in the house and Elaine quietly reading a magazine that Cinda had cannily brought and left around to further her own purposes.

It was after supper that Elaine tried a new line with her sister: "Lexie, I suppose you are tired and I hate to ask you to do anything more tonight, but *would* you run across the road to one of the neighbors and phone Mr. Thomas? I have something very important to tell him, and I think he would come out tonight and see me if he knew. Would you just say that I have a matter of importance to tell him that he ought to know tonight?"

Lexie looked at her aghast for an instant, and then a sudden remembrance came to her that she was not alone. God was with her. His Presence was there, even if Elaine couldn't see it. But *she* knew He was there, and she would be strong in *His* strength.

Then Lexie smiled pleasantly, but her lips took on a new firmness, her voice an assurance that was not too natural to her.

"No, Elaine, I'm sorry to seem unaccommodating, but I cannot have anything to do with that man!"

"Now, Lexie, don't be silly. You will just be carrying a message for me, your sister. He needn't even know who you are."

"No," said Lexie. "I do not care to approach him in any way, even as an unknown."

"But that is silly! It's childish!"

"No, it's not silly. I do not like the way he speaks to me, and I do not intend to give him another chance to insult me. It's useless to argue, Elaine, I simply *won't* do it. If you want to have dealings with him, you'll have to do it without me. And now, would you like me to help you to get ready for bed, or shall I wait till the children are in?"

"Oh, don't trouble yourself!" said Elaine coldly. "I'll get to bed somehow. Though I'm not going yet. But if you can't do the one thing I want, I shall have to hire somebody to do it for me or else go myself."

"Sorry," said Lexie briefly, "but what you ask is out of the question for me." Lexie went quietly out of the room and upstairs to get the beds ready for the children.

Cinda was Elaine's next choice of a messenger. She called Cinda in and endeavored to wangle her into carrying the message to the telephone across the street, but Cinda had been listening to the conversation between the sisters and was prepared with her answer.

"Now, you know, Miss 'Laine, I'd like to accommodate you, but I'm that shy of a telephome, I just couldn't do it. No ma'am. I can't get over it. I'm what they call mikerphome-shy, only with me it's telephome-shy. Besides, those folks across the street have all gone to the movies. I heard 'em go, an' their house is locked up. I saw 'em lock it. An' no ma'am, I wouldn't care to go down to the drugstore this evenin'. I'm that tired I thought I'd go right to bed an' get rested up for tomorrow. Don't wantta play out on you. You can ast me most anythin' to do fer you but phome. I jest can't learn to phome."

So Elaine had to resign herself to writing a letter to her lawyer asking him if he carried the little book away with him. While Lexie was putting Bluebell to bed and Cinda was clattering the dishes in the kitchen, Elaine snuck out herself and went down to the corner where there was a mailbox. She mailed her letter, but she took pains when she got back to see that both Lexie and Cinda knew that she had gone to the mailbox, that she was worn out in consequence and was sure she was going to be sick that night from the exertion and the chill, damp air. She also complained of having twisted her ankle crossing the street.

Lexie went to bed early that night. She didn't want to enter into any more discussions. She lay in her quiet room with little Bluebell by her side and wondered how long this sort of thing was to go on. She felt almost like a criminal, not telling her sister that the little book was in safekeeping where she would not find it again, but she knew this was the wise way. It was her book, not Elaine's, and she had a right to put it beyond use against her.

But in the dark room, as one by one the noises of the street toned down, the neighbors came home and went to bed, and the light around went out, somehow she had a stronger feeling than ever that the Presence of the Lord was in the room and that He was going to watch over her and guide her. If it had not been for this, it seemed to her she could not have gone on into days that would of necessity be filled with bickering and strife. Yet she must, and if He was there, was it true that His Presence could protect her? She would see.

Chapter 12

About the middle of the next morning there came a telegram from Lawyer Thomas.

> I DO NOT HAVE THE BOOK. YOU WILL PROBABLY FIND IT IF YOU SEARCH CAREFULLY. IF NOT I SUGGEST A REPRODUCTION FROM MEMORY OF AS MANY PAGES AS POSSIBLE. LET ME KNOW AS SOON AS YOU HAVE COMPLETED IT.
> B. THOMAS

Cinda found the telegram in the wastebasket when she took it out to empty it, and she relayed the contents to Lexie, which caused her to sigh heavily and finally run down to the drugstore and call up Judge Foster's office again.

When the secretary answered, she said: "This is Lexie Kendall again. Am I troubling you very much if I ask how Judge Foster is this morning?"

She was thrilled to hear the answer:

"Oh, you are Lexie! I was about to write you a letter since you have no telephone listed. Judge Foster is quite better this morning, and he has been asking for you—at least he has several times murmured your name with a worried look in his eyes. The doctor wondered if you would care to come down to the hospital and see him for a minute or two. He seems to be worried about you in some way."

"Oh, that's very kind of you to tell me. Of course I'll come. Just when and where should I come?"

The secretary gave the necessary directions, and Lexie hurried back to get ready to go. As she passed through the dining room she caught a glimpse of Elaine at the desk nibbling the end of her pen and looking perplexedly at the paper before her. Ah! Elaine was taking her lawyer's advice!

All the way to the bus line she was puzzling to know if there wasn't some way she could stop Elaine from doing this preposterous thing. Oh, if only Judge Foster was able to talk and she could ask him what to do! But of course they wouldn't let her do anything but just step into the room and say she was so glad he was better.

She trod the marble halls of the hospital with her heart beating wildly, because in spite of her desire to see Judge Foster she was frightened at the idea of visiting a very sick man. She was afraid she might do or say something that would make him worse, and she read herself a great many warnings as she walked sedately toward the room to which she had been directed.

She tapped at the door and waited. The nurse opened the door and she asked in a soft voice if that was Judge Foster's room, and the nurse's face brightened.

"Oh, are you Lexie Kendall?" asked the nurse. "He's been asking for you. I'm glad you've come!"

It was nice to be welcomed. She went in shyly, and there was the judge looking every bit as friendly and judgelike as when he was sitting in his office. But his face was white, and there were worn lines that gave him a gaunt appearance. Her heart smote her that she had come hoping to get help from him, but of course that was impossible. She must be very careful with what she said.

She approached shyly and put her hand in the big white one he held out to her.

"Well, I'm glad you've come, little Lexie," he said, his voice almost natural in its cordiality.

"Oh, I was so glad to be allowed to come. I was terribly worried when I heard you were in the hospital."

"Well, they're fixing me all up fine here," he said with a smile. "I think I'll be ready to go home pretty soon." He smiled.

"Oh, I hope so, Judge Foster!" said Lexie earnestly.

"But how about you, child? As soon as I came to myself I began to think about you, and to worry lest I wouldn't be able to help you as I had planned. How has your affair come out? Did you go to college?"

"Yes, I went back," said Lexie cheerfully, "and they were very nice. They said if I found I had to return here that they would arrange for me to take my examination here at the university, and they gave me papers, credits, and letters to people of the university. I went there today and it's all to be arranged next week."

"But why did you come back, child? I thought you were planning to stay away from that lawyer."

"Yes, I was, but—well, Cinda telephoned me I *ought* to come back."

Lexie hesitated, and looked worried.

"But I oughtn't to trouble you with my small worries," she said, trying to look exaggeratedly cheerful. "It's nothing, I'm sure, and I guess it will be all right. But I thought I ought to return."

"Child, you needn't be afraid to tell me. They won't let you stay long, I know that, for I heard what the doctor said, but it's best that I should know all, for I've been worrying about you, and if there have been any new developments I want to know them."

"But I know you ought not worry about me. I want you to get well. I'll tell you all about it when you are better."

"No!" said the judge in his most judgely tone. "You will tell me *now*. I am your father's friend, and I *must* know *at once*!"

"Oh, well, I guess it wasn't anything to worry much about, but I did want to ask you if I did right. Cinda telephoned that Elaine had gone up in the attic and pulled out all my mother's things, her private papers and everything, and when I got home I walked in the back door and overheard her talking with that lawyer. She had found Mother's private diary, and she showed it to him. There were little items about the money she had earned and how she wanted to give some of it to Elaine and some to me, and they twisted it so it seemed as if she was referring to something Father had said to her about

Elaine, about saving up and having money to send us both to college."

The judge nodded.

"Yes, that was your father's desire," he said with a sigh.

"Well, the lawyer read the diary nearly through, and then he showed Elaine where she could write in words that would make the meaning entirely different. Elaine has always been clever at imitating writing and she agreed to do what he suggested, and then he went away. Cinda was in the dining room and overheard the whole thing, and I heard most of it. But they didn't know that I was home yet, nor that Cinda was where she could hear them. They wouldn't have thought she mattered anyway. But she was very bright. She told Elaine she needed to lie down and rest. She brought her lemonade, and took her into the bedroom and tucked her up. Then as she came out she picked up the diary, brought it out to me, and told me to go quick to the bank and put it into a safe-deposit box before my sister knew that I had come home. And so I did. Do you think it was wrong? I hurried across the fields and got to the bank just before it closed, and the book is safe in the bank now. Elaine doesn't know where it is. Do you think that was a wrong thing to do, to let Cinda take that book, and for me to hide it and not tell Elaine?"

"Certainly not. You did just right. And now, this puts things in a little different light. What was Elaine's reaction to the loss of the book?"

"Oh, she thought the children had taken it first, till she found out they hadn't been home. They were across the street playing. She asked Cinda, but Cinda said she never took notice to anything belonging to *her*, so there was no more said. But when I came she tried to get me to call up her lawyer, and I declined to do it. I told her I didn't like the way he talked to me and I didn't want anything further to do with him, and then I walked away. Was that right?"

"Yes, that was right. Keep that up. Don't let him get any chance to talk with you if you can help it. And now, if anything more happens and you need help, I wish you would go to my friend Mr. Gordon. He is a fine man and a keen lawyer, and I have told him about you. I felt it was necessary someone else should be wise about you. I spoke a few words to him on the phone again this morning, so he will understand. Now, I wish you would go right down to his office. Here is the address. I asked the nurse to write it, and this card with my name on it will admit you to his office right away without waiting a long time. I am talking rapidly because I think the nurse is coming back and she will drive you out. But I'm so glad to have had this talk with you. It's relieved my mind a lot, and now I can rest better. I seemed to have a psychic warning that you were still in trouble."

The nurse entered quietly and came smilingly to stand beside the bed.

"Now," she said looking apologetically at Lexie.

"Yes, I'm going," said Lexie, smiling and rising. "Good-bye, Judge Foster, and you've helped me a lot. I'm relieved to think you feel I did right."

"Yes, you did perfectly right," said the judge happily. "And now, will you go at once to Mr. Gordon's office?"

"Yes," said Lexie, "of course."

"Well, please tell him everything, the whole story. He knew your father slightly, and I want him to get every detail you have. And if anything further occurs report it to him *at once*! That is, until I am back in my office. Gordon's telephone number is on the card. You will find him most sympathetic and helpful. Now, good-bye, little girl. Come and see me again soon. And please call up occasionally. I might have a message for you about something, you know."

"Oh, thank you," said Lexie, a bright, pleased color in her cheeks. He was so pleasant, so fatherly, it almost brought the tears.

"I hope I haven't tired him," she said to the nurse as she got to the door.

"No, I think not," said the nurse with a quick glance at her patient. "I believe he almost looks more rested. He worried a lot about you that first night. You seemed to be on his mind."

So Lexie went on her way to Mr. Gordon's office and found her talismanic card opened the way to him almost at once. He proved to be all that the judge had said he would be, a man of keen eyes, quick understanding, and a friendly smile. When she left, Lexie felt a great burden had been lifted from her shoulders. God had sent her an adviser to whom she could go! Oh, she would still go to God with it all first, and then if an earthly adviser was needed, here was Mr. Gordon who would if necessary talk it over with Judge Foster, and she wouldn't have to bother Judge Foster with things that he didn't need to know.

So Lexie went back to the house feeling that whatever had happened she was fortified to stand it.

Cinda was washing the kitchen floor, with a face like a thundercloud.

"Them childer," she murmured as Lexie came in the back

door, "they went out an' jumped up an' down in a puddle of black oil some old truck left in the road, an' then they come in here to me nice white floor just scrubbed yesterday, an' they walked all around makin' what they called patterns on my floor, an' crowin' over it to beat the band. Even that oldest kid, that 'Angel-child' you call her, she was walkin' around makin' circles of her footprints, an' runnin' out to the road to get more oil on her shoes when it got dim. So I up an' spanked her, good, an' she screamed for her mother, an' that neighbor-lady across the street come over to see was she hurt ur sompin', an' then they all howled so I spanked eh other two. I guess I spanked pretty hard, fer their mom she come out from her nap, an' she was pretty mad an' said I was to stop hurtin' her childer, an' then she fired me! *Me!* She had the nerve to *fire* me. An' then I up an' told her I wasn't workin' fer her, I was workin' for her sister an' I wasn't fired till *you* fired me an' fer her to git outta me kitchen, ur I'd swash some water over her feet. So she got, but she said when you come home she'd tell you ta fire me, an' I might as well go git packed, fer it wouldn't be many minutes 'fore you'd come home an' give me the gate. So, Miss Lexie, you better go right in there an' git yer orders, an' then I'll know what ta do."

"Oh!" said Lexie in dismay, and the *"Oh!"* with a little laugh at the end of her breath. "Well, Cinda, don't you worry, I'm *not* giving you the gate. Not unless you feel you can't stand it here any longer. I wouldn't blame you, of course, but I'm sure I don't know what I would do without you."

"All right, me lamb, don't you worry none. I'm workin' fer *you*, an' ef you still want me, here's where I stay."

"Oh, that's good, Cinda!" said Lexie. "Now, tell me the rest.

What else happened, and where are they all?"

"Well, Miss Elaine, she's on her bed cryin' her eyes out, an' groanin'. Can't ye hear her? The childer are acrost the street as usual. That Angel-child is probably tellin' all that happened. Drat her! I could whale her good ef I got another chancet. But whut else happened? Well, that fat lawyer come back, and he had words with my lady. It seems she'd writ a whole lot more an' signed yer mom's name to it, an' he said she'd got ta get you to okay it or somepin', so it would carry more influence, an' she tole him she *couldn't* get you to do *anythin'*, an' he said there was a *way* ta *make* ye. He ast her did you have a lawyer, an' she said, 'Oh no,' you didn't have any lawyer, an' he said well in that case maybe she better go easy an' coax. But he tuk her ole papers she'd been writin' all mornin' an' said he'd see what he could make out with them. An' he ast her wasn't there some rich relative she could borry of ta pay the advance fee, an' she cried a lot more an' said *every*body was against her an' she didn't know what she was goin' ta do, so he just tuk her in his ole fat arms an' hugged her, an' kissed her three four times, an' petted her like she was a baby, an' said he'd do his best to get her the money somehow, an' then he went away. An' then those childer come over an' worked that oil-act on my nice clean floor, an' that's how 'tis. Now, I'm sorry fer you, but I guess you better go in an' settle with her, an' after you're done if you really think you better fire me, why, I'll go quietlike an' not make you any trouble."

"Oh, bless your heart, Cinda. No, I'm not going to fire you. I'm much more likely to fire myself. This certainly is an awful household, and I don't wonder you'd like to leave, but please don't, Cinda, for I just can't go on without you."

"Okay!" said Cinda with a crooked, triumphant grin. "I'm here fer the duration, so put that on yer pianna an' play it. Run along now, an' don't lose yer nerve."

So Lexie put aside her outer wraps in the dining room and went into the living room and over to the bookcase, where she selected three or four books, and sat down to run over some of the work she would likely be tested on at the new university.

But Lexie didn't have long to study. She heard Elaine's studied sobbing being audibly wound up, heard stirrings in the region of the bed, and then slippered footsteps, and the door opened.

Lexie sat very still, absorbed in her study until Elaine spoke: "Well, so you've finally got home *at last*! Where on earth have you been?"

"Oh," said Lexie, looking up pleasantly, "why, I had a few errands to do. Did you want something?"

"I certainly do," said Elaine. "I want you to go out in the kitchen and fire that outrageous, impudent woman you hired. She is simply insufferable! I can't stay in the house with her another night! She is not fit to have around. I'm afraid to trust my babies near her. Do you know what she dared to do? She *spanked my children*! *All three* of them! Imagine a girl as old as Angelica being subjected to that! And the whole neighborhood was roused by their screaming! So, Lexie, I won't stand another day of that insolent woman. I told her to go. I told her we didn't want her here another hour, but she said you hired her, and she was working for you, and nobody but you could fire her. So now for pity's sake go out there in the kitchen and fire her, and then you go downtown to the best agency there is and get a real servant. Offer good wages. You simply can't get anybody worth her salt unless you promise to pay for it."

Lexie looked up with mild, troubled eyes.

"I'm sorry you've had such a time, Elaine," she said, "but perhaps you don't know what the children did to make Cinda spank them."

"Oh, she's been blabbing to you, has she? I thought so. And of course you take *her* side. I might have known you would. You always go against me if there is any possible way to do so."

"Listen, Elaine. Did you know that Cinda had just scrubbed the kitchen floor the last thing last night, and the children found a puddle of dirty black oil in the road and they all stepped in it and then came into the kitchen and walked around making patterns on the nice white floor? You don't think that was right, do you?"

"Oh, the idea! A little trifling thing like that, and she gave them the most cruel chastisement I ever saw. She left the imprint of her ugly coarse hand on their tender little pink flesh. It was terrible. I had to anoint them with oil, and the poor little things were in agony! Simply *agony*! And I demand that that woman leave this house at once! I wouldn't feel safe another day with her and my babies in the same house together! Now, go, and fire that creature, and then come back and I'll tell you what I suggest we do next."

Lexie looked at her sister steadily for a minute, took a deep breath as she had prayed she might remember to do when a time of stress arrived, and then answered quietly: "I'm sorry, Elaine, I can't do what you ask. You see, Cinda is the only one we could possibly get without wages for the present, and neither you nor I have money to pay a trained servant. Besides, I told you I went carefully into that matter before I went away, and I could not find a single servant who was willing to come out to this suburb where this is so little bus and train service. I talked with several applicants at several agencies because you had insisted and because I did not know for certain that you might have some secret source of money that would change things. But I simply *couldn't* find a single servant who would come out here. And I thought you felt you *had* to have somebody when I am away."

"Away! You're not still thinking of going away again, are you? I thought you had gone up to college to close that business all up."

"Oh no, I didn't close it up. I tried to arrange to take the rest of my work nearer by, and I may be able to do so, but even then I would have to be away a good deal, and you are not able to do the housework yet, are you?"

"*Yet? Me* do the housework? Well, I should *say not*! So! You thought you were going to be the scholar and I was to be the household drudge! Well, you've got another guess coming, and if you think that I'm going to fall for any such idea as this, you're badly mistaken! You can go out there in the kitchen and fire that vampire and then come back and I'll tell you what to do next."

Lexie took another deep breath and looked at her sister steadily.

"Elaine," she said, "I'm neither expecting to be a scholar nor have you slave for me. I'm just trying to get my diploma because in these days one is not sure of any job that's worth anything unless they have finished college. So, as there are only three months of hard work now to finish my college course, I am going to stick to it and do the best I can. And to that end, I intend to keep Cinda here. I haven't any money to pay a maid or a nurse, and we shall have to get along with Cinda even if you don't like her. That is, unless you can lay down enough money to cover the weekly wages of a better maid. Even then you'd have to find the maid, for I've exhausted my resources in that line."

"The idea!" snorted Elaine. "What have you done with all that money of mine? That's what I want to know. *Some*where you have it stored away, and now you are trying to get money out of me to run this house, and you're not going to get it! Do you hear? You're not going to get a cent more out of me for anything."

Lexie drew a weary breath.

"I'm sorry, Elaine, that you have such a mistaken notion. I can't think where you got it. But you evidently think it is true. And it isn't! Really it isn't. I have only a very little money that I have earned in hard work, saved to get myself a graduating dress because I didn't think it was fair to the other girls in the class for me to go on the platform in a dark dress when they were all in white. I didn't have a single thin dress left that wasn't simply in rags."

"Oh, *really*! What earthly difference would that have made? You probably would never see any of those girls again, and they would never hear of you. I declare, Lexie, you seem to have gotten very worldly. I'm sure your mother would never have approved of that. But whatever you have become, I really don't credit that story of yours about having no money except enough to get a simple white dress. So you might as well understand it, and it is time that you came across with some of the money that belongs to me. You said you had fifty dollars that Mamma left you and that you would give it to me, but I haven't seen it yet. Suppose you go and get it for me now. I need a new dress myself, and I want to go to a beauty parlor and have a facial and a shampoo and a permanent. I am ashamed to meet my lawyer looking like this."

"I'm sorry, Elaine, but I've spent every cent of that fifty dollars on you and your children since you came, to get food for you all to eat, and I haven't any more to spare. And now you'll have to excuse me. I don't want to continue this discussion. It only brings hate in our hearts, and it isn't good for the children to hear bickering all the time. They are coming in now."

"Oh yes, you are very clever to get up excuses to change the subject, but you'll soon find out that it would have been much better for you if you had come through and told the truth, because if you go on like this you'll not only lose every cent of the money yourself, but you'll find yourself sadly in debt for interest on all that money. You see, my righteous little sister, I have definite proof now. We know pretty well just where you have parked that money, and are going to have no trouble in getting possession of it."

"Yes?" Lexie asked, lifting her eyebrows. "Just what evidence could you possibly find of something that doesn't exist and never has?"

"Says you! Well, my dear little sister, I have evidence in your own mother's handwriting stating the whole thing, when and how she took possession of the money, and what she did with it. But of course you know all about that."

"No," said Lexie steadily, "I do not know anything about

any such thing, and I don't believe you do either. I'm sorry to speak this way to you, but I know what I am talking about, and I'm quite sure if you keep on in this way I shall have to take steps that will make you know also just what you are doing. You know I am not entirely without friends, even though I haven't much money. If you persist in acting this way to me I shall be obliged to appeal to them to put an end to it. Certainly I'm not going to stay here and run this house for your benefit, and feed you and take care of your children when there is need, if you are going to persist in being unfriendly. I would rather go away by myself than to live in continual bickering. I'm willing to forget what you have said without formal apologies, and to try to forget what you have said about my mother, who was as kind and good to you as she was to me, her own child, if you will try to be decent to me. But to stay here and take insults like this is unbearable."

"Oh well, if you are going to take that attitude, of course you will have to bear the consequences, but I was just trying to warn you that it is a great deal simpler to come clean and tell what you know. You will be treated with far more leniency than if you persist in lying about it and won't tell what you know."

"Very well," said Lexie quietly and got up to go out of the room, but Elaine detained her.

"Wait a minute, Lexie, there is something I want to ask you. Do you remember a friend of Father's, a Mr. Harry Perrine, a financier who made investments for Father?"

Lexie looked at her sister thoughtfully.

"Yes, I remember a man of that name who *wanted* to make investments for Father, and Father wouldn't have anything to do with him. He said he was rotten and not fit to handle money for anybody, and Mother couldn't bear the sight of him. He was always coming here at mealtime and hanging around to be invited to dinner, and coaxing Father to invest in this and that."

"You're quite mistaken, Lexie. He was a successful financier, and my father put some of my money with him at your mother's suggestion. I have had this investigated, and he owns that Father put money with him intended for me, and after his death your mother drew it all out and invested it elsewhere. He has all the papers to prove it, and he knows just what your mother did with the money after she drew it out to use for herself."

Lexie was very angry by this time, but she knew she must not let this be seen. Her talk with Mr. Gordon had fortified her for such a scene as this, so she closed her lips and turned toward the door again.

"Oh! You haven't anything to say to that!" taunted the angry woman. "I thought that would finish you. There is nothing further you can say!"

"No," said Lexie gently. "I just felt that I would rather not talk any more about this matter lest I might say something unpleasant to you, and I don't see that would do anything but make you more angry. I think if this has to be talked about any more I will let you talk to my lawyer."

"Your *lawyer*!" laughed Elaine. "Since when did my kid sister have a lawyer? Send him on. I'm sure I can give him a few facts that will astonish him, and he will certainly wish he hadn't taken you on as a client."

The sentence ended with a hateful, taunting laugh, but Lexie had gone quietly out of the room, shut the door, and did not hear the meanest part of it. She hurried upstairs to her own dark room and stood for a long time looking out into the starry night, wondering if God really cared for her and was going with her through all this.

And then she bowed her head on the window frame and prayed softly, "Dear God, help me to trust even when things are like this. Help me to remember You are here, walking with me every step of this hard way."

Chapter 13

The letter that Benedict Barron had written to Alexia Kendall reached her the morning after her fiery talk with her sister and almost precipitated another.

In fact, Lexie almost didn't get that letter at all. Elaine had been watching for the postman as *she* expected a letter from one Harry Perrine, and she was close by the front door, ready to fly out before anybody in the house knew that he was there. But Lexie had been watching for the postman also. She had written a letter to Lawyer Gordon as she had promised she would if anything arose at home that she felt he ought to know, and she wanted to get it off in the next mail. She was worried lest she ought not to have let slip those words about her lawyer. Maybe it could do no harm, but she must keep watch on her tongue and not let an angering word break her silence.

Lexie had hurried out from the kitchen door by the side entrance with her letter as soon as she sighted the postman, and met him at the gate. So she got her letter first.

But all these days since that letter had started on its way, Ben Barron had lain on the hard little cot of the ramshackle place they called a hospital, slowly recovering from a serious wound and its resultant illness. The depressing condition had been brought about by his long exposure and the lack of food and rest, following his unremitting fighting of fire and fiends without any assurance that they would sometime reach safety.

Most of the convalescing time he had dreamed and slept by turns and in snatches. He had eaten a little of whatever they gave him apathetically, slept some more, and waked again to dreams of the past. But sometimes there came to his mind the thought of the letter he had sent out so blindly into his old world to a girl who did not know him, and whom he scarcely knew at all. He would wonder if it would ever reach her, and if it did, whether she would be minded to answer it.

Of course it had been a crazy, unconventional thing to write that letter. If he had waited until he was really well and strong he never would have written it at all. Though in these war times, plenty of girls were writing bright, cheery letters to boys they had never seen nor heard of before. They were just given an address by somebody, and asked to write to a lonesome soldier. So he hoped this little Lexie-girl would be moved to answer his letter, if it ever reached her.

He sometimes dreamed of what she might think or say or do if the letter reached her. But as the days passed by, the letter faded into the past, and new thoughts about going back to the fight again began to take form in his renewed brain as his body slowly healed. The letter took on less significance. It had been a vagary of his sick mind, out here in that fiery field, a brief respite from the heat and terror. God's cool mountain with the dew on the grass at the roadside, and one of God's children smiling and swinging on a little white gate—just a symbol of home it had been, but he still was glad he had written the letter, if only to get it off his mind.

❧❦❧

Lexie, holding that letter in her hand, seeing her own name in an unfamiliar handwriting written on it, noting the strange foreign stamp with the war insignia upon it, wondered. She read her name again to make sure and slid it into her apron pocket, one hand safely guarding it as she turned to go back to the house.

Then Elaine's sharp voice interrupted her.

"Give that letter to me!" she said, stepping out to the small front portico and holding out her hand. "How *dare* you put it into your pocket and take it in to examine!"

Lexie looked up in surprise.

"But it isn't your letter," she said sweetly. "It is *mine!*"

"*Your* letter! That's a likely story. I was expecting an important business letter, and I don't want to be delayed in reading it. I *demand* to see that letter instantly!"

Elaine was very angry, and was talking in loud, piercing tones. Lexie was aware instantly of furtively opened doors and windows from neighbors' houses. They would be too polite to stand around and listen, but they could not fail to hear that an angry altercation was going on between the sisters, and pursed lips and shrugs would be exchanged between those women who heard. Oh, this was terrible!

"Why certainly, Elaine, look and see my name on the envelope," she said, and held the letter up where she knew her sister could easily read her name.

Elaine leaned over the porch and looked, reached out her hand for the letter but did not quite touch it.

"Give me that letter!" demanded Elaine again. "There is some trick about this! You are as sly as can be. You've exchanged the envelopes or something, and you're trying to open my letter and find out what I'm writing to my lawyer about. Give me that letter, I say!"

"Why no, I won't give you my letter," said Lexie. "Why should I? It's my letter, not yours. Oh Elaine, why will you go on acting like this? You're fairly driving me to leave. Is that what you want me to do? It would be much easier and cheaper for me to go than to stay here and submit to all this from you. It is shameful for you to act this way, and there is no point to it. What is your idea anyway?"

"Who is that letter from?" demanded Elaine. "I insist that you tell me at once. I don't want any more underhanded business. After all your threats yesterday, are you doing some foolish thing, writing to some man and trying to get help?"

Lexie laughed.

"Why no, Elaine, I haven't been writing to any man, and I don't know yet who wrote me the letter. You haven't given me a chance to go into the house and open it. It's probably from someone I met at college."

"It's from a *man!*" insisted Elaine. "That's a man's handwriting! You went to a *women's* college."

"Yes, but we had men callers, several men teachers, and often met men in the town and at games and so on."

"Now don't try to tell me that you had some incipient lovers out in that dull college town of yours. You aren't the kind of girl that attracts men, and never will be."

"Oh," laughed Lexie amusedly. "Does this look like a love letter? No, I didn't have any lovers out there that I know of, but I did have a few friends, and this is probably from one of them, or it might be from the dean."

"No!" said Elaine sharply. "That's an overseas envelope. I know their look, you know."

"Oh yes. It is overseas. But there were a number of the girls' brothers who are overseas of course. It really isn't important, though, I'm quite sure," and Lexie slipped the letter into her apron pocket again, with her protecting hand over it.

"Give me that letter! I want to see for myself that you're not fooling me."

"No!" said Lexie firmly, and sudden as a bird in flight she flew down the path to the kitchen door and fled up to her room, where she locked her door and sat down to read her letter.

She did not, however, stay upstairs long. She knew that to make much of that letter would only be to continue the controversy with Elaine. She must make light of the whole thing. With fingers that trembled just a little at the thought of a letter from anybody for herself, she opened the envelope and unfolded the letter. Later she would read it more carefully, of course, but just now it was as if she must take the whole thing in at a glance and be ready to be composed about it if Elaine should venture to climb the stairs and try to investigate.

Lexie had a trained eye, used to taking in a good deal at a glance, and the whole lovely idea of the letter burst upon her mind like a sweet picture. That boy, with his books in a strap and his handsome, laughing eyes—yes, she remembered him! Of course! She even remembered his asking her if her name was short for Lexicon. She laughed and swept her eyes downward to the quiet, wistful, respectful closing, and then folded the letter and locked it quickly inside her old suitcase under the bed. She ran downstairs and began to help Cinda in the dining room, making out a list of small necessities that must be ordered from the store.

Suddenly Elaine entered like a frowning nemesis.

"Who was that letter from? I insist on being told."

"Why should you be told?" asked Lexie innocently. "It was from an old friend I used to know in my school days. He's in the armed forces now, and he was just sending me a greeting the way all the boys in the army do. It isn't important."

Elaine gave her an angry, suspicious look, but Lexie went out the back door and down the field to the store. Then Elaine went back to her own scheming. On her way Lexie had an opportunity to think over this remarkable surprise, remember more definitely the boy who had accosted her on her white gate so long ago, and try to think just how he had looked. A nice smile, a twinkle in his eyes, pleasant words—to just a little girl! And to think he had remembered it all these years!

When Lexie came back from the store with the yeast cake Cinda had sent her for, there was a look of unexpected brightness in her pretty, wistful face that quite gave old Cinda pleasure. She knew there had been some sort of a quarrel between the two sisters, and she was glad to see that Lexie no longer looked as if she had been crushed. There was a lightness and a brightness that was more of what Cinda would like to see in Lexie's face.

And all the morning as Lexie went on her sunlit way across the meadows and did her other errands at the store, and back again, she was thinking back to the day she had swung on the gate and seen the nice, big boy! And to think he had written to her! Remembered her all these years, and thought of her when he was under fire! He said that the memory of her face had helped him bear the heat and fire and terror. Thanked her for just being herself, a little girl with a smile in her eyes for a stranger boy.

As soon as lunch was over and the children started off to their play again, Elaine retired in a huff to her bed and a nap. Lexie stole upstairs to her room and locked the door, and there in the quiet she read that letter over again. Read it several times, and reveled in the fact that she had a letter from a young man across the sea who remembered her.

When she knew the letter by heart she took her fountain pen out of her handbag, hunted up some stationery from her little old desk in the attic, and wrote an answer to that letter. Somehow it seemed to her that she must answer at once, that a letter like that demanded an immediate reply. A lonely soldier boy who turned back to his childhood for a bit of comfort! She would let him know that she remembered, too.

Dear Sergeant:

Yes, I remember you. You were a tall boy with curly black hair and a nice smile and twinkles in

your eyes. I was wonderfully surprised that you
noticed me, just a little girl.

I remember what you said, too. You asked
me if my name, Lexie, was short for Lexicon. I
laughed over that a lot all by myself, afterward.

But I am very much surprised that you
thought of a little girl when you were under fire,
and quite pleased that the thought of my mountain
helped you through hard places. Dew on a hot forehead would be pleasant, and I'm glad I was that
to a brave soldier, for somehow I know you were
brave. You looked that way the day I saw you.

Your letter came to me here at the little white
house, down by the white gate where I went to
meet the postman. I just happened to be here or I
wouldn't have got the letter. I'm glad I came.

I've had some hard times, too. Your letter came
on one of the hardest days and made a bright spot
in what would otherwise have been a very dark
day. I thank you very much for taking the trouble
to write me.

Someday perhaps the war will end and you will
come home, and then perhaps you can come to the
hometown. I would like so much to see you again.

Your little-girl-friend,
Lexie
(Alexia Kendall)

Lexie slipped out the back door and whisked across the

fields to the post office with her letter, and when she returned she went straight up to the attic to put things right. She hadn't had time before, and Elaine hadn't even gone back to attempt clearing up the mess she had made. Lexie was appalled. Blankets and pillows and papers and books spread out in a heterogeneous mass, papers and old letters all scattered over the top. She stood still for a moment, angry tears springing into her eyes.

Then she remembered.

Her Lord was with her. He would know how hard this was for her to bear, seeing her mother's precious things that had been so carefully guarded and put away in such lovely order, now all crumpled up and thrown around, some of them crushed in balls and thrown under the edge of the eaves.

Lexie dropped down in the midst of all the disorder and struggled with her tears. "Dear God," she prayed softly, "please, help me now. Help me to forgive her, and not to let her know I am angry."

Then she lifted her head and went to work.

First of all, the precious letters she gathered into a neat pile. The box they had been packed away in was sprawled at the other end of the room with its sides torn down, and its cover bent in two. Elaine was evidently angry because she couldn't find what she was searching for, perhaps. Well, why think about it? Just get things in order as quickly as possible, and then put them all under lock and key and hide the key or keep it always about her. That would be the only safe way. She would probably have to go down to the hardware store and buy some more locks. Or perhaps a hammer and some nails would be better. That ought to make things safer, for she was well aware that Elaine could never pull a nail out of a board, and it wouldn't be easy for her to open a box that was nailed up. She must be prevented from pulling things to pieces again.

So, carefully, thoughtfully, she put her precious belongings into safekeeping, and finally nailed up the boxes securely.

She was almost done with her work when the stair door opened and Elaine's shrill voice complained: "What on earth are you doing upstairs, Lexie? Here I lie down to rest and just get to sleep, and you set up the most unearthly noise right over my head! It seems to me that you are just doing this to be disagreeable, and you know how easily I get one of those awful headaches. I feel one coming on now, and I just know I'll have it all night."

Lexie stopped in dismay.

"Oh, I'm sorry, Elaine. I thought you were still sitting out on the porch."

"But what are you doing?"

"Why, I was just nailing up some boxes so things won't get all over the place."

"You mean you are nailing up boxes you don't want *me* to look into. That makes me quite certain you have something more that you are afraid I will find."

"No," said Lexie sadly. "I just wanted to put things away. It looked terrible up here. I'm only straightening up. But I'm quite sure there is nothing up here you would want to find. Oh Elaine, I wish you wouldn't be so unfriendly. You give me the feeling that you are just here to fight me."

"Really? Well, if you want me to treat you differently, you know what to do. Come clean. Tell me all you know about that money. Then I'll be as friendly as I always used to be." Lexie sighed.

"I've told you all I know already and you won't believe me. What is the use of talking anymore?"

"Well, there isn't any use. Not if you keep to that attitude, of course," and the stair door closed with a slam. Then she could hear Elaine's footsteps clicking back to the living room.

Lexie took a deep breath and, turning, went on with her work. But she drove no more nails at that time. There was no need to make her sister angrier than she already was.

When the attic was in neat order again, and all traces of the onslaught were removed, Lexie went quietly downstairs and marshaled the children home from the neighbor's sandpile, which had become the unfailing rendezvous of attraction to them. Their mother seemed to pay no more attention to them than if she had never heard of them, unless she thought somebody else was finding fault with them or attempting to punish them, then she roused to a scathing sarcasm. But Elaine, after her tempestuous outburst, had gone back to her bed and was soundly asleep at last, an old mystery-story novel lying open by her side. So Lexie was free for the time being. After the children were fed, she coaxed them off to bed by telling them a couple of stories while Cinda reluctantly prepared a special tray for Elaine, to tempt her to relax and stop tormenting Lexie.

But after the tray had been administered, Elaine still refused to be on good terms with Lexie, to Cinda's great disgust, and went back to her bed and her novel. So Lexie sent Cinda off for a walk, and a little time to visit an old friend in the neighborhood. Lexie sat on the quiet porch and had opportunity to think over the remarkable letter she had received. A soldier in the midst of the fire! She likened his situation to her own. For in a way they were alike. Although no physical harm was coming to herself, she was in no danger to her health, she had no pain nor actual fear to endure, yet on the other hand, what could be hotter than her sister's scorching words? What could be lonelier than this existence, day after day in company with one who apparently hated her, and lived only to do her harm, to subjugate her?

But she must not get to pitying herself. Her soldier boy was not doing that. He was drawing comfort from a distant picture of mountain strength, dewy grass, and a child's small cool hand. And *she* must find the comfort that surely was somewhere about for her. And if she didn't find it she must press on anyway. Oh yes, there was comfort, there *must* be comfort in the thought that God was with her, and God cared, had promised to be with her through water or through fire. Yes, this lad from her childhood past had helped her just as he claimed that she had helped him. The thought of him was pleasant, like something out of a story, when all had been unhappy prose before the letter came. It certainly was a strangely beautiful thing for that grand boy to have grown up and yet to have remembered her, an insignificant little girl, remembered her well enough to take the trouble to write her a letter.

There was one thing that made her sad for him. He must feel strangely alone in this world that he should bother to write to a mere thought-shadow of a child he had seen but once. There must be something almost occult about this. Lexie couldn't understand it, but she liked it. Perhaps God had made him do it! What a wonderful thought!

And then she heard Elaine groaning, heard her flinging

her book away upon the floor and bursting out into heart-breaking sobs.

Lexie hesitated for just a moment. Should she go to her? And then she heard her calling Cinda petulantly like a child's wail, and she hesitated no longer. Stepping to the bedroom door she said gently: "Is something the matter, Elaine? Are you feeling worse? Can I do anything for you?"

Elaine stopped her sobbing and looked up.

"Oh, it's *you*, is it?" she said in a voice like an icicle. "I didn't call *you*, I called Cinda. I wouldn't want to trouble *you*, who are so utterly unaccommodating. Where is Cinda?"

"Cinda went out for a little while," said Lexie pleasantly. "Tell me what you want, Elaine. I'll be glad to do anything I can for you. I don't want to be unaccommodating."

"Oh, you *don't*, don't you?" taunted the unhappy woman. "Well then, come clean and tell me what I want to know about that money!"

"I'm sorry, Elaine. I've told you all I know. You don't believe me. There is nothing else to say!"

"Oh, *be still!*" snapped Elaine, kicking her slipper off at her. "I'm sick of such lying prattle. I wish you would go upstairs and let me alone. Here I am, a widow if there ever was one, or worse than a widow perhaps. The only man I ever loved, either dead or a prisoner of war, and I all alone having to battle my way with an unfriendly world, and penniless, having to fend for my poor, dear little children. And my only sister, instead of showing sympathy and kindness and being ready to sacrifice some part of the fortune that she has been enjoying, remains silent and smug and refuses to divulge what has been done with the booty!"

Elaine was working herself up to a fine fury now, and turned to Lexie fiercely. "Get *out*!" she cried. "I say, *get out*! I don't want to see you again, *ever*, *anymore*!"

Lexie quietly stepped out of the room and said no more.

What was she to do with a situation like this? There seemed to be no possible way of making Elaine believe what she had told her. How could she go on from day to day under conditions like this? Certainly she couldn't hope to do much worthwhile studying.

But then, this wasn't any worse than that soldier over on the other side of the world had it. There was no actual fire here. And God let that young man go through that, probably for some reason she wasn't wise enough to understand. And He wanted her to go through this, and walk worthy of Him, worthy of having God for her Companion, Christ for her Savior. Could there possibly be glory in this walk? Would any witness she could manifest be a testimony, to her unbelieving sister, for instance? What and if somehow by her life she might show forth to Elaine what Christ wanted to be to *her*? It didn't seem possible that anything she could do would do any good, but if it did, wouldn't it be worth doing? Of course she could never do it alone. It would have to be Christ living in her, and not herself.

Then she knelt down by her bed and talked to the Lord about it, and it really seemed as she knelt in the dark room that the Lord Himself stood there and showed her how this might be, if she would yield herself utterly to Him.

Chapter 14

When Ben Barron received Lexie's letter, he was sitting up in a very crude deck chair on the meager little upper veranda of the tiny hospital, a building hastily assembled from what material could be found in the vicinity.

He had had a long hard siege, a bad time getting well, and perhaps little heart to help the doctors who were doing their best with the supplies at hand and within the necessary limitations of the war. But now it seemed fairly certain that he was to recover, and to that end he was ordered out in the chair to do nothing, which wasn't very helpful to a person of Benedict Barron's eager, restless temperament.

For Ben Barron was lonely. Definitely lonely. This wasn't like being among his comrades in camp, or on the march, or even under fire with a lot of friends who had grown to be closer than brothers because they had fought together, had bled together, and some of them had died. His clan had grown during this season of war to be a part of him. But now there were none of them here. The few who had come to the hospital when he came had either got well and gone or died from their wounds. He had no one here. He was looking forward to going away himself very soon, he hoped, yet he had no special place to go unless they would let him go back into action. The doctor had said that must not be for some time, if ever. He would have to await developments in his recovery. So, he had to sit here and try to build a new philosophy of life.

When his thoughts turned back to home they seemed to come up against a blank wall. His father had died three years before he went to war, and his mother died in the hospital while he was fighting fire. He would never see her again on this earth. The thought of his native country was gloomed with sadness because she was gone. There seemed to be no one left over there whom he wanted to see just now, no one who would really care whether he lived or died. Oh, there were a couple of aunts and an uncle, several cousins. The girls had written a letter apiece to him after he entered the army, just stupid sort of formal letters because they had a duty toward all soldiers, and he was moreover their cousin. One of them had recently written him that she was married to a flier and described her elaborate wedding in detail, said she wished he had been there to add his uniform to the procession. Another one had joined the WACs, and still a third was an army nurse and going overseas. They were enthusiastic and eager over the war as if it were a new game. They spoke of their uniforms and training as they used to tell him about their new permanents and lipsticks. They were giddy girls full of rollick with no thought for serious things, though perhaps if they got into the real war it might put some sense into them. But they and their crowd were not interesting to him now. He might get over this feeling during the years perhaps, but just at present he was not interested in them at all.

There had been another girl, a girl he had almost decided to take for his girl. Then, one day just before he left for camp, she came smiling to him to show him her new ring. She was engaged to another soldier. He had waited too long. He had lost out! Or had he? He hadn't been sure she was the girl he wanted, until somebody else got her, and that put a gloom on things for a while until he got interested in war. He had nearly forgotten about her now, the way she lifted her sunny lashes, the dark look of her big, soft eyes. But it had closed one volume of the book of regret for him when he went away from his own land. Perhaps that was why it had been so easy to take the thought of a little child in a blue dress from long ago to think about out there on that dark hot field of fire when memory needed a relief, instead of some girl of his own age who had been a companion. That girl who had shown him her new ring had been a friend of years, yet she had turned so easily to the new soldier who had only been in town a week or two visiting some of her friends, when she got that ring. He felt she had been rather faithless to him. But perhaps she had never counted him as closer than just a playmate. Well, he had a feeling that women were rather undependable. And so after he had waited for several weeks since writing his letter and sending it out into a world that had likely forgotten him, he had come to class Lexie with all other girls. She wouldn't likely even bother to acknowledge his letter. She was grown up, maybe married, no longer a little girl, and never really knew him anyway. So he must forget that letter. He had acknowledged his debt for her little memory, and that was that. It had been a crazy idea to write to her anyway.

And that was what he was thinking when the nurse brought him the letter. Her letter. Little Lexie!

He gave a quick glance around after the nurse had handed him the letter to see if anyone near was looking at him. But the man in the next chair was sound asleep, and the two chairs on the other side of him were vacant. Somehow he felt half silly getting a letter from a little girl, and on his own initiative.

He had known at once that it was her letter, partly because there were so few others who would be likely to write to him now as the relatives had all done their kindly duty, one letter apiece; and partly that he had sensed the familiarity of the postmark even before he was able to read it clearly.

So, slowly, carefully, he tore open the envelope and pulled out the sheet of paper, folded so neatly, traced over with such characterful handwriting. He was conscious of being glad that the letter was not too short. He must savor every line of it, for whether it was pleasant or not it was the only letter he had had in a long time, and he wanted to enjoy it, even if it was a cold haughty rebuke from a grown-up young woman who did not like it that he had written to her, recalling such a childish thing as that she had been swinging on a gate!

"Dear Sergeant," she had written, familiarly, pleasantly, like any girl in a social center, being friendly with a soldier who was lonely!

He read on eagerly now. Yes, she remembered him. She recalled what he had said and had laughed over it by herself! Bless her little heart! Then the next paragraph—yes, he understood the strain he had been under. She knew what dew on a hot forehead would mean. She did not resent it that he had thought of her and acknowledged that she had been a help to him.

As he read on, he was thrilled to think she had answered, glad that he had written her. He had acted on a hunch and he was glad he had. He shut his eyes for an instant, and now he could see her in a blue dress, walking down to the little white gate to meet the postman.

She had just happened to be there or she would not have gotten the letter. Then she must have been away. Where? Had she moved away? Or been away to school, or working somewhere like everybody else?

He opened his eyes and read on. Would the rest of the letter tell where she had been, and why she would not have received his letter if she had not been there?

Ah! She had had hard days! Poor child! She was going through some kind of fire, too, though she didn't say what kind of fire it was. Her letter really told him nothing about her daily life and circumstances. Yet it did give the general background of a common experience, hard times, dark days, a life under fire that had to be gone through with. She acknowledged that his letter had made a dark day bright for her, and that was as good as making a fiery day cool and restful for him.

He drew a long breath of pleasure and reflected to what a pass he had come that a letter from a young unknown could bring such pleasure to him. He read on to the end. She hoped the war would end and he would come home someday, that she would like to see him. Well, that settled it. He would go home when he got that promised leave that the doctor had hinted might be in the offering for him if he continued to improve as he had been doing lately. Yes, he would certainly go home and seek out the little white house with the white gate, and the little girl with the blue eyes, and they would get acquainted, get really acquainted. That would be something to look forward to.

He lay back in his chair with his eyes closed and the letter held tight in his hand, and when the nurse came padding along on her rubber heels with his glass of milk, he did not hear her. His thoughts were absorbed in what he was going to write back to the little girl.

Yes, he was going to write back at once! He wouldn't need to wait for courtesy's sake because a letter took plenty of time to travel across the world and get there without putting unnecessary time between. He would start tomorrow morning and write a good, long letter this time because her letter would likely be longer if he made his long. He needed good, long letters to get through these days until he could go home.

So the next day he wrote a really long letter, taking it at intervals as the nurse would allow, and writing as if he had known her always. It was quite plain from everything he said that her letter had been a great delight to him, and so he wrote:

> *Dear Lexie:*
>
> *You don't mind if I call you that, do you? Because you know you told me that was your name, and I'm not so well acquainted with the Kendall part; and it doesn't seem right to call you "Miss," though*

of course you must be by this time.

I can't tell you how glad I was to get your letter, for you see, I had worried a good deal lest you would think me presuming, now you are grown up, to dare to write to you, right of out of the blue, when you weren't the little girl I remember anymore. But you see, I felt as if I had a proper introduction because you came to me in my troubled vision of you that dark night among the fire and pain. So when the nurse brought me your letter, I was really glad. And when I read the letter I was doubly so.

I am sitting up now a little while every day. I was in a deck chair on a sort of scaffold they call a porch when your letter came, and it seemed to me the sky looked bluer, and the few trees around were greener after I read it. I suppose that may sound childish to you, but after you've been in a hard, narrow bed for weeks and weeks, and wondered if you would ever get up, and after you've wondered if anybody would know or care if you didn't, a voice from the faraway home-place seems very sweet, and very nearly puts one out of his head. So, thank you for the letter.

It would be nice if you had sent me a little snapshot of yourself. I'd like so much to see how you look now you've grown up, so I will know you if I ever get home and have a chance to see you. And I'm sending you one a fellow took of me in London before we came out here. I've been keeping it just as a sort of souvenir of London, but I'd like to send it to you. It will be more as if we were talking to one another. I'm not sure they will let it get by the censors, but if they don't, it won't be much loss, so I'm sending it.

This letter is getting pretty long, but there's one more thing I'd like to tell you before I close, because I'd like somebody to know about it, and there is no one else I'd care to tell it to or who would likely understand. But I have a feeling you will.

It's about an experience I had while I was lying out in that hot dark field with fiery pain in my shoulder, and more planes bringing more fiery bombs coming on and on. One had just exploded near me, and I was thinking that the next one would be the end for me.

And then suddenly there was a great stillness, and I wondered if perhaps I was dead after all. But then I heard a voice speaking. It said "I am here with you!" And I looked up and saw that it was the Lord!

I had never seen Him before, of course, but I knew Him by the nail-prints in His hands, and by the great glory-light in His face. I wonder if you have ever seen Him, or heard His voice? Please don't think I'm crazy. I'm just an ordinary fellow, but my mother used to talk about Him, used to read me stories from the Bible. A verse I had learned from my mother came back to me then. "When thou passest through the waters, I will be with thee; and through the rivers, they shall not overflow thee: when thou walkest through the fire, thou shalt not be burned."

I had been through a river, a deep wide river, but it did not overflow me, though I had thought at one time it would; and then I had been through fire, fire after fire, but I was still alive! I had not been burned. I was startled. That verse had come back into my life, spoken just for me, spoken by the Lord Himself! It wasn't anything I had just imagined. I had heard His voice speaking the words! You don't know what it did to me. It is something I can never forget. And because you are the only friend in touch with me now, I want you to know about it. Do you mind?

Just today I got to thinking those words over that I heard Him say to me, and I asked the nurse if she knew whether there was a Bible anywhere that I could read for a few minutes. She said yes, there was a chaplain in the next ward now who had one, and she would borrow it for me. So she did, and I looked up that verse, and then I read on. A little further on there was another verse, almost like a signature to a letter. It said, "I, even I, am the Lord*; and beside me there is no savior."*

So, I have that to think about. He is the only Savior. He saved me from fire and water. There'll be other things further on that I'll need saving

*from, too. He saved me when they thought I was
dying from my wounds, so there'll be other times
ahead when I'll need saving. I'm going to trust
Him from now on.*

*I wonder, do you know Him? Did you ever
see Him? Do you trust Him, too?*

*Forgive me if I sound crazy, but I wanted to
tell you. I'm going to investigate this, because I
know it's real.*

Please write to me again.
Your friend,
Ben

The letter went off, and then Ben began to worry himself
lest it would sound crazy to her when it reached her. People
didn't talk about seeing the Lord in the workaday world where
she lived nor where he had lived either. People didn't have such
experiences as he had had every day. They didn't go through
such fire, they didn't stay alive afterward, and they didn't meet
the Lord. It wouldn't make any difference how long he lived
afterward, nothing, nobody, could even make him believe the
Lord had not come to him. If they didn't believe it, they just
didn't know, that was all. Well, he had given the story to Lexie,
and this would be a sort of test of what she was. If she made
fun of him, he probably wouldn't write again, at least not more
than once or twice. He would know she just hadn't met the
Lord and couldn't understand until she did.

So he tried to put the matter out of his mind, but he had
a sunny feeling in his heart continually, that he was no more

alone in a strange land with no place anywhere that wasn't strange. He had the Lord with him continually. He had found another verse in that borrowed Bible before he sent it back to the sick chaplain. A verse that said, *"Lo, I am with you always, even unto the end of the world."* So, what did it matter whether he had anyone else or not?

Perhaps Ben Barron wouldn't have come so fully to believe in what he had been through if life had always been full of fun and joy to him, but the loss of so many things he had cared for when he was younger and the terrible strain through which he had passed had opened his mind to receive. And then, too, that vision had been very vivid.

So the days went on, and the patient was docile and quiet and content. He was not restless, though he knew that as soon as the doctor felt he was able to travel, and the journey could be arranged, he was to be sent home to America on furlough. It was wonderful to look forward to, but he was not impatient because secretly he wanted to wait until there could be a chance of another letter from Lexie. But when he realized this he told himself he was a fool; she was only a child. Well, grown-up of course, but nothing to him but an idea, a vision. And why should he care whether she wrote again or not?

And then one night, in the still darkness, it came to him what was behind this whole feeling, but it came to him clearly then, and he acknowledged to himself what it was. It was because he was troubled that perhaps he should not have told that sacred, tender experience to anyone, even a girl who was in his mind but a child with innocent, lovely thoughts. Perhaps it was a desecration of his Christ that he should have told that experience at all. And why did he choose that memory-child to hear it?

But the days went on and the doctors watched and rejoiced over this patient who had seemed at first so hopeless. He was really getting well, and he was being very docile and doing everything he ought to do willingly. That was an unusual state for a patient to be in. Most of them were so impatient to go away, to get home, but he seemed content to lie here and wait.

Then one day the nurse brought him another letter, and she studied it as she carried it across the hall to his room where he was lying down resting. It must be from a girl. It was a girl's handwriting. And when she handed it to him she had the pleasure of seeing a brightness in his face, lighting up his handsome features. He was thin and somewhat wasted of course, but he was still handsome, and she wondered what the girl was like. Or would she be his sister? Perhaps. But he only thanked her and smiled. And she had to go her way without having her curiosity satisfied.

Ben Barron sat up on his cot with interest and opened his letter. It was from Lexie. She *had* written again! And out of the envelope as he opened it carefully, there fell a small unmounted photograph of a lovely girl. Yes, it was the same little girl with the sweet eyes and the charming, innocent smile. She hadn't thought him quite a fool or she would never have sent him the picture, and there was a look in those eyes of trust and understanding, just as he had hoped there would be, just as he had seemed to read in her child-eyes so long ago. He had taken a girl on trust from memory and now he was looking into the pictured face of that girl, and she came fully up to what such a child should have been. He was thrilled with the picture.

Then suddenly he thought to himself that he had not read her letter yet, and he unfolded the pages. Yes, it was a good long letter, and he felt a joy. Just why he didn't understand, only he had been so lonely, and now there was someone who was interested enough to write him, interested enough to take hold of the slender invitation he had thrown out and respond to it. He was crazy of course, but he was very glad. He had been waiting, and the letter had come before he was gone. So he read.

Dear Sergeant Ben,

It was wonderful to get your letter from such a far land, and I was so glad to have the little snapshot you sent. It is just like what you were when I saw you. I'm sure I remember you well. Looking at the picture made me sure. Your nice smile is just the same. And I think it was such a good idea for you to send me the picture and ask for mine because it sort of identifies us for each other.

So I am sending you a little picture that was taken for our class book in college, and I happened to have one left over. It's not a very wonderful picture, but it will give you some idea of what the little girl swinging on the gate looks like now. You see, I've been very busy lately, and I haven't swung on the gate for a long time of course. So I don't know whether my smile has changed or not, but you can imagine the picture is smiling at you because I am so pleased that you wrote to me.

And now you have told me a wonderful thing

about your experience that night of so much fire. I
am glad to know, because it makes me sure you are
a Christian, and your experience matches something that has happened to me. I'd like to try and
tell you, if you don't mind.

You see, my father died, and then my mother,
just a little over a year ago while I was still in
college, and now I am on my own. There hasn't
been much money, but I found some work and
was getting through. I've just a few weeks more
to go now before the end with a nice job promised
when I finish. But my half sister telegraphed me
her husband was reported missing in action, and
she was very sick and was coming home with her
three little children.

I couldn't stop her. She didn't give me time,
and the house is half hers. Of course I knew I must
stay and help her out. Things haven't been easy.
I haven't been through fire, but sometimes sharp
words can burn your soul very much like a flame
of fire. I've had to give up going back to my college,
but I have been able to arrange to finish and take
final examinations at the university in our nearby
city. Still it is not going to be easy to stay here. My
sister does not approve of my finishing college. She
feels I ought to go to work. But I can get a better
job if I have a diploma.

Things have been rather awful sometimes, and
one night when I couldn't get to sleep, thinking it
over and wondering how long this kind of thing

could go on, suddenly I seemed to feel the Presence of the Lord in the room, and to realize that I wasn't alone in this. God was here, and He knew why it had to be. If I trusted Him, it would all come out the way He has planned.

You see, though I've never seen the Lord the way you describe, I've known about Him always. When I was a little girl I took Him for my Savior. But I'm afraid I haven't done much about it since. Of course I've prayed and sometimes read my Bible, and gone to church when I could, but I haven't taken the trouble to get better acquainted with Him. And while I lay there with the feeling of that Presence in my room, it came to me that God was letting all this happen to me to call my attention to Him, and to His love for me. While I had had comforts and good times, I had practically forgotten Him, and it seemed there was nothing would call my attention back to Him but trouble and sorrow. And it even took a lot of that. So I began to see it all, that He really loved me, and wanted my loving service.

My sister wasn't ever interested in religious things. She didn't join the church when I did, and never wanted to go to Sunday school, and she used to taunt me saying I thought I was so awfully good because I went to church, whenever I did anything she didn't like. And I began to see that perhaps the thing that I had to do was to show her how I had a Savior who could help me through hard places. I knew I hadn't been doing that at all. And somewhere I had heard that the only thing God has put us here for is to witness for Him.

So I knew, there in the darkness, with the feeling of God's Presence in the room, that henceforth I was going to try to do that.

But I knew I could never do it of myself. It would have to be Christ living in me, instead of myself, and living my life for me.

So that's how it is with me now. I've just started, but I'm trying to let Him have His way in me. That's why I'm glad you told me about meeting the Lord, for if you hadn't, I never would dared tell you all this. What you have told me has made me feel that we are really friends because we both belong to Christ.

I've never talked about such things to anybody else but my mother now and then, and she was very shy of it. So maybe I do not know how to say such things, but it certainly makes me glad to know someone who can talk the way you do.

I am so glad you are getting better, and I do hope you will not have to go back and fight under fire anymore. But I know if you feel that it is needed you will go. But God will be there, and nothing can hurt you. You may not always be able to see Him, but He will be there, and I am glad.

Your friend,
Lexie

There was a grave, sweet look in Ben's eyes as he finished the letter, and then he thoughtfully turned back to the first page and read it over again. In his heart there was chiming a pleasant thought. *"Dear little girl,"* it said. *"I never knew a girl could be like that."* And later when he thought it over again, he said to himself: "If Norine had been like that, she never would have done what she did to me. That is, she never would have led me on to believe she cared the way she did when she didn't really care at all, only wanted me for an added trophy."

Ben Barron had read the letter through three times before the nurse came back, and he had such a renewed, happy look that she could not help but notice it.

"Well, I guess you must have had good news in your letter," she said as she handed him his glass of orange juice.

"Why, yes, thank you. I did. By the way, when is that doctor coming again?"

"Well, he said he was coming in tomorrow. Why, don't you feel as well?"

"Oh sure! I feel as if I could go into the fight again."

"You do?" she said with surprise. "But I think you're due for a furlough before you go into any more fights. At least that's what I heard the doctor say the last time he was here."

A happy grin dawned on Ben's lips.

"Suits me all right," said Ben. "I'm getting right fed up on lying here in a hospital."

"Well, you've been a pretty good patient, and we'll all feel sorry to have you go. Not sorry for you, you know, but sorry for ourselves. We're going to miss you."

"Thank you," said Ben with satisfaction.

"Do you know what I think about you?" said the nurse,

lingering a moment with misty eyes upon her patient. "I think if there ever was a real Christian, it's you, even if you *are* a soldier."

Ben Barron looked startled.

"Oh!" he said embarrassedly. "I'm not much of a Christian. I never claimed—"

"No, you didn't claim to be, but you just acted like one. You don't always have to go around talking about what you believe to make an impression. It's when you stand pain with courage and don't get mad when you can't have everything to eat you want. It's when you speak kind to the nurses even if they bring your bathwater too hot and forget to bring you cold water when you're thirsty. You live like you know God. Not just having been brought up polite, but as if you had a real gentleness in your soul like they say Christ had!"

"Yes?" said Ben Barron, wonderingly. "Well, that's extraordinary of you to say that, because I just had a letter from a friend I used to know in America, and she talked something like that, but not about me, you understand. She was talking about some of the hard things she had to bear, and it seemed to be her idea, too, that it wasn't all in profession whether one was a Christian or not. She seemed to think a Christian had to go through fire, like a soldier, to prove the Lord was his Savior."

"Well, there's soldiers and soldiers. Plenty of them are brave to stand fire, but not everyone can keep a civil tongue in his head when he's suffering. It takes something more than human nature to do that at times. I know for I've seen plenty of 'em."

"Yes?" said Ben Barron, thoughtfully. "I guess it does. It takes a divine nature. And if you've seen anything like that in me I guess it was because I met the Lord out there on the field of fire."

"You—*what?*"

"I met the Lord. He came and stood beside me. He spoke to me. And I guess it's up to me, since then, to act a little different from what I used to act when I was just on my own and acting out what I felt."

The nurse stared.

"That might make a difference! You certainly are different. I am sorry to see you go! We need more like you. You're a loyal soldier if there ever was one," and brushing away the mists from her eyes she hurried out to get another man's orange juice, another man who definitely was *not* a Christian.

But Ben Barron sat still with his glass of orange juice in his hand and stared into the distance. She thought he was a Christian! Lexie thought so, too. *Was* he? He certainly had not known he was. He certainly had done very little about it in the past. And yet he had given a testimony to that nurse! Was it all because he had met the Lord out there in the fire under the stars? Well, it was time he did something definite about this! When he got somewhere where they had such things, he would buy himself a Bible. That ought to help!

Chapter 15

Lexie was enrolled now in the university, and very busy every day with her study, and doing what duties she could find time for between about the house. Elaine found a great deal of fault with her, and hindered her in every way she could. When she would discover Lexie studying she would demand some service from her—lemonade made, or cakes brought, and would she please go across the street and see what the children were doing, and bring them home and give them baths and dress them up?

Lexie made protests now and then, urging a heavy schedule at college, and examinations imminent, but this only brought scorn from Elaine.

"Such silly nonsense! A great big girl like you going to school at our age! You ought to be back at home getting the meals and cleaning the house and helping me with the children."

"*Helping* her!" Lexie complained to herself. "As if she ever lifted a finger for those children, except to scold them, or protect them against others' protests!"

But what was the use of protesting? Elaine always won in the end, unless, as on a few occasions when there was a great stress in her own work, she simply ignored Elaine's request and went on with her study. But she always paid bitterly for this in reprisals and sharp words that scorched her very soul. Oh, it was not easy to live this kind of a life, and so far as she could see, she was getting nowhere in making any impression on her sister. She only grew sharper day by day, and more exacting. She complained continually, and Lexie's nerves were on edge all the time. Oh, would this ever be over?

The one bright spot now in the happenings of the day was the occasional letters that came from abroad, from Benedict Barron.

Sometimes Lexie wondered what her mother would say to her keeping up a correspondence with an utter stranger. Yet somehow she couldn't help but feel that it was all right and her mother would approve of the letters that passed between them. He was so very respectful, and he was a Christian. He seemed so sincere, and so sort of lonely, just as she was. And yet she sensed through it all that there was danger in such sort of blind friendships. He was lonely now, and so was she, but sometime, when he would perhaps come home, and meet his old friends, and get into his old life again, would he forget her, and was she laying the foundation for sadness and disappointment in her life?

Well, suppose she was. People had to have some sorrow

in their lives. Hadn't God sent her this friendship? She wasn't counting great things on this, just a nice, pleasant—perhaps passing—friendliness. As free on the one side as on the other. No lovemaking nor any foolishness. Why should she not enjoy it? Why not be glad about it? She hadn't much else of earthly pleasure to enjoy. Even her college where she had a number of casual friends and acquaintances had been taken away from her. Had that been right? Ought she not to have fought to keep that college life until it was over? And yet Elaine had seemed so helpless, and it had been borne in upon her that for their father's sake she must stay here for a while. Perhaps Elaine wasn't really sick. Perhaps she was perfectly able to work, to keep house and care for her children, to even get a job to support them. But it had seemed so heartless to charge her with that, yet continually it came to her that her sister was acting a part and wasn't really sick at all.

But, sick or well, she couldn't leave the house and all its sweet belongings to Elaine's heartless rule. There were things so inextricably connected with her mother that she could not bear to have them mishandled by her sister, who had never cared for any of the old family furniture, and she had no other place to store them if she tried to go away. Besides, it would make endless complications. Elaine would probably sell half of her mother's things if there was any way to get money out of them. And if she tried to take them away, there again would be trouble. Also, this continual threat of a lawsuit was something that must be settled before she dared go away anywhere. She must be there near her friends. Judge Foster and Mr. Gordon had promised to help in case Elaine really carried out her threats, but they advised her to stay by the house and try to carry on in a sane and quiet way, as if nothing of the sort was proposed.

There had been a cessation of hostilities along these lines from Elaine for the past five or six weeks while Lexie had been studying so hard. But the real cause was that Bettinger Thomas was absent on a business trip, and he had promised to get the evidence in shape while he was gone. So Elaine had relaxed and was waiting. She had written all the suggested sentences into the little book that the lawyer had selected for her, which was a very good match in size, shape, and color to the original book belonging to Lexie's mother. She had done her part and been highly commended for the delightful way in which she had imitated her stepmother's handwriting. She had produced several letters written to herself during the years by her stepmother, and these had been good examples of the script. The lawyer had had an expert's advice on the subject, or said he had. So Elaine felt she had done her part and had only to rest now and wait until her expert lawyer should arrive and produce results.

"Lexie, can you spare ten dollars for me?" she asked one afternoon when Lexie arrived home after her final examination, tired to death, and very much in doubt as to whether she had passed the test because the ways of the university were somewhat different from her college life.

"Ten dollars?" said Lexie, wearily lifting tired eyes to her sister's face. "I'm afraid not. I had to use the last ten I had for college fees and I'm just about cleaned out. I didn't know there were any big necessities ahead. We have enough in the house to eat for the rest of the week. What is the matter, Elaine? Is it anything I can do for you?"

"No! Certainly not!" said Elaine. "I wouldn't have asked you for ten dollars if anything else would have done. I've *got* to have ten dollars, and if you don't fork it over, I'll go upstairs and take some of your mother's old rattletraps, send for a second-hand man, and *sell* them, for I just *must* have it!"

"Elaine! What is the matter?" asked Lexie, really alarmed, and trying to think what of her mother's precious relics would be pitched upon for this sacrifice. "Has something happened I don't know anything about? Some bill that has to be paid at once?"

"Don't be absurd!" sneered Elaine wearily. "Of course not. But my lawyer is coming back early next week and I've got to get a permanent and a wave and a manicure, and get myself in some shape so that I won't be a disgrace in court. Then I can sit up and feel some self-respect again. I thought I would send for a taxi and get them to take me into town and go to my old beauty parlor. They always turned me out looking like a million dollars!"

"I see!" said Lexie sadly. "Well, I'm sorry. I really haven't the ten dollars. You'll have to go to some of our other friends to borrow it, for I don't know how to get it."

"Oh, now, Lexie! Have a heart! You know I haven't any friends around here now, and you needn't pretend you haven't any money, for I know you have. You see, we are almost to the time, and you better get over your nonsense and come across. You can have your choice. Hand me over that ten dollars, or go up in the attic and bring down that quaint little writing desk of your mother's and take it down to Nerokian's. I sent for him last week and told him about it; he's very much interested in buying it. So you can run down to him with it and bring me back the ten dollars. If you can get any more out of him, you can keep the extra for yourself. You see, I'm quite generous."

Lexie stood still a moment looking at her sister, and her lips began to tremble. Two tears formed in her eyes, and she turned quickly away from her sister and walked out of the room with her head up. Gently she closed the door into the dining room and turned toward the stairs. She hurried up to her own room and closed and locked the door, thankful that the children were still outside playing hopscotch on the sidewalk. She dropped on her knees beside the bed and turned her heart to her Lord. It was the only source of help she knew.

"Oh, my heavenly Father! Show me what to do! Don't let me have to lose Mother's dear lovely desk, the one her mother gave her when she was a girl. Please help me, dear Lord."

One moment she paused to get quiet, and then it came to her what to do. She had no doubt but that the Lord had put the thought in her mind.

Quietly she got up, unlocked her door, and went up to the attic. Far over in the corner under the eaves she had hidden the desk. Now she saw it had been pulled out and the contents spread over the floor. She had locked it when she put all the things away, and taken the key downstairs with her. But the lock had been broken, smashed in with a hatchet. The hatchet lay near at hand as if in defiance of decency.

Tenderly she picked up the desk, gathered up the papers and letters, put them safely inside, and then found an old straw suitcase, of the type that used to be called a "telescope," put the desk inside, covered it, and fastened the leather strap firmly about it. Then she went down, stopping long enough at her room to get her hat and purse. As she passed through the kitchen she said in a low tone to Cinda: "You need not say anything about where I've gone, not to anybody. I probably won't be back in time for supper, but it's all right. Can you carry on while I'm gone?"

"Sure thing, Miss Lexie! I'll carry on! She been putting the screws on you again? I thought so! Okay. You can depend on me."

So Lexie slipped out the back door and made her way down through the meadow and off to Mr. Gordon's house, first stopping to telephone and ask if he was at home and could see her.

His cordial voice encouraged her, and helped to still her wildly beating heart as she hurried along to the bus that would take her within a couple of blocks of the Gordon city house.

She would much rather have asked this favor of Judge Foster, but Judge Foster had been taken away to the mountains for a thorough change and rest before he returned to his duties at court. She would not trouble his family. They probably knew nothing of her affairs. So she went with great temerity to explain, deciding on the way that she must tell him everything that happened since she last saw him. She must tell him of that Mr. Perrine, and find out if that complicated the situation, and whether she ought to go away for a time until this was over, or what she ought to do.

Of course if he said she ought to sell the little writing desk and give the money to Elaine, she would do it, but she sincerely hoped he would not. It didn't seem as if even God would want her to do that. It seemed a desecration of her mother's property, and being a Christian didn't mean that one had to lie down on the floor and be a doormat for someone to walk over. Or did it? She was troubled about that. Of course if she was sure it was right she should give it up, if she thought God wanted to do so, she would do it. But it did not seem the right thing to do.

It was a great relief to her to find Mr. Gordon at home ready to see her, and glad to take charge of her precious package. Moreover he told her absolutely not to give up her mother's treasures for any such foolish reason. Also he asked some very pertinent questions concerning the man whom Elaine said was going to testify about her mother's disposal of money that was falsely charged against her. He said he would investigate, but he was almost certain a Harry Perrine had been involved before in false witnessing.

And when the interview was over—for Lexie had sense enough not to stay long—Mr. Gordon said: "You'll be glad to learn, I know, that Judge Foster is much better and that a letter received from him today asked after you and made some suggestions concerning your affairs that may put a decided crimp in Bettinger Thomas's plans."

So Lexie went gravely back home, just as dark was coming down, and found Cinda had fed the family, put the children to bed, and happified Elaine with a new magazine. She was keeping Lexie's supper hot, and insisted on her eating it before she answered Elaine's imperative demand for her presence.

So Lexie ate a nice supper and then went quietly in to find her sister trying on some of her dresses, and deciding what alterations were necessary to bring them up to date.

"You wanted to see me, Elaine?" she asked, coming in quietly.

Elaine turned with a smirk on her face from the mirror, and held an artificial flower in her hair, as her eyes demanded admiration from the despised Lexie.

"Becoming, eh, don't you think, Lexie?"

"Very nice," said Lexie, trying to keep her voice from being cold and disapproving. "You wanted to see me, Elaine?" she asked again.

For answer Elaine turned and slowly, amusedly surveyed her sister. When she spoke her voice was derisive.

"Well, naturally I did, of course. What report have you to give me? You certainly took long enough. How much did you succeed in getting for that desk?"

"Desk?" said Lexie slowly. "Oh, I wouldn't care to sell the desk, it was very precious to Mother and is therefore precious to me."

Elaine shrugged her shoulders.

"As you please, of course. I'm sure I don't see what good old, outdated, worn-out rattletraps are, if that's your idea, and you have other resources. Hand over my ten dollars, please. I want to use it in the morning. And while you're about it, you better make it fifteen. There are one or two other items I forgot to mention."

"I'm sorry, Elaine. I told you I hadn't any money. Was that all you wanted of me? If it is, I think I'll go to bed. I'm rather tired. I had my last examination today, and it was a hard one."

"So silly and useless!" sneered Elaine. "But Lexie, I've simply *got* to have that money. You can get it whatever way you please, but I'll only give you till ten o'clock tomorrow morning, and then if you don't hand it over I'll take some treasures of yours in the attic and sell them myself. The desk will be the best bet because I really have a buyer for that."

Lexie was still for a minute, and then she said sadly: "Good night, Elaine. It really seems useless for me to talk to you. Perhaps it would have been better for me to have stayed at college and the job I had. I don't seem to be of much use to you here."

"No, you don't!" said the older sister. "You certainly have changed. I used to think you were very kind and accommodating, but you have grown utterly selfish and insolent."

Then into the electric atmosphere of the house came Angelica's voice, sharply like her mother's, complaining: "Aunt Lex, I wish you would come up to bed. Bluebell is crying herself sick for you. She says you are the only one who can tell bedtime stories and get her to sleep, and she keeps getting out of bed and coming over and pulling my hair and pinching me."

Lexie smiled.

"All right, I'll come, Angel. Tell her I'll be with her right away!"

"Yes, go! Steal the love of my children away from me, too, with all the rest you are doing," sneered Elaine, "but you get that money for me in the morning or you'll wish you had."

But Lexie had escaped, and was rapidly preparing for bed, to nestle down beside Bluebell and comfort her baby sobs.

After a little the house quieted down, and even Cinda could stop sniffing and get a bit of rest. And in the still night watches Lexie's tired prayers arose. She and that soldier over on the other side of the world somewhere were both praying to a God they knew, who was close beside them all the way, and as Lexie was dropping off to sleep she wondered if ever in the years ahead she would see that soldier again, and if they could talk over these things they had passed through. Well, anyway, perhaps in heaven. Somehow there didn't seem to be much prospect of anything pleasant happening to her on this earth.

Chapter 16

The university commencement was the next night and Lexie's dress that she had ordered at the other college with the girls of her class, which was to be forwarded in plenty of time, did not arrive until the morning of the day. Lexie had been wondering what she would do if it didn't come. Stay at home entirely, or go down in her old blue voile, which was the only dress-up garment she possessed that was at all in keeping with warm weather. And it was warm! But that last morning the big pasteboard box arrived by parcel post, and eagerly Lexie carried it up to her room, thankful that Elaine was still asleep and wouldn't be demanding to see what had come.

But she reckoned without knowledge, for Elaine was not so soundly asleep that she had not heard the postman come and she had been at the window looking out behind the curtain.

Lexie scarcely had the box open before the stair door opened and Elaine called up the stairs, "Lexie, what was that package that came in the mail? Wasn't that for me?"

"No," said Lexie pleasantly. "It was just some things that I didn't bring from college."

"Oh! Things! So you have some more old togs, have you? I should have thought they wouldn't have bothered to send any more such worn-out duds as you have."

Lexie made no reply, and so Elaine closed the door and went back into her room. But well did Lexie know that she hadn't heard the last of this yet.

However, she was soon engrossed in opening her new dress, and hanging it up where she could examine it.

It was white organdie, sheer and fine. Those girls who did the ordering for the class were wealthy girls and they knew how to select good material. Lexie's eyes reveled in the sheer lovely folds, the delicate lace with which the ruffles were edged, the lovely lines of the whole garment. And to think it was her very own! How nice it would have been if she might have graduated with the rest of her own class in the college where she had worked so hard, among those girls she had come to know so well and some of them to love.

Then she began to put her fingers on the folds shyly, to smooth the skirt down softly as if it were a baby's skin. There were a few creases in it where it had been folded too sharply, in order to get the cover of the box on. Ought she to iron it, or would just hanging up in the air take the creases out? Perhaps that would be better.

She took one of her hangers, padded it carefully with cotton, and covered it with white cloth, and then she hung the dress on it and placed the hanger where it would get the breeze from the window. The air was a little damp from the rain last night and that would surely take the musings out!

So, with quiet step and careful hand she went out, closing her door. There was no point in locking it of course, for that would only arouse Elaine's suspicions and start her on the warpath again, asking uncomfortable questions.

Lexie hurried downstairs and began dusting the living room, softly humming a happy little tune, until suddenly Elaine appeared in her bedroom doorway.

"Mercy!" she said, scowling darkly. "Do you have to *screech*? I can't imagine why. Stuck here in this horrid hole of a town, working hard to make both ends meet! But oh, I forgot, you are counting on the fortune you are saving till all suspicion blows over and you feel you dare come out in the open and flaunt your riches!"

Suddenly Lexie felt as if she simply couldn't bear another word.

"Oh don't, Elaine, please don't talk that way! You know that isn't any of it true, and you are just saying those things to be hateful. Isn't it enough to make me glad and want to sing to think that after all the hindrances I've had I've really finished my college course and am getting my diploma tonight? That certainly is enough to make me feel lighthearted. But I'm sorry if I disturbed you. I didn't know you had gone to lie down again. I thought you were dressing."

"Oh, it's of no consequence of course. But dressing? What would I dress in? I need a new dress. I haven't a rag fit to put on my back, and today that noted financier is coming to talk with me. I'm sure I don't know what to do."

Lexie was silent. There really wasn't anything she could say to that harangue. And so Elaine was going to bring that other obnoxious man here to the house along with the disgusting lawyer! Well, perhaps she had better get out for a while. How would it be for her to run down to the store now, as soon as she had this living room dusted, and call up Mr. Gordon? He had asked to be told when either of those two came to the house, and promised if he found it out in time to do something to help her relieve the situation. Besides, he said he wanted to get a view of Perrine, and make sure he was the one they were after before he could do anything.

So Lexie hurried through her task and started down to the store, but as she came down the stairs from her room, where she had lingered a moment to note that the air was taking the few wrinkles out of her new dress already, she heard Elaine calling.

"Yes?" she answered, opening the dining room door a crack.

"I wish you would scrub the front porch!" ordered the lady. "It looks as if the pigs lived here. I can't have gentlemen coming to see me with a porch like that!"

Lexie smothered a desire to tell her sister that the only pigs that lived there belonged to her, as her children had been eating bread and jam out there the night before and had smeared jam and an overripe banana over everything. But she took a deep breath instead and endeavored to answer steadily.

"Sorry, Elaine, I can't do it just now. I have to go on an errand. Perhaps when I get back there may be time. I'm rather busy this morning." And then she went out and closed the door before Elaine could say any more, and was speeding down across the meadow before Elaine had roused to keep her from going.

A little talk with Mr. Gordon brought calm into her troubled soul. He thanked her for letting him know, and said he might come out himself during the morning if he decided that was a wise thing to do.

So Lexie went home a trifle relieved, and wondered if she really ought to go out and scrub that porch. Of course Cinda would eventually do it, but she wanted to make things as easy as possible for Cinda. She decided that if there was no limousine parked before the door she would see that at least the jam was washed off the chair back and porch. She didn't want even an obnoxious lawyer, nor a crook, to find things actually dirty.

So Lexie hurried into the house and was about to go in search of a pail and scrubbing brush and cloths, when she met Cinda coming in from the side door carrying them.

"I just been out to scrub her highness' porch," she said with a comical grimace. "I heard what the likes of her said, and I would not have lifted a finger to help, savin' I knowed you would do it when you got back, and I didn't want that to happen. So it's done."

"That was sweet of you, Cinda, but I think you have enough to do without that. Anyway, those two men she said were coming aren't worth any effort. But thank you for your thought of me." And Lexie went smiling into the house to make sure she hadn't left her dust cloth in the living room.

But when she opened the door, she saw Elaine seated at the desk writing, and she was wearing a delicate white dress.

Lexie stared at her sister for an instant, and then she recognized the fine lace on the edge of the ruffles, and it all came over her. That was her commencement dress! Elaine had gone up and got it and put it on! Oh, and she would muss it all up!

Lexie was suddenly very angry, so angry she was petrified. She couldn't speak!

Then Elaine looked up from her writing; caught a glimpse of her sister's face and was startled. She hadn't expected Lexie to return so soon, and she wasn't prepared for the look of utter anger and despair in Lexie's eyes.

"Oh! So you *did* decide to come back in time to scrub that porch! Well, you needn't have bothered. I made Cinda do it. She's a lazy good-for-nothing anyway. She ought to do it without being told!"

But Lexie had no ears for anything about the porch just then. She was struggling to regain her composure and trying to speak in a pleasant, compelling manner.

"Oh Elaine! That's my commencement dress!" she said in a cross between a wail and a protest. "Won't you please go and take it off quick? And, *please*, be careful. I've nothing else to wear tonight! You had no right to go up and get my dress—!"

"*Right? You* talk of *right*? Why didn't I have a right to do anything I wanted to do with what you claim as fortune and refuse to tell where it is?"

"Oh Elaine, please, *please* stop talking like that. You know I haven't any fortune. And won't you please get up quick and take that off? Let me help you off with it right away! Please be *careful*! Oh, if anything should happen to it I don't know what I could do!"

"Get away from me, Lexie. Take your hands off my shoulder! No, I will not take the dress off. I'm expecting callers any minute and this is a perfect negligee. It's nothing extraordinary anyway. Just a white nightgown affair. I have two old white dresses myself that will do well enough for you to march on a platform with a whole lot of other people. I intend to keep this on now; I haven't time to change and you can rave all you want to, but it won't do you a bit of good!"

Elaine waved her hand determinedly and her white arm swept out across the desk and took the ink bottle in its path, landing it directly in her own lap, where it turned over and spilled a large wide path of blue-black ink down the front of the cherished dress!

For an instant there was a dead silence in the room as both girls were horrified at what had happened, and then Elaine, gathering anger as she spoke, said: "There! Now see what you have made me do? Ruined my costume, and devastated your own dress! But that isn't all," she said as the enormity of what had happened came over her. "I had on my own best silk slip. The pink one that matches my only evening dress, and it's *ruined*. And that's *all your fault*! I know you can't buy real silk things anymore and I never could match this again. Oh, what *shall* I do? Why don't you help me get this terrible dress off quick. Take the scissors and cut it off. You can't get it off any other way. There are the scissors over on the table. Cut it off quick before this vile ink gets all through my undergarments!"

True to her nature Lexie froze into composure with an emergency. She took charge of the frantic woman and made her obey just by the force of her own will.

"Stand up!" she said quietly, and took hold of her sister's arm firmly. "Wait! Don't stir! Let me get this waist unfastened."

No one noticed when Cinda came in, a basin of water in her hand and several large clean rags. She went quietly over to the excited, weeping Elaine.

"There, dearie," crooned Cinda in perfect acting form.

"We'll fix ye all up in good shape before yer comp'ny comes. Just stand still and shut yer eyes. Hold out yer right arm. Yes, that's right. Pull it off gently there. And now the other. There, the waist is off! Now we're through the worst. Wait, suppose I take off yer pretty slippers. They're too nice to get spoiled. Stand very still!"

Lexie knew enough to keep her own mouth shut and let Cinda carry on. She knew that her voice would only excite Elaine. So she worked with careful, quick, frightened fingers, unzipping and pulling off the skirt cautiously down over the slim angry hips, zealously guarding the back and sides of the skirt from all contact with the tainted front breadth until the skirt lay in a billowy circle about the feet of the distressed Elaine. Then suddenly Cinda rose and put her strong arms quickly about the slim waist of the young woman, lifting her body out from the dress and setting her down fully two yards away from it. As she did so, Lexie gathered the blackened front breadths closely in her hands and drew the whole skirt out of the room. It was deftly done, and perhaps no one who had not so much at stake could possibly have accomplished the feat, but there it was, out in the dining room, with sides and back unmarred. Now, what could be done next?

Lexie was quick and clever. She knew exactly the pattern of that dress, and even while she had been rescuing what part of it was still untouched by ink, she had been trying to contrive how she would yet wear it. So now as she laid it down on the floor for the moment, she knew just what she had to do. If only the ink did not reach too far, it might be possible to rip or cut out that marred front breadth and let out some of the gathering in the full skirt. But she must get rid first of that inky section or somehow it would contaminate the rest. The scissors were the quickest way.

She stepped to the kitchen and got the pair of shears that had always hung under the shelf by the dresser. Kneeling, she cut swiftly, ruthlessly, through that beautiful garment that only an hour before had been such an object of delight to her tired, worried young soul, really the prettiest dress she had ever had.

But she must not stop to think of that now. There was not a great deal of time in which to bring this garment into usefulness for her immediate need, and she must not waste a minute in useless repining. So with a steady hand, she cut from the hem straight up to the belt, on each side of the stain, and then with a glance at her hands to make sure they had no ink on them, she gathered up what was left and carried it up to her room, laying it on the bed and locking the door to make sure no intruder arrived to hinder her.

A quick examination showed the shirring around the waist was very full indeed, and surely it would do no harm to take one small piece out of all that fullness!

So she went to work trying to steady her trembling hands, trying not to think of what her ruthless sister had done to her as she carefully ripped the shirring loose from the belt, and then examined it again to calculate just how far she would need to rip out the shirring to make the skirt wide enough to go on the band again. How fortunate it was that the belt had not been touched by the ink!

And down in the living room, Cinda had a problem all her own. The angry, bewildered woman who had been so precipitately lifted out of her borrowed garments, and placed trembling in the corner wearing a ruined pink slip with a great black stain down its front breadth, stood staring stupidly down at the devastation she had wrought, too bewildered to utter a word, which was a state to which she had seldom in her life been brought.

And just then, while Cinda wiped the small rivers of ink from the otherwise neat floor, they both heard that elegant limousine drive up to the door, and Elaine came sharply to her senses. Her callers had arrived, and she in a shocking pink slip with ink stains all down the front and over one white arm was standing unprotected in the opposite corner of the room from the door to her bedroom, and nothing between her and her callers but a worn old screen door!

Cinda was on her feet with the basin and rags in her hand. She gave a glance out the front door and saw the men getting out of the elegant car.

"Yer callers is here," she announced grimly. "Ye better beat it an' get some cloes on. I'll open the door for 'em," and she flung open the bedroom door. As Elaine scuttled across the room into her haven, Cinda went and stood guard before the screen door watching the two men come up the path.

But Lexie, upstairs, had no time to more than glance out the window, though she sensed what must be going on. Well, she had her work cut out for her, and she needn't take time to go down unless Mr. Gordon came, in which case Cinda would surely tell her. Thank the Lord, Cinda, downstairs, let the two men in, scanned them thoroughly, classified them according to her wide knowledge and keen discernment, and then took her implements of service into the dining room, where she took care to leave the door open a crack, and where she had beforehand carefully set her stage so that she could come and go and get on with her work, and hear all that went on without seeming to do so.

She lumbered up the stairs and touched Lexie's door with the tips of her fingers, giving a high sign, and Lexie softly unlocked the door and let her in.

"Them men is come!" she announced in a solemn whisper. "An' ef one cud look worse'n t' other, he *does*. Seem like I've seed him 'afore, too, but I wouldn't trust him with me dog's bone!"

Lexie managed a one-sided grin in the corner of her mouth that was not filled with pins.

"You'd oughtta seed *her*, scootin' acrost the room in her inky slip. It was a sight fer sore eyes! How ya gettin' on with the dress? Can ye do anythin' with it?"

"Yes, I think so, but it will take time. Don't call me down unless Mr. Gordon comes, though I'll listen for him."

"Okay! Well, is there any sewin' I kin do fer ye?"

"Not yet, I guess, Cinda. By and by I'll want you to see if it looks all right. I just took out a length in front and let out the shirring. That ought to look all right, don't you think?"

"Sure thing!" said Cinda. "It sure was a shame I didn't find out what that brat of a woman was doin' 'afore this happened, but I was tryin' ta get things in order early so you wouldn't do no work, an' here look at what come!"

"Never mind," said Lexie. "I guess I can wear it. There isn't but one little blot on the waist, and that's where I can cut the blot out and paste a bit of the organdie over it. I think I'll get by all right."

Lexie had run up the two seams of the skirt quickly, and adjusted the gathers about the waistline. She was just about to try it on when she heard a car drive down the street, and then another from the opposite direction, but when she looked out there was only one and it went on by and stopped across the street on the other side. Could that be Mr. Gordon's car?

She opened the door and listened. There seemed to be several voices downstairs, but she didn't hear Mr. Gordon's yet, and she did not want to go down until Cinda called her. Elaine could make trouble enough without charging her with coming in where she was not wanted. So she closed the door and went back to her sewing, but she had an uneasy feeling that something was going on that she did not understand.

Then she went to her window again, and looking out toward the side of the house she saw a man going like a shadow, silently, and disappearing out behind the kitchen. Quietly she opened her door again and slipped down the hall to the little window that opened out toward the back, and there she saw two men standing, looking toward the house, talking in very low tones, more as if they were whispering or using sign language. A horror came with the memory that the lawyer had suggested they might arrest *her*. How dreadful if they were really going to try that on her, and Elaine was going to let them do it, the very day she was to graduate! Would Elaine be as mean as that?

Then she heard Cinda coming up the stairs and she slipped back to her own room, followed by Cinda, who came in after her and held the door closed while she whispered: "That there Mr. Gordon you was lookin' for is in the kitchen. He says for you *not* to come down just yet till he sends you word. He's brung a lotta cops and got 'em all standin' around, an' he says tell you you was right, that's the man. An' it'll all be over in a few minutes, but you're to stay up here till I come after you."

Cinda vanished, and Lexie remained by her door listening. She heard measured steps below the stairs. Through the dining room three figures passed showing up sharply against the sunlight in the opposite dining room window. They were policemen! In uniform! What could it mean? And did Cinda say that Mr. Gordon was down there, too? Or was he out in the kitchen? Oh, surely she ought to go down! But Cinda had been so sure that Mr. Gordon wanted her to stay upstairs until he called her. Then the door into the living room was swung open. She hadn't noticed before that it had been shut. But it swung so silently as if a deft hand had swung it, and she could hear low talk, then Elaine's rippling, apologetic laughter almost like a giggle. She did that when men were there, especially that outrageous lawyer of hers. And then—a sudden silence! A breathless silence it seemed, as if everyone in the room was suddenly suppressed, a frightened silence, though none had made a sound since the talking ceased.

Then a strange voice spoke. "Harry Perrine, alias Waddie Dager, alias Mike Gilkie, you are under arrest for forgery. I must beg your pardon, madam, for interrupting your conversation, but this man has been wanted by the state for more than a year and we can't take chances! Handcuff him, Officer!"

Elaine gave a little childish scream. Lexie could almost envision how she would be shrugged down in her chair with her pretty, slender, manicured fingers pressing over her eyes.

Lexie could hear the other two men step forward to someone who sat in a chair just inside the living room door, and then a well-remembered voice that she had always disliked came tremblingly out: "But, Officer, you have made a mistake. I am not the man you are looking for. My name is not any of those names you spoke. I am James Bradwell, and I'm a respectable citizen. I have never been in any criminal trouble." "No, Jimmy Brady, we haven't made any mistake. You can call yourself Bradwell, or Brady, or Tanzey Brown if you like, or any one of a dozen other aliases that I have on my list, but you're still the same old Harry Perrine you used to be when you got away with that big forgery game, and we're not running any chances."

"But I'm a respectable citizen," whined the culprit. "I can prove that I am innocent of any crime. These people are merely my friends and I was making a business call, offering them an investment that is worth its weight—"

"Oh yes?" said the officer. "Your friends are fortunate that I met up with you before they signed any of your rotten papers. Come, Harry Perrine, let's get going. You arrived in a limousine but you will be going away in a police car. You're sure none of the rest of you feel you'd like to go with us?" Lexie could well imagine his glance at Lawyer Thomas as he said it.

But there was only an ominous silence, and then the policemen marched away to their car with their reluctant prisoner in their midst.

Lexie remained at her door, wondering what would happen next, wondering if the next thing would be a call for herself to come down and see Mr. Gordon, but after the police cars had gone she heard another car going away, and stealing into her own room she saw it was the car that had been parked across the road a little while before. Yet she lingered, uneasily, and then she heard Lawyer Thomas say: "Well, Elaine, I guess that about finishes our interview for the morning. You can readily see that I've got to go at once and see what can be done to release our star witness."

"But I thought you were going to tell me this morning where that money is to be found. That is the point I was so anxious about," wailed Elaine.

"Well, of course I was not anticipating any such happening as has just occurred. I can't understand this. Just who did you tell about this witness? You don't suppose that sister of yours has found it out and told the police, do you? You didn't tell her about this witness, did you?"

"Certainly *not*!" lied Elaine firmly. "And if I had, my sister wouldn't think of going to the police. She is not that kind of a girl."

"Oh, isn't she?" queried the lawyer. "I understood that you felt she would stoop to almost anything to carry her point and keep this money. And besides, I'm afraid you're going to have to let me have a little more money right at once. It is going to cost quite a sum to get this witness free, I'm afraid. And you know it is essential that we get him. If you could spare, say, fifty dollars, right away I'll hurry down and see if I can get him off. You know he is really the only one who can tell you where that money is. If you'll get the money, I'll go at once and see if I can set him free."

"But I haven't any money. I couldn't possibly give you any today."

"What about that tightwad of a sister of yours? Can't you work something on her?"

"Oh no!" groaned Elaine. "I can't do a thing with her. Not now, especially. Oh, this has been an awful day!" And Elaine burst into loud weeping.

"Well, there, there! Don't cry. We'll manage somehow for a

day or two, but I really must go at once. I shouldn't care to have these police get me mixed up in this sort of thing! Good-bye. I really must hurry!"

"*This* sort of thing?" screamed Elaine. "What do you mean? Are we mixed up in something terrible? Oh, I don't know what the neighbors are going to think with police coming here and taking a man away. This has always been a respectable neighborhood! Oh, you said you would take care of my affairs and I would have no trouble!"

"There, there, Elaine," soothed the hurried lawyer, "don't go getting excited. Just take it easy and everything will come out all right. Now, good-bye for the present. I've got to go and see what I can do about that witness, you know."

With oily tones that were almost funny because he seemed so excited himself, he got himself out of the house and went plunging down the walk to his limousine, and away in a whirl around the corner and out of sight.

"Good riddance to him," breathed Cinda, coming softly up the stairs. "An' yer Mr. Gordon said he would be coming again some other day perhaps, but you had done good work, an' not to worry. He had to go away to some sort of a hearing in court, he said. An' I come to ast you could I do something about the dress, or would you want me to see to the likes of her, an' get her quiet? But beggin' pardon, Miss Lexie, my advice is to leave her be awhile till she comes to. She's had a good hard shake-up, an' it'll be awhile 'afore she gets her balance again. I'm hopin' it'll do her good."

"Thank you, Cinda, for all you've done, and I guess you're right about Elaine. Perhaps she won't be wanting to see either of us for a while. Suppose you come in and let me put on my dress and see if you think it will do at all, before I finish it up. I've got it on the belt, but I'm not sure it hangs just right. If I can get this so it's wearable I'll be able to think about other things."

So Lexie put the dress on and Cinda got down on her knees and measured the distance from the floor to the hem all around and then held an old mirror off so that Lexie could get a view of herself. They finally decided they had done the best they could.

"And it's really pretty an' becomin', Miss Lexie. Maybe I ain't no judge, but I don't believe there'll be another dress as purty in the whole bunch. Now, Miss Lexie, you just don't worry another bit. You take that dress off an' hang it up an' I'll finish sewing them gethers fer ye, an' you go lay down an' rest. Goodness knows, you've hed it hard enough this day, let alone graduatin', an' you need ta get some rest."

Lexie gave a breathless little laugh and shook her head.

"No, Cinda, you've plenty to do, and I'll finish this myself. There isn't much more since you're sure it hangs all right. But I'd appreciate it if you would see if Elaine's all right. You know she's apt to get into one of her spells of hysterics after a time like this. And there'll be plenty of work for you today without sewing. And, by the way, isn't it almost time for the postman? I wonder if you couldn't head him off this once and get anything there may be for me. I've been getting notes from my former classmates, and I wouldn't like one of them to fall into my sister's hands in her present state. I'd never see it, I'm sure, if it did."

"Okay!" said Cinda. "An' then agin there mought be some letter from foreign lands again, ye never can tell."

"Oh no," said Lexie. "Not so soon again. You know I just got one last week."

"Wal, we'll see!" said Cinda with a sly wink, and thumped heavily down the stairs. There were times when Cinda could walk featherlight and again times when she defied the world with her stride. This was one of them. Her young lady had come through the fire and her graduating dress was still intact and quite wearable. So Cinda sailed downstairs, and peered cautiously into the living room, but there wasn't a sign of her ladyship in the room, and the door of her bedroom was wide open. A casual glance in there showed a dismal little silent heap on the bed, face buried in the pillow. Elaine was too stricken even for sobs. Besides, there wasn't any audience.

Chapter 17

Elaine's collapse lasted all through the day and into the next, which in a way was a relief to Lexie because she had enough of her own concerns to attend to without trying to deal with her sister. And it was of no use whatever for Lexie to try and coax her out of her doldrums. It would only be a waste of time. So Elaine continued in her discouraged heap, woebegone to the last extent. She refused anything to eat, even shook her head at the cup of coffee Cinda grimly offered. The whole collapse of her arrogant schemes was upon her and she could not creep out from under it even long enough to drink that cup of heartening coffee.

Perhaps, as the lonely day went on, and there were no sounds of more than light footsteps in the house, for the children had been invited across the way to lunch outdoors with their playmates, it may be that some sense of her own fault in all this disaster came upon her, though it is doubtful, for Elaine had never been one to see anything wrong with herself.

She was still arrayed in the street suit she had put on so hastily at the approach of her visitors. She hadn't troubled to take it off when in her despair she threw herself on the bed, and Cinda hadn't bothered to go and coax her into a bathrobe. Cinda felt that this was Lexie's day, and whatever she did, beyond absolute necessity, must be done for Lexie. So Elaine had her room and her quiet entirely to herself, and whether she waked or whether she slept she was undisturbed. But it must have been brought home to her mind as the day wore on and there came no word from her lawyer that she had got about to the end of her rope with him. He hadn't given her much hope when he left that if this arrested witness should fail them, they had a chance to win a case. And Elaine was really a bright woman when she stopped thinking about herself long enough to exercise her brains. She was beginning to see that she was beaten. And if she couldn't get any money out of Lexie, what was she to do? Sit still and make Lexie support her? Maybe she might do that if she ever got up her ambition again. But how terrible. Lexie couldn't even make enough to support her in the style she had lately been used to, and now that her husband was gone, who was there to care? And what was Lexie going to be like after that dress episode? Of course she could perhaps persuade her that the ink part was her own fault. That if she hadn't come in and startled her she never would have jumped and knocked over the ink bottle. But Elaine was at last so low in spirits that she couldn't even rouse a lead like that.

If only Cinda would come in and say that Bettinger Thomas

had sent a telegram or a message to say that his witness was free and everything was going to be all right, why, then she could rouse up and even forgive Lexie for having been the cause of her ruining that lovely silk slip, the slip of the only really imported dress she ever owned. But as it was, perhaps, she would say nothing more about that slip for the present.

So Lexie stayed in her room and put her dress in perfect order, and Elaine stayed in her room and finally slept, and at least there was peace in the house, if not harmony.

Cinda had brought up a tray for Lexie and on it was a note she said she found on the kitchen table. It was from Mr. Gordon.

> *Dear Miss Kendall:*
>
> *Sorry not to have seen you, but later I hope to explain fully.*
>
> *Meantime you have helped to do one of the neatest pieces of detective work I have seen in a long time, by making it possible to put into custody one of the slickest criminals in this part of the country. I am only thankful that we could get him before he put over any of his frauds on your family.*
>
> *Let me know if there is any way I can be of immediate service at any time, and I shall be seeing you again soon.*
>
> *Sincerely,*
> *R. Gordon*

Lexie read the note over carefully and then after due deliberation she tore it into small bits and put them where they could never be read. She wondered as she was doing it whether she would ever be able to trust that sister of hers again, or would she have to go on living in danger of perpetual annoyance?

Lexie went early to the city, for she had an uneasy feeling that if she stayed in the house a moment beyond getting ready that something might happen to upset her plans and perhaps either spoil her dress again or keep her at home. Elaine was perfectly capable of staging a near-to-death scene if she thought that in some way she could hurt Lexie. Lexie was running no risks. She didn't even go out the front gate, for the children, if they should spy her all dressed up, would be altogether likely to rush across the street and make an outcry that would bring the attention of the neighborhood, and they would probably embrace her with sticky, dirty hands, and ruin her dress once more. So, gathering her dress up carefully, and getting Cinda to help her over the fence, she went carefully down across the meadow, the voluminous billows of her skirt gathered up on either side so that it would not come in contact with grass and weeds. At last she stepped safely on the sidewalk of the highway, and could stand in quietness and peace, waiting for the bus she knew would be there very soon to bear her to the city.

So at last Lexie was started, and could get her breath before the ordeal of the evening began, and just be thankful that the various disasters of the day had not been permitted to prevent her from coming to commencement. There in the quiet of the country road, under a tall elm tree, as she waited for the bus, she bowed her head and closed her eyes, and murmured softly: "Dear Father, thank You for being with me all day long.

Please be with me tonight, too, and keep me when I get back home. Please look after all the rest, and don't let Elaine make any more awful trouble for us."

Then the bus came, and she was on her way.

There were few people on the bus, and she took a seat at the back where she could lean her arm on the window seat, put her head down on her hand, and close her eyes. She suddenly realized that she was very tired. It had been a hard day, and it was almost done. What was it going to feel like to be through with college? Well, it didn't matter much now, since none of her friends could be with her, and her pleasant anticipations had all to be transferred to another institution. But at least she would be in a position to get a good job, even if Judge Foster wouldn't be well enough to need her. She still had much to be glad about.

The next thing on the docket to worry about was that lawsuit, which if Elaine carried out her plans might upset everything else she had hoped for. But she simply would not think of that tonight. God had taken care of her so far, and she could surely trust Him for the rest. How great it was that the awful Perrine was in custody. "Oh, dear God, please keep him where he cannot do us harm by telling lies."

She was almost asleep when the bus reached the university and people were getting off all around her. Slowly she made her way out and entered the great gates that led from the street up to the auditorium. Somehow she couldn't seem to realize what she was about to do. Graduate? Yes, but why had it seemed so important? The nicest thing about it all was that she was away from her troubles for a little while and felt almost rested. She hadn't felt as rested since Elaine came back. And if she had only known it, she *looked* rested, and more than one passer on the street turned and looked at the pretty girl with the sweet eyes who had such an expression of utter peace. Dewy-eyed she was from just those few minutes with her eyes closed.

When she entered the hall she found a great number of students in gala attire, and the graduating class in their white dresses. Her own dress was not *just* like theirs, but she felt happy and inconspicuous among them. And then, just at the last minute before the class would march up on the platform, one of the ushers hunted her up.

"There's a box of flowers here for you, Miss Kendall," he said and handed her a small box. "It says they are to be given to you *before* the exercises. You'd better open them here. They are probably for you to wear." He grinned as he went on his way.

"Oh, but nobody would send me flowers to wear," said Lexie to herself. "Even those crazy girls in my old college wouldn't think of it. I was really nothing to them, only a girl who worked hard and belonged to their class."

With trembling fingers she untied the knot, turned back the soft folds of green wax paper, and there nested three of the most gorgeous gardenias she had ever seen, fastened with silver ribbon, and all equipped with pearl-headed pins to fasten them on.

"Oh, how lovely!" exclaimed one of the other graduates, smiling gaily at Lexie. "Gardenias! Aren't they spiffy! Here, let me help you fasten them."

"Oh, but I don't think I'm going to wear them," said Lexie shyly.

"Why, sure you are. You wouldn't let such gorgeous gardenias as that go to waste. Sure! Put them on. We want all the honors in our class that are coming. Who is he anyway? Not your family?"

"Why, I haven't looked yet," said Lexie, her cheeks as rosy as if they were painted.

"Well, look quick! Here's the card. A soldier, as I live! Benedict Barron! That's some name. Where is he?"

"He's overseas," said Lexie softly, her eyes starry with a new kind of joy. What a wonderful thing to come at the close of this awful day. Now, *now* she could go through the evening calmly!

It was not until the class was seated on the great platform with all the dignitaries and professors and speakers in their places that Lexie was able to get her thoughts in order and begin to wonder how her soldier had gotten those flowers to her for this particular night. Yes, she had told him *when* her commencement came, but only a word or two to explain how busily she was working for her examinations. And here he had figured it out and somehow got word to a florist to send those wonderful blossoms to her in time for her to wear them. She held her sweet head up proudly, and looked down at the flowers nestling among her lace-edged ruffles. She laid her hands in her lap over the front seam at which she had worked so hard that morning with her dress. In fact, the whole morning—obnoxious lawyer and lying witness, policemen, arrest, and Elaine's collapse—had become a blank for the time. She was sitting here in this great throng, living through the thing she had dreamed about for years, the night that she and her mother used to talk about and plan for, and she had no thought for anything else, except the wonderful soldier friend who had sent her beautiful flowers for the crowning touch to her festive evening. It was all very wonderful, and she must not let other thoughts get tangled up with it, for she wanted to remember everything just as it happened. It would be the shining evening of her young life. Other girls might be looking forward to going into society, and then marriage, but so far as she could see now there would be only plain days of work for herself. And grateful enough she would be for even that if she could be free from such incidents as "suits" for money she had never had, and contact with unholy, dishonest lawyers. At least she had a God who was protecting her! Look how He had spared that dress so she could wear it, in spite of her sister's ruthless unkindness. Look how He had sent those policemen to arrest that criminal witness! Look how the lawyer had been frightened away! Might not God always frighten away her enemies who were trying to plot for her downfall? Oh, she would be willing to work hard all her life if she might just have peace, and now and then a little pleasantness. And this assurance she now had of God's caring for her was wonderful.

But the exercises of the evening were beginning, and her interest was caught away from the troubles of the day. Music and speeches and well-dressed young people made a pleasant combination. How pretty some of the girls looked! Lexie did not know that she herself was as pretty a girl as any on that platform. But she was not thinking of herself except as she was thrilled by being a part of this great pageant.

For a little time she was lost in the program, as if it were a ship on which she had embarked, sailing down the evening. Then the sweet breath of the flowers on her shoulder would speak to her, mingle with her consciousness, and make themselves apparent, and a thrill would come over her. She was like other girls. She had a friend. She was wearing flowers,

flowers a man had been thoughtful enough to send her! Oh, of course there was nothing loverlike about it. He was just a friend. A friend "of the years," that was it. That sounded well, if Elaine should ask her. For she would have to wear the flowers home. She couldn't just lose them by her sneers and questions. She must make them last as long as possible. Her first flowers from a young man! Even if the sender of them was half a world away from her, it was nice that he should have thought to do it.

She tried to think it through. She had only told him about the commencement in her last letter. He must have cabled for the flowers to get them here so soon.

Then she remembered the card she was clasping tightly in eager fingers. She hadn't read it yet. But of course he could only cable the words. They would not be in his handwriting. Her eyes sought the card. It said:

> *With best wishes to Lexie for a happy commence-*
> *ment. Wish I could be with you.*
> *Benedict Barron*

It seemed to Lexie as if she had never been so happy as now, when she sat there with that card in her hand and those gardenias on her shoulder. At least not since her mother died. And how she longed just then to be able to tell her mother all about it.

But then perhaps she knows. Perhaps she sees the flowers, and is glad for me, she thought to herself.

So in a daze of joy she sat through the evening.

Then at last came the diploma for which she had worked

so long. Brimming over, that evening was, just *brimming* over with nice things, even enough to offset the awful morning that had passed.

And then as if that were not enough there were more flowers, afterward, different personal gifts to the graduates from friends. That was something in which she would not share because she was a stranger among them, she thought, but lo, they brought her three! First a great basket of lilies and blue delphiniums from her class at the dear old college, and the inscription, "For our dear Lexie from her own old class," and all their names signed. How lovely of them to do it! She hadn't thought they cared about her. Then there were beautiful pink roses from Judge and Mrs. Foster, and an exquisite purple and white orchid from Mr. Gordon. How kind they all were!

And by this time, Lexie was so tired that the tears were very near the surface of her starry eyes. What a lovely, wonderful evening it had been, to have come after all that troubled morning!

She looked down at her pretty white dress, and saw it was as crisp and trim as when she started away from home.

And then suddenly it was time to catch the bus and go back to all that there was to call home. But the joy and the thrill lasted all the way home, and she didn't let herself worry about what Elaine would say, or whether she would try to tell her about her flowers, or what would be coming the next day. She just sat quietly and enjoyed her evening over again. There might not be any more such lovely times coming to her ever again through her life. This might be the last one, but she would therefore cherish it, and sometimes go back to it in memory and enjoy it all over again.

She found Cinda waiting for her at the corner when she got off the bus, and they walked slowly back to the house, Cinda carrying the basket of lilies and the box of roses and the orchid, Cinda gazing at her young lady and reveling in her sweetness in the dim moonlight. Cinda rejoicing that the gardenias had come from the soldier, and that people who had good taste and judgment had sent her flowers of distinction.

It was Cinda who unfastened the gardenias and arranged and sprinkled them in their box for safekeeping over night, and it was Cinda who saw that the other flowers were sprinkled and cared for. It was Cinda who insisted that Lexie get to bed right away, and then lingered to look at the wonderful diploma and talk some more.

She answered Lexie's anxious questions.

No, Elaine hadn't eaten any supper, just drank a cup of strong tea. No, no lawyer had come that evening, but a telegram had arrived from Lawyer Thomas, and Elaine had made her read it to her because her own eyes were so swollen from weeping she couldn't see. It said: "Impossible to contact witness at present time. I advise calling a halt in proceedings for the present. Am suddenly called away to West Coast for an indefinite period, and cannot do anything more for you at present," signed B. Thomas.

Lexie looked at her in wonder.

"Oh!" she said, and, "Oh, *isn't* God *wonderful!*"

"Okay, Miss Lexie, only I don't just follow you."

"Never mind, Cinda. I was just thinking aloud," said Lexie, smiling. "But how did Elaine take this?"

"Well, I can't say she took it so good. First off, I thought she was fainted dead away, an' then she bust right out cryin'" somethin' fierce. But after whiles she got calmer, an' now I think she's asleep. I guess she was just plain exhausterated from all her carryin's on. But now, Miss Lexie, you *must* get to bed."

So Lexie went to bed. She thought she was too happy to sleep, which wasn't so at all, for she was soon sound asleep and dreaming of a land where the fragrance of gardenias was all about her, and a dark-eyed soldier was smiling at her across a great distance.

Cinda was up early next morning. She had arranged it so that Bluebell had a little bed by herself near Angelica, and Lexie had her own room to herself. In the morning she skillfully suppressed the noisy children by promising to make cherry tarts for them if they would be good and quiet. So when she got them off for their morning play she went to Elaine, cheerily tidied up her room, and herself, and talked affably just as if the grumpy lady was all interest, though she wasn't, but she heard the elaborate account of the evening in silence, and never spoke except to say, "*Gardenias?* Of course you don't mean gardenias, Cinda. Nobody would send Lexie gardenias. They must have been snapdragons!"

"No ma'am, they was gardenias. Great thick white leaves, an' the most heavenly smell you ever smelled! It filled the whole room when she came in. I'll go get the box an' let you see 'em. An' then there was a great wonderful basket of lilies an' blue delphimium, that was from her old college classmates back in New England. An' then some pink roses, an' a funny-looking orchid from other town folks, I don't rightly know their names yet. But they was swell flowers all right." Elaine lay and listened hungrily, jealously, unable to believe that her little sister whom she chose to consider "plain" had been received with so much attention, and she finally retired into more tears and spent hours in vain regrets.

But it was a gloomy-eyed sister that Lexie met the next morning when she took her breakfast tray in to her, and Elaine vouchsafed no reply to her pleasant "good morning," except a fresh burst of tears. So for several days this went on, Elaine eating almost nothing, drinking strong coffee, refusing to talk, until Lexie began to feel that her sister was really ill now, and ventured to suggest that she send for a doctor. But Elaine only shook her head and wept again.

So Lexie turned her attention to the children and began to coax them to stay at home. She taught them pleasant games, and some that were also useful, resulting in swept sidewalks and little garden plots. She offered prizes for picking up crumbs dropped, and keeping the rooms in order. Sometimes the prizes were privileges, sometimes stories, and sometimes little homemade articles that she had contrived herself for them out of scraps of bright cloth from the attic.

Little by little Elaine came out of her shell and transferred herself from the bedroom to the living room, lay silently on the couch watching what went on, seldom smiling, seldom speaking, a great gloom over her face. She seemed like an utterly cowed, disheartened dictator who had come to an end of his schemes and couldn't seem to get hold of life anymore. She had made money a sort of god, or rather what money would buy, and she could not seem to bring herself to take an interest in a life that was not full of luxury.

But after a little, she began to watch Lexie, to see her kindly forgiveness, her utter lack of resentment for all she had tried to do to her, her happy expression, her willingness to serve whenever she could, and somehow her own life and ways began to stand out in sharp contrast. It wasn't apparent that this was happening, of course.

Lexie was praying for her sister now. Halfheartedly at first, perhaps, but as the days went on, with more faith. And this had much to do with the way Lexie lived her faith. Elaine couldn't make it out, and more and more her selfish soul was condemned.

Then one morning, there came a special delivery letter from Judge Foster's office, saying that he was back at work again and he had a job for Lexie if she was still free. Would she call at the office as soon as convenient?

So Lexie went flying across the meadow to the bus line quite early the next morning, neatly and simply attired, and was at the office almost as soon as Judge Foster arrived. When she came back late in the afternoon her face was shining with contentment. She told her sister that she had a job now and things would be a little easier for them all.

Chapter 18

There was one thing that troubled Lexie, as the days went on and she was continually happy in her work at the office, and the resultant money in hand, and that was that although she had written the day after commencement to thank her soldier for the wonderful flowers, she had not received any more letters from him. Was he done with her, and had those gardenias been a lovely gesture for good-bye?

Well, if that was it, at least she was glad that she had had those gardenias and his delightful letters.

And then a new thought came to trouble her. Was he worse again, unable to write? Perhaps near death's door?

But when her heart trembled at that thought she carried it to her Lord. He was in her Lord's care. He loved him. He would take care of him and so she was able to throw that care away.

Of course, too, there might be another explanation for his silence. He might have been sent into action again. He had hinted in his letters that there was such a possibility, and that he would like to go back, even if it meant being under fire again.

The thought made her catch her breath, and then she remembered that God would be with him, even if he went under fire again. God had brought him through before. Surely He would not desert him now. She could rest on that. But even if he should be wounded or die, and she never have the privilege of seeing him again on earth, there was something comforting in the thought that he was God's own child and that she would surely meet him in heaven. And they could talk all this over sometime. That would be nice. Only there was a great wistfulness in her heart, for she did so want to see him now on earth. She did want to be able to tell him with her own lips how happy he had made her by sending her those gardenias, and how his letters were being treasured by her. And sometimes at night, after she had read her Bible, she would get out his letters and read them over. It seemed to help her to feel she had some Christian fellowship with someone. Of course if she never had anything else of this sort in her life, she at least had had this knowledge of a Christian friendship.

Lexie went to church as often as she felt she could be spared from the difficulties at home, and sometimes she could coax some one or the other of the children to go with her. But they were not churchly minded children, and Elaine utterly refused to allow them to go to Sunday school because she had not the money to dress them in what she considered "suitable" clothes.

But the church in their little suburb was a rather coldhearted place, more interested in church suppers and social affairs, or, at best, war work, than in getting near to God, and so there was not much real spiritual comfort to be found there, except as all real Christians can feel they are worshipping God when they come to His house. But Lexie felt very much alone, except when she was in the office where the mere nearness of Judge Foster comforted her. She knew he was a good man, a Christian man, and her father's friend.

The rest of her fellow-workers in the office were very pleasant, and Lexie felt that the lines had fallen to her in pleasant places as far as her work was concerned. Sometime she remembered how distressed she had been to give up the job she had been promised in her college town. This work in the judge's office was so much more desirable, and much better pay, besides being among such congenial people. It was wonderful what God can do for one when He decides to change the background of one's life, and takes away cherished hopes and plans, He always seems to be able to give His yielded ones something better when the right time comes. Something like that idea floated through Lexie's mind occasionally as she voiced her daily prayers of thanksgiving.

And yet, there were fires to endure at home, even now. Elaine had so far roused from her stupor of gloom to be quite insistent about certain little things, and could fly into a rage as easily as ever, and fill the house with more gloom. She could still incite her young children to open rebellion against simple household rules made for the comfort of all of them, and she could still sneer coldly, angrily, when Lexie told her firmly how much money she could afford to spend on the household, and utterly refused to lend her money for beauty parlors and new dresses or to write any letters for her to Bettinger Thomas asking when he was coming home.

But fortunately these flares on the part of Elaine were not now *daily* occurrences, or nobody could have survived it. And Lexie could see that each time they happened her sister was more and more discouraged about any suit she was going to bring for nonexistent money. Less often she spoke of any such possibility as there having been money intended for her, and now and then she even said something pleasant about her stepmother. Nothing important. Just little sentences that gave Lexie a happier feeling toward her sister. Sentences like, "Your mother always had such good taste in dress, Lexie," or "Nobody could make such nice desserts as your mother. She had a hand with her cooking."

But such little breaks of sunlight in the mental attitude were of course few and far between, and the daily routine was often like going through fire with no hope of a letup ahead.

Then one day, after Lexie had about given up hope of ever hearing from her soldier again, a letter arrived. The envelope was very much battered up and had evidently been missent, or held up. The envelope was full of different directions. The wonder was that it ever reached her at all. She opened it almost in fear, like a message from a dead friend it seemed.

The letter itself was brief.

Dear Lexie:

I am suddenly being taken away from this location, perhaps on furlough, or else to return to the

*front. It will be as God wills. I have no time to
write, the order is imperative, and I do not yet
know my destination. Will let you know as soon
as I have opportunity.*

*I hope you had a happy commencement and
that my flowers got there in time.*

*They have come for me and I must go. May
God be with you to bless and help.*

*With my love,
Ben*

The letter was dated a long time ago. It must have been
written around the time of her commencement, but apparently
he had not yet received her own letter of thanks. And where
was he now? Oh, there were so many terrible possibilities. He
might have been in one of those transports that had been sunk,
or in the clipper plane they said was missing, or his body might
be lying at the bottom of the sea. He might have been captured
by the enemy and in an internment camp somewhere, or have
been shot, or—

Stop! ordered her conscience. *Haven't you and he a God?
Didn't your God promise to be with you both? Hasn't He done it
before? And won't He do it again? What right have you to antici-
pate horrors that may never be in God's plan for either of you? Let
God work it out. Just trust. That's what he said he was going to do.
You must not fall down on your job and go around looking glum.
God does not forget, and He knows what He has planned for your
good! When He has tried you He has promised that you shall come
forth as gold.*

Lexie was learning a great deal from her Bible in these days, and she was growing closer to her Lord through prayer than she had ever been before. Somehow the things at home that used to seem like the hottest fire to her shrinking soul, did not seem so important now. They were merely experiences through which to pass. And she must pass through them bravely.

But day after day Lexie kept looking for another letter. And still the days went on and none arrived.

Morning after morning Lexie scanned the newspapers, noting the disasters reported to transport ships and other modes of soldier travel—a mail plane crashed and burned, all other possibilities—and then breathed a prayer that her soldier might not be involved. But though she scanned the lists of names of killed and wounded whenever there were any, still she found no Benedict Barron. But what had become of him?

Of course there were ways of searching out what had happened to missing soldiers, and perhaps she could write somewhere in Washington and find out—perhaps, but had she, a young stranger practically, and not a relative, nor even a friend of long standing, a *right* to go to headquarters asking for his whereabouts? Perhaps he was tired of his correspondence with her, and had taken this way to vanish out of her life entirely. Well, perhaps—but certainly she would not feel justified in going to any government headquarters to trace out knowledge of him. Just an acquaintance was all she could possibly claim. There was just one place, one all-powerful Person to whom she might go, and that was her God, and his God. She would have to let it rest with that. After all it was

God who was managing this whole thing, and He knew what He was doing.

There came a bright, beautiful Sunday morning after a day of heavy rain, with a cool crispness in the air so heartening after the heat of the week that was just past.

Lexie was wearing a new dress, just a cheap little blue dimity she had seen when she went to the store to get a few things for the children, and her preference now was always for *blue* dresses because she felt that it brought her back to the days when she used to swing on the gate, and the soldier had noticed that her dress was like her eyes. It was silly of course, and she often reproved this tendency in herself to buy blue things, but still they seemed to draw her irresistibly. And now she was wearing the dress for the first time.

The children had been invited to go to some kind of a children's Sunday school celebration with their playmates across the road, and they had cried to go, so Lexie had brought home some simple garments for them bought at a sale. Their mother had rather contemptuously allowed them to wear them and go.

So it was very still around the little white house. Only the sweet notes of some wood thrushes could be heard now and then, and the mountains in the distance had on their smiling, holy look as if the night's rain had brought them comfort and serenity. The neighborhood was quiet, for they had all gone with their children to see the exercises in which some of their little ones were to have a part. The day seemed perfect.

Elaine had retired to her room to weep, after she had watched her children in their new cheap garments trip happily away. Lexie sat down on the porch with her Bible, gazing off at the mountains, and taking in sweetness of the flowers that were blooming along the little front walk down to the white gate. And then she heard footsteps, brisk footsteps, coming up the street. Turning, she saw it was a soldier, tall, good looking, well set up, his uniform gleaming with its touches of gold emblems and brass buttons.

Of course she watched him. Soldiers were always interesting to everybody now, during wartime, and especially to her, for there was one soldier that she longed very much to see. She made no excuses to herself about that now. He was her own soldier. She cared a very great deal about him. But of course, she probably never would see him again.

The soldier came on, walking straight toward the white house as if he knew the way, had been there before, and had an aim in coming. He paused by the little white gate and looked at her with a nice smile. A smile she remembered from long ago.

She started to her feet, and dropped her Bible on the chair. It was her soldier! It was Benedict Barron in the flesh, looking just like that picture she had of him up in her room. Smiling and looking as if he might ask her what her name was. And then he called it, and his voice was just as she remembered.

"Lexie!" he said. He didn't put a question mark after it as if he wasn't certain about her. There was assurance in his tone.

"Yes?" she said and flew down that path to the gate straight as a bird to its nest.

When she reached the gate she stood there looking radiantly up into his face as he was looking down into her eyes with a deep, sweet, searching gaze as if he wanted to make sure it was really the girl he knew. Then he put his hands out and laid them on her slender shoulders, looked down deeper into her eyes, and said: "May I kiss you, Lexie?" He stooped and laid his lips upon hers, and it seemed to her as if all heaven looked down and held its breath in joy as their two souls came together at last.

"You're just the same," he said at last, lifting his head and looking down at her. "My little Lexie! I'd have known you anywhere. The same eyes, the same smile. Oh my dear! To think I'm here again at last! And it's *really you*!"

Her eyes went up to his, full of delight.

"And you're the same, too," she said softly, letting her eyes caress his face. "Oh, I'm so glad you've come! I thought I never would see you again. I was afraid something had happened to you!"

He smiled gravely.

"Something did, my Lexie! Our transport was torpedoed, and a couple of us floated for days before we were picked up and carried all around the globe until finally we got to a place where we could contact the right parties. But that's a long story and I haven't so much time just now. I've got to get back to Washington this afternoon. The army trucks are passing the highway at exactly four o'clock this afternoon, and I've got to be waiting for them, for they haven't time to wait for me. But I'll be back later, in a week or two, or maybe sooner if I can find out what the plans for me are. And then we can tell the whole story. In the meantime, let's make the most of this little time. Where were you going this morning before you saw me? I see your hat up there on the porch, and you must have been going somewhere."

"Oh, I was just going to church, but it isn't necessary this morning. I want to hear all about you."

He smiled appreciatively.

"I'd like to go to church with you," he said tenderly. "Is it time?"

"No, not for an hour yet," she said.

"Then there's time to take a walk first," he said. "Or, was somebody going with you?"

"Oh no," she said with a laugh. "I usually go everywhere alone."

He looked down at her tenderly.

"Not anymore," he said. "Not when I get home to stay! Now come, let's go. Do you have to tell anyone you're going?"

"Why, no," said Lexie. "Only, you'll have time to come back to dinner, won't you? I ought to tell Cinda, though she's liable to have seen you and have something ready."

"Let's not bother with dinner today, we haven't time," he said. "I'll come again later. Get your hat and Bible, and we'll take our walk and find a church before we get back."

So she got her hat and Bible from the chair, and was back at his side. He drew her hand within his arm and they walked off together, she with her hat in her hand and he with her Bible under his arm.

"There used to be woods up this way. Is it still there, or have they cut it down yet?"

"It's still there!" said Lexie.

"Then we'll go there," he said. And side by side they walked away to the woods, while Elaine stood peering out of her bedroom window watching them eagerly, taking in every item of his uniform, noting a decoration or two, noting his smile, and the way he walked, and everything about him.

And out of her kitchen window that looked toward the woods Cinda was watching.

"That'll be him," she said delightedly to herself. "An' ain't he the soldier man! He'll do fer my bairnie. He has it written all over him. Good an' brave, an' a looker besides! Wonder what I oughtta do about dinner? Well, there's fried chicken enough. I don't needta save any fer meself. It'll be all right. An' that cherry pie turned out real good ef I do say so as shouldn't."

But the two who were sitting under a great tree in the woods with their feet resting on a bed of velvet moss, and the songs of the thrushes overhead, were not thinking of what they would have for dinner, not even intending to come back for dinner, not today. They were getting acquainted, and looking into the years of eternity ahead of them. Two people who had met God, and trusted Him utterly because He had been with them through the fire and flood and circumstance.

Eventually they went to church. But before they left the woods, they sat hand in hand and read a few of their precious verses from the Bible, and then bowed their heads together and prayed a few words. Shy words, they were. Neither of them was used to formal prayer before others.

"But, you see, I love you," said Ben Barron as he lifted his head with that grave, sweet smile on his face, "and we had to have some sort of a ceremony or dedication or something to mark it. We belong to each other, now, in God's eyes, don't we?" And he searched her face.

"Oh yes," said Lexie, drawing a deep breath of joy. "I am so glad! Now I won't ever have to worry again, thinking you don't care. I was so afraid if anything should happen to you I would never find you if you cared at all."

"You dear!" he said stooping to kiss her again, and gathering her in his arms, holding her close. "But I don't see how you cared when you didn't really know me. When you hadn't seen me but once."

"Oh, but I *did*," said Lexie. "I grew into loving you before I knew I was doing it, and I was so worried lest I had not right."

"Precious child!" said Ben. "But you were only a child."

"Yes, I was only a child!—but—you say *you* loved me!" She gave him an endearing look.

"Well, yes, of course I wasn't conscious of it when I first saw you, for I wasn't grown-up either, you know, but something caught in my heart, and came back to me in the fire that night, and I guess God had this planned for us all the time."

So they talked, and they very nearly didn't get to church on time. If Ben hadn't been a soldier used to timing himself, they wouldn't have.

But they walked into church just as the first hymn was being sung, and were given a hymnbook and stood and sang together:

> *"Mine eyes and my desire*
> *Are ever to the Lord;*
> *I love to plead His promises,*
> *And rest upon His Word."*

And their eyes as they met told a story of love and trust that the watching, eager churchgoers read and interpreted.

"My, don't they make a swell couple!" said one envious girl

as she watched them go down the aisle together at the close of church.

"Yes, and did you get on to the way they sang, as if they really *meant it*!" said another.

"Oh, *that*!" said a third girl. "Their looks were for each other, not for the words they were singing."

"No," said another girl, "they *meant* it, I *know* they did. You cannot fake *real* things. Not like that!"

"Oh, piffle! There *aren't* any real things anymore!" said the first girl, whose lad had gone off to war without saying the word that counted.

But the two who were walking in heavenly ways went happily on with their brief, short day, treasuring every second of it for sweet memory.

They took a brief lunch at a little place along the way they walked, for they could not take time out for formalities. Lexie then went with her soldier over to the highway, where they sat under a tree together to wait for the army truck to come. And quietly, just before he had to get on, Lexie started up the lane that led home to the little white gate, and when she got to the turn of the lane, where a tall tree arched over her, she stood, a slender figure in a soft blue dress and a big white hat, waving a small handkerchief toward the great dark army truck that was moving down the highway toward Washington. He was gone, but he was *hers*! Her heart thrilled with the thought. And she was wearing his ring! A sweet, dear ring, its bright clear diamond sparkling on her finger, filling her with continual joy. To think that she should be wearing his ring! And she had a tender thought for the first owner of that ring, Ben's mother. She must have been a wonderful woman. And

Ben had worn that ring on a slender chain around his neck ever since she died. He had worn it all through that awful experience in the fire. It was almost like having something that was a part of him.

She walked slowly home in the quiet of the late Sunday afternoon, and thought what wonderful things God had been preparing for her all these years when she had thought things were so very hard and never would be any different. And now heaven seemed to have opened before her and all around her.

And then she got home, and there was Elaine out on the porch looking fretful and impatient!

Chapter 19

Well, so you've got home at last! Where on earth have you been all day Sunday? This is something new for you!"

Lexie looked up and smiled with that dreamy smile that shows one has been far away in a heaven of one's own, and for some reason, it made her sister angry and jealous.

"Oh, have you needed me?" said Lexie. "I'm sorry. But I've been having a wonderful time. We went to church, and then we took a walk."

"Oh, you took a walk, did you? All this time? You couldn't have come home and told us what you were going to do, could you?"

"Why, no, I couldn't very well," said Lexie, with a winsome look in her eyes.

"Well, who was the man? Someone you picked up on the

road? I didn't think you were that kind. Your mother certainly wouldn't have approved of that."

Lexie laughed.

"No, I didn't pick him up. I've known him a long time."

"Oh, you *have*? And why did he never turn up before?"

"Why, he's been overseas," said Lexie. "We've been corresponding for a long time. He's just home on leave, and he doesn't know if he may soon be ordered off again. He thinks, though, that he can come back at least for a few hours before he as to go anywhere."

"Oh!" said Elaine. "So he's coming back!"

"Yes, he'll be back," said Lexie joyously.

Elaine gave a sharp look, and then she said: "Whose ring is that you're wearing? I never saw you have that on before. Is it a real diamond, or just paste?"

"Why, it's my ring," said Lexie, lifting her hand proudly. "It was his mother's, and he's worn it next to his heart all through his war experience. And, oh yes, the diamond is real. His father bought it at Tiffany's in New York when he and Ben's mother were engaged."

"It's not very large," said Elaine sharply. "They can't be very rich."

"I don't know," said Lexie. "I never asked anything about that. I really didn't care."

"No, you *wouldn't*!" said Elaine contemptuously. "Well, I hope you're happy. I thought I was once, but it didn't last."

"But this will," said Lexie with a grave, sweet smile, "because we both love the Lord Jesus, and whatever comes, we are both His."

"Oh, *religious*, is he? Well, that *would* be the kind you'd pick. Well, I'm sure I wish you well."

"Thank you, Elaine," said Lexie brightly, and she went over and kissed her sister on the forehead, which was the only part of Elaine's anatomy that she presented for the salute.

Then Lexie went in the house and out to the kitchen to find Cinda and show her her ring.

But Elaine sat still on the porch into the deep gloaming of the evening, and let the slow tears course down her cheeks unchecked.

The days that followed brought great joy to Lexie. Ben came back within the week to tell her that he had been put in charge of an important training camp for a while because they felt he must not go back to fighting until he was in better shape physically. And besides, they felt his experience would be more worthwhile in training others just how to fight as he had done than in going back again to fight. Incidentally he was wearing a decoration of honor for his valorous deeds under fire, and several times he was called to speak on the radio, giving a little sketch of the experiences of soldiers fighting fire. It was all very wonderful to Lexie, and she took great pride in him in her shy, sweet soul. Especially when she saw the honor Judge Foster and Mr. Gordon gave him and heard their words of commendation.

And all this had a great deal of influence with Elaine. She treated Ben with the utmost deference, and actually changed in her habitual manner toward her sister when he was present, until Lexie almost cried with joy at the sweet way she spoke to her.

It happened a few days after all this that a letter came to Elaine from the war department stating that her husband was still alive. It was found that he had been taken prisoner, placed in an internment camp by the enemy, and had been there so long that his health was greatly undermined. But he had at last managed to make an escape, and after various thrilling experiences in which he almost lost his life and, more than once, his freedom, he had managed to reach this country and get into contact with the proper authorities. They had placed him in a hospital in Washington, for he had not been fit to travel farther, and now he wanted his wife. Could she come to Washington at once to see him? He was in a very weak condition and his life was hanging by a thread. But the doctor thought that his wife's presence might materially aid in a possible recovery. Could she come at once? Cinda sniffed when she heard this.

But it was a new Elaine that came in excitement to Lexie with her letter, and asked most humbly if there was any way she would lend her a little money to go. She was no longer weak and helpless. She was alert and eager, and ready to start at once without going to a beauty parlor or purchasing any new clothes.

"But, are you *able* to go?" asked Lexie, looking at her in surprise.

"*Able!*" she said sharply. "Of *course* I'm able. Don't you understand it is my *husband* who needs me, and he may be dying! It is my husband *whom I love*! The only man I ever really loved. I *must* go, and I must take the *first train*. Will you find out how I can quickest get there?"

"Of course!" said Lexie, and she went to work.

It was Lexie who arranged it all, who took her sister in a taxi to the station, asked her if she didn't want her to go with her, gave her all the money she would need, told her to let her know if she needed more, and then promised to look after the children while she was gone. As they waited for the train to be open, Elaine suddenly spoke:

"Lexie, I've been a fool. I may as well tell you before I go because something might happen and then I never could. I knew better than to torment you the way I did. I practically knew I was chasing a fool's hope when I tried to get money out of you. But I met that Thomas lawyer and he was telling how he found a fortune for one woman, and I began to tell him about my father and how he once said he wanted to leave a small fortune to each one of his girls. Then he got me all worked up to think that perhaps this was really so. He's an old robber himself, for he got an awful lot of money out of me at one time or another while that was going on, and he promised me that it would be no trouble to make you and me both rich. But I was a fool to believe him. And I owe you a great apology. I hope you'll forgive me!"

"Oh, that's all right," said Lexie with a sigh of relief. "I'm so glad you know at last that I was telling the truth."

"Oh, of *course* I knew you were telling the truth all the time, but he kept telling me if I worked it that way you would fall and I could get a part of some of my father's old holdings out of people who owed him. But I was a fool."

There were sounds about now that the train was ready to go, and Elaine picked up her suitcase, and then lingered an instant.

"And Lexie," she said in a low, hurried tone, "I want you to know that I think you're wonderful. If there ever was a Christian, you're that! The way you've stood all I've put upon you was something great. If they gave decorations for things like that, I'd vote for one for you, and someday, maybe I can be your kind of a Christian, too. I never wanted to be one before until I watched you under fire."

Then she gave Lexie a quick kiss and hurried onto the train, and Lexie went back home with happy tears in her eyes.

She went and told Cinda about what Elaine had said, and Cinda listened, and sniffed unbelievingly.

"Humph! Pretty Christian *she'd* make! Wull, I s'pose God *ken* do *any*thin' He *loikes*, but I shouldn't advoise His wasting His toime on such poor material. Well, it may be so, but I'll believe it when I see it!"

But a few days later when Ben Barron came down to talk over plans for their wedding in the near future, she told him of Elaine's words, and he listened gravely.

"The Lord knows how to work, doesn't He, and bring glory out of shame. My dear, there are going to be many surprises in heaven when the decorations of honor are handed out to the quiet saints who have been under fire for years without complaint. I was reading in Timothy this morning: 'Therefore endure hardness, as a good soldier of Jesus Christ. No man that warreth entangleth himself with the affairs of this life; that he *may please him* who hath *chosen* him to be a soldier.' I guess, my dear, we're going to find that all the fires we have to go through are worthwhile when we come to stand before His Presence."

All Through the Night

Chapter 1

$\mathcal{D}$ale Huntley finished labeling and tying the last of the packages. The expressman had promised to call for them before ten o'clock. Dale gave a quick glance at the clock, and finding it was only half past nine, she sat back with a sigh of relief and closed her eyes for just a second.

It had been a hard time, and she had not stopped for a moment to think of herself or her own feelings. But now, were all the little nagging duties accomplished that Grandmother had left for her to do before the relatives should arrive? With her eyes still closed, she went swiftly down the list that was sharp in her mind.

Put all personal gifts, jewelry, heirlooms, private letters in the safe-deposit box in the bank. That had been done last week while Grandmother was still alive and alert to all that was going on around her, intent on leaving her world all in order for her going, interested in each item as if it were a game she was playing.

"You know," she told Dale with one of her old-time twinkles that gave her such an endearing look, "those cousins of yours that have been anything but cousinly in their actions are liable to turn up as soon as they hear that I am gone, and they'll do their best to search out anything that could possibly be interesting to them and make your life miserable if they think you want it, so it is best not to have anything around to make trouble for you."

Grandmother was always so thoughtful for everybody.

But she must not think about that now. This was going to be a hard day, and she would not be able to get through it if she gave way to tears at this stage. At any moment those relatives might arrive—the telegram had said Tuesday—and she must not have traces of tears on her face. Oh, of course, tears were natural when one had lost a dear one, but she was in a position where she must be more than just another relative. She must carry out Grandmother's plans. She must meet the cousins quietly and with some measure of poise. That would be the only way to offset any arrogance and desire to manage, on their part.

Dale had not seen these relatives for years. Not since she was a small child, too young to be noticed by them. Young enough to be calmly swept aside for the pretty, spoiled cousin, Corliss, who had to have everything her little heart desired, even if it upset everybody else in the house. Corliss had taken great delight in making Dale the butt of all her tantrums. It was natural, therefore, that Dale did not look forward to the reunion with pleasure. Still, she told herself, perhaps she was not being fair in feeling this way. After all, it was a good many years ago, and Corliss had been only a baby then, some months younger than herself. There was a good chance that through the years Corliss might have changed and would perhaps be a charming young woman by this time; it might even be quite possible that they could be friends. Though from Grandmother's description of her when she last saw her, Dale did not think so. Grandmother had at times given little word-sketches of her grandniece, witty and sarcastic but altogether good-natured. However, those sketches were clearly given in the way of warning, so Dale would not be taken unawares and thereby lose out.

It was for that reason that Dale was dreading the arrival of these unknown relatives and had carried out the little details of Grandmother's plans most meticulously, schooling herself to a calmness that she was far from feeling. Not until these relatives had come and gone could she relax and give attention to her own personal plans. By that time, perhaps, she would be used to the fact that the dear grandmother was gone and that from then on she was utterly on her own.

She was interrupted in her troubled thoughts by the sound of the doorbell.

Quickly assuming her habitual quiet demeanor, she hurried to the door, giving a worried glance toward the little stack of packages waiting for the expressman. Oh, if only it was him instead of the dreaded relatives. Then she opened the door and glimpsed with relief the express car parked by the curb.

"Oh, you've come, Mr. Martin! I'm so glad! I do want to get these packages off on the first train."

The expressman grinned.

"I told ya I'd come, didn't I? I always keep my word when I can. Especially in a case like this where there's a funeral. I always like to help out. Especially when it's an old friend like Grandma Huntley. I know she ain't here, but somehow I think where she is she'll know."

Dale's face lit tenderly. "Yes, I think she will," she said softly.

The old expressman got out a grubby handkerchief and blew his nose violently, then turned on his grin again. "Okay!" he said, pulling himself together. "Where's yer packages?"

"Oh yes. Right here by the dining room door. All of them."

"And you want these here things all prepaid, you said, didn't you? Okay. You can stop by the office and settle the bill when you come downtown again. I'll have 'em weighed and be ready for you."

Dale drew a breath of relief as she watched the truck drive away. Now, no matter when Aunt Blanche and Corliss came, there wouldn't be anything for them to question about. Grandmother had made it quite plain that they would likely resent her giving anything away before they arrived, if there was any evidence around that it had been done.

So Dale was free now to go about the arrangements for the day and her undesired guests, realizing that she was going to need great patience and strength before this visit was over.

Hattie was in the kitchen, Dale knew. Dear old Hattie, who loved Grandmother so much and whose lifework from now on was merely to be transferred to the granddaughter whom Grandmother had loved so well.

Hattie had had experience in former years with the coming relatives and would know how to deal with them. Grandmother had talked it all over with Hattie and prepared her, made sure that she fully understood and could arrange an adjustable firmness, with courtesy, so that no clashing would be necessary. But when Dale came into the kitchen and found Hattie standing disconsolately looking out the window into the kitchen garden, the old woman said sorrowfully, "I dunno, I dunno, Miss Dale! Grandma said I was to be real sweet and polite and not stir up no strife. But if you had knowed them people the way I did, you'd know that wasn't just physically possible. I'd like to carry out your grandma's wishes, an' I'm sure I'll do my best, but I know I can't really do it. I've tried before and it didn't work, and I don't seem to believe it'll work this time, but I'll do my best."

"Why, of course you will, Hattie. You'll be all right. And don't you worry about it. If they say anything you don't like, just put it aside and don't think about it."

"Yes," sighed Hattie, "that's what Grandma advised me. She said I was to remember that the Lord was listening to me, and He would know what was going on and would be expecting me to act to please *Him*, not them."

"That's right, Hattie," said Dale with a little tender smile on her sweet lips.

"Miss Dale, if that's so, and the Lord can watch an' see what I do, do you s'pose perhaps *Grandma* can see, too? If I thought *she* would be watching I could do a great deal better."

Dale smiled.

"Why yes, Hattie, perhaps she will be able to see. I think it would help us both to think of her watching, and I'm sure the Lord will care and will be watching and be pleased if we do the right kindly thing."

"Okay, Miss Dale, I'll remember that. I'll do my best to

please the Lord, and *her*!"

It was a busy morning after that. There were orders to give, telephone calls to answer, telegrams and letters to read, and the dinner to plan for the possible guests that evening. There were callers to meet, old friends of Grandmother's to talk to, a hundred and one questions to answer. The minister came to talk over the arrangements that Grandmother had made with him. There were flowers to receive and arrange for keeping, and there were tender, precious messages from friends. Everybody had loved Grandmother for years, and she was going to be greatly missed.

Then suddenly, late in the afternoon, when the company dinner was beginning to give off delicious odors, there was a stir in the street, and a taxi pulled up at the door ostentatiously. They had come! The waiting was over.

Dale cast a quick look out the door, caught a glimpse of a golden-haired, haughty girl with very red lips, and drew a deep breath to quiet the sudden thumping of her heart. She knew that it would not do to yield to excitement, for if she did there would be no poise and no quiet dignity in her meeting with her guests, and she must remember what Grandmother had desired.

With another deep breath and a lifting of her heart for help above, she went to the door with the nearest to a real welcome in her eyes that she could summon. She came down the walk to the little old-fashioned white gate to meet them.

Aunt Blanche was having an argument with the taxi driver about the fare and didn't notice her at first, and Corliss, who was engaged in gazing around at the neighborhood, did not at first see her either.

But finally the aunt finished her argument with a sharp bit of sarcasm and flung herself out to stand on the pavement and look around.

"Oh, is that you, Dale?" she said as she almost tripped over her niece. "Why, you've grown tall, haven't you? I expected to find you short and fat the way you used to be."

Dale had been prepared to greet her aunt with a brief kiss, but it appeared the aunt had made no provision for such a salutation, so she contented herself with a brief handshake and turned to Corliss.

But Corliss was standing there staring at her. Apparently for some reason she was not at all what Corliss had expected, and it required some adjusting of her preconceived ideas to help her correlate the facts. It had not yet entered her mind that any form of definite greeting would be required between them, so Corliss took no notice of Dale's smile or the hand held out in greeting. She simply stared.

And behind her loomed a boy whom she knew must be Corliss's younger brother, Powelton. How cross he looked! Such frowning brows! She sensed on the boy's lips the grim distaste for the errand on which they had come. She tried to reassure him by smiling, but he only summoned a wicked grin.

Dale spoke pleasantly. "You are Powelton, aren't you?" she said with real welcome in her voice. "I haven't seen you since you were a baby."

"Aw, ferget it!" said the insolent youth. "Just call me Pow. That's what I prefer."

"Now, Powelton!" reproached his mother. "You promised me—"

"Yes, I know, Mom," said the boy, "but that was when you

said there was going to be a lawyer here. You can't make anything out of this little dump, I'm telling ya!"

"Powelton! Be still! Driver, you can bring the luggage into the house."

"No ma'am, I can't! I ain't doing that no more. These is wartimes, and I can't take the time to lug in suitcases. I put 'em on the sidewalk and you can lug 'em in yourself, or let that spoiled boy o' yours do it. I gotta get back to the station. I'm overdue already." And he started his car defiantly.

"Oh, we can manage the luggage," said Dale pleasantly, gathering up three of the smaller bags. "Come on, boys and girls; each of you gather up a handful and we'll soon be all right."

The annoyed aunt stood in their midst and protested, but Dale had started on with her load of bags, and there was nothing for the rest to do but follow.

As they came up the steps to the white doorway, the boy flicked his cap over the exquisite, delicate lilies that were fastened to the doorbell.

"Why the weeds?" he said contemptuously, turning a sneering glance at Dale.

"Oh, please don't!" she said, planting herself in the way of a second thrust of the ruthless cap.

"Well, of all the silly customs," sneered the young man. "Mom, I wouldn't stand for that if I were you. Tying a whole flower garden on the house we're expected to stay in all night."

Dale took a deep breath and tried to summon a calm expression. "Take the suitcases into the living room," she said quietly. "Put them right on the floor by the door and then we can easily sort them out for the different rooms."

"Okay!" said the lad disagreeably, and he dropped the luggage he was carrying and turned to walk into the living room and look around. "Some dump!" he commented disagreeably, casting a contemptuous look at the old steel engravings and ancestral portraits. He gave a semblance of a kick toward the fine old polished mahogany sofa with its well-preserved haircloth upholstery.

But Dale paid no attention to him. She put down the bags she was carrying and hurried out to the walk to get more, though she noticed that nobody else was like-minded, for they were surging into the house and staring around.

"Heavens, Moms," said Corliss, "I don't see what you wanted of a shanty like this! It really wasn't worth coming all this way over for."

"No," said Powelton, "it wouldn't even make a good fire."

His mother cast a reproving look at him.

"You'll find it will sell for quite a tidy little sum," said his mother. "You see, I didn't come all this way over here without knowing plenty about the situation. I found there is a project on to build a large munitions factory right in this neighborhood, and a few strings properly pulled can make it possible for this place to be included in the center of things. A little judicious maneuvering will bring us in a good sum if we hold out just long enough."

Dale, coming in with the final load of bags, happened to overhear this last announcement, although her aunt thought she had lowered her voice. But Dale put down the baggage with no more sign than a quick pressure of her pleasant lips into a straight line.

"Now," she said, looking up at her aunt and endeavoring to

speak pleasantly, "will you come upstairs, Aunt Blanche, and see what arrangements I have made for you? Perhaps Powelton will bring up the bags you want right away."

"Not I, my fair cousin," responded the boy. "I've carried just all the bags I'm going to carry today."

But Dale thought it best to ignore that remark. Let his mother deal with her boy. It wasn't her business. So she led the way upstairs.

A straight, easy flight of broad, low steps led to a landing in a wide bay window, overlooking a pleasant landscape. The sun was just setting, and the scene was very lovely. But Dale was in no humor to pause or to call her aunt's attention to the sky decked out in glory. She hurried up the stairs, trying to make her voice steady as she spoke. "I thought you would like the old room where you used to be when you last visited here."

"Oh! Indeed! I really don't remember anything about it," said the aunt in a chilly voice. "I'll see what you have arranged and then take my choice; I'm rather particular about my surroundings."

Dale threw open the door at the head of the stairs and indicated the room within.

"I hope you'll be quite comfortable here," she said as pleasantly as she could over the anger that made her voice tremble.

The aunt cast a cold look over the pretty room with its starched muslin ruffles, its delicate old-fashioned china, and its polished mahogany.

"Hm!" said the woman. "I don't remember it. Have you anything else?"

Anger rolled up in a crimson wave from Dale's delicate throat and spread over her face, and for an instant she thought she was going to lose control of herself. She was being treated as if she were a servant in a rooming house. Then it suddenly came over her that Grandmother had drolly described what her daughter-in-law was like and given her clues to just such actions, and she caught her breath and gave a little light laugh.

"Yes," she said brightly. "I thought the next room would be nice for Corliss."

"Which one? That next door?" asked Corliss sharply. "No, I won't have that. It only has one window! I want that room down at the far end of the hall. It looks out to the street, and I'm sure it's much larger and sunnier." She turned and sped toward the room she craved, and Dale caught her breath and cried out softly, "No! No, you couldn't have that. That is Grand-mother's room."

"Nonsense!" said Corliss sharply. "What's that got to do with it? I say I want that room." And she hurried down the hall, her hand already on the doorknob before Dale could reach her, and she was only deterred from flinging open the door by the fact that it was locked. "What's the meaning of this?" she almost screamed. "What right have you to lock the doors? I suppose you are keeping this room for yourself because it is the best room, obviously. Answer me! Why have you locked this door?"

Dale was by her side now, and her voice was low and sweet as she answered gently, "Because Grandmother is lying in there."

Corliss let go of the doorknob as if it had been something terribly hot. She turned frightened eyes on her cousin.

"What do you mean?" she almost screamed. "Do you mean that you have kept a dead person in the house and then let us come here to stay? Why, how perfectly gruesome! I think that is ghastly! I couldn't think of staying in the house, going to sleep, with a dead person in the next room. I should go mad! Mother, are you going to allow this to go on? I won't sleep here. I simply won't. Not with a dead woman in the house. You'll have to do something about it!"

Then Aunt Blanche came forward.

"Dale, you don't mean that Grandmother's body has not been taken to the undertaker's yet? Why, I cannot understand such negligence. Who arranged all this anyway? Did you, a young girl, presume to do it?"

"No, Aunt Blanche, Grandmother made all the arrangements. She said she wanted to stay here till she was taken to her final resting place, and she sent for the undertaker herself and made all the arrangements."

"How horrible!" said the aunt. "Well, it's evident we shall have to get another undertaker and have the body taken away at once. We can't let this go on. Corliss is a very nervous, temperamental child. The doctor says she must not be excited unduly. Suppose you call up another undertaker, and I will talk with him and have this thing fixed. We'll have the funeral in some funeral parlor. I somehow knew I should have come yesterday."

But Dale stood quite still and looked at her aunt. "I'm sorry you feel that way, Aunt Blanche, but it will be impossible to change the arrangements."

"Nonsense! Leave it to me. I'll cancel the arrangements quick enough. I'll just tell the man we'll not pay him, and he'll get out quick enough."

"He is paid, Aunt Blanche. Grandmother paid him

herself. She wanted to save us from having any trouble at the end, she said."

The aunt turned a face of frozen indignation. "All paid! How ridiculous! Grandmother must have been quite crazy at the end. She had no right to do this. I shall refuse to let this house be used for the service."

"I'm afraid you wouldn't have the right to do that, Aunt Blanche."

"Not have the right? What do you mean? The house will of course eventually be mine. I certainly have the right to do what I will with my own property, and I do not intend to have any funeral here to spoil the sale of the house. You see, I have found a purchaser for it already. Someone I met on the train, and he's coming here tomorrow morning to look the house over. We certainly can't let him see a funeral and dead people here. He would never want to buy it under those circumstances, so gruesome."

A wave of color flew up into Dale's cheeks and then receded suddenly as she remembered her promises to her grandmother not to get angry in talking with her aunt, but to remember to take a deep breath and lift her heart in prayer when she felt tempted. Grandmother had been so anxious that all things should be done decently and in order, and she must have known, too, just what provocative things might be said. So Dale drew a deep breath with partly closed eyes for an instant and a lifting of her heart to God for help.

"Why, the house isn't for sale, Aunt Blanche," she said quite sweetly, in a pleasant tone.

"What do you mean?" screamed the lady. "Do you mean to say that the house has already been sold and Grandmother was only renting it? I always understood that it was her own."

But just then Corliss raised her voice from the foot of the stairs. "Mother, if you stand there and chew the rag with Dale any longer, you won't get anything done, and I simply won't stay in his house tonight the way things are. I feel as if I was about to faint this minute. Where is my medicine? I'm going to faint. I am! Come quick!" And Corliss slumped down on the stairs and dropped her head back on the step above, rolling her eyes and gasping for breath.

Her mother flew wildly down the stairs, wafting back angry words to Dale: "There, see what you've done now! You'd better send for a doctor. These spells of hers are sometimes very serious. Powelton! Powelton! Where are you? Go out in the kitchen and get a pitcher of cold water, and a glass and spoon, and then look in my black bag for Corliss's medicine. Be quick about it, too."

Corliss was presently restored to sufficient consciousness to talk again, and she began to whine at her mother. "Moms, you've simply got to get things going. You can't have night coming down and all this funeral stuff around. I simply would die to be in a house with a dead body."

Then Dale stepped up quietly and spoke with dignity and sweetness. "Corliss, if you would just come up into the room and see Grandmother, how sweet and pretty she looks, just like a saint lying there with the soft lace around her neck and her dear hands folded and the loveliest smile on her gentle lips, you wouldn't feel this way."

But Dale's plea was interrupted by a most terrific scream of utter terror that must have been heard throughout the neighborhood. "No! No! No! I won't! I won't ever see her.

How perfectly horrid of you to say that. Take me out! Take me out of this house!"

This was followed by a quick exit to the front porch and a flinging of the girl's body down in a chair, where she sat moaning and wailing in a tempest of hysterics.

Then her mother came back into the house to Dale. "Dale, you'll have to tell me someplace where I can take her until you can make other arrangements. Corliss will be a wreck unless we can get her out of here."

Dale, with a quick uplifting breath, thought rapidly.

"Perhaps you would like to take her to the Inn," she said coolly. "I think they might have a room there. At least they would have a reception room where she could lie down on a couch till you could find a room that would do. I'm sorry I don't know of a boardinghouse that is not full to the brim with defense workers just now. Or it might be one of the neighbors would let her lie down in the parlor till she gets control of herself. But certainly it is impossible to make any different arrangements here in the house. These are Grandmother's own arrangements, and I intend to see that they are carried out. If Corliss cannot get used to the idea, she might stay at the hotel or down at the station till the service is over. Now if you'll excuse me, Aunt Blanche, I think I'm needed in the kitchen. The dinner will be ready in about a half hour. Perhaps Corliss will feel better after she has had something to eat."

"No!" screamed Corliss, uncovering her sharp ears. "I'll not eat a mouthful in this house! I'm going to the hotel."

But Dale went into the kitchen to face an indignant old servant.

"Let her go to the hotel!" said Hattie furiously. "We don't

want her screaming around here, desacratin' Grandma's house for her when she ain't fairly out of it yet. We don't want 'em here. Let the whole kit of 'em go. We don't want to house 'em or feed 'em or nothin'."

"There, there, Hattie," said Dale. "Remember what Grandmother said."

"Yes, I know; only Miss Dale, it ain't fair for you. You workin' an' slavin' to get ready for 'em, an' then they act like this! It ain't reasonable."

"Yes, I know," said Dale wearily, "but it will soon be over and they'll be gone."

"Yeah?" said the old woman. "I wonder, will they?"

And then Dale could hear her aunt calling loudly for her, and she went back into the living room to see what new trouble might have arisen.

She found her aunt most irate. "Dale, what in the world was that you said about the house just as Corliss was taken ill? Did I understand you to say that you thought this house was not for sale? What did you mean by that?"

"I meant just what I said, Aunt Blanche," said Dale firmly. "The house is definitely not for sale."

"But how could you possibly know that?" asked the aunt sharply. "Grandmother didn't rent it, did she? I always understood that she was the full owner."

"No, Aunt Blanche. Grandmother did not own the house at all. It was just to be her home while she lived, but she had no ownership in it."

"Well, she did own the house once, I'm sure of that. I remember perfectly well. I think my husband engineered that. I think he paid part, or perhaps it was the whole price for it. And of course it was to be mine after Grandmother was gone."

"I'm sorry you have misunderstood, Aunt Blanche," said Dale quietly, "but that was not the case. Grandmother never owned the house, or even a part of it. The house is mine. My father bought it for me before he went away on business. Later he was killed, and there was a proviso that Grandmother was always to have a home here as long as she lived. The house was left in trust for Grandmother and me until I should come of age, and that happened just a year ago, you remember."

"How ridiculous! That's a pretty story for you to concoct out of whole cloth. I suppose the real truth of the matter is that you coaxed Grandmother into signing some papers and giving the house over to you, but a thing like that will be easily broken. And of course it will not be hard to prove that your father never had any money before he went to war. He was a sort of a ne'er-do-well, as I understand it, and couldn't have bought a house if he wanted to. As for you, you were only a babe in arms when he went away. I don't believe that even Grandmother could have helped to make up a story like this, much as she disliked me."

"Aunt Blanche, don't you think perhaps we had better leave this decision until after dinner? Hattie has just told me that the dinner is all ready to be served, and I'm sure you must be hungry. If Corliss doesn't care to eat in the house, would she like to have a tray brought out to the side porch? It is pretty well shaded with vines and nobody would be likely to see her, and wouldn't it be good for us to sit down now and postpone this discussion until tomorrow after the service? You know a little later the friends and neighbors will be coming in to see Grandmother, and we wouldn't want to be eating then."

"Oh for heaven's sake! Is that going to happen, too? I think we better go over to the hotel right away. This certainly is an odd reception you are giving us."

"I'm sorry, Aunt Blanche. We have a nice dinner, and surely you must be hungry!"

And just then Hattie swung the kitchen door open, letting in a delicious smell of roasted chicken. Powelton arrived in the doorway and spotted two plump, delectable lemon meringue pies on the sideboard.

"Oh gee!" he said. "Let's stay, Mom. I'm clean hollow, and if you don't stay, I'll stage a scene, too, and then see where you'll be!"

So Dale seated her recalcitrant guests around the table that had been stretched to its fullest extent for the occasion, and there was a sort of armed truce while they ate.

But Dale felt as if she scarcely could swallow a bite as she sat trying to be sweet and pleasant and not think of what was going to happen next. Perhaps she should have insisted that they go to the hotel. But she wasn't entirely sure there were rooms there, and certainly the neighbors would think it very strange that Grandmother's relatives would be sent off to a hotel. Still what would they think if a public argument about the house, and the funeral in general, should be staged that evening in their presence? Well, she couldn't help it. What had to come must come. But she prayed in her heart: *Dear Lord, please take over, for I can't do anything about it myself.*

So they were soon served, the visiting aunt under protest, though she was hungry. She sat down with a face like Nemesis, as if she were yielding much in doing so, and snapped out her sentences as if she were a seamstress biting off threads.

Outside on the pretty white porch sat the petted, unhappy

Corliss, accepting ungraciously the plate of tempting food, surveying it with dissatisfaction, and tasting each separate dish tentatively, with a nose all ready to turn up and lips all ready to curl in scorn. But after the first taste she gobbled it all down in a trice and called out for more.

But before anyone heard her outcries, her roving glance suddenly lit on the lovely spray of lilies that was fastened so gracefully to the doorbell, and she rose from her improvised dinner table with a clatter that rattled all the dishes. She flung down her knife and fork and spoon noisily to the floor; she pranced angrily over to the front door, where her frantic fingers wrenched the beautiful flowers from their moorings then, snatching them up, marched into the dining room.

"So you thought I'd eat my dinner beside a lot of funeral flowers, did you? Well, I *won't*, and that's *flat!*" she finished and flung the lovely blossoms across the room.

There was an instant of utter silence while the angry girl stood surveying them, frowning, and then Dale rose from her seat and slid quickly over to pick up the flowers and vanish into the kitchen to determine how much damage had been done. These flowers were sent by Grandmother's close friend, Mrs. Marshall, the lady who lived in the finest house on the hill above the town and had her own conservatories and wonderful gardens. They must go back in place and must not be missed for a moment by the neighbors or anybody in town.

Dale found that, fortunately, the blossoms were reinforced by wire around their stems and had not been badly broken by their rough treatment. She straightened them carefully and, going out the back door, went around to the front and put the lilies back in place again. Then, just as she fastened the last bit of wire and felt that the flowers were going to be all right after all, Corliss appeared in the front door with a dish of Hattie's exceptional apple pudding brimming with delightful hot sweet gravy. With thunderous fury on her brow, she stood and screamed. "You *shan't* put those horrid flowers back on that door. Not till I've finished my dinner!" And she stamped her dainty foot resoundingly. Then she followed her wild words by another piercing scream, which brought her mother to the door at once.

"Well now, what are you doing, Dale Huntley? You certainly act possessed! Are you determined to make my little girl suffer?"

Dale turned as calmly as she could, though she was trembling from head to foot. "I'm sorry, Aunt Blanche, but these flowers were sent by Mrs. Governor Marshall, from her own conservatories. She cut them with her own hands for Grandmother, for she loved her very much, and she is due to arrive here any minute now, for she was anxious to see how the flowers look, and I could not let her see that they were not in place. I'm sure you will understand that, Aunt Blanche. And—here she comes now!"

A shiny limousine pulled up in front of the door, driven by a uniformed chauffeur, bringing a lovely lady of unmistakable breeding.

Aunt Blanche stared aghast and then suddenly turned and vanished inside the house, herding her children together and out to the kitchen.

Chapter 2

Mrs. Marshall's car had been gone only a short time when a handsome naval officer came slowly down the street with a package in his arms, looking carefully at the numbers of each house.

Corliss emerged from her hiding in the kitchen just in time to see him in the near distance. She remained within sight to watch him. Such a personable young man in uniform she had not seen since she came East to attend this awful funeral of a grandmother she had seldom seen and had not been taught to love.

Corliss went nearer to the open window to see him better and wondered if it would be too obvious if she were to go back to the chair in which she had eaten her only half-finished dinner.

But the young officer was stepping more quickly now and was actually turning in at the gate. He was coming *here*! What was he? A florist? Surely not, as he was in uniform! Of course not.

Corliss gave a quick pat to her golden curls, adjusted a smile of come-hitherness on her fierce young features, and got ready to go to the door when he should knock. She had no intention of letting an opportunity like this pass her by.

But Corliss was reckoning without her hostess, for Dale had lingered on the porch to straighten out the evidence of the recent meal served there before more people should arrive, and she went forward with a quiet little smile as the officer came up the steps saluting her.

"Is this where Miss Huntley lives, Miss Dale Huntley?" he asked with a grin of recognition. "I thought I'd find you. You wouldn't remember me, would you?" And there was a wistfulness in his voice that it was most fortunate that Corliss was not outside to hear. "I'm just the guy that helped you wipe dishes about a month ago at the Social Center. I had another short furlough, and I thought I'd stop by and see if you were still on the job."

"Oh yes, I remember you," said Dale with a sudden lighting of her eyes. "You are David Kenyon. Isn't that so?"

"That's right. You've got a wonderful memory. All the fellows you must meet at that center."

"Oh, but that night you were there was the last night I've been to the Center. You see, we've had sickness here, and death—"

"Yes, I know," said the young man with a sudden gentle sobering of his expression. "They told me. They said your grandmother was gone. And I remembered how you spoke of her. You've lived with her for a long time, and it seemed as if you must love her a lot. I thought perhaps you wouldn't mind if I brought a few flowers, just to show my sympathy."

He held out the florist's box he carried, almost shyly.

"Oh, how very kind of you," said Dale, quick appreciative tears springing to her eyes at such thoughtfulness in a young stranger. "Do you know, I told Grandmother about you when I got home that night. She had been a little worried about my staying out so late, and she was so grateful that you had walked home with me. Of course she wanted to know what kind of a man you were, and I told her how you came out in the kitchen and helped me wash up the last dishes after the other helpers had gone. She enjoyed hearing what we talked about, and she said, 'If you ever meet that young fellow again, you tell him I thank him for being helpful to you and for bringing you home. And tell him I like his name, David!'"

"Say! I appreciate that," said the young man. "You described her so pleasantly I was quite disappointed when I heard she was gone. I had hoped I might be able to find you and perhaps have the pleasure of meeting her. You know, my own grandmother died while I was overseas the first time, and she was the last of my family, so I have missed her greatly this homecoming."

"Oh, I'm sorry you couldn't have met my grandmother, then. She would have loved it, I know. She was so sharp and sort of young for her years. She could enter right into con-versation with anyone and seem to understand them. Would you—care to—see her now? She looks so sweet, lying there, just as if she is glad to be seeing heaven."

"Yes, I'd like to see her," he said gently. "That is, if you don't feel I would be intruding."

"Intruding? Why, of course not! I'd love to have you see her. We'll take your flowers up and give them to her. Come!"

She brushed bright tears away and led him in the front door and up the stairs. Right past the curious Corliss, who had quickly and arrogantly arranged herself where they would have to brush by her and could not, she was sure, fail to see her in her recently repaired makeup.

But David Kenyon did not cast an eye in her direction, although he passed so near he almost had to *push* by her, following Dale up the stairs. Dale had not even noticed that she was there until she had started up the stairs, and then she could only pray in her heart that her young cousin would not be moved to scream or otherwise mar the quiet atmosphere of the home from which the moving spirit had fled.

Corliss stared up after them until they vanished toward the room where the grandmother lay, and then she flounced out onto the porch and met her brother, who had just come whistling up the walk from the street.

"Hi, Cor; didn't I see a navy man coming in here? What's become of him, and how come you're not flirting with him with those big, wistful eyes of yours?"

"Oh, get out! You're a pest if there ever was one! That navy man is a flat tire. He's gone upstairs with Dale, acts as if Gram was *his* relative. It makes me tired, all this carrying on about a dead person. When you're dead you're dead, and that's the end of it, isn't it? Then why all the shilly-shally? Where've you been? Isn't there a movie theater around here where we could go see a picture or something? I'm simply fed up with all this funeral business. And where is that hotel Dale talked about? I think it's time we found it and moved on. Go find Mother and tell her to come out here. I can't see going into that house again. It makes me sick to smell those flowers. I'd like to pull them all down and scatter them on the sidewalk. I wonder what Dale would do if I did, now that her precious Mrs. Marshall has been here and seen them. I believe I will."

"You better go easy, Cor; that's the undertaker coming now. He'll give you ballyhoo if you touch 'em, and he looks as if he could wallop you good if he got mad enough."

"Oh, get out, you bad boy! You know perfectly well he wouldn't dare!"

"Wouldn't he, though?" mimicked the loving brother. "Wait and see! Just you wait till I tell Mother what you said about those flowers. Now she's seen the dame that furnished 'em she wouldn't let you get by with an act like that!"

So the bickering went on out on the porch, with rising angry voices floating around the neighborhood.

"Isn't that perfectly awful!" said little Mrs. Bolton next door, peering out behind the curtains and then pulling her window down sharply with a bang to let the young people understand she was hearing them.

But upstairs Lieutenant David Kenyon and Dale Huntley were standing quietly before the sweet dead face among the flowers. The sun was slowly sinking behind the distant hill and made a soft rosy light on the quiet, lovely face of the old lady, lighting up her silver hair and giving a glory that was not of earth, as if God's sun would touch her brow with a hint of the heavenly glory that her clear soul was wearing now.

"Why, she's beautiful!" said the young officer in surprise. "I've seen a lot of death lately, but I never saw a face glorified like that. I didn't imagine death could be beautiful!"

"She is beautiful, isn't she?" said Dale softly. "She was like that in life, lovely of expression. Only there's something different about it now. Something not of earth. Something heavenly. Doesn't it seem that way to you?"

"It does," said the young man reverently. "It seems—" he hesitated, and then went on, "it almost seems as if she were standing right in the Presence of God and had just looked at Him for the first time. Only I suppose she must have known Him well before she went away."

"She did!" said Dale, brushing the quick tears away. "Only I suppose it is different when one gets there and really sees Him in His beauty. 'The King in His beauty.' She used to say that sometimes, smiling to herself, those last few days. 'The King in His beauty!' I wonder what it will be like when we first see Him."

"Well, she's seen Him now," said the young man with conviction.

"Yes, there's no doubt about that!" said Dale, with a smile like a rainbow through her tears. "Oh, I'm so glad you stopped by! It's good to have someone who understands. A great many loved her, but very few knew her as she really was. She was reserved and quiet, just a touch of fun and a twinkle in her eyes. She had a great sense of humor, too, but they didn't all understand how real Christ was to her. But you are a Christian then, aren't you? I didn't know."

"One could scarcely be anything else where I've been for the last two years," he said gravely, "unless one turned into a devil and grew hard. Coming near to death every day puts a different light on life and what it means. You find out that you need a Savior when you are surrounded by death. But somehow I never realized that death could look like this."

They talked a few minutes while Dale opened the box and took out the lovely flowers he had brought.

"Lilies of the valley!" she said. "How lovely! And Grandmother was so fond of them. But I thought it was too late for them."

"I guess it is late," said the officer, "but somehow they seemed the fitting thing for a grandmother gone home. I could not send flowers to my own grandmother's funeral because I did not know in time, so I thought I would like to bring them to this one."

"Oh, that is so kind of you!" said Dale, lifting a lovely smile to his eyes. "It seems the most beautiful thing that anyone could do. We'll put them in her hands. I can imagine just how she would have held them in her lifetime."

Dale lifted the white hands that were folded across the breast and put the mass of delicate little blossoms in them, just as the dear old lady might have picked them up and held them to her to smell their exquisite perfume, and then the two stood back a little, looking at the sweet picture it made.

"It seems," said the young man, "as if there must have been somebody else's flowers that should have priority over mine; as if I were stealing in where I have no right to be, so very close to her. I am only a stranger to her, you know."

"No," said Dale quickly, "you are not a stranger. You are someone whom God has sent, and it comforts me to see your flowers there, because you understand. And there are no flowers she loved as much as those lilies of the valley."

"Thank you," he said. "I'm glad I could help a little."

And then there were sounds from downstairs of more people coming, and the young man drew back, feeling that their quiet time together was over.

"When is the service?" he asked wistfully.

"Tomorrow afternoon at two o'clock," said Dale. "I wish you could be here. Grandmother arranged it all. She wanted the service to tell the story of salvation, if there should be somebody here who did not know the way."

"I shall be glad to be here," said the young man, "if I won't be intruding. I am afraid this may be my last leave before I go back overseas, but I have till midnight tomorrow night. I was hoping I might have another word or two with you before I leave, but I suppose you will be very busy."

"Not too busy to talk to you. I shall be so glad if you will come to the service, and I can give you time afterward. You will help to tide me over the first hard hours knowing that she is gone."

He looked down at her tenderly and smiled. "Thank you," he said quietly.

And then they could hear those other people coming up the stairs with Aunt Blanche's clarion voice leading them on self-consciously, as if it were entirely her funeral, glory and all, although she had not as yet come upstairs to see the grandmother.

David Kenyon put his strong, warm hand on Dale's with a quick clasp like a benediction.

"Thank you, and good-bye till tomorrow. I'll be praying for you all through the night, for I know it will be a hard one for you."

Then with a smile like a blessing he was gone, down the stairs alone, out the door, and into the street before Corliss realized that he was coming. He vanished so quickly that she looked down the darkening street in vain to see a stalwart officer, whom she had fully intended to accompany on his way to get a little better acquainted with him.

"What happened with that navy guy, Cor?" asked her brother, looking up from the funnies over which he had been straining his eyes in the fading light.

"That's what I'm wondering," answered Corliss surlily. "I thought I was watching him every minute. I was going out to speak to him, but he just came down from the porch, swung out that gate, and disappeared before I could tell he was even there. He must wear seven-leagued boots. I never saw anybody go into nothing as quick in my life. It certainly wasn't very flattering to the family, when he must have seen us all sitting here on the porch."

"Mebbe he had to catch a train," said the boy. "Say, how long is this line gonna last? I'm about fed up with it. Why can't we go to the movies somewhere?"

"No," said his mother sharply. "We've got to wait till Dale comes down and arranges for us to go to the hotel. She'll have to send for a taxi, and I do wish she'd hurry up. All these fool neighbors coming in and staying so long! I can't see any sense in it."

"Well, why can't we go and find a taxi ourselves? Can't you phone for a taxi? Ask that servant out in the kitchen. She'll know where to get a taxi."

"No," said their mother. "It's better to stay right here till I can have it out with Dale. I've got to find out about that funeral, what time it is set and when I can have the man here to see the house. I'm afraid she's going to be hard to handle about this. She seems to think the house is hers, and it isn't, I'm quite sure. I'll have to find that lawyer our Mr. Hawkins told me about and look into things tomorrow."

"When are we going home, Mom?" asked the bored boy. "I'm fed up with his funeral business, and if you are going to hang around here any longer, I'm going home by myself."

"No!" said the mother firmly. "You are not going home alone. You are not going until the rest of us go. I may need you here to carry these things through. You aren't of age of course, but there is nothing like having the family visible. We may be able to make some money out of this. You'll be glad of that, I know. And if there *is* any money, we don't intend to be cheated out of it. I'm quite certain that your father told me he had furnished the money to buy this house for his mother, and if that's true, the house is mine."

"But I heard Dale say it was hers."

"It doesn't matter what she said. She's probably made that story up herself, or else Grandmother has told her some fairy tales. Of course even Grandmother may not have known where she got the house. She may have thought it was from both brothers, but I've always heard that Dale's father was sort of a ne'er-do-well. I really never knew him, you know. He went overseas before we were married and just before your father went, and Dale's father never came back. He was killed, you know."

Just then there was the sound of footsteps coming down the stairs, several people, and Dale's voice could be heard gently. Aunt Blanche stopped talking and sat up abruptly.

"*Now*, we'll see," she murmured in a low voice to her children, and promptly there was an arrogant question in the very atmosphere, so that it was almost visible to the neighbors who came slowly down the stairs and out to the porch.

The neighbors lingered several minutes on the porch, just

last tender words about the woman they loved who was gone from their midst. Aunt Blanche and her children, in spite of their avid curiosity, grew more impatient before the last kindly woman said good night and went out the little white gate.

Then Aunt Blanche, without waiting for them to get beyond earshot, rose to her feet and pinned Dale with a cold glance from her unfriendly eyes. "And now, if you have got through with all the riffraff of neighbors that seem to have so much more importance in your eyes than your own blood relations, just what are you going to do with us?"

Dale turned troubled eyes toward them. "Oh, I'm sorry," she said gently. "I suppose you are tired after your journey. Would you like to go up to your rooms now?"

"No!" screamed Corliss with one of those piercing shrieks with which she had lorded it over her family since she was born. "No! I will *not* sleep in this house, not with a dead person here! My mother knows I won't do that! Not *ever*!"

"Well, in that case, what do you want to do? Go to a hotel? I didn't know you hadn't already arranged to do that. Of course you knew I wasn't able to get away just then."

"I don't see why!" said her aunt sharply. "I should think guests in your house would be of the first consideration. But I don't suppose you've had the advantage of being brought up to know good manners from bad ones and ought to be excused on that score. But how would you suppose I could do anything about a hotel? I don't know any hotels around here."

"I'm sorry," said Dale again, "but I thought you would probably ask Hattie about them. She would know, and any hotel in this region would be all right, of course, provided you could get in. You know, this region is rather full of defense workers, and most hotels and boardinghouses are full to overflowing, just now in wartime."

"So you would expect me to go to a servant for information, would you? Well, that is another evidence of your crude manners. However, now you are here, what are you going to do with us?"

"Well, what would you like me to do? Your rooms are all in readiness upstairs, of course, and since you do not choose to occupy them, I wouldn't know just what to do. Would you like me to order a taxi to take you around to the different hotels, to see if you can find a more desirable place for the night?"

"No, certainly not," said the irate aunt. "After I've come a long journey, I'm not going around hunting a place to stay. I'm too tired for that. I think it's up to you to find me a place."

"I'm afraid I don't think so," said Dale firmly but pleasantly. "However, I'll be glad to call up and inquire whether there is room anywhere. I can call the Oxford Hotel. It's rather expensive, but it would be very nice, if they still have room. And being expensive they might be more likely to have a room left. Or would you rather I try the cheaper places first?"

"I should think that would be entirely up to you, whatever you want to pay. We are your guests, you know."

Dale stared at her aunt in slow comprehension. "Oh, I see," she said slowly. "Well, I don't see that it's my affair at all. If you are my guests, you will occupy the rooms I have arranged for you. But since they do not suit you, I think the choice would be all your own. I couldn't afford to pay hotel bills, you know."

"Then you could have sent for the undertaker and had Grandma taken away. It isn't too late to do that now."

"No," said Dale, "I can't do that. But if you won't stay here,

I can call up and find out if there are any accommodations left anywhere. Or, if you and Powelton are satisfied to stay here, I can ask one of the neighbors to take in Corliss. The old lady who just went away asked if she could do anything for me. She has a little hall bedroom that is plain but immaculate, where I think Corliss could be very comfortable. I could call and ask her. Would you like that, Corliss?"

"Me? Go *alone* to some little old *stranger's* house? Not on yer life!" said Corliss hatefully.

Dale gave her a steady look and then turned into the house and went to the telephone, followed by the three guests.

"What are you doing to do?" asked Corliss impertinently. "You needn't think you can force me into anything like this. I'll *scream*! I'll make a scene! You haven't really heard me scream yet!"

Dale did not answer. Instead she called the number of the Oxford Hotel and asked for the manager, while the three invaders stood in a semicircle around her belligerently. Dale, as she caught a glimpse of their three unpleasant faces, could not help thinking what a contrast they were to the sweet, placid face lying upstairs with the glory of heaven upon it.

A few clear-cut questions she asked, showing that she was well versed in making business arrangements. "You have a room? Only *one* room? What floor is that on? The second floor? What price? Ten dollars a day? Is there a double bed? Twin beds, you say? And where would the young man sleep? The fifth floor, you say? A small hall bedroom? Five dollars a day. Oh, you say there is another larger room on the fifth next to the small one? The price is seven-fifty a day? Thank you. The lady will probably be around there to look at them. Yes, it's a lady and her daughter and son." Dale turned. "You heard what he said, didn't you? Would that be satisfactory, or do you wish me to ask at other places?"

"Yes," said Aunt Blanche. "It's best to find out what is available. Yes, call up three or four more hotels."

Dale smiled. "I'm afraid I don't know that many hotels anywhere near here. There is the Longworth and the Kenmore. No others this side of the city. Unless of course you want to go all the way in town, and that would cost you a good deal in taxi fares."

Dale turned back to the telephone and called up the Longworth but was told curtly that they had no available room at any price. Then she tried the Kenmore and found one large double room, where a cot could be put in for the young brother.

Dale gave the result briefly and then said, "Now, please excuse me a minute while I talk with Hattie. There are some plans for tomorrow she will be waiting to know, and you can talk this over and see what you want to do. When I come back I'll call a taxi for you."

Then Dale vanished into the kitchen.

"The very idea!" said the indignant aunt. "Well, I guess she'll find she'll have to pay for this. I'll have all bills sent to her."

Dale returned and ordered the taxi. She was relieved to get her unaccommodating guests off finally and be alone in the quiet of her sorrow.

"They ain't no kind of relatives for a dear lady like our Grandma to have," grumbled Hattie as she locked the back door and turned out the kitchen light. "I'm right glad they're outta the house, so I am, and I wish they didn't have to come back. They don't care nothing about *her*—just what they can get out of it!"

"Well there, Hattie, don't let's think such thoughts about them. That wouldn't please Grandmother, and I'm quite sure it won't make it any easier to get along with them while they are here."

"Yeah. I know that. But human nature can't stand *everything*, you know."

"No, but we haven't had to stand everything, Hattie. And besides, Grandmother's Lord can help us to stand even everything."

"Oh, you is just a saint, Miss Dale, an' no mistakin'," sighed the old woman. "I couldn't never be as good as you, no matter how hard I tried."

"Well, just tell the Lord about it, Hattie, and then forget it. Do you know, I don't believe they know the Lord, and that's what's the matter with them. But if we act unpleasantly to them, they won't have much opinion of the way we serve the Lord, either. We've got to think of that, you know, Hattie. Grandmother always said our business on earth was to witness for the Lord."

"I know, Miss Dale. Yes, I know well enough, but I ain't so much on the doin'. Say, Miss Dale, do you reckon they will come to breakfast?"

"I don't know, Hattie. I told them breakfast would be at eight and we were having lunch at half past twelve to get everything cleared away in time for the service, but Aunt Blanche didn't answer, so we'll just have a simple breakfast and lunch, and if they come we can always cook another egg. Dry cereal, coffee, toast, jam, and orange juice. Then that nice soup you made for lunch, and hot muffins with applesauce. If that doesn't suit them, they can go back to their hotel. But I don't much believe they will come till lunch, or perhaps only in time for the service. However, don't worry about it. Just plan simply and have enough so if they do come we don't need to be embarrassed. Now, good night, Hattie, and thank you for the way you've carried on today and made things easier for me."

"Oh, you blessed little lady, I ain't done nothin'. I just wish I coulda made things easier. Good night."

And then the two went quietly to their beds to rest for the day that was ahead and to ask keeping all through the night and the days that were to follow.

Chapter 3

The next day dawned brightly, a fitting morning for an old saint to leave this earth on her way to her heavenly home. Dale rose quite rested and ready to face the trials that would undoubtedly come to her that day.

She had a passing wish that she could go in there and stand by her sweet grandmother and tell her all that had passed, for somehow she felt her beloved presence was still here. Well, she knew that if she were here she would only laugh at some of the things that happened and press her lips and shake her silver head at the whole attitude of those unwelcome relatives, and she would finally say, "Didn't I tell you, Dale dear?"

Then she knelt by her bed and thanked the Lord that her grandmother was away out of it all, not here to hear the unpleasant words, nor guess at the insinuations that Dale was having to bear. *I thank You, dear Lord,* she prayed, *that You have taken her home, out of all the unpleasantness of earth. And please help me to keep calm and sweet and bear everything gently as You would have me do.*

She went down the stairs slowly, singing softly to herself the words of a little chorus that the soldier's words had brought to her mind, a song she had often sung in young people's gatherings.

> *"All through the night, all through the night*
>   *My Savior has been watching over me.*
> *He saves me so sweetly, so fully and completely,*
>   *And washes in His own atoning blood;*
> *My sins are all forgiven, I'm on my way to heaven,*
>   *I'm walking in the smile of God."*

Hattie looked up from her work at the stove and smiled. "You-all feelin' better, Miss Dale?" she asked in her most motherly tone. "You look real rested. Now sit down and eat your breakfast. You ain't got no call to wait to see if them relatives come. They'll surely understand that people will be comin' and goin' and you couldn't wait around to be stylish."

Dale glanced at the clock. "Yes," she said thoughtfully. "I believe you're right. They'll probably like it better that way anyway. And then, you know, they may not come."

"I surely hopes they don't!" breathed Hattie, almost like a prayer, as she slammed out into the kitchen to bring in the coffee and toast, and Dale felt her soul echoing an *Amen* to that prayer.

But they came. All three of them. With an eye to Hattie's delectable cooking they remembered. It was a quarter to nine before they got there, and the table was all cleared off, except for the cloth. But when Hattie heard them say they hadn't eaten yet, she whisked the dishes on and remembered to keep a pleasant face as she had promised Dale she would do.

There was orange juice for them all, coffee, and toast in plenty.

"Is this all?" asked Powelton insolently. "We should've stayed at the hotel. If I had known—" But Hattie hurried out into the kitchen, thus moving the audience to further insolence.

Hattie returned presently with a platter of neatly fried eggs and set them down with finality. Powelton surveyed them unpleasantly and asked, "Haven't you got any bacon? I like bacon with my eggs."

But Hattie in a greatly controlled tone said quietly, "Not today, we ain't. We couldn't have the smell of bacon when there's folks coming and going."

"Nonsense!" said the boy in his imperious voice. "Go cook me some bacon."

Hattie looked at him calmly an instant, with close-shut lips, and then marched back to the kitchen, shutting the door definitely. She did not return, and Powelton finally finished the eggs and went out to the front porch to smoke endless cigarettes, growing more and more peeved at the idea of the funeral that was imminent and from which his mother had absolutely refused to let him absent himself.

"You know you have got to make as good an appearance as possible," his mother had said. "The will hasn't been read yet, and it may mean something to you if the lawyers are in your favor."

So the spoiled boy sulked on the front porch and smoked and watched the undertakers bring piles of folding chairs into the house. And when he went into the house to get a drink of water, he found them taking the leaves out of the dining room table, closing it up, and shoving it to the far corner of the room.

"Hey!" he said arrogantly, standing in the doorway. "You can't do that! We've gotta have lunch here before the funeral!"

The undertakers glanced at him curiously and looked to their own boss, who answered Powelton curtly. "Those were the orders, young man," he said and paid no further attention to him.

So the guests discovered—when Hattie called Aunt Blanche to the hurried meal—that lunch was to be served in the kitchen. A couple of small, neat tables covered with snowy napkins were set in the far end of the kitchen, with steaming bowls of soup for the three, cups of coffee, a pitcher of milk, plenty of bread and butter, and applesauce with a plate of sugary doughnuts. But Dale was nowhere to be seen.

"She's in the livin' room, fixin' the flowers," explained Hattie when questioned. "She said she couldn't come now."

Aunt Blanche stiffened and sat down in the neat chair after inspecting it to see if it was really clean.

"Well, if I'd known I was to be treated so informally," she signed, "I certainly shouldn't have come."

Hattie pursed her lips grimly together and refrained with effort from saying, "I wisht ye hadn't uv."

But they ate a good lunch, and not a crumb of the big plate of doughnuts remained, for Powelton and Corliss made a business of finishing them, meantime going outside to observe developments.

"Well," said Aunt Blanche arrogantly, as she rose from the kitchen chair, "that's the first time I was ever served a meal in the kitchen in any place where I was visiting."

But Hattie again made no reply, and very irately and a trifle uncertainly the guest withdrew.

They found when they entered the hall that the casket had been arranged in the living room opposite the door, and the sweet silver-crowned face was visible among the flowers.

Corliss gasped and, ducking her face down in her mother's neck, got ready one of her terrific screams. But her mother, well knowing the signs, put a quick hand over her mouth and uttered a grave order: "Shut right up! Do you hear? There are ladies coming in the front door. And there comes a sailor!"

It was that word *sailor* that stopped the scream in its first gasp. Corliss lifted her frightened, angry eyes and caught a glimpse of a uniform coming in the front door.

Wide-eyed, Corliss ducked behind her mother, slunk into the corner out of sight of the doorway, and shut her eyes. If she had to endure this torture, at least she would make it as bearable as possible. She wouldn't *see* any more than she *had* to see of the horror of death.

The people were stealing in quietly now, going into the living room for a solemn look at the face of the old friend who was lying there and then, with downcast eyes, sitting down in an unobtrusive seat. A few of them stepped across to the open dining room. It seemed to be quite a sizable gathering, mostly old ladies, a few uninteresting-looking men, thought Corliss, as she peeked out between the fringes of her lashes and observed Grandmother's friends contemptuously. The seats were almost full and the minister was arriving, according to a somber whisper of the woman who sat just in front. And then suddenly there came more people, hurrying in as if they knew they were late, filling up all the chairs in sight. Behind them came a good-looking young man in a gray business suit, who walked straight out of sight over to where the minister had gone, by the foot of the casket. Corliss wondered who he was and stretched her neck to try and see him, wishing she had taken a better seat while there was still room. But there wasn't a vacant chair in sight, and even if there were she couldn't get by, the chairs were crowded so closely.

Then, just at the last minute like that, came the officer, the same one who had been there the night before with the flowers that they had put in Grandmother's hands, they said. She hadn't seen them. She wouldn't go and look. Silly lilies of the valley, what you gave to a baby!

But the officer walked quietly in and one of the undertakers placed him in a chair in the doorway, where he could see into the living room and, best of all, where Corliss could watch him. She decided that this funeral wasn't going to be so stuffy after all and straightened up in her chair, opening her eyes as effectively as she knew how.

Then gentle notes on the piano startled her into attention, and a wonderful voice began to sing. It seemed to Dale as she sat quietly by the casket as if an angelic voice were announcing the arrival of a soul in heaven, and a sweet smile hovered over the lips of the girl who was being so terribly bereaved.

"Isn't that Grandma's song?" whispered an eager neighbor to Hattie who was standing up just behind Corliss.

"Yes ma'am," Hattie whispered audibly. "Mr. Golden always sang it for her when he came to see her. She just loved to hear him sing."

"Open the gates of the temple,
Strew palms on the victor's way,
Open your hearts ye people,"

sang the golden voice, thrilling triumphantly through the rooms and causing even Corliss to listen. That man really had a voice if he only would sing something decent. But this song was quite an old chestnut. Why didn't they pick out something real? Why, there wasn't a word about heaven even in that song. Or was there?

Then suddenly the golden voice brought out the tender triumphant affirmation:

"I know. I know. I KNOW that my Redeemer liveth!"

Oh, so that was it, was it? Religious stuff! Of course that would be it. Grandmother was that way. Corliss turned back to lean against the wall and close her eyes again.

But the golden voice went on, bringing out the words with such conviction in the tone that Corliss had to listen, had to know that there was really something in this song that others beside Grandmother believed in. A hint crept into her heart that it might somehow be true, at least to a certain extent. It was conceivable that she herself *might have* to pay some attention to such things *some* time. But not now. She was young. When she got to be as old as Grandmother it might be all right, if people still believed in such things as a Redeemer. She wasn't at all sure *she* did. Yet the voice of that good-looking young man sounded as if *he* did. That golden voice like a piercing blade of a golden sword that was cutting deep into her soul and frightening her, in spite of all her opposition, in spite of all her unacknowledged sin!

Suddenly she turned toward the officer sitting across from her, sitting where he could see into the room with the golden voice and the casket. Was he taking it as some sort of mockery, just mere words? Or even a joke? She hoped he was.

But no, the man was looking straight toward the voice, sympathy and conviction in his face. It really was quite attractive in a serviceman, a look like that. She hadn't thought it would fit with a uniform, but it did. And he didn't look like a sissy, either. He looked as if he could fight hard if he tried, throw bombs, and shoot, maybe dance and have good times. Corliss sat back and studied him through half-closed lashes. She decided he looked pretty nice, and she would stick around and see if she couldn't date him for the evening. It oughtn't to be hard to do. If she only could get out of riding to that old cemetery!

The service was going on all this time, but without benefit of Corliss's attention. She was studying the young officer. Maybe she could work it around for him to ride in the same car to the cemetery, if he went. If he didn't, she would stay at home herself and see if she couldn't follow him down the street and pretend to sprain her ankle or something. She was determined to get to know him. Maybe make him take her to a movie or a dance tonight.

Wonderful scripture was being read that Grandmother Huntley had herself selected, but it made no impression upon Corliss. She was studying the profile of the splendid-looking officer. But the man was giving interested attention to the service and was utterly unaware of the girl who was watching him.

Corliss was disappointed that he didn't ride in the same car with them. Instead, he was put with Dale and the minister and the young man singer. That was mean of Dale to manage it that way. And there was some old woman in the car with her mother and brother and herself. If there hadn't been so many people around, she might have tried the screaming act, but on account of the good-looking singer and the navy man, she didn't consider it. Perhaps there would be some way to get to talk to him after this ride was over. So she gloomed through the remaining ceremonies and was glad indeed when the car drew up at the house again and she saw that the navy man was getting out and going into the house with Dale. He probably wouldn't stay long, and she would plan to talk to him somehow. So she settled herself on the porch to wait for his departure. He seemed to be over by the desk in the living room writing something for Dale. What in the world could he want of Dale? Some business probably connected with the funeral. He certainly couldn't be interested in her. She was awfully plain and not stylish at all according to Corliss's tastes.

But Corliss grew impatient before the meeting at the desk ended. Dale was writing something, too. Some address probably, or maybe signing a paper. Only they seemed so awfully interested in what they were saying. A sharp, jealous look went over her young face. It had always been this way with Dale, thought the young cousin. She seemed to think because she was older she could manage everything.

But at last the two young people rose from the desk and came to the door. Corliss rose precipitately and scuttled to the other side of the door, where she could easily slip down the steps after the man when he should go; and so she missed the look in his eyes when he took Dale's hand briefly and said good-bye.

Then he was gone, with a quick, bright smile back at Dale standing in the doorway. But Corliss missed getting the full effect of even that, for she was hurrying down the walk nonchalantly ahead of him, sliding behind two old ladies, who were going into the house next door, and nearly knocking one of them over in her haste. Her main object was to catch that "navy guy" before he should vanish again as he had last night, for he was walking now with long, quick strides and looking at his watch as he went, as if he was afraid he was going to be late somewhere. She mustn't appear to be walking too fast, either. She mustn't dare to run, or her mother would say something. She had already endured one long, sharp lecture from her mother on the subject of decorum at the time of a funeral. But as soon as the two old ladies went into their own gate, she pressed by them and hurried on, dismayed to find how far ahead the man had already gone. Then, as he turned a corner, she did begin to run. She wasn't going to let him escape this time. A moment later she caught up by his side, quite out of breath, and accosted him.

"Oh, I say, what's your rush?" she panted. "I've nearly run my legs off to catch you."

"Oh, I'm sorry!" he said, coming about-face and looking at her, startled. "I didn't leave something, did I? Was there some message from Miss Huntley? Should I go back?"

"Oh no, no such luck," laughed Corliss. "I just wanted to talk to you. I like servicemen, and I especially like you. I wanted to ask you if you wouldn't make a date with me for this evening. We could go to the movies first, and then you could take me dancing. I'm just sick to death of all this funeral business and I want to have a little fun. I thought you would show me a good time."

The young man gave her a puzzled look. "That would be impossible," he said. "I have to catch a train back to the barracks."

"Well, miss your old train, then, and stay with me. There are always more trains. Besides, I want you! I'm fed up with all the solemnity, and I've got to get out and see some life. Miss your old train. Come on!" There was wheedling in the blue eyes lifted to his, but there was only firmness, almost severity, in the eyes of the young officer.

"Haven't you heard that there is a war?" he said. "When one is in the service one does not miss trains. Here comes my bus. Good night!" And he was gone.

Corliss—baffled, angry—stood and watched the bus disappear around the next corner and then went furiously back to the house to see what other deviltry she could think up.

Meantime Dale had dropped into a chair near her aunt, getting ready to take over the burden of this uncongenial set of guests, hoping against hope that they would see their way clear to going home on the midnight train yet not daring to believe that they would.

But her aunt broke the momentary silence: "Who is this naval officer who seems to be always around?" she asked, withdrawing her gaze from the place where her daughter had disappeared in pursuit of the uniform.

Dale came to attention at once, bringing back her mind from a consideration of what she ought to do or say next.

"Officer? Oh yes? Why, he's just a friend."

"Oh! Only a friend. He must be a very special friend to go

out of his way to come to a mere funeral."

Dale hesitated. How should she explain?

"It was kind of him, wasn't it?" she said pleasantly. "You see, he was interested in Grandmother. A great many people were interested in Grandmother, you know."

"So it seems," said Aunt Blanche sarcastically, as if the fact annoyed her. "You certainly had a mob here today. One wonders what satisfaction people like that get out of a funeral. It must be just morbid curiosity."

"Curiosity?" said Dale with a perplexed frown. "What could they possibly be curious about? They were most of them very dear old friends who have been here constantly during the years and who loved Grandmother very much."

"Oh I see!" said the aunt dryly. "Well, I suppose the poor things have very little else to do. But I can't understand a young naval officer coming. He must have seen plenty of death in a more dramatic form, if he *really has* been overseas."

Dale's eyes suddenly flashed, but she turned her face away so her aunt would not see, and taking a deep breath, she suddenly rose to her feet, changing the subject sharply: "Now, what are your plans, Aunt Blanche? Are you returning home tonight, or do you wish to go back to the hotel? In which case, would you like me to send for a taxi?"

The aunt looked at Dale with an annoyed manner. "I don't see any rush about it," she said, offended. "I thought perhaps we'd stay here now and take those rooms you prepared for us. Corliss, of course, thinks she would like to have Grandmother's room. She is sure that is the best room in the house, and the view is much pleasanter. I suggest you send Hattie up to clean it thoroughly right away and open all the windows wide."

Dale paused and looked at her aunt steadily. "No!" she said firmly. "Nobody is going to occupy Grandmother's room at present, and certainly not Corliss, after the way she acted. I wouldn't like Grandmother to be dishonored that way."

"*Dishonored?* What do you mean? Can't you understand a young girl being afraid of death? Don't let's have any more argument about it. Just call Hattie and tell her to thoroughly clean Grandmother's room and put it in order for use. If you don't, I *will*. I'm not going to live through another night like last night, and Corliss is all upset. Will you tell Hattie, or shall I?"

Dale drew another long breath and looked at her aunt quickly. "Hattie isn't here," she said.

"Isn't here? Where is she? She was at the funeral, wasn't she? I saw her myself. I thought it was awfully strange, too, letting a servant come in with the family. Where has she gone now?"

"She has gone to see her sick sister. I told her to stay as long as she thought it was necessary, that I would get along all right. She has been wonderfully good staying here through it all, though her sister really needed her. But she wouldn't leave me alone till the funeral was over."

"Oh! She wouldn't, wouldn't she? And you actually *let* her go while *we* were still here?"

"Why, I wasn't sure whether you were here or not. You have been staying at the hotel, and I never heard you say whether you were going back west right away or not. But anyhow, that made no difference; Hattie *had* to go. I think she did a good deal to stay till the stress was over."

"*Stress?* Well, I'm sure I don't know what you mean. We're still here, and since the objection to staying here is now removed, I don't see why you should jump to the conclusion that we were going to the hotel. Of course having come so far to look into business matters, I shall not be going back until I am finished. And now, what are we going to do about that room? It *must* be cleaned *thoroughly* or we never can get Corliss to enter it, and I cannot blame her. Is there someone else you can get to do this cleaning, at once?"

"I am sorry to disappoint you, Aunt Blanche, but that room is not an option. It has already been thoroughly cleaned, of course, but it is *not* to be used at present, by Corliss or anyone else. I have other plans, which I am not willing to change. And please, Aunt Blanche, I am very tired tonight. It has been an exceedingly hard day. Suppose we don't talk any more about such things. I am not going to get another cleaning woman, and there is no house-cleaning to go on here, either tonight or tomorrow."

"But Dale, you are unreasonable. I told you that the man who is thinking of buying this house is coming to see it. I reached him last night on the telephone and told him to come tomorrow morning at eleven instead of today, so whatever has to be done toward cleaning *must* be done tonight."

Dale turned suddenly and faced her aunt. "Listen, Aunt Blanche," she said firmly. "Nobody is going to look at this house tomorrow or any other day with an idea of buying it. The house is definitely *not for sale*! I thought I made you understand that yesterday."

"We'll see about that!" said the aunt hatefully. "You are not beginning very well for the favors I was planning to give you. I had decided to ask you to come and live with us. I know you have no money to live on, and you are scarcely prepared to earn your living in any way, so I thought it was really my duty to look out for my dead husband's only niece. But you certainly do not give the impression of being very good-natured or adaptable, and we shall have to have a thorough understanding before I can go on and make the offer I had intended. But this first thing must be understood: *I* am taking over in this matter about the house. It will eventually be mine, and I do not intend to lose the opportunity of a sale to a man who is willing to pay a good price."

Dale faced her aunt with steady calmness. "You will do nothing about this house, Aunt Blanche, because you have no right to do anything. Tomorrow morning my lawyer, Mr. Randall Granniss, will be here at ten o'clock, with all the papers to show you how impossible your claims are. I called him last night and arranged this, and he said he would bring all the data relating to the house."

"Oh *really*! You presume to have a lawyer? Well, that's ridiculous! A girl of your age having a lawyer."

"He is the lawyer whom my father left in charge of my affairs," said Dale quietly.

"Yes? Well, you'll find you'll have to prove all this."

"Yes, certainly, Mr. Granniss will bring the proof."

"Well, if you are going to such lengths, I shall certainly have to call up the lawyer to whom I was recommended. Just excuse me, and I'll call him."

"Certainly," said Dale calmly and then sat down and covered her tired eyes with her hands. How right Grandmother had been when she had warned her about this aunt and had prepared for all such contingencies as were happening one by one.

Out in the hall at the telephone she could hear her aunt's

sharp voice demanding to speak with a certain Mr. Greenway Buffington. Then the voice lowered into a confidential scream. But Dale resolutely held her weary eyes shut and, in her heart, began to pray: *Oh God, be with me. Protect me through all this unpleasantness. Help me not to be a false witness. Help me to show these people, who in a sense belong to me, that I have a Savior who is able to keep me. Guard my tongue that it may speak the truth in quietness and peace, and not let anger come into the conversation. Keep me calm and trusting.*

In a little while, Aunt Blanche came back into the living room and announced, "My lawyer will be here tomorrow afternoon. That will make it possible for me to expose to him all the machinations of the man you say is your lawyer."

"Very well," answered Dale quietly, without opening her eyes, and her aunt flounced down into a rocking chair and fairly snorted in anger. After a few minutes, Dale heard her get up and go upstairs. She heard her walk the length of the hall to Grandmother's room and try the door but failed to get in, though she rattled and shook it. Dale sat still. She had locked that door and had the key in her pocket. Moreover, she had gone through the adjoining bathroom and *bolted* the door from inside and then locked the bathroom, so it was impossible for her aunt to enter the room without actually breaking down the door. She sat still for a few minutes and then went up to her own room and lay down on the bed. She was very tired, and it just did not seem she could stand any more argument.

She was awakened a few minutes later by a loud, determined knocking on her door.

"Yes?" she said, sitting up sharply and trying to get her senses back from the deep sleep into which she had fallen.

ALL THROUGH THE NIGHT

It was her aunt's voice that answered her: "Aren't we going to have an evening meal? Or hadn't you thought of that?"

Dale got to her feet and staggered to the door. "I'm sorry," she said, putting her hand to her eyes and trying to make her voice pleasant, "I should have told you. I didn't realize I would fall asleep so soon. I really was very tired, you know."

Her aunt gave her an unsympathetic glance. "We *all* are!" she said coldly. "And of course we *are* guests, so we couldn't do anything about it."

"Well, if you don't mind foraging for yourselves this once," Dale said pleasantly, putting her hand up to her forehead, "there are sandwiches and salad in the refrigerator, also a pitcher of iced coffee and plenty of milk. You'll find an apple pie in the pantry, or if you prefer custard, you'll find some in the refrigerator, and there's a sponge cake in the cake box. I think if you don't mind I'll just sleep this off. I'm rather dizzy."

"Oh!" said the aunt ungraciously. "Well, I didn't expect to have to do the housework when I came, but if you're *really* sick, of course we'll do the best we can."

With a deep sigh, as if she were being ill treated, Aunt Blanche summoned her children, and they went out to the kitchen and certainly made a mess of Hattie's neat kitchen and pantry and refrigerator. But for once, Corliss had a chance to sample everything in sight.

347

Chapter 4

Dale went back to sleep, being thoroughly worn out by the strain of the last two days and the sudden realization that her beloved grandmother was gone from her and she was now on her own. But she was too near the breaking point to do any more connected thinking now, and hearing only dimly the sounds of the slamming refrigerator door and the breaking of a dish or two, she sank quickly into a deep sleep.

It was several hours later that she awoke suddenly to a realization that a tremendous storm was in progress—lightning, thunder, wind, and rain—and the wind was blowing rain fiercely from the open window into her face. The lightning made her room bright as day.

Dale brushed her wet hair away from her face and hurried wildly across the room to shut her window. Then, turning, the lightning shivered blankly into darkness for an instant and she glimpsed a line of brightness under her door and realized that there must be lights on and perhaps windows open in the rest of the house.

She unlocked her door, flung it open, and stood listening an instant before another thunder crash came. There was no sound except the thunder, but there was a tremendous draft pouring up the stairs. She hurried down the stairs, noting that the lights were on everywhere and that the front door and all the windows were open just as she had left them when she went upstairs. "Aunt Blanche!" she called as she hurried down. "Corliss! Where are you all?"

But there came no answer.

Then the clock struck solemnly. "One! Two! *Three!*"

Dale's startled eyes went wonderingly to the clock. Was it right? Could it be three o'clock in the morning? Could she possibly have slept all this time? And where were her guests? Asleep upstairs?

She cast a quick glance back and upward, but all the bedroom doors except Grandmother's were standing wide open. Surely they wouldn't have gone to bed and left their doors open that way, left all the lights burning and the doors and windows open.

Another gust of wind, another crashing clap of thunder, and she hurried down and shut the front door, then went from one window to another closing them quickly. In the dining room and kitchen she found a hopeless clutter of dirty dishes and half-eaten food. The big serving plate that had been piled high with delicious sandwiches was empty. Absolutely. Not a crumb left! The pie was demolished and half the bowl of custard gone. The iced coffee was gone also, and some of the milk, while half-filled milk bottles were standing around, indicating that the cream had been drunk first and the rest left out of the refrigerator. In fact, further investigation showed that the refrigerator doors were both standing wide open.

Vexed, Dale pushed them shut, gave a hopeless look around the devastated rooms, then walked on to the living room and looked around. That room was as bad as the others, for everything that could be lifted by the wind had been tossed about. Several comics and joke books were on the floor, torn and crumpled, blown here and there. A game of Chinese checkers was blown from the little end table where it had been used, the pieces all over the floor. Three or four books were lying open, facedown on the floor, and two more had pages torn and crumpled by the wind. Her guests had evidently eaten everything within sight, tried all the forms of amusement they could discover, and then gone their ways.

Dale looked around in vain for a note they might have left, but found none. If there had been one, it must have blown away. Well, evidently they had gone to the hotel for the night. A glance at the kitchen clock confirmed the hour again. And there was nothing she could do about it. It was too late to call up the hotel and wake everybody there, and what end would it serve anyway?

Dale sat down and looked around, considering what she ought to do. In her indignation she would have liked to lock the house up and refuse admittance when they came back for breakfast, but she knew that would not be Grandmother's way; and, too, it would not be God's way. God, who had cared for her in all that storm and wind, lying asleep and unprotected in an open house that was lit from top to bottom with wide open doors and windows. Yes, God had been watching over her. Well, this was the challenge she had to meet, and she must go through with it.

God, help me to do right, and please protect me from having to meet with more than I can bear.

Then Dale got up and went to work.

She took off the pretty dress in which she had lain down in her weariness and put on a cotton housedress from the hook in the kitchen. Then she went to work in the living room first, quietly, swiftly pulling down the window shades to guard against curious, puzzled neighborly eyes, if any chanced to be awake. She gathered up all the papers and scattered things from the floor, swept the checkers into a drawer of the table, piled the books and stowed them in the bookcase, taking care to lock the bookcase and place the key in safety. She gathered the plates and cups that evidently held snacks from the evening meal and carried them to the kitchen. Then she came back and turned out the living room lights and the hall lights and closed the doors to the dining room and kitchen.

The enemy might not return very early the next morning, but it was just possible that Hattie might, in case she found her sister much better, and Dale did not want Hattie to know what had been going on. For Hattie needed no more fuel added to the fury of her indignation. Hattie was already irate, and she would find it difficult to restrain a bitter tongue if she once got started telling the relatives what she thought of them. So it was up to Dale to obliterate the traces of what had happened, and that meant doing thorough work in both kitchen and dining room.

The dishes were all marshaled into the kitchen first; then she went to work with broom, dishpan, and carpet sweeper. It was too late at night, or too early in the morning, to use the vacuum cleaner and startle the neighborhood. She must work quietly.

When the sweeping and dusting were done, she gathered the tablecloth for the laundry bag. It had been shining clean when Hattie set the table for the evening meal and departed. But now it was smeared with three different kinds of jam, which had been taken from the pantry shelves and sampled. There would have to be a clean cloth and napkins for breakfast, in case they had to serve a company-breakfast. And of course they would. There was no chance of the unwanted guests leaving for their home until they were entirely satisfied about a will or property they had hoped to get by coming to this funeral. Dale sighed and wished Grandmother hadn't thought it necessary to send for these unlovely folks. But of course it was right that they should know of her death.

Dale's weariness came back upon her when she was about half through washing the mountain of dishes that the intruders had managed to soil, but she plodded steadily on, working so quietly that even a curious neighbor who might have gotten up to look out her window would never know that dishes were being washed. She was thankful that the kitchen windows were guarded by shades that had a dark green back and therefore no light would shine through to the outside world. Thankful also for the storm that continued to thunder noisily on to cover any unavoidable noises she might make. She did not want those dear, friendly neighbors to know what had happened in Grandmother's home the night after she had left it. Dear Grandmother!

The dawn was beginning to creep into the sky when at last Dale wiped and put away the last of the dishes and washed and hung up her dish towels to dry. She was very weary, but it did her good to realize that even if her visitors should return now they would see no signs of the devastation they had wrought. It was all in order again, lovely quiet order. And if their consciences did not reproach them for what they had done, she would not be the one to do it. That was as Grandmother would have wanted it.

She cast a quick glance into the plundered refrigerator. There were enough eggs. They could be scrambled for breakfast. And there was enough dry bread to make toast. That with coffee should be enough to give them. She would make no apologies.

Wearily she turned out the lights and climbed the stairs to her own room again, undressing in the dark and getting gratefully into bed. She would sleep just as long as she pleased. If they came back before she was up, they could sit on the porch until she got up. There were plenty of porch chairs there. They might be damp from the storm, but she couldn't do anything about that now. She *must* get a little more sleep, for she felt certain that tomorrow was going to be a hard day. And of course she must be up and rested in time for her lawyer who was coming. She was so glad that she had called him up the night before and told him all about the situation. She knew he could be counted on to look out for everything. He had been her trusted guardian for years.

So she went to sleep again, and the day began slowly, widening into brightness after the storm.

Dale dressed rapidly. The day would be a hard one—it could not help but be—but she must not allow herself to give way to the weariness that threatened to sweep over her now and then. She had not had enough sleep. That was true. She had been through a great strain. Yes. But she was expected to go through this. God would take care of her. How He had helped in small, quiet ways all the way through these hard days. *She* must not fail Him.

She went downstairs and began to get breakfast ready. Not that her unwelcome guests deserved it, but she would not let any failure on her part be the cause of unpleasantness. Soon they would be gone—that is, she *hoped* they would—and she did not want to spend her time afterward regretting any sharp words she might speak. After all, they were related to her, and her cousins' father's *first* wife had been her own mother's beloved sister. She must not let the fact that Aunt Blanche was a second wife influence her. And she had a very pleasant memory of her uncle, their father, when she was a very little girl. Once he had brought her a peach, the very first peach she had ever had all her own. And once he had sent her a funny postcard. But that was so very long ago, and her thoughts faded into precious memories of her own father, whom she had dearly loved.

Well, these people were all she had left, and not at all precious at present. But she would have one more try at doing her best to like them and make them like her.

So she squeezed glasses of orange juice and prepared delicate slices of toast, piling it in front of the toaster so it would not dry up and still keep warm. She made the coffee with the greatest of care, put as many ice cubes in the glasses as they would hold, set the table with nicety. Laid out eggs for scrambling when the relatives should come, and then having drunk a glass of milk herself, she hurried upstairs to put herself in battle array for the day that was going to be so filled with perplexities.

She had scarcely had time to change into a clean white morning dress and to smooth her hair when the telephone rang. With a troubled frown, she hurried to answer it. Would that be Hattie? Or Aunt Blanche?

But it was neither. Instead, it was a man's voice—young, friendly, courteous.

"Good morning!" it said. "You are Miss Huntley, aren't you? I thought I recognized your voice. This is David Kenyon. I wanted to thank you again for letting me in on that wonderful service yesterday and to ask if you are all right after the hard strain you must have had." There was such genuine friendliness in the words that just hearing his voice comforted her. He was almost a stranger, of course, but somehow she felt a kinship with him. He seemed to have such an understanding of the things she had been brought up to believe.

"Oh, David Kenyon! How kind of you to call," she said in a truly welcoming voice. "This will make my day seem more friendly and pleasant. And I certainly think it was wonderful of you to go out of your way when you were on leave and come to a funeral of someone you did not know, when you might have been enjoying yourself somewhere."

"You forget," said David Kenyon, "that you were very kind and friendly to me the last time I came to town, and I was an utter stranger to you. But now I sort of feel as if we are friends; that is, if you don't mind."

"*Mind!*" said Dale happily. "Why, I'm delighted that you

feel that way. And of course I'm glad to have you for a friend. Only I'm just sorry that I had to be so busy while you were here and we had no chance to talk. But then I felt you understood."

"Of course I understood. And I was glad that you took me right into your household that way and let me be a part of things as if I had known you always. I liked that part the best. You know, I haven't anyone who really belongs to me on this earth anymore, that is, not around here anyway, and it was nice to get that home feeling. You see, I took a great liking to you that first night I met you, and I felt I'd like to know you better. You were somehow *different* from so many of the girls I met. And I'm partly calling up now to ask you whether—in case there *is* another opportunity for me to come up to your city—you would mind if I came again to see you. I'll be going back overseas pretty soon, I suppose, and I'd like to have another pleasant memory to take along with me. Do you mind if I come?"

"*Mind?*" said Dale again, almost breathlessly, her heart giving a little pleasant twirl and the color dancing up into her cheeks. "Why, I would just be *delighted* to see you. When can you come?"

"I don't know yet. It may not be possible at all, but if it is I'll call up and find out if it is convenient for you."

"I'll certainly *make* it convenient," said Dale joyously. "It will be something nice to look forward to. I've got a hard few days ahead of me just now—relative-guests, business to talk over and settle, some unpleasantness to face perhaps—and this will be a pleasant something to think about and look forward to in the intervals, something to be glad about."

The voice at the other end of the wire was warm and glad.

"That's nice," he said. "You've made me feel as if I would really be welcome. I shall look forward to it myself and only hope I may not be disappointed about being allowed to come. Now, I won't take any more of your time. If you have guests you are busy, I know. I'll hang up now, but I'll be ringing you up pretty soon perhaps. Good-bye."

Dale turned away from the telephone with a smile on her lips and a sudden joy in her heart. She wondered why a little thing like that should make her so exceedingly glad.

Then the doorbell pealed through the house, as if manipulated by a cross, impatient soul, and she hurried to the door. She hadn't had time before to open it. This would be her guests, of course.

She swung the door open and summoned the smile she had been readying herself all the morning to give.

But there was no answering "Good morning."

"Doesn't your royal princess of a maid ever sweep the front porch?" snapped Aunt Blanche. "Usually maids are very careful about front porches and sidewalks, and ours looks *scandal*ous."

"Yes?" said Dale, trying to keep her cheerful manner. "It does need attention. But I just haven't been able to get to it yet. I'm afraid I overslept."

"Well," said the aunt hatefully, "I should think Hattie was the one to do it. You better send her out right away. It looks terrible here for the lawyers—and the purchaser—when they come."

"Sorry," said Dale, summoning her strength, "I'll do the best I can. But I've been concentrating on getting some break-fast ready for you before the lawyers arrive. I'll get to the side-walk as soon as you sit down. The breakfast is all ready but the eggs. Will you come right in?"

"Why, of course! That's what we came over for. I'm half starved. You must remember that we had no dinner to speak of last night. But why should *you* have to go out and sweep the porch? That doesn't look at all good to the neighbors the day after a funeral. Send Hattie. Lazy thing! She ought to have done it without telling."

"Hattie is not here," said Dale quietly.

"Not back yet? Well, the idea! I should think she was taking advantage of you. You better let me get after her; I'll soon whip her into shape. But meantime, you'll certainly have to get someone else for the time being, and if she turns out to be better than Hattie, you better dismiss Hattie and keep the new one."

Dale took another deep breath and tried to steady her voice. "I'm sorry, Aunt Blanche. You just don't understand. Hattie is like a part of our family. I couldn't think of dismissing her. And of course *I'll* do anything in her place that has to be done until she gets back. She is having trouble herself and has always stood by me when I was in trouble. She'll be back as soon as she possibly can come. I'm sure of that."

"Yes? You're very sure of yourself! But remember, you are young. You haven't learned yet that servants are *never* dependable. They *pretend* to think a lot of you, but then when the stress comes, they take time off and go and visit with their friends. You take my advice and get somebody else."

Dale gave a half smile. "There wouldn't be anybody else to get," she said gently. "They've all gone into defense work. And anyway, your breakfast is getting cold. Won't you all come right in and eat?"

"Who said eat?" said Powelton noisily. "I'm starved, and

that's a fact! I hope you have beefsteak and hotcakes. I remember we used to have those when we came to see Grandma."

But Dale led the way quietly to the dining room and made no reply. She motioned to the table and went on toward the kitchen door.

"Sit down, and I'll bring the cereal and eggs," she said sweetly and vanished into the kitchen.

"I don't want eggs!" complained Corliss, shouting after her. "I just *hate* eggs. I prefer bacon or creamed beef."

But Dale went on to get the cereal and paid no further attention. Let her mother deal with Corliss. She had enough to do to keep other things going.

Presently she brought in the cereal and a large dish of golden scrambled eggs, piping hot and very tempting looking, and then she hurried out of the room and upstairs as Corliss continued to wail that she didn't like eggs. What was she going to do if this kept on for many days? Just ignore it and provide what she could and let it go at that? Well, what else could she do? And she must not carry this matter as a burden during the day, either. She would just do the best she could and then take what came of blame or faultfinding. They didn't need to stay if they didn't like it. And she wouldn't go and complain to her heavenly Father, either. After all, He had allowed these things to come into her life, and He must have some good reason for it.

The doorbell interrupted her thoughts, and she glanced out the window. Could that be Mr. Granniss already? He was ahead of the time he had said he would come. Ten minutes. That wasn't usual with him, for he was a busy man. He must have something to say to her before he was ready to read the will. She hurried downstairs, and there stood her lawyer-friend.

Chapter 5

"Am I too early, Dale?" he said apologetically. "There are a few questions I want to ask you. Have you a copy of the last interview we had with your grandmother?"

"Oh yes," said Dale and, turning, swiftly closed the dining room door where the relatives were all agog listening for all they were worth. Dale led the lawyer into the living room and closed the door opening into the hall, which maneuver definitely quickened the tempo of the breakfast that was being eaten to the last crumb.

Aunt Blanche wasn't long in appearing, and when she found the door to the living room closed, she promptly turned the knob and came in, gazed at the strange man sitting by the table leafing over a pile of papers, and then said sharply, "Oh, excuse me! Have I interrupted a conference?"

The lawyer looked up, and Dale rose and came forward. "It's all right. Come right in. We were just about through. Aunt Blanche, this is Mr. Granniss, my former guardian and now my lawyer. This is my aunt, Mrs. Huntley, Mr. Granniss."

The lawyer rose and bowed courteously, glancing at the lady with a keen appraising look, which caused Mrs. Huntley to draw her shoulders up and stick her chin out assertively. She was not accustomed to having anyone look at her with question in their eyes, as if she might not really be all that she asserted herself to be. So in turn, Aunt Blanche put more haughtiness into her own glance, a look that almost *dared* the lawyer to differ from her.

"Won't you sit down, Mrs. Huntley?" he said courteously and brought forward a chair for her.

The lady sat down as if she were doing him a favor and kept her belligerence in evidence. "Just how long have you been associated with my niece?" she asked arrogantly.

The lawyer did not smile. He answered in clear, clipped tones. "Well, practically ever since she was born," he said coolly. "Her father and I were close friends before he was married. Then after her mother died and her father found it necessary to go abroad on confidential business for the government, he asked me to take over for him."

"Really! I never heard that my brother-in-law was connected with government work. Are you quite *sure* of that?"

Mr. Granniss looked at her with lifted eyebrows. "I beg your pardon," he said. "It is a matter of record. If you want that verified, you might write to Washington. I'll give you the address." And he took out his fountain pen and wrote an address on a small pad he took from his pocket, and tearing off the page, he handed it to the lady. "Of course the matter was not generally known, as it was confidential business," he added, "but I supposed his own family would be likely to know the fact. However, I suppose you may not have been interested in the matter at the time, and Mr. Huntley was not one who blazoned widely matters of business."

Aunt Blanche was a bit taken aback by the calmness of the lawyer's statements. She had expected *him* to be awed by *her* cold manner. She was not by nature very well versed in matters of business and was not capable of doing much logical thinking for herself. But she had always depended upon this haughty manner and her sharp tongue to overawe people in any matter of business with which she had to deal. It had been her experience that if most men were treated in her peculiar style that they would give in on any point they considered "minor" rather than to continue to deal with her longer.

But Mr. Granniss was not one of the superficial kind of businessmen, and he was not overawed by her.

"And now, Mrs. Huntley," went on the lawyer, "are we ready to read the will? Are your children here? Should we call them?" He looked toward Dale.

"Yes, yes," said Aunt Blanche, rising quickly, certain that Powelton would never answer a summons unless she pressured him. She cast a quick, triumphant look toward Dale as she went out. Perhaps, after all, this lawyer was going to have sense enough to realize that she knew what she was talking about. The will? Yes. She had been exceedingly anxious to hear that will read. She hadn't been quite sure whether there really was a will, until now.

She came back into the room with a firm hand on an arm

of each of her offspring and ushered them to chairs near her own. "Now," she said, "we're ready. And kindly get at it as quickly as possible. I have callers coming, and my own lawyer will be here soon."

Mr. Granniss looked at her with surprise, but he did not hurry with the business. "I think there is one more to come, isn't there, Dale? Hattie Brown? Isn't that her name? Your grandmother's old servant?"

"Why, the *idea*! What on earth would a *servant* have to be here for?" snapped Aunt Blanche. "I insist that you don't wait any longer. I have important business that cannot be delayed."

"I am sorry, Mrs. Huntley," said the lawyer, "but I would prefer that the servant be called. Dale, will you call Hattie Brown?"

Dale rose anxiously, about to explain that Hattie had been called away by her sister's illness, but suddenly a shadow darkened the doorway.

"I's right here, Mr. Granniss," said Hattie as she slung off her hat and sat down in the chair by the door.

"But I don't understand!" said Aunt Blanche indignantly. "Why should a mere servant be present?"

But Mr. Granniss's calm voice rose above the indignant scream of the aunt. He went right on with the business in hand, ignoring the visiting aunt with a dignity that made Dale admire him even more than she had learned to admire and trust him during the years. An instant more, and the solemn phrases of the law broke upon their unaccustomed ears, until everybody, even the aunt, hushed down.

The reading of the will did not take long. The entire amount of the grandmother's estate was only a few thousand. Of that she had left a thousand apiece to each of her three grandchildren—Corliss, Powelton, and Dale. At that the aunt looked sharply, suspiciously, at Dale, as if Dale had had something to do with this. As if she did not believe that was all Dale had received. As if she felt there was some crookedness about it somewhere and her children were being cheated out of their just rights. But she sat back with pursed lips and listened for the rest. But there wasn't much else at all. Just a gift of five hundred dollars to the old servant Hattie and a few smaller bequests to the man who had worked in the garden and other people who had served her in various lesser capacities. Then the lawyer folded the paper and said quietly, "And that is all."

Aunt Blanche sat up with a snap. "Why! *Why!* I don't understand. You haven't mentioned the house."

"The house?" said the lawyer with raised eyebrows. "What house?"

"Why, *this* house. Wasn't that mentioned in the will?"

"Oh no," said the lawyer. "Why should it be? Mrs. Huntley never owned this house. She was only given a life residence in it, the privilege of living here all her life."

"But I'm sure you are mistaken!" snapped Aunt Blanche. "I am quite sure my late husband purchased this house, or at least helped *largely* to purchase it for his mother's residence during her lifetime. I was given to understand that it would come to us as next in line. I am quite sure there must be papers somewhere to that effect. Unless—of—course—they have purposely been *destroyed*. But in that case, of course, there'll be some way to prove that and to find out the criminal."

"I do not understand you, madam," said Randall Granniss with that stern, authoritative manner that had won so many cases for him before famous judges. And before that look even Aunt Blanche stopped—astonished, startled—and her belligerence oozed out of her like gas out of a balloon.

"Well, I wasn't of course making my remarks personal. I am simply saying that if there *has* been any crooked work going on, of course *you* would be able to detect it and trace it to its source."

Mr. Granniss's steely glance became no less severe, and his voice lost its soft geniality as he answered her. "My dear madam," he said, "there has been no crooked work in connection with anything about this house. It was bought the year that Dale's mother and father were married. The down payment was made by Dale's father, Theodore Huntley, and I myself negotiated the sale for him. His endorsed check, endorsed also by the trust company that was in charge of the house for the estate of M. J. Eaton, the former owner, is now in the bank, in the safe-deposit box belonging to Dale Huntley and can be examined by you at any time that you would care to come down to the bank with me. Your husband's name does not appear anywhere in connection with this sale, and there were no checks from anyone else but Theodore Huntley in payment for this property. I have some of the original papers here with me, and if you or your lawyer would care to look further into the matter, I can arrange for a meeting at the bank where you can see them. I have with me, however, the bill of sale and several other documents that ought to be sufficient proof to you of the truth of what I have said. Moreover, madam, as I understand it, your marriage did not take place until after Theodore Huntley had gone abroad, for I remember he was unable to attend the ceremony because his business was very insistent, and that was two years after this property was purchased. I have here on this paper the dates relative to the matter and shall be glad to have you examine them at your leisure. You will note that the clause concerning Dale's ownership and her grandmother's life-occupation of the house was not added until five years later, at the time of the death of Mr. Huntley's wife, when he returned to this country to make arrangements to leave his young daughter with his mother. Those are the facts, madam, and I shall be glad to substantiate any of them that you do not understand. Also, if you wish to go to the city hall and look into the records of property owners, you will find that the house is now listed under the ownership of Miss Dale Huntley."

Mrs. Huntley gave a startled, almost frightened look that merged quickly into a firm, determined one as she heard footsteps on the porch and realized that it must be her own lawyer.

Then the doorbell pealed through the house, and they could hear Hattie going to answer it. Dale sat quite still and quietly watched each person in the room as the other lawyer entered. The tense, strained expression on her aunt's face; the amused grin on Powelton's disagreeable mug; the bored contempt of Corliss; and the quiet assurance of Mr. Granniss. He was not worrying about what was going to happen, because he had the facts and proofs against all the trifling claims of the pretenders.

In fact, it seemed utterly absurd to Mr. Granniss that any sane woman would try to put over such an unfounded claim. He had told Dale that she need not worry.

And as for the lawyer Aunt Blanche had secured, Mr. Granniss had said that he was so notorious that he was not to be taken seriously. He was a big bluff who had a way of deceiving gullible women and outtalking any serious questioners.

Dale knew Mr. Granniss felt it would be a bore, but for Dale's sake he must listen to it and then, when it was over, bring forward some convincing proof that he had with him, which would upset all the other man was planning to do. Mr. Granniss was a conscientious lawyer who went clearly to the bottom of things and left no room for clever roundabout ways.

It was at this stage of affairs that Powelton decided to speak up. "Oh heck!" he said, yawning audibly. "I can't be bothered with all this bologna! I'm gonna beat it! See you later, Mom!" And Powelton vanished with a slammed door behind him.

And next, Corliss began to wriggle and writhe and sigh audibly and finally changed her seat until she was close to the french window that opened on the porch. It wasn't long before Corliss, too, was absent from the family group, though nobody but Dale actually saw her edge behind the curtain and depart.

There followed a tiresome rehash of what had gone before, listening to pompous questions asked by the newly arrived lawyer, and Mr. Granniss's quiet, brief answers. Finally Greenway Buffington rose and, clearing his throat, ominously said, "Mrs. Huntley, it will be impossible for me to give you an adequate idea of what can be done in this matter until I have opportunity to go down to the city hall and verify some of these statements that have been made. Would you like to come with me now? I think we would have time to look into this before the lunch hour."

"Certainly," said Aunt Blanche, rising triumphantly and looking around at her two adversaries, as if she was already assured of the rights she had been claiming.

Aunt Blanche was not long in getting ready, and meantime her lawyer sat in imposing silence while Dale and Mr. Granniss talked in low tones about the service of the day before and who were the singer and speakers. Nothing whatever that could possibly be connected with the matter of the property.

After they were gone, Dale drew a long breath. "I'm glad that session is over. Do you think that lawyer can do anything?" she asked with a troubled look.

Mr. Granniss looked at her and smiled. "Not possibly," he assured her pleasantly, "except to charge her a big fee, perhaps. He will probably string the matter out as long as he dares before giving her the final word that he can do nothing. Of course the property is yours entirely, and her husband never had anything to do with it. You need not worry. Your property is as safe as property could ever be, and in the end your aunt will find that out to her sorrow, I'm afraid, for Buffington has the name of never doing anything for nothing. Is your aunt intending to leave soon?"

"Oh, I don't know," said Dale with a weary smile. "She hasn't said anything about it yet. If her lawyer leaves her with any hope, she will probably stay indefinitely, and it just seems as if I could not stand that."

"Of course not, child," said the lawyer comfortingly. "We'll try to contrive some way to get her interested in going home. Don't worry. We'll find a way. And now, what are you planning to do, little girl? I suppose you talked that over with your grandmother?"

"Oh yes. We planned it all out together. I'm going to stay right here in the house, and Hattie is going to stay with me. I'm thinking of looking after some little children while their mothers are working in war plants. Grandmother suggested that, and I know there are several mothers around here who

are greatly troubled because they cannot find the right place
for their children while they are away. In fact, one mother has
already asked me to take her twins, and I'm sure I'll love the
work. It will be sort of a school, you know."

"Splendid!" said the lawyer. "And you should be able to get
a good price for such work. You know, the mothers have good
wages where they are working."

"Yes, so I have heard. I'm glad you approve. Grandmother
heard of this through a friend of hers who came to see her, and
she thought it would be a lovely way to use my home. At least
for a time."

"Fine!" said the lawyer. "Are you planning to start right
away?"

"I'd like to," said Dale with a troubled look, "but I can't
really do anything about it while my relatives are here. In fact,
I wouldn't want them to know about it. They would try to talk
me out of it. My aunt would like me to go home with her and
do housework for my living."

"Housework! *You?* Absurd. They'd better go home and do
their own work. Better hurry them off."

"I don't know how I can hurry them. I can't just *ask* them
to go, can I? I don't want to be rude. Grandmother wouldn't
want me to do that."

"No," said the lawyer thoughtfully, "but there might be
other ways. I'll think about that. I might be able to find a way
to get them started sooner. We'll see. Perhaps the result of today's investigation may be sufficient to make them see that
they have got all the financial assistance they can get out of
this episode. Suppose you let me know if there is any change in
the status of things when your aunt returns. Better phone me

from the drugstore, then there'll be no danger of your being overheard."

"Yes, of course," said Dale. "Thank you so much for your advice. It makes me feel so much safer."

"Has this aunt always been so unpleasant in her ways of talking?" asked Mr. Granniss.

"I've never had much to do with her. She came to visit when Corliss was about five, and we had a terrible two weeks while she stayed. Then she and Grandmother had a talk and she went away in a huff, and it's been a long time since we heard from her until about three months ago when she wrote a very sweet letter and wanted to come for a visit. Said she heard that Grandmother wasn't so well and she got to worrying that her children didn't know her better. Grandmother didn't answer that for a long time, but finally she wrote a nice little note and said she wasn't in any shape at that time to have company, but she would send word later. That was when she told me to write the letter about her death and have it ready to send as soon as it happened, putting in the date and time of the funeral. That was why she insisted that they should be notified. For Grandmother was always courteous, although you know she had an odd sense of humor at times. She felt that she must make up for not having them visit her at the time they had asked by inviting them to her funeral. She knew they would be interested in the will, and she had that quaint little grin when she said it. But you don't know how I have dreaded this visit. In fact, Grandmother gave me reason to dread it in little bits of warnings. That is why I am so glad to have you here now, and why I am depending so much upon your advice."

"Poor child!" said the lawyer. "Don't worry. I'll see you through this. We'll wait till your aunt gets back from her investigations. Then we'll devise a pleasant way to get her out of the picture so you can go on with your plans. Now, I'll run down to my office for a little while, and I'll be there when you get ready to phone me."

"But won't you stay for lunch? I'm sure Hattie will be glad to hurry it up so you won't lose any time."

"No, child, no. I'll get right down to the office and have a tray sent in. I often do that, you know. It saves a lot of time, and while I do always appreciate Hattie's cooking, I think this way is better for today. Tell Hattie I said so. Remember you may have your guests all here to feed in a little while, and they may even bring the other lawyer along with them again, too. But if they do, you send Hattie to the store to phone me, and I'll come up at once."

"Oh, thank you, Mr. Granniss," said Dale, her eyes full of grateful tears. "I shall never forget all that you have done for me all the years, and especially today, for I have been so tried and so disheartened."

The old friend looked at the pretty girl tenderly and patted her shoulder. "There, there, Dale! Don't get that way. Don't you know your grandmother's Lord always provides someone to look after His dear children when they are tried and in need? And this time He just chose me to look after you. Now, get upstairs to your room and lie down for at least a few minutes. You certainly look all in, and you need to relax a little before the next stage will begin. So go rest, and don't worry. Trust me, and the Lord!" he ended reverently, as he took his leave.

Dale hurried down to the kitchen and had a little talk with Hattie, who also implored her to rest. Hattie promised to prepare a good, substantial lunch that could be served whenever the erratic guests should choose to arrive and to make enough for Mr. Buffington, too, if he came back. So Dale did go and lie down with closed eyes for at least five minutes trying to pray her way through to quietness and peace. And she succeeded so well that there came a little gleam of brightness to her face. Then she remembered David Kenyon's possible coming sometime in the near future. Oh, she hoped so much that if he did come her aunt and cousins would be gone by that time. She couldn't bear the thought of having this bit of pleasantness spoiled by their presence, for she knew just how Corliss would behave.

Please find a way for them to go home, dear Lord, before he comes, she prayed softly in her heart.

And then there came the sound of feet flying up the front walk, stamping into the house, and Corliss's clarion voice calling loudly, "Dale! Oh Dale! Have you got any tennis rackets? We want to play tennis. We've found a tennis court that's not in use, and we want some balls and rackets."

Dale rose with a weary little sigh. She must answer. Of course tennis was a harmless amusement. It would be a good thing if those two could get interested in something absorbing. Yes, she had a couple of rackets that she and a dear friend, now married and gone to Africa as a missionary, used to have when they were in school together for a year. She hadn't played herself since her friend left; there hadn't been any opportunity, for she had come home to stay with her grandmother, who was beginning to be very feeble. But she had kept the rackets and balls and put them away as carefully as keepsakes of her girlhood, which she recognized was about over so far as games were concerned. She hated to give them up as they were precious for old times' sake, but she didn't need those rackets, would probably never use them again. Was that right? Why should she hang on to them when she would likely never have any use for them? Why not let these unlovely cousins get a little fun out of them? This was what Grandmother and God would likely want her to do.

"Yes," she answered pleasantly. "Yes, I have a couple of rackets. It's been some time since I had a chance to use them, but I'm sure they are in good condition. I oiled them before I put them away. I'll get them."

"Well, make it snappy! We want to get back before anybody clsc snitches the court."

Dale was back in a moment, unwinding the soft tissue paper wrappings as she came down the stairs. But Corliss did not wait for her to get down. She sprang up the stairs and snatched the rackets from her, casting the wrappings in a heap on the stairs and almost tripping herself as she tore out the door and away, waving the rackets in the air, whacking the furniture and the door frame as she passed. "You'll be careful of them, won't you, please?" Dale called after her as she went.

"Okay, I'll be careful of the old relics," she jeered. "They don't look like they'd be able to play more than a set or two without passing out! About the model they made before the ark, aren't they?" She yelled all this up the street at her, and several elderly women came to their front doors to look out and see what it was all about. Dale felt sure they turned away pitying her for having such ill-mannered guests.

Dale sighed and turned back into the house, almost regretting that she had loaned her precious rackets. Yet how silly that was. What difference did it make if they did spoil her rackets? It was just sentiment, and that, of course, was silly.

So Dale put aside that burden as unworthy of her and thought no more about it until after dinner that night when her cousin said carelessly in answer to her query of how the game went, "Oh gee! I forgot to go back for the rackets. But it won't make any difference. They're neither of them fit to use again. They're both broken!"

In spite of herself, Dale's quick indignation rose. "Where did you leave the rackets?" she asked sternly.

"Oh, up around behind the bushes over at the end of the tennis court."

"Come with me and show me," Dale said authoritatively.

But Corliss only laughed. "It won't do any good to go after them. Some kids were having a fight with them when I left. They won't be any use now."

Dale gave her a withering glance and, turning, went out the door and down the paving to the street, walking with swift steps toward the country club and the tennis courts that crowned the rise of the winding drive off to the left. Could she find her rackets? Well, she would try. But at least she would walk until she had her temper under control.

She went swiftly down the street and turned on to the road that led up to the country club. On, on, up the smooth, wide road, up the hill, up the drive that swept around in front of the country club, to the courts, on beyond the high stop nets at the end where the shrubs and bushes grew, down to the edge of the little winding brook that went with soft steps and glittering blue like a lovely ribbon, making pictures of itself in every nook and corner where it twinkled.

She stood for a moment letting her eyes follow the bright water down the hill, the soft sky above with white, fluffy clouds floating lazily. How lovely and sweet this scene was and how far from the ill-natured struggle of the day that had done so much to her tired nerves. She took a deep breath and let the scene creep into her senses, storing up the beauty. Just as she had so often done to carry the picture of the outside world to Grandmother.

She sighed as she turned away and thought sadly that now she had no one left to describe such things to, for she couldn't think of going home and trying to tell Aunt Blanche about the scene. And she could hear her two cousins shouting with sneering laughter if she attempted any such conversation. Then her thoughts went to her new service-friend, David Kenyon. Yes, she could think of telling him about this scene. Perhaps when she met him again, she would remember to tell him. But that would be foolish, too, describing a scene in her local vicinity to him, a stranger. He had probably seen a lot more interesting ones. But it was lovely, and the sight of it had calmed her spirit so that she could go back and meet her careless cousin without frowning at her, she hoped.

Then she turned to go back home again and there at her feet she saw the rackets, lying in a heap just under the edge of a large bush that reached out over the brook. And the strings were gleaming wet as if they had been plunged into the water. Some of the strings were badly broken.

She picked them up, wiped the water away with her handkerchief, and tucking them under her arm, went swiftly home, entering the house by the back way where she would not be seen, going upstairs, and hiding the rackets in her own room.

Then she heard voices in the living room, a strange voice and a loud voice. Smoothing her hair, she hurried down to find out what had been happening during her absence.

Chapter 6

As Dale came downstairs she could hear the pompous voice of Greenway Buffington boasting as he stood up by the front door, in the act of departing.

"Now, you don't need to worry anymore, Mrs. Huntley. I'm quite sure we'll come upon some definite evidence in a day or two. And if you can find those letters you spoke of, that would certainly clinch the matter. You might try long distance to your banker and have him look in your safe-deposit box. He'll have a key, of course, and then he can send the letter on by airmail, and it won't take over a week to work this thing out. I'm confident I can get the judge to arrange it to come on the docket soon and get the whole matter settled up in no time. And now, thank you for this retainer. Of course I'm accustomed to getting at least twice that for a retainer, but since it is you and since you bring a recommendation from my friend in Chicago, why, we'll call it all right for the present. And of course when you get home, you can send me the rest. Well, good evening, Mrs. Huntley. You do that telephoning, and let me know the result. Good night."

The door closed at last on the obnoxious lawyer, while Dale stood desperately on the stairs and tried to realize that there were perhaps days and days ahead of her filled with all sorts of incalculable discomforts. *Oh God, help me, all the way through,* her heart prayed, as she tried to gather up her courage and go forward. *Oh, if they will only go before David comes,* she thought to herself. And then her cheeks grew hot in the darkness of the dining room. She was thinking of him as David now. And he was coming again to see her, if only the government didn't send him away before he had an opportunity to come. Well, she would have to take it all as it came, of course, and surely her God could bring all things to work together for good for her, and for the rightness of everything.

To Dale's relief, Hattie rang the bell for the evening meal, and they all trooped into the dining room. Dale slipped into the kitchen for a hurried whispered conference with Hattie.

The lunch had been a sketchy affair, partaken of by Powelton and Corliss while Dale was out hunting for her rackets.

The cousins were seated at the table with an air of annoyance that there was any delay in the service when Dale came in, and they kept up a conversation among themselves, scarcely speaking to Dale except to ask her to pass the butter or order more ice water or coffee. And once her aunt told her that she really ought to speak to Hattie about putting so little shortening in her piecrust. "It's really quite tough, you know, Dale," she said, making a great show of having to work hard to cut the crust of the delicious apple pie she had just been served.

But Dale smiled good-naturedly. "We're having a war, you know," she said gently. "We can't get as much fat as we might like to use."

"A good cook can make tender crust without so much shortening," said the aunt in a superior tone. "Why doesn't she use cream if she can't get lard?"

"We can't get cream," Dale said with a smile. "Won't you have another cup of coffee, Aunt Blanche?"

"You always have an impertinent answer ready, don't you?" said the aunt as she passed her cup for more coffee. "Well, the time is coming fast when you will sing another tune. I've found out a good many things this afternoon that will make you open your eyes in astonishment." She flung this out as she rose from the table; then she went into the living room and took up the evening paper.

Corliss and Powelton soon sauntered off to a movie, and Dale was free for a little while. Then she was called to the telephone. It was Mr. Granniss.

"Is that you, Dale?"

Her voice was low and could not be heard in the living room, she was sure.

"Yes. This is Miss Huntley," she answered pleasantly in accordance with his instructions.

"Is there anyone nearby to listen?"

"Possibly," she said composedly.

"All right. Just answer yes or no, or very briefly. Has anything important developed?"

"No."

"Are you worried?"

"A little."

"Well, it isn't necessary, everything is going to be all right. Forget it all and get a good night's rest. I'll be over in the morning."

"Thank you."

"Good night."

"Good night."

It was a simple conversation, but somehow it lifted a load of worry from Dale's heart, and quietly she slipped from the telephone and went to the kitchen to help Hattie with the dishes and plan for the problematic morrow. Meantime she was wondering just what her aunt was planning for the night. So far, the guests had taken possession of the house pretty thoroughly for whatever purposes they chose, without any by-your-leave, except at night, and so Dale was left in doubt. But she did not intend to ask any questions. This visit would likely be at an end *some*time, and she wanted if possible to have no twinges of conscience lest she had not acted with perfect courtesy.

But there was no use in hoping that there would be any settlement of this question until the cousins came back from the movies, so she took a bit of sewing and a book in which she was interested and went into the living room. She would endeavor to be sociable if her aunt was so inclined, but if not, then she could read.

Mrs. Huntley seemed to be doing thorough work of the evening paper, for she read on and on, studying every page as if she were deeply interested in it, and Dale sat there with her book, trying to concentrate on it, and yet continually wondering what her aunt had been doing downtown all that day.

But at last the cousins came storming up on the porch, and without further ado and very few words, the guests took themselves away to the hotel, saying with an air of condescension that they would be back in the morning for breakfast and demanding that it be an early one, as their lawyer was coming again.

Then Dale, with a deep sigh of relief, locked the house and went to bed, after the long, long day. But as she was drifting off to sleep, her thoughts went happily to the telephone message from that officer this morning. She found herself wondering about it. Why had he taken the trouble to call her? He must have plenty of friends in camp, plenty of people who would invite him to spend a day or a weekend, and yet he had chosen to call her. That was wonderful. Of course they had had a very pleasant hour together that first time she found him sitting alone at the U.S.O., reading a much-thumbed newspaper. She had made hot tea for him and found some doughnuts, and then he had come out to the kitchen and helped her wipe dishes. She had been taking the place of three women who all had good reasons to be absent from the center that night, and it was getting late. Most of the fellows had gone away. He alone had been left. Why? Didn't he care to go to the places they chose? Or was he not feeling well? She hadn't bothered to ask him. He had just said he was a bit tired. But not too tired to wipe dishes. That was strange. Well, she had decided he was homesick and wanted to talk to some woman, so he had smiled at her and wiped dishes. They had had a nice little talk and he had walked home with her when she closed up for the night and left. Just being kind. It was nice of him. And the reason he came to the funeral and brought the flowers? He was sort of doing that for the sake of his own grandmother whose funeral he had not known of overseas even in time to send flowers.

That the young man came because he was attracted to her never entered her head. Dale wasn't a girl who was self-centered. She had grown up in a healthy atmosphere, never realizing that she had a beautiful face and an unusually lovely expression. Never dreaming of great things that might come to her. Thinking only of love in the abstract, as a miracle that might come to anyone sometime, but not planning to go out and get it for herself. There was too much to be done for others in this world to leave much time for thoughts of self. And she had been so quiet and shy in school, and what college she had had, that she had not made many boy friends. She was just good friends with all who came her way. She didn't wear lipstick or paint her fingernails or dress in the latest fad of fashion to make people look at her. She was just a healthy, happy girl doing her duty as far as she knew it and enjoying the doing of it. So, though the telephone message from the young officer that morning had pleased her mightily and set her heart thrilling pleasantly, she did not immediately go to planning to marry him or do anything about it except to be a pleasant friend to him in the last hours before he should go overseas again and perhaps to meet death. He knew the Lord. She was glad of that. They could talk more understandingly together because of that fact. And it was nice to have this pleasant memory of the day.

❦

A few miles away in the base, the young officer was staring up at the moon that shone through a window of the barracks and thinking of the immediate future and what it likely held for him. He had finished his quota of missions and been duly decorated for them. He was proud of his work in the past. He would like to go back and fight some more, but from what the commanding officer had said to him briefly the day before, he had reason to believe that something else was being shaped up for him. He didn't yet know what it was, but he didn't want changes. There was emptiness and desolation enough in his life already, and he didn't like the idea of a new background, new companions, new duties. Oh, doubtless they were honors, but somehow he had lost heart. His last two months in the hospital recovering from the raids in which he had participated prominently and now this trip home had filled him with a great desire to get back to that fighting line and help get this war over. What he wanted was for the world to return to the old life that he had known and enjoyed before he went to war. He wanted a home and a real life. He wanted some friends, a family, perhaps a place to come home to at night and someone to welcome him. But of course that could not be until this was over, so he was impatient to get into the active part of the fighting again and be responsible for definitely wiping out as many of the enemy as possible. They need not think they could put him on any office job and count that his due. If they tried that he would definitely protest. Such jobs might be all right for fellows who were really sick and who loathed the thought of battle, but he somehow knew that battle was his place until all this war was over. He could never be content to settle down and do office work, important as that might be to the whole effort, while there was a job requiring courage and a willingness to face peril. That was what he would ask for if they let him have any choice.

But of course they might not. And he must not dwell on it. Tomorrow morning he was to meet his commanding officer and hear more about it, and he must be ready to yield his wishes to what was ordered. But if there was any chance to choose, he certainly would choose to go back and help get this job done quickly, this job of setting the world free for peace and quietness.

So he told the moon, as he turned over and sought to go to sleep.

Then came that girl's face, the face that had attracted him so much when he had first seen it—a clean, happy, peaceful face, lovely in something above the look he saw in most other girls' faces, a face without "illumination" as he jocosely called makeup. A face that had an inner illumination coming from a beautiful soul. Or would it be a beautiful spirit? A lovely inner life. That was it.

He had known from first sight of her that it was such a girl he would like to know and make her a part of his own life sometime when he should return to the world, if such a time was really to come for him.

So he lay now and watched her face in memory as he reviewed the few little times of contact he had had with her. Every one of them fit. He could see her now as they stood beside her grandmother's casket while she arranged his lilies in the white hands. There was no despair in her eyes, only a glad look as if she were preparing a loved one to go to some great festive occasion. Not getting her ready to lie in the ground. Not bidding her farewell forever. There had been hope and trust in her eyes, in the set of her lovely lips, and as he thought about it, his own hope and trust for a life hereafter seemed to strengthen.

He thought of the few minutes of hurried talk they had had at her desk while he wrote his address for her and the way his hand had touched hers as she gave him the pen. It thrilled him now to think of it. And how her voice had sounded over the phone when she recognized him and seemed glad. The thought of that thrilled him, too.

But this was no way for a man to feel when he was going into the thick of battle again, perhaps. He should not wish a love and a sorrow together like that on any lighthearted girl. Had he been wrong to call her and ask for himself these few hours of joy before he went?

There it was again! That uncertainty. He didn't even know yet that he was going, or that going, his would be a time of peril. He didn't know a thing about it. Suppose, on the other hand, they should want him to stay here and do something important. Suppose there was a chance he might love and marry and have a home with a girl like Dale. How his heart thrilled to even think of it. And yet—and yet— He simply must not bank on anything like this. For if that came he knew in his heart that his inner soul would not be satisfied unless he went out first with the rest and faced the peril and the fire and won through. He simply must not let himself desire such home things now. He must yield his life to God. For he had a God in whom he believed and trusted. God had some plan for his life, and it had to be as God wanted it. That was what his inner soul desired.

Then somehow peace came into his heart. The future days were bringing changes. Perhaps this problem would be settled for him. Meantime, at least he had made pretty sure that if he were permitted to stop over in the city he had at least paved the way for meeting Dale again for a little while and talking with her. And if he was able to call her up and arrange for their meeting, wouldn't it be all right to ask her to bring along a little snapshot of herself that he might be able to look at her face sometimes when he was far away again? Surely there would be no harm in that, even if he decided that she didn't care about a friendship herself as much as he did. Surely she would not object to having a fighter carry a snapshot of herself over the seas with him, just in memory of the pleasant times they had had. At least he would ask her, when and if he telephoned.

Chapter 7

Dale awoke the next morning to the disturbing thought of planning menus for the day. The larder was getting low, and she really ought to go down and order a lot of things. There would need to be vegetables, of course. But everything was expensive now when one considered buying for four guests. She simply couldn't provide expensive fare if these relatives were going to stay indefinitely. If she only knew how long this was to go on! Well, perhaps she must just begin to cut down quietly on the food and say nothing about it.

She hurried downstairs early, and together, she and Hattie went through the stores already on hand. They finally decided on oatmeal, toast, coffee, and pears for breakfast. If the guests didn't like it, well, that was all she could do about it now. If she should go on serving fine meals she would presently be bankrupt, and they would just go on growling about her arrangements. So perhaps it was as well to do only what she could afford and let the results be what they would. She would not apologize. She would treat her menus as if they were the best that anybody could desire.

And what should she have for lunch? Perhaps some lettuce sandwiches and canned soup. If it did not please her boarders they could always go out and buy food not far away. She didn't want to seem mean, but she must not run over her budget. Perhaps they would understand without an argument. But she had little hope for that.

And what should she have for the main dish at dinner? She had no more red stamps with which to get meat. It would be two days more before others were released, and her guests had produced no ration books to help her out. Well, there was still a glass jar of tongue, and there were some lovely big flakes of codfish. What would Corliss say if they had creamed codfish for dinner that night? Well, she would try it. Of course it wouldn't be so good if Mr. Granniss had to stay to either meal. She didn't care about the lawyer Buffington. She felt almost guilty at the plans she was making. But then she knew she could depend on Hattie. Hattie would present codfish, or in fact anything, at its very best. It would be delicately flavored, delightfully attractive, and appetizing, really almost interesting, on the table. There were apples, too. There could be applesauce and cookies for dessert.

Then Dale went up to her room and knelt down by her bed.

Dear Lord, I'm doing the best I can. Is this right? Should I make some further sacrifice, sell something I want to keep, in order to buy something more expensive? If You want me to, please show me. If not, please give me courage to keep calm in the midst of any storm that arises. And please don't let us have trouble with the relatives or about the property. Please make a way for them to go away soon.

This last sentence was like a young child's cry for help in utter despair. She went downstairs again to meet the day with more assurance in her heart than she had felt when she awoke.

But the day did not enter smiling. At least the guest part of the day did not. It was almost as if the enemy understood how this child of God was beginning to rest and trust in her heavenly Father's care, so he summoned all his wildest young demons to meet her and demolish all her defenses. They waltzed into the house along with the relatives and began to battle even before any good-mornings were said.

"I certainly hope you've got a good breakfast this morning," flung out Corliss as she slammed into the room. "I was just sick all day yesterday whenever I thought of those horrid eggs I had to eat!"

Dale tried to speak reassuringly, with a bright little wistful smile: "No eggs today," she said. "They were all eaten up yesterday. I haven't had time to go to the store yet."

"Well, that's a good thing," said Corliss. "I don't see what eggs were made for, anyway. If I had my way there never would be any."

"What would you do for floating island and lemon meringue pies, then?" said Dale, smiling.

"Oh, *those*! Well, I suppose it would be all right to have a few eggs for lemon meringue pie. I'm not so keen about floating island."

Dale did not go out to the dining room with them. She said she would run down to the store right away before so many others had to be waited on, as there were things they needed.

"Well, get some beefsteak," shouted Powelton.

"No, get roast beef. Prime ribs, you know," called Corliss.

"Sorry," said Dale pleasantly, "I can't get either of those. I haven't any more red ration stamps, and you can't get steak or roasts without red stamps. We'll have to go easy on the butter, too. We have only a quarter of a pound left, and no more stamps will be released yet for two days."

"Why, that's ridiculous!" said Corliss. "I'll bet Hattie has been eating up the butter."

But Dale went on about her business, realizing that if she got out of hearing Corliss would stop talking and Hattie would not have to hear her. Poor Hattie! It was hard enough for her to keep her temper without also being charged with eating the butter. So Dale went on to do her shopping, hoping and praying that the breakfasters might get through without too much growling and that Hattie would be able to carry on until her return.

But the relatives at the dining table were anything but happy. "No orange juice! Just three measly little pears!" said Corliss.

The aunt rang the bell, and Hattie appeared in a leisurely manner.

"You've forgotten the orange juice," said the aunt sharply.

"There aren't any oranges," said Hattie grimly. "You'll have to make out with them pears."

"I just hate pears," said Corliss with her face all snarled up.

"Well," said the aunt, "you may bring the rest of the breakfast."

"That's all there is this morning," said Hattie, with a sort of triumphant note in her voice and a finality that appropriately preceded the closing of the kitchen door.

"Well really!" said the aunt, surveying the table with its neat and ample pile of toast in front of the glowing toaster where it would keep hot, the small portion of butter at each plate, and the glass dish of blackberry jam. "Well, what's the idea? It seems we are being put on rations. I should think it was time Dale took a little thought for running her house. She certainly can't expect that inefficient Hattie to do it all. And no cream, either. That's all nonsense. They ought to take more milk then and skim the tops off all the bottles. And *oatmeal!* The idea! How could anybody possibly eat that old-fashioned stuff? And without cream! Wait! I'll ring for some dry cereal. That would at least be tolerable."

But when Hattie finally decided to answer the summons, she vouchsafed that all the dry cereal was finished and that was one of the things Miss Dale had gone after.

"Well then, we'll wait till she returns. We can't possibly eat oatmeal, and certainly not without cream."

"She said she wouldn't be back in time. She said as how you were expecting some lawyer. Oatmeal ain't as bad! Even without cream. Some eats it with butter! You better try it. It's pipin' hot, and butter tastes very good."

"I really couldn't endure the thought," said the lady. "Butter on oatmeal! I really think that I shall have to hunt a place to board while I am obliged to stay here on business. I wonder if you can tell me who in the neighborhood takes boarders. How about that house over across on the opposite corner? That large house with stone pillars. That looks like a pleasant place. Perhaps they could be persuaded to let us board there. You wouldn't know what they charge, would you?"

"What, that mansion over there? Not they. They's quality folks and they'd drive you off the place if you dared suggest such a thing. Why, they's an old family. No ma'am, there ain't anybody around these parts takes boarders. They's just private families, and most of um's pretty well fixed for theirselves. You'd have to go down in the village to get board. I believe there's a room or two over the drugstore and the grocery, with mebbe a kitchenette where you could do light housekeepin', if you wanted that."

"*Mercy* no!" said the aunt with disgust.

"I should say not!" said Corliss with contempt.

Hattie made good her retreat to the kitchen and left the unhappy breakfasters to finish everything edible within sight.

❦

Mr. Granniss was on the front porch reading the paper when Dale got back to the house, and she sighed with relief as she recognized him. Now, whatever happened, he would be there to answer her questions.

Mr. Buffington drove up in his limousine a few moments later and requested to see his client alone, so Dale ushered him into the living room and went back to talk to Mr. Grannis on the porch. But Mr. Buffington's voice was loud and penetrating, and most of his conversation came booming through the open windows, so they were well informed about the position of the relatives before he left. The gist of the whole matter seemed to have resolved itself in Lawyer Buffington's mind into the fact that there was so far nothing to prove that Mrs. Huntley's claims about the property had any foundation and that unless she could go home at once, or at least telephone her lawyer, and get hold of letters showing that her dead husband had ever put money into the purchase of the house in question, he did not see how he could possibly undertake the case. Of course if she insisted, he might undertake it, but the expense of the matter would be greater and the retaining fee would be doubled.

Listening, Dale took heart. Perhaps God was going to answer her prayer this way, but she must not think too much about it, nor get her plans made for their going away. There was no telling what her aunt would finally do.

It almost seemed as if Mr. Granniss had read her thoughts, for he began to talk about her plans for the little school she was thinking of starting and suggested that it might be good to arrange a definite date for its opening and tell her aunt that she would need the house from that time on.

Then suddenly the talk in the living room ceased. The pompous lawyer came out and went away. With a few low-spoken words promising to be ready to help in any need that might arise, Mr. Granniss also went away.

And now what ought she do next? Would God show the way?

And then the future, as if in answer to her thoughts, began to open up before her.

Her aunt appeared in the doorway and looked out, saying coldly, "I should like to use your telephone. It will be a long-distance call and may take some time. I thought I better ask you if you have any immediate necessary calls first, because I cannot be interrupted once I begin."

Dale looked up pleasantly, wondering what was coming. "Why certainly, Aunt Blanche. Use the phone as long as necessary. I won't interrupt you," she said cordially.

Without even a thank-you, the aunt turned, swept toward the telephone, and called long distance.

Dale went swiftly into the dining room and began to rearrange the setting of the table, not for any special reason except to listen and discover if she could what her unwanted guests were going to do next.

It was a bank that was being called up and an official who evidently knew her aunt. There ensued a rather frantic conversation in which it appeared that the gentleman in question would not have access to the lady's safe-deposit box without a letter from her giving him authority and the key to open her box.

But the lady did not stop with the one try. She insisted on getting the address of the bank president, who was absent on vacation, and then did not hesitate to call him up and insist on a reply as soon as the man came in, no matter how late it was. After that, with ominous sighs, she flung herself down in a chair and snatched up a book.

Dale tried to busy herself around the house, not to seem to be listening, but occasionally her aunt would go to the phone again and sharply question long distance.

But at last there came an answer from the man she had called, and then Dale almost felt sorry for him, for such a list of questions as were poured across the line. Did he remember anything about her husband having bought a piece of property in the East, property in which his mother was to live? Over and over again in different phraseology she asked the question until the man, trying to be courteous, must have been exasperated. The upshot of it was that he did not remember any such transaction and that if Mrs. Huntley wanted her personal letters gone through for a matter of evidence of any kind it would be wiser if she were to come home herself and go through her own papers. He did not feel that anyone else should take that responsibility. And anyway, he was off for a time of rest and was not sure how soon he would be back. If he did as his doctor advised, it might be several months yet before his return.

At last the interview was over, and Dale drew a long breath, for it was evident that there would be a large charge for that call, and it was most unlikely that her aunt would stop to inquire how much it was or ever remember to ask for the bill when it came in and pay it. Dale was not penurious, and if even a large telephone bill would open the way for her guests to go home soon, she would not begrudge it, but she was appalled at the expenses that were mounting up daily. Grandmother had warned her, but somehow she had not been able to comprehend how true it would be.

And now, noting a cessation of loud talk, Hattie opened the kitchen door and signaled that lunch was ready to be served whenever Dale desired. So she gave the signal and the boarders trooped noisily in.

"Oh boy, but I'm empty! After that measly breakfast I could eat a whole cow," said Powelton, slamming himself into his chair.

"Yes," said his mother. "Dale, you certainly did give us a slim meal this morning. Or was that Hattie's planning? If it was, I think she ought to be dealt with about it. It was simply horrid."

"Oh, I'm sorry, Aunt Blanche," said Dale quietly. "No, it was not of Hattie's planning. I did the best I could with what was in the house. You know, I was pretty well occupied yesterday and didn't get my usual shopping in."

"Well, I can't understand why you couldn't have sent Hattie down for what you needed early this morning."

"Well, that didn't just seem to be convenient, either," said Dale with a quiet dignity.

Then Corliss entered and stood a moment behind her chair, surveying the table with disgust. "Sandwiches!" she sneered. "Made of lettuce, too! My greatest abomination! As far as I'm concerned, you can take them away. I want something real. After that sketchy breakfast we had, I think we rate something better than just sandwiches."

She slumped down in her chair unhappily, and just then Hattie entered with a salad of grated carrots and pineapple.

"Oh, for heaven's sake!" said Corliss. "You can't feed me carrots! I simply *won't* eat them, and that's all!"

"Get me some peanut butter, Hattie!" ordered Powelton.

"I'm afraid there isn't any peanut butter in the house, Powelton," said Dale apologetically. "I didn't know that you were especially fond of that. I'll get some the next time I'm in the store."

Hattie brought in the plates of hot soup, the disgruntled boarders settled down deprecatingly to eat it, and quiet was restored for the moment.

Then the pudding came in, a nicely browned bread pudding made in Hattie's best style, with a nice little cup of hard sauce to eat with it.

"What is it?" asked Corliss with her nose in the air. "*Bread* pudding? Heavens! No! You can't get that down me, nor Pow either. We told our family long ago not to try any of that on us."

"Sorry you don't like it," said Dale. "I'm very fond of Hattie's bread puddings." But she made no further apology.

"Well," said the mother at last, after picking among the array on her plate, "I'm sure I don't know how you children are going to last till dinnertime. You haven't either of you eaten enough to keep a bird alive. Here! I'll give you some money and you can go down to the drugstore and get some ice cream."

She handed out fifty cents, and the brother and sister departed. Then she sat back surveying the table dishearteningly. At last she spoke. "It seems too bad to let your table run down this way," she said, looking sadly at Dale. "If you haven't time to go to the store and you can't trust Hattie, would you like me to take over the ordering and running of the house while I am here?"

"No, thank you," said Dale sweetly. "I'm afraid I just wouldn't be able to pay the bills. You don't realize, Aunt Blanche, that I have only one ration book of my own to depend upon."

"Now, Dale, don't begin to talk that way. You had a good dinner the night we came. And the next day. I'm sure if you understood running things right you could have good meals all the time without any more ration stamps. We didn't bring our books along, of course. It never occurred to me that it would be required when we were *visiting*."

"Well, I'm sorry you feel you are not well fed, but you know we do have to have ration stamps for meats and butter and lots of things, and one book of stamps doesn't go so very far. You see, that first day I had enough because I had been going without meat and butter for some days, and a lot of things that took stamps, saving up for your coming. But those saved-up stamps are all gone now, and I'm really doing the best that I can. And of course I haven't a very large budget of money to go on either, you must remember."

"Well, Grandmother left you that thousand dollars," said the aunt, almost contemptuously.

"Oh! And would you think I should use that right up for the table? And when it is gone, what would I do then?"

"Oh, I guess Grandmother gave you plenty more, if the truth were known," was the contemptuous reply. "And besides, I offered you a job that would cover your board and keep, which you turned down most ungratefully."

"Yes," said Dale gently. "I have other plans. But I am not expecting to use up my small inheritance in furnishing the table. Not at present. I'm sorry, of course, that my table doesn't please you, but it's the best I can do at present, and of course there is always the hotel and the drugstore if our table isn't satisfactory."

"Well, I think you are getting pretty impudent. I know of course Grandmother must have left you a large sum besides what was named in the will. I don't know how she got around the law, but she certainly must have had oodles of money, and naturally you got all you could out of her."

Dale was quiet for a moment trying to control her temper, and when she had been able to steady her voice, she looked up and smiled. "I'm sorry you have any such an idea of Grandmother," she said. "I may as well tell you that she had nothing whatever of her own but her small annuity, which ceased at her death. Out of that she has through the years saved a little here and a little there, until she was able to put aside enough to cover her funeral expenses and to give the few small bequests that were named in the will. She did not give me money other than was named. Now, shall we go in the other room and make our plans for the day?"

Dale rose with gentle dignity and led the way into the living room, and there was nothing left for her aunt to do but follow; that is, if she wanted to keep up the conversation.

"Now, what are you going to do this afternoon, Aunt Blanche?" asked Dale. "Is there any way I can be of service to you? Is your lawyer coming out again today?"

Her aunt gave her a sharp look, as if she suspected she might have been listening to her telephone conversations. "No," she said sharply, "he isn't. He's much too busy to devote so much time to one client, he says, but goodness knows he's being paid enough. I think he ought to give up everything else and attend to one client until he gets things started. This is unendurable, hanging around this way. Your father certainly messed things up terribly, insisting on putting everything in his own name. I don't see what right he had to do that anyway."

Dale lifted her chin a bit haughtily. "I would rather not discuss what my father did, Aunt Blanche. I have entire confidence in his actions, of course, and I think you will find that so have all the people who had to do with him in a business way."

"Oh, of course you would feel that way," said the aunt disagreeably, "no matter *what* he did."

Dale went over to pick up a book that had been dropped on the floor, and after a moment, her aunt continued: "Well, I'm certainly disgusted with everything, especially all business matters, and of course if I felt that you were willing to accept my offer and come home with us, to help run our household, I would promise to be entirely responsible for your board and keep, and we would just forget this house and wait until a good opportunity comes later to sell it. But you are determined to be stubborn, and I feel responsible for you. I've always told dear Grandma that I would look after you when she was gone and she needn't worry about that."

But Dale turned and spoke firmly. "No, Aunt Blanche, you needn't feel that way any longer. I am of age and fully able to take care of myself. I have my plans all made. I discussed them with Grandmother, and she heartily approved of everything, so you can cast aside any responsibility you have been feeling on my behalf and just make your own plans."

"But I should like to know just what your plans are. I really can't give up the burden of my responsibility for you unless I can know and approve what you are thinking of doing."

"Well, I'm sorry to disappoint you, Aunt Blanche, but my plans are not ready to be divulged yet. It is enough for me that Grandmother and my former guardian approve of them, and it is better that no one else should know anything about them yet."

"Indeed!" said her aunt. "I see you are still stubborn and impudent, and I am sure the time is not far off when you will have to regret this. I think you will find that Granniss lawyer is a fraud and is pulling the wool over your eyes."

"No," said Dale, "I am sure I will never regret it. And now, if I cannot do anything to help you in any way, I will ask you to excuse me. I have some errands downtown, which I should do this afternoon, and I think I'll go now so that I shall not be late for dinner." Dale hurried out of the room.

She went first to a store from which she could call up Mr. Granniss and report on the state of things without being overheard at home, and she received comfort in so doing.

"Buffington is just stalling for time," he said. "He hasn't a leg to stand on and he knows it. But don't worry. This will all come out right in good time. I only wish I could find some way to send your unwelcome guests home, but that might only mean they would return again, so perhaps it is better to get it all done at once."

Dale went to see three of her grandmother's old friends, who were confined to their homes or bedridden and hadn't been able to get even to the funeral. She stayed a little while with each, giving them dear little last messages from their old friend and a few little tokens, like a handkerchief, a devotional book, and a small testament Grandmother had designated for them. And when she came back to the codfish dinner, not anticipating a happy time, she was at least calm in her mind and resolved to keep sweet no matter what happened.

❦

It was quite early the next morning, before the relatives had come over for breakfast, that the telephone rang and there was David Kenyon, her officer-friend, calling her.

"Is that you, Dale?" he asked, and his voice was eager.

"Yes, David." Her heart was singing that he had called her so early before there was anyone around to listen.

"Well, my orders have come. Are you busy today? Can you meet me at the station when my train gets in, and can we have the day together?"

"*Today?*" she said joyously. "Why yes, today, of course. What time does your train get in? Eleven o'clock? Yes, I can make it.

And what time do you have to leave tonight? Ten? Yes, I can do it. I'll be there by the train gate. And if by any chance you can't find me, go to the traveler's aid desk and wait for me. But I'll be there. Good-bye."

Chapter 8

With a radiant face, Dale sat down to plan her day. She must make out the best menus she possibly could for her time of absence. There was no point in making Hattie endure the grim remarks of the relatives, which would, of course, be directed against Hattie in her absence, as if Hattie had perpetrated the whole idea. What could she have? An omelet for breakfast, *jelly* omelet? That was one of Hattie's great dishes. Dry cereal, orange juice, and raisins. For lunch, some of Hattie's delectable rice pancakes with honey; for dinner, fried chicken, mashed potatoes, and an apple pudding. That ought to be a good enough dinner for anybody, and they couldn't complain that she had run away for the day and left them without enough food.

She would start right away. She would get the chickens and anything else necessary, and hire the little Talbut boy to bring them so that she could go into the city and not have to return and explain where she was going or how long she was staying.

She went down and told Hattie what she was having for the meals. She told Hattie a friend who was passing through the city had called and asked her to come down and stay for lunch and maybe dinner. She would be back in the evening sometime. Would Hattie carry on?

Hattie's face shone with willingness.

"Sure thing, Miss Dale, I'll carry on. And I don't know one thing about where you is goin' or what you is doin'. Don't you tell me neither, and then those nosey people can't get nothin' outta me. I'm so glad you is gettin' some rest. I hopes you have a good time. Your grandma would just like that, and I hope you get all that's comin' to you. Them relatives, they is just too snooty and disagreeable, and there's no reason why you should have to dance 'tendance on them every minute. Now you just set down and eat a good breakfast, and then go get yourself all prettied up, and go off before they gets here. Then they can't get up any hindrances, for I'm just sure they would if they knowed about it. They is just folks that don't want no other folks to have a good time."

So with Hattie's help, Dale was fed, got herself dressed up, wrote menus for the day, and departed out the back door and down the backstreet before her guests arrived for their breakfast.

Hattie had agreed to explain to the aunt about her sudden telephone call, so Dale went off with all her burdens laid aside for the time being and her heart ready to take in the joy of a day's pleasant companionship.

Not until she was seated in the bus on the way to the city,

with the hometown in the background and the day before her, did she let herself think much about what the day was to bring. Then she found herself visualizing the young officer and her heart quickening over the memory of his pleasant face. Would he look as handsome to her when she met him as he had when she had first seen him? Of course he would. How silly! But still, the other recent encounters with him had been so brief and so filled with cares and duties that she had scarcely had time to study him or really to know how he did look. However, she was sure she would know him, even if he came in company with a lot of other servicemen.

It was funny to her, Dale Huntley, who had never had much time to accept attention from men, to be going out to meet a young man whom she would have all to herself for the rest of the day. Would she be able to make it interesting for him all that time? Wouldn't he soon get bored and wish he hadn't asked her to meet him? Wish he had merely called, so he could go away at any time if his interest flagged? Well, he *hadn't*, and so it was up to her to make the day interesting for him. And how should she do that?

Should she plan to take him to see the notable places in the city? Would he like that? The museums, the historic buildings?

But it was silly to try to plan until he came. He would likely know what he wanted to do, and he should be the one to choose.

Dale looked very pretty that morning. The cares and annoyances that had been with her ever since her grandmother's death were lifted from her for the time being, and she was going out to be a real girl and just have a nice time. Grandmother would have loved that for her. Dale wondered briefly if Grandmother was where she could see her and be pleased about her day.

She was wearing a simple cotton dress of blue with white printed flowers in a delicate design and a plain, little white sailor hat, not new enough to be exactly stylish but very attractive. She had always liked it and felt at home in it. Its band was a simple black velvet ribbon tied in a neat bow a little to one side on the front. There was a soft pink flush of excitement on her cheeks, her eyes were starry, a sweet smile was on her lovely lips. More than one fellow traveler in the bus looked at her with admiration, and looked again because she made a pleasant picture and was very lovely. Dale would have been amazed if anyone had told her that she was. Perhaps that was what gave the perfect touch to her loveliness, that she was utterly unaware of her own beauty. But with that bright anticipation in her eyes she was really very beautiful.

Then suddenly they were at the station, and she saw by the clock on the tower of the station that it was almost time for her navy friend's train to arrive.

She got out and hurried up to the train floor, searching out the right gate, making sure by reading the sign over the gate, asking a question of the gateman. She found that the train was on time, and though the clock on the wall said it would be there in just two minutes, those two minutes seemed each an hour long.

It was coming! She could see it down the track, a mere speck in the distance, rushing toward her. Then it had arrived, and she stood behind the gate, watching as the passengers poured from the train and crowded up to the gates.

Dale studied each face as the uniformed men came up, but

none of them was the right one, and her heart began to sink. Now the crowd was thinning; most of the passengers had entered the gates and gone on into the city. There was just one man down the length of the train, talking to a redcap, handing over some baggage, and paying some money. Could that be David? And if it was, what was he doing? And now the redcap was running toward the gate, carrying some bags, and dashing over to the checkroom. Her quick mind grasped the idea at once, and she looked back at the man. Yes, that was David. Her heart thrilled at his fine bearing, his brisk military walk. He was coming to her. He had gotten rid of his baggage for the day so that he would be free to go with her!

Her face was beaming, radiant; there was a banner of welcome in her eyes as she stood there behind the gate and looked out, and David saw her and came forward. How beautiful she was! How had he dared call her up and make a date with her?

He came to her quickly and swung inside the gate, came and took both the hands she held out to him with his own, warmly clasped, and drew her aside by the gate entrance where a few stragglers were still coming through. He held her hands an instant and looked down into her eyes, and the look he gave her set her heart to thrilling and brought the color sweetly into her cheeks.

They almost forgot that there were other people around and that some of them might be watching, for each was so engaged in reading the look in the other's eyes. But just then a group of people rushing to catch another train came bumping and elbowing by, and they had to draw farther aside. But David did not let go of the hands he was holding. He drew one of them up through his arm, and laid his other hand on the soft little hand that almost seemed to nestle on his arm. Was he imagining all this, or did she really feel as he did? He looked down at her sweet, shy face, but it was a glad look she wore. She was not annoyed, nor embarrassed. Just a great gladness seemed to envelope her, and he knew he mustn't let her know what he was reading in her eyes, not yet, anyway. Perhaps she wasn't conscious yet of her own reaction to his touch. Bless her! And he mustn't startle her with it. He mustn't run any risk of losing even a fraction of this wonderful thing that had come to be between them.

But both these young people were trained to be ready in all situations, and so it was scarcely a minute before they came to themselves and realized that they were in the way of a lot of hurrying people and must get out of it.

David smiled down into her eyes and kept his hand closed over the hand on his arm. "Come!" he said and led her across into the main station room and to the elevators. As they went slowly down, his eyes were upon hers, their glances locked in a look of delight, as if each glance were a new discovery to the other.

The elevator came to a stop, and they went out with the other passengers.

"This way," said David.

Dale smiled and turned her footsteps as he led. "Where we going?" she asked, like a pleased child in a dream.

"Do you care?" he asked, smiling. "Had you someplace you wanted to go?"

"Oh no," said Dale. "I wasn't sure just what you were planning to do, or where you would want to go."

"Then that's all right," said the young man. "The last time I was in this city I picked out a place where I would like to take you if I ever got the opportunity, and now we'll have a try at it. If you don't like it, we needn't stay there. We can easily go somewhere else later. In fact, we probably will, *later*. But—do you like the woods?"

"Oh, I *do*!" said Dale with happy eyes. "I used to think a day in the woods was the next thing to heaven when I was a little girl. And after all I've been through, this is going to be wonderful!"

"I'm glad of that," he said, pressing her fingers under his hand. "Here! Here is a taxi." He helped her in, explained to the driver where he wished to go, sat down beside her, and they were soon on their way. But the young man lost no time in quietly possessing himself of her hand again.

It seemed amazing to Dale that just a quiet handclasp could become such a wonderful thing, going to the heart of her being and bringing her closer to this almost stranger than she had ever imagined anyone could be to another.

She found her own fingers clinging to his hand and caught her breath at herself. Yet it seemed so right. Was she in a dream, and would she soon wake up and find it all had not happened? Could she be losing her head?

They whirled through the soft greenness of the park—tall trees arching overhead, wide drives and banks of shrubbery on every side, breath of the sweet out-of-doors wafting in at the open window, here and there a little cottage with some historical legend painted on a board at the side, beds of fall flowers, glimpses of the sky above, arches of a large bridge spanning overhead. It was like going into a new world. And David knew a lot about all these places. He had purposely come here on his last trip to find out about it, so that it might be of interest to them both. He was telling her now what he knew with animated words, but his hand was still warm around her own, and his eyes were telling pleasant, friendly, happy thoughts to her heart. She couldn't quite place herself in all this delight. It wasn't anything she could withdraw herself from, as her dignified life training would have admonished her at another time to do. This was a real friend, telling her good things, in a gentle, friendly way. A Christian young man. Couldn't she trust herself to be happy over it?

They climbed a hill now and dismissed the taxi, and then they turned into the deeper, higher woods until they came to a pleasant sheltered clearing where they could look out over the far world that seemed so distant and yet was so near that Dale drew her breath in delight.

They stood together for a moment, looking out across the world, David still holding Dale's hand, quietly, warmly, as if it belonged there, and then he turned and looked down at her, straight into her beautiful eyes that were looking so earnestly, so questioningly up into his, and it suddenly seemed as if their whole brief acquaintance was climaxed in that wonderful moment. David's other hand slipped out almost reverently toward her, as he bent his head and drew her close within his arms.

"Dale!" he breathed softly, in almost a whisper. "Dale! My darling! I *love* you! I love you with my whole heart! I've loved you since I first saw you. And because we've had so little time to get acquainted and I have to go away so soon, I've brought you here to this lovely spot so near to heaven to tell you about it. I pray that God will help you to forgive me for being so abrupt about this. But Dale, darling, I love you."

Then he drew her reverently closer and bent and laid his lips upon her own.

There swept over Dale such joy as she had never dreamed could come to a girl on this earth as she surrendered herself to his embrace, and her soft lips answered his caress.

They soon came to themselves, and he drew her down to sit beside him on the broad, pleasant bench that was placed comfortably behind some young hemlocks. His arms were around her, and he gently put her dear head down on his shoulder.

"Have I rushed you too much, my dear?" he asked tenderly. "I know it's a very short time to get you used to such a great love as I want to give to you before I go away, but this was all the time I had, and there hasn't seemed any other way. I love you, and when I come back I want to make you my wife—that is, if you're willing to wait for me. To take a chance that I will live to come back. Am I being too presumptuous to dare to hope you could love me?"

Dale nestled her head closer on his shoulder and her hands in his clasp. "Oh, I do love you," she murmured. "It doesn't take time to love."

"Dearest," he breathed, "perhaps that is true. As soon as I saw you, I loved you. The first time I looked at you, I said to myself, 'That is the kind of girl I would like to marry. How can I get to know her? When will there be time to win her? If I go back overseas will there ever come a time for me to be with her? How can she be willing to trust me?'"

"Trust you?" said Dale. "Oh, I trusted you the minute I saw you. But I never dreamed that you would ever love me."

"And I haven't even asked you the question that I have been

so afraid to ask. Is there someone else in your life that you love? Someone who loves you and has a right to your love? I should have asked you that first."

"Someone *else*!" laughed Dale, with a sweet little ripple of amusement as she looked up into his face. "Why no! Don't you know I've never had time to love anybody? I've never had much time to know boys and go out very often. I was in school, of course, and then there was Grandmother. She began to fail, and I had to be with her whenever I could. I loved Grandmother, you know. But oh, she would have loved you, and she would be so glad to have me love you, glad to know you love me. I think perhaps God will let her know about us."

Then he drew her closer within his arms again, and they sat quietly listening to the sweet fall sounds of nature. A few birds calling, some purple grackles crying to one another, a rusty-throated cricket rasping sharply in the thicket below them. And every sound seemed to be counting to the moments that were so precious, the moments that they still had together.

But they lived hours during those carefully dealt-out minutes. They touched on many things in their past lives, and the hours chimed dimly from some distant city tower.

And at each hour, realization would come, their hands would clasp closer and their glances would clash sadly.

And then when the distant clock struck a solemn one o'clock, David looked up suddenly and grinned at Dale. "It's time for mess," he said brightly. "Aren't you hungry?"

"Oh, I never realized," said Dale. "It's been so wonderful to be with you!"

"You sweetheart!" said David with one of his gentle looks that made Dale feel so protected and beloved.

"But I should have brought a lunch along," she said, appalled. "I never thought. I lost my head. I was so engaged in planning menus for my relative guests, so I could get away before they came to breakfast. So they wouldn't know where I had gone. And it never occurred to me I had a social obligation to us. If I had only known you were coming to a wonderful place like this!"

"Ah, but this was *my* party," said David. "You see, I invited you, so the social part was entirely up to me."

"But you had no way to get ready a lunch," said Dale. "A base wouldn't have facilities."

"Wouldn't they?" David said, grinning. "But, you see, I had other facilities besides. Wait till you see." He reached over to the end of the bench where he had parked his overcoat and pulled out packages from its ample pockets. "What do you think of that? I got those sandwiches on the diner of the train coming up. I found the fruit at a station where we stopped five minutes. And this box of candy I bought in the Washington station. I found these little paper cups there, too, and I discovered the other day that there is a little spring just around the knoll below us here. Wait, I'll bring the water while you spread out the eats."

He was gone only a minute or two, and Dale arranged the food on the bench between them as attractively as she could. The sandwiches were in neat paper wrappings. She opened the fruit bag, and there were peaches, pears, two red apples, and two bananas. He seemed to have thought of everything. She smiled to herself in admiration of his cleverness.

Then he appeared between the trees, walking cautiously, two brimming cups of water in each hand, intense attention on his face.

"There!" he said with a relieved sigh. "I didn't spill any of them. And now, would you like to have some lemonade?"

Reaching into his pocket, he produced a lemon and an envelope of sugar in triumph. "I saved that sugar from my coffee at the base for a week," he said.

"Oh, how lovely!" cried Dale. "You have thought of everything! This is a real picnic lunch."

"Yes?" he said comically. "But not as good as the lunch you would have prepared, I know."

"Oh, but you don't really know. You've never eaten any of my lunches."

"You're wrong," said the soldier positively, with a twinkling grin. "Have you forgotten the cup of hot tea you made and the doughnuts you wrestled for me at the U.S.O.?"

"Oh," said Dale, a lovely flush flaming over her sweet face. "No. I haven't forgotten. I loved doing that."

"And you didn't know me at all then," said the officer with satisfaction.

David went and stood over her and, stooping, kissed her forehead. "And you're mine now. And we feel as if we'd known each other for years."

"Oh yes!" said Dale softly.

Eventually they got down to earth and managed to eat all the sandwiches and a great deal of the fruit and to drink cups of lemonade.

And then shadows on the grass in front of the bench began to grow long, while they talked and laughed and loved each other with stars in their eyes. And finally they picked up their cups and their paper bags and the banana peels and left the lovely hidden bench behind the hemlocks. They went slowly down the hill hand in hand, knowing that they were going into the world again where there would be no cool green retreat and where they could not stop and kiss. But still as they loitered with their fingers linked together, David's arm now and again around Dale's waist, he would stoop in the shadow of some foliage and touch his lips to hers.

At the broad winding road they stopped a moment and turned back, looking up to the sheltered nook where they had been, as if it were somehow a hallowed place.

"It's been a wonderful day," said Dale wistfully, almost sorrowfully. "I wish it were just beginning!" And a bit of a sigh escaped from her lips.

"Yes," said David. "It has. And it's going to be a wonderful time to remember when I that is, when we are" he hesitated.

"Yes, I know," said Dale bravely. "I know. Don't put it into words. We'll just put the memory of this day into the place where words come that we cannot bear to speak."

They walked slowly on, keeping to the grassy side of the road where cars would not come too near.

But all too soon the walk was over and they had come to the highway and a taxi.

Seated in the taxi, Dale came to herself enough to ask a few questions. When did his train leave again? How much did he know of his destination, and could he tell her anything or must she just wait and trust? How soon, how often could he write? Oh, there were so many questions, and the afternoon was gone. She ought to have asked them before. There would come a long, lonely time when her heart would be all questions, and no way to ask them.

For answer he smiled. "It's all right, dearest," he said. "My train is supposed to leave the station at ten. Shall I take you home first, or can you find your way back alone safely after I leave? Ten o'clock is not late, and I thought I could put you in a taxi before my train comes in."

"Oh no," said Dale, "I'm used to going around alone, and ten o'clock is early. Besides, there is a bus that passes the station that comes right up to our street corner. I'm staying, please, until you leave, if you don't mind."

"That's what I hoped you would do. I want to be able to watch you out the train window as we start off. And now, here" he handed her an envelope filled with papers—"inside that envelope you will find all the addresses and the answers to as many questions as I am permitted to answer. It isn't very much, but I knew you would understand. And I'll be writing you almost at once after leaving. I couldn't do otherwise. There are so many other things we haven't had time to say. After I got my bags packed yesterday, I spent most of the time getting these things together and trying to think of everything that might come up to trouble you after I am gone. I hope I haven't forgotten anything. But if I have, we'll be able to write, and you can trust God with it. It's such a comfort that you know God and are not frivolous like so many girls I've met! I'm so glad you're the kind of girl you are. How I love you for it."

There were thrilling glances between them, even when they were where they could be overheard and could not talk privately. Dale was conscious of storing the glances away in improvised corners of her memory where she could take them out and exult in them afterward. Perhaps David, too, had visions of a time ahead when he would need such memories to help him through hard days.

He took her to a quiet restaurant where they could talk without interruption and where the food and service were of the best. He had not been idle during his days in the city and had carefully selected this place because he felt that it was to be a memorable night. He wanted everything to be the best for the sake of its memory. After all, it just might happen that it would be the only festive supper they could ever have, at least for a long, long time, and he wanted it to be happy all the way through.

They were not either of them in a mood to be very hungry and at first began to eat indifferently, but after all, they had spent the greater part of the day in the open air in the woods and that made for good appetites. So they soon began to enjoy the wonderful dinner.

"Oh David, this is going to cost a lot," protested Dale, as he kept on with his ordering.

"I hope it does," said David with a stubborn grin. "After all, it's got to stand for all the times I'll be *wanting* to take you out and can't in the next weeks, or months, or whatever it is."

"But you are ordering as if I were a princess."

"Aren't you my princess?"

"Oh," said Dale, putting shy hands up to her crimson cheeks, "I never thought anyone would call me that!"

"But why not?" asked David, watching her with happy eyes. "You are very lovely, you know."

The dinner was good, and the room was fairly quiet. They could sit there and talk. They searched out each other's innermost thoughts and rejoiced in one another. And so at last the hours sped on until it was time to hurry to the station, time for David to retrieve his checked baggage and answer the call of the train.

There were other servicemen standing there with friends, mothers, and girls, and some fathers. Tears on averted faces, earnest last words. But Dale and David had no eyes for others. They were taking those last looks at each other.

And then the final call. David stooped and kissed her now, as if he had the right before all the world to own her as his, and she dared to put her arms around his neck for one brief instant.

"It is night now," he whispered as he held her close, "but it will be day, by and by. And 'All through the night, my Savior will be watching over you,' my darling!"

One more kiss and he was gone, flying down the platform with other last ones, swinging on the train and waving his farewell. And then the train chugged out of the station and into the darkness of the night. He was gone!

Dale turned and went back into the empty station, her heart suddenly crying out for him. Then she heard his whispered song words: "*All through the night, my Savior will be watching over you,*" and she continued on, her heart comforted with the thought.

Chapter 9

All the way home, Dale was reveling in the things that had come to her and thrilling with joy over them. Life could never again be the same to her. Someone loved her! Someone wanted her, needed her. Come life or death that would always be something to rejoice over. And she did not once think what else was before her except the great empty space until her love's return, nor once remember the problems she had left behind her in her own home, problems that had loomed so large last night. Not until she got out of the bus and saw her house standing in its usual place up the hill a little way and remembered that there were other people perhaps waiting for her in her house who felt anything but love for her and who could well engender hate if one wasn't on guard continually. But all through the night her Savior would be watching over her. And He would also be there in the day, too, when problems thickened and storms arose.

Then she turned into her own street and walked up the hill and was surprised to find her home ablaze with light. Lights in every window, even up to the third story. Someone must have been rummaging. Of course Hattie hadn't discovered that yet or the lights would have been promptly turned off. But what could be the occasion of the other lights? Every room visible from the front and one side had a light in every window. Only the windows in Grandmother's locked room were dark. She was thankful for that. She had worried a little about Corliss. There was no telling if she would not even get the ax and break the door if she took the notion. She was that way, and she was so determined to take possession of that particular room, just because it was forbidden, perhaps. But Dale was greatly anxious to protect the room from desecrating prying hands and to keep it as far as possible just as Grandmother had left it. She could not bear to have it disturbed, not yet.

But now Dale hurried on, for the sounds that reached her were a bit hilarious, as if a party was under way. But who were the people?

As she reached the gate, it became apparent that the crowd in the house was not only jovial but decidedly boisterous, and one voice sounded actually *drunk*! Oh dear! Now what could be going on?

There were two men on the front porch smoking long cigars. There was a noisy bunch of youngsters on the side porch, glasses and plates in their hands, talking in loud screaming voices and beside themselves with laughter.

Unholy laughter it sounded like. But of course she must

not judge them. They were young. That was Corliss's style. But oh, it didn't sound like Grandmother's house! What should she do? Did she have to stand this?

A glance toward the living room showed her several tables set around the room, and two separate groups were sitting around the tables playing some kind of a card game, between times taking sips from glasses that contained some dark liquid. Well, it looked like a party all right, whoever the people might be, and the sounds of hilarity that boomed out from the simple old house did not seem in keeping with the atmosphere that Grandmother had always had there. Somehow it shocked Dale. Not that she disapproved of laughter and merrymaking; of course not, and neither had Grandmother. But this was not just simple-hearted merrymaking. This was more hilarious merrymaking than seemed in keeping with a beloved place where death had just been to take a dear one away.

With distress in her eyes, Dale slipped softly around to the back of the house to find Hattie, if possible, and discover just what was going on.

She did not have far to search for Hattie, for she stood in the deepest shadow just around the corner by the kitchen door, evidently watching for her.

"What is it, Hattie?" she whispered.

"Oh Miss Dale, I'm certainly thankful you've come at last. Such goings on! I did my best to stop it, but she said it was none of my business, so I took myself off where I could watch and not be seen. They think I've gone to bed, but I couldn't sleep with the likes of this goin' on, and I'm just certain they've broke into the sideboard drawer and took the best napkins, and they're usin' the Spode plates Grandma liked so much and only got out for her lovingest company," wailed the woman in a subdued whisper.

"Never mind, Hattie; don't let them hear you. Who are they, do you know? People who called to see Aunt Blanche?"

"Naw. They's just a pick-up crowd. Some that old Buffington brang along and some she brang over from the hotel! She come out into the kitchen and says they was gonna have a party and if I wanted to make some cakes and wait on her company, she'd give me a whole dollar for the evening. I said no, I worked for *you*, and I couldn't do nothin' you hadn't told me to do, and anyhow I was tired and half sick and I was goin' to bed. So I went off and 'tended like I was goin' up to my room. But I come right down soon as I heard tell what she was doin'. She went to the telephone, and she called up a lotta numbers, and she got a case of liquor sent over from the hotel and a lot of cakes and ice creams and things, and then she rafted round the furniture till you wouldn't never know the place. And Miss Corliss, she went out and searched up a couple'a soldiers and a drunken sailor, and that brother of hers brought three of the toughest girls I've seen in this town, besides one boy, Greek Lufty, who has just come home from reform school! Listen to 'em sing them sickenin' songs. It worse'n ever anythin' comes over the radio. Now Miss Dale, what ya goin' to do? We can't have no goin's on like this is Grandma's place, now she's gone."

Dale had been thinking rapidly as Hattie talked. "No," she said thoughtfully. "Wait. Let me think! I'll tell you, Hattie. Suppose you run over to Mrs. Relyea's back door—I see there's a light in the kitchen there yet—and ask her if you may call up somebody on her telephone. Tell her there's so much noise over here with my aunt's friends that we couldn't phone without them all hearing. And then you go in and call up Mr. Granniss's number and ask him if he and Mrs. Granniss can come over here quickly, that I need them both in a hurry."

"Yes ma'am! That's a good idea."

"If he wants to know what it's all about, tell him my aunt has a very noisy party here and I don't know how I can quiet it down. He'll understand, and he promised to help any time."

Dale stood still in the darkness of the backyard and tried to think how this thing was going to work out. Suppose Mr. Granniss was not at home? Suppose Hattie came back having failed to reach him? What should she do? There wasn't a neighbor she cared to bother to help her. Indeed, they were mostly quiet women or shy men. They wouldn't be able to get anywhere with that crowd in there. It would take a person with some degree of sophistication to deal with a problem like this. In fact, there were only a few lights downstairs in any house along the street, indicating that her neighbors were going to bed at this hour. They were early risers, most of them war-workers in some way. Poor things! They must have been annoyed at the unusual tumult on their quiet street. Her cheeks burned with mortification as she thought of explanations she would have to give to a few who were always wondering about anything unusual.

Then suddenly Hattie was beside her, looming out of the darkness, all out of breath from hurrying over the rough grass so her footsteps would not be heard on the walk. By the party.

"He's comin'," panted Hattie, "right away, he said, and he said to tell you not to worry. It'll be all right. He's bringin' somebody with him, and he'll see that they understand the situation. Mrs. Granniss is comin', too. Now, what all you want I should do?"

"Well, I think *I'll* have to go in and do something," said Dale with a troubled glance toward the house. "Suppose you slip in and stay where you can hear if I need you. Is there anything around in the kitchen that needs clearing up? Just seem to be busy, you know."

"There's plenty," said Hattie grimly. "There's a whole lot of bottles in some kind of a contraption, right in the middle of my kitchen floor. They come out as big as you please and open up their bottles and cut their cake, and they took our best dishes and broke one right before my face, when they first asked me to serve, and they was mad 'cause I said I worked only for you and under your orders. They was hoppin' mad."

"Well," said Dale, "I'll go in and see what I can do. Perhaps they will go home of their own accord and we can phone Mr. Granniss not to come."

"Not them, they won't. They ain't that kind! You'll see!"

So Dale went into the house the front way and paused in the living room door. "Oh," she said with well-feigned surprise, "you have guests, Aunt Blanche. It is nice that you were not lonely. I didn't know that you had friends living near."

Dale looked around with her sweet engaging smile and hoped her hands were not trembling. She did not know how very sweet and young and beautiful she looked, with the quick color in her cheeks and her eyes so starry bright. The guests looked up in amazement, and one sophisticated woman from the hotel asked, "Why, who is this, Mrs. Huntley? I did not know you had a young niece. Won't she come and play with us?

That will just make up for Buff, if he really has to go."

Aunt Blanche froze into haughtiness and performed a few reluctant introductions, beginning with, "Oh Dale, is that you? I understood you were to be quite late tonight."

Then the men drew near, including the lawyer Buffington, quite openly admiring the pretty newcomer. There arose a clamor for Dale to take off her hat and join them in their game, and one of the men hurried to her with a glass of wine.

"You'll have a glass of wine first, won't you, Miss Huntley? And shall I get you a piece of cake?"

Looking up, Dale caught a glimpse of an angry, jealous Corliss scowling, but somehow she was enabled to keep on smiling as she shook her head courteously. "No, thank you. Nothing to eat or drink. And I don't play cards, so I'm sure I wouldn't be any addition to your number. But now, if you've all quite finished your refreshments, I'll have Hattie remove the plates and glasses, if you don't mind. You see, I have some friends coming to see me shortly. So I thought it would look a bit tidier if we just got rid of the dirty dishes."

"Oh for heaven's sake!" said the aunt, rising in anger. "You have people coming here at this hour? You have no right to do that, right in the middle of my party!"

"Sorry, Aunt Blanche. But you didn't tell me you were having a party." Dale smiled.

"Oh for Pete's sake!" Corliss shouted furiously. "Can you beat that?"

"Well Dale, you know now, so go to the phone at once and call them. Tell them they can come tomorrow night or some other time but you find it isn't convenient now."

"I can't very well do that Aunt Blanche, for they are just

arriving at the door now."

"Oh, certainly you can! I'll send Corliss or Powelton out to inform them the house is occupied and they'll have to come again."

Powelton quickly dodged around the corner of the porch out of sight and remarked aloud to himself or to Corliss, who had also dodged out of sight, "Well, for crying out loud! Can you beat it?"

But Dale paid no heed to her aunt's admonition. She was at the door now, her hands extended cordially and a little lilt in her voice as she said clearly, "Oh Mrs. Granniss! I'm so glad you were able to come! And how lovely that you brought the Bonniwells with you. This makes it just perfect!"

But behind Dale the former guests sprang to their feet in consternation, with a shower of playing cards all over the floor at their feet where they had fallen from the hand of the one who was dealing.

So the guests entered, five of them. The Grannisses and the Bonniwells and their charming daughter, the latter in a gorgeous evening dress.

"You must excuse our formal dress," said Mrs. Bonniwell, entering cordially into the room and not seeming to notice what was going on. "We have just come from the Newell wedding, you know, and the Grannisses simply insisted that we join them here. I do hope we're not intruding."

But Dale turned graciously, looked at the dismayed group behind her, and began her introductions with pleasant poise, more than she likely would have had if there had not been the interval out in the darkness of the backyard to prepare herself and gather strength from above.

"This is my aunt Mrs. Huntley, Mr. Bonniwell. I think you, Mrs. Granniss, have met her before, haven't you?"

The incoming guests were full of courtesy and graciousness and appeared not to notice the distraught look of the formally jovial crowd. Of course they couldn't know how funny they were, caught all unawares with that ridiculous shower of cards at their feet and that guilty look over them all. The strangers from the hotel were impressed with the newcomers. The Grannisses were always distinguished-looking people, and the elegant simplicity of the Bonniwells, even the young daughter, was demanded attention, and they looked the Bonniwells over thoroughly and realized that these were people from another world.

But it was Greenway Buffington who seemed the most uncomfortable and made the first move, with a troubled glance at his watch. "I'm afraid I must be moving on, Mrs. Huntley. You know I told you my time was limited." And with a hurried bow toward that embattled lady, he turned to slide out by the dining room door, thus sidestepping any contact whatever with that Granniss man, of whom he was not at all enamored, was in fact at present almost afraid. At least afraid that here was one who would upset his own plans for personal aggrandizement with this rather promising client.

Now Hattie had been quietly, deftly stepping around the living room, picking up and removing first the precious Spode plates, which she had placed safely on the dining room table, then the glasses. She had just gone through the dining room door and was carefully turning around to avoid hitting a chair in her way when Lawyer Buffington barged through the door, coming full tilt against her tray, which was more than overloaded, some of the glasses having just been refilled and Hattie trying to keep them from slopping over.

But Lawyer Buffington was coming full sail with plenty of power behind him, and he hit the loaded tray squarely and knocked the glasses everywhere, not only making a great crash but also a widespread splash, for the wine sloshed all over his immaculate white suit, streaming down in ugly dark rivulets and up into his face, even in his eyes, utterly putting him out of commission for the moment as far as sight was concerned.

Meanwhile the whole tray of glasses went down on the dining room hardwood floor with a mighty crash, and Hattie could do nothing about it. But before she tried to pick anything up or even to exclaim over what had happened, she did have presence of mind enough to reach out and close that dining room door, thus shutting the other guests out of the scene of disaster and shutting them into their own utter undoing.

The first impulse of the strangers caught in the general melee was flight.

"I really think we should be going, too," spoke up the woman from the hotel who had suggested the way to get the wine and had drunk deeply of it already. "You know, my dear, we are greatly indebted to you for this delightful party." She turned to Aunt Blanche hastily and gave her a hurried little pat on the shoulder. "And you have made it so delightful for us that the time has passed for us before we knew it. Do you realize how late it is? I am afraid the band has finished my piece that I especially requested for tonight, and I promised I would be there to applaud. Come friends, we must 'scram' quickly, isn't that what the children say? Good night! See you in the morning!" And the visitor scrammed.

It was really very funny when one was looking on. The guests that Aunt Blanche had brought in through Lawyer Buffington made brisk adieus and vanished. Aunt Blanche and her two guests from the hotel decided they, too, must leave. The young people had disappeared.

And when the sound of the hurrying cars that they had come in was dying out in the distance, the Grannisses and the Bonniwells and Dale by common consent sat down and laughed.

"Well," said Mr. Granniss, taking off his glasses and wiping them on his immaculate handkerchief, "that was about the easiest job of ejection I ever was called upon to do."

And then they all laughed again.

In the sudden silence that followed the second laughter they could hear a broom plying in the dining room and the tinkle of broken glass as Hattie hurried to clear away the traces of disaster.

Then Dale rose and opened the door. "Don't you want more light, Hattie?" she asked. "There are bits of glass on this side of the door, too. I saw them fly under through the crack."

"Yes ma'am, Miss Dale," said Hattie in almost a sob. "I spec's somehow this whole thing was somehow my fault, but there didn't seem no way I could have prevented it. Here's only just one thing to be thankful for. There ain't none of them Spode cups your grandma laid such store by broke, not a one. And I got money enough to buy new glasses, so you needn't worry none, Miss Dale. I was only tryin' to get outta that old galoot's way, and he come bargin' right in on me."

That started the group laughing again, and Dale had to go right up to Hattie and tell her she was proud of her, and she didn't mind it happening, and it would be all right, and she needn't pay for the glasses—they were only cheap ones, anyway— and they all knew it wasn't her fault. And then Hattie recovered so that she was able to come into the living room and laugh with the rest. It might be that if Aunt Blanche had seen that—Hattie in the best room laughing at her crowd and hobnobbing along with the elegant Mrs. Bonniwell—she would have passed right out. Dale was thankful she wasn't there and need never know it.

"I can never thank you enough for coming to my rescue, Mr. Granniss," said Dale. "I was perfectly appalled when I got back here and found what was going on. And I don't know what the neighbors are thinking of it yet. They are such quiet, respectable people and such dear friends of Grandmother's. It would seem to them such a desecration."

"I don't wonder, my dear," said the old guardian. "And I'm glad you called on us. Do it again as often as there is need. Of course you understood that I would tell the Bonniwells all about the circumstance and they were delighted to help."

"Well, it was wonderful. And it was all the better that they were wearing such lovely garments. I could see the evening dresses went over big. One diamond speaks volumes to my aunt and cousins."

"You dear child! Well it's good the diamonds can be of real use somewhere," said Mrs. Bonniwell, smiling. "And I'm sorry, dear, that you are having such an uncomfortable time—just after your recent sorrow. But don't worry. This sort of thing doesn't last forever, and someday it will pass. I'm so glad to have had an opportunity to help in a small way, and of course you understand I'll say nothing about all this to anyone."

When they were gone, Dale felt a surge of relief and a return of her joyous thrills as she remembered David Kenyon and the day they had spent together.

She turned out the porch light, gave a quick comprehensive glance around the disheveled living room, and then turned toward the open dining room door where Hattie stood, her face drawn into the most disapproving expression she knew how to wear.

"Well," she said with a tone like a punishment, "now will you do something about her? *Now* will you see what I mean and send her off?"

"Listen, Hattie," said Dale, still with that lilt in her voice, for somehow she was sensing that there was a new joy to revel in, in spite of all her annoyances. "What would you think I should do?" Dale said, smiling. "You know, after all, Grandmother wouldn't want me to be rude to her. But I think there will be a way, somehow. I think God will do something about it."

"*Rude!*" sniffed Hattie. "I should say *she* was being rude to you."

"Well, perhaps that doesn't matter, Hattie. I'm a Christian, and I must be sure not to do anything the Lord would not approve."

"Now, Miss Dale!" sniffed Hattie indignantly. "You *know* the Lord couldn't never like such actions as was goin' on here tonight. Drinkin' and shoutin' crazy things so all the neighborhood could hear. Desecrating the home of one of the holiest woman that ever lived on this earth."

Dale drew a trembling, troubled breath. "I know, Hattie. It was rather dreadful, wasn't it? I'm sure we shall hear from the neighbors tomorrow in some way. I think they must have been shocked. No, I'm sure it wouldn't have pleased the Lord, but the Lord never set me to judge other people's wrong actions."

"Well, I ain't so sure," said Hattie. "This here is *your* house, ain't it? Nobody else can say what shall go on here, but *you* can. And surely you don't think the Lord wants such doin's in a Christian home. You don't think that's honorin' Him, do you?"

"No, I suppose not," said Dale thoughtfully. "But I'm not just sure yet what *I* should do. I'll think it over, and I'll pray it over, and I'll ask the Lord to take charge. Of course if it's only a matter of annoyance to *us*, or even embarrassment, maybe we are supposed to be gentle and forgive and stand it."

"No *sir*, Miss Dale, not in your own house! If you was a man, you'd just tell her it couldn't go on. Of course I know you be young and it ain't easy to speak up to a humbugger like that aunt, but I guess somehow you gotta do it."

"I'll pray about it," said Dale, smiling and patting Hattie's shoulder. "But now, come on and let's go to bed. You lock up the kitchen, and I'll lock up the front."

So the two went to work and soon were up in their rooms preparing for rest.

As Dale turned out her light, she paused a moment by her window in the darkness and looked at the sky. Dark, dark blue set out with stars, many of them. And off somewhere under those stars David was in a train hastening away from her into another world. He hadn't said which way after New York, but she had a feeling it might be west. But she knew in her heart he was thinking of her wherever he was. And she stood there thanking her heavenly Father for the wonderful love that had come so unexpectedly into her lonely young life.

A little later she lay down on her bed, her heart at rest. All through the night her Savior would be watching over her. She was content to trust the annoyances and necessities to Him. He would know how to control this thing, and she would leave it to her heavenly Father.

Chapter 10

The morning mail brought a brief letter for Dale, sent special delivery, mailed on the train. How had he managed to get it sent in time to reach here so soon?

My precious Dale:

It seems incredible that I have the right to call you mine. Only just this morning I didn't, you know, and my heart is full of rejoicing that you have given me this right.

Oh my darling, I thank my God that as I go out into the unknown I may carry the knowledge of your love with me and leave my love with you.

And I am deeply grateful for the lovely little

*picture of yourself you gave to me. I shall carry it
close to my heart, all the way, wherever I go.*

*And there is another picture of you that I
shall carry in my memory. The lovely vision that
you were as I met you this morning. It is fixed in
my thoughts indelibly. Did I tell you how beautiful you looked to me? But perhaps there were too
many other things to say and the time was too
short. So I will save it up in my mind, for every
detail of the blue dress and the charming little
hat that seemed so fitting for you is stored away
in my heart so that I can take it out and look at
it, and I shall be writing you from time to time
and telling you about it. There isn't time now, for
I want to go back to the mail car and see if I can
wangle this into the mailbag that is thrown off
when we meet the express pretty soon.*

*I love you, my sweet, and I had to tell you
again before I slept. And may the dear Lord be
close beside you continually to comfort and guide
you all the way, till we meet again.*

*Yours,
David*

Dale went hurriedly up to her room, hugging the thought
to her heart that this letter had reached her before Corliss arrived, for if she had been here she would have been sure to
meet the postman and sign for the letter and been sure to examine it thoroughly before she brought it to her. Perhaps she

wouldn't even have brought it. That was a thought. She must do something about her mail. There would be other letters, she hoped. She could not have them at the mercy of Corliss. Of course she could take a box at the post office and have all her personal mail held there. It would be best if she did that at once. Meantime, she must meet the postman herself until she was sure this had been done. Corliss was a little vandal. She wouldn't hesitate to destroy mail before it had been read if she got the chance, or if she thought it would annoy her cousin. Besides, she would delight to try and find out personal matters and annoy her by speaking of them at most inopportune moments. She must lose no time. With a quick glance at the clock, Dale hurried down to the post office and arranged for a box. This wasn't going to be a bit convenient, but it was going to be necessary as long as her relatives were with her. With a sigh, she wondered if she would find out anything that morning about their plans.

But when she reached home again they had not as yet come over to breakfast.

"Maybe they had too much last night," said Hattie with a grin. "Maybe they decided to leave today."

Dale shook her head. "No such good luck, Hattie," she said with a smile. "There are a couple of suitcases upstairs in the room where Aunt Blanche takes her naps, and a lot of their other belongings."

"Well, I wouldn't put it past 'em to telephone you to pack 'em up and send 'em on," said Hattie. "Want I should tell you what I think? *I* think they're ashamed to come back after the way they acted last night. They know the whole neighborhood would be roused up against 'em, after yelling and screaming the way they did in Grandma's house just after she's gone."

"No, I'm afraid not, Hattie. They have no such shames. In fact, I don't believe they were ashamed. I think they were only angry because I brought Mr. Granniss here when that other lawyer had brought his friends. They are staying away now to punish me, perhaps. Or else they stayed up so late last night that they haven't got up yet."

"Well, whatever it is," said Hattie grimly, "I s'pose you'll forgive 'em and be as sweet as a peach to 'em. What you goin' to give 'em to eat today? Roast turkey or pheasants' breasts? Me, I'd give 'em another dose of codfish, and even that's too good for 'em."

"Was there enough chicken left to make a few sandwiches?" asked Dale.

"Couple a wings and a few scraps. But you forget. The princess don't care for sandwiches."

"Well, that doesn't matter, I suppose. But perhaps you better cream it and put it on toast. It will go further that way."

"Okay," said Hattie affably, "and we'll have a gelatin pudding. There is some extra milk oughtta be used up."

"That's all right, Hattie. And fix a little salad of some kind, too."

"Oh, all right. It'll piece out. But you just baby those folks, I say. After they acted like they did I should say it didn't matter if they had anything to eat or not. But I'll make it."

Hattie went away with a chastened look on her grim face, and Dale smiled after her and went upstairs to write an answer to her letter and send it immediately so it would get to her beloved at the first possible moment.

So she sat joyously down and began to write.

It was quite a good deal later that Dale heard a sputtering of angry voices, mounting to a perfect tornado of sound that bore the accents of Hattie in her most indignant mood. And then haughty indignation from her aunt, interspersed by screaming denunciations from both Corliss and Powelton.

Dale smiled, half-amused, and went on with her writing, but she drew a sad little sigh. It was scarcely possible to continue writing loving words when arguments were going on so near to her. She folded her letter, locked it away in the little secret drawer of her desk, and took out fresh paper. There were other notes she must write. She would get those done now while her mind was likely to be distracted. She could not bear to write to David out of the midst of annoyances. He would have enough battles to think about without getting even a hint of her own home-front battles. He must not even get the subconscious atmosphere of distress.

So she began to write thank-you notes to people who had sent flowers to Grandmother's funeral and to some who had written beautiful letters of condolence. She soon grew interested in getting as many as possible ready for the mail. She had no wish to go down into the atmosphere she was sure she would find in the dining room. So she wrote on.

But after a little while she heard footsteps coming up the stairs and then became aware of someone standing in her open door, looking severely at her. But even then she did not stop writing or look up.

"Oh, so you *pretend* to be *very busy*!" said the sharp, querulous voice of the aunt. "You have no apologies to offer for the outrageous way in which I was treated last night."

Quietly Dale looked up, her pen poised for the next words

she was about to write. "Apologies?" said Dale with a surprised lifting of her brows. "Apologies for what? Or—did you mean *you* came to apologize?"

"*I? Apologize?*" screamed the aunt. "Why should *I* apologize?"

"Well, I am afraid I wouldn't just know what you would consider a sufficient reason for apology," said Dale, speaking gently, almost as one would speak to a child who had misbehaved. "Perhaps you did not realize that the whole street, who are all very dear friends of Grandmother's, were greatly scandalized at the sounds of hilarity that proceeded from the home where she had lived, so soon after her death. You see, the people around this neighborhood are quiet, respectable people who are not in the habit of attending nightclubs and getting even slightly tipsy, and to hear such sounds coming from Grandmother's home shocked them. But you are a comparative stranger here, of course, and did not know those people who came here and probably thought you could not help what your guests did. I felt rather mortified for you."

"*What?*" screamed the aunt. "*You* felt mortified for *me?* You outrageous little baggage you! And what did you think of yourself, coming in to *my party* and bringing a lot of old fogies and practically sending my guests all home? Have *you* any apologies? Oh no! You turn on us, your guests. It is a pity that Grandma couldn't have lived long enough to know just how rude you were to her nearest relatives."

Dale looked at her aunt steadily. "Aunt Blanche, what did I do but come to my own home, where I had a perfect right to come, and expect quietness and respectability, and introduce my friends who are among the finest in our city? I am afraid I do not see any reason for apology in anything I did. And now,

Aunt Blanche, since we are coming to some understanding I think I should go on and explain that I am starting a school for the children of defense workers here in the house and that after next week I shall not be free any longer to entertain guests. I am sorry to have to seem inhospitable, but the matter has been all arranged, and I have promised to undertake it without any further delay. I don't know what your plans are or whether you were arranging to stay in this region longer than next week or not, but if you feel that you would like to stay I think I can suggest several nice places down farther toward the city where you might secure board."

"Well, *really!*" said Aunt Blanche, rising and snapping her furious eyes. "So we are being turned out of the house, are we? Well I shall certainly remember that."

"But I haven't meant it that way, Aunt Blanche. You see, I have a regular job, at least for the duration. Grandmother helped me plan it. Besides, Hattie is going to the hospital for an operation pretty soon, and I can't possibly look after twenty children and cook meals for a family besides. I'm sure you must see how it is."

"No, I don't see how it is at all," snapped her aunt. "In the first place, you never had to take a job like that. And certainly you don't need to begin it while we are here. As for Hattie, she isn't the only working woman left in the world. And I'll engage to get you another as good or better than she is. Certainly I'm not going to leave here to accommodate Hattie. Not until my business is finished, anyway."

"I'm sorry, Aunt Blanche, but you can't run my life for me. I'm of age, and this is my house. I'll do all I can to find a pleasant place for you to board. I'm sure there must be one that wouldn't cost you as much as you are paying now at the hotel."

"*I* am paying!" screamed the angry woman. "It was not *my* idea going to the hotel, in the first place. It was *you* who suggested it, and therefore the paying was *your responsibility*. I told the hotel manager when I went there that they might send the bill to you, and it will probably be here in a day or two. I understand they send bills at the end of the week, or perhaps month. I don't know which. But you'll find out."

"Aunt Blanche, I'm not going to argue with you, but certainly I am not responsible for your bills at the hotel, and I shall not pay any of them! You had no right to tell them I would. I shall certainly make that plain to their management. But I'm sorry you do not understand. I am not doing this to be disagreeable. I am only telling you what my present obligations and plans arc. And inasmuch as you arc not staying hcrc nights, anyway, I didn't think it would make so much difference to you where you ate. Besides, you haven't seemed satisfied at all with our food. Certainly you wouldn't want to be coming to meals with twenty children running all over the place, would you?"

"*Twenty* children! That's ridiculous! What right did you have to take twenty children into the house, especially when you had relatives visiting you? This is the most absurd thing I ever heard of, and you might as well understand *now* as anytime that I *am not* going anywhere else. I am staying *right here*! We are the wife and children of Grandma's son, and that at least gives us the right to stay in her house, even if she did see fit to leave it to you. And while we are talking about it, you may as well understand that Corliss is going to have Grandma's room from now on. If you don't unlock that door I shall get a carpenter this morning to do so, and you can't do anything about it. I'll see if I have to stay in a hotel because a little up-start of a girl like you takes a notion to be disagreeable. Now, I hope you understand. I'm going out for an hour, over to the hotel to get our suitcases. And when I get back, if Grandma's room isn't open I shall phone for a carpenter at once to knock down the door!"

Then Aunt Blanche rose with a grand gesture and left the room. Dale's heart went down with a thud. What was she going to do about this?

Suddenly she got up, locked her door, and knelt beside her bed.

"Dear Lord, I'll just put this all in Your hands. Will You please help me and show me what to do. Please don't let me have to fight for my rights."

For some little time after she rose from her knees she stood by her window looking out. Was she wrong? Could it possibly be required of her to let the vandal relatives into Grandmother's precious room? Was she making too much of this? She did not worship that room in any sense, but it was a dear place to her with precious memories. Even now in her mind she could see Corliss jeering at the little framed sampler hanging on the wall that Grandmother's little-girl hands had wrought: "*The LORD is my light and my salvation; whom shall I fear? the LORD is the strength of my life; of whom shall I be afraid?*"

She could see the sneer that would curl Corliss's lips, the ugly antipathy that would register in her expression as she read that. She could see Corliss's hands snatching the poor old sampler down and stamping on it, smashing the glass that protect-ed it, if she were ever allowed the freedom of that room. She could see the derision that would greet the quaint old picture of Grandfather, with his old-fashioned haircut and the stock around his neck. Corliss simply wouldn't be able to comprehend how anybody who looked like that picture could possibly be dear to anyone, and she would never stop her vandalism because somebody else reverenced the object of her scorn.

The quaint little vases on Grandmother's bureau, with their guilt edges and their hoop-skirted maidens and old-time suitors. They would all come in for her contempt.

Grandmother's old rocking chair with its patchwork cushions made of the pieces of family dresses of bygone days. Grandmother's pretty little desk that Grandfather had bought for her, with its small bundles of precious letters and papers, every one of them heirlooms that under Grandmother's direction had been left there for Dale to read over and put away among the other heirlooms. There hadn't been time for her to go over everything since Grandmother's last attack that brought her death. And she must do it quietly, without stranger's eyes looking on. There was no use. She simply couldn't let Corliss into that room. Not unless everything was first moved out, and there wasn't any place to put the things if she were to try to do that.

She thought of the neat piles of Grandmother's garments and the little gray dresses hanging in the closet, including the shining gray silk to be worn with the lovely white lace kerchiefs in the top drawer of the bureau. She thought of the fine silk shawl with long handsome fringe that Grandfather had bought for Grandmother on their first wedding anniversary. She imagined how Corliss might stretch it around her and sail out even into the street dragging it behind her as if it were an evening dress. Corliss was capable of all sorts of things like that. She remembered the groups of much-loved photographs of Grandmother's old-fashioned family, even the daguerreotypes of her two boys, now dead. Oh, she couldn't have Corliss laughing at their strange clothes, their little copper-toed shoes, as they stood sturdily beside the photographer's chair, one hand stiffly outstretched to grip the plush arm. Oh, surely it wouldn't be right to let the relatives in there, to destroy all that belovedness that Grandmother had meant to leave for her memory. They had often talked about it. So she wasn't being just selfish. And it wasn't as if it would have done Corliss any definite good to sleep in that room. It was just a notion she had taken, which would probably pass. Probably the only reason she wanted the room was because she knew that Dale treasured it, and she had always enjoyed being unpleasant to Dale.

However, of course she was not going to allow any carpenter to knock the door down. That was absurd. She would do her best to settle this matter peaceably, but if not, she would have to resort to—well, what could she resort to? Of course she might appeal again to Mr. Granniss, but she couldn't bear to trouble him with such trifling matters of bickering. Well, she had told the Lord about it, now what was there else for her to do?

But down in the kitchen Hattie, who had hung around at the foot of the back stairs listening and had heard the whole conversation between Dale and her aunt, decided to take matters into her own hands. So she called up the back stairs to Dale: "I'm just goin' down to the drugstore to get some more pills. I took the last one last night and I need some more. Is there anythin' you want, Miss Dale?"

"No Hattie, not unless—why yes, we need some peanut butter and some cinnamon. You might get a yeast cake, too, and make a few cinnamon buns."

"Yes'm," said Hattie. "Okay by me," and then under her breath, "though what you want to pamper that old battleax and her brats for I don't see!" So Hattie made her hurried way to the drugstore and called up Mr. Granniss. She felt that he was a tower of strength at all times.

"Mister Granniss, sir, I hope I's not interruptin' your work, but there's a question I like to ask. Is there any way you can stop a relative from tearin' down a door when she wants to get in a room where you don't want her? 'Cause that old battleax of an aunt has gone after a carpenter to break down a door of Grandma's room so her girl can have that for her room. And is there any way to stop her?"

"Why yes, I think there is, Hattie. Does Miss Dale know you are calling me? Did she ask you to?"

"Oh no, sir, Mister Granniss. And don't you go tell her, neither. I just overheard a conversation, and I thought maybe I oughtta do somethin' about it."

"Well, don't you worry, Hattie; I'll look into things. I don't think she'd dare go that far anyway."

"Oh yes she would. You don't know that woman."

"All right, Hattie. I'll look after it."

"Okay, thanks, Mister Granniss!" And Hattie hung up and went for her pills and cinnamon.

What Mr. Granniss did was to call up the police headquarters that wasn't far from the Huntley home.

"Is that you, Mike? Well, glad I caught you. This is Granniss. I think I want your help in something. It's rather a difficult matter, and as usual I'm butting into affairs that don't perhaps rightly concern me. So I thought I better rope you into it. You remember Dale Huntley, the little girl you used to look out for when she went to school?"

"Sure thing I do," said Mike heartily. "Her Grandma died the other day, didn't she?"

"Yes, she did, and she's having a stiff time of it just now. Some in-laws came to the funeral and don't seem to know enough to go home. The woman is the widow of Dale's uncle Harold, and she's a handful. She's trying to make it appear that she ought to inherit at least a part of that house, and she's making life miserable for Dale. She hasn't, of course, a leg to stand on, for the house is Dale's out and out, but while she's trying to see what she can work, she's doing everything she can to make herself unpleasant. Just now I hear she's taken a notion she wants her daughter to have Grandmother's room, and because Dale has locked the door and doesn't want it opened—wants to keep it just as her grandmother left it—the aunt has gone off to get a carpenter to break down the door. Can you manage to stop that, Mike? You see, Dale doesn't know I know. Hattie, the maid, phoned me. I wonder if you can't invent a reason for hanging around and helping out if it really comes to a showdown."

"Sure thing, Mr. Granniss. I'll find a way. Dale used to be a little pal of mine in her school days."

The big policeman asked a few more questions and promised to do what he could to keep an eye on the house, and when he had hung up, he gave a few terse directions to some of his men and then went out, walking in the vicinity of the Huntley house, first encircling it at a distance until he had pretty well taken in everything that was going on. From different points he did some watching of the house, and it was how he came to finally see Aunt Blanche approaching purposefully up the street with a shambling, ancient carpenter carrying a small chest of tools in her wake. She had the appearance of towing him, like a truck and a trailer. Mike smiled grimly behind his hand and changed his position somewhat so that he could take in the whole situation.

Aunt Blanche came briskly up the steps of the house and let herself and her workman into the living room, not pausing to look for anybody but mounting the stairs determinedly, the carpenter obediently following her.

Mike, by this time, had crossed the road and put himself within hearing distance, for just then Aunt Blanche had her hands full and was not listening for rubber-shod footsteps behind her.

Dale stood at the head of the stairs, blocking the way to Grandmother's room effectually.

But the aunt's voice was determined and clear as she pointed to the closed door down the hall. "That is the door we want opened," she said forcefully. "Someone has locked it, and we need to get in."

But Dale stepped up in front of the carpenter. "No," she said firmly, "we do *not* want that door open, Mr. Moxey. My aunt is mistaken. This house is mine, and I definitely do not want the door open. I locked it myself and do not wish it interfered with."

"But lady, you said the *owner* wanted it open—" said the old man, turning puzzled eyes to Aunt Blanche's angry face.

"You don't understand, carpenter. I am really the owner of the house, though there are some legal matters to be attended to before I take possession, but I *must* have the door open at once, and I'll pay you double what you asked if you do it at once without further discussion. Step aside, Dale, and let him pass. I simply won't be interfered with."

But it was not Dale but the policeman who did the stepping. He strode up the two remaining steps of the stairs and planted himself right in the way between Aunt Blanche and the closed door.

"Sorry, madam, I'll have to interfere. This house belongs to Miss Dale, and she's the only one who has a right to say whether her doors shall be open or not. So, Moxey, you better scram! You don't do any carpentry work on this home unless Miss Dale Huntley hires you to do it. So scram! And do it quick if you don't want me to take you to the station house."

"Now look here!" said Aunt Blanche. "Who are you, I should like to know, and what business have you butting in on my affairs?"

"I'm the chief of police, ma'am, and this doesn't happen to be your affair. It is entirely Miss Dale's affair, and she says she doesn't want her grandmother's door open, so it doesn't get opened. I've been asked to look after Miss Dale's affairs and keep an eye on her house, and I'm doing it. I've known Miss Dale since she was a baby, and I don't intend she shall be put upon. I don't know who you are or what right you have in this house, but if you don't belong here, *you* better scram, too."

"The idea! The very idea! I'm Dale's aunt, and I've come here to look after her affairs for her since her grandmother died. So, you see, she doesn't need your care any longer. *I'm* here to do that."

"No ma'am. You made a mistake. You ain't Miss Dale's guardian, and I happen to know she's of age and don't need no guardian no more. I'm just here to look out she ain't bothered, not even by a so-called relative."

"Oh! So that's the idea," said the irate aunt. "Dale sent for you, did she? And she asked you to protect what she chooses to think is her own. Well, Dale, I didn't think you'd descend to sending for the police, but since you have, I shall have to send for my lawyer."

"Send for all the lawyers you want, lady," said the imposing policeman, "but you'll still find you're up against something bigger than lawyers, and that's the law. But you're wrong about Miss Dale. She didn't send for me, and I didn't know just how she felt about this door till I come up the stairs and heard her say she didn't want it tore down, so I thought it was time for me to get to work. And now, lady, I'll thank you to walk downstairs and to look out that you don't make any more attempts to tear down this door or else I'll have to take you to the station house."

"Why, you—*you*—out*rageous* creature. To talk to a lady like that! I shall certainly report you and have you ousted from your job!"

Mike grinned. "Sorry, ma'am, I just made one mistake in this here transaction. I shouldn't have called you a lady, I see, but we'll let it go this time. Would you like me to help you down the stairs?"

"You let me alone. You take your hand off my shoulder this instant!"

"Okay, ma'am, just as soon as you scram!"

Aunt Blanche, as she felt the iron hand of the law tighten on her shoulder, scrammed rapidly, so that she almost fell full-length down the stairs, except for the firm hold of the policeman, which steadied her safely to the hall below.

Mike steered her to a comfortable chair, sat her down, and stood ominously before her.

"Now, ma'am," he said grimly, "if I hear of any more doings like this, you may expect me around to escort you to the station house. I hope you understand!"

Then getting no answer from the frightened woman he turned and went out into the hall, where he addressed the anxious Dale who was coming down the stairs.

"Now, Miss Dale, if this so-called lady pulls any more pranks like this, just you send word to me. You still got Hattie, haven't you? Well, you can have her call me on the phone if anything like this happens again, and I'll be here before you can count to ten. I guess maybe it wouldn't be a bad idea to have your lawyer tell this person that you own the house, and if that doesn't do the trick, I'll take her down to the city hall myself and show her who owns this house. And now, is there anything more I can do for you before I go? I just stopped around to get a line on how many folks you had here. We had a report on some very noisy doings around here a couple a nights ago. I thought I better understand what to count on. Grandma never had such doings here, and I couldn't rightly understand it. Thought I better come and ask you."

Dale's cheeks flamed scarlet with embarrassment. "Why— it was just some guests, strangers to me, who came to see my relatives. They brought some liquor with them. But they soon went away."

"Well, Miss Dale, if anything like that happens again, you better call me up as soon as it begins. We're tryin' to put a stop to such doings in this township, you know. Well, thanks for the information, and call me again if you need me. Good morning!" And Mike tramped out the door and down the walk in his rubber soles, making a vague sound of law and order.

Dale did not go into the living room, where she saw Aunt Blanche getting ready for a showdown of words. Instead, she went quickly into the kitchen and almost fell over Hattie who was well placed by the crack of the partly open door in a position to hear all that went on in the front part of the house.

Quietly Dale steadied Hattie to a firm stand, and closing the door softly behind her, she then came near Hattie and whispered, "Hattie, did you telephone the police headquarters for Mike?"

Hattie opened wide innocent eyes. "Oh no, ma'am, Miss Dale. I never telephoned to no police headquarters. I'd be scared to death to do that."

"Well, I wonder whatever started him here," she murmured more to herself than to Hattie, but Hattie hurried over to turn the burner down under the stew she was concocting to hide a knowing glint in her innocent eyes. Was this the way Mr. Granniss had taken care of the message she had confided to him?

A few minutes later, Dale heard the front door open and close and footsteps going down the walk to the gate. She hurried over to the door and called, "Are you going far, Aunt Blanche? Because lunch is almost ready, and I know you like it really hot. And are the young people coming soon?"

Aunt Blanche's voice came back coldly. "I'm sure I don't know when they will be here. Whenever they please, I suppose. As for me, I'm going down to see my lawyer! I'll see if this kind of thing can go on any longer."

Dale closed the door softly and, leaning back against it, drew a deep breath and lifted her heart in thankfulness. Whatever was coming next, Aunt Blanche wouldn't be likely to be here for lunch, and it would be good to have a little interval for anger to subside before there had to be any more family conversation.

But if Dale had known what was coming next, she might not have felt so relieved.

Chapter 11

Powelton and Corliss came rushing in an hour later, shouting to know if lunch was ready, and Hattie appeared quietly in the kitchen door and said that it was if they would sit down right away. She didn't know that Dale was coming downstairs. She knew that she must be very much upset by what had gone on that morning, and of course these two young people had not likely heard of it all, unless they had met their mother, which didn't seem likely. They were talking eagerly about the golf course where they had been playing that morning, and it didn't sound as if they had been with their mother. They must have all taken whatever breakfast they took at the hotel. Perhaps only coffee. They were like that. And they had been at the party the night before, so they might have felt shy about coming to the house, not quite knowing how they would be received.

But the two youngsters were not shy, not they. They swarmed into the house as if they owned it and shouted out their wants. They chattered and they clattered, and Dale, hurrying downstairs to prevent any new kind of an outbreak, marveled at them, how easily the night before might have embarrassed them if they had any fine feelings at all. Apparently they had none, for they greeted Dale quite hostilely and demanded strong coffee and pie.

Dale had determined to try out a new system with them and see if she could not possibly win them to some kind of friendliness, just because she could not bear to have them go away with a feeling that she was their enemy. So she sat down, smiling, and asked them where they had been that morning, what they had been doing, and did they make good scores in golf? Asked about their hometown, what sports they liked best, where they went to school, and what studies they enjoyed the most, at which last question they hooted. Imagine anybody enjoying anything by the name of studies!

She did not attempt to enter into an argument on the subject, just skated on to other topics until finally she was rewarded by actually making them laugh at a story she told, and they looked at her with surprise that she could possibly be interesting when she talked. The haze of hostility that had up to this time surrounded their personalities began slowly to melt and the brother and sister grew almost voluble in telling their cousin several jokes and funny stories about their pranks in their school, and they laughed excessively.

Dale did her best to laugh with them, though there were a number of somewhat questionable pranks that really deserved a severe rebuke. But this was not the time, and she was not the person to administer it. Her object just now was to gain their friendship and find some congenial point of contact.

The climax was reached when the lemon meringue pie came in—a really dressy pie it was with piles of meringue in fancy forms—and the two young people received it with whoops of joy and almost seemed to be having a good time and to be glad they were there. They did their duty by the pie, each demolishing two more-than-normally large pieces and sighing that they were unable to hold a third. Then they sat back and talked some more on school and the things they were and were not going to do next winter when they went back.

It was while they were laughing and talking and Dale was taking a deep relieved breath that they had gotten through one meal without a single combat that the telephone rang.

It was Corliss who jumped to her feet and demanded to be allowed to answer it. But when the message began to come through she grew panicky. "What? Where are you speaking from? The Mercy Hospital? *Where?* Who *are* you, anyway? A *nurse?* Well, why are *you* calling *us* up? What? Yes, I'm Corliss Huntley. What do you want of me? Why should a nurse in a hospital want to speak to me? I guess it's my cousin Dale Huntley you want, isn't it? What? You say someone is hurt? Someone who knows me. Who is it? You say she was hit by an automobile? But *who* was it? My *mother?* But that can't be so. She just went out a little while ago. She went down to her lawyer's, they say. No, I don't think she was in the neighborhood of that hospital. I don't think she ever heard of it. You're haywire. You've got your numbers crossed. *What?* You say it was Mrs. Huntley? Yes, Mrs. Blanche Huntley. Yes, that's my mother's name. Won't you ask her when she is coming home?

Tell her we are all through lunch! *What?* You say she is badly *hurt?* She isn't *dead,* is she? Oh, she *couldn't* have been run over by a car. She's very careful crossing streets. What? You say she wants *me?* She wants *us, both* me and my brother? Yes, he's here. But wouldn't it be better for her to take a taxi and come back home? Oh *Powelton,* what shall we *do?*" And with a shriek that for once wasn't planned for effect, Corliss flung the telephone from her and threw herself on the floor in a spasm of frenzied tears and screaming.

"Oh my mother, my *mother*! I just know she'll *die,* and what shall we *do?* We shouldn't have come to Grandma's funeral. I knew it was bad luck when we started, and now Mother's going to die, and what'll become of *us?* Oh, they say there are always three deaths in a family after one has come, so one of *us* will have to die, and it *can't* be *me,* for I'm *scared!*"

Wildly Corliss was carrying on, screaming so that the sound could be heard all up and down the street. Dale reached over to her aunt's place where a clean napkin was set by the plate, and unfolding it, she quietly dipped it into the glass of ice water and then went over and knelt beside the frantic Corliss. Talking gently, she put the cold, wet napkin on the girl's hot forehead and eyes. Quickly she washed her face till the girl gasped and finally ceased to scream so wildly.

"There, there, dear," she was saying, "quiet down, little girl. We'll call up and find out just how your mother is. Maybe it isn't as bad as you think. It's always hard to understand anything over the phone, especially when you're excited. But you'll have to stop crying before I try to call, or I can't hear what they say."

"Aw, shut up, Corrie," said Powelton, suddenly rousing to the fact that he was the man of the family and ought to do something about it. "Shut up, Corrie. Shut up till we find out!"

And at last the screaming ceased entirely, and Dale went to retrieve the receiver and discover if she could what nurse had been talking to Corliss. But by that time, of course, the hospital had hung up and the operator was calling: "Won't you please hang up your receiver?"

But at last Dale got the right nurse and a small amount of information, enough to know that they could not tell yet how badly Aunt Blanche had been injured. They had just taken her to the operating room and wouldn't be able to give more definite information until the doctor came back from the operation. And, anyway, the woman's relatives had better come to the hospital as soon as possible, as they might be needed. If she rallied, she might want to talk to them.

At the word about their mother having gone to the operating room Corliss went into another fit of terrible weeping, and Dale had to put more ice water on her face and soothe her like a child to bring her back to normal again.

"Aw, shut up, can't ya!" wailed the boy, almost as overwrought as his sister.

"Come on," said Dale. "We'll have to go right down to the hospital and see if she wants us for anything, and you two mustn't be weeping when you go in or they'll put you right out of the place. And you know your mother might need you very badly for some reason. Come, grow up and be a man and a woman for this emergency."

So she coaxed them along until she got them to go upstairs and prepare for going to the hospital.

"Corliss," she said, "I've got a pretty pink bed jacket. Come over to my room and see if you think your mother would like you to bring it over for her. And wouldn't she want some pretty nightgowns? Go to her bureau and pick out a couple. I know she won't like wearing those hospital gowns they have, not after she begins to get better."

So she distracted the child from her horror and fear over her mother's possible fate and got her interested in preparing to please her mother, a thing she had hardly ever gotten her interest off herself long enough to even think of. Then again she talked in a soothing way. "Come, cheer up. You don't want to go weepy when you get there. Your part will be to act cheerful. That will help her to get well quicker."

"Oh, do you think she'll ever get well?" It was Corliss who cried out again.

"Why yes, of course," said Dale with more hope in her voice than she actually felt sure of herself. And in her heart she began to pray that the Lord would intervene and help them all. Then finally, with the aid of Hattie, who appeared helpfully at the right minute, they finally got started to the hospital.

Out in the street, Corliss seemed to put aside her fears and became interested in the people she was passing, but the boy walked gravely along, scarcely speaking at all. Dale wondered if he really was touched by his mother's condition. And what kind of a scene would they make when they reached the hospital? Corliss, who was used to letting her feelings govern her actions. Would she realize that they wouldn't stand for her tantrums in a hospital? Once she tried to explain to them that they must remember they would have to be very quiet when they got there, because there were a great many sick people there, some of whom were in a most critical condition.

"Well, I guess my mother's as sick as anybody, and why

should I think about other people when I'm feeling bad about my mother?" put in Corliss.

"But why would you want to make other people suffer? It won't hurt your mother any for you to be kind and thoughtful for others."

"I won't worry about other people. I'll feel bad about my mother if I want to. And you can't stop me. I'll scream if I like, no matter what you say." This from Corliss.

"I'm afraid you would have somebody more unpleasant to deal with than myself," said Dale quietly. "The hospital authorities wouldn't allow you to stay there if you should make an outcry. They would have the orderly put you out."

"Put me out! They wouldn't *dare*."

"Oh yes they would. It is their business to keep the hospital quiet for the sick people for whom they are responsible. Your mother is one of their parents, and for *her* sake, at least, you would not want to make a disturbance. Your mother might hear it, and it would make her worse."

"Oh, she knows me. She wouldn't mind what I did," said Corliss.

"Well, I don't believe you would enjoy being put out of the hospital because you wouldn't keep the rules, and not be allowed to enter it again while your mother was there."

"They wouldn't *dare!*" said Corliss indignantly. "I never heard of such a thing. I would certainly tell them where to get off. I would get my mother's lawyer to go and tell them. I guess they would be afraid of a lawyer, wouldn't they?"

"I'm afraid not, Corliss," said Dale sadly. "You see, they have their patients to look out for. You wouldn't want them to let any harm come to your mother, would you?"

"Oh, there couldn't any harm come to her that way. She knows me!"

"Aw, shut up, you little fool, you," said Powelton, "and if you dare put on one of your acts at that hospital I'll wallop you, and I don't mean maybe."

Corliss gave a half-frightened gasp and glanced at him sideways. It was evident she had experienced one of her loving brother's wallopings in the past and had no desire to have another. Not this time. So they continued on their way in silence, and Dale felt almost sorry for the naughty girl who kept giving her brother speculative glances from time to time. When they reached the hospital, Corliss paused at the steps of the large building.

"I'll just wait out here," she said, "while you go in, Dale. I'm scared to go in until you find out how Mother is."

"No," said Dale firmly, "you'll have to go in now with me. You might be needed at once, and there might not be time for me to come out and hunt for you."

"Whaddaya mean?" she asked with bated breath, a gray look coming over her face. "You don't think she's dead, do you?"

"No, no, Corliss," said Dale quietly. "I trust not. They told us to come at once, so we must go in."

"Oh-h-h-!" began Corliss with every evidence of a tantrum nearing. Dale cast a hopeless, troubled look at her and wondered desperately what she should do next to prevent an outbreak, but to her astonishment Powelton stepped before his sister and looked into her eyes.

"Now, Corrie, you just pipe down and behave yourself. Understand?"

Corliss dropped her glance and ducked her head and went,

beaten, up the steps. She dropped gratefully into the seat where Dale placed her, while Dale went up to the desk and found out where they were to go.

They had to wait a little while to get any information at all about the invalid.

"She's still in the operating room," was all the information they could get at first. But after a long, long wait, a white-starched nurse came rattling down the corridor and told them they could come up and look at her for a moment but that she was not yet out of the anesthesia and they could not stay.

They followed the nurse, filled with awe and horror as they passed open doors with glimpses of white beds and white faces on the pillows. And then they arrived at the ward with rows of beds and more white faces on pillows.

As they entered the doorway, Corliss stopped stock-still. "But that is the *ward*," she said to the nurse. "You can't put *my mother* in the ward. She would be *furious* at being put in a ward."

The nurse gave her a sweeping glance of contempt. "Sorry, miss," she said calmly, "it was the only place we had left in the hospital. We are overcrowded, as you can easily see."

"Well then, you should have sent her to some other hospital," said Corliss, sounding so much like her mother that Dale looked at her in astonishment.

"That wouldn't have been possible if we wanted to save her life," the nurse said. "She was bleeding and unable to say where she wanted to go even if we had had time to ask her. There was no one with her, of course, to answer for her. But anyway, we had no other room or bed."

"Well, you must have her moved at once into a private

room. No matter what it costs."

"It isn't a matter of cost, miss," said the nurse, with another withering glance at the girl. "There *isn't* any other room."

"Then we'll have her taken to another hospital at once," said the spoiled child haughtily.

"That would be impossible," said the nurse stiffly. "She has been operated on, and it would probably be a very serious matter to move her at present. Besides, all the others are full to overflowing. But anyway, you would have to see the doctor. And now, if you want to look in you'll find your mother in the third bed from the far end." And then the nurse turned coldly away and left the three standing alone in the doorway.

It was Dale who went forward, and after an instant of hesitation, Powelton followed her solemnly, walking gravely, as if at a church, feeling that the walk he had to take was miles in length, with all those white staring faces from pillows on each side of him.

But his going left Corliss alone, and Corliss, looking around on the unfamiliar scene, was frightened. Her haughty insolence faded suddenly away and left her trembling and ready to cry. Suddenly the tears came down, and she opened her mouth to scream, but the head nurse appeared at her side and, taking firm hold of her arm, steered her out into the hall.

"You mustn't make a disturbance in there. There are some very sick women in there. One has just been brought from the operating room. If you frighten her, she might die."

Corliss held her scream in the middle and stared at the nurse defiantly. "I'd like to see anybody stop me!" she gasped desperately. "How could you stop me?"

The nurse put out her hand and touched a button by the

door. "I have called the orderly. When he gets here, which will be at once, if you haven't stopped, he will muffle your mouth and carry you out instantly. We do not permit anybody in the hospital who cannot control themselves. If you make a disturbance now, you will not be admitted to this hospital again."

"But—my—mother—is here!" quivered Corliss.

"It is for your mother's sake, and others, that we make these rules," said the nurse. "You wouldn't like your mother to die because she heard you scream and couldn't get up and go to help you, would you?"

Corliss stared at the nurse with frightened eyes, and then suddenly the elevator in the hall arrived and a man in uniform came to the head nurse and saluted. "You sent for me," he said, and his eyes suddenly looked questioningly at the pretty girl with bleary eyes.

"Yes," said the nurse crisply, "I sent for you to carry this weeping girl away. But perhaps she has conquered herself. If she has, you won't be needed." The head nurse looked questioningly at Corliss, and suddenly Corliss straightened up and lifted her chin bravely.

"Yes, I'll be all right," she quavered.

"Well, that sounds better," said the nurse coldly. "But Jasper, you better stay around and see if she keeps control."

Corliss put on her haughty air and started down the aisle after her brother. "I'll be all right," she said with much the air her mother assumed to master people.

The head nurse watched her with an amused smile. She was a clever student of human nature and had an aptitude for conquering hysterical women who disturbed the peace.

Powelton and Dale were standing beside that third bed

from the far end of the room and had for the moment forgotten Corliss, or else it might have been a lesson to them
how to stop Corliss's tantrums another time. But they were
not watching and did not see her taking that long solemn walk
alone. They were looking down at that stiff figure on the bed,
swathed in bandages, her restless hands—wrapped in more
bandages—were folded under the sheet; her arrogant face was
unrecognizable through the sheltering gauze, only her lips visible and one arrogant eyebrow. It was almost as if she were
dead. That was their first impression, for they were so little
used to sickness and death. It was a ghastly sight to them to
see this woman who had always carried all before her in any
situation lying there so silent, so subdued, so almost frozen in
a still helplessness.

Dale was startled to think a few short hours could bring
about a phenomenon like this.

But Powelton seemed suddenly to have grown up. His face
had lost its spoiled baby-boy roundness and seemed to be grav-
en into a new, more dependable maturity. It was as if to him
there had been shown a vision of the briefness and solemnity
of life and what it was meant for, and a startling revelation of
the fact that life wasn't just meant for fun and one couldn't get
away from it no matter how hard one tried.

Then came Corliss, closely but unobtrusively shadowed by
the head nurse, with the orderly openly watching her from the
doorway. The question was, how would Corliss react to that
white, still, swathed face, that rigid figure?

As Dale looked up and saw them both, she had a vision of
what might be ahead for herself and for those two—in fact for
those three—if Aunt Blanche came out of this and lived. And

yet they had not been told the possibilities, and Dale began to wonder how all this was going to affect her life. Only a few short hours ago she had been planning how to send these relatives away so that she might go on with her plans and have her home and her school. But it was obvious now that this could not be at once. It might be some time before her aunt was able to leave the hospital if she recovered at all, and she could not, of course, refuse refuge to the cousins with such calamity upon them. Her heart sank as she recognized the possibilities ahead. Of course not. And if Aunt Blanche got well, what then? There would likely be a time of recuperation, and of course it was natural that she would expect to be cared for by the only relatives in that area. There was no use in arguing these matters now, however, or even shrinking from the possibility. This thing had not come upon her through any fault of her own, and being upon her, the teaching of her faith was that whatever came was sent, or at least allowed by the Lord, and therefore was to be accepted sweetly, knowing that there was some purpose in it for her good and for the Lord's glory. What was it that the Bible said about His purpose for each of His children, that they should "be *conformed* to the image of His Son."

So, if that was the Lord's purpose for her, the only way He saw to bring her to be conformed to the image of His Son, then her heart must accept His way and yield herself to it until His will for her was complete. Meantime, she must remember that her business in this world was witnessing for Christ, and that could not be done if her attitude was hostility. Was it then her work for the time being to try to witness to these two unlovely cousins? Well, she would have to learn to love them, then, learn not to see all their unloveliness.

So Dale stood and looked at Powelton and saw the new manliness dawning in the saggy boyish lines of his face and wondered if it would last, or if every step of the way would have to be a battle.

Then there came the thought of David, now far on his way to some unknown destination, someone who belonged to her and who would pray for her. He might not know what her trials and tests were, but he would pray for her. He would know it was something hard, even if she did not feel she ought to tell him about all she was going through, but he would pray.

They did not stay long in that awful silence. Down at the other end a woman was wheeled out, and a little later a slight disturbance off at one side showed a new cot being wheeled in. There were other sufferers in this strange new world of a hospital. The new patient was moaning, and a nurse hurried to place a screen around the bed to which she was being transferred. Corliss caught a glimpse of it all, caught her breath, and bit her red lips with her little white teeth, but she did not scream. She had also seen the side view of the head nurse and cast a quick, frightened glance back at the orderly still standing in the doorway. Yes, Corliss had been thoroughly frightened for once in her life.

And then, very soon, the head nurse suggested that they had stayed long enough for now. It would be several hours before their patient would be able to recognize them.

So they walked solemnly back through that awful length of aisle with suffering on every side, leaving a mother behind them, a mother who had never been very motherly toward them but still had been the only power over them, that had dominated their young lives thus far.

Down at the desk they had a few words with the desk clerk and then met the doctor who had treated the patient. He spoke gravely, saying it was rather impossible to tell just how serious the injuries had been yet. There was a broken arm, two fractured ribs, and a concussion, of course, but it would not be possible to tell further until all the X-rays had been developed. There must be absolute quiet for her for several days. He hoped there was a good chance of her ultimate recovery, but there must be no excitement whatever, of course—absolute, cheerful quiet when they came to see her, preferably not too often. Meantime they could keep in touch with the nurse and find out how she was coming on; and in a day or two she would be more able to see them and to recognize them.

It was then that Corliss lifted her phenomenally long golden lashes and used her big beautiful blue eyes on the grave doctor.

"But she'll just hate that ward," she said earnestly. "She won't stand for it for a minute when she comes to herself. She'll simply *have* to have a private room or go to another hospital."

The grave doctor studied the spoiled child a moment and almost smiled. "My dear young lady," he said almost wearily, "she will have to be satisfied with whatever she *can get*! Every hospital in this city is overcrowded, and they are even putting cots in the main hallways in City Hospital. But even if there were rooms elsewhere, the patient would not be able to be moved. It would be as much as her life was worth to attempt it at present."

"Oh!" said Corliss, suddenly drooping like a deflated balloon and following Dale as they made their way home in a sad young silence.

Chapter 12

It was Corliss who at last broke the silence as they turned onto their own street and could see the house just up the hill. "Well, what are we going to do now?" she asked in a tone more humble than any Dale had ever heard her use before.

"Well," said Dale, trying to speak cheerfully, "I think the first thing to do is to get some dinner, don't you? We can't go through hard things without food. And then we've got to sit down and plan just what is to be done next. Do you happen to know what your mother did this morning about her baggage? She said she was going over to the hotel to get it, before she went out. She didn't do it, did she? Because I didn't see any arrive. Although, of course, I was upstairs and might not have heard a taxi drive up."

"No," said Powelton, "I don't think she did. She told me she was going out to get a cheaper boarding place, that she couldn't stand that hotel any longer, and when she got back I would have to go get the baggage and take it somewhere, or else bring it to the house."

"Well, of course we don't know what she did, and we can't ask her till she is well enough, so I guess after we have had dinner you better go over to the hotel and get the things. Are they packed in suitcases, do you know, or will you have to go and pack? Corliss, do you know? Did she pack before she came over this morning?"

"No, the things were hanging in the closets and lying on the bureau."

"Well then, we'll all go over together and get them packed. We'll go just as soon as we've had dinner, or if you aren't too hungry we can go now. It probably won't take long if all of us go."

"Let's go now," said Corliss dolefully.

"All right," said Dale pleasantly, "perhaps that would be best. And, anyway, Hattie will know to hold dinner for us till we get there."

"I don't want any dinner," said Corliss, her eyes brimming with tears. "I don't ever want to eat again."

"Oh yes you do, dear," Dale said, smiling. "You can't go through hard things without food. Come now, don't get to crying. You've been a brave girl. This is something we've got to go through bravely. Courage always helps at a time like this, and we'll try to be just as cheerful as we can."

"But where can we go?" wailed Corliss. "We don't know what place Mom found."

"Well, just go to our house, of course. You'll stay there till your mother gets well enough to say what she wants to do.

You'd like that best, wouldn't you?"

"Yes," said Corliss sadly. "I don't ever want to see that old hotel again."

"Well, here's a taxi," said Dale. "We'll take that and get the packing and moving over at once."

So they went to the hotel, and Powelton marched over to the desk and got the keys.

"He says Mom paid the bill here and said she'd be back today to check out," he said thoughtfully.

So they went sorrowfully up to the rooms and began their work.

It didn't take long. Aunt Blanche had folded a good many of her things into the suitcases before she left in the morning.

Dale organized the work.

"You pick up the little things—brushes, combs, powder, and so on," she said to Corliss, "and I'll fold up the things that are still hanging in the closet."

So they were soon done and went to help Powelton but found he was just locking the suitcase. They rang for the porter and soon were on their way back to the house, quiet and thoughtful, trying to think what was coming next.

"Where am I going to sleep?" Corliss asked. "I don't want that Grandmother's room any more, not since I've seen how Mom looked in the hospital. I said I wanted it, but I don't now. I'm scared of it."

Dale drew a relieved sigh, for she had feared a battle on that subject.

"Why, I think you better take the room where your mother took her naps, don't you? Then Powelton can have the next one, and there's a door between. You can leave it open if you want to."

"Okay," agreed Corliss listlessly, "that will be nice. I'd like that."

"It's okay by me," agreed the newly grown-up brother.

Then they went in to a nice dinner that Hattie had all ready for them—a tasty hot soup and a meat pie with vegetables. It was hot and appetizing, and there was a peach pie. The young people ate and were heartened and then rose and offered to help clear off the table. Probably because they felt shy and awkward and did not know what to do next, not feeling in the mood for either games or reading.

Later in the evening, Dale telephoned the hospital and got the latest news, that the patient was sleeping quietly and less restless than she had been. She was doing as well as could be expected at present. So finally the brother and sister went to bed and were soon asleep, worn out with excitement and worry. And at last Dale was free to go to her own room, read over her precious letter, and go on with the answer she had begun earlier in the day.

Somehow her heart cried out greatly for this newly found lover whom she had known so short a time and yet who seemed to be the only one to whom she could unburden her heart.

Dale sat down and read over her unfinished letter and, after a moment, began to write:

> *Dear, this is rather late at night. Something*
> *happened. We've had an exciting afternoon. My*
> *aunt—I think you met her the day of Grand-*
> *mother's funeral—went out on an errand and*
> *was run over by an automobile. They telephoned*
> *us from the hospital and we went right over. We*

saw her, but she was still unconscious and didn't see us, of course. We came home and got dinner, and now the brother and sister are asleep. The word from the hospital tonight is the patient is doing as well as can be expected. A concussion, a broken arm and ribs, some facial cuts are among the injuries. We don't know all yet, of course.

So now I am wondering what is coming next. I think I told you that the aunt has not been easy to get along with, and her children have been rather impossible. But of course now I must be all I can to these cousins, for they haven't anybody else, and I've been thinking that God wouldn't have sent this to me if there hadn't been some good reason. I think perhaps I needed to learn to love them, for I never have, I'm afraid. Of course I haven't seen much of them, but when I have they have always looked down on me and been just as disagreeable as they could. However, perhaps some of that may have been my fault, too.

Perhaps I ought not to be telling you all this, for you will soon have enough unpleasant things of your own to think about. But you are all I have now, and it is sweet to know I have your sympathy and prayers. I'm sure God is going to somehow bring good out of this experience. But for the present, at least, I shall not be able to go ahead with my plans about the little children till I see the outcome of this. So I shall be glad to think you will take this to the Lord for me, too.

*And now I am going to read your dear letter
once more and pray for you, and then I am going to
sleep. God be with you, my dear. How I wish I might
be looking forward to your coming back to me soon,
but it will be according to His will. Good night.*

Dale

Dale was very tired and was not long in getting to sleep in
spite of all the questions that came up to torment her. But in
the middle of the night she was awakened by a slender figure
in frilly silk pajamas standing by her bed and putting a cold
little hand on her cheek.

Dale started awake and saw that it was Corliss.

"Why child, dear!" she said gently, for she saw that the
young girl was trembling like a leaf. "What is the matter? Haven't
you been to sleep?"

"Yes, but I had a terrible dream. I dreamed my mother was
dead. Oh Dale, do you think my mother will die? She looked
so terrible, all done up like that!"

Dale reached out warm, comforting hands toward the
formerly unpleasant cousin and drew her down on the side
of the bed.

"Why no, dear, I don't think so. You know the nurse said
she was doing as well as could be expected," she said, holding
the cold little hands in her own. But Corliss only trembled
more.

"Oh Dale, I'm—*frightened*!" And the pretty gold head went
down on the cold hands and the girl began to cry as if her heart
would break.

"I went to my brother, but he was sound asleep. He wouldn't wake up."

Then Dale put her arms around the cold, trembling shoulders and drew Corliss close to her.

"Get in my bed with me, Corliss," she said gently. "You are all in a shiver. Let me get you warm. Cuddle up to me and you won't be so frightened. It was only a dream, you know."

Corliss promptly slipped inside the covers and shivered up to Dale's inviting arms, and it wasn't a second before she was weeping right into Dale's neck, shaking with great sobs.

Dale let her cry for a while, and then she began to talk in low tones. "Poor little girl," she whispered. "I'm not much of a substitute for a mother, am I? But you just cry there till you feel better. It will do you good to get all the cry out. Poor little girl!"

"Don't pity me!" cringed the child. "I can't bear to be pitied!"

"Oh, I'm sorry! You see, this is something just a little out of my line, and I don't really know you so awfully well yet, you know, but you cuddle up close and perhaps I'll learn."

"Oh, you're all right!" gasped the unhappy girl. "I'm just not used to being coddled. But—I guess—maybe—it isn't so bad!" Corliss snuggled a little closer, and Dale's arm held her close. How was this coming out, this sudden affectionate episode in the middle of the night with this strange child?

But she began to pat the soft young shoulder, and soon the shivering and trembling ceased and the hands she held grew warm. A few more minutes and the breath came softly, regularly. She thought the girl was asleep. Should she try to slip away now? No, that seemed too unfriendly, and if she should wake again, she might be even more frightened. No, she must see this night through. It might mean all the difference between winning or losing Corliss. Maybe this was why the Lord had let this unhappy experience come to them all, to bring them nearer to each other. For after all, they were kin.

Dale wondered if it was going to be possible for her to get to sleep again, so close to another. She had always slept alone. But she, too, was very weary, and it wasn't long until she was asleep herself.

She awoke very early, and lying still because she did not wish to wake Corliss, she had the probable day spread out before her. How was she going to get through with it? Certainly she could not do it alone. She must have help from on high. And so lying there with the sleeping Corliss in her arms, she began to pray. And certainly Corliss had never been so near to prayer in all her rebellious young life. Would she have been frightened if she could have known how near she was to an open line to God?

As the morning sun stole in from the window, slanting across the gold of Corliss's pretty curls, Dale glanced down at her and thought how pretty the girl was now, asleep, with the hard selfish lines erased in slumber and the little mouth without its lipstick, all sweet and innocent. What a pity the child couldn't be trained to want to be sweet and pleasant and right. What a pity that in all probability, if her mother lived, she would have to grow up just like her mother. Was Aunt Blanche ever sweet and childlike herself? And would there be any possible way of her being changed? Of course God could do anything. He could change what He had made in the first place, although it wasn't likely Aunt Blanche was *born* disagreeable, at least not any more than all humanity was full of sin and determined to go in selfish ways. But how could one ever get a person like Aunt Blanche, or even one like Corliss, to know their need of God and turn to Him? As far as she herself was concerned, it seemed an utterly thankless, useless task to attempt it. It would only bring scorn and derision upon her.

Well, a new day was at hand, and what was it to bring forth? There would have to be a visit to the hospital, of course, by them all. Judging Corliss by her nervous state last night, there was no telling what she would do. Perhaps she might even be capable of refusing to go to the hospital, which might make trouble with her mother, in case her mother was well enough to know. However, she would have to decide on that question when she came to it.

The first question that was nearest to Dale's heart just then was whether there might be a letter in her new post office box for her and how she was going to manage to get it without being questioned about why she was going to the office. Really what she thought to do was to somehow manage to slip out of bed without waking Corliss, pick up her clothes, and make an escape to the bathroom to dress. Could she do that?

She gave a quick glance around the room to see just what she would need to take with her, for she must plan not to return until it was time for Corliss to wake up. She silently memorized the things she must remember to collect. The garments she had taken off the night before, her shoes, her brush and comb, her purse and keys. Then she focused on the task of getting away from Corliss without disturbing her. Almost finger by finger, muscle by muscle she moved and waited between each stealthy withdrawal, breathless, to see if she had stirred Corliss's deep sleep. But the steady, quiet breathing went on, and at last she was free from the covers and outside of the bed, standing on the carpet, pulling the warm covers up over the girl. Then for an instant Corliss stretched slightly and drew a single sighing breath, as if the relaxing was a comfort.

Dale stood for several seconds, watching her cousin, thinking again how pretty and really sweet-looking she was in her sleep and how one could love her if she would be like that more often.

Then carefully she slipped across the room and let herself out, closing the door noiselessly. She slid into the bathroom, where with swift fingers she donned her garments, then hurried downstairs and went to the kitchen for a word with Hattie, who was just beginning to get things ready for breakfast.

"Don't hurry, Hattie," she whispered. "I don't want them to wake up very early, for they can't go to the hospital till visiting hours begin, and it will just be a restless time to get through. I'm running down to the store now to get a few things. I'll be right back, but is there anything else you want besides the yeast you said you needed for hot biscuits tonight?"

"Why yes," said Hattie. "We need mustard and vinegar and cinnamon and salt. Can you bring all those?"

Dale laughed. "Did you think I had grown weak, Hattie? Sure I can bring them, and a bit of fruit of some kind, too. Maybe some grapes. Well then, you carry on till I get back. If the cousins wake up, tell them I'll be right back and then we'll call up the hospital. It's too early to do it now. But I don't think they'll wake before I'm back."

So she hurried away and was rewarded by finding a nice thick letter in her new letter box. She went on to the store and got a few necessities and hurried back to the house.

It was all quiet there yet. Hattie reported that nothing had been heard from the two, who were likely accustomed to sleeping late, and Dale drew a happy sigh of relief and sat down by her desk to read her letter, remembering that she couldn't be sure of long privacy and so must merely skim over it the first reading and read it slowly later when she was assured of more time. But as she opened the letter, she thrilled anew that he had written again so soon. Her love! Her letter! It was all so wonderful. So like a fairy story she used to dream when she was just a little girl.

My dearest:

I pause and wonder at myself for daring to write that, but you are mine, aren't you? I rejoice at the thought. It thrills me anew every time I think of it.

And I have been sitting here in the train, flying along to a far and unknown destination, on my way to follow out orders, and as I sit here alone I think of you and wonder what it would be like if you were sitting by my side. How wonderful it would be! And so I try to kid myself that you are here. I turn and look down at where you might be and smile at you, just vaguely. If any were noticing me they might wonder, but no one in the car would mind. In fact, if they knew they would probably all understand. For every fellow in this car has likely left some beloved one behind him.

And when I think of that and the way I used to feel, looking enviously at the other fellows with snapshots and photographs at which they took furtive glances, I feel triumphant. I used to envy all the other boys, and even those who only had sisters or just friends, and I hadn't even a mother left.

But now I'm filled with joy. For I have a girl who beats them all, I'm sure. A girl so beautiful that I wonder any of them should possibly have left her free for me. They just never met her, that's all, I'm quite sure.

Did I ever take time to tell you how beautiful you are to me? You thought perhaps that I never noticed the little details about you, but I did. I was just so pressed for time on the important things that had to be said before we parted that I saved it up to write about instead. You may think I would have forgotten, but I haven't. I can close my eyes and see your exquisite face, even the very rose tint of your cheeks and your lips and chin. The soft curves of your sweet lips, the lines they make when you speak and when you smile. Even without closing my eyes I can bring them all back to mind, so that you seem to be conversing with me, smiling at me. I can see you as you were sitting against the hemlock green, the sunlight shining on your hair. It is all dear, very dear. I can see the little curl at the back of your sweet white neck when you stooped over to pick up the little beechnuts that fell at your feet from the beech tree over at our left. I can see the very color of your dress. My girl, who says she loves me and doesn't mind that *we haven't known each other very long, because somehow God has introduced us and made us to be sure about one another. After all, that is the main thing, isn't it? That we both know and love our Savior? And when I think of that I find it again so very wonderful that I should have walked into that social center and found you.*

I wasn't looking for you then. I wouldn't have gone to anything with the word social *belonging to it to find my dream girl. Because I had found so many of the girls in such places were just pretty, dressed-up dolls, and that wasn't the kind of girl I wanted. Not if I never had one, did I want a fashionable doll, no matter how pretty she was.*

But now that I have found her, I defy anyone to find a more beautiful girl anywhere, than my dear girl. And I want you to know it. I'm sure that wherever I go, and however many girls I see, whether beautiful or sensible or very lovely, none will ever look or seem to be as lovely as my girl.

And so I have described to you the girl I love. The girl, who one day, please God, is to be my wife.

There was more of the same sort, deeply sweet and earnest. Wonderful talk that Dale had never dreamed of having written to her. Precious sentences that seemed almost as if they must have been formed in heaven. At least formed by one to whom heaven was very real.

And when she had finished reading she folded the letter

tenderly and slipped it safely inside the blouse she was wearing. Such letters were not for the public eye. Precious, precious!

And then she heard footsteps upstairs and realized that her day had begun. There was only time to breathe a prayer for help before Powelton came down, and she could hear Corliss hurrying around to follow him.

So she rose and went out to the kitchen to tell Hattie she might as well get ready to serve breakfast.

Chapter 13

The young people came down to the dining room very much subdued in manner and sat down at the table quietly, as those might do who had met with a great awakening of some sort.

Corliss even flung a little shadow of a half smile toward Dale, like pale sunshine, and Dale felt again that wonder that the girl could change so overnight. Was it because she remembered her fright of last night? Was she still afraid of that dream of hers?

But Dale sat down cheerily smiling and said, "Good morning," as if she were any hostess.

It certainly was astonishing to see how quietly they ate their breakfast. Though they did not seem as ravenous as they had been before. But there was no complaining, no snarling, no demands for food not on the table. Hattie looked at them wonderingly and even smiled at Dale when she asked for more cream.

"Have you called the hospital yet?" asked Corliss shrinkingly.

"No, I thought we better wait till the doctor was there. Then we could really find out how things are going. But perhaps I might call now and get the nurse's viewpoint."

"Yes," said the boy suddenly. "It seems an awful long time since last night."

"Yes," said Dale, springing up. "I'll call right away."

They followed her to the telephone and waited solemnly for the nurse to be called. But when the nurse came there wasn't much new. She said Mrs. Huntley had spent a fairly comfortable night, but she would not be able to give them any definite news until the doctor arrived. Yes, they might come at any time to see her now, but about eleven o'clock would be best. She had, of course, suffered a good deal of shock from the accident, and they must be prepared to realize that she would not as yet be very responsive. She might not even recognize who they were.

They turned solemnly away from the phone, and Corliss went over to the window and stared out unseeingly. Dale, looking at her furtively, saw her wiping away big tears and went over to put a comforting arm around her.

"Come on, dear," she said pleasantly, "don't let's worry yet. We'll have to expect she won't be quite herself yet, but the nurse seemed to feel she was doing as well as could be expected. So let's run up and get the beds made. That will help to keep our minds busy, and then we'll get ready to start for the hospital."

The boy stared at her in a troubled way. "Is there anything you'd like me to do, Dale?" he asked unexpectedly. "I don't suppose I'd be much good making beds."

"Why yes," said Dale brightly, "you can wind the clocks, one in the upper hall and one in the living room. And there's a door upstairs that needs a drop of oil. It squeaks horribly. Hattie will tell you where the oil can is. It would be good to have all squeaks oiled up before your mother comes home. We don't want anything around to make her nervous."

"Oh," said Corliss brightly, "will she be coming back here, do you think?"

"Why, of course," said Dale, trying to make her voice sound cheerful over the thought. "That is, of course I can't be sure what *she* will want to do, when she is able to get around again, but I should think this would be her natural haven while she is recovering, and we want to be ready for her."

"Then you think she is really going to recover?" asked the son anxiously.

"Why, I should think so, from what the doctor said last night," said Dale. "He didn't seem to feel there were going to be any serious complications. But of course we can tell better after we have seen him again this morning."

Somehow Powelton seemed to have taken on a new character—silent, subdued, solemn, and a bit anxious. Dale rather liked him in his new role. He seemed almost attractive now.

Upstairs Dale and Corliss made lively work of putting the rooms in order, one on each side of a bed, smoothing the covers neatly. Corliss seemed never to have tried bed making before and said she thought it was almost fun.

Then they got themselves ready and started for the hospital.

Dale could not help pitying Corliss as she glanced at her while they went up in the elevator. Corliss's hands were gripped viselike and stuffed so tightly into her chic little suit jacket that the knuckles showed through the material. Poor child. She was frightened again. It wasn't just fear for her mother's safety, was it? She had never *seemed* really to love her mother, although that mother had always given her everything she wanted. But it seemed more a fear of possibilities, gruesome things, like suffering and death.

Corliss's lips were closed tight, her teeth even shut tight, making her soft little mouth into something firm and hard. And her eyes were frightened eyes.

She slipped over to stand by the girl and slid her hand inside one firmly stiff young arm. "Don't worry, Corliss," she whispered. "It's going to be all right pretty soon, I'm sure."

Corliss gave her a troubled searching look. "Are you *sure*, Dale?" she asked fearsomely.

"Yes, I'm quite sure," said Dale reassuringly.

Then they were at the doorway of that long room filled with beds, and sick or dying people in those beds. Corliss gripped Dale's hand as they walked down to her mother's bed, gripped it so hard that it hurt, but her pursed lips let out no sound. Corliss had really grown a lot in the last twenty-four hours.

The sick woman lay, almost as yesterday, not seeming to notice anything, until the nurse came up.

"Well, here are your family come to see you, Mrs. Huntley," the nurse said in a pleasant tone, and the white image in the bed turned her eyes toward them and looked them over oddly as if they were strangers.

The sick woman's quick, bright eyes surveyed them one at a time, and there came no welcoming look, nothing but critical survey.

"You haven't got your tie put on right, Powelton," was the first thing she said.

The boy's hand went quickly to his tie, but his face got painfully red, and he cast a quick deploring look around to see if the nurse or anyone else had noticed his mother.

"Do you feel any better, Mother?" asked Corliss in an unsteady little voice, so evidently trying to say the right thing, as if she must have thought it out beforehand.

"Better?" snapped her mother. "Why should I feel better? Have I got any reason to feel better? Stuck away in this awful white room? My arm all tied up, my face all tied up, and I can't do anything about it. What does it all mean, Powelton? Why have you let them do this to me? After all, I'm your mother, you know."

The boy got white around his mouth and, stooping, tried to explain in a gentle voice that surprised Dale: "Mother, there was an accident, and you got hit by an automobile. They had to bring you to the hospital, and they are going to make you get well. You just be patient, and you'll feel better pretty soon."

"Oh, you think you can lecture me, do you? Why, you're nothing but a child! I guess I know when to be patient, and this isn't the time for that. I'll have them know I won't be kept in this hospital *ward*. I can afford to pay for a private room if I'm really sick, but I don't think I am. They have just got me all tied up this way to amuse themselves, those doctors and nurses."

She chattered on meaninglessly, showing that she was not altogether herself, and then her eyes caught a glimpse of Dale, and she fixed her with a hateful glance. "Oh, so *you* thought you had to come, too, did you? Well, you can *go*! I don't want you hanging around and gloating over me. And if you do anything unkind to my children before I get back I'll see that you pay for it, do you understand?"

But Corliss, coming close, whispered earnestly, "Oh Mother, Dale's been wonderful to us. She's just as sweet and kind as can be! She's taking care of us."

And Powelton came closer on the other side. "Dale has been awfully good to us," he said firmly. "She has taken us home with her and made us just as comfortable as can be. She couldn't be better. You must not talk that way about her. She is sweet and kind."

"Oh, she *is*, is she? Well it's the first time in her life, then," snapped the woman on the pillow. "But she'll turn you out when she gets ready. Don't trust her."

Then the nurse came near and said in a low tone, "She doesn't rightly know what she is saying yet. She's still under opiates, somewhat, and hasn't got back into the world yet. But I think the next time you come she'll be more like herself."

Oh, thought Dale sadly, *she's quiet like herself. You just don't know her, that is all.* But aloud she said: "Of course. I know."

The invalid's sharp eyes had closed, and the visitors began to think it was time for them to leave, but suddenly she opened them, and looking straight at her son, she snapped, "I want to see my lawyer. You go down and explain to him what they are doing to me, keeping me here in this ward, and tell him to come right up and get me out of here. Do you understand?"

The young man looked at his mother disapprovingly. "I don't think the doctor would approve having your lawyer come to see you now. You will have to wait till you are better. Just be patient, Mother. It will all come right."

"Oh, you think you can *manage* me, do you? Why, that's ridiculous! Nurse! Help me get up. I've got to get out of this bed right away."

The nurse came quickly, administered some medicine, and said gently, "Just you lie still for a little bit, Mrs. Huntley. Everything's going to be all right."

Then the sick woman turned her eyes toward her daughter. "Where are you going now, Corliss?"

"Why, I think maybe I'll play a little tennis," said Corliss with a quick understanding. "You take a nice little sleep, Mother, and then we'll come and see you again."

Already the medicine was taking effect, and they were able to slip away without further talk, but the nurse followed them to the hall to reassure them. "You know she'll be quite different from this in a few days. You needn't feel worried. The doctor seemed to think she was doing as well as could possibly be expected yet."

They got themselves silently out of that hospital and down into the sunlit street, their faces utterly sad and disheartened.

"Now," said Dale suddenly when they were out from any chance of being overheard, "I think we've got to plan to do something pleasant, don't you? It wasn't a cheerful session today. In fact, I was afraid it would be just that way, because I've heard before that when people have had concussions and shocks they are very vague in their minds. But they come out of it. Don't you worry. In fact, the head nurse told me that things were going very much as the doctor had hoped, and he thought if nothing further developed later that we might be very comfortable about the patient. So, the idea is to try to be as cheerful as possible. Have you any suggestions? How about it, Corliss? You said something about playing tennis. Is that what you'd like to do?"

"Oh, I don't know," said Corliss with a desolate look. "I don't suppose Pow will be willing to. He said the last time we played that I wasn't playing as well as I used to, and he was fed up with playing with me."

Powelton turned, annoyed. "I didn't say just that, Corrie. I said we ought to try and get some others to play with us. I said you were getting stale just playing with me and that if we had a foursome you'd get back to your game."

"Well, isn't that the same thing?" said Corliss sullenly.

"No," said the brother quietly, "not quite. But anyhow, now, I'm glad to play."

Dale wondered what had come over Powelton, but she smiled encouragingly. "That's fine of you, Powelton," she said, "but if you want a foursome I think I could find one for you. In fact, I might play awhile myself if we can't find anybody else, and I'm sure Dick Netherby would help out. He's young, but he's rather a wizard at the game, I understand. Anyway, let's try it. I'll call him up and see if he's free."

Neither of the cousins was particularly overjoyed at the idea of strangers, but they were on their good behavior just now, it seemed, so they said nothing except, "Oh, all right." And Dale went to the telephone. When she came back, she said it was all right, that Dick could come, and he was going to bring over another racket for her to use, so they would all be able to play.

"Who is this Dick?" asked Corliss rather grimly. "Is he just a kid? Because kids can't really play our game."

"Wait till you see," said Dale, smiling. "They send for him

everywhere to play because he's really a sort of champion. But suppose we come on and eat our lunch now and be ready when Dick comes. He may not be able to stay long this time. He's working somewhere in the late afternoons."

So they went in to the nice lunch that Hattie had ready for them, and the atmosphere became a trifle less doleful.

But Dick as a tennis player turned out to be a great success. He arrived early, and they heard his sharp whistle while they sat waiting for him. They went off happily together, Corliss studying this bright-faced homely boy with the engaging grin and wondering why it was she couldn't seem to make him look at her admiringly, the way the high school boys at home did. But there was a sort of dignity about Dick that, in spite of his youth, made him seem older than he really was.

Hattie watched them going off together, Dale swinging her racket as cheerfully as any of them, and she said to herself, *Miss Dale, she is a real livin' saint, that's what she is! Just fancy her goin' off to play with them brats after the way they treated her before this.*

Chapter 14

It was a golden day in the late fall, and as they started out for the tennis courts, the leaves of the trees seemed just beginning to flame into deeper color, especially the maples, some of which had brought out a lovely coral pink that seemed almost as if they were trying to aim at the new fall fashionable shades. Dale took it all in, to paint it over again in words for David when she had an opportunity to be by herself and write him again. Up in a tall tree a little bird was voicing its joy in the continued mildness of the weather and announcing its intention of going south soon for the winter.

Somehow the problems of the immediate future grew less staggering to her mind as she went out into the sunshine to try and help two other despairing souls to keep their footing in their new uncertain world.

But there was something else besides the sunshine and the singing of the birds that gave Dale a song in her heart as she went out for a real playtime; and that was her love, going somewhere—out into danger, far away from her—but *loving* her, with a love that she felt would last even into another life, if God willed that he might not come back in this one. But oh, how she prayed that he might come back! And so David in mind went out with her, and she thought much about him and perhaps played better because of her thought of him.

That afternoon set the pace for a steady life for the two, little more than children, who were suddenly cast upon the mercy of an up until then unloved cousin. They all had a good time, even the girl who was giving up her time and thought to help the two cousins.

They came home to another good dinner. Hattie was all for what her young mistress was doing, now. These wild young visitors were showing some sense and allowing themselves to be led in right ways. Well, she would help all she could. So the dinner was full of little pleasant surprises that only Hattie knew how to make, and yet it had not been costly, either in money or ration stamps.

That evening Dale got out a large jigsaw puzzle, and so well had she proved herself an equal in tennis playing that the other two were interested to inspect the puzzle. Before long they were all working away happily at it, spurred on by trying to get their portions finished as soon as their cousin finished hers, which proved to be some contest, for Dale was skillful at jigsaw puzzles as well as tennis.

Dale hustled them off to bed at ten, realizing she had a letter to write yet before she slept and wondering if Corliss would repeat last night's act again. She asked her if she would like to sleep in her room again, but Corliss sheepishly declined. Dale had caught a glance between the brother and sister, showing that the brother had been making fun of his sister for what she did the night before, probably scolding her. "I'll be all right," she said with a pale little smile, and then added, "but thank you just the same."

"All right," said Dale in a matter-of-fact tone, "but come in anytime, night or day, when you feel you need company." And a smile passed between the two girls that was far different from any glance they had ever shared before.

The jigsaw puzzle, left on the table in a corner all night, proved an incentive to get up early the next day and go at it, and Dale began to feel that if she could just keep these two busy and a little interested, half her problems would be solved.

So the days fell into a pleasant routine—the visits to the hospital beginning each day, sometimes another in the late afternoon, all brief and bringing very little satisfaction.

As the mother recovered, more and more she fell into the habit of bewailing her fate and somehow trying to blame Dale for her accident. If Dale hadn't been so trying, she said, she was sure she would never have gotten so confused as to let herself get run over.

Dale avoided such issues as much as possible and responded by bringing a few lovely late blossoms from the garden, until Aunt Blanche waved them away one day and called them weeds. "Take those weeds away!" she snarled disagreeably. "They give me the creeps. They make me sneeze, and they might have worms on them." So then Dale brought a few roses from the florist's and made Corliss give them to her mother. But it made little difference in the woman's attitude. She was determined to complain. She took a dislike to all the nurses and demanded others. She kept up a continual outcry about being put in the ward and kept demanding a private room. But no private room was given her. There was the same excuse, "We have no private room to spare. The private rooms are now occupied by two or three patients at least, because of war conditions."

But that kind of talk had never stopped Aunt Blanche, and she kept right at it, harping on it whenever her children came to see her. Blaming Dale for not doing something about it. But the most Dale could say was that she would speak to the doctor about it.

And then she began to clamor again to see her lawyer. But when the nurse tried to reach him, he as always out of town. The plain truth being that he did not want to see her, for having gotten all the money out of her that he reasonably could, he felt it was time to be away from the vicinity. And neither Dale nor the children made any response to Mrs. Huntley's requests to see her lawyer. They were not in sympathy with her on this subject. The son, at least, had reached the stage where he began to see just what kind of a man this lawyer was. He could not argue with his mother now, while she was sick and unable to leave the hospital and look after her affairs, so he said nothing. That had been his habit in dealing with things he did not like in the past, always to ignore them, so now his mother was not surprised at his attitude. But she spoke to him bitterly about his unwillingness to help her, and sometimes Dale could see that it was very hard for him to hear her faultfindings. Just once he did say, "Mother, I don't have much faith in that lawyer," but his remark brought about such a torrent of abuse and scorn that he did not venture to oppose her again. Dale could see he shrank from hearing his mother shriek out, "Powelton! Stop! How dare you speak that way about my lawyer?"

It was on the day that that happened first that the boy was very silent on the way home, until they got quite near to the house, and then he said quietly, "I wish you folks would begin to call me by my right name. I just hate that name Powelton! I wasn't rightly named that, anyway. Dad wanted me named after himself, George Harold, and I want to use George now. It sounds more like something real, and not that sissy name of Powelton."

"All right," said Dale. "I'll call you George. I like that name. But—will your mother mind?"

"I expect she will," he said bitterly. "Powelton was her maiden name. But I'd rather have my father's whole name."

"I think you have a right to be called what you want to," said Corliss unexpectedly. "I know Mother used to want to call me Clarissa, and I wouldn't stand for it. But now she seems to like Corliss. Anyhow, I think you can do what you like. Mother won't be around for a while till we get used to it. I like George best, too."

The lad looked pleased and nothing more was said, but they were careful after that to call him George.

After dinner that night, Dale brought out a new jigsaw puzzle and they grew almost happy at times as they worked over it. They were beginning to really enjoy each other's company, and since the mother was away there was no one to find fault.

So the days settled into a quiet routine, and it was good for Dale that she had something pleasant to occupy her mind, for David's last letter had intimated that he was being sent off on some mission from which he would not be able to write to her, perhaps for a long time.

Nightly she read over that last precious letter and prayed for him, wondering where he was, trusting him to the care of the heavenly Father, and then reading a few verses in the Bible, verses they had agreed together to read at night while he was gone.

So they got through the days, wondering always what was coming when the invalid recovered and was able to walk. Would she come to the house that Dale owned, where they were staying? And what would it be like if she did?

It is safe to say that all three of these young people thought a great deal about this subject. Dale knew that of course she must invite her aunt if she seemed to want to come but that it would bring dissension on every side. Corliss and George both knew that this quiet time while they were waiting for the recovery of the mother was heaven compared to what it would be if she returned. Then there was the subject of a nurse. Corliss knew *she* would never be able to take care of her mother, for there would be no satisfying her ever with anything. Oh, it was all a sore subject, and none of them liked to think about it. And only Dale could throw it off by laying it all in the keeping of her heavenly Father. "All through the night," and all through the days, also.

Of course Dale was the one who dreaded it most, perhaps, for she would be the butt of all the faultfinding, and she would be the one who would have to sweat and bear it as if it were nothing. Could she do it? Yes, but not in her own strength. In the strength of her Lord she could lie back and take it sweetly, remembering that it was not herself who was bearing the responsibility but her Lord who had promised to undertake for her. She had put her all in His hands, and she must only be careful that she did not interfere in the matter but let her Lord manage it all for her.

It was very still in the room for a few minutes, with only the soft sound of the flickering flames in the fireplace, where a quiet wood fire brightened the dusk in the corners of the room, mingling with the silvery beam of the new moon shining across the floor as if to meet and caress the firelight.

Troubled thoughts were going through the minds of the young people as they sat working over the new jigsaw puzzle. At last Corliss broke the silence. "What are we going to do, Dale, when Mother begins to get well? I tried to ask her today while you went to speak to the nurse, but she looked at me so strangely and just said, '*Stop!* Don't torment me with questions like that when I'm sick.' And then you came back with the nurse and I couldn't say anything more, but what *are* we going to do?"

"I think the way will open somehow when the time comes," said Dale with a sweet smile. "There's really nothing to worry about, you know. There will be a way."

"Yes, but we can't stay here," said the boy. "You want to start a school or something, and we are taking up all your time and your house. And goodness knows it will be work when Mom comes here with a nurse in the bargain. We ought not to put you out this way."

It was a manly speech, and it thrilled Dale's heart to think her cousin had had kind thoughts for her comfort.

"But I'm not worried, George," she said pleasantly. "Maybe that school wasn't in God's plan for me just now, and certainly having you here was, for the present, anyway. And somehow I think it was nice that you stayed here and we got better acquainted with each other, don't you?"

"Swell!" said George heartily. "I never knew you were so nice, and I'll always be glad I got to know you. You've been wonderful to Corrie and me. You couldn't have been better. But all the same, that's another reason why we ought to get out and let you have your house to yourself."

"No," said Dale earnestly. "You mustn't think that way. I'm just glad you are here, and I know we're going to have a nice time together, in spite of worry and anxieties and maybe some discomforts in the days ahead. But I'm sure there's something good coming out of it all."

"What makes you so sure?" asked the boy curiously.

Dale hesitated for an instant. Should she tell him? Would he understand? Yet she felt she must. "Because my heavenly Father is managing it all, and I have trusted my life with Him. I know He will work it out right for our best good. You see, what He wants for us all is to make us like His Son, Jesus Christ, and if He sees that hard things will accomplish that for us in a better, quicker way than anything else would, then that is what He will do for us. I know, for I have told Him I want to rest my life with Him entirely."

"But you couldn't have any fun or good times that way, could you?" asked Corliss in wonder.

"Oh yes, definitely so," said Dale. "You know He loves us, wants us to be happy in Him. So He would want to give us happiness as well as hard things. And I believe He truly loves me. He has given me a great deal of joy in many ways. Sometimes my heart is just thrilled to running over with the things

He has handed out to me."

Corliss looked at her curiously, studied the radiant look on her sweet face, and wondered at it. "Well, I wish I could feel that way about missing things and seeing uncomfortable things coming ahead. But I can't," she said.

"Well, perhaps that is because you do not know my Lord Jesus yet. That makes all the difference in the world. When you know somebody well, you know whether you can trust him or not. Do you see?"

"No, I'm not sure I see at all," said the girl. "What about all those people over in the war and all those people in Europe? Don't you suppose there are any of those who know God? Don't *they* pray and trust Him? And He doesn't do anything for them, does He?"

"Oh yes," said Dale quickly, "there are a lot of God's children over there, and a lot who are trusting Him, too. I know. I have a few friends, some among the fighters, some among the people who have lost their homes and their dear ones, and they are just *resting* in the Lord and waiting patiently for Him to set the world right. They believe He will do it. And while they are suffering, they are trusting, too, and they understand that this is all going to work out in the end for righteousness and for good to all."

"Well, I don't see that," said Corliss. "I couldn't trust that way, not with things going wrong the way they are. It doesn't seem kind in God."

"But you see, dear, you just don't know Him, and you don't understand what He is working out for the world. There is the question of sin that is everywhere, sin that has to be conquered. Sin for which He died to make a way for us to escape. And just as if *He* had sinned instead of us, He deliberately took our sins upon Himself and bore their punishment as if they had been His sins. We've nothing left to do but believe that He did it and accept what He did and take Him as our personal Savior, and we are free from it all."

The boy had stopped working with the puzzle and was looking at her, taking in all that she said, weighting it, pondering it. "I'd like to hear more about that," he said at last as he turned back to his puzzle. "It sounds reasonable, but not very likely. I don't know anybody that would do that for people. *Die* for them. Is all that in the Bible? That's a book I've never read. Just heard a snatch or two now and then read in school. But does it have real things like that in it?"

"Oh yes," said Dale with shining eyes. "I'd be glad to show you some of them if you would be interested."

"I think I would," said the boy.

And then suddenly the doorbell rang and Dale went to see who had come, although both the young people started up anxiously as if they thought they should go, and Dale realized that they always had in the back of their minds now the possibility of some change coming to their mother, the anxiety of what might happen next.

"It's all right, George," she said as she hurried to the door. "Probably some neighbor. I would likely have to go anyway." But they followed to the hall and hovered in the shadow until they heard it was a special-delivery letter, and as they couldn't possibly figure out how that could have anything to do with their affairs, they went back to the jigsaw puzzle again.

They heard Dale tear open the envelope, saw through the doorway how she paused eagerly to read the brief letter, and they looked up curiously to see the bright color in her cheeks and the glad, yet sorry, look in her eyes. But she went quietly over to her chair and sat down. "It's only a note from a dear friend who is probably being sent overseas, or somewhere, on a dangerous mission. He wanted me to know that he was starting, though he cannot tell me where. It is just sort of a good-bye, for the time being."

The two young people were very quiet for a long time, and the jigsaw puzzle grew into a semblance of the story it was to tell when finished. At last Corliss asked a question. "Does he—the one who wrote that letter—know God?"

Dale looked up with a bright smile. "Oh yes," she said happily. "He knows Him *very well*, and he is trusting in the Lord to help him through, whatever way He will, either to bring him back home or to his heavenly home."

"Do you mean there is any fighter, a *young* man, who feels that way about war and dying and all that?"

"Yes, I know a good many. Somehow didn't really trust God before they went over, but who have come to need Him and cry out for Him since they have been surrounded by death and terror. But this man especially really knows and trusts and is *happy* in the Lord."

It was just at that point that the kitchen door opened and Hattie walked in with a tray bearing three cups of hot chocolate topped with whipped cream and a heaping plate of delicious sandwiches. The young people pounced upon the food eagerly, and the subject for the time being was forgotten. Or was it? Did the two cousins, after they had retired for the night, lie awake pondering these things, which they had never known or thought of before? And Dale knelt long beside her bed praying for them.

But once more before she turned out her light she read the precious letter over again, then folding it she put it under her pillow before she lay down.

The letter was very short.

> *Dearest:*
>
> *Only a minute to write. Orders have just come through. We are about to leave for an unknown port and probably no opportunity to write again for some time. Be praying, and so will I. Remember, "All through the night" our Savior will be watching over us, and "Joy cometh in the morning." Trust on, beloved.*
>
> *David*

So when she lay down and closed her eyes, the bright words of faith from that letter illuminated her dark room. Out there beyond her window was the dark night and the hovering images of fears that might be threatening her beloved, but those words of trust made the difference in what might have been a message full of fear. So Dale, trusting, slept sweetly in spite of tomorrow, and more tomorrows, looming large and portentous ahead in a dreadful future, could not disturb her sleep because her faith was fixed upon the Rock, Christ Jesus.

Chapter 15

And while they slept, a long way off a ship slid out on the ocean, beginning its perilous way into the night.

David Kenyon had not expected this change to the new duties to which he had been transferred. He was ready to be an unimportant cog in the machinery of this war he had already given many weary months and much bravery to for the cause of righteousness. But to be put into a position of trust in place of a notable man whose health had failed in a crucial time had not been within the possibilities of his thought. Yet here he was, ordered to have charge, for the time, of a convoy transport, which there was every reason to suppose would be followed and bombed by the enemy from both under and on and over the sea. He had not known definitely just what his orders were to be when he wrote that note to Dale, yet now as he thought about it with the full responsibility of the new duties upon him, he was glad he had written as he had. It was his farewell to her for the time, and together they would be praying and trusting their all.

He watched the dim lights of the harbor disappear into blackness and wondered if he would ever see them again. It seemed a solemn time to him, almost like standing at his own deathbed, watching himself die. It was going to be his duty, presently, to watch for the enemy. Would he be equal to the task? He thought of the lives that would be dependent upon him, of the responsibility that would be his, and then as he went below to the bunk room to prepare for the night's duties, it came to him that it was not only his own deathbed that he might be set to watch but that of all the others, who were his comrades. He did not know them all very well yet, for he had been with most of them for only a few hours on the train across the country, but those other fellows were his responsibility, too. It might be their deathbeds also, as well as his own. And were they ready to die? With him it was right either way, for his heart was fixed on the eternal.

He cast his eyes around on the fellows in the bunk room. It was comparatively quiet. Only an occasional attempt at a joke, for all seemed thoughtful, suddenly brought to realize what might be before them that night. They were all getting dressed for their coming duty, a night on deck.

Some of their young faces looked hard and bitter, some careless, trying to whistle and laugh off the solemn thoughts that must come at a time of stepping into a night of peril.

There was one, a young lad, younger than any of them, who had recently come among them, and he looked exceedingly blue. The others had been kidding him, trying to find out what made him look like that, but the boy's face grew only more desperate. Somehow it reminded David of the way he used to feel when he had his first taste of danger. The other fellows had all had experience, too, though he could see that some of them were grave with apprehension even yet, whenever they were still long enough to let their thoughts take over. But this young lad touched David's heart deeply.

"What's the matter, kid?" he asked pleasantly. "Scared?"

He spoke with a heartening grin, but the boy lifted that desperate face to him and did not smile.

"Sure." he said solemnly. "Aren't you?"

"No," said David firmly, "not scared. Feeling a little solemn, perhaps, because this thing we're in is real, not just a game that doesn't matter, and of course death is stalking these waters, underneath and overhead as well. But we knew that would come sooner or later when we joined up with the outfit, and I don't feel that God is dead. I know He's looking after me."

"How'll that help you when the bombs begin to fall?" asked the boy. "I guess they're all good and scared, if they'd just own it, aren't you, fellows?"

Several of the men lowered their glances and gave a shamed assent.

"What I'd like to know," said the boy, looking straight at David, "is why you're not scared? Is it just because you've been in battles before? Have you got used to it and don't mind it anymore, or what?"

David shook his head. "No, Phil," he said gently. "It's because I have a Savior in whom I trust. I know He'll do the best for me, whatever comes. He's wise and powerful, and He's watching over me continually."

"Aw, that's all bunk," sneered an older man. "Nobody that was a God would be bothered watching over a lot of tough fellows that didn't give a hang about Him or never had paid any attention to Him. You just got brought up that way, Dave, and swallowed a lot of old traditions, that's all. But you can't tell me when you see bombs coming your way that you ever think about God or that your beliefs ever help you get by without being scared stiff."

"But it isn't like that, fellows," said David earnestly. "You've got it all wrong. In the first place, it isn't a lot of traditions. It's a Person whom I know and love and whose love has been with me through a good many years, in a lot of other troubles, so I know He'll not forget me now, and whatever He does for me will be the best that *could* come to me."

"Yes, but you see, I haven't got any such friend as that," said Phil, in a sort of contemptuous quiver. "I wasn't brought up with traditions. My folks never even went to church. And you can't just rest down and trust somebody you don't know and you're sure don't care a hang about you."

"Oh, but He does. He cares very much about you, Phil."

"What gives you that idea?" sneered the boy.

"Because He's said so, and all you have to do is believe it. He loved you so much that He gave His life for you, so that you might know you could be saved forever."

"I don't know how you could possibly know that."

"Because He has said so in the Bible, and I believe it. 'For God so loved the world. . .that *whosoever* believeth in him should not perish, but have everlasting life.' Then, there's another: 'He that heareth my word, and *believeth* on him that sent me, *hath* everlasting life, and *shall not* come into condemnation; but is passed from death unto life.' There are a lot of other proofs. I can show them to you if you care to read them, but aren't those enough for a start?"

"I suppose so, if I was sure He said it. If I was sure He was God and able to carry out His promise," said the kid miserably.

"Yes—well," said David thoughtfully, "if you were driving through an unknown country and lost your way and you came to a road that had a sign on it directing you to the place of your destination, would you stand there and debate and say, 'How do I know this is the right way? How do I know that somebody hasn't put this sign up just to fool me? Just to lead me into trouble? Or how do I know that it isn't a joke somebody is trying to play on me?' Would you go around looking for another road? Or would you turn down the road and try it out and see if it led to your city?"

"Well, I don't know. Maybe I'd looked for another road first."

"So?" said David. "Well, have you looked for another road yet? Is there any other way in a time like this when danger is on the way? Do you know any other way to meet God and not be afraid?"

"I suppose you can just trust to luck," said another young fellow dismally. "I suppose if you're going to get through you will, and if you aren't there's nothing you can do about it."

"That doesn't sound very hopeful, Sam. Do you think it does? Just swing out into the blackness and trust to *luck*?"

The boys sat earnestly, thoughtful, their heads bent. One caught his breath in something that sounded like a suppressed sob.

"Luck's no good. It's nothing to trust to," said another gloomily.

"Well, at home I used to go to Sunday school every Sunday for years, and just before I left home I joined the church to please my mother," said another tall boy with a tentative question in his voice.

They were all looking at David, so after a minute he answered, "Are you satisfied to offer that as your entrance ticket into eternity, Jim?"

The tall fellow sank down on his bunk and collapsed, burying his face in his crossed arms. "Oh, I don't know," he answered. "I don't feel sure about anything."

"Isn't it safer to take the condition Christ offers? He says, 'He that *believeth*.' If you're going to trust something, better get the conditions straight. Couldn't you just accept that offer of His and swing off and trust *Him*, and let Him prove it to you? That's what trust or belief really is. Letting God have the chance to prove it to you. I took it that way ever since He's given me peace. He'll give it to you, too, if you'll take it and try Him out."

There was a great silence for a long moment broken by the distant sound of an explosion. They had been hearing those at intervals all day, but somehow this one seemed to deepen the silence.

"We may not have much time ahead to accept that offer," suggested David.

The lad called Phil suddenly looked up, his eyes wild with fright. "*I'll* do it," he said with sudden conviction. "What do you have to do?"

"Just tell Him so," said David, coming close to the boy and

drawing him down on his knees beside the bunk, kneeling with his arm around the lad, and so he began to pray for him: "Oh God, our Creator, who loved us all and sent Your own Son to take our sin upon Himself and die the penalty for it, as if He had been Himself the sinner, we are coming to You, because You have said You love us and want to save us, and we do not know any other way to be saved except to believe what You have said. We know that we are going out in a few minutes into what may be sudden death for us all, and we know no power on earth can help us. So we are casting ourselves on You knowing that You will do the best for us that can be, because You love us and have died for us. So take us, and make us, whether in life or in death, Yours to all eternity, because You have promised and we have believed that promise and are trusting ourselves to it."

There was a brief pause, and David sat quietly. "Now, Phil, will you tell Him you accept Him as your personal Savior?"

Another pause, and then Phil's low, solemn voice, scarcely heard above the sounds of engine and waves: "Lord, I'm believing You and I'm taking You for my Savior now and forever. I've done a lot of sinning, but You said You'd take care of that. Thank You. And now, whatever comes, I'm Yours, Lord. Amen."

It had been very still there in the dim narrow bunk room. But one by one the other five fellows that were there had knelt down, and in a kind of group, with their faces buried in their folded arms. And as the two remained kneeling after their prayers, there came other voices.

"Lord, save me, too. I want my sins forgiven!"

"Lord, I'm afraid to die. Stay with me. Help me!"

"Oh God, I haven't been very good. I haven't pleased You, but won't You forgive me, too?"

"Lord, I'm scared stiff! Get me ready to die, too, please."

The man called Jim who had said he had no friend in God was the last to kneel down, and when he tried to speak his voice was broken with sobs: "Lord, I've been an awful sinner, and I've never believed or thought anything about You before, but here I am, and if You can do anything with me, Lord, save me!"

Then David's clear voice took up the prayer: "Lord, we believe. Help our unbelief and save us in the midst of all this terror. To live, or die, Lord, we commit ourselves to You."

Then from above them came a signal. It was time to go on duty. They all sprang up, a new look on their solemn faces, almost a smile on the face of the lad Phil as he brushed away a tear and gripped David's hand, saying fervently, "Thank you!" and dashed away to take his place in the line of duty.

And the others, with frank tears still on their faces, came by David Kenyon and gripped his hand. "Thanks, Dave," said one, "I'm all right now." And they all felt, as they moved out to meet what the night had in store for them, that there was a bond between them that nothing would ever break, in time or in eternity.

And suddenly a great joy came to David, such as he had not dreamed there could be on a night of peril like this one. He felt as if the blessing of the Lord had been bestowed upon him. For there had never been a joy like this one, to know the wonder of leading those needy souls to know Him, to know what it was to have the Lord with them. They joy that came to his own soul to have all fear of death removed, and then to know that, living or dying, all was well with those other fellows, too.

Was that what was meant by "the joy of the LORD" in the Bible? Was it that He allowed His children to share in His own joy in saved souls who had accepted His wonderful salvation? His heart thrilled and thrilled again as he made his way out to the place where duty called him, praying as he went, *Oh Lord, help me to give the right orders at the right time. Show me how to do my whole duty tonight. And please order the outcome according to Your will.*

Chapter 16

All that night the boys were out on duty under the sky, looking for enemy lights, and thinking. Now and again they looked up into the sky and sent their thoughts out to find God, to wonder at Him for making a way for them to be safe forever.

They walked the deck as if it were a sanctuary. For some of them, it was the first realization of a personal God that had ever come to their consciousness. As they met one another on duty, there was a grave, shy smile in their eyes, as if they belonged to some secret order. And later, before they took their rest toward dawn, they knelt in the dimness of the bunk room and then lay down to sleep, over the enemy-infested sea, with a quietness in their hearts that they had not known before.

Late in the next day, the enemy was sighted more than once, and when night came there were distant flashes and sounds of planes, vanishing and coming again.

The night was very dark. As the hours dragged by, not even a single star could be seen in the blackness above. David Kenyon, alone for the moment looking down at the deck, saw his comrades pacing back and forth and his heart rejoiced to think of them as they had knelt to His Christ. And they had all meant it, he was sure. Now, whatever came, he felt sure of seeing them all in the Father's house above. His thoughts paused tenderly when he remembered that someday he might tell this all in a letter to Dale. Or perhaps tell her face-to-face if it pleased God to let him go home. Just now, of course, there was no opportunity to even send letters. His duty was imperative and all-absorbing. But how he would enjoy telling of those buddies of his and their surrender to his Savior!

Suddenly there was a signal. A light! A sound! A plane coming on! More lights! More sounds! More planes! The enemy was here at last and coming strong!

With one swift look above, David turned to give commands, lifting a quick prayer with a passing wonder what it was going to be like to be suddenly ushered into the Presence of God. He was conscious of a lifting of his heart as he went quickly into action to meet the oncoming test.

"God by my side," he said softly to himself, "all through the night."

Suddenly bombs splintered the blackness of the night and a shudder came from the sea beneath. Great geysers of water spouting within a hundred yards, downpouring, were flooding the decks, drenching everything, and then sucking back to the sea, taking all in its way with it. It washed the men from their feet, sending them sprawling against the rails, barely saving themselves. *Oh God, are You there? Yes. Thank You! Seven men all safe so far. Phil? Yes, clinging to the master yonder.* Boom! Another blast! This was the night they had known was coming when they first prayed. The night they had trusted the Lord to be with them. To live or die! Unafraid? Unafraid, because God was there!

David gave his orders in firm, crisp tones as the noise died out for an instant. His men looked up, and their eyes answered his. What would it be like in heaven, if that was where they were going now? Yet, they would all have liked to finish their job for victory before they left. But God had His plans. *Ready, Lord! What will You have me to do?*

There came another bomb! And another of those shuddering undersea attacks! Another geyser more torrential than before. David called a sharp order for his men's protection, and the enemy came again.

More planes overhead, more bombs dropped. Then a terrific explosion and the forward part of their ship was shot away, *gone*! He could scarcely believe his eyes. Absolutely sliced off and disappeared! That meant the men that were on that part were down under the sea? Who were they? And the radio? *Gone!* The smoke and storm obscured the atmosphere. It was of no use to look for his buddies, even if he could see through the smoke. There was no time. It was only a question of moments— seconds even, perhaps—before they would all go down.

There came another geyser. A great plume of water close at hand plunging down, greater than any before. A real inundation. Even David was swept over, though he had tried to anchor himself. And when it was past, he looked around for the rest of his men. The fellows that just a little before this happened had been kneeling together to commit themselves again to the care of the Almighty. Where were they? And as he looked the wash came back violently from the top side of the tilted ship, and the men with it, and swept them all into the sea! *His men!* He looked aghast. Down into that inferno of burning oil and tossing water! His men! Going into glory by *fire!* The boys he had been working with. The boys who had prayed with him that morning. Somehow they had all prayed with him that morning. Somehow they had all seemed to feel this day was the end of things.

The enemy was coming in thick and fast now. There was fire in either end of the ship. Some of the brave men were putting it out and fighting also, and David, as he turned around to give an order, saw the enemy coming on again in full force. Planes and ships and submarines working together against them. Was there time for one more effort before he, too, must go? He called an order that instantly started what guns they had left. *Oh God, keep us true. Make us brave to the end.*

Another great explosion; two more geysers shot up almost beside him and descended in torrential floods. His buddies were gone, washed out to that awful frothing, flaming sea and disappeared! Bless God, they had gone *Home!* But there were still some gunners left. Another chance before all was over.

He gave the command and the guns spoke sharply, quickly.

Something struck David on his head. Fire and darkness came upon him. He did not see the enemy turn to flee in panic. He did not know that his last effort had turned the tide of battle. He felt the ship turning over, and he reached out to take hold of something, anything that he could hold on to as he went down to join those buddies of his whom he had led to know his Lord. This was God's will, now, that he should go. God's will was best, and he was content.

For an instant, he roused to remember Dale. If only he might have written her farewell. But she would know where he had gone. It would be hard for her. But perhaps they would find the little note he had written and fastened in his Testament over his heart, a note he wrote when he first started on this unknown expedition. A last word in case he did not come back. God keep her, his dear girl!

Once he roused enough to know someone was trying to lift him. He tried to tell them not to bother. It was too late, and then all got black again. The explosions seemed very far away. He was now definitely on his way to God.

Did it always take so long to die, or was it only a moment after all? So many thoughts could press upon his brain and flash a meaning to his fading soul. His ship! What of his ship? He was responsible for what was left of his ship! Shouldn't he do something about that, or was it too late? He had distinctly felt it turning over, hadn't he? Felt the sea beside him, close beside him so that he could touch it, or was that the hallucination of a brain under strain? But would God look after his ship for him? Yes of course, if God was taking him Home. It was God's ship, and he would be answerable to God now, not even to the navy. God was above the navy. Only David wanted to have done his duty bravely, in his fight for righteousness. But God was the captain, and God would look after the outcome of the battle. Would perhaps explain it all to him when he got over there at Home with his captain.

Then he drifted into a dream of Dale, sitting against the hemlocks, holding his hands, and giving sweet promises, her lips upon his, her smile for his eyes. Dear Dale! Perhaps one day up above they could talk this all over and understand why it had been this way. Dear Dale! She would be praying for him now, perhaps.

The sea was very close to him now. He felt as if he were riding Home. Would be meeting his comrades, perhaps before they entered glory? Would they all go in together? Well, it would be all right however it was. They had taken his Lord for Savior. They would not be shy meeting Him. And it was very dark now. The end! There would be glory soon and no more regrets. All peace and blessedness. Dale would be coming, too, someday. Good night! God would be with her all through the night.

≈≈≈

Back home, Dale was kneeling *then*, praying that God would be with David wherever he was, on land or sea, perhaps by some strange telepathic influence feeling that he was in special peril.

When the morning came there was another day, with its own problems, so far remote from the exaltation of the night before when she had felt for a time so very near to David.

Now, this morning David was far away somewhere on the sea probably, going through hard things, in peril, perhaps. He had expected that if he was sent out again. And she, Dale, had homely duties to perform, common details to look after, questions to settle. There, for instance, was that meeting in her church that she had promised to attend. It was a meeting sponsored by her Sunday school class of girls. They would feel aggrieved if she was not there, and there were little details that they would expect her to advise them about. Yet how could she conscientiously leave her cousins? They were desolate and seemed to depend on her. Of course they could go to the movies again, probably, but somehow she felt that was not the place for them, now in their uneasy, restless state of mind. They were just beginning to be strangely dependent upon her, to look to her for entertainment and ways to while the anxious hours away. Little by little she was growing to feel that their unhappiness was not altogether on account of their mother's illness. They had come to believe what the doctor had told them—that she would presently be well again and quite all right. But there was something more to their uneasiness, she was sure. She must find out what it was if possible and try to discover a remedy for it. She must not lose her weak hold over them, now when they were just beginning to turn to her and trust her. What was she going to do about it?

In the end she went to her Lord in prayer and laid the whole burden down at His feet. *Dear Lord, here's something I just can't do anything about. Please manage it for me.*

Then she went downstairs and found the two cousins working hard at the puzzle they had not quite finished the night before, and they greeted her cheerfully, quite as if she was a real pal. She marveled at the change that had come upon them in these few short days while they were going through trying times.

They had a cheery breakfast, and while they ate the telephone rang. It was one of Dale's Sunday school students, consulting her about the meeting that night, and with her mind still undecided about whether she ought to go, she answered the girl briefly: "Yes Doris, I *hope* it is going to be possible for me to be there. I have been trying to plan all the week for it. But Doris, if I *shouldn't* be able to make it, I'll be sure to call you beforehand. And if that should happen, suppose you get Margaret Dulles to take my place and greet everybody."

"Oh Miss Huntley!" came a dismayed voice over the telephone, so loud in protest that the two cousins could not help but hear. "We can't possibly get along without you. And besides, Margaret Dulles has gone to her cousin's wedding in New York and she won't be back for over a week. You just *must* come. There isn't anybody else to take your place. That old Mrs. Gromley will want to take over, and she always makes everybody so mad. It just won't do!"

"Well, why not take it all in your own hands, Doris? I'm sure you could be a very nice hostess."

"Me? Oh! *No!* I never could do it! I should just die if I had to take over responsibility that way. I really *won't.* And you know all the girls would be deadly jealous. They always say I try to get in the limelight. Miss Huntley, it'll be a regular flop if you don't come. What's the reason you can't? You are *sick*, are you?"

"No," said Dale thoughtfully, "I'm not sick, but you know my aunt had an accident and is in the hospital, and my two cousins are here. I really don't like to leave them just now when they are under such a strain."

"Oh, but can't you bring them along? I'm sure they would enjoy it. The speaker is perfectly marvelous, they say. He's been in all the major battles in the Pacific, and he tells about it very vividly. And the singing will be swell. I've heard the quartette myself, and it's perfectly spiffy. Would it do any good if I were to come around and invite them? I think I have time."

"Oh, that's kind of you, Doris, but I don't think that will be necessary. I'll see what I can do about it. I'll let you know later. I'll arrange *something* for you, anyway. Don't worry."

When Dale came back to the table, the cousins looked up.

"What is it, Dale? Anything we can do for you?" asked George.

Dale's eyes brightened. "Why, that's awfully thoughtful of you, George," she said. "There *is* something you could help me out with if you don't mind, but I'm afraid it might bore you."

"What is it, Dale?" asked Corliss eagerly. "You've done a lot of things for us that must have bored you. I guess we could stand being bored a couple of hours or so for your sake. Is there really something you want us to do? It might even be interesting, you know."

"Yes, that's quite true," said Dale thoughtfully. "I'm told the program is very fine. But of course they will all be strangers to you. Though I don't want to leave you here without anything to do a whole evening."

"Forget it!" said George loftily. "We aren't infants. And anyway, what is it? We can stand anything once."

"Well, you see our church is interested in a young college that has only been going a few years, and my Sunday school class of girls has undertaken to have their college quartette and glee club come and give us a performance and tell a few words about the college. You see, one of our own boys from the Sunday school has been studying there for three years, and now he's overseas, and everybody wants to help his alma mater for Jan Hooper's sake. So this is the night they are coming, and I promised to be there and meet them and perhaps say a few words about our boy who is now in combat. But I was going to try and get somebody else to take my place. Since your mother was hurt, I didn't feel as if I wanted to leave you alone."

"Leave us alone, *nothing*! We're *going*, Cousin Dale," said Corliss unexpectedly. "We'll go with you, of course; won't we, George?"

"Sure we will," said George. "Besides, if you're going to speak, we wouldn't miss it for the world. Even if the program isn't good. Tell us about it. What time do we go?"

"Well, that's certainly nice of you," said Dale appreciatively. "The meeting is at eight o'clock. We'd have to leave here around seven. Well, that takes a load of my mind. I'll call Doris and tell her it is all right, I'll be there. And now I think it's about time for us to go to the hospital."

But when they reached the hospital they found the patient in a most difficult mood.

"Powelton, I want you to go down to the city right away and find that lawyer of mine. I positively *will not* be put off *another hour*. I've simply *got* to see him. It's very important, and you'll be responsible for making me a lot worse if you don't get hold of him at once. Do you understand? And don't let them put you off by any of these stories they've been telling the nurse, that he is out of the city, because I'm sure he's not, and I won't stand for his treating me this way another day. Now that's your job, Powelton, and I want you to start at once."

The lad gave his cousin one despairing look and then quietly answered his mother. "Why yes, Mother, I'll do the best I can. But I still think you are making a great mistake getting mixed up with a man like that. I don't believe he is an honest man. He doesn't sound like it to me."

"Be still, Powelton, and do as you're told. You're not grown up enough to be a suitable judge of people, and anyway, this is my affair. Go!"

"Very well, Mother," said Powelton, with so little of his usual disagreement that his mother stared at him in surprise. "Shall I report back here after my errand is done?"

"Why certainly! You may bring the lawyer back with you just as soon as possible."

Without another word, and with only a sweeping glance toward Dale and Corliss, George turned and marched out of the hospital, and the two girls by Mrs. Huntley's bed stood silently, with averted gaze, both understanding just how unpleasant this errand was going to be for the boy, for he had expressed his views about the lawyer more than once.

It was finally Corliss who broke the silence after George left. "Mamma, when are you coming back to the house? Aren't they letting you get up pretty soon? What has the doctor said?"

The mother looked at Corliss languidly. "The doctor? Oh, he never says anything. Just tells me I'm getting along as well as could be expected. I've told him again and again that I never shall get better until I have a room to myself, but he says that's something they don't expect to have in the hospital, not till the war is over. That's ridiculous, of course. They're just trying to get me to offer some enormous sum for a private room, but they've overstepped themselves. I shall not offer a single cent more until they actually move me to a good big room. That stuff about not having a room is ridiculous. A great big institution like this and no private room for a woman who is willing to pay for the best they have."

"But, Mother, you're mistaken. We know, for we've been all over the hospital, and every nook and cranny is filled with cots and patients, even the hallways. We came in the back door today, and we could hardly get by to the elevator."

"That may be true about the common halls where the poor people are put, but you didn't open the doors and look into all the private rooms, did you?"

"Why yes, Mother," said Corliss eagerly. "Dale and I talked it over, and we thought we would just go around all the halls and see if we could discover a room that wasn't occupied, so we did. You see, we thought perhaps somebody was being moved home or something, and we went all around and looked in all the rooms, for you see, this was the time when most of the doors are standing wide open, or if they are not we could ask a nurse. But Mother, there wasn't a single one empty, and *all* of them had two beds and sometimes three in them. And there were three emergency cases this morning, accidents, and they don't know where to put them. There isn't another spot where they can put another bed, and I heard the head nurse say there was nothing else to do but to send a few cases home before they were supposed to go. That's the reason I asked you whether the doctor had any idea of sending you home today."

"Well, I certainly am not going to let them send me home until it's time. I'm not going to be cheated out of my rights by some petty accident case. That certainly wouldn't be fair. Besides, I haven't any home to go to. I couldn't, of course, go back out west when I am not about to take care of myself yet, could I? And I've no other place to go. I have been distinctly told by Dale that I'm no longer welcome in what she calls *her* house, so until I can get some sort of settlement about that house from my lawyer, I couldn't leave here at present."

"Oh, but Aunt Blanche," said Dale earnestly, "you are mistaken. I did not *ask* you to leave. I told you I was going to have a school, and I was afraid it would not be comfortable for you with a lot of children in the house. But that is all changed now. I have given up the idea of having the school for the present. I have found another girl who has taken it over, and so we shall have plenty of room for you as long as it is convenient for you to stay, and we will, of course, do our best to take care of you and make you as comfortable as possible. And I have only been waiting until you were feeling a little better and able to make your plans to tell you this. My cousins and I have been getting on very pleasantly together, and I'm sure we have all been looking forward to your coming back to us as soon as you are able. There will be room for a nurse, too, as long as you need her. I thought maybe we should be inquiring about that, for they say nurses are very hard to get, and I know they have been terribly short on nurses here. Of course if worse come to worst, Corliss and I might be able to make you comfortable. I'm not exactly ignorant about nursing, for I've had a short course in it, and then I've had a good deal of experience taking care of Grandmother. But I suppose you will be a little happier if you can persuade one of the regular nurses here to be with you, at least for the first few days of your homecoming. Have you spoken to your nurse yet to see if that would be possible?"

"Spoken to her? No, certainly not. I wouldn't have one of these nurses on any account. They are abominable. But of course you would be no better. I fancy that taking care of your grandmother was a very trifling matter compared with my case. And in any event, I shouldn't think of troubling you. Not after what you said. I certainly could not be comfortable there, not after the way you have treated me and my children."

"Mother! You mustn't say that," put in Corliss. "Dale has been perfectly wonderful to us all through this horrible experience. She has been just lovely. She's played games with us and bought jigsaw puzzles for us, and we've had a grand time. If it hadn't been for you being sick and us not knowing what was going to happen, we would really have had a lovely time. I like this place; I really do."

"That will do, Corliss. Don't go into hysterics about this. If you could enjoy yourself while I was suffering I suppose I ought to feel glad, but I can't say I relish your attitude. And no, certainly I'm not coming to that house! As soon as the doctor comes, I will ask him if he can't send us up to your Aunt Evelyn's in Connecticut. We'll take a nurse along, maybe two, for the journey. I'll risk it, but I can get plenty of nurses when I get up, and I think I shall get up today. I'm not going to be kept down any longer!"

Corliss gave Dale a frightened look. What had she done by starting this subject? But perhaps the doctor would be able to straighten her mother out on a few things.

Then the nurse came in and announced that it was time for the patient to take a nap.

"But I'm expecting my lawyer," snapped the patient. "I simply can't take a nap till I get my business settled. After that I'm going away, and you can't tell me anymore when to take a nap, for I'll be my own mistress again."

But the nurse went quietly about her duties, gave the patient her medicine, arranged the blanket, plumped up the pillows, and adjusted the screen around the bed. And in the meantime Dale and Corliss slipped away and went home.

Chapter 17

Very solemnly the two girls walked along, not talking until they were some distance from the hospital. At last Corliss spoke. "Why do you suppose my mother acts like that, Dale? Is she sort of out of her head, do you think?"

Dale gave a troubled sigh. "No, I don't think so, dear. I think she's probably just hurt and worried with a lot of things. I'm afraid I hurt her by telling her about my school. I didn't mean to, of course, but I just didn't know how to plan, and I had promised the committee I would start the school."

"Of course," said Corliss. "And now you have given it all up just for us, and Mamma talked that way to you! I can't bear to think *my mother* would be that way to you after you've been so nice and kind to us."

"Well, don't worry any more about it, dear. I guess I must

have been to blame the way I spoke. I should have waited till she got ready to tell me what she was going to do, only I had to tell the ladies before they had their next meeting. I guess I didn't tell the Lord about it and ask Him to look out for it. When I don't do that, I usually get into trouble."

Corliss looked at her in wonder. "Do you always talk to God about everything you do?" she asked.

"I should," said Dale, "but sometimes I get going my own plans and forget that the Lord knows better what He wanted me to do. I'll have to ask Him to straighten this out for me."

"I suppose that would be a wonderful way to live," said Corliss thoughtfully. "I always plan to do what *I* want and not bother about anything else. But I guess maybe that's why I always get into so much trouble. I wonder if my mother knows how to live this way. Sometime maybe I'll tell her about it, but I don't know. It might only make her furious. She never likes me to know anything she doesn't know."

"Well, but we can pray for her, that God will show her. After all, that might be better than telling her about it now, though sometime God may show you a way to tell it. And now I'm wondering how George got along with his errand. I won-der if he got hold of the lawyer and persuaded him to come to your mother. If he didn't, I'm afraid George will have a pretty bad time when he gets back. But never mind. We'll pray about that, too."

"Do you think my prayers would do any good?" asked Cor-liss after a minute of silence. "I've never been very good myself, and I'm sure God doesn't think much of me."

"Oh yes, God loves you. He wants you to take what He has done for you in dying on the cross and taking your sins on

Himself, and if you'll take Him as your Savior that means you are born again and are His child. Surely, pray, but first pray for yourself; tell Him that you are sorry for your sins and that you will accept Him as your Savior. Then when you are His child you can ask Him for other things. Now, here we are home, and probably lunch is ready. Shall we wait for George, or do you think he will get lunch in the city?"

"He won't bother to wait for lunch. He'll get back to the hospital and then come home. And perhaps Mother'll be asleep when he gets there so he won't have to wait. I think he'll be here soon. But let's sit down when Hattie is ready. I can save something for him if he doesn't come in time."

But George arrived soon after they had sat down. He was breathless from a rapid walk, and his eyes were troubled. "I didn't go back to the hospital," he said worriedly. "That lawyer is not to be found. They say he is gone up to Canada on business and won't be back for several weeks. I don't much believe it. I think he doesn't want to talk with Mom anymore, and he just tells his secretary to say that. I even went to his apartment, but the housekeeper had the same tale, and they wouldn't even give me his address. They said he was off for his health and couldn't be bothered with business. So there! What was I to do? I knew if I went back to the hospital, I'd have all kinds of time with Mom, so I just telephoned the nurse and told her about it. Told her to ask Mom what I should do. But she said Mom was asleep and she shouldn't wake her now, but she would tell her after she had her lunch and phone us if there was any message. I don't know if I did the right thing or not, but I couldn't help being glad that bum wasn't there. I don't trust him. I think he is putting it all over on Mom."

"Yes," said Dale. "He hasn't a very good reputation. But perhaps your mother will forget about it this afternoon and there will be a little more time to work this out."

"She says she is going to write Aunt Evelyn, George, and we are all going there as soon as she is able to get up."

"Not *me!*" said George. "That's an aunt I never want to see again if I can help it. She is worse than Mom about finding fault, and she thinks I'm the world's worst. I simply won't go there!"

"Well, don't worry about that now, George. Wait till the time comes and maybe there'll be a way to work it out," said Dale.

"There sure will as far as I'm concerned," said George.

"What if we go upstairs for an hour or so and see how we can fix up a nice room for your mother to come back to as soon as she is done at the hospital. Then we can tell her it's all arranged, and maybe she will be pleased," Dale suggested.

"Oh *yeah?*" said George unbelievingly. "I never saw her pleased yet at anything anybody did for her. But of course we can try it."

"George, you ought not to be so hard on your mother," said Dale, with a troubled look. "After all, she's your mother, and she's sick and suffering."

"Okay, I know it," said George penitently. "I guess I'm sort of a heel, but it certainly makes me mad the way she finds fault with everybody. That pretty little nurse at the hospital was almost in tears about her when I talked to her on the phone. But I guess I shouldn't act this way, of course. Only nobody is going to make me go to Aunt Evelyn's, not on your life they aren't."

"No," said Corliss, "and I won't go either. But we'll have to wait till Mamma is better before we can say anything about that. Maybe she'll be pleased after all if we fix up a room here, only it will be hard on Dale."

"No," said Dale, "I *want* her to come. I wouldn't feel right if she didn't, and perhaps if she comes we can make her have a nice time and get a better feeling between us all."

George grinned. "Wishful thinking!" he commented, and then added, "Well, mebbe! I sure hope so."

"Listen!" said Dale. "Let's make a game of this and get really interested in it. Let's go upstairs right away and see what you think about which room we should prepare."

"Oh, I know which room she will want, if she takes any," said Corliss. "She'll want the room you gave to me, the one where she used to take her naps, and George's room would be just right for the nurse while she is here. George and I can park anywhere, down in the living room on the couches, if you don't mind."

"Oh, that won't be necessary," said Dale. "You can come in my room with me, Corliss, and George can go up in the front third-story room, if he doesn't mind. It isn't very large, but there is a comfortable bed up there. I used to sleep there myself sometimes when Grandmother had company. There is a bureau, too, and a chair, so I guess you could be comfortable."

"Sure I can. I'll get along anywhere. That will be swell."

"Well, come on up and see what you think," said Dale, and they trooped happily upstairs.

"You can put your things in the hall closet, Corliss. It's all empty. I took everything out of it yesterday and packed them away in trunks in the storeroom upstairs, and Hattie cleaned it, so it's all ready for you. Do you want to move your things now? I think it might cheer your mother up if she knew we had everything ready for her and the nurse."

"Sure, I'll move them right away. I think this is going to be fun," said Corliss. "Are you going to move upstairs now, George?"

"Okay," said George. "It *might* have some effect on Mom if she knew everything was all fixed. And we could get used to it. Then Hattie can get everything ready for Mom and the nurse."

"All right, but here is something else I want to tell you first," said Dale. "There is Grandmother's room, of course, and if you think your mother would rather have that I can take Grandmother's things out of the room and pack them away, and I will if you think your mother would prefer that. Or, if either of you would rather have it than the other plans I suggested."

"But I thought you said you didn't want anybody to have that room, Dale. I thought you said you wanted to keep everything just as she had left it." This came from Corliss, spoken thoughtfully.

"I know. I did want to keep it just as she left it for a while," said Dale. "But perhaps I was wrong to feel that way. If you think I should give it up, I'll be glad to do so. I want your mother to be comfortable. Or, Corliss, if *you* still would like to have that room, I can arrange that. I don't want to be selfish."

"No," said Corliss sharply. "I don't want the room, and I don't much think mother would. Anyway, I don't think she should have it, not after the way she's acted to you."

"No," said George. "She shouldn't, and neither should Corliss. You have been awfully good to us, and you have a right to do what you want to with your own house. No, I think the other arrangement is much better."

"Wait," said Dale, taking a key out of her breast pocket. "I want to show you the room, and perhaps you will understand why I felt almost as if it was a sacred place. But I guess that was silly, and if Grandmother's room is going to make things easier, why here it is, and it shall be up to you who is to have it."

Dale put the key into the lock and flung the door open, and the two cousins stood solemnly in the doorway and looked around, wide eyed and interested.

"Why, it's sweet," said Corliss, two great tears gathering in her eyes. "I don't wonder you didn't want me to come barging into this room. It looks just like I remember Grandmother."

Suddenly Dale reached over and kissed Corliss softly on her forehead. "You're a dear!" she said. "I'm so glad you feel that way. I was afraid you would want to make fun of the quaint old-fashioned things, and I just couldn't stand that. And now since you feel this way, I don't mind if you come in here to sleep. I really don't, Corliss. And I think Grandmother would like it, too. That will likely be more comfortable for you than sleeping in my room me."

"No," said Corliss, shrinking back. "I'd love to share your room. I really would. I'd like it a lot. But I'm glad you let me see this room. It somehow seems to be a real place, and I think I understand you better for seeing it."

"Yes," said George, huskily. "I'm glad you showed it to us. And I don't blame you for wanting to keep it as she left it. I know just how you feel about it. And I'm glad Corrie thinks so, too. If anybody sleeps there, it ought to be you, Dale. Grandmother would like that better, I'm sure. But anyway, Mom wouldn't choose it for herself, I know, because she told me that other room where she took her naps was the nicest in the house, she thought. It wasn't as noisy as Grandmother's. That fronts on the street, and she said you could hear all the children crying and shouting and playing. No, Dale, you better just keep that room as it was. Open it up sometimes if you want to, but don't give it to any of us. Not now. Come on and let's get Mom's room fixed. Anything you want carried anywhere, Dale? I'm strong and able."

"Thank you," Dale said, smiling. "We'll see. Now, let's fix your mother's room first. What needs moving out? Corliss, have you heard your mother say she didn't like anything in this room?"

Corliss looked around with troubled eyes. "Well yes," she said reluctantly. "Mother never liked that bureau. She said the one in the room you intend for the nurse was much larger and more roomy. She liked the big mirror, too."

"Why, that is easily changed," said Dale. "Come on, George, let's get to work. We'll move the other one out of the way and then there will be a place to put this. And Corliss, what else did she want changed?"

"Well, she said she'd rather have one of the overstuffed chairs from the living room, instead of that straight-up-and-down one that had long rockers to fall over. But I don't think you ought to change that. The big chair belongs in the living room, and this rocker wouldn't fit there."

"Oh, nonsense," said Dale. "What difference does that make? A chair is a chair, and they are easily changed. Anything else?"

"No," laughed Corliss, "only that engraving of the Lord's Prayer in the gold frame. She said she didn't like it, and she always turned it around to face the wall when she lay down. She said she didn't want to always be confronted by religion.

I'm ashamed to tell you this, but you asked me."

"That's all right, Corliss. We'll have those things changed in a jiffy. Are you sure there was nothing else she didn't like?"

"No, that's all, except the big pincushion. She said it was all out of style to have cushions like that."

"Well," said Dale, laughing, "if that's all, I guess we can get by."

"But I don't think this is right, Dale," said George, "to make all this trouble for you, and when she may not come after all. I don't think it is a bit polite of Mom to want it."

"There, there, George. We want to get this room so she will like it, don't we? Well, don't let's stop on little things like that. Let's make it nice for her, the way she wants it, and maybe she will be happy about coming. And say, I've been thinking. Suppose you two go to the hospital without me now, and then you can tell her about it and not feel hampered with having me around. Then she can tell you just what she really wants. I think that will be better, don't you?"

"But we'd rather you went along," said Corliss.

"Next time, dear," promised Dale. "Besides, I have to go to that committee meeting about the school and tell them what I had planned and introduce the girl who is to take my place. It really is better this way just for this time. Now come, let's get this furniture in place and get it done so it looks pretty and you can draw a word-picture of it for your mother."

The young people worked with a will and soon had the two rooms in lovely order. Dale went to her store of pretty linens and selected two of her nicest bureau doilies and some of her best towels and the rooms looked pretty as pictures.

"We'll get a rosebud or two for the bureau, and I'll put my

bud vase in here," said Dale as they stood surveying it all when it was finished. And even Hattie came to stand in the doorway and look.

"I'll take the curtains down, Miss Dale, and wash 'em," said Hattie. "It won't take long to iron 'em and get 'em up, and when you come back you'll be surprised."

"Thank you, Hattie," said George suddenly. "And Dale, I'll take that engraving up to my room. Do you mind? I seem to feel I'd like to have it where I can look at it for a while. It's very old, isn't it?"

"Yes," said Dale. "It belonged to great-grandfather, Allan Dale, and that's one reason why I have always liked it. Yes, take it to your room. I'll be glad to think you are looking at it sometimes. And now, it's getting late and you two ought to be going. Remember, you have a very important mission, and I'll be praying for you while you are gone. Good-bye."

They separated, and the brother and sister went solemnly on their way, planning together their campaign.

"We'll have to settle that matter of her old rat of a lawyer first," said George. "I'll have to make her understand that he is gone absolutely and we can't possibly get hold of him, and then you can start in and tell her about the room if you want to, Corrie, and what we've been helping Dale to do. Don't forget to tell her how she offered you Grandma's room if you wanted it. That'll make a big hit with Mom."

"I don't know if she'll listen to anything I say about the room. She got pretty mad at me this morning when I tried to ask her when she was coming back home. She said she had no home to come to, and a lot of other things, and then Dale spoke up and told her she never meant to hurry her away and that of course she wanted her to come here now, that this was the proper place for her to be getting well, and she was as nice as could be. But it didn't do a bit of good. She just told me I needn't get into hysterics on that subject, and you know, all that old stuff she always shuts me up with."

"Well, never mind, you go ahead, Corrie. I'll back you up, and we'll try to work it out."

"All right, I'll try again," sighed the girl, and they walked with discouragement up the steps of the hospital to their appointed task.

Chapter 18

When the two walked timidly into the hospital and up to their mother's bed, she was partly sitting up against her pillows and eyeing them as if they were a couple of criminals plotting to keep her from her rights.

"Well," she said, looking sharply at George, "where is my lawyer? I thought I told you to bring him with you. Where is he?"

The boy braced up bravely and looked at his mother courageously in the eye, a slightly apologetic smile on his lips.

"Sorry, Mother," he said courteously, "so far as I can find out, he has gone out of the country. The nearest suggestion I could get from his office or his home either, is that he went to Canada to spend a few months in the woods and try to recover from a severe nervous breakdown. And he has ordered his secretary and what there is left of his family not to disclose his address to anybody. I've done my best to get some other answer, but there doesn't seem to be any way to get any further information."

Mrs. Huntley's face was stony cold and the look she gave her children was as if she suspected them of making up this story. But after a few minutes of characteristic storming and questioning, she began to cry. Just big stormy tears pelting down her angry cheeks and her lips trembling almost pitifully.

Corliss looked around with a worried expression to see if the nurse was near, for if she was she would undoubtedly send them away for making her patient weep, and this really must be stopped.

Corliss got out a crisp little handkerchief, softly wiping her mother's tears away, as gently as if she had been a baby, and the mother looked up astonished, the action was so unprecedented. Corliss had never been known to do the like before.

Then Corliss began to talk softly, quietly, as a mother might comfort a little child. "There, Mamma, don't feel bad. There'll be some other way. Don't you worry. Listen. We've got some nice things to tell you. We're getting ready for you to come home to the house. Dale and my brother and I have been working at it ever since lunch, and we've fixed it all up so prettily. We've moved the bureau you didn't like, and got the nice big chair in your room and taken the old rocker out, and the picture you didn't like is gone, too. We had a lot of fun doing it. Dale didn't mind at all. In fact, she thinks it looks lots better. And she got out her very prettiest bureau doilies. And the curtains are being washed, all crisp and nice, and everything is going to be lovely. And we've fixed up the next room for your nurse, and we wondered if you couldn't be allowed to come home in a day or two. It would be lots nicer for you there, and then we could talk about plans and things without having a lot of people listening the way they do here."

Then the son spoke up. "Yes, Moms, I think that would be better. I thought I'd go down now and have a talk with the doctor and see what he says, and then we could get the ambulance and take you very comfortably."

"No, no, *no!*" exclaimed the sick woman. "I can't go till I see my lawyer. He's taken all my money and he hasn't done anything about it."

"Never mind, Moms, we'll see about that after we get you to the house—"

The mother stared at this boy who had always been bored at any planning for herself and didn't know what to make of it all. "But I can't go to Dale's," she mourned, more tears coming down.

Corliss got up and dabbed at the tears again. "Don't worry, Mamma," she said coaxingly, "we're looking after you, and yes, you *can* go to Dale's house. She *wants* you. She really does. If you could have seen her going around with her eyes so bright, smiling and planning to put pretty things in your room, you would be sure she wants you. You'll like it there. And Hattie has been planning to make some spoon bread for you. Come on, cheer up, Muv, and let's have a happy time. And when we get you home and you're really well, then we can talk over plans for what we'll do next."

So they kept on coaxing, and the mother, amazed to have some real loving comfort offered her, finally settled down and ceased her objections. George, delighted at the outcome, began to think of Dale's promise when they came away, to be praying for them. Did prayer really ever do any good?

The two young people were greatly comforted themselves that they did not have to go back with ugly refusals ringing in their ears. The nurse had told them she thought the doctor would think their mother might be well enough to be moved in a few days now, and the mother almost put on a watery little smile for them. Was that the effect of Dale's prayers?

So they went home to Hattie's nice dinner and then hurriedly to Dale's meeting with her, wondering whether they really hadn't made a mistake promising to go with Dale. Would they be bored after all? But they had promised, and they couldn't go back on Dale after all she had tried to do for them.

They started early, for Dale had duties to perform before the talent arrived, and while she was organizing her girls who were to be ushers, the brother and sister sat together conversing in low tones about what their mother would likely do after she was well enough to travel and what *they* wanted to do.

"There's one thing I *won't* do," said Corliss stubbornly. "I won't go near Aunt Evelyn's. Do you know what I'm going to do? I'm going to college somewhere if I can manage it, or else I'll get a job in some defense plant."

So they quietly and unhappily plotted, knowing that any plan they could make would likely be swiftly overthrown by their mother when she got back to her normal self.

Then presently the talent arrived, several young men and a girl, and Dale brought them over and introduced them to her cousins.

George was interested at once, and Corliss sat looking them over, filled with interest. They all were bright faced and well dressed, though plainly, and she couldn't quite place them socially. There were a few in uniform—some soldiers and some sailors. One was introduced as the dean of the college, though he seemed quite young, and he and George fell at once into conversation. Corliss wondered what it could be about. Something about the college she judged, though she caught only a word or two of their conversation.

Then the meeting began with a burst of song from the audience, followed by a chorus from the glee club, and a number by the quartette, who were publicly and informally introduced to the audience. George and Corliss were interested from the start.

There was a brief talk from the young dean about the college, especially stressing its Christian character, which for the moment somewhat dampened George's ardor. But he soon forgot that aspect and grew interested in the personality of the different speakers and singers. For the young men sang solos and gave testimonies about what the college had done for them, until George grew deeply interested. Religion, of course, wasn't his specialty, yet these fellows didn't look like sissies.

Then suddenly a very tall sailor from the navy was introduced as the speaker of the evening, and immediately the audience was breathless, enthralled with the young man's story.

He had been a student in the college before he enlisted in the navy. Three years he had been out in active duty on the sea and had participated in all but one of the great naval battles.

Simply, unostentatiously, he told his story and made those terrible battles live before his audience.

And the strange thing about this story was that the young man constantly spoke of the Lord as his companion all the way through. And he talked so naturally and easily and enthusiastically that one could not possibly think he was proud of his own achievements, or even that he was dragging in the religious aspect.

He spoke of his first impressions of the college and how surprised he was that every day began with prayer, prayer meetings of groups in their rooms, an atmosphere of prayer and dependence upon God. It opened a new view of life to the brother and sister who sat listening in wonder.

When the service was over they all gathered around the young talent and talked, especially with the young navy man who had spoken. Corliss lingered nearby listening to every word he said. Corliss had never heard a young man talk this way, as if he knew the Lord personally and yet wasn't afraid of Him.

But George was talking to the dean, asking questions, accepting a bunch of printed material, looking at the papers in his hand and then asking more questions, and when they all finally parted at the church door, the dean and George seemed like old friends, and the dean's last words were, "Well, Huntley, glad we met, and I'll be looking for you next week. Good night."

It was on the way home that George spoke. "I'm all kinds of glad, Dale, that you took us to that meeting tonight. I'm going to that college! What do you think of that?"

"I think it is simply wonderful, George! I couldn't ask anything better for you. I've known a lot about that institution, and it's great!"

"Oh," said Corliss aghast, "but—what will Mamma say? Will she let you go? And what will you do for money? She'll never let you have any if she doesn't like the college."

George was still for a moment, and then he said, "I'm not

going to ask Mother, not till I get everything arranged. I'm going to *work* my way through. The dean said they had an arrangement for that, and that speaker said he did, you know. That's what I'm going to do."

"Oh, but George, you can't go away and leave me," said Corliss pitifully. "I just can't stand it! You know Mamma won't let me do a thing if you're not with me, or else she'll send me away to some stuffy girls' school, and I'd *die*. I'd just *die* without you."

"Maybe you could go to this same college, kid? Girls go there, you know. There were all those girls there in the glee club. Don't girls go there, Dale?"

"Oh yes, but would your mother let you go there? Perhaps she does not believe in coeducational schools."

"No, I don't believe she does," said Corliss. "And besides, I never finished the last year of high school. You can't go into college without credits. You know that."

"Oh, we can fix that up somehow. You can get a tutor and catch up. There are always things you can do. We'll see. But don't you say anything about this, not to Mom or anybody else, till we find out more. I'm going down to that college and see that dean again, and I'm going to telephone to my old principal at high school and get him to send by credentials. And then, you know, Grandmother left me that thousand dollars. I suppose I could use that in a pinch, couldn't I? Dale, don't you think Grandmother would like me to use it that way?"

"Why yes, I think she would. But George, I don't just know how that was left. Haven't you a guardian or something? Perhaps you could get his permission. We might ask Mr. Granniss. He drew up the will. Probably he could tell us all about it."

"Yes, would you mind doing that?"

"Not at all. Mr. Granniss is very nice. If there is any way you can use it, he will know. When are you of age, George?"

"Oh bother. Not for two years yet. But when that comes, then I'd have to go into service if the war's still on. Of course I wouldn't mind that, but that's the reason Mom wouldn't want me out of her sight. She wants to keep me young so they can't get me. But I've been figuring to get into the marines somehow and then be with that crowd who are in college at first, until they are called. I tried to get Mom to let me go into a college that way. But she had nine fits. She doesn't want me to go to war, and she says anyway it will soon be over," the boy said glumly.

"Well, don't worry. We'll find out just what rights you have, and then when your mother comes here perhaps there will be a way to get her consent."

"Consent nothing!" said the boy. "She'll never do that. But she can't tie me to her apron strings all the rest of my life. I've got to be a *man*!"

"There'll be a way, George," said Dale comfortingly. "Don't let's worry about it tonight. But I can't tell you how glad I am that you feel this way about this grand college. You don't know what it will do for you if you go there. I've known a lot of boys and girls, too, who have gone there and they have all been rather wonderful."

Corliss looked up sadly. "Yes, Dale, I can see it is a wonderful place, but just for that reason Mamma wouldn't like it. She would never consent, not for anything."

"Well, Corliss dear, suppose we hand this over to the Lord and see if He will do anything about it for you. Meantime,

George, when are you going down to the college?"

"Next Tuesday. I hope that's not the day the doctor picks out to send Mom home. I'd like to get this settled before she gets here, for something tells me there won't be much chance after she comes. She'd find some other college right away. She wouldn't think this was swell enough, I'm afraid," said George dejectedly.

"Well, don't worry about it. Things may work out your way yet," said Dale cheerily.

"Fat chance!" said Corliss dejectedly.

But George set his lips firmly. "They are *going* to work out the way *I* want them for *me*, anyway," he said. "I think I'm old enough to say where I'll go to college, and I mean to do it. If I have to work my way through, why then all right, but I'll choose the college, see? This is the first college I ever heard of that appealed to me, and I don't mean to let it go for any other, no matter how noted the other is."

Dale smiled quietly to herself. This was better than she had hoped. If George did get to go to such a college, he would surely learn what the Lord could do for him in his life. But then, on the other hand, it might make a lot of trouble for him in his home life, and would she be blamed for it? Probably. But what of that if it worked out for George's good? Well, this was one more thing to be prayed about and put in God's keeping.

Dale sat up a little while that night after the others had gone to bed. Somehow she felt as if she must write and tell David about what had happened that day. He might not get the letter for weeks or even months, and of course he might not ever get it on this earth, but still it helped her to bear the long absence and the terrible possibilities if she kept in touch with him by writing, even if he could not answer her. That she was prepared for. He had told her it might probably be a very long time before he could send a letter out to her. But it comforted her to talk to him on paper.

So she wrote a long letter, telling of all the problems about her aunt and how she hoped some of them were working out. Thanking him for the prayers she knew he was putting up in their behalf. And then she wrote of the wonderful Christian college and the interest her young cousins were taking in it. Another item for his prayers. Perhaps the Holy Spirit would guide his prayers for her problems.

It was quite late when the letter was finished, and she slipped quietly into her room and got into bed, so quickly and silently that she hoped she had not woken Corliss. But after she had cautiously settled herself in her bed, Corliss's hand came stealing over and clasped hers, squeezing her fingers, and then Corliss whispered, "Oh Dale, this has been a perfectly wonderful evening. I'm so glad you took us. And oh, I do so want to go to that college!"

"Dear child!" said Dale tenderly, "I hope you can."

"I was thinking, Dale, if Mamma should go up to Aunt Evelyn's perhaps, just *perhaps*, she might let me stay here a little while and study. Wouldn't there be a tutor around here I could get, or couldn't *you* help me get ready to pass an examination so I could go to that college, too? I could get a job somewhere that would only be part-time and I could pay you for teaching me—"

"Corliss, dear! I wouldn't want any pay, if I would be good enough. We'd have to find out about that, of course, in case there was such a chance. But you wouldn't need to get a job. I could give you one. Not a very lucrative one, of course, but one that would give you a little spending money. I thought perhaps you could help me with that little school I'm likely taking over when the way is clear. How would you like that?"

"I'd love it. But wouldn't I really be in your way, Dale? Wouldn't you hate having me here for several months till I was allowed to go to college?"

"No dear, I wouldn't hate it. I would love it. You have grown to be very dear to me since we have been through so much together, and I'd love having you. But of course that would all have to depend on your mother and what she is willing for you to do. But I'd love teaching you if I know enough. I'd have to find out the requirements, of course, maybe I could. If I couldn't, there would be somebody else, I'm sure."

Talking quietly, their voices presently faded into silence, and then Dale heard the soft even breathing of Corliss and knew she was asleep and for the time being out of her perplexities. It was strange, wasn't it, how pleasant it had been to have Corliss want to stay with her? And such a few short days before, what a trial it would have been. She wondered what had made the difference. Was it because she had been trying to make it pleasant for them, and how she seemed to have come to love them?

Ruminating over the wonder of a God-given love where there had been natural dislike, it was not unlike the God-given love of her young man. Softly she fell asleep praying for her beloved, so very far away. What would she have thought could she have known that her beloved was not alone on a wide, turbulent sea, tossing in a little toy of a lifeboat, even though the man who had rescued him and put him there had gone back for some cans of provisions and met a bomb instead. A rescuer who had lost his life! And a rescued man who had been struck by a falling spar was delirious, alone, on the wide ocean, under a dark, starless sky, burning with fever, with no provisions and no companion, with a wounded shoulder, full of pain, too far gone to know his own situation. Now and again a scrap of a song from out of his past floated out hoarsely from the little boat into the night. "All through the night, all through the night, my Savior has been watching over me."

Was David taking his last journey, on his way to meet his God?

Chapter 19

$\mathcal{I}$t was a sunny, bright day when they brought Mrs. Huntley from the hospital, in the very best ambulance the institution boasted, with two of the choicest nurses in charge. The nurses had not been the choice of the hospital, but the patient had made such a terrific uproar about the matter that, rather than have the uproar kept up, the hospital arranged to give her what she wanted on the way over. However, the nurse who was to remain with her for a week or two was not the one she had asked for and expected to have, but a younger nurse, a recent trainee, because they could not spare the best nurses from the busy institution. The nurse who was to remain was sitting in front quite meekly with the driver and pledged to say nothing about it until the patient was well settled in the new bed and the other two had disappeared around the corner where the ambulance would be waiting for them. Then she was to arrive at the bedside and take up her duties. It was not going to be easy for either the nurse or the family, to say nothing about the patient.

So Mrs. Huntley, arriving back in the house she had made so uncomfortable before she left, a little weary from the excitement of moving and the trip, was settled comfortably in the delightful guest bed that had been the pride of dear Grandmother's heart. She rested back on the smooth, shining linen away at last from the hated sights and sounds of the hospital, closed her eyes and, without intending it, fell into a delightful sleep and never knew until her waking that she was now at the mercy of an entirely new nurse.

The afternoon waned, and the family tiptoed around carefully to preserve the utmost quiet. A single rosebud in a clear glass bud vase touched the atmosphere with delicate, luxurious fragrance, and later there came stealing through the house the delicious odors of fresh baked bread and roasting meat, even penetrating to that quiet room upstairs and speaking to the sleeping senses of the woman who for long weeks had been on hospital fare. Of course it had been a fine hospital with the best of fare, but that was not exactly home cooking, and certainly not Hattie's cooking. And strange to say after all her grumbling, here was Hattie working hard, determined to do her best for the woman whom she had despised and to have such a dinner as would tempt the appetite of the most particular guest. She was at least determined not to let her dear Miss Dale outdo her in kindness toward the woman who in her heart she looked upon as the most hated of enemies. And yet she was doing her best to produce a delightful dinner that would interest and tempt an invalid's appetite.

It was later when the invalid at last awoke, the new nurse standing by her side and offering a cool washcloth and a spoonful of medicine and then arranging the delightful tray that Dale brought up with a smile.

Mrs. Huntley did not at once discover that the nurse was new. She was just a trifle bewildered at being in a strange bed with new surroundings, Dale coming in so smilingly, her children there as if they really enjoyed having her. Perhaps it was something as heaven may surprise some of us who have not been living in great anticipation of it. But at least she did not rise to her usual rebellious attitude, and George and Corliss began to hope that perhaps things were going to be different now and their mother was going to live a happy life like other people and not find fault with everything.

Corliss hovered around her and offered to feed her the dessert, which was Hattie's specialty—a confection of eggs and gelatin and cream in a most delectable form of charlotte russe, and was eaten with cream and crimson raspberry jelly. The invalid, in a kind of wonder, accepted her daughter's ministrations, a bit ungraciously perhaps, but still accepted them. So all went smoothly until it was time to prepare the invalid for the night and the new nurse appeared on the scene again and began to get her ready for sleep. Then she recognized her strangeness and demanded the other two nurses, and when she was told that they had gone back to the hospital, as they could not be spared any longer, she raved wildly, declined to let the nurse touch her, and demanded that her daughter telephone the hospital and have those nurses sent back to her. When the son and daughter both declined to accept that commission, saying that the head nurse had told them it would be impossible, she went into a storm of tears and mourned her helplessness and the cruelty of the doctors and nurses, and declared she would make that institution known as a dreadful place from one end of the country to the other so that they would have no patients any more. And at last she sent for Dale.

Dale, with a heart lifted for help, went quietly in to her aunt and tried to reason with her, and when she found that did no good, she offered to do the nursing herself; but that, too, was most summarily declined. On the whole, it was very late that night before the invalid was at last composed and drifting off to sleep and the family could take heart of hope and try to get a little rest themselves.

Dale's last thought as she drifted off to sleep was for her beloved far away. *Oh Lord, keep him safely all through the night.* And as she closed her eyes and fought back the weary tears that stung to blind her, she wondered when, if ever, she would see him again.

❧❦❧

It was two days later, hard days every hour of them, that the message came for the War Department that Captain David Kenyon, naval bomber pilot of note and recently transferred to the command of an army transport, was missing in action.

Somehow it seemed to Dale at first as if she could not bear to see the sun shine when she thought of her beloved, with that calm trust in his eyes, that sunny smile on his lips, gone from her. Dead, perhaps, or even something worse. Missing in action! Didn't that usually mean they were taken prisoner? Oh, it seemed as if her heart would break. Yet of course she mustn't let it. She had known when he went away that this might happen. He had known it, too. And they had the sure knowledge that they would meet again. They both were saved, born-again-ones, and they were going Home to meet. She must not give way to this awful goneness that crept through her very being. She had work to do, souls to win, guests to make comfortable. And they did not know of her loss. She must not betray her sorrow. She must go on about her duties knowing that her Lord was keeping her and would live her life for her if she would only let Him. So, not even sorrow must be able to get her down.

And she could not weep even at night. Corliss was sleeping next to her and she must not let her know she was in trouble. Corliss did not know about David.

Then the thought would come that perhaps he was not dead. Sometimes those who were missing in action were found, sometimes they were able to escape from their prison camps. At least she could pray, and her Savior would be watching over her beloved, day and night, and he was loved by her Lord. She remembered how they had prayed together "in life or in death, Lord." Yes, she must be brave. She must be as brave as if she, too, were fighting in action.

Then it came to her that she had a home front to fight right here in her house. She had to try to win her household to know the Lord.

But neither did life in the home move smoothly. It was hard for everybody. The invalid, when she found the nurses of her choice were out of the question, accepted the new one only under protest and made the poor thing's life miserable with millions of unnecessary errands, demanding this and that which could not be had, and making many outcries and protests when she was frustrated; and she made the lives of her son and daughter very unhappy.

Perhaps it was because of this that Corliss began to see herself as she had been—selfish and proud and cruel—and began to try to have some self-control.

George, meanwhile, had made a couple of trips to the college of his choice and secured all the necessary details about what would be necessary for both himself and perhaps later for Corliss, also, to enter, though they had no present inkling of how this wish of theirs was going to be carried out.

But Corliss, as soon as she found a little free time when her mother would not suspect, went downtown and procured certain books upon which she would have to be examined if she tried to enter college. With Dale's encouragement, she began to do a little study by herself, helped out by suggestions from Dale, who was busy indeed just at present assisting the new nurse and taking her turn with the invalid whenever it seemed wise to do so.

Life was looking pretty bleak to Dale just now, with the heavy burden of anxiety upon her heart, the thrilling joy that had been hers suddenly turned into fear and sorrow, and a lingering anxiety. It seemed to her as if her every breath was a prayer.

The days dragged by, each moment filled with some difficult duty or some knotty problem to solve. Sometimes as she passed the door of her grandmother's room, which stood open always now, like some glimpse into a quiet prayer room, her thoughts went back longingly to the sweet days when

Grandmother had been there, slipping from her quietly day by day. But they seemed in contrast with this hectic time like a little glimpse into heaven. Still, she had not had David in those loved days, and now whether he was dead or alive he was hers. If still on this earth, she might still pray for him and his return. But if in Glory, surely he was doubly hers then. So she must not be despondent. Besides, the rest of the people in the house knew nothing of her own special heartache, and so she must carry a sunny face always. They must know that she had a Lord who was able to keep her from falling. Able to give her a sunny smile in the midst of trying circumstances.

Yet in the midst of these hard days, often as she sought the quiet of her grandmother's room for a little while to pray, she gradually became possessed with the thought that she must pray with all her heart for David. She had a strong feeling that "missing" in this case might not mean death, or even imprisonment. There were stories coming in now and then of those who had been sent out on missions and their ships had been lost, but somehow they had floated for days and finally been picked up. There was one notable case like this, a man who had found God through those days of panic and almost death. Might not David be somewhere safe in God's keeping?

Meantime the date of the opening of George's college was coming on, and George was determined to begin if possible. They got hold of Mr. Granniss and, at his suggestion, called up George's guardian who had charge of his finances and found that he could and would give consent to the arrangement until such time as the boy's mother should be able to look after his affairs more carefully. So George arranged to go down to the college and start, returning as usual in the evening to talk with his mother and keep her satisfied that he was all right. She never had been one to greatly concern herself over the daily doings of her children. If they were enjoying themselves somewhere, she was usually satisfied. So for the present, George was able to say he was getting acquainted with the surrounding neighborhood or he was reading or studying, and she did not question further. Although they all knew this could not go on indefinitely and he would soon have to account for his absences.

Corliss, meantime, spent as much time with her mother as seemed acceptable, always with a book in hand, trying to study when her mother slept. And more and more Mrs. Huntley was becoming dependent upon Dale and Corliss for attention, preferring to have their ministrations rather than the nurse's to whom she had taken a dislike.

And so the days settled uneasily down to a routine, and the invalid seemed a bit more content than when she was in the hospital, but kept on with her daily demand for the lawyer. Then one day she asked Dale if she supposed her Granniss-lawyer might be prevailed upon to come and talk with her about trying to get back the money she had paid the fraud of a lawyer, Buffington.

Mr. Granniss very kindly came and let her talk but told her that he was afraid, since she had given cash both times in paying him and had received no receipt for the amount, that it was hopeless to try and get it back. She had nothing to show for the transaction, and that lawyer had the reputation of conducting such affairs in a shady manner. After he went away, Mrs. Huntley wore a desperate look, and Corliss found her crying when she brought her supper that night.

The girls did all they could to cheer her up, told her she didn't need the money now. When she got well, she would have another check due from her regular income, and so why bother? But the lady did not cheer up easily. And the bills began to come in from the hospital, and finally the doctor told her that he wished she would go for a few weeks to a certain hospital up in the mountains. That he felt it would not only build her up wonderfully but that she might even find help for a more rapid recovery through a noted specialist who was working up there. And when she told him she could not afford it, he told her that his sister was driving up that way to take another patient and they would be glad to have her go with them. There would be a nurse along, and it need not be such a hard trip, nor very expensive, and she need not be in a hurry about paying his bill.

He was very kind, and most surprisingly the invalid was intrigued by the idea and decided to go.

So the household was all in a twitter getting her ready and off. She even sat up for an hour or two and felt no worse for it.

And then Dale came to her with a check for five hundred dollars. "Aunt Blanche," she said earnestly, "I want you to take this to pay your bills and perhaps have a little left over for necessary expenses when you get there."

Tears sprang unbidden to the invalid's eyes, and she stared at Dale, unable to believe that Dale wasn't doing this for some disagreeable reason. "I can't take your money, Dale," she said in a broken voice. "I'm afraid I haven't been very pleasant to you about the house."

"Oh, that's all right," said Dale happily. "I'm glad I have the money to help you out. Your own money won't be here in time, you said, and there's no reason why you shouldn't use mine, for the present at least. I don't need it just now."

"But you are taking care of my children, Dale, and that has cost you something. And I really ought not to go away now. I ought to arrange to send my children home, or put them in a school somewhere before I leave."

Dale caught at the idea. "Oh, don't worry about that now. Just you go and get well," she said. "Corliss and her brother will be all right here, and I'll promise to find a school for them both where they will be interested till you come back for them. You wouldn't need to worry at all on that score. What you should do is to get well first, and then everything can be settled up."

"But they could go up to my sister Evelyn's, only they both dislike her so much they will make a terrible fuss about it."

"Well, never mind. I think they'll enjoy it here more, and I'll love to have them."

Her aunt looked at her for a minute in wonder. Then she said thoughtfully, "But you wanted to start a school."

"Well, perhaps I will after. And if I do, I'll let Corliss help me teach, perhaps. Anyway, we'll manage nicely."

And so, though there wasn't much gratitude expressed openly, the matter was arranged, and the next morning saw the aunt carried carefully out to the big comfortable hospital car in the arms of a strong man, one of the hospital nurses, who knew how to handle broken bones without hurting. The family stood on the sidewalk and watched her happily away.

"Now," said George, "do you figure it was all our prayers that brought this about, so I could go on to that college without expecting a hurricane every time I came back?"

"I shouldn't wonder," said Dale, smiling. "And now, Corliss, we can really get to work at your studies so you will be able to take those examinations sooner. Perhaps if you are both already entered in that college when your mother gets back, she may consent to let you stay. At any rate, you can have a chance to find out if you really like it."

"Oh, I like it all right," said George, "and I'm sure Corrie will, too."

"Of course," said Corliss. "Oh Dale, I think you've been perfectly wonderful to bring all this about for us."

"There, there," Dale said, smiling. "Forget it, and come let's get to work. What comes first? Latin or mathematics?"

"Latin!" said Corliss. "I simply adore that, and I like to get the easiest things out of the way first."

So they settled down to regular life, doing good work, and being fairly happy.

It wasn't really very different from Dale's life the last few years, perhaps, but she hugged the thought of her wonderful beloved to her heart and still prayed for him day by day, hoping against hope that some word might someday come from him.

And every night when George came home to dinner, he had pleasant things to tell of his college, and she could fairly see him grow into another person from day to day.

Chapter 20

$\mathcal{D}$ale was getting to be a good teacher. She was enjoying the study herself and enjoying Corliss's quick mind, enjoying the game of getting her ready for a quick examination. But while she was working with her hands here and there around the house she was continually praying for David, that if it was God's will he might come home to her sometime. That she might not have to live out her life without him.

Now and again she would read in the paper that some soldier or sailor boy who had been reported missing had come home, and her heart would leap over the thought of what joy his family must be feeling on his return. Would such joy ever come to her?

It was as if she were living his life out with him wherever he was, in prison, or suffering, or distress of any kind.

Her Savior watching over David, and she keeping continual watch for answer to her prayers. Of course most people would tell her she was a fool to keep on hoping, for now days and weeks had passed since the word had come, and nothing further came. She was glad that nobody knew of her beloved, for now they could not pity her. She would hate to be pitied. For they would not understand what was strengthening her in such a sorrow. They would think she did not care, and she could not bear that. And they would never understand how an idea, a trust in an unseen being could keep her bright and sunny. She must not bring her Lord into shame by not trusting Him, and she knew He was able to keep her, even though He did not see fit to give her back her beloved.

There came letters from Aunt Blanche, not written by her own hand, because her arm and wrist had not yet recovered strength to write, or at least she thought they hadn't, which amounted to the same thing. But she had found a nice nurse who would write very neat letters for her, and she described the hospital where she was and all its lovely views and the people, some pleasant and some disagreeable. But she said that she had found a few friends who were very good bridge players, and therefore she was happy, for she simply adored bridge.

She said that her usual check had come through and she was sending Dale twenty-five of what she owed her and would hope to be able to repay her in full before too long. Meantime she thanked her for being so kind to the children, and she was so glad that they had found suitable schools where they were happy, and she hoped they would do their best to behave and not get into trouble anywhere as she wasn't there to get them out.

Dale did not wonder that neither of her cousins mourned

much for the absence of their mother. They had been greatly broken up when she was hurt, but more because they were afraid of suffering and death than because of any deep love for her. Nevertheless, they were greatly glad that their mother was happy and had decided to stay where she was for several months, until she was thoroughly well and could go home and attend to her own affairs as usual, for they were both very much in love with their college and wanted above all things not to be taken away against their wills.

At last Corliss was ready for her examinations and was hoping to be allowed to get into classes before the year was over. And suddenly Dale felt that if she did, life was really going to be quite dull for herself without either of her bright young cousins. For now they had all grown to be very dear to one another, and whenever there was a chance for George to get away from his work, he would run home for an hour or two to report on how things were going with him. And then one day he came in a great hurry and said he could stay only a minute, that he was tutoring another fellow in geometry and had promised to be back before supper to help him.

"But there is something I want to tell you. Dale, I knew you'd be interested, maybe Corliss, too. Anyway, *I've found the Lord*, and I thought you'd be glad! It's wonderful to know I'm saved, and I never was so happy in my life. I don't know what Mother would say to it. Sometime I'll have to tell her, when I've had a chance to live it a little and let her see I'm different. It isn't a thing I'd know how to write to her about. She'd be taking me right away from here and sending me to some worldly college. She's horribly afraid of anybody getting religious. But now, Corrie, I'm praying for you, and I want you to get saved, and then we'll begin to pray for Mom."

He scarcely gave them opportunity to tell him how glad they were. Even Corliss seemed glad, though she didn't altogether understand the matter and after that day often asked Dale many questions and sometimes consented to read the Bible with her. But Corliss was more interested to pass her examinations now, and she was working very hard.

And at last she did pass them, and Dale went with her to enter the college, and they were all very happy about it.

But when Dale went back to the empty house, it seemed very desolate without either of her cousins, and she wondered if she ought not to think about taking over her school, although it seemed to be getting on nicely without her, and she wondered if that was what the Lord would want her to be doing now. She seemed to have arrived at a place of pause, where she must think things through and know how she was going to order her days.

And then that very night there came a letter from the War Department that Captain David Kenyon had been found and brought back to a base hospital, where he was under the best of care. A letter was enclosed that had been found in his Testament in his breast pocket. He had been wounded and was not yet in a condition to tell all that had happened to him, but it was known that he had floated for a number of days on the ocean in one of the small rubber boats, that he had been picked up by a pilot who had seen him far from land and had taken him to his own outfit. He was wounded and not in very good physical condition when found, but now the doctor gave every hope that he would eventually recover.

There followed an address where she could write, and Dale,

tears of joy streaming down her face, hurried up to her lonely room and began to write a letter. Perhaps he would not be able yet to read much of a letter, but she would put what was in her heart for him just in a few words at first. And later she would write all that she had wanted so say for all the lonely weeks he had been away.

But the first letter she wrote came from the depths of her heart.

My precious David:

The letter has just come that says you have been found. After all these weeks when you were missing in action, now you are found and in the hands of nurses and doctors who can help you.

My darling, I cannot thank God enough that you are safe and I can know where you are. I've been praying hourly for you. I know you were always safe, because our Savior has been watching over you.

Now I shall get this down to the post office at once so that you may have word from me as soon as you are able to understand it, but I'll be writing all the time now, every day, and if they are too much, just let the nurse put them away to keep for you till you are well.

Good night, beloved,
Dale

She looked up to find Hattie standing in the doorway

looking at her with troubled eyes.

"Why Hattie, I thought you had gone to bed," she said.

"No ma'am, Miss Dale, I couldn't go to bed till I knowed you was all right and ready to rest. I thought you'd be lonesome, maybe. But you look real happy, Miss Dale. Are you glad you got rid of them children?"

"Oh no, Hattie. I love the children, and I shall miss them very much, of course, but I am happy, Hattie. Something wonderful has just happened to me. You heard the bell ring a little while ago? Well, it was a special delivery letter from the War Department, telling me that a dear friend of mine, whom I love very much and who has been missing in action for several weeks now, has been found. He was floating for a long time, several days, perhaps, on the ocean in a little boat, and a pilot saw him from the sky and picked him up and took him to a base hospital. They are taking care of him, and they think he may get well. Yes, I'm happy, oh so happy and thankful to God."

"That's great, Miss Dale. And do I know that man?"

"Why, I'm not sure. He was here several times. Do you remember a man in naval uniform at Grandmother's funeral?"

"Man with a gold bar on his shoulder and gold wings on his chest?"

"Yes, that's the one, Hattie. His name is David Kenyon, and we were engaged before he went away. He's been made a lieutenant commander now. Oh Hattie, I'm so happy!"

"Well, you got a good man, I am positive. He's the very handsomest man I ever saw, and that's certain. Does anybody else know about this?"

"No Hattie. You're the first one. I'll want to tell the cousins, of course, when they come back for the weekend. But how I wish I could tell Grandmother. How she would love it!"

"Don't you reckon she already knows it, Miss Dale?"

"I think perhaps she does," said Dale softly, with a golden look in her eyes.

After that, Dale wrote every day to her beloved, who perhaps was not yet able to even hear the letters read, but she had to write them, or else her heart might have burst with the messages it contained.

And when the cousins came home for their first weekend, they looked at her for a minute and then they said, "What's the matter? What's happened? You look as if something wonderful had come to pass."

"It has," said Dale with a great illumination in her face. "My very dear commander, to whom I am engaged and who has been missing in action for a long time, has been found and is in the hospital, with a very good hope that he may get well and come back to me."

Then Corliss lifted up her voice—a new, happy voice— and screamed for joy. "Oh Dale, you darling Dale, I'm so very glad for you," she cried and embraced her cousin around the neck and administered some very definite kisses. "Who is he, Dale? Is it that perfectly darling uniformed man that came to Grandma's funeral? David Kenyon, wasn't that his name? Oh, I'm so glad, so *glad.* I thought he was wonderful!"

And then George spoke. "Well, I'll say, you put one over on us all this time. You never let on all these weeks that we've been so close to you! And you didn't wear a ring or anything."

Dale laughed. "We didn't have time to think of rings or anything but each other, he had to go away so soon."

"That's the talk," said the boy. "Rings are just doodads,

anyway. And besides, in wartime people aren't thinking of things like that. Say, but I'm glad for you, Dale, only I hope you won't go far away from us where we can't see you anymore. You don't know what you mean to Corrie and me. We were talking about it on the way up today. You are family to us now, and I don't know how we'd ever get through all of life that's ahead if you go so far we can't get to see you often. You can just tell Cousin Dave that we won't stand for him taking you away to China or anywhere afar off, and that's not maybe."

Dale laughed. "I'll tell him," she said happily. "But you might as well know that your cousin David is very much interested in you and has been praying for you while he was away. Yes, he has, and I've written him a lot about you, too, although I'm not sure he ever got those last letters, for he wasn't allowed to write after he went off on this last assignment."

They sat down and wanted to know all about him, and Dale got out her pictures. They really got acquainted with their new cousin and quite approved of him.

And then after a time they got back to talking about their college and all the things that had been happening there and how they enjoyed the Christian fellowship.

"And Corrie does, too," said George eagerly. "I guess you'll find she's saved now, too!"

Corliss nodded her head. "Yes," she said, "one couldn't stay there very long and not be. They all just live in an atmosphere of salvation. And it begins little by little to seem more and more real to you, till you want it for yourself."

"Oh, I'm so glad!" said Dale. "So very, very glad!"

And then all three cousins knelt down and thanked God for His wonderful salvation.

Chapter 21

Day after day Dale watched for more news, though her common sense told her that there might be a long delay. The first announcement had left her to suppose that David's condition was more critical, and if he was still delirious of course he would not know what message had been sent her, nor have strength to frame a personal message to her. How long would she have to wait, she wondered? Of course until he could talk to the nurse or to some comrade, no one would know how to get in contact with her, except the War Department, and they had already done their duty in letting her know her man had been found and was doing as well as could be expected.

Night after night she went to bed praying, and morning after morning she arose with new hope in her heart that there might be some word that day. Hattie, too, was on the lookout every time the telephone rang or every time the doorbell sounded.

Dale laughed as she met her rushing to the front door in answer to a ring and called out, "He couldn't be coming yet, Hattie. He's away on the other side of the world somewhere, and he's been too sick to even send a personal word, so there is no use in expecting him to come and ring the doorbell."

"Aw, but Miss Dale. He might have flew, mightn't he?"

"Well, not likely in the condition they gave me to understand he was in."

"Aw well, you can't always tell what may happen in wartimes," said Hattie, nimbly excusing herself and grinning at her mistress.

Dale grinned back.

Three days later there came a telegram, brief and to the point but from David himself.

BELOVED DALE: SAFE IN HIS CARE. ALL MY LOVE, DAVID

Dale sat down and laughed and cried for joy into that telegram. It told so much and yet so little. He must be better or he could not have worded it. It rejoiced with her and called her to rejoice with him that he had been saved from great peril through their Savior who had watched over them "all through the night." It told all his love. He had not forgotten her, and she apparently was his first thought when he came back to life and self again.

She had much to tell the cousins when they came again, and they all rejoiced together that David was getting well. For there soon came letters from David's nurse and from a comrade now and again, giving a few more details of his progress. His shoulder was healing nicely. His hands were getting stronger. The sprained wrists were so much better he would soon be able to write her a letter "under his own power" and not have to wait for a secretary to take dictation.

There was nothing about the hardships he had gone through, except one sentence:

> *I'll tell you all about it when I get home. God speed the day.* "Joy cometh in the morning."

The two eager young cousins who were so interested in her romance exulted in all these messages, which Dale let them read because she enjoyed having someone to talk them over with. And they just reveled in knowing what a wonderful man was coming back to their dear Dale someday.

But now brief letters in his own hand began to come more often, and Dale began to take new heart of hope that soon he might be coming home. He hinted now and then that there might be a chance, though the doctor had not yet told him his release was coming soon.

Of course like all soldiers and sailors who had been in combat, David wanted to go back and finish up the job, but when he suggested it, his doctors and nurses shook their heads. Definitely no. He had been through too hard a time, and his physical strength was not up to such things yet, perhaps never would be. He had earned his ribbons and his stars and other decorations, what else did he want?, they asked him, and so he let his heart relax and began to look forward to seeing his beloved once more. Oh, would she think the same of him? He asked himself that a thousand times a day, yet kept on praying and hoping.

But Dale began definitely to get ready for his homecoming.

She wanted the house to be in perfect order, though with Hattie's willing help there wasn't so much to be done in that way. The house was always in order, for Hattie took pride in keeping it so. But there were a few curtains to be washed, a few little things that needed mending, and it was happy work to be doing, in between the Red Cross work she was doing now and the occasional groups of children she supervised during part of each day while their mothers were away at war work. Some of Grandmother's geraniums and pots of ivy needed trimming and coaxing into early bloom so the house might be bright and attractive when he came.

And often as she sat sewing or reading, only half her attention was on her work. She was remembering her beloved as he had been with her on that one long, beautiful day among the hemlocks out under God's wide sky before he went away. And now was it really true that he was coming back to her? *He* had hoped that God would let him; *she* had hoped and prayed about it and given up her will about it again and again. But God had been so very gracious to save him from that awful fate alone on the sea. No, not alone, but alone with God on the sea.

Again and again precious thoughts like these went through her mind until her heart became a continual hymn of praise. And now she was so often watching for his coming, for he had at last told her it might be soon and unannounced. He might be brought home in a plane when there was opportunity. There were so many things that had to be considered in sending wounded soldiers home, so many men to be sent back and forth.

Quite often now, when Dale was alone sitting at her desk or under the light reading or resting in a comfortable chair, she would get up and go out on the porch, just to look down the road and see if anyone was walking up the street, just to look up to the night sky and imagine how he would be coming, like that great plane that sailed across the house above her at a certain time each night. And sometimes the moon would be rising—a lovely golden crescent, or later in the month, a great round silver orb in the wide deep blue of a sky punctuated here and there with white stars—and she would think, *What if he should come now, tonight, while I am standing here, and we could be here together watching this night. Sometime we will perhaps. Sometime he will be here and will not go away, but we shall be together, shall* belong *together. How great and wonderful that would be!*

She went over all her pretty anticipations. How she would telephone Corliss and George to come home and meet him. Or wait—perhaps it would be better for David to take her down to the college. Ah, that was something that must wait until he came, to see how well he was and whether he was able to take trips like that.

Then she would chide herself for planning so far ahead when she was not even sure yet that he was to be allowed to come home at all at this time. He might even be considered well enough to be sent on another assignment, and there might be another long period of waiting and trusting ahead of her yet. Well, even so, the war must be won, and if their Lord had planned it that way, they must be content.

Then she would chide herself for making up so many possible disappointments when it was all in her Lord's hands and she could perfectly trust that He would do His best for her and for David.

One night she came down to supper in a new dress, all bright and colorful with small knots of giddy little flowers scattered over it and outlined here and there with cords of scarlet among the bright knots of flowers. It was a pretty dress, and she wished he were there to see it. And then she got up and went out to take her nightly observation of the sky and see if there were any planes coming over the house, just to carry out her whimsical fantasy.

She had looked long into the face of that great moon and counted the stars around it and finally turned away. And then suddenly she heard a car. It was coming up their street. It came on quickly. It was the town taxi, and it was coming straight to her door! Could it be? Oh, it wasn't Aunt Blanche coming back to take her cousins away from their beloved college, was it? For an instant, her heart stood still, but then she saw a tall man in uniform was getting out, paying the driver, picking up his bag from the curb where he had dropped it while he hunted out his change. He turned and looked toward the house, saw her standing there—her bright dress fluttering in the evening breeze, the moonlight on her beautiful hair—and then she knew him. It was not just her imagination. He was there in reality. She could hear the taxi that had brought him going down the street, turning onto the highway below. It was all real, and David had come home!

It was then she turned and flew down the steps and went to meet him, went straight into his arms, right there in the dusk of the evening with all the neighbors' quiet little houses around her watching, holding their breath to tell it to the nightingales.

And David dropped his bag and folded her in his arms, laying his cheek against her own.

"Dale, my darling! Oh, I have you in my arms once more. God has answered my prayer and brought me back to you again!"

And Dale nestled into his arms just as she had been dreaming she would do and felt her heart overflowing with gladness and thanksgiving.

There was another watcher besides those neighboring houses. Hattie had heard the taxi, and Hattie had tiptoed softly into Grandma's room and peeked out between the curtains. She caught the gleam of the streetlamp on the bright bars of the uniform, she saw the bag, she measured the stranger's height and knew the lost had returned at last! And then Hattie went back to her room, got dressed in a jiffy, and went to brewing among her pots and pans until she produced a tray of delightful, tempting edibles, topped by cups of fragrant tea and little delectable frosted cakes with cherries on them. Little sandwiches and scrambled eggs such as no one but Hattie could make and season just right. And then quite innocently, she came sailing into the living room with her tray, as if a bell had sounded and she had been sent for.

"I thought you might like a little bite to eat, Miss Dale," she said wistfully and then paused and eyed the tall uniformed man, liked his face, and heartily approved of him.

So Dale roused smiling, drew a little away from the strong arm that encircled her shoulders, and spoke: "Oh, thank you, Hattie, that was nice of you. David, this is Hattie. She's a part of us, you know, and she had been helping me watch for you."

"Oh yes, I've heard of Hattie, and I'm glad to meet her at last!" said David as he got up from the couch where he had been sitting and took Hattie's two work-hardened hands in his own big ones and gave them a warm pressure.

"Oh, thank you, sir," said Hattie with her best bow. "And now you children set down an' eat your 'freshments 'fore they get cold. I sure is glad you have come at last, Mr. Captain, and I hope they gets this war over now you've come back so you won't have to go away no more."

Laughing and happy, they sat down to the ample tray and ate as they had not eaten since that day on the mountaintop that seemed so very long ago. And yet now that David was here, was only the other day.

They had eaten it all, every crumb, and Hattie had taken the tray away and left them to a happy talk. Then quite suddenly there was the sound of a car, a clatter of young feet on the walk outside coming up the steps, and there came the cousins, barging in cheerfully. They paused an instant at the doorway, abashed; then George roused to the occasion. "Oh, excuse us, Dale. Are we interrupting? A fellow was coming up for the weekend and we got a chance to ride up with him in his car. We thought you wouldn't mind. But gee, we didn't know you had company. If we're in the way, we'll go back. But, say, isn't this Cousin David? How are you, David? We're glad you've come at last, and we hope you'll like us. We like you a lot already just from your picture, you know."

Then David Kenyon got to his feet again and took the two new cousins by the hand, one hand in each of his own.

"Well, I certainly like that," he said genially. "That's the nicest welcome you could have given me, and I sure am going to like you two just as much. I've been hearing all about you in letters, you know. And I'm so glad you both are saved and we can all be happy together!"

"There! See that?" said George to his wide-eyed sister. "I said he was all right, and he is, Corrie, and I guess we've got about the greatest family a fellow and a girl could have. How about it, Dale? Do you mind our coming home this first night he's here?"

"Oh no, I'm glad you've come. I want you to know him right from the start."

Then Hattie appeared in the doorway and summoned the younger ones.

"They all had a little supper," she said, "but they done et it all up, so I guess you two better come out in the kitchen and tell me what you want to eat, and I'll fix it up for you."

So laughingly the two disappeared into the kitchen, and Hattie felt she had accomplished great things to leave the dear girl and her returned soldier alone together.

Promptly David's arms went around Dale and drew her close to him, her head on his shoulder, his face against hers, where just their lips could touch.

"My darling!" David said and drew a long, deep breath of satisfaction. "Oh, it's so good to be with you again!"

Once more his face went down to her and his lips met hers, and then he raised his head and looked into her eyes.

"How soon can we be married?" he asked her earnestly. "I want you for my own for always. I kept wishing all the time I was gone that we had had time to get married before I left. But of course I couldn't help it that we were going so soon. But how soon, dearest?"

"Why, right away," said Dale joyously, with a lilt in her tone. "The sooner the better."

"That's perfect," said David. "We'll hunt up a license tomorrow. How long do you have to wait to get a license in this state?"

"Why, I really don't know, but what matters a little bit of time like a day or two? You are here now, and all time will go fast. But I'd like the cousins to be here."

"Of course," said David. "They're rare! I'm glad they are nearby. But oh, my darling! To think I have you in my arms at last! It seems too good to be true." He drew her close again and touched his lips to her eyelids. "My precious!" he said. "What did I tell you, 'Joy cometh in the morning'? This is our morning."

Dale smiled softly and then added in a low tone, "And my Savior kept you safely all through the night."

More Than Conqueror

Chapter 1

A tall young soldier swung off the bus at its terminal and walked briskly up Wolverton Drive.

He was a handsome soldier, though he did not seem at all conscious of it. He had strong, well-chiseled features, heavy dark hair, and fine eyes. He walked with a kind of grave assurance, as if this was something he had fully made up his mind to do, though not as if this broad avenue were an old haunt of his; more as if he were driving himself to a sacred duty.

Oh, it wasn't the first time he had walked that way, of course. In his school days he had passed up that road, had carefully studied its substantial houses, admired them each, and later come to search out and be interested in one particular house. He had never stepped within one of them, for his life had not been blessed with wealth and luxury, but he had admired a girl in school who lived here, and he had taken pains to find out where she lived. Not that he had a personal acquaintance with that little girl in the grade school. Oh no! They had been only children then, with but the passing acquaintance of classmates as the years progressed. But he had been interested enough to find out where she lived, and when he had found her house he had been glad, as his eyes took in the lines of the fine old stone mansion. There had been no envy in his glance. He was glad she had a background like that. It was satisfying to know it. It seemed to finish out the picture for him. But he had known then, and equally he knew now, that *he* did not belong in this setting. He even knew that the circumstance that had brought him here now might not be recognized by anyone belonging to her as justifying his coming. Nevertheless, he had come, and having started he was not to be turned back now at the last minute by any qualms of reason or conscience that might have made him hesitate in the past.

At the third corner the soldier turned sharply into a broad driveway sweeping up in a pleasant curve to the old gray stone house that gave evidence of having been built a goodly number of years before.

As if he were accustomed to treading this way, he walked quickly without hesitation, mounted the stone steps, and passed within a stone arch.

As he stood awaiting an answer to his ring, he cast a quick comprehensive glance up and down the broad veranda, with a look in his eyes as if the quiet elegance of the place was pleasant to him. There was satisfaction in his expression.

As he stood there he looked as if he might fit into that setting very easily. There was courtesy, strength, grace in his whole bearing, and the elderly servant who opened the door did not seem to see anything incongruous in his being there. These were days when men of the army and navy were honored guests everywhere. Moreover, his attitude and manner showed the culture of one to the manner born.

"I would like to see Miss Blythe Bonniwell," he said, stepping into the hall as the servant swung the door wide and indicated a small reception room where he might sit down.

"She's still in," said the woman. "She's gone up to get ready to go to her Red Cross meeting."

"I'll not keep her long," promised the soldier understandingly.

"Who shall I say is here?" asked the woman.

The young man turned on her a winning grin.

"Why, you can tell her it is Charlie Montgomery. I'm not sure she'll remember the name. It's been some time. Just tell her I'm an old schoolmate and I'd like to see her about something rather important. That is, if she can spare just a minute or two."

"*Mr.* Montgomery, did you say?" asked the woman with dignity.

"Yes, I suppose you might call it Mr. But I doubt if she would identify me that way," said the soldier with a grin. "It wasn't the way I was known, but it's all right with me if she remembers."

"Just sit down," said the woman, with a disapproving air. "I'll call her. She'll likely be down in a short time."

The young man entered the room indicated and sat down in the first chair that presented itself, dropping his face in his hands for an instant and drawing a quick breath almost like a petition. Then he straightened up, but he did not look about him. This was her home, her natural environment, that for long years he had often wished he might see, but he did not wish his mind to be distracted now. He must be alert and at attention when she came. This was probably a crazy thing he was doing, and yet he felt somehow he had to do it.

He heard a light step, and glancing up he saw her coming down the wide staircase that he could just glimpse through the open doorway. She seemed so like the little girl she had been long ago. The same light movement, as if her feet had wings, the same curly brown hair with golden lights in it, the same ease and poise and grace of movement.

She was wearing a slim brown dress that matched the lovely brown of her eyes, and there was a bright knot of ribbons in her brown hair, green and scarlet, that looked like berries and a leaf. It was like a jewel in a picture. His heart quickened as she came, and he felt abashed again at the errand that had brought him here.

She entered the room eagerly, and an interested smile dawned on her sweet face.

The soldier rose and stood awaiting her. A salute—*that* was her due, yet he didn't want to flaunt his position as a soldier. But she was putting out her hand, both hands, as if she had a warm welcome for him. It occurred to him that perhaps she did not remember him—had possibly taken him for someone else. Or was it her habit to welcome all soldiers in this war-hearted gracious way? But no, she just wasn't that free kind of a girl. She was welcoming him as someone she knew intimately and was glad to see.

The look in her eyes, the warm touch of her hand, seemed so genuine that his own plans for distant courtesy seemed somehow out of place. And so for a moment he could only stand there with her hands in his and look down at her as she spoke.

"I'm so glad to see you!" she said. "It's a long time since we met."

"You remember me?" he asked in wonder. "You know who I am?"

"Why, of course!" said the girl, with a happy little lilt in the turn of her voice. "You're the boy who sat in the very last seat in the first row in our senior high school year. You're the one who always knew all the answers all the way through our school years. Because you really studied, and you cared to know."

He looked at her in astonishment.

"Did I seem like that to you?"

"Oh yes," she said, drawing a happy little breath. "You seemed to be the one student in our room who really cared. I wondered whatever became of you. Did you go away to college, or go to work, or what?"

"Oh, I went to college," he said modestly, not even showing by so much as a glint in his eyes what a march of hard work and triumph that college course had been. This young man was one who took the next thing in his stride and did his best in it as he went.

"And now you're in the army," she said, her glance taking in the insignia on his uniform. "You're—?" She paused and gave him a troubled look. "You're going overseas pretty soon?"

"Yes," he said, coming back to his purpose. "Yes, if it hadn't been for that, I would scarcely have ventured to come to see you."

"And why not, I'd like to know?" asked the girl, lifting her lovely eyes and bringing into her face all the old interest she had had in this fellow-student who had been so much of a stranger to her, bringing a light of genuine understanding and admiration.

"Why not?" He laughed. "Why, I had no acquaintance with you. You belonged in a different class."

"Oh no," said the girl, with a twinkle in her eyes, nestling her hands in the big strong ones that still held hers. "Have you forgotten? You were in my class all through school. And what's more, you were the very *head* of the class. It was my main ambition to try and keep up with you in my studies. I knew I ever could get ahead, but I wanted to be at least second in the class! So don't say again that you weren't in my class."

He laughed, with an appreciation of the way she had turned the meaning of his words, and the fine color rolled up into his face gorgeously.

"You know I didn't mean that," he protested. "I knew you were the lovely lady of the class, and that you gave me a wholesome race as far as studies were concerned. But even so, that didn't put me into your class. You, with your lovely home, and your noble father and mother, and your aristocratic birth, and your millions, and your fashionable friends."

"Oh," said the girl, with almost contempt in her voice, "and what are they to separate people? Why should just *things* like that have made us almost strangers, when we could have been such good friends?"

He looked at her with a deep reverence.

"If I had known you felt that way, perhaps it wouldn't have taken me so long to decide whether I ought to come to you today."

"Oh, I am so glad you came!" she said impulsively. "But come, let's sit down!" Blythe, suddenly aware that her hands were still being held closely, flashed a rosy light into her cheeks as she drew the young man over toward the couch and made him sit down beside her.

"Now," she said, "tell me all about it. You came for some special reason, something you had to tell me, Susan said when she announced you."

"Yes," said the soldier, suddenly reverting to his first shyness and to the realization of his appalling impertinence in what he had to say. "Yes, I have something special to tell you. I know I'm presuming in speaking of it, and perhaps you will think me crazy for daring to tell you. I'm sure I never would have dared to come if it hadn't been that I'm in the army and that I have volunteered to undertake a very special and dangerous commission about which I am not allowed to speak. It is enough to say that it means almost certain death for me. And that's all right with me. I went into it with this knowledge, and it's little enough to do for my country. But when I came to look the fact in the face and get ready for my departure, which is probably to be tonight, I found there was something I wanted to do before I go. There was just one person to whom I wanted to say good-bye. And that was you. I have nobody else. My mother has been gone two years. She was all I had. My other relatives, the few that are left, live far away and do not care anyway. But there was just one person whom I wanted to see before I left, and that was you. I hope you don't mind."

"Mind?" said Blythe, lifting dewy eyes to his. "I think that is wonderful! Why should I mind?"

"But we are practically strangers, you know," he said with hesitation. "And in the ordinary run of life, if there were no war and things were going normally, we would probably never have been anything but strangers. I am not likely ever to become one whom your family would welcome as one of your friends—"

"Oh, but you don't understand my family," said the girl, putting out an impulsive hand to touch his arm. "My family is not like that. They are not a lot of snobs!" She was speaking with intense fervor, and her eyes implored him to believe.

"Oh no," he said, "I would not call anything that belonged to you by such a name. I don't want you to think that, please! It was never even in my thoughts. I have only thought of them as being fine, upstanding, conservative people, with a high regard for the formalities of life. It would not be natural for them to pick out a 'poor boy' as a friend for their cherished daughter. But I thought, since this is probably the last time that I may be seeing you on this earth, it would do no harm for me to tell you what you have always been to me. You have been an inspiration to me from even my little boyhood when I first saw you in school, and I have loved to watch you. And in my thoughts I have always honored you. I felt as if I would like to tell you that, before I go. I hope it will not annoy you to be told, and that you will remember me as a friend who deeply admired—and—yes, *loved* you from afar, and who for a long time has prayed for you every night. Will you forgive me for saying these things?"

Impulsively he put out his hands, laid them upon hers again, and looked at her with pleading eyes. But her own eyes were so filled with sudden tears that she could not see the look in his.

"*Forgive!*" she said in a small, choking voice. "Why, there is nothing to forgive. It seems very wonderful to me that you should say these things, that you should have felt this way. And of all the beautiful thoughts, that you should *pray* for me! Why,

I never knew you even noticed me. And I'm glad, *glad*, now, that you have told me! It seems the loveliest thing that ever came into my life. But oh, *why* do you have to go away? *When* do you have to go?"

He gave a quick glance down at his wristwatch and said with distress in his voice, "I ought to be on my way now. I have things to do before I take the noon train. I waited on purpose until the last minute, that I might not be tempted to stay too long and annoy you."

He sprang to his feet, but her hands clung to his and she rose with him.

"Oh, but I can't let you go like this," she pleaded, her eyes looking deep into his, her face lifted with the bright tears on her cheeks. "I *can't* let you go. You have just told me that you love me, and we must have a little time to get acquainted before you go. I—oh—I think I must have been loving you, too, all this time." Her own glance dropped shyly. "There was no one else ever who seemed to me as wonderful as you were, even when I was a little girl. Please don't go yet. *We must* have more time to get our hearts acquainted."

He looked down at her, his very soul in his eyes, his face deeply stirred, and then suddenly his arms were about her and he drew her close, his face against her tear-wet cheek, his lips upon hers.

"Darling!" he breathed softly.

She was clinging to him now, trembling in his arms.

"Darling, if I had dreamed it could be like this!"

Again he held her close.

"God forgive me! I've got to leave you. I'm a soldier under orders, you know."

"Yes, I know," she said softly. "I must not keep you. But oh, I wish you had come sooner, so that we might have had a little time together."

"I'm afraid my coming has only made you unhappy!"

"No, don't say that! It is a beautiful happiness just to know what you have told me. And you know—*I* shall be praying, too. May God take care of you and keep you and bring you back!"

He took her in his arms again, and their farewell kiss was a precious one to remember. And then suddenly a clock above the stairs with a silvery chime told the hour, and he sprang away.

"I must go at once!" he said.

"Yes, of course," gasped the girl sorrowfully.

It was incredible how hard it was to separate when they had only just come together. It was breathtaking.

Hand in hand they went out to the hall, to the front door, trying to say many last things for which there wasn't time, things that had just begun to crowd to their attention.

"But you will write to me?" said Blythe, lifting pleading eyes. "You will write at once?"

He looked at her with a sudden light in his eyes.

"Oh, may I do that?" he asked, as if it was more than he had dared to hope. "I hadn't planned to hang on to your life. I don't want to hinder you in any way. I want you to have a happy time, and—to—well, *forget* me. Think of me just as somebody who has gone out of your life. I mean it. I don't want the thought of me and of what I have said to hinder you from having friends and going places. I want you to be your dear happy self, just as you have been all through the years before you knew I cared. That will be the best way to keep me happy and give me courage to go through with what I have undertaken. I mean it."

Her hands quivered in his and clung more closely.

"How could you think I could forget you and go on being happy? You have told me that you love me, and it has—well, just *crowned* my life!" She looked up at him with a kind of radiance in her face that beamed on his heart like a ray of sunshine and warmed him through and through. He had been so humble about telling her, that he hadn't dreamed it would bring this response. It thrilled him indescribably.

"Darling!" he breathed softly and caught her to him again, holding her close.

Then upstairs another clock with a silvery voice chimed a belated warning, and they sprang apart.

"You must go!" It was the girl who said the word. "You mustn't let me make you late. And—how can I write to you? We have so much to say to one another."

"Oh, yes, I forgot!"

He plunged his hand into his pocket and brought out a card.

"A letter sent to this address will be forwarded to me wherever I am. Good-bye, my precious one! You have given me great joy by the way you have received me, and you haven't any idea how hard it is for me to leave you now."

He touched his lips reverently to her brow and then dashed out the door.

She watched him flashing down the street, her heart on fire with joy and sorrow. Joy that he loved her, sorrow that he must go away into terrible danger, or what he was supposed to be going to do, but he had spoken as if it were plenty. "Probable death!" he had said, and yet even that terrible prospect had not been able to still the joy that was in her heart. Whatever came, he was hers to love, she was his! Whatever came there was *this*, and for the present she could only be glad. By and by she knew that anxiety would come, and fear, and anguish perhaps, but still, he would be hers.

How strange that she should feel this way about that boy with whom she had scarcely had a speaking acquaintance. A word, a look, a hovering smile, all the most formal, had been their intercourse thus far. And yet he had loved her so that he could not go away into possible death without telling her how he felt. And she had loved him well enough to recognize it at once, though she had never used that word even in her thoughts with regard to him. It seemed as if it were something that God had handed to her as a surprise. Something He had been planning for her all through her life, and she hugged the thought to her heart that she had always admired him, even when he was a little boy. He had beautiful, intelligent eyes that always seemed to understand, a tumble of dark curly hair, and a way of disappearing into thin air as soon as the business of school was over for the day. He never seemed to take part in social affairs of the school—he just vanished. But his location in the room had always seemed to Blythe like a light for the whole class. Something clear and dependable to give their grade tone. It had been that way right along through the grades.

Just once in those years they had stood side by side at the blackboard working out a problem, their chalk clicking, tapping along almost in unison, driven by sharp brains, quick fingers—and they had whirled around with lifted hands almost at the same instant, the only two in the class that had finished. They had given one another a quick look, a flashing smile, and that smile and look had lingered in Blythe's memory like a pleasant thing, and helped to complete the picture she had of that wise young scholar with a well-controlled twinkle of merriment in his eyes.

The memory flashed at her now as she stood on the steps of her father's house and watched him stride down the driveway. She followed down to the end of the drive and watched him away down the sidewalk. Then she saw the bus coming. Was he going to make it? She held her breath to watch. Oh, had she made him late to something most important? That would be an unhappy thing to remember, if she had.

Then she saw him swing on inside the door just as it was about to close. Was he looking back? He was too far away for her to see.

But there were footsteps. Was someone coming? There were also tears on the verge of arrival. She turned like a flash, hurried up to the house, and vanished inside just as one of her friends reached the gateway and called out to her. But she was gone. She couldn't, *couldn't* talk to anyone now. Not after what had happened. Idle chatter of friends and neighbors would put a blur over the precious thoughts that were in her heart, if she allowed them to come now, before they were firmly fixed in memory. The morning was too rare and precious to be mingled with the commonplaces of life. She must get away by herself and savor this wonderful thing that had come to her.

So Blythe sped to her room and locked her door on the world that might have interfered.

For a moment she paused with her hands spread behind her on the closed door and looked about her. It was the same room it had been a few minutes before. There lay her coat and hat across the chair, just where she had dropped them when Susan told her she had a caller. There on the bureau lay her handbag.

She had been all ready to go down to that Red Cross class, and of course she ought to be going at once. But she couldn't just walk out and go down to sew, until she had a chance to catch her breath and realize what had happened. Anyway, there were women enough there to run the class without her. It would be all right for her to wait just a few minutes and get her poise again. If she went down at once there would be a kind of glory-shine in her face that everyone would see. She was sure some of those catty women who had so much to say about other girls would ask her about it. They never let any little thing go by. It seemed sometimes as if they were putting a magnifying glass over her to study her every time she came into the room. The questions they asked were impertinent questions about her home life, her family and friends, just so they would be able to tell about it afterward. "My friend Miss Bonniwell went to the orchestra concert last night. Yes, she went with young Seavers. You know. They run around together a lot." She could fairly hear them saying things like that. In fact, she had overheard some of their talk that ran a good deal after that fashion, and she couldn't bear the thought that they should look into her face today and, by some occult power they seemed to possess, search out that grand and glorious thing that had happened to her this morning.

She sank into her easy chair and put her head back happily. This was her own haven. No one had a right to call her out from here.

Then she closed her eyes and drifted back to the moment when she had gone downstairs, scarcely able to believe the message Susan had brought, that Charlie Montgomery, her childhood's admiration, was really down there and had come to see her.

Oh, she had thought, it probably wasn't anything that mattered—some technicality, perhaps, about the business of their alumni. Though she couldn't remember that he had been interested in their plans about the alumni, but perhaps they had drawn him into it in some way. Those had been her thoughts as she hurried downstairs with her hands out. Had she been too eager, shown her pleasure too plainly at first?

But no. He loved her! He had come to tell her that he loved her. Amazing truth! That anything so unforeseen should have come to her. The joy in her heart seemed almost to stifle her.

And then she went over the whole experience, bit by bit. Her delight when she recognized him. Her instant knowledge of her own heart, that he was beloved! Her hands held out to greet him, the touch of his hands, the thrill! Was she dreaming, or had this all been true? Oh, if he could but have stayed a few minutes longer. Just so that they might have talked together and gotten their bearings. And he was going away, into what he seemed to think was pretty sure death! Could it be that they would have to wait for heaven to talk together? Oh, the joy and the sorrow of it! The memory of his arms about her, his lips on hers! It was wonderful! It was beautiful!

And it wasn't anything she could tell anyone about! Not yet, anyway. Not even her mother. Her mother wouldn't understand a boy she never had known telling her he loved her. She couldn't bear to bring the beauty of that newfound love into the light of criticism. And that would be inevitable if she tried to make it plain. They would only think he was one of those "fresh" soldiers, as her mother frequently disapproved of some of the very young, quite exuberant boys at the canteen. And her mother would never understand how she could have so far forgotten her upbringing as to let a stranger kiss her, hold her in his arms, even if he *had* gone to school with her years ago. No, this was something she would keep to herself for the present. Herself—and God—perhaps. She didn't feel that she knew God very well. She would want to pray to Him to guard her beloved as he went forth into unknown perils. She would have to learn to pray. She would want to do this thing right, and she did not feel that she knew much about prayer, that is, effectual prayer! Oh, of course she had said her prayers quite formally ever since she was a tiny child, quite properly and discreetly. But seldom had she prayed for things she really needed. She had seldom really needed anything. Needs had always been supplied for her before she was even aware that they were needs. But now, here was a need. She wanted with all her heart to have Charlie safe and to have him come back to her. She wanted to feel his arms about her again, to see him look into her eyes the way he had done when he told her so reverently that he loved her—that he had prayed for her.

Where could she learn to pray right? Since she could not tell anyone else of her need, would God teach her?

And just then Susan tapped at her door.

"You're wanted on the telephone, Miss Blythe," she said, and Blythe's heart leaped with sudden hope. Could it be possible that Charlie had found a way to telephone her?

"Coming, Susan," she sang out, springing from her chair and hurrying to the door.

Chapter 2

Charlie Montgomery, striding down Wolverton Drive, was quickening his pace with every stride until he was fairly hurling himself along, straining his eyes toward the highway. Was that the bus coming? Yes, it was. And he must catch it! He couldn't possibly do all that was to be done before he left unless he did.

But the glad wonder was in his heart even though he hadn't time to cast a thought in its direction. Was he going to make it? He scarcely had breath for the shrill whistle that rent the air and arrested the driver as he was about to start on his route, but it reached the driver's ear, and looking around, he saw the soldier coming. One had to wait for a soldier these days, of course.

Just in time Charlie swung onto the bus and was started on his way; and not till then, as he dropped into the seat that a smiling old gentleman made beside him, did his mind revert to the great joy that he was carrying within him.

He had come this way full of fear and trembling lest he was doing the wrong thing. Lest he would be laughed at, scorned, for daring to call on the young woman upon whom his heart had dared to set itself. She had not only received him graciously, warmly, gladly, but she had listened to his words, had owned that she loved him, had let him hold her in his arms and kiss her. That much was the theme of his joy-symphony. It was enough for the first minute or two till he got his breath.

"Well," said the kindly old gentleman next to him, "you going back to your company?"

Charlie suddenly became aware that someone was addressing him. He turned politely and gave attention.

"Why, yes," he answered hesitantly, recalling his thoughts from the house up Wolverton Drive and the girl he had gone to see.

"Where are you located?" asked the old man with kindly interest.

"I've been in Washington taking some special training," he said evasively.

"Yes? That's interesting. What special service are you doing?"

Charlie twinkled his eyes.

"I'm not supposed to discuss that at present," he said. "Sorry. It's kind of you to be interested."

"Well now, I beg your pardon, of course," said the old man, and he looked at the young soldier with added respect. "But I—I really didn't know that a question like that couldn't be always answered."

"It's all right, sir," said Charlie, with his charming smile. "It's not my fault, you know. And, I beg your pardon, this is where I change buses. You'll excuse me, please." He swung off the bus as its door opened and tore across to another that was standing on the opposite corner. Fortunate that he could catch this one. He had been expecting to have to wait ten minutes more for the next one, and that would have given him little time to pick up his luggage and catch his train.

And now, when he found himself almost alone in a bus, with time to get back to his happy thoughts, it already seemed ages since he had left the girl he loved. He began to wonder if it had surely happened? Perhaps he just dreamed that he had been to the Bonniwells's and talked with Blythe. And then suddenly the sound of her voice whispered in his heart, her eyes seemed to look into his, the feeling of her lips on his! No, it was not a dream! It was real. Joy, joy, joy!

Just at present, in the midst of his tumult of realization that memory brought, the possibility of his own probable death in the offing, the fact that had loomed so large before he had dared to come to her, seemed not to count at all. He was simply rejoicing in the unhoped-for love that had been given him, and could not think of the days ahead when earth would probably come down and wreak its vengeance. He was just exulting in the present, with no thought or plan for the future, as a normal lover would have done. It was enough for the present moment that she loved him and was not angry that he had told her of his love. It made her seem all the dearer than he had dreamed; it gave a glimpse of what it might be to have her thought, her love to carry with him on his dangerous mission. It was enough that he could sit back in that bus and close his eyes and remember the thrill of holding her close in his arms, his face against hers.

With such thoughts as these for company, the ride seemed all too brief, till the bustle and noise of the city brought him back to the present moment and its necessities. Tenth Street, yes, here was the corner where he must get off and pick up those packages he had ordered yesterday over the telephone, to be ready this morning. And over on Chestnut Street was the place where he had promised to stop and pick up a book some kindly stranger had offered him. He didn't think he would be likely to want the book, but he did not like to hurt the man's feelings, for the man had a few days ago gone out of his way to get an address for him that he wanted. Well, it wouldn't take but a minute. He glanced at his watch. There was time. He could give the book away, or conveniently lose it if it proved a bore. He didn't at all know what the book was. The kindly friend had not told him. Just said it was a book he might like to have with him, and it was small, wouldn't take up much room. So, well, he would stop in case the first packages were ready on time.

And then to his surprise the packages were not only ready but waiting near the door for him, and a smiling proprietor handed them out with a few cheery words, and it suddenly came to Charlie to realize how exceedingly kind everybody was to men of the service now. The world had really taken on an air of kindliness. Was it only for the soldiers and sailors, or was it everybody?

He hurried over to his other stopping place and was handed a small, neat package with a letter strapped on with a rubber band. The man himself was out, but the salesman handed it out smiling. More kindliness!

He put the little book in his pocket, thankful it was not large, and went on his way. A glance at the clock told him he had plenty of time to telephone. Should he, dared he, telephone Blythe? He hadn't dared think of that before, but now the longing to hear her voice once more was too much for him. Passing a place where there was a telephone booth, he went in and looked up her number, even now hindered by a shyness that had kept him for days deciding whether to go and see her before he left. Perhaps someone else would answer the phone—that dour servant woman, or even possibly her mother. What should he say? Was this perhaps the wrong thing to do? Was there a possibility that it might spoil his happiness? But no, if such a thing could be possible, it would be better to find it out now than to go on dreaming in a fool's paradise. So he frowned at the number and dialed it quickly before he could change his mind, for now the longing to hear her speak was uncontrollable. It was going to be simply unspeakable if she was gone anywhere and he couldn't get her in time.

It was the dour Susan who answered.

No, Miss Bonniwell was not in. She had just gone out to her Red Cross class.

He felt as if the woman had slapped him in the face, but of course that was foolish. There was an instant's silence, and then Susan asked, "Who shall I tell her called?"

Charlie came to himself crisply. "Montgomery is the name. Is there any way that I can reach her at that Red Cross class?"

"I suppose you might," said Susan disapprovingly. "She's always pretty busy though. Still—if she chooses, of course—

the number is Merrivale 1616."

"I thank you," he said with relief in his voice. "It's rather important. I'm leaving in a few minutes. I wouldn't be able to call her later."

He began to dial Merrivale 1616 as if it were some sacred number.

Of course, he did not know how reluctant Blythe had been to go to that class. How eagerly she had flown to the telephone a few minutes before, hoping, praying, that it might be him calling, although he had not said he would—and of course he wouldn't have time, she knew.

"Who is it, Susan?" she had asked eagerly, as she passed the servant in the hall, dusting.

"It's one of them Red Cross women," answered Susan sourly. "They act as if they owned you, body and soul. They said they had to speak to you right away that minute."

"Oh," said Blythe in a crestfallen tone. "I suppose I ought to have gone to that class, but they had so many, I thought they could get along without me for once."

"And so they could!" encouraged Susan indignantly.

"I suppose I could send a message by you that I have something else important to do this morning."

Blythe lingered on the stairs looking hopefully at Susan, for the woman had often helped her out of unwanted engagements, but this time Susan shook her head.

"No, Miss Blythe, you couldn't. I asked them did they want me to give you a message, but they said no, they must speak with you. They seemed in some awful hurry."

Blythe gave an impatient little sigh and hurried down to the telephone in the library.

Chapter 3

Mrs. Felton and Mrs. Bruce had arrived early at the Red Cross room, had hung their wraps in a convenient place and settled down in the pleasantest situation they could find.

They arranged their working paraphernalia comfortably and looked around with satisfaction.

"I wonder where Blythe Bonniwell is," said Mrs. Felton as she took out her thimble and scissors and settled her glasses over her handsome nose. "She's always so early, and she seems so interested in the work. It's unusual, don't you think, for one so young and pretty to seem so really in earnest."

"Well, of course, that's the fashion now, to be interested in anything that has to do with war work. They tell me she's always at the canteens evenings. She's very popular with the young soldiers," said Mrs. Bruce, with pursed lips. "She won't last, you'll see. I'm not surprised she isn't here."

"Well, somehow, I can't help feeling that Blythe is somewhat different from the common run of young girls. I don't believe she'll lose interest," said Mrs. Felton, giving a troubled glance out the window that opened on the street.

"Well, she isn't here, is she? You mark my words, she'll begin to drop out pretty soon. They all do, unless they have really joined up with the army or navy and *have* to keep at it. This is probably the beginning already for Blythe."

"I hope not," signed Mrs. Felton. "I'm sure I don't know what we'll do if she doesn't come today."

"Why is she so important?" demanded Anne Houghton, who had just come in and was taking off her hat and powdering her nose. "I'm sure she doesn't do so much more work than the rest of us." There was haughtiness and almost a shade of contempt in Anne's tone.

Mrs. Felton gave her a quick inspecting glance.

"Why, she put away the materials last night, and I don't see what she has done with the new needles. I can't find them anywhere, and we can't sew without needles. The one I have has a blunt point."

"Oh, I see!" said Anne. "Well, I should think she was rather presumptuous, taking charge of all the needles. She sat down in the third best chair in the room. "Who does she think she is, anyway? Just because she's Judge Bonniwell's daughter and has plenty of money and has Dan Seavers dancing attendance on her at all hours. I can't think what he sees in her, anyway, little colorless thing, so stuck on her looks that she won't even use the decent cosmetics that everybody else uses. She'd be a great deal more attractive if she would at least use a little lipstick."

Mrs. Felton gave Anne another withering glance and went to the sewing machine to oil it and put it in running order for the day, not even attempting an answer.

"Well, what do you suppose she can have done with those needles?" asked Mrs. Bruce, rising to the occasion. "My needle has a blunt point, too. I don't see how so many of them got that way. They can't be very good needles."

"Well, if you ask me," said Mrs. Noyes, who had just come in, "I think it was that child Mrs. Harper brought with her yesterday. He picked up every needle and pin he could find in the place and drove them into the cake of soap they gave him to play with—the idea! *Soap!* For a *baby*! And scarce as soap is now in wartimes!"

"Well, but soap ought not to make needles blunt," said Mrs. Felton.

"Oh, he didn't stop at the soap," said Mrs. Noyes, with a sniff. "He had a toy hammer with him, and when he got his cake of soap all full he started in on the table and the floor and tried a few on the wheel of the sewing machine. I declare, I got so nervous I thought I should fly. I was so glad when she decided she had to take her child home for his lunch. I don't know why he needed any lunch, though. He had bread and butter and sticky cake and chocolate candy and a banana along, and he just ate continually, and kept coming around and leaning over my sewing and smearing it with grease and chocolate. I had to take that little nightgown I was working on home and wash it out before I could hand it in. I don't think we ought to allow women to bring their children along. They're an awful hindrance."

"But some women couldn't come without them. They have

no one to leave them with at home," said another good woman.

"Let them take their children to the nursery then," said Mrs. Noyes, with a pin in her mouth. "Mrs. Harper thinks her child is too good to go to a nursery with the other children!"

"What I want to know is, what are we going to do about those needles?" said Anne Houghton. "Here I am ready to sew, and *no needles!*"

"I think I'll call up Blythe Bonniwell and ask what she did with them," said Mrs. Felton. "I've looked simply everywhere, and I can't find them. She must have taken them home with her."

And without further ado Mrs. Felton went to the telephone, while all the room full of ladies sat silent, listening to see what would happen.

"What did you do with the new needles last night, Blythe?" asked Mrs. Felton severely, getting so close to the phone that her voice was sharp and rasping. "I've looked simply everywhere for them. And you know we can't work without needles. You must have taken them home with you."

"The needles? Why, no, Mrs. Felton, I didn't take them home. They are right there on the shelf where you had them before," said Blythe pleasantly.

"The shelf?" said Mrs. Felton more sharply. "What shelf?"

"Why, the shelf right over where you were sitting yesterday, Mrs. Felton."

"Well, you're mistaken, Miss Bonniwell. There isn't a needle in sight, and I'm looking right at the shelf."

"Oh, Mrs. Felton. But I'm sure I put them right there in plain sight. Someone must have moved them."

"No," said Mrs. Felton coldly. "No one could have moved them, for there hasn't been anyone here to move them, and we have looked just everywhere. I wish you would come right over and find them. You know we have simply *got* to have those needles, for there is not another one to be had in this town, and we haven't any of us time to go into the city after them. You know needles are scarce these days. I wish you'd look in your handbag and see if you didn't take them home with you."

"No, I didn't bring them home," said Blythe decidedly. "I know I didn't."

"Very well then, come over here at once and find those needles! I shall hold you personally responsible for them."

"All right," said Blythe indignantly. "I'll be right over!"

So Blythe caught up her hat and coat, snatched her handbag from the bureau where she had put it last night when she came in, and hurried away, calling to Susan that she was going to her Red Cross work.

When she walked into the Red Cross room, the ladies were all sitting there in various stages of obvious impatience. They had purposely so arranged themselves for a rebuke as soon as Anne Houghton announced, "There she comes at last! My word! It is high time!"

But Blythe was anything but rebuked as she entered with that delightful radiance on her happy face, for she had been thinking about her new joy all the way down, and her thoughts had lent wings to her feet.

So, as she entered, the ladies sat in a row and blinked, for perhaps the brightness of her face dazzled them for an instant.

"Well, so you've come at last!" said Mrs. Bruce disagreeably. "Now, get to work, and find those needles if you can. We've looked everywhere."

Blythe's glance went swiftly to the shelf over Mrs. Bruce's head.

"But—why, there they are! Just where I told you they were!" she said triumphantly.

"What do you mean?" snapped Mrs. Felton. "I don't see any needles."

"Why, in that blue box. Don't you remember, we took the whole box because we were afraid we wouldn't be able to get more later when we needed them."

"That blue *box*?" said Mrs. Felton, jumping up and going over to seize the box from the shelf. "Why I supposed those were safety pins. I don't understand."

She took down the box and opened it, and her face took on a look of utter amazement.

"My word!" she said slowly. "I certainly don't understand. I supposed, of course, these were safety pins that Mrs. Huyler brought. Well, then, where are *they*?"

"She took them home again when she found this wasn't a nursery," said Mrs. Bruce grimly. "She said she would take them to a place she knew *needed* them."

"Well, upon my word!" said Mrs. Felton again. "I guess you're right, and I was the one to blame. I certainly ask your pardon, Blythe."

"Oh, that's all right," laughed Blythe, swinging off her coat and hat and taking the first empty chair that presented itself. "Now, where do I begin? Do you need more buttonholes made, or shall I run a machine?"

"Make buttonholes," snapped Anne, handing over the baby's nightgown she had been set to finish. "I just hate them, and anyway, I always make them crooked. I don't see why *poor* babies have to have buttonholes anyway. Why can't they use safety pins? I'd rather buy a gross of them and donate them than have to make a single buttonhole."

"Oh, I don't mind buttonholes," said Blythe pleasantly. "That was one thing I learned to do when I was a little girl. We had a seamstress who made beautiful ones, and she taught me."

"Well, I'm sure you're welcome to do them all for me," said Anne disagreeably.

And it was just then that the telephone rang, and Anne, being on her feet, answered it. She always liked to answer the phone. It gave her a line to other people's business, and that was usually interesting.

"Yes?" she drawled as she took down the receiver. "Red Cross Sewing Class. *Who?* Who did you say? Miss Bonniwell? Yes, she's here. Who shall I say wants her?"

But Blythe, with cheeks like lovely roses, was on her feet beside the telephone.

"I'll take it," she said smiling, as she gathered the receiver into her hand.

"Well, you needn't snatch it so," said Anne, turning angrily away just as she was trying to identify the voice as Dan Seaver's.

"Oh, I'm sorry," said Blythe, her cheeks flaming crimson. "I didn't mean to snatch."

But Anne turned away with her head held high and went over to select a needle for her own use.

So the room held its breath to listen to the telephone conversation.

"Yes?" said Blythe quietly into the instrument, though she couldn't keep the lilt out of her voice, for she hoped she knew just who was calling her, though, of course, it might be her mother or Susan from home.

"Is that you, Blythe?" The voice on the wire was cautious, tentative.

"It certainly is," said Blythe, with a light ripple of a laugh.

"Are you alone?" Again the voice was very guarded, low. Even the most attentive listener could not have understood what came from the other end of the wire, for Blythe was cupping her hand about the receiver, which was most annoying to Mrs. Bruce. She severely shook her head at Mrs. Felton, who ventured to interrupt the performance by asking a question about which buttons were to go on the little nightgowns they were making.

But Blythe's voice was clear, without confusion.

"Oh no, I'm sorry!" she answered brightly. "But—you weren't late, were you?"

"No, I got here in plenty of time. The train was late, I found I had a few minutes to spare, and I wanted to hear your voice again, even if we couldn't speak privately."

"Oh, that's nice of you!" said Blythe graciously. "Don't forget to write that down for further reference," and she rippled out her bewildering laughter again.

"No, I won't forget," came the man's voice, louder and clearer than before. "I'll write that down as soon as I get on my way, and I'll see that it gets to the proper person. And by the way, will you kindly think over what I told you, and see if you can possibly respond to my suggestion?"

"Oh—yes—I'll do that," said Blythe in a matter-of-fact tone. "I'll take pleasure in doing that, and I'll let you know later what I think."

Blythe was talking in a very off-hand tone, and she had a feeling that her eyes were twinkling over her words and across the space between them, as if he could see her and understand why she was speaking in such veiled language. But her heart was warm and happy over his voice, even though she had to strain her ears to identify every word.

"That's good of you," said the man's voice, falling into the game easily. "I'm glad to have had this little talk with you—this chance to explain."

"Yes," said Blythe, smiling into the receiver. "It was so good of you to call. But how did you know where to find me?"

"Oh, I called the house first and the servant gave me the number," he explained.

"Oh, yes, of course," said Blythe, letting her voice linger, glad to have the brief interlude drawn out to its utmost, knowing the listeners would not understand. "Well, it was nice of you to take all that trouble to find me and let me know."

'Oh, it was a pleasure, I assure you," spoke the young man. "And you are sure you won't forget?"

"Oh no, I won't forget," lilted Blythe. "And—I hope you—are successful!" Those last words were spoken guardedly, very low, her tone full of feeling, as she gave a quick glance about the silent room full of women, sewing steadily without a word.

Suddenly the man's voice spoke sharply, almost breathlessly:

"Well, I hear it coming! I must go! Is there any chance you might be at home later in the day or evening, if I had the opportunity to call again?"

"Oh yes," she breathed softly, "after two o'clock and all the evening. Yes, I'll be at home."

"Of course it *may not* be possible for me to call, but I'll try. Good-bye—*dearest!*"

Could that last whispered word be heard by the audience? Blythe held her head high and didn't care. What did all these women know or care about her and her precious, beautiful affairs?

Then she hung up the receiver, and walked steadily over to Mrs. Bruce.

"Have you one of those buttons I'm to make buttonholes for, Mrs. Bruce? I must get to work and make up for lost time."

She took the proffered button and went smilingly over to an empty chair, without a sign of the lovely tumult in her heart.

Then those frustrated women sat and sewed away, and occasionally lifted baffled eyes and glared at one another, as much as to say, "Does that Blythe Bonniwell think she can get away with a thing like this as easily as all that?"

And at last Anne lifted her head with a toss and sang out clearly for them all to hear. "Well, who *was* your friend? It was Dan Seavers, wasn't it? I was sure I knew his voice. Are you and he going to the benefit concert at the arena tonight? I suppose that's what he called up about. I don't see why you had to hedge about answering him that way. I'm curious to know if he succeeded in getting tickets after waiting all this time. And I think I know where he could get a couple if he didn't. I know somebody who has some who has to leave town tonight. Do you think he would like them?"

Blythe looked up with a distant little smile.

"Why, I wouldn't know, Anne," she said. "That wasn't Dan calling."

"Well, who was it then, with a voice so much like Dan's?"

"Oh, it was just one of my friends in the air corps," said

Blythe easily. "I don't think you would know him. He was only here on a brief furlough."

Anne looked at her curiously.

"Oh, *yes*?" she said contemptuously, but Blythe was too happy to be ruffled by her contempt and went on making buttonholes with a radiance upon her lovely face that defied the scrutiny, furtive or open, of all those women. She went happily through the morning, thinking her pleasant thoughts. True, Charlie Montgomery was going from her, but he was leaving his love in her heart, and for the present that was all she needed to give her joy.

And thus, thinking her happy thoughts, Blythe's morning went forward with its business, and at last was over, so that she was free to go on to her home and wait for whatever might be in store.

Dearest. Had he really said that? She hugged the memory to her heart.

But back in the room she had left, where the other women were purposely idling about, putting on their wraps, and getting ready to leave, there was a significant silence until the sound of her footsteps died away in the distance and the ordinary routine noises of the street assured them that Blythe was well out of hearing. Then they relaxed almost audibly.

"Well," said Mrs. Bruce grimly, "she certainly has more brass! Imagine her sitting here sewing after she had been through that playacting on the telephone. Was that really Dan who called her, Anne?"

Anne Houghton shrugged her shoulders.

"Well, I certainly thought it was. But why on earth she considered she had to tell a lie about it, I'm sure I don't know. It wouldn't of much importance, would it? We all know she runs after him day in and day out."

"I don't think she does," said Mrs. Felton. "She's too well bred to run after anybody. Remember, Anne, her mother is a lady."

Anne shrugged again. "That's not saying *she* is one," she said.

"What makes you hate her so?" asked Mrs. Felton, looking gravely, steadily at Anne.

"Oh, I don't hate her," laughed Anne. "I don't give the matter that much importance. I merely think she's so smug, and she does like to give big impressions about herself. See today how determined she was to let us think that was some soldier she was talking to, one of those soldiers she's hostess to up at the canteen. She wants us to think that she can flirt around like the other girls."

"She doesn't flirt at the canteen," said Mrs. Stanton gravely. "I go there every night, and I've never seen her do anything out of the way."

"And I guess you'll find that Blythe is busy some nights doing evening hospital work or something of that sort. Isn't she? I'm sure I heard that," said Mrs. Felton.

"Oh, *really*? I think you must be mistaken. I saw her out with Dan Seaver last night and also the night before." That from Anne.

"Well, I suppose she must have some nights off. Most of them do, don't they?"

"I'm sure I wouldn't know," said Anne coldly. "But for heaven's sake, don't let's talk about that girl anymore. I'm fed up with her. She gets on my nerves every time I see her. Just say she's a paragon and let it go at that. If that's what you like in a girl, then that's what you like. Good-bye. I'm going out to lunch and I'm late now." Anne slammed out of the door, her high heels clicking as she hurried away.

Mrs. Felton and Mrs. Bruce walked slowly down the street behind Anne and watched the arrogant swing of her shoulders till she vanished around the next corner. Then after a pause Mrs. Felton said, "Young people are awfully rude nowadays, don't you think?"

"I certainly do," said Mrs. Bruce, with a heavy sigh. "It's the one thing that makes me glad my daughter died when she was a child, so she wouldn't have to live to grow up in this impudent age."

Mrs. Felton uttered a sympathetic little sound and walked thoughtfully on until they parted.

Chapter 4

The telephone was ringing as Blythe entered the front door, and she hastened to answer it, wondering if it could possibly be Charlie again so soon. But it was only a tradesman calling up about something that had been ordered that he couldn't supply yet, and she turned away with a sigh.

Upstairs, her mother met her in the hall, smiling.

"Oh, you're back, Blythe," she said. "I didn't think you'd be here for a half hour yet. Well, I just made a tentative engagement for you for this evening. Dan Seavers called. He wanted you to go somewhere with him tonight. I forget where. But I told him I was sure you'd be glad to go."

"Oh *Mother!*" said Blythe in dismay. "Not *this* evening! I really can't go this evening."

"Why, why not, child? If it's that hospital-office work, I

think you give entirely too much time to that. It isn't good for your health, after you have sewed all the morning. And you really ought to take some days off and not slave *all* the time, even if it is wartime. The government doesn't want to kill anyone, and there's no need to go to excess, even in a good thing."

Blythe was silent and thoughtful for a moment, then she looked up.

"Is Dan going to call up again?"

"No, I think not," said her mother. "He's going to be away this afternoon, but he said you could call and leave word with the butler what time you would be ready. And he'll be here as early as you say."

"All right," said Blythe after an instant's thought, "I'll attend to it."

Her mother turned away, smiling, satisfied. After all, Mother didn't know, couldn't understand, why she must stay at home tonight. She better engineer this thing herself. Later, when she could talk about this, she would tell her mother all about Charlie Montgomery. But not now, not till it was more a part of herself so that she would be able to answer questions and make her mother fully understand.

She watched her mother get ready to go out to her war work, watched her down the street, and then she went to the telephone and left a message with the Seavers's butler.

"Please tell Mr. Dan that Miss Bonniwell cannot possibly accept his kind invitation for this evening. Something else was already planned. Thank him for the invitation."

Then Blythe went contentedly to her room and sat down to await the ring from the telephone. Would Charlie call? *Could* he call? She was sure he would if he could.

And it was then she had her first uninterrupted time for going over, step by step, the beautiful experience of the morning. It was then she could close her eyes and visualize his face when he rose from his chair to meet her as she came downstairs. That fine lifting of his head, the sparkle in his eyes, the old humble, yet assured manner he had as a boy in school. Charlie! The same Charlie she used to watch and admire as a lad in school days. Charlie, come to tell her that he loved her! It was almost beyond belief! He had never seemed to look her way before. How did he know that he loved her? He had seen her so seldom.

All the sweet, hurrying, eager questions rushed upon her, each demanding to be answered at once, yet none of them shaking her faith in his love, even for an instant. The breathtaking memory of his arms about her, folding her close. Why, she had never dreamed what love like this could be!

She had read many beautiful love stories of course, had delighted in them, yet none of them came up to the sweetness of those all-too-brief blissful moments while Charlie was with her. Her own beloved!

There would come a time, of course, when she must bring all this out in the open, must tell her mother and father. Or would there? *Must* she? If anything happened to Charlie, if he did not come back, she would keep it deep in her own heart. Never would she allow even her dearest ones to speculate on what Charlie was, and what he had intended to do about all this. That was her part, and for the present it must be kept so. Precious. Just between themselves. And so, whatever came in the future, this afternoon was hers to be with Charlie in her thoughts. To knit up all the years that had been so empty and barren for them both before the knowledge of their mutual love had come to make it shine like a light.

And then she turned in her mind to face that other thought, that terrible thought, that perhaps he might not come back. Not *ever*! He had spoken as if that was a sure thing. In fact, it was the only reason, apparently, that had given him the courage to come and tell her of his love, as if it were just a kind of spiritual thing that could last through eternity but could not be used on this earth. It seemed a beautiful, awesome way to look at life, to reach such heights of sacrifice that he could smile as he said it. Would she ever reach that height, too? Oh, she could not, must not, think of that now. She must only think how he was going to try to call her up sometime, today, or this evening, and she *must* be at home and be ready for it. She must have heartening words ready at the tip of her tongue, for his time to talk with her might be very short, if it came at all. Just between trains, or a stop at some station for connection or some needed repair. She must think of all those things and be ready not to waste the time. She must have a pencil and paper ready in case he wanted her to write down an address or something. But she must have some brief sweet messages ready for him to take with him in his memory; things he would like to hear her voice saying, ringing in his heart sometime when he was far away and needed comfort or strengthening.

And so she sat and dreamed it out, as if she were communing with him, knitting up those past years when they had never talked except a few scant words concerning an algebra problem.

It might have seemed to an outsider like a monotonous

little round of thoughts to be so sweet and absorbing, but they were precious to the lovely girl who sat and thought them. Like some potent charm that works a change on words written long ago brings out clearly what was invisible before, so these tender thoughts were painting over the past years and bringing out the meaning of a young love that had grown up unknown and unacknowledged. And now she could remember glances, furtive shadowed smiles, little acts of kindness and courtesy, like picking up her examination paper that a breeze from the window had caught and fluttered across the aisle down to his vicinity. She could read the look in his eyes, the flush on his cheek that before might have only meant embarrassment, shyness. Oh, it was wonderful, this thinking, in the light of the knowledge of that confession of his that he loved her!

Into the midst of these happy dreams, that were as yet not consciously tinged with the coming fears of possible pain and sorrow, there came the ringing of the telephone.

Blythe sprang from her chair and hurried to the instrument across the hall in her mother's room, lovely anticipation in her face. Could this be Charlie?

But no, it was only some tiresome woman who wanted to persuade her to undertake the management of a play to be given for the benefit of a day nursery.

Feverishly, because she didn't want the telephone to be in use when Charlie called—if he called—she tried to decline, but the woman only urged the harder.

"But such things are not in my line, Mrs. Basset. I never got up a play in my life, wouldn't know how to go about it, and besides, just at present I'm doing all the war work I can possibly manage, without undertaking anything else. No, I'm sorry. I can't possibly do it. Think it over? No, I'm sorry I can't promise to do that even, for I wouldn't, under any circumstances, undertake to put on a play anywhere, and I'm quite sure there are more important things to do for the war than to get up a play. No, Mrs. Basset, you'll have to count me out."

She hung up at last with a sigh and glanced at the clock. Five whole minutes wasted that way! What if he had tried to call during that time, and might have no other opportunity! But there! She must not get hysterical over this.

Quietly she went back to her room and read over the notes she had been writing down. Why, they were almost a letter, for the words came directly from her heart! She would go on writing, and when he did call, she would tell him she was just writing him a letter.

With this thought in mind she went back to her writing, a light in her eyes and a sweet smile on her face.

The next interruption was from her mother, calling to say that neither she nor Blythe's father would be at home to dinner tonight, as they had met an old friend who was leaving town at midnight and wanted them to dine with him at his hotel so they could have an old-time visit.

"Why don't you call Dan and ask him over to dinner with you tonight? That will probably just fit in with his plans," said her mother.

"No," said Blythe sharply. "I don't want to, Mother. I've got letters to write and a lot of other things to do. I'll be all right, and I'll tell Susan. You needn't worry. What's one dinner, after all? And I'm tired, I really am. Have a good time, Mother dear." Then Blythe went back to her pleasant thoughts and her first happy letter.

It was five minutes of six when the telephone rang again and Blythe flew to answer, sure now it must be Charlie. But instead she heard Dan Seaver's angry voice.

"What in the name of time is the matter with you, Bly? *Can't* go? Of *course* you can go! I've been planning to take you to this picture for weeks. You know I've spoken of it several times."

"Oh," said Blythe, "I'm sorry, Dan, to disappoint you, but you said nothing about going *tonight*, and I really can't do it. I made other plans!"

"Plans! *Plans!* What are your plans? Change them, then! Call off whatever you've promised to do. This comes first, and I won't take no for an answer."

Blythe drew a weary little sigh and looked with anguished eyes toward the clock. Suppose Charlie should call now? It might be likely. It would be so near the dinner hour, surely his train would stop somewhere at this time, or would it?

Her mind was turning this subject over and over while she tried to be half listening to Dan and wondering what she could say to him that would make him understand she meant what she said and that she was not available this evening for *any-*thing but her own plans.

"Bly, you're not listening! I say I'm coming right over there and get you. We'll go somewhere and get dinner, and then take in the first show."

Blythe roused.

"No!" she said. "*Positively no!* I simply *can't*. I thought I sent you word in plenty of time for you to find someone else to go with you."

"No, Blythe, you don't mean that! You know you don't want

me to take someone else."

"Why, yes, I certainly do, Dan," she said sweetly. "I'm sure you can find somebody."

The altercation lasted some minutes, and Blythe drew a breath of relief when Dan finally grew angry and hung up the receiver with a slam, furious because she wouldn't tell him where she was going or what engagement she had that she would not break for him.

Annoyed beyond measure at the time he had kept the telephone occupied, Blythe tried to get back her happy serenity, but try as she would, she was worried lest Dan had made her miss the few treasured words she hoped to hear from Charlie. Of course, he hadn't been sure he would be able to call, and this was probably but the beginning of a long weary hopeful waiting. But she put the thought from her. She must not allow her mind to dwell on the possibility of future unhappiness, not on this first day of her new joy. Sorrow and anxiety might come, but she would not dwell on them ahead of time. And this was a day that must be remembered as having been all joy.

It was an anxious evening for Blythe. She was beginning to worry lest Charlie hadn't been able to telephone at all, and perhaps there wouldn't be any way she could hear his voice again, ever! She was also beginning to be afraid the call might come so late that her mother and father would arrive in the midst of it, and there would be questions perhaps, and she might have to explain at once, so that the beauty of Charlie's words might become dimmed before she could savor them fully.

But there she was, being silly and hysterical again! Why couldn't she be sensible? This whole thing was something that had come to her right out of the blue as it were, nothing she had solicited, nothing that any act of hers had brought about, and if it was something sent to her, she ought to be able to trust, and not get excited about it.

It was not until a little after ten that the call did come, and she tried to go to it calmly, so she would not be out of breath to talk.

His voice was very clear in the quiet room.

"Is that you, Blythe?"

"Oh yes, Charlie!" she said joyously. "It is *you at last!*"

"Yes, beloved," he said. "Are you alone?"

"Yes, I'm alone, and so glad to hear your voice!"

"My precious girl! How wonderful to hear *your* voice!"

"I was afraid you couldn't make it," she breathed.

"Yes," said the young man, "our train was late and we had to make up time. New orders. And now, I've only a few minutes to talk, so we mustn't waste time. But I've written you a letter, and you may get it in a day or two. It has to go through the regular routine now of course, I think, and you won't know where I am nor where I'm going. But don't mind about that. I just want to say again that I love you. I love you more than I ever dreamed I could love anyone. You opened the way into a heaven of delight when you told me you loved me. I hadn't counted on that. I hadn't thought you ever noticed me. I know I'm going to spend a lot of time rejoicing in your words, in the memory of you in my arms, your face against mine, your lips on mine. It is a greater joy that I ever had hoped could be mine. Even though it must likely be a brief joy, since I have a rendezvous with death."

"Oh Charlie! *Don't* say that!"

"Well, it's true, beloved! You know I told you if it had not been for that I would never have presumed to tell you what I did." He spoke gravely.

"Well, I'm glad that anything made you tell me," said Blythe happily. "But oh, I pray that it may only be a brief absence and that you will soon come back to me."

"I shall be glad of your prayers, but don't be arbitrary about them. My mother used to say that God must have His way, and it was of no use to try to force any other. I believe God knows what He is doing, don't you? And I've committed myself to this thing, you know. I think it is right. I know it is patriotic."

"Yes, I know," sighed Blythe, "but oh, *don't* take it *for granted* that this is going to be *the end*!"

"No," said the young man's voice, with a clear ring to it, "we won't take anything for granted now, but just our love. Shall it be that way, beloved?"

"Oh yes!" said the girl breathlessly. "And I like the way you say 'beloved.' I shall remember your voice saying it, *always*—till you come again."

"That's very precious of you to say. Yes, till I come again—somewhere, sometime. For I do believe there'll be a 'somewhere' of meeting, don't you? *Don't you?* No matter what happens?"

"Yes, of course," said Blythe. "But—I'll believe—you will come back. Oh, Charlie! Why didn't we know each other better before? How much time we've lost out of our childhood days!"

"Not enough to keep us from loving, my dear!" His voice was very tender. "Please don't mourn over that or anything else. It is enough for me for the present that I can carry your love with me, your permission to receive my love. You are not angry that I told you. That gives me great joy and strength for my mission. It is more than I have ever dared to ask of life. Will you pray for me that I may be brave as I go forth to my duty? Forget that it is terrible, and think of it as something that *must* be victorious. Will you do that?"

"Oh yes, dear. Of course."

"Then I shall go armed with courage, feeling that whether I live or die, I shall *conquer*. And now, I've only a few seconds left to talk, and how can I possibly say all that I have in my heart in that time? But I want you to understand that if you hear nothing from me, perhaps for a long time, or even perhaps *never*, still I have loved you with all my heart. They have not told me what are to be our circumstances or location, but I feel that communication with our home world may hereafter be greatly restricted, certainly limited, possibly entirely forbidden or impossible, and you will not let yourself grieve about that, will you? You will say in your heart it is all right. You will know I have not forgotten, nor changed. You will remember that?"

"I will remember!" Blythe breathed the words softly, choking back the sobs that kept rising in her throat.

"Dear girl! It was selfish of me to do this to you, and make you unhappy, even for a day. I should have kept my love to myself."

"No, no, don't say that! Please don't!" she pleaded. "Your love is the greatest thing that ever came into my life. I am glad, *glad* that you told me! I shall be glad always!"

"You *dear*!" he breathed softly. "You wonderful, beautiful dear!"

There was silence for an instant, and then suddenly a far

call, and the young man's voice alert, almost agonized, "They are calling me. I have to go! Good-bye, my precious girl. God keep you!"

And then as he hung up she could hear his voice answering to the call. "Coming!"

Chapter 5

For a brief interval she stood still before the instrument, staring hungrily into it, hoping against hope that there would yet be perhaps one more word from her beloved. And then she was suddenly aware of her mother standing in the doorway watching her, astonished.

"Why, my dear!" said the mother. "How did it happen that you came home so early? Dan told me you would probably be late!"

And suddenly, the long wait of the evening with its precious thrilling climax was swept away, as if it had all been a dream, and she was back in her everyday life again, with the usual things and people surrounding her.

"Oh," she said dazedly. "Oh, why no, Mother, I didn't go."

"You *didn't go?* But, my dear, I told him I was sure you

would be delighted. I am afraid you must have been very rude, for he was quite insistent about it, and I understood him to say that you had known about this for some time. Didn't I make you understand that I had promised you would call him? It certainly was very rude of you if you did not."

"But I did, Mother. I called him right away after you went, and left word for him that I couldn't go tonight. I left word with their butler, and then Dan called up himself later and I explained that I couldn't go tonight. I had something else to do that was important."

"*Important?*" said her mother, eyeing her bewilderedly. "What was it, dear? I don't understand. I thought this was your free evening. I told him that."

"Yes, Mother, but this was something that came up that you didn't know about. I had promised to be at home all the evening for a phone call."

"A phone call! Why, who was calling that you felt was important enough to make you miss going out with Dan? When you had practically promised him you would go with him?"

Blythe's face flushed.

"But I hadn't promised Dan, Mother. He had never made a definite date for this, and he can't expect me to dance attendance every time he speaks. I have a few other friends and interests."

"Oh," said her mother significantly. "I thought you considered Dan's wishes would be paramount. I thought you were especially fond of him."

"Oh, not *especially* fond, Mother. He's just a good friend. But I wasn't rude to him, really, Mother. I left word I couldn't go tonight, and when he called up I tried to explain to him that something had come up that I felt I *ought* to do."

"But who was this person who presumed to ask you to stay at home all the evening? Couldn't you have called him up and told him that you found you could not be here?"

"No, Mother. I had no way to reach him till he called. He was a soldier friend who was leaving—for the front—and he had asked if he might call me to say good-bye when he left. I said yes, I would be at home all the evening."

"But a soldier boy, just one of those soldiers at the canteen? Strange boys you don't know very well? It couldn't possibly have made any difference with him. I think, Blythe, that sometimes you confuse your obligations and let trifles hinder more important things. In fact, I've been a good deal worried at the number of hours you are spending in that social service down there at the canteen. Of course I want you to be patriotic and all that, but you are just sticking in the house and working hard almost every minute of your life, and it is time you had a little brightness and fun, or you will wither up and get to be old before your time."

"Oh, Mother!" protested the girl. "I—you—you don't *understand*. This was a special soldier, going into danger, and his mother had died. He wanted somebody to say good-bye to before he went."

"Oh, yes," said her mother a bit sadly. "They're all going into danger, of course, and of course we all feel sorry for them. But you, Blythe, can't take every one of those soldier boys on your heart and feel sorry for them. There are plenty of people over there at the center, good, motherly women, who would be glad to give a boy good advice before he leaves for the front. That's what they are there for. He didn't need to pick out a young girl and hold her up for an evening just to say good-bye. Those boys haven't always got good sense. I have no patience with them. It is all right, of course, for you to play games with them and make them have a cheerful time, but I do think you ought to hold your home time free for your own friends. Blythe, I'm really worried about you. I don't want you to go to extremes in anything, and you know these boys in their uniforms may be very attractive and all that, but when they get across the water they'll forget all about the girl that sacrificed what she wanted to do just to humor them."

But Mother, it wasn't like that! I didn't *want* to go with Dan tonight. I really didn't. I was tired and wanted to stay at home and get caught up with several things, and I had some letters to write. You see—"

Blythe hesitated and looked troubled. She was almost on the verge of telling her mother all about Charlie Montgomery, only somehow this seemed no time to bring out that precious experience and tell it in every detail. Her mother was in no mood to sympathize and understand just now. She was evidently too much annoyed about her failing Dan Seavers.

"You see," said Mrs. Bonniwell, "I had a long talk to-day with Mrs. Seavers. She is so pleased that you are going so intimately with Dan. She says it has made her feel so safe and happy about him, so content that he is in good company and not getting in with a wild set. She has been greatly troubled about a girl who sings at one of the nightclubs, in whom he has been interested, and she was so relieved when he took to asking you to go places. I do think you ought to consider other people as well as those young boys in the soldiers' canteen. You know it would be really worthwhile to help a young man like Dan Seavers. A young man in his position would have a great many temptations, and a young girl with right principles can often strengthen her young men friends by her friendship and be doing something really worthwhile. You know Dan is in line for an officer's commission, and what he *is* will be an influence on all the soldiers under him. If I were you I would consider how wonderful it would be to help anchor Dan to the right kind of people."

"But Mother, that's just it. I don't like the kind of men and girls that come around Dan. More and more it is getting so that I feel uncomfortable in his company. I don't think you would like them either, Mother, if you could be with us sometimes."

"Well, that's unfortunate, but don't you think a good girl can usually dominate a situation wherever she is and show them how much better a right-minded girl is than one who is loud and coarse and common?"

Blythe looked troubled.

"No, Mother, not always. I used to think so, but lately I've been places with Dan where I felt as if I were being soiled and trampled underfoot."

"Blythe!" said her mother. "You don't mean Dan would allow anybody to be rude to you while you were in his company?".

"I don't think Dan feels the difference. He doesn't understand why I don't enjoy going places with people like that."

"Oh, my dear! I'm sorry to hear that. But don't you think you might be able to win him away from that kind of people?"

"I'm afraid not, Mother," said the troubled Blythe sadly, thinking in her heart that there were going to be a lot of questions to settle that she had not thought of yet. How was she going to make her mother understand? Oh, this was something she had to think out before she talked any more about it, even with her mother. But for the present her inmost heart told her that she had no taste nor interest in going anywhere with Dan or any other young man, now that she knew of Charlie's love, and while he was off engaged in a terrible undertaking for the cause of freedom. Oh, of course, she would have to go about as usual and be pleasant and interested in life as it had to be lived here on this side of the world, but good times were not the chief aim of her existence anymore. Something had happened to her since Charlie Montgomery had told her of his love for her and the great undertaking to which his life was pledged. To a large extent that undertaking must be hers, too, hers for interest and prayers. Hers to place first in the list of daily plans. Hers to cherish as the greatest possible undertaking. Because she and Charlie were one in heart now, they must be one in purpose, too. And if, in the working out of that purpose, it came about that Charlie had to die to accomplish it, well then, it was her part to die, too, to a lot of interests that had up to this point been a part of her life.

But she couldn't tell all this to her mother now. Mother would protest and tell her she was crazy. Mother didn't know what it was to love someone who was going out to die. She would say Blythe was morbid. She would turn heaven and earth to get her interested in the world and get her out among the young people again, make her stop her delightful work among the nursery babies, and maybe make her stop even the Red Cross classes. Mother would tell people that Blythe hadn't seemed well lately and she felt her daughter needed a rest, maybe insist upon her going away somewhere, to the shore or the mountains or down to Florida. There was nothing in life that Blythe wanted to do less than to go away from the home where Charlie would write if he had any opportunity to write at all. Oh, what should she do?

Of course, if worst came to worst, she could tell her mother the whole story, tell of Charlie's coming and how she had always admired him. But could she make Mother understand now, after all this excitement? Evidently her mother was thoroughly on Dan's mother's side and willing to have Dan take her out anywhere, just so that his mother's worries might be appeased. But Mother just did not understand, and how could Blythe make her see it in the right way? Mother had always been so sane and reasonable. She wouldn't for a moment approve of things Dan did and said when he was out among that crowd whose company he seemed to enjoy so much. Was it possible that Dan could be turned back to a more refined crowd? Was it really right that she should try to help him in this way? How the thought of it irked her, in the light of the wonderful love of a real man!

Well, she would have to think this out, try to find out what her duty was, and of course if it was duty, she must do it. But it need have nothing to do with the new joy that had come into her life. That was something secure, that was hers. So far, hers in secret, but *hers*, and it was something that nothing, *nobody* could ever take away from her. Not even death, because it was that rendezvous with death that had set his heart free to come to her and tell her of his love. Oh, death could be cruel, *cruel*, and the fear of death could bring agony—the death of a beloved one! But death with all its stings could not take her beloved's love away from her. Somehow that thought bore her along over the immediate present with its problems and bravely into the dim future that loomed ahead with so many terrible possibilities. She must sit down and think this thing all through and see what was the right thing to do. Oh, if she only had somebody to talk it over with.

Of course her mother, normally, would be the one, the only confidante she had ever had. But how could her mother judge aright in this thing? She would be too horrified by the unknown. Charlie would mean nothing to her now but a menace. She would not at first realize what a difference death made in the conventions of the world. Even if it was only a *rendezvous* and didn't reach a final end, it did make a difference, and by and by when this matter of pleasing Mrs. Seavers was past, she was sure it would all be perfectly understood by her mother. Anyway, it wasn't really hers to tell—yet. It was their precious secret, hers and Charlie's.

All these things flashed through her mind like a message she was reading to herself, while her mother talked on.

And then her mother, watching her daughter's changing expressions, finally dropped wearily into a chair and said, "Oh Blythe! What *is* the matter with you? It is not like you to be so regardless of others' needs. Why will you not give the help you can so easily give? If you could have seen his poor mother!"

Suddenly Blythe put on a resolute look.

"Why, of course, Mother, I'll do all I can to influence Dan for the right things, but you don't seem to understand that he practically wants to *own* me, to order me around, and insist I shall go whenever he commands."

"Oh my dear! I don't think he means it that way. He just likes you very much, and really wants your company."

Blythe's face grew serious.

"Well, perhaps," she said hesitantly. "But tonight I didn't want to go, and I felt I had a right to say no. Bedsides, Mother, people are beginning to talk as if Dan and I were engaged and we're *not*. I don't *want* people to get that idea! I don't like to be watched and talked about!"

"Nonsense!" said her mother. "Nobody is talking about you. That's just a sign you're getting self-centered. I don't believe anybody has ever thought of such a thing."

"Yes, they have," said Blythe firmly. "I heard them myself today as I was going into the Red Cross room."

"You heard someone talking about you? Who in the world would dare to do that?"

"Oh, it was only Anne Houghton, and she's always been disagreeable and jealous, but she was talking to Mrs. Bruce, and *she* assented to everything Anne said, and I just felt as if I wanted to get out and get away from them all. I won't desert the work I've promised to do for the war. But I do think I'd rather not go out quite so much with Dan. Oh, I'll go sometimes, of course, but please don't urge me when you see I'd rather not."

"Why, of course not, dear," said her mother anxiously, "but I wish you would tell me what they said that has made you feel so uncomfortable."

"Oh, Anne was just saying that I thought I was so great because I had Dan Seavers tagging around with me everywhere, that I wouldn't let him out of my sight, and things like that. Mother, I don't like to be talked about that way. It takes all the joy out of life."

"Well, of course it isn't pleasant," said her mother thoughtfully. "But, after all, that wasn't such a dreadful thing for her to say. She's probably jealous. Maybe she admires him herself very much. However, I don't want to urge you to do anything that does not seem pleasant to you."

"Thank you, Mother dear," said Blythe, coming over to her mother and kissing her tenderly, and as she stood so with her mother's arms about her, she felt a quick impulse to tell her all about Charlie Montgomery. And perhaps she would have done so, except that her father came in just then with some news about the war that he had just heard, and the time seemed again not to be just right for the story. Perhaps she should wait and think it over a little more, plan out in her mind just how she would make them understand what kind of a boy Charlie had always been, introduce him to them as it were, bit by bit, so that they would see the beauty and tenderness of his nature. So that they would not be shocked by the abruptness of what he had done in telling her, an almost stranger, that he loved her.

Then her father turned on the radio and there came a session of reports of what had been going on in some of the war zones: men sent on secret missions behind the enemy lines to get certain information and to spy out the enemy's plans; others flying straight into death to accomplish some great necessary destruction of the enemy's works. They were almost like a suicide squad.

Blythe caught her breath, and one small hand flew to her throat involuntarily.

"Oh!" she breathed softly under her breath, and looked aghast at her father and her mother. But they were not noticing her then. They were only looking pitiful and sad over the terrible state of the world in these wartimes, never dreaming that one of those young men whom they were distantly pitying *might* be the lad their cherished daughter loved, and who was even now hastening on to such a death somewhere. "A secret mission" he had called it. Oh, was this what he was going to do? Blythe did not know, could not know, perhaps would never know till the war was all over and the missing ones were counted up.

So, the moment passed, with Blythe's heart suddenly overwhelmed with understanding, and a terrible sadness settling down upon her which kept her silent. Then suddenly they were all roused to realize that it was getting late and the morrow had duties early in the morning. So they said good night and hurried away to their rest.

Back in her own room, Blythe settled down in her chair, her knees still weak from that sudden startled realization of Charlie's peril. She looked about her. Was it only this morning that she had gone downstairs to hear him tell her that he loved her? It seemed that she had lived years since the morning dawned and she went happily down to pleasant duties, without a thought that this war was coming into her life. Really coming. Not just by forcing her to go without a few luxuries, doing a few unusual things, economizing—less candy and sugar and coffee, fewer beefsteaks, walking miles instead of using her car. The war had struck to the center of her being now, through the boy she had watched over the years and greatly admired, and who had suddenly become beloved beyond anything that had ever touched her life before.

For some time she sat there quietly and relaxed in her chair, trying to think it all out.

And would the morrow bring her a letter? No, for that would scarcely be possible. Her soldier had said all mail would have to go to headquarters before it could be forwarded to her, that is, after they had really started on their mission. And now that she was beginning to understand a little what terrible possibilities loomed before such missions, her heart trembled at the thought.

But oh, how she longed to get a word from him, his hand-writing written *to her*! How wonderful that was going to be! A letter from Charlie Montgomery, all her own! She must get to sleep to hurry on another day, to bring that letter nearer to her.

Quietly, with her light turned out because she didn't want her mother to come in and ask her what was keeping her up, she got ready for sleep and, creeping into her bed, lay thinking over all that had happened since morning. But though she had been good friends with Dan Seavers for years, not one thought of him came to spoil her bright vision.

Chapter 6

Charlie Montgomery, back in his train again, his heart warm with the sound of his dear girl's voice, tried to settle down and compose himself for rest, for he knew the journey ahead was likely to be strenuous the next day. But the joy surging over him was like a bright sunshine shining in his face, and how could he sleep when he could bask in its warmth and brightness? To think that wonderful girl was really his beloved, at least for the little time he had ahead to live. And, after all, that was all that anybody had of joys, for death *might* be waiting just around the corner anywhere for anybody.

But somehow since he had talked with Blythe, and begun to sense all the joy that life might have held for him if he had not committed himself to this war enterprise, the whole thing took on a gloomier aspect. The exaltation of willingly giving himself to a great duty seemed suddenly to have faded, and his heart was beginning to cry out to have it all done with, to go back, and live like a normal human being.

With a sudden closing of his firm young lips, he straightened up and took himself to task. This would not do. The preciousness of what had come to pass for him must not be allowed to spoil the greatness of the undertaking to which he was committed. He must not allow himself to sink into gloom over this. He must go smiling to the doom he firmly expected, and he must not falter.

All his life Charlie Montgomery had had to be doing something like this. Even as a child, his father and his mother had wisely trained him to know that his first concern should be to conquer himself. His father once told him that half the battle was won if he once was sure he could conquer himself. His mother taught him that this must also be done at no expense to the gentleness and beauty that was meant to shine in his life, but that he must learn to put his own wishes and plans aside, lay them away carefully in his heart, if there was something else that ought to come first. So, now, as he thought things over, he could almost hear his mother's voice saying, *"First things first, son, and don't let personal wishes cloud over the brightness of your judgment or make your will waver in what you ought to do. The precious things of life can wait. They will not perish. There will come a time, either here or hereafter, when their beauty will be yours in all fullness."*

Yes, those words of hers were graven on his heart, and he wished with great longing that she might be here now, that he could tell her about Blythe and see the look of love in her eyes as she understood. For she would have understood, he knew.

She had been like that.

But Mother had God. He was very real to her, and she drew great stores of wisdom and strength from Him. And he did not have God. At least, he had never consciously drawn much strength from any slight contact he had had with his Creator. Oh, he used to go regularly to church in the days when his father and mother always went. And he went through the form of joining the church when he was quite young. He had been brought up to read his Bible and pray every day when he was a child, and he had eagerly taken in the Bible stories then. But somehow they had never taken hold of him, and he had never drawn any help from his connection with the Almighty. He supposed now, with death in the offing so definitely, that perhaps he ought to do something about this. But he wasn't quite sure how to go about it. He hadn't for a long time read his Bible, and it had never meant much to him. Prayer had been a sort of routine, a formality. Not a definite coming of his soul into the conscious presence of the Most High. Well, he ought to do something about that before he reached the end. Perhaps if they stopped at some camp for a day or so he could look up some chaplain and ask a few questions, sort of get him to intercede with God for him, for his soul that was so soon to go out at the end of this life. Since his mother wasn't here to do it, surely he could find someone to pray for him, though to tell the truth, his idea of chaplains was that most of them were more or less what the fellows called "stuffed shirts." However, perhaps there would be an exception, and he must make that a definite engagement, to look up some contact with God before he finally left.

So, having settled that, he composed himself to rest. He told himself that at least until he reached the next stopping place he might allow himself the dear privilege of thinking exclusively about Blythe, just as if he might be coming back someday to her. No, that wouldn't do, for the letdown would be too great when he remembered the present duties of life. He must not get a gloomy slant on what he had to do. He could never do good work in any way if he was filled with personal gloom. But at least he could rejoice in her attitude toward him, in her precious words, the look in her dear eyes, her smile, and her voice over the telephone.

Sinking into sleep with these thoughts in his heart, the night was amazingly brief, and waking in the morning, it came to him sharply that he was another day nearer to his doom.

Soon after breakfast the train halted at a station and took on a lot of soldiers, also quite a number of officers. Some of the officers were most distinguished-looking men. About mid-morning Charlie was summoned to an audience with the officer he had been advised would give him more definite instruction in what was before him.

Charlie had written a letter to Blythe that he had mailed at the time he had last telephoned her. And now as he returned to his seat after his interview with the officer, he reflected that he was glad he had done so; for he had learned, among other things, that hereafter, while he was in this special service, all communications with the outside world would have to pass through the censor. It gave him the feeling that from now on they were in the eye of the public, and they might not exchange their precious intimate thoughts, for which circumstances had given them so far little opportunity. The great separation had begun! Only the most impersonal matters might be discussed from now on, and of course, a little later, he might have no assurance that he could write at all.

With all these things in mind he had made that letter a kind of added farewell, a summing up of all the matters they had not had time to discuss. So now as he thought about it, he prepared to write even another letter. Just a brief one now. One that he wouldn't mind having any censor see. Blythe would understand, of course. It gave him a kind of a hopeless feeling. War! *War!* Why was it?

Yet he must not go out to a duty such as his with a feeling like that in his heart. He must somehow find a chaplain and get into conversation with him. Surely a man who had come out to war on God's service would be able to clearly point him the way to God. But though he searched through the train several times, he did not find a man to whom he felt drawn enough to seek help from him.

Just what was he looking for? he asked himself. A saint? An angel? A man with a holy face? No, that wasn't what he wanted. He tried as he stood at the front end of the train where he had a good view of all the faces he saw, to think what he was searching for, and he decided it must be a man with a face of quiet wisdom and strength, a man with a happy face, as if he were possessed of something that ordinary people lacked, yet wise and true and tender, even when merry-hearted. Was there any man like that in the train, or in the army anywhere? There ought to be a great many. If there were any such men in the whole wide world who had something real to impart to men who were going out to die, they ought to be in the army.

He got to talking to another soldier, and they touched on the topic that was on Charlie's mind.

"Yes, I've seen one or two like that," said the soldier who was a private, and owned that he was scared—afraid—to die. "Of course, there are a few great ones, like the man we had at the first camp I was sent to. He was swell. He really *believed* all he said, and he knew how to put it so you found yourself believing it, too. I wish I could have stayed there long enough to have gotten all his dope. I heard he was going out to visit different camps, and believe me, he was really popular with the fellows. He used to talk about Jesus Christ as if he had really met Him, as if he knew Him kind of intimately, you know, and when he preached you could see it all acted out there before you, like it was a play. You felt as if you had been there and seen the miracles done. I really was sore when we had to leave him. But I heard he was going around to other camps preaching. Perhaps we'll run into him yet somewhere. His name is Silverthorn. If you get a chance to hear him, don't miss it. He gives you great stuff! You feel like you've met God after he gets through talking."

Charlie stood a long time talking to this young private who had evidently been so deeply impressed by this preacher.

"I'll hunt him up," said Charlie, "if I ever get within hearing distance of him."

After that, because his heart was sick and sore with longing for the love he had found and lost so soon, Charlie went back to his belongings, hunted out pen and paper, and wrote another brief note.

Dearest:

I've just heard of a man who preaches real things and might tell one how to die courageously. I want to be more than just a conqueror. It's got to be something greater than courage, because I'm not afraid to die. Dying is nothing in itself. A little pain, a little oblivion. But then what? My mother wasn't afraid to die, and she was not physically so courageous. But she had something bigger, something that lifted her above any physical fear. It is not fear of the pain of death that makes people afraid to die; it is fear of what comes after. I am not afraid to die, but I wonder if I know much about what comes after. Do you? For, after all, whether in war or in peace, we all have to die, and we all need to understand and be ready for what comes after.

If you and I expect to spend eternity together, we should look into this and be ready, the way we used to have to prepare for a lesson or an examination that was coming. You and I always used to be prepared, didn't we? Perhaps you are ready for what may be ahead, but I don't feel that I have been, so I'm studying. Will you think about this? Because we don't want to take any chances of missing the great things that are ahead for us who love one another. Will you think about this, too, so we shall be one in thought? We'll only be preparing for an eternal joy; and together, I trust,

*dear love. Don't let this make you sad. It was just
something I felt ought to be said between us. You
have all my love.*

*Yours,
Charlie*

Afterward, as he thought it over, he wished he had not
written that last letter. Would it seem desperately gloomy to
her, put a damper on her ardent joy? Yet, of course it was something he wanted her to know, his feelings on this great subject
of death about which they had said so little. But it was too late
to do anything about the letter now. He had put it in with the
rest of the mail as soon as it was written, and he did not wish
to go through the routine of trying to get it out again. No, he
would write her another presently, in the morning perhaps. A
happy letter, without a reference to death, and try to dispel the
gloom.

So, he drifted off to sleep again, wondering what the future
was about to hold for him and for his beloved.

And the next morning, as soon as it was light enough to
see, he wrote briefly:

Dearly Beloved:

*I want you to be happy, bright and cheerful, and
happy every hour of your days. Every day of your
years. Do not grieve for me, for I shall be in the
way of duty, and I shall be glad that I am counted
worthy to serve my country and the cause of right.*

*And if letters cease, you will know that I am on
my way. Trust God for the rest.*

Yours,
Charlie

And then, toward evening, the train drew into a camp where he learned they were to spend the night, awaiting other men who were joining their company. And there in the darkening dusk, a name sprang into the sky in brilliant lights, "SILVERTHORN," and below it, flashing an instant later, "Hear him tonight!"

His pulse quickened. Could that be the same man the private had told him about? He would go and see.

Chapter 7

Blythe came down the next morning with dark rings under her eyes and a worried wrinkle on her brow. Her mother, looking up from the morning mail, smiled at her cheerfully.

"How would you like to run down to Florida for a few weeks, dear?" she asked quite casually, and Blythe knew that the campaign was on.

Blythe tried to smile when she looked up, and shook her head.

"Oh no, Mother dear! I just couldn't spare the time. I'm so interested in the work I am doing. I wouldn't interrupt it for anything."

"But I know you are overworking, dear. I was talking to your father about it last night after you went to your room, and we decided you ought to get away from it all for a while, at least, and get rested. You've got dark circles under your eyes, and we can't have you going into a decline, you know. Remember you've been working hard in college, and it's time you had a real rest."

"But I don't want a rest," said the girl earnestly. "I want to stay right here and do all the nice things that I am doing. I just love the babies I am working with in the day nursery, and the hospital class is so interesting. And besides, I've undertaken a lot of things at the Red Cross class. No, I couldn't *think* of going away now. I'm having the time of my life!"

"Well, you certainly don't look it this morning," said her mother, scanning her face thoughtfully.

"But Mother, don't you know what makes me look that way this time? After you gave me a regular scolding for not going out with Dan Seavers, you got me worried."

"For pity's sake, child! Why should that worry you?"

"Well, I just don't like going out with him anymore the way I used to do. I don't like the crowd he goes with, and I don't like the way he talks and acts. I think you are mistaken about my having a mission to change him. I know I *haven't*. Of course I'll be as nice to him as I can when we are thrown together, but I don't see that I should take him over to bring him up."

A puckered frown came on her mother's forehead.

"Why no, of course not, dear. I didn't mean anything like that. But I can't see why you can't make it plain to him why you don't care to go with such people. Let him see that if he wants your company, he'll have to choose a different group."

"Oh, yes, I suppose I can do that, if the occasion offers," sighed Blythe. "But I'm really not much interested. You see, Mother, he doesn't want me to make him over. He's trying to make me over to suit his own plans. And I don't care to be made over."

"But Blythe, you don't want to be left without *any* escorts, do you? You know, so many of your old friends have gone overseas or to the camps, and there aren't so many men that you can afford simply to turn a respectable one down. I wouldn't like the idea that you had *nobody* to take you out."

"Mother, if I were in the army, a WAC or a WAVE or something, or if I were working in a defense plant like a lot of the other girls, I wouldn't have to have an escort. I'd be going places by myself."

"Blythe! My *child*! *You* working in a defense plant?"

"Well, why not? Of course I'd rather be doing what I'm doing than trying to be a riveter, but that is a perfectly respectable job, and lots of nice girls are doing it. And in these wartimes, girls haven't time to go around to parties and have escorts and be so formal. There isn't time for frivolity. And do you know, Mother, somehow it doesn't seem good taste to be running around to parties and entertainments when so many of our friends and acquaintances are facing death to make our world safe for us."

"Why, Blythe, I didn't know you felt that way. You never seemed particularly interested in the boys in the army or navy."

A flash of color went over Blythe's face.

"Oh, but am *now*, Mother! The more I see of those young boys going out from their homes before they are really half grown up, and the more fine-looking older men in uniform I see, the more I feel what serious business this war is. It doesn't seem the thing for us who stay so safely at home, to run around trying to amuse ourselves like a parcel of children."

"Blythe! What a strange thing to say! You don't want everybody to sit around and be gloomy, do you?"

"No, certainly not. I think we ought to be bright and cheerful for the sake of the young soldiers who are lonely and sad about giving up their lives at home, and looking forward to no one knows what terrible futures."

"But, my dear! What a gloomy view to take. I shouldn't think you would be much help among the soldier boys if you talk as if they weren't any of them coming home."

"But I don't *talk* that way, Mother. Of course, a lot of them *are* coming home—I hope—and of course we must make it as cheerful as possible for them. I'm only saying that the ones who do not have to go, who have duties that keep them at home, ought to put aside any childish desires they may have to amuse themselves, and try to make the ones who have to go have good times while they are waiting to be called."

"Well, I don't see your line of reason, but it does seem to me that the boys who are staying at home to do important work for the war have as good a right to have a good time now and then as the ones who are going over."

Blythe drew a long breath that had a little note of almost despair in it.

"Well, Mother, perhaps you are right, but somehow I don't seem to have much respect for the boys at home who have to be babied, when a lot of their own age have set their lips, and their wills, and have gone out to face whatever comes, even death. It is like people trying to have a dance while they are waiting to find out how many of their friends have been killed in some great disaster."

"Well, my dear, it is sweet of you to be so sympathetic, and it shows a beautiful maturity and gravity of thought in one so young, but I do think that everyone, both young and old, ought to keep just as cheerful as possible. And then, of course, there are boys at home who are not physically able to go and fight."

"Why, yes, of course," said Blythe, weighing each syllable carefully to be sure it was true in her own heart.

Yet there was a gravity in Blythe's face that made her mother uneasy.

"Well, if you feel that way, we'll wait a little while and see how you look. If you continue to have those dark circles under your eyes, something will have to be done about it. But there is one thing I shall insist upon. I want you to stop that work in the Red Cross class right away. You can call up and tell them that you can't come anymore, and they will have to get someone else to take your place, for I won't have you spending so much time in the company of people who dare to talk about you."

Blythe laughed.

"Why, Mother dear, you mustn't feel that way. Everybody talks about everybody else when they happen to want to, and I can't get out of every place where they talk. I'll just be careful not to give them anything to criticize, if I can help it."

Her mother looked troubled.

"I'm afraid you can't do that, Blythe. You know when people get started talking, they just make up things to say without realizing it. I would rather you didn't go there another time. Out of sight you'll perhaps be out of mind, and so free from their gossiping tongues."

"No, Mother, they'll just call me a quitter, and I'm not going to have them say that. Besides, I've just undertaken to make the buttonholes on a whole lot of the darlingest little nightgowns for babies, and I can't leave till that's done. You know I love to make buttonholes. No, Mother dear, I'll just stick by the work I've promised till something really worthwhile needs me. I'm quite content with what I'm doing for the present."

"But you really need some young company, and I can't bear to have you forlorn and alone. If you are so determined that you can't go with Dan anymore, you'll just drop out of everything, and have no friends at all."

"Oh no, I won't," said Blythe with a happy little smile. "Don't you worry. I'll be all right. And please don't go and get up trips to Florida and things like that for me, for I really don't want to go anywhere just now. I would rather stay here and do just what I'm doing."

"Very well," said her mother with a sigh, "if you want it that way of course. But I hate to feel that you are holding aloof from everyone, all your young friends."

"Don't feel that way, Mother. I'm quite happy with the friends I have, and there will be others, too, someday," and a sweet little fluttering smile flickered over her face.

And then, if Susan hadn't come into the room with a message from the grocery man, it is possible that Blythe might have started in to tell her mother about Charlie Montgomery. But she still dreaded so her mother's worried look when she told her that a perfect stranger to them all had told her that he loved her; had dared to tell her that and then go off to war. Her natural reaction would be to resent his daring, and Blythe felt that she could not quite bear that yet.

"Well," said her mother with a sigh, as she rose to answer Susan's questions and get a list for the tradesman, "I suppose if you feel that way, perhaps it's as well for you to go this once, but if I were you, I would get out of that work just as fast as possible and let us find some more congenial work for you. And Blythe, I wish you wouldn't go today, at least. You look so very tired."

"No, I think I'd better go," said the girl. "And Mother, the boys at the front don't wait for some more congenial work. This is war, you know, and we must work where we are bidden. You're doing it, and I must do it, too. Don't worry about me. I'll be all right. And now I must go. I don't want to be late at the class again. 'Bye, Mother dear!" Blythe jumped up and gave her mother a soft little kiss and hurried away.

It was true that her heart was a bit heavy this morning, for she had just begun to realize that Charlie was going farther and farther away from her now, and into the dread possibility of death. Would he ever return? Would any earthly joy ahead come out of this beautiful sorrow that had come to her? And would she be able to bear her cross all through the long uncertainty?

So, setting her thoughts on the fact that Charlie loved her, and had told her about it before he went, she breezed into the Red Cross room with a fairly good imitation of happiness and greeted them all as if they were her dearest friends. She had no idea that any of them had ever dared to say unpleasant things about her.

"Good morning, everybody," she lilted out. "Isn't this a lovely day? I was afraid it was going to rain again, but it certainly has cleared off beautifully, hasn't it? Now, where are my buttonholes? How many of them ought I to get done this morning? I always like to set a goal for myself. It's so much more fun to try and finish what I plan."

Anne Houghton looked up, astonished. She had taken

pains to find out that Blythe had not gone out with Dan Seavers the night before, and she could not understand her being so joyous. What did she have up her sleeve now? Some new man who hadn't yet been seen in town?

"You seem to be very cheerful about it," she said contemptuously. "Almost as if you had private information that the war was over."

Blythe looked at her, a bright smile kindling on her lovely face.

"Wouldn't it be nice if I had?" she said with a twinkle in her eyes. "Wouldn't I just enjoy telling you all about it, bit by bit, and speculating about the difference it would make in our poor, tired world? Why couldn't we pretend that it was so this morning? Wouldn't it seem a bit more cheerful? For someday, likely, that *may* happen you know. I always did like to play 'Let's pretend.'"

"I'm afraid I haven't much imagination," said Anne coldly. "I never saw any advantage in kidding yourself along, because the truth always catches up with you sooner or later, and the letdown is too great!"

"Oh, do you think so?" said Blythe. "I can't help feeling that there is a decided advantage in keeping cheerful."

Some of the others cast significant glances at one another, and a few, of whom Mrs. Felton was the leader, gave her an approving smile.

There was a quiet little woman sitting at the far end of the line, sewing with all her might—swift firm stitches, neatness and precision in every angle of her trim, slim body, and the set of her fine thin lips—who took no part in these pleasantries and did not even cast an eye in her direction, and Blythe took note of her attitude. She seemed to have no acquaintance with the other women, did not speak, and was not spoken to. Her garments were plain and her hands had the look of being work-worn. Yet there was about her an air of intense purpose, as if this work she was doing meant something to her. Meant more, perhaps, than it did to these other women, some of whom, at least, were merely here because it was an easy way of discharging a war duty and gave pleasant publicity to their efforts. Not that it wasn't important enough, of course, but most of them had the languid air of not caring much about what they were doing. Blythe wondered what made the difference, and when a little later the woman who had been sitting next to the quiet one vacated her chair to go out on an errand, Blythe quietly went over and took it, giving a bright little smile to the busy woman, who barely glanced up when the newcomer arrived next to her, as if it made little difference to her who sat there.

A fleeting smile crossed the gravity of the silent woman, and Blythe followed it up. Quietly, so that the attention of the other woman would not be called to her words.

"Mind if I sit by you?" she asked pleasantly. "I think there is a little more light by this window, and I thought you looked as if you would be a pleasant person to sit beside."

The little woman looked up, surprised.

"Why, you're quite welcome of course," she said cordially. "But I'm only a very unimportant person. I'm just Mrs. Blake, and I don't live in a very fashionable quarter of the city. In fact, I think my house is just over the edge in this section, and I don't really know these ladies. I've thought perhaps they rather resented my being here. I don't know. But this was where I was told to come, so I came."

"Why, of course," said Blythe, with a tone of merriness in her voice. "And why should anybody resent anybody else in the world, no matter on which side of an imaginary line they live? We're in a war. We have no time for silly trifles like that. Do you think we have?"

Mrs. Blake looked up, astonished again.

"Why, no, I don't suppose we have, but you can't change the way people think about such things just because there's a war, can you?"

"I don't know why not. It seems to me when almost everybody has some dear one in that war, either far away or on the way somewhere, that we all feel for one another and love one another, at least a little bit more than we used to do. Isn't that the way it should be?"

Blythe lifted her eyes and Anne Houghton came into her range of vision, and it came to her suddenly that she didn't love Anne Houghton, or feel for her a bit more than she used to do. In fact, she was in a fair way to hate her because of the way she was acting. Well, she'd got to check herself up on that. But she went on with her conversation with the quiet little woman by her side who somehow interested her greatly.

"Yes," said Mrs. Blake with a quick-drawn sigh, "I guess that's the way it ought to be, but I'm not sure it is always, even yet."

"Perhaps not," said Blythe thoughtfully. "But I think we *ought* to be that way. Now take yourself. I'll have a guess that you have somebody in the service. You seem so interested."

Mrs. Blake was still for a minute, and then she said with another sigh, "Yes, I've got somebody in the war. I've got three somebodies in it. In fact, there were four till my husband got hurt in the munitions plant where he was working, and that laid him aside in the hospital. But he still hopes to get well and get back to his job. He thinks it was sabotage that caused the accident that put him on his back, and it's hard not to hate the people who would do a thing like that, isn't it?"

"Why, of course," said Blythe. "I guess that's the kind of thing we were meant to hate, isn't it? That's devilish. That's just what the war's about."

"Yes, I feel that way," said little Mrs. Blake, snapping off her thread and putting a knot in the end for another seam.

"But you said you had four somebodies in the war. Who are the other three?" asked the girl, starting in on another buttonhole.

"Yes," sighed the mother. "There's Floyd. He's in Guadalcanal in the hospital. But they say he's getting better. He's hoping to get back into the service soon. I don't know where they'll send him next. And there's Johnny, he's in Africa; that is, he was the last time we heard. And there's Walter, he's in camp, getting ready to go somewhere. He thinks maybe it will be Iceland. But they're all fighting in the war, thank God, and so I come here the only free time I have to sew a little while. It's all the time I have free to give. You see, I work in a munitions plant myself afternoons and evenings, and I have to take a little time to keep our two rooms tidy for me and my little girl who is in school yet. So when I come here, I have to work hard and fast to get as much done as possible."

"My dear, I think you're wonderful!" said Blythe, with true admiration in her eyes.

"Oh no, I'm not wonderful! I'm just a common wife and mother doing her best to help her family keep right and brave and with the war. But tell me about you. They say you make wonderful buttonholes, but something tells me that's not all you do. Have you got somebody dear to you over in that war?"

Blythe's cheeks flamed rosy for an instant, and a very sweet look came into her eyes as she lifted them to the new friend she had found in this unpopular corner of the room.

"Yes, I have," she said softly. "Somebody *very* dear!"

She paused a minute, and then added in a still softer tone, "He's not a father or husband or son, nor even a brother. He's just a friend. A very dear friend."

"I see," said Mrs. Blake understandingly. "I used to feel that way about Jim, my husband, before he was my husband. When he went away to France in the last world war. I know just how it is. And—does he know you care? Or perhaps I ought not to ask that. Excuse me for being so forward."

"There's nothing to excuse," said Blythe gently. "Yes, he knows. And *he* cares, too!" she added softly.

"That makes it nice," said Mrs. Blake. "You've something to look forward to."

Blythe was silent a moment, and then she lifted sad eyes.

"I'm afraid not," she said sadly. "You see, he's gone on some very special mission. And he thinks it is pretty sure death! He seemed to think he might not come back. In fact, he was sure there wasn't a chance. I don't know where he is. It's a military secret."

"Oh, *my dear!*" said the little woman sadly, with a great tenderness in her voice and eyes. "I'm sorry for you!"

"Thank you," said Blythe, with a catch in her voice. "You're the only one I've told about this—but I knew you wouldn't say anything."

"No, of course not, child. But I'm greatly sorry for you, and

I'll be praying for you—and him!"

"Oh, thank you!" said Blythe, brushing at a quick tear that was trying to get out. "I'll remember that always!" And suddenly her lovely smile bloomed out like a rainbow in the rain.

The gathering broke up just then, everyone hurrying away to lunch.

"I must go," said Mrs. Blake. "I mustn't be late to my job. But I'll not be forgetting to pray for you—and *him!*" And she hurried away.

Blythe smiled sweetly at her and then looking up, saw Anne Houghton's scornful glance upon her.

"Getting quite chummy with our slum-lady, aren't you?" she sneered. "Not trying to hire her for something, are you? I'm sure I don't see why they put a woman of that sort in with our crowd. She just doesn't belong, and she really lives out of the district. Somebody ought to write to headquarters and have her sent to another group."

"*Don't!*" said Blythe sharply. "She's very sweet, and Anne, she has three boys in the service."

"She would, of course, but they're just the common herd, children of a woman like that! That's all those common boys would be fit for, anyway, to go out and fight."

Blythe looked at the other girl, appalled, and could not think of words to express her indignation, so she turned and walked away, wishing she knew how to make Anne understand what an utter snob she was, but realizing that utter silence was probably the best rebuke she could give her.

On her way home Blythe began to wonder at herself for telling this strange woman about the sweetest thing in her life, her love for Charlie. How was it that she could tell this stranger, and she hadn't yet mustered courage to tell her own dear mother? Oh, if she could only be sure that her mother would take it in the sweet sympathetic way that the stranger woman had listened. What made the difference? Not just the fact that Mrs. Blake lived on the wrong side of the township line, or wore plain clothes and worked hard for her living. Was it because she had children in the war, and knew what war possibilities were? Oh, war did make a difference. And maybe her mother would begin to realize that soon, and she could bring her sweet secret and share it with her precious mother.

And then she went into the house and found there a letter from her beloved, the first one he had written and mailed just after talking to her on the telephone that first time. She was glad that there was no one about, not even Susan, and she might, unquestioned, steal up to her own room and read her letter undisturbed. Her first wonderful letter!

Chapter 8

Blythe was trembling as she settled down in her chair to read her letter, grasping it tenderly as if it were something fragile, something almost elusive that might take flight from her hand even yet.

Carefully she opened the envelope, studying the formation of her own name in Charlie's handwriting. It seemed so much like a miracle that he should be writing to her. She laid her face softly against the folded letter and closed her eyes an instant, with a soft little smile on her lips. Then she unfolded the letter and began to read:

To the most wonderful girl in the world.

My Dearly Beloved:

I am filled with an almost heavenly joy to be writing to you, with your permission, and to know that you are letting me love you and take your own love with me as I go out into a world of sin and death and uncertainty, with practically no chance that I can ever return.

But I want this to be a happy letter, because you have given me so much joy by taking my intrusion into your life in such a beautiful way. So, may I go back through the years and tell you what you have meant to me?

The first day I went to school in your city, I looked around the room, and saw you almost at once. You wore a yellow dress, and there was sunshine on your curls that gave them a golden glow, and sunshine in your happy smile. I thought you were the most beautiful little girl I had ever seen. I went home and told my mother that you looked just like an angel. If my dear mother were living on earth now she would delight to tell you about that.

It wasn't many days before I discovered that you were a very bright little girl who always knew your lessons and could answer the questions the teacher asked, quickly, as if you understood what she was talking about. It made me eager to study and do my best, too. I didn't want you to think I was dumb. You see, you were a great inspiration to me. Though I had no idea I would ever get to know you or have an opportunity to

tell you these things, of course. You were just like a
beautiful angel living up near heaven somewhere,
out of my world.

I shall never forget the day when we were
both sent to the blackboard to work out a problem
in algebra, and stood side by side for a little while.
We were told to compare our work and explain it
to one another. I was so thrilled at being so near to
you that my brains would scarcely work, and to look
into your beautiful eyes and hear you talking to me
with your sweet voice made my heart beat so that I
had hard work to control my own voice to answer
you. Just thinking this over afterward brought me
great happiness. And once when you stood near me
in class, you dropped your little scrap of a handkerchief and I picked it up and handed it to you, and
as you took it, your fingers touched mine and swept
the most wonderful thrill of joy over my soul. You
wouldn't have noticed that touch perhaps, but it
meant a great deal to me, and I thought of your
lovely hands with the utmost reverence. Your touch
seemed to me like the breath from an angel's wing.

Do you think all this language is silly? But
I wanted to let you see into my heart and know
what you have been to me all these years, even
from very early childhood. It sort of explains, and
perhaps just a little excuses, my temerity in coming
to tell you of my love at this, the last minute. My
heart somehow ached to let you know.

For, you see, when high school days came, and

you and I were even further apart than we had
been as children, there was less opportunity even
to see you, for social life, in which I had no time
to take any part, had come in to make a greater
separation.

But I can recall the lovely vision of you that I
had in those days, brief glimpses. You wore enchant-
ing garments and seemed a picture in each one. I
used to rejoice that you were not all painted up with
lipstick and rouge like so many other girls. You were
fine and different.

So that was the background for my great love
for you, which grew and grew through the years,
even after I went away to college and didn't see you
anymore. Till one day it came to me that I loved
you, with a great deep love that filled all my being.

Yet I never presumed, even in my mind, to
look forward to having you for mine. Your people
were cultured and wealthy, and mine were poor,
and what culture they had was not from worldly
advantages. I was a poor boy, and while if the
war had not claimed my services, I might have
tried to get up in the world and do something
worthwhile, I never dared to hope that I would
be in a class where your people would like to have
me for their daughter's intimate friend.

So that was how it all began for me, and I
think you have a right to know, and to know that
I have always thought of you as one for whom I
was trying to keep myself fine and pure and true

in my daily life; that I might be worthy to love you, even from afar, even though you might never know it.

I do not think this is much of a love letter, yet I felt you had a right to know all this.

And now, because this may be the last letter I can write that I am sure will go uncensored, I must tell you again of my great love for you, which has been growing and growing for so long, that it finally drove me to find you and tell you about it before I went away.

I want you to know how your sweet presence is going with me, wherever I am, and the joy of your precious lips on mine will thrill me again and again when things grow hard and fearful. My hungry arms will remember how it felt to hold you close, with your dear face against mine, your lovely hair touching my cheek. It will be a precious memory that I shall hold reverently as long as I live. I have always looked upon you as very sacred, have always had the utmost reverence for you. My mother used to tell me when I was just a small kid that someday God might send a girl who would seem that way to me, and I must take care that I kept myself fine and clean for her in spirit as well as in body. Perhaps almost unconsciously I have remembered that, and I have definitely kept it in mind several times when you seemed to me to be high above all other girls.

Well, and that's what you seemed to me all

through our school days. Do you wonder that I
dared at the last minute before I said good-bye to
my native land, to come to you and lay my love at
your feet, as a tribute to what you have been to me?

But there is one thing I want to make clear,
and that is that I do not want my love to be a
hindrance to you in your life in any way. And if
I do not come back and the future should bring
you another love, do not feel you must send him
away because you have told me that you love
me. The joy of love is that the loved one shall
be happy. Only this way can I go contented to
whatever my duty has in store for me. I am sure
you will understand that I had to say this, even
though for the time being it may sadden you.
But don't be sad. Be glad that we had the joy of
one another for at least a few moments.

If in any future letters I do not speak of my
love so plainly, remember that I am conscious of a
censorship that seems to me a sort of desecration of
our precious love. But you will understand.

So, to bring my letter to a finish, I am closing
my eyes and feeling your lips upon mine, my arms
about you, my darling!

Yours forever,
Charlie

Blythe finished the letter slowly and then buried her face
in it for a moment or two. Such a precious, precious letter!

Why, this was a letter that she could show to her mother and father. It was a real picture of the story of their love. It gave a true account of their first knowledge of each other; it showed what Charlie really was. Mother and Father could not help understanding how fine he was from that letter. Oh, she was glad he had written it! Yet, would he like her to show it to even her nearest and dearest? He had written this because he knew that there was censorship ahead, and he wanted his letter to come to her before any other eyes had seen it. Well, she had it now, as it came straight from himself, without any alien eyes between. Yes, it was hers to use as she felt was right. She was sure Charlie would agree with her. She would think about it. And she would read it over and over and get it into her heart. She would be able to tell in time whether she wanted to share that letter with her parents.

Happily she began to read the letter again, reveling in every word, following his memories and matching the time with her own. How he had felt just as she had done again and again. It was almost like having him there. How she could envision his speaking face as she read! How she could thrill with the memory of his arms about her, and the tenderness of his kiss!

She was just starting to read the letter over for the third time when she heard her mother's voice downstairs.

"Oh!" She caught her breath. She didn't want to be interrupted in this third reading of the letter, and she hadn't decided yet whether or not she was willing to show it to her mother. She listened for an instant and heard another voice. Ah! Mother had brought someone home with her, and there would not be opportunity to talk with her alone at this time anyway. So with a quiet smile on her face, Blythe went through her third reading of that precious first letter.

A little later she heard the summons to lunch, and she went down to find a friend of her mother's was a guest. So, her secret was her own for another little while at least, but she sat through the meal with such a happy smile on her face that the guest could but remark on how well Blythe was looking. Blythe was hugging to herself the thought of this first letter of Charlie's, and already she was planning how she might answer it and make plain to her lover how his words had rung bells of joy in her heart, even though the censor's eagle eye might keep him from writing another like it. Oh there would be ways to write that a mere censor would not understand, words that yet would convey a depth of love and trust each to the other.

And Mrs. Bonniwell, watching the happy face of her dear girl, was relieved to see that the dark circles under her eyes were gone, and that there was a healthy flush on her cheeks. She must have been very tired the night before, or else upset about her words concerning Dan Seavers. Strange that young people took such strange notions about each other when they began to grow up. Dan had always been such a handsome boy, rightly born and rightly bred. His people were intimate friends of the Bonniwells, and their children had been educated in much the same way. She could not think that Blythe was right in what she thought of the way Dan had changed. Very likely this was only a whim, and would pass. Dan and Blythe would presently be as good friends as ever, perhaps, and she wouldn't worry about it. There was one good thing about it. Blythe wasn't fond of any other young man, she was sure of that.

So she put away the worried thoughts she had had and entered into a discussion of the best way to conduct the new War Bond drive that they were planning. Soon after lunch Blythe escaped upstairs to write to Charlie, her first answer to his first love letter to her.

Meantime, downstairs in the library, Blythe's mother and her guest, Mrs. Corwin, had settled down before the open fire to have a nice talk and plan the War Bond drive.

"What a charming daughter Blythe has become," said Mrs. Corwin. "She used to be so tall and gangling, but she seems to have filled out beautifully, and is really lovely now. I'm so glad to have seen her again. And why did she go away? Wouldn't she like to sit in on this conference? I'm sure we could give her something to do. She is so ornamental, she ought to be sitting in one of the best positions to reach the right people, say, in the bank, or one of the big department stores. Why don't you call her down?"

Mrs. Corwin was one of those who could always spoil any complimentary remark she tried to make by some unfortunate word like "gangling," and as that word had never described Blythe's slim loveliness, it rather annoyed the mother. Blythe had always been lithe and graceful as soon as she got out of actual babyhood.

Mrs. Bonniwell looked up sharply.

"No," she said decidedly. "Blythe already has too much war work to do. She has no time at all to relax and have a little social life. I wouldn't think of letting her get into this."

"Oh, of course, if you feel that way," said the guest petulantly. "But she is so lovely, and would make a grand drawing card, I'm sure. But of course a young girl should have amusement. I suppose she goes out evenings a good deal and stays up too late. I hear she's very popular."

"We haven't encouraged her going out very much," said Mrs. Bonniwell. "After all, she's just got through her college course and the last year is always so strenuous. But Blythe is doing some hospital work in the early evenings among little children, and other days she works in the baby day-nursery."

"How sweet of her!" said Mrs. Corwin. "So many girls wouldn't bother to do a thing like that. It's very strenuous."

"She loves it," said Blythe's mother, bringing pencils and paper and settling down ready for work.

"Well, that's all very well for a little while," said the guest, "but I suppose her young friends will soon clamor for her release. I think you are so fortunate to have her at home again, and to have such a delightful companion for her in Dan Seavers. So many of the young men are gone overseas, she is fortunate to have one so good-looking and so devoted to stay nearby. Has he received his commission yet? I understand he had been asked to take over some very important work for the government. Is it arranged yet where he will be stationed?"

"Why, I wouldn't know," said Mrs. Bonniwell coolly. "I haven't heard the matter discussed."

"Oh, *really*?" said the guest, lifting her stylish eyebrows. "Why, I should think you would be one of the first to know. They're engaged, aren't they? I suppose if he is stationed nearby they will be married before he goes and she will go with him?"

"Engaged?" said Blythe's mother, lifting a haughty chin. "Of whom are you speaking? Who are engaged?"

Mrs. Corwin rippled out a musical little laugh.

"Why, I'm speaking of Dan Seavers and your charming daughter, of course," she said with a daring little smile. "I understood the engagement was to be announced in a few days. Isn't that so?"

"Engagement?" said Mrs. Bonniwell severely. "Between my daughter and Daniel Seavers? Certainly *not*! They have no idea of being engaged, and never have had. Where in the world did you get that idea?"

"Why, my dear, I have heard it everywhere. Everybody has been saying what a delightful match it is and how simply perfect for you to have your daughter marry a young man you have known so long and so well and one who is such an admirable fellow. Simply everybody is saying that. You certainly surprise me."

"Indeed!" said Mrs. Bonniwell. "It is quite amusing how people can make up stories out of whole cloth with nothing to go on but a few scattered appearances in public together. They are good friends of course, have been for years, but nothing more. I am afraid Blythe would be quite annoyed if she knew that her world was parceling her off in this wholesale manner, without even asking her if it is true."

"But Alice! You surprise me! I had no idea I was speaking of affairs that were not yet in the open. I do hope you will pardon my speaking beforehand. Of course I felt you were an old friend, and I would be expected to congratulate you. I didn't understand that something must have happened, and the engagement was off."

Mrs. Bonniwell gasped.

"But, my dear, you don't understand yet! There *never* has been an engagement, and *nothing* has happened, and therefore there is nothing to 'be off,' as you say. Now, forget it, please, and shall we get to work?"

"But my dear, I'm so embarrassed. I didn't think you'd be so secretive with me!"

"Why, Clarice, the idea! I'm not being secretive. I have nothing to be secretive about. There is *nothing* in this at all. I can't understand who could have told you a thing like this. But please, *please* put the matter entirely out of your mind and let us plan this drive."

After much persuasion Mrs. Corwin stiffly agreed to drop the matter, but her manner retained its stiffness, and she had the air of having been deceived about something. Deceived, and intentionally left out of something important.

So, amid an undertone of hurt and suspicion the two ladies went to work, and perhaps even more was actually accomplished than would have been if there hadn't been a dignified restraint in the atmosphere.

The work had progressed to the stage of two very neat complete lists of names, two sets of programs finished, and two notebooks with various items listed that must be attended to later. Suddenly they heard Blythe coming lightly down the stairs humming a bright little tune, and Blythe's mother rejoiced that her child sounded happy and lighthearted. Mrs. Corwin couldn't possibly go out and tell people that Blythe was wasting away because Dan Seavers had jilted her. But there was no telling. Mrs. Corwin had certainly proved herself this afternoon to be capable of getting up almost any story out of nothing.

"Blythe, is that you, dear?" called her mother suddenly. "Are you going out this afternoon?"

Blythe appeared promptly at the door, her cheeks beautifully rosy and what looked like stardust in her eyes, a letter in her hand.

"Why, Mother, I'm just running down to the post office with a letter I want to get off in a hurry. I think it will go more quickly if I take it down. Can I do anything for you?"

"Why no, dear, I think not. Will you be going out after dinner?"

"Yes, Mother, I'm on the evening shift at the hospital tonight, but I shall be done by eleven. Would it be convenient to send the car, or are you using it somewhere else? I can come back on the bus if you are."

"Why no, dear. You don't need to do that. I have to run over to Mrs. Haskell's a little while to get her ideas about this War Bond drive, and suppose I stop at the hospital and pick you up. Eleven, you say? All right. Do I go to the side entrance? Very well, you can plan for that. Now run along with your letter, dear, and leave us to our work. We're almost done, and we simply must finish this and get the lists off to the printer."

"Well, I'll say good-bye, Mrs. Corwin," said Blythe, pleasantly. "So nice to have seen you." She smiled on the lady and flitted away like a bright bird of passage.

"She certainly looks happy," said Mrs. Corwin provocatively.

"Yes, she's a very happy child," said Blythe's mother. "She seems so glad to be at home again. Her father asked her this morning if she wouldn't like to take a trip somewhere, but she said no, she wanted to stick by her war work in the day nursery."

"Well, that's certainly commendable," said the lady stiffly. "And now about the list of people who are to work the suburbs. Do you have Mrs. West's suggestions for the district around the northwestern part of the city?"

"Yes, here it is. I looked it over and it seems very good to me. See what you think." And so the work went rapidly on to the finish, Mrs. Corwin presently went away, and Blythe's mother drew a long breath of relief. Was this kind of thing what Blythe had meant? Well, it was most annoying. Nothing bad, nothing that would do any harm to her dear girl, of course, and yet it was most trying. No girl liked to have her affairs settled by a committee of the town, nor pried into. And if Blythe stopped going with Dan abruptly, everybody would say he had deserted her. But there, what was the use of worrying? So long as Blythe could bring such a happy face around, no amount of gossip could really hurt her. Her mother smiled indulgently and went slowly upstairs to her room to snatch a few minutes' rest.

What would she have thought or said if she had known about that first real love letter her daughter had received and answered that day? What would she have thought about Charlie Montgomery?

Back in her own room Blythe was standing by her window staring out across the lawn with a look of distance in her dreamy eyes. She was feeling as if she had just been talking with Charlie, and was reflecting that it was only a few hours ago that he was actually with her and now he seemed so far away. She must not lose sight of that wonderful first visit of his. And now, as soon as her mother woke up, she probably ought to go and talk it all over with her. She must not have the blight of any burden on the joy of her heart. It was burden enough that very soon Charlie was going into awful danger, and how she was going to bear that when the time came, she did not know. But she simply must not let her present happiness be spoiled. It was something so perfect that it must not be touched by gloom.

And then, just a few hours apart, Charlie's other letters began to arrive, a dear procession of them, and she seemed to be living in his company, all the way of his journey, although of course she had no idea just where he was going.

Chapter 9

As Charlie Montgomery went from the train into the camp where he had been given to understand he was to await further orders, he looked about him at the men who stood watching the newcomers, and then suddenly he heard a voice calling out.

"Hello, Charlie Montgomery!"

He turned sharply and looked into a young face that seemed familiar even in the army outfit. Eager gray eyes searched his face, and he heard a doubtful, hesitant voice.

"You *are* Charlie Montgomery, aren't you?"

"Sure!" said Charlie, in turn searching the boy's face.

"Lieutenant, I mean," said the young soldier, turning red and saluting apologetically.

"Why, sure, but—who are you?" said Charlie. Then his face broke into a grin. "Walter Blake, as I live! You don't mean to say you're in the army *already*?"

"Oh, sure," said the lad, straightening up and trying to look old and experienced. "I've been in this camp two months already. I think they're sending me off somewhere worthwhile pretty soon."

"You don't say!" said Charlie, astonished. "But surely you are not old enough yet?"

"I was seventeen three months ago, and Mom signed up for me," said the lad. "She said there was no use trying to hold me any longer, and both my brothers are in."

"Well, I am surprised. Why, kid, I don't see how the home ball teams are going to get along without you. You haven't finished high school yet, have you?"

"Sure!" said the lad. "I took summer school, and then they gave some of us examinations and allowed us to graduate. We could either go into college, engineering, or the service. I chose the army."

"Good work, kid. Do you like it?"

"Yes, it's swell! I like it a lot, but I'm about ready to get into some real work."

"I see," said Charlie, smiling. "Well, I suppose that's what we all feel."

Walter looked up wonderingly.

"But *you're* in!" he said with a glance at the insignia Charlie wore. "You're a lieutenant. Do you feel that way?"

"Sure I do," said Charlie. "What do you suppose I'm here for? Amusement?"

There was new respect, almost adoration in the lad's eyes. "You are wearing—wings!"

Charlie smiled.

"Where are you going?" He breathed the words eagerly. "Or must I not ask?"

Charlie smiled again.

"I wish I could tell you, but—"

"It is a military secret?" the boy asked. "It is, then, something quite important. I was sure you would have something of that sort. Oh, if it might be that I could go *with you*!" The boy's words were almost like a prayer.

But when Charlie Montgomery spoke, his words were quite commonplace.

"I wish it might be, lad," said the former football star, smiling down on the younger man most kindly. "I would like nothing better than to have you for my companion. But I'm afraid that would be out of the question. Mine will probably be a solitary way. But I'll be thinking of you. I hope you'll have some great needful part in this war, and I'm sure you'll do as good work, whatever it is, as you used to do on the field in the old days."

The younger man flushed, and there was a pleased light in his eyes as he marched in step with Charlie.

"It seems to me I used to see you at some of our college games," said Charlie.

"You sure did!" said young Walter. "I used to come to all the games in our city whenever your college played the university. I stuck by you and cheered you for all I was worth."

"Good work!" said Charlie. "I guess that's why we won so often when we came to the home city. But it seems to me you came to one or two other places where we played, too. Wasn't that so?"

"I sure did. I used to work overtime to get money to follow

you around wherever you were playing, if it was at all possible. You were always my hero. That's why I'd like to get transferred to your outfit if I could." The boy's tone was wistful.

"Well I certainly appreciate that, Walt, and I wish it could be managed, but I don't see any chance at present. Maybe we'll run up against each other again."

"I sure hope we do!" said young Walter sadly. "Say, are you thinking of going over to the meeting tonight? Ever heard that Silverthorn? He's swell! All the fellows like him. I'd like to go with you if you do."

"Silverthorn! Why yes, I've heard *about* him. All right, I'd like to go with you if I find, after I check in, that I am free this evening. It's nice to see somebody from the hometown, you know. Where shall I find you? What time?"

"Oh, I'll stick around and show up when you're ready."

The two parted and Charlie went in to make his arrangements and get his orders. A little later, after mess, he came out to find Walter Blake waiting for him shyly, and together they walked over to the auditorium that was already filling up fast.

The place was brilliantly lighted and a burst of song greeted them as they stepped inside and found seats.

There was something heartening and thrilling in the music from so many men's voices. For an instant it almost seemed to Charlie as if it might be a church service at home where he used to go with his mother when he was a youngster, and something constricted his throat and brought a sudden mist to his eyes as he remembered the past. Only this singing had more volume and power, more enthusiasm than they ever had in those old days at home. He gave a quick look around and noticed with how much fervor most of the men sang, as if they loved it. As if they meant every word they were singing.

It was an old hymn they were singing, and presently Charlie, noticing that Walter was joining in with a clear voice, found himself singing, too.

> "*Rock of Ages, cleft for me,*
> *Let me hide myself in Thee:*"

He could almost hear his mother's voice quavering through the words. Those last weeks when she was with him, after her long illness, her voice was soft and unsteady. And sometimes she could not sing very loud, just a sweet little quaver, a tremble. She hadn't really been well enough to go to church, but she had insisted upon doing so. She said she needed the strength she drew from the service. He was glad that the last few times they went he had managed either to borrow a car to take her, or to get a taxi. That was just a few weeks before her last illness and death, and as Charlie sat there with that old song his mother had loved surging about him, he felt the tears stinging into his eyes, and a great longing came into his heart that he might find his mother's refuge, which he was sure she had.

> "*Let the water and the blood,*
> *From Thy wounded side which flowed,*
> *Be of sin the double cure,*
> *Save from wrath and make me pure.*"

That part of the song didn't mean much to Charlie. He wasn't conscious of being a sinner. At least not much of a sinner. He had been taught to be clean and true by his wonderful mother, and had always been too busy to break laws and carry on the way most boys did, which was what sin meant to his mind. But this was the good old-fashioned Gospel, of course, that his mother had taught him, and he had accepted it without a thought. So it wasn't sin that was troubling Charlie. He wasn't exactly sure what it was that troubled him, only that he was presently going out alone to meet death, and he felt he needed *something*.

The singing went on. Many old hymns, new choruses, too, in a little red book, and he enjoyed using his voice and being a part of the swelling melody that was filling the hall.

Then there came upon the platform a young man in uniform walking easily, assuredly.

"That's him," murmured Walter in his ear. "That's Lincoln Silverthorn."

"But—he's in the *service*?"

"Sure! He's a chaplain, s'posed to be! But he's different from a lot of them. He's real!"

And now Lincoln Silverthorne was speaking.

"Good evening, fellows," he said in his clear, pleasant voice that seemed to be speaking personally to each one in the room. "I've got a pleasant surprise for you. Just a few minutes ago a good friend of mine who has worked with me for several years walked in on me. He has a great voice that can sing to your heart, and he's going to sing for you and strike a keynote for my message tonight. Fellows, this is my buddy, Lieutenant Luther Waite, and he's doing a very important work for our war. Go ahead, Lutie!"

And then a big redheaded fellow, also in uniform, came forward, grinning.

"Glad to meet you, fellas," he said, and then began to sing.

It was a rich, full voice, and it held the audience from the start, every note clear, every word distinct:

> *"I was just a poor lost sinner,*
> *Till Jesus came my way.*
> *He smiled into my eyes and said,*
> *'Come walk with me today.'"*

Probably some fellow who was reformed in some mission or other, thought Charlie, as he settled back under the spell of the song.

But as the song progressed, the singer's eyes seemed to seek out Charlie and tell his story directly to him. There was something about the way those true fine eyes held his attention and made him listen to every word, on through several verses, that made the singing a story of the man's life, the story a testimony of what the Lord Jesus Christ had done for him.

And when he came to the last four lines, those earnest eyes, which seemed to have been piercing Charlie's soul, looked deep into Charlie's eyes again as if they were alone and were having a conversation.

> *"Me! A sinner! A poor lost sinner!*
> *I'm telling you it's true!"*

The singer's manner was most impassioned.

> *"He died upon the cross for me!*
> *He's done the same for you!"*

Charlie was startlingly aware of being charged with something that he had never before felt was true. "He's done the same for you!" seemed to be aimed directly at himself, as something that had been done for him, of which he had never been aware before, and for which he never made any acknowledgment to the Donor. He was filled with a sudden compunction, a kind of new shame.

And then at once his self-esteem began to assert itself, that he *wasn't* a sinner. Not a sinner like that, who needed *saving*!

It was strange that almost upon that thought came Link Silverthorn's words, announcing his theme.

"*All* have sinned and come short of the glory of God. . . . The wages of sin is death."

There was a tense silence that gripped every listening heart. Even the protest that was beginning to form in Charlie Montgomery's heart, the outcry against being called a sinner, was silenced, as everyone waited for the next word about this hopeless situation in which they had all found themselves to be.

"The greatest sin, *all* sin, is not believing in Christ, who took all our sin on Himself, and paid the price with His own blood. Unbelief is not accepting what He did, not accepting it for ourselves."

The speaker was very still for a moment, letting them take that in. Then he went on.

"Some of you think you are not sinners, don't you? But you are. That's not my idea. You look pretty fine to me. But *God says* you are. Ever since Adam sinned we were all born sinners. God told Adam that there was but one law to keep. He must keep that one law or death would come into the world. Adam broke the law, took the forbidden fruit, and since then we are all born sinners, and are all under condemnation of death for our sin. But God loves us, and He made a way for condemned sinners to be saved through accepting what Christ His son did for them.

"Did you ever think of Christ as having come voluntarily away from heaven and glory to live down here and be crucified in your place, just as if He had been the sinner, not you? Have you ever considered Him there upon the cross in your place, where *you* belonged, bearing upon His sinless self every thought and word and action, and even that indifference of yours, just as if they had been His sins, and bearing it even unto death?"

As the young chaplain talked, he seemed to be possessed of a supernatural power to create a picture of what he was saying, so that as he went on, with simple words like strokes of an artist's brush, there appeared a vision before the listeners' eyes of the Christ, standing before His persecutors; standing before Pilate and those unbelievers who would stone Him, kill Him, anything to get rid of Him. Somehow Charlie began to feel himself one of those unbelievers who had not accepted the Christ for what He was willing to be to him, and a great desire came into his heart to align himself with the followers of Jesus, and not with the unbelievers. He felt it so keenly that he longed to be able to go up to that silent figure standing alone and tell Him he wanted to follow Him. It was not pity he felt, for somehow that quiet figure of the Savior of the world, who seemed to be standing up there on the platform alone, had a majesty about Him that defied pity.

And now came the cross, and Jesus, lifted up with all that sin—sin of the whole world—upon Him, and all the world's death punishment to bear! Never before had Charlie Montgomery felt that he himself had had anything to do with hanging the Son of God upon that cross. But now he suddenly saw it. Charlie Montgomery, who had always been so proud of himself that he had gone through school and college against such great odds, always so smugly sure that he was doing the right thing, and always would do the right thing, he had been one who had helped to crucify the Son of God when He was dying for him!

It was very still in that big hall. The speaker had utmost attention. Perhaps all those young men were seeing that same vision of Jesus, up there suffering for their sins.

Once Charlie gave a quick glance around and saw the deep interest in all eyes. Even the boy by his side was all interest. Jesus, the Savior of the world, was holding them all, and Charlie Montgomery felt that he had found what he had been seeking—a Person. Jesus the crucified was what he sought. It was his mother's Christ. He had a strange feeling during the closing prayer that he wanted to slip up to that platform and tell the Christ who had been dying there for him that now he believed. That now henceforward through what days were left for him to live, he wanted to walk with Christ. He bowed his head quietly and found there were tears on his face.

As the petition at the close of that wonderful message came to an end, the big man with the great voice and the red hair began to sing.

> *"I would love to tell you what I think of Jesus,*
> *Since I found in Him a friend so strong and true;*
> *I would tell you how He changed my life completely,*

He did something that no other friend could do."

How that voice stirred the throng of young men! And then Charlie felt himself to be a part of a company of astonishingly saved people. There was no reasoning it out. Jesus Christ had been up there before them all, dying for them, and Charlie had found out he was a sinner, too, with all the rest of them. The singer went on giving his testimony.

> *"No one ever cared for me like Jesus,*
> *There's no other friend so kind as He;*
> *No one else could take the sin and darkness from me,*
> *O how much He cared for me!"*

When it was over they stood there looking toward the platform.

"Wantta go up and speak to him?" asked Walter shyly. "He don't mind. He likes the fellas to come up, and he's swell about explaining things he's said. The fellas all call him 'Link.'"

Charlie gave a thoughtful look at his young companion.

"Have you been up before?" he asked.

"Sure, I been up a coupla times. I like ta hear him talk."

"All right! Come on!" said Charlie, and followed his young guide up to the front, where Link Silverthorn was talking interestedly with a lot of the men, as if they were all intimate friends. So they drew nearer and nearer to the eager group around the speaker, until they could hear, and became a part of the innermost group. At last Charlie came to be in the forefront, listening, with keen eyes on Link Silverthorn.

And then suddenly Link's eyes caught Charlie's glance,

and he came down the steps of the platform and stood beside the young lieutenant, placing a kindly hand on Charlie's arm and reaching down to grasp his hand.

"Are you saved, brother?" asked the young chaplain.

Charlie looked steadily into Lincoln Silverthorn's eyes, with no reserves in his own glance.

"I'm not sure," he said slowly. "I'd like to be. I'm going out in a few days on a commission where there is very little likelihood that I shall ever return to my own world. I've always believed in Christ and His dying for the world, but it never, somehow, seemed to have anything to do with me personally. Tonight you made me see Him. What do I have to do?"

The young chaplain smiled with a great light in his eyes.

" 'Believe on the Lord Jesus Christ, and thou shalt be saved,'" he quoted, "but that means more than a mere intellectual belief. It means a real heart belief. It means accepting Him as your personal Savior. Accepting what He has done for you. Are you willing to do that?"

"I am," said Charlie steadily.

"Then let's tell Him so," said Link, and the two slipped down on their knees beside the wooden bench, while Link prayed.

"Lord Jesus, here's a seeking soul who wants You. He says he is glad to accept what You did for him, in taking his sin upon Your sinless self and suffering the penalty of death that was rightfully his. We're asking You now to fulfill Your promise when You said, 'He that heareth my word, and believeth on him that sent me, *hath* everlasting life, *and shall not* come into condemnation; but is passed from death unto life.' Take him now, dear Lord, and show him how to walk with Thee."

"And now, brother, will you tell Him, too?"

Charlie was still for a moment, and then he spoke, his eyes closed, his head bent low and resting on his lifted hand.

"Lord, I believe. Forgive all the years of my indifference. Stay by me, and show me the way."

Neither Charlie nor Silverthorn had noticed young Walter kneeling down beside them, his head reverently bowed, his eyes closed.

The gathered groups around the platform had drifted a little farther away, talking in low tones, mindful of the ones who were kneeling. As the two arose, Walter rose with them, stepping back shyly. It was only then that Silverthorn saw him and put out his hand to touch the lad.

"And how about you, buddy?" asked Link Silverthorn. "Don't you want to be saved, too?"

"Yes sir," said Walter, his eyes lighting up. "I *am*. I did it yesterday."

Link's eyes shone.

"Are you glad you did it?"

Walter flushed, and he lifted brightening eyes.

"Yes sir, I am. A lot, I am! It's easier to go on now, sir."

"That's right, fella," said Link, giving the boy a hearty grasp of his hand. "Are you two fellows—brothers?"

Walter shook his head.

"We're from the same hometown," offered Charlie, with a warm lovingness in his tone that made Walter's face flush again and his eyes lighten.

"He's the best quarterback in football you ever saw!" burst out Walter enthusiastically.

"Oh, so he's your football hero, is he? Well, that's great!

And now, I hope you're both going to be the best Christians this army ever saw, and win souls for Christ wherever you go."

"Okay!" said Walter. "That's what we—that's what *I* want, too."

"Here, too," said Charlie, smiling. "I guess it was his doing that I came here tonight, and I'm glad I came. I thank you, sir, for the help *you've* given me. I think I can go out now without worrying."

"Oh, I'm glad to hear you say that. I certainly am, and I'm glad to have had a little hand in it. I'll remember you fellas, and I'll be praying. I'll be praying that if it's God's will, He'll bring you both safe home again, alive and sound and well."

Then suddenly he motioned toward the big redhead who had sung.

"Here, Lute, I want you to meet these two fellows. They've just found Christ, and one of them's going out on a hard assignment that doesn't give much hope of returning. I want you to remember these fellows and pray for them, and when we pray together, remind me about them specially, will you, Lute?"

"That I will," said the big man, with a wide genial smile. "Praise the Lord! He's able to keep you true all the way through, fellows, and able to bring you back again, too, no matter how great the odds. But if instead He calls you Home, why, that will be all right, too, won't it?"

Charlie gave a grave sweet assent to that, and Walter nodded with a seraphic smile. Walter knew what he was doing and was content. And for the first time since Charlie had left Blythe, a great peace came to dwell in his heart.

They walked along together, with a ring to their footsteps, and finally separated.

"Isn't he swell?" said Walter at last, really thinking aloud.

"He certainly is," said Charlie. "I'm glad you took me there! And I'm glad you *belong*, too. That makes us sort of buddies in a special sense, doesn't it?"

"It sure does! Good night, I never thought I'd ever have anything as grand as this in my life, not in the army anyway. Having you come to Christ along with me! I didn't think I'd ever be tied in any company as fine as you. And to have you find Him, too, at the same time. It'll be something to remember always. Gee, but Mom'll be glad when I write her about this. You don't mind if I tell her about you, too, do you? She knows who you are. She's always been glad to help me get away to one of your games, and she'll be awful pleased that you're a Christian."

"Mind?" said Charlie. "Why, no, I'm glad! I only wish my mother were at home now and I could write to her about it. She'd be glad, too."

And then they parted for the night with a heartier handclasp then even football would have brought about.

Chapter 10

The next three days were a time of great strengthening for Charlie Montgomery in many ways. The morning found him summoned to an audience with an instructor in the special mission that was to be his in the near future, and his heart swelled with the tremendous import of what each move he was to make would mean toward victory in the great task he had undertaken.

Yet he found that the thought of it did not appall him as it might have done, now that he had taken the Lord Jesus Christ for his Savior. When he had time to think of it all, it was as if he were going out hand in hand with God's Son, they were yoke-fellows in this work to put down evil that had a grip on the world. God *must* want it stopped, and had put it into the hearts of men to go out and stop it, to put an end to the selfish ambitions of men who did not consider God, men who were out to destroy all good thoughts and motives and even to destroy the thought of God, if they could. Somehow as he thought of it, it seemed to him that God was going to use him for His own purposes, and he was solemnly glad. And glad, too, with a light heart, because his heart was right with God. Whatever came now, whether life through a hard way, or the death that seemed to be the inevitable outcome of this undertaking, he was safe, a child of God! Saved through His blood!

As the day waned and the time for the evening service drew on, Charlie's work with the instructor finished for the day, and his thoughts went more and more to the decision he had made the night before, and he seemed to have a revelation of himself. Only a few hours ago he hadn't thought of himself as a sinner at all, or as one who needed saving. His only concern about this matter had been somewhat in the nature of going through a form of preparation for a change from life to death, as one would get a passport for a journey, or a reservation on a train, or register in the army.

What was it that had made the difference in him? Could it be that it was that one evening's glimpse of Christ, as the man Silverthorn had described Him, and that had made the change in his whole point of view? He had *seen* Jesus with the eyes of his spirit. He felt as if he knew Him now. Was it possible that that one short view of Christ had acted as a measuring rod to show him where he was lacking? Had that brief transaction, on his knees, when he handed himself over to the Christ and took Him for his personal Savior, shown him how mistaken he had always been when he thought of himself as having no sin?

Of course he had not been conceited about himself. He was sure of that, for his mother had dealt determinedly with every possible showing of conceit in his nature, but he had thought of himself as a pretty fairly good fellow. Oh, a few imperfections of course, as anyone might have, but nothing to be alarmed about.

And now, why! Thoughts, feelings, even attitudes of mind, began to crop out and take the form of sin when seen in the light of the eyes of God, and of His Son, Jesus Christ.

Why hadn't he known all this before, with a mother like his to teach him? A mother who loved God and lived her life as in His Presence? And yet he had never taken more than the mere head knowledge of a few facts that he had accepted without thought! And that wasn't the way he had taken any other subjects that he had been taught. The difference must be that now he had seen Jesus, and before he had merely *heard* about Him and swallowed the knowledge as a fact to which he need give but small concern.

There were two or three invitations to go places from other men—officers, and some men he had met before, old college mates, but he put them all aside and went to the meeting with Walter.

They sat up very near the front this time, and received welcoming glances from both Silverthorn and Waite, who was still there, and it seemed sometimes to Charlie as if parts of the service were arranged for his own help, though of course there must be others in the same situation as himself. But his soul was hungry for this knowledge of holy things that was being given out here, and he was drinking it in eagerly. And again the preacher brought the Christ in vision before them all, and

Charlie seemed to look into His eyes and get a recognition from those wise and loving glances, so that he came away from that meeting with a sweet assurance in his heart that he was Christ's and nothing could harm him; even death could not take him out of the continual presence of his Savior.

It was after Walter had left him for the night that it came to him to wonder if Blythe knew the Lord in this way?

Oh, she must be a Christian. He had seen her going to church several times. He knew which church her people attended. But did she know Jesus Christ as Savior? Had she ever felt her need of a Savior, or was she careless about it all, as he had been?

Quite early the next morning, before the day's routine called him, he wakened and wrote a very brief letter to Blythe, telling her of his experience. There came to his heart a solemn anxiety for her. Would she understand what he meant when he tried to tell her, or would she be hurt and think he was discounting her fineness and belovedness? He found himself shyly asking God to help him write that letter so she would understand, and so that no thought of any censorship could detract from its meaning.

Two days later Charlie got his order to move on, and with a parting blessing from Link and Luther Waite, and attended to the train by Walter Blake, he took his way again into the unknown.

There was a few minutes' delay at the train, and the sorrowful Walter tried to think of all the things his bursting heart would like to say.

"I—wish I—was going—with you," he choked out, blinking back the unbidden tears. "You—kinda—seem like—*home* folks!"

Charlie gave him a pitying glance and owned that he felt that way, too.

"I'll tell you, kid, you might get a furlough pretty soon. Do you suppose you might get home at all?"

"I can't tell," said the boy. "I might! Depends on where they're sending me. If I go overseas pretty soon they might let me stop off home for a day or so."

"Well, say, kid, if you do get home, and it doesn't take too much time from your family, I wonder if you'd deliver a greeting for me to a friend of mine?"

Charlie was merely figuring to take the lad's mind off their parting, and he reckoned rightly, for Walter's face brightened.

"Sure. I'd be proud to. Who is it? Your family?"

"No, they're all gone. It's—a friend of mine. Did you ever hear of the Bonniwells?"

"Sure I did. I useta deliver papers there, and they always bought magazines from me."

"Then you know where they live?"

"Oh, sure! Big stone house on Wolverton Drive. Got a daughter name Blythe. Useta go to our school when you and she were in high school. She the one?"

Charlie grinned.

"You're right, kid. How'd you know?"

"Oh, I've seen her around. Saw her at a coupla your football games. Saw her watching you play."

"Well, that's something!" said Charlie, realizing that was something he and Blythe had not had time to talk about. Of course he had seen her there, but he had not been aware of her watching him. She hadn't been one of his crowd, and he hadn't even ventured a greeting to her at those games.

"Well, think you could give her a message? Here, I'll write just a line. Of course, if you lose it before you get there, it won't matter. You can read it and repeat it."

The engine screeched a warning, and Lieutenant Charles Montgomery, standing on the bottom step of the car, seized his pen and notebook from his pocket and wrote.

"You'll havta make it speedy, pard," said Walter, forgetting his army manners. "She's about ta start."

"Beloved. I'm off. God bless you. Love, Charlie."

The engine gave a lurch and then a warning whistle.

"Make it snappy, Lieutenant," breathed Walter anxiously.

Charlie folded the paper and put it in the eager hand, even as the train began to move.

"Good-bye, kid. Keep it safe, and if you have a chance to talk with her, tell her how we met and all about it. If you don't get home, well, never mind! Take care of your faith, kid, and don't forget to pray."

"Oh, sure, you know I won't!" shouted the boy-soldier, as the train moved away beyond his following feet.

Two days later Walter was moved on, *without* his furlough home. He had wrapped the precious slip of paper in a bit of cellophane and fastened it between the pages of the Testament his mother had given him when he left home, which he always carried over his heart. That meant that Charlie's message would never get lost and would *sometime* be delivered, unless the young soldier was lost himself. This commission from his hero was his only consolation for the sorrow that he would not go with Charlie through fire or death or whatever was to come to him. And his prayers every night for Charlie and for the girl to whom he had sent his farewell, were most fervent, and never forgotten.

Two days more Walter had, following after Silverthorn and his friend Luther Waite, and then they went on to another location; but the boy-soldier had learned much from sitting at the feet of these two servants of the Lord, and he carried a lighter heart as he went out into the great unknown future that was to be his. His hand was in God's hand; his strength was the joy of the Lord.

But as he went he thought often of his friend and hero Charlie Montgomery, and sent up a prayer for him. For though he had no idea what Charlie was going into, he was sure it was full of danger, more than most soldiers and fliers were destined for, and his heart would fail him sometimes as he thought that perhaps he would never see Charlie again on this earth. But he was glad, glad that he was sure of that meeting in heaven. There would be no doubt or anxiety about that.

And then, at his first opportunity, Walter wrote a long letter to his mother.

> *I met a fellow from home, Mom. He was with me in camp for three days. He's the football guy I used to talk about so much, do you remember? His name's Montgomery, and he's a prince, he sure is. More of a prince even than he used to be. He's a lieutenant, but he wasn't a bit stuck up for his rank. He went around with me a lot, and we went to a wonderful meeting together. That chaplain named Silverthorn was here, and he preached swell, and we went to his meetings every night, and both of us took Christ as our Savior. I*

thought you'd like to know that. And I mean it, Mom! And I feel a lot better about going into war since I did it. So did Montgomery. He's something special, going out on a separate commission. Something pretty high up, and pretty dangerous. It's a military secret what it is, and of course he didn't tell me, but I judge from what he said he doesn't expect to come back. But I'm glad I met him. He's swell, and I guess we'll meet in heaven, anyway. I said I'd like to go with him, and if I get a chance to get transferred to his location, I sure will accept. So, I'm telling you, Mom, if anything happens to me, you can know it's all right with me and Christ is my Savior. So, Mom, don't you feel bad. And tell my sister Peggy I've sent her a little pin like the one I wear.

Mrs. Blake cried tears of joy over that letter and prayed for the two who had gone their separate ways, and in due time went to her Red Cross sewing class, from which she had been absent for a couple of weeks on account of extra time at the plant where she worked. When she came into the room, Blythe noticed that there was a look of peace on her face, and a light in her eyes that she had not seen before.

As usual the other ladies paid little attention to her except to nod a cold good morning. Only Anne Houghton remarked hatefully:

"Oh, *you're* back, are you? I thought they'd got you transferred."

But even that didn't disturb the calm of Ms. Blake's tired little face.

Blythe had been sitting at the other end of the room when Mrs. Blake entered and had distinctly heard the disagreeable greeting. She made an excuse, presently, to change her seat and take the one beside Mrs. Blake.

"I've been missing you from the class," she said sweetly and quite distinctly, so that everyone could hear. "Have you been ill?"

"Oh no," answered the little woman pleasantly, in a very quiet, refined tone. "I had extra work at the plant and couldn't get away, but I came back as soon as I could."

"Oh, I'm glad you weren't sick," said Blythe, beginning on another buttonhole. "So many people have had colds this time of year. And then I thought of your little girl, and wondered if she was sick. All the children in our neighborhood have had the measles."

"No, Peggy's quite well," said her mother. "She's been joining that Junior Red Cross group they've started at school, and she heard me telling what wonderful buttonholes you make, so she wants to learn how, and I told her I'd watch you if I got the chance and see if I could give her some help. I never was very good at buttonholes myself, but maybe if I watch you I could teach her."

"Oh, let me teach her, Mrs. Blake! I'd love to. That would be fun."

"Why, would you be willing to? That would be wonderful. But I'm afraid that would be a lot of trouble for you."

"No, I'd love it. What time does she get home from school? Could she stop at my house on her way home a few times? We'll make a fine little buttonhole maker of her."

Mrs. Blake fairly beamed.

"Well, I'm sure I never can thank you enough for being so

kind. It's just beautiful of you to offer."

"Oh, please don't get the idea I'm doing anything great," said Blythe, smiling. "We're in a war, you know, and everybody is supposed to do everything they can to help along. I'm sure if I succeed in making Peggy a good buttonhole maker, why, then she can help to finish more garments, and so we'll be doubling our output. Isn't that good reasoning?"

So they laughed about it, and little Mrs. Blake's face took on a very sweet look. If Charlie Montgomery could have seen Mrs. Blake, he might have said she looked like her youngest son, Walter. But Charlie Montgomery was not there, except in the thought of one dear girl whose mind was always hovering about his memory.

"This is a happy day for me," said Mrs. Blake, "you offering to do this for Peggy, and I know she'll be so happy about it. And then I had a letter from my Walter this morning. I was almost late getting here, stopping to read it. In fact, I haven't read it all yet, but I must read one sentence near the end where it was folded that said he had met with somebody from home and it made him very glad. He went around with him for a couple of days, and it's evidently braced him up a lot."

"Oh, that is nice! Poor boys. It must be very hard for them to be torn away from their homes and families this way and compelled to grow up suddenly and go out and fight! It's hard enough for the older ones, but for the very young ones it must be terrible. Didn't you tell me he was only seventeen?"

"Yes, just turned seventeen," said the mother, sighing.

"Oh, why did you let him go yet? Couldn't you have kept him at home for one more year?"

"Well, yes, I suppose I could, but it would have been like

holding wild horses in. He was just raring to go, and he really felt kind of ashamed, his two brothers both gone already. You know the boys feel it."

"Yes, I suppose they do! Poor kiddies! They don't realize what it is, but I suppose there are some good things about it."

"Yes, perhaps," sighed the mother. "Well, one thing in Walter's letter made me real glad anyway. He says he's been getting to know the Lord." She said it shyly, with almost a hush of shame in her voice, as if she wasn't used to talking of such things, and she didn't know how this girl from the aristocracy would take it.

"Oh," said Blythe embarrassedly. "Why, that's kind of wonderful, isn't it? I suppose war does make the boys thoughtful. They aren't always sure how they are coming through."

"Yes," said Mrs. Blake, "I suppose it does. Though before they went that was one thing I worried about. I was afraid they would get into bad company and get to cursing and swearing and doing all sorts of dreadful things. You see, I always tried to bring my children up to be Christians, though to tell the truth, when they went out from home and were with other children, they kind of got away from it. They'd make any excuse to stay away from church, you know. But now Walter says he and this fellow from home went to a meeting every night and that some chaplain who's very interesting has got them to thinking real seriously."

"Well, I guess you ought to be very glad over that," said Blythe. "Maybe there are going to be some good things come out of this war after all. Of course, it's going to be awfully hard for their families, a lot of sorrow having them gone and not knowing if they'll come home safe, but it's good there is a brighter side."

"Yes," said Mrs. Blake. "If I thought my boys would get to be good Christians and be right ready if they had to die, I wouldn't worry so much. And that's why I'm so glad over Walter's letter."

And then suddenly the sewing class broke up, and they all went home. Blythe and Mrs. Blake lingered just long enough to make arrangements about Peggy's coming for her button-hole lesson, and then Blythe hurried away, for somehow Mrs. Blake's telling of the letter from her son made her eager to get home and see if there might be another letter from Charlie.

And sure enough there was, the letter he had written that early morning after he had given himself to the Lord the night before.

Chapter 11

Mr. Bonniwell, busy in his office that morning, had received a telephone call from Dan Seavers, asking urgently to be allowed to see him at once. Blythe's father, annoyed, had put aside some very important telephone calls he had planned to make right away, and told him he might come, if he would make his business brief, as he had but ten minutes to spare. Young Seavers agreed, and presently presented himself at the office.

There was no humility in the bearing of the brash young man as he entered the Bonniwell office smiling, almost condescendingly.

He was in officer's uniform, and looked very handsome and domineering. Mr. Bonniwell suppressed a definite dislike that he of late had experienced whenever he saw this young man. Even the stunning new uniform did not dispel this feeling, and the older man struggled against it and tried to be decently cordial. His own prejudice dated back to when Dan was ten years younger and Mr. Bonniwell saw him do a very unfair thing to a schoolmate who was even younger, and definitely not as well dressed as himself. But of course, he tried to tell himself, the fellow was grown up now, and had likely got over those snobbish tendencies. Anyway, he would give him the benefit of the doubt. He was Blythe's friend, of course, and she must see something good in him or she wouldn't be off with him so much. "Good morning, Dan," he said, trying not to be stiff in his manner. "Won't you sit down? Sorry to have to hurry you about time, but I am a good deal rushed this morning. Now, what's on your mind? I see you're in uniform. Does that mean you are going to leave our town soon?"

Daniel smiled proudly.

"Yes, I suppose so. I just got my commission, and I'm getting matters arranged for my departure. And that's why I wanted to see you without delay, so I can begin to get everything shaped up. You see, it is not quite settled yet where I am to be stationed, but the order may come through in a few days, and I don't want to have a lot of things to attend to at the last minute, and have to rush, you know."

"Yes?" said Mr. Bonniwell, lifting puzzled eyes to the young man and trying to understand what his glib speech could mean. "And how do I come in on that?"

The young man gave a self-conscious laugh.

"It's about Blythe, sir. My mother brought me up to feel that it was the proper thing always to ask permission of the father before one formally asked a girl to marry him, and I came this morning to get that over with. I know it's rather old-fashioned to assume that the parents have anything at all to do with the modern marriage, and it isn't done much anymore, but I know that both my mother and Blythe's mother are rather sticklers for the old-time formalities, so, as I want to do everything up right and please everybody, I came this morning to formally ask you for your daughter's hand in marriage."

Mr. Bonniwell sat there and stared at the young man, suffering a distinct inner revulsion, and he stared so long that Dan grew slightly impatient. He had expected a smiling acquiescence, at the very least. Was he not honoring this man's daughter? The man ought to be very grateful that he had even troubled to ask his permission. Most fellows wouldn't think of stooping to do that nowadays.

"You see," he said uneasily, to bring the matter to a head, "if I should have to go suddenly, it would be well to have the wedding over with and not have to be rushing through everything. One has to prepare in plenty of time to avoid confusion at the end, you know, and I hate above all things to be rushed. Half the beauty of a stately and magnificent wedding is to have it without any appearance of hurry, just calm and perfect. Don't you think so, sir?"

But Mr. Bonniwell was not considering the stateliness and perfection of wedding ceremonies. Instead he was looking sharply at the young man who was talking, wondering if it was just his prejudice and imagination that made him suddenly feel that there was a great weakness in Dan's chin. A weak chin! And that man with a weak, selfish chin and conceited eyes wanted to marry his little girl!

Then he noticed the lazy voice. "I was trying to do the

proper thing according to the old-fashioned acceptance of that term. That is why I came to you first. That, and because I felt that I would be in a stronger position with your daughter if I brought your okay with me, and also would save much trying discussion of a matter that I have already worked out to perfection. I didn't want to run the risk of having to wait around for formalities, so I'm taking them ahead of time and arranging things for myself. That is why I came to you to get your consent right from the start."

Mr. Bonniwell continued to look the young man over carefully, sadly. And at last he spoke.

"Why do you want to marry my daughter?"

"*Why?* Well, that's some question. You act as if it was a surprise to you. Surely you've seen us going together for years. I've been coming to your house in and out since I was a child. Everybody has always known we were meant for each other, Blythe and I have gone together so long. We're pretty well used to one another. It's rather late for you to be asking *why* I want to marry her, isn't it?"

"Perhaps so. Nevertheless, I'm asking you. Just why do you want to marry my daughter?"

Mr. Bonniwell looked keenly into the young man's eyes. His own mouth was very firm, and it was evident he wanted an answer.

"Well," laughed Dan, "if you insist, of course. Why, I decided she was the one best suited to my needs in a wife. She's good-looking and graceful and well bred. She has an easy manner and will make an excellent hostess. I would never need to be ashamed of her when I chose to entertain, even royalty. She knows how to dress well. Her education is all right, and she's very adaptable. Besides, she isn't set in her way. She wouldn't be always insisting on having her own way. And then, she has—we both have—plenty of money. We wouldn't be troubled financially. I could always be proud of her in any situation. Say! Isn't that enough reasons why I want to marry her?"

"No!" said the father, suddenly straightening up and turning his eyes to the window, looking off as if he were seeing a vision of other days. "No, that isn't enough! You've left out the main thing. You talk of her looks and her education and her money, and her position and breeding; you talk of her ability to exercise social duties and to yield her own wishes to yours, and you think on the strength of just that that a marriage can be made! No sir, young man, you are all wrong. I'm older than you are, and I've lived through a good many years of marriage, and if I had had only what you have named, it would have been a mighty poor chance of happiness I'd have had. You've got to have more than that, boy, before I'll ever endorse your marriage with my daughter. She's worth more than that. This isn't a mere commercial transaction, you know. No true marriage is. There's got to be something more than that, or you'll go on the rocks for sure before many years."

Dan looked at the man whom he desired to make his father-in-law haughtily and in some perplexity.

"I don't understand you," he said in a tone of annoyance. "Is there something more that you require?"

"Yes, there is," said the father, shutting his firm lips with decision. "You haven't said anything about your personal feeling for my daughter, and true love is the only foundation for a successful marriage. No father would be willing to see a beloved child go into a loveless marriage. Dan, do you love my daughter?"

"Oh! *That!* Why, of course, that goes without saying," said Dan amusedly. "I've always been nuts about Blythe, and I'm sure she's crazy about me. But that is entirely a matter between Blythe and myself, isn't it? At least, she's always seemed very happy in my company. I don't think you need have any hesitation on that score. Of course I'm very fond of her."

"That isn't enough," said the father decidedly. "No, boy, just being fond, or even 'being nuts' isn't enough. It's got to be more than that. It's got to be something that will stand when trouble comes; tribulation and poverty, and death."

"*Poverty!*" laughed Dan contemptuously. "I guess there's no danger of that!" And he lifted his patrician chin haughtily.

"It's quite possible to have poverty come to anyone," said Mr. Bonniwell soberly. "Things happen in this world, and you can't ever be sure any of them won't come to you. And when they come, I'd want to be sure that there was gentleness and loving-kindness and tenderness and a world of protection for my girl. Sickness and suffering, too, may be anybody's lot."

"Oh, I'll take the chance," said Dan, with a shrug and a laugh.

"But that isn't enough. You've got to be sure you will be all that my girl needs to help her weather these things, if, or when, they come. I don't want my girl to take a chance."

Dan smiled in a superior way.

"Oh, don't be a pessimist!" he said. "You don't need to worry about that. I'll look after her. She'll be all right. Come, Mr. Bonniwell, don't let's draw this thing out. You know you can bank on me all right. Give me your okay now, and I won't bother you any longer."

Mr. Bonniwell straightened up with that firm set of his lips that his business associates knew meant serious disagreement and shook his head.

"Sorry, Dan, I can't comply at present. I've got to have time to think this thing over, so you needn't go any further in your plans until you hear from me, and that's final. I'll bid you good morning now, for I've got to get back to work."

"But—Mr. Bonniwell—" began Dan, leaning forward with a wheedling manner.

"No buts, Dan Seavers! I meant what I said."

"Mr. Bonniwell, you wouldn't like it very well if Blythe and I *eloped*, would you?" asked the young man, flashing his eyes with a look that he meant to convey dangerous threats.

"No," said Blythe's father, "but my daughter would never do that."

"I wouldn't be so sure of that if I were you. Your daughter might do just that thing if the right arguments were brought to bear upon her. If I know her at all, I'm sure she would if you made it necessary by withholding your consent."

"If my daughter did that, young man, she would have to take the consequences. Now, I will bid you good morning again, and this is final."

While he was speaking he pressed the buzzer on his desk, and his secretary promptly appeared at the door, pencil and pad in hand, ready to take dictation. She took her regular seat near Mr. Bonniwell's desk, and the business magnate swung around, reached for a letter tray, and began to dictate a letter, so Dan Seavers perceived that the interview was ended, at least for the present. He rose and stood hesitantly a moment, but perceiving no further notice as to be taken of him, he spoke again, in a quiet, rather haughty tone:

"When can I hope to have that answer from you, Mr. Bonniwell?"

The father finished the sentence he was dictating and then said, lifting his eyes briefly to his persistent caller, "I will let you know when I have had sufficient time to think the matter over." And then he went on with the letter he was dictating.

Dan Seavers turned angrily toward the door, and then with his hand on the doorknob he flung back, "I think you will be sorry, Mr. Bonniwell, that you have taken this attitude."

This time Mr. Bonniwell did not even lift his eyes as he answered almost meditatively, "It may be so. And then again, I might be even more sorry if I should take any other."

Furious at the failure of what he considered a stroke of genius calculated to put his future father-in-law forever in his debt, Dan Seavers stalked from the room and closed the door forcefully. Mr. Bonniwell went calmly on with his dictation, though he was by no means calm within himself. This idea of his little girl grown up and somebody trying to marry her in a hurry and take her away, was entirely a new thought to him, and that somebody a young snob with a weak chin and a way of trying to act superior! What did it matter that he was handsome and had a lot of money in his own right? The young scoundrel hadn't even had the grace to say that he loved her! Bah! Was it possible that Blythe had had so little insight into character as to fall in love with that poor excuse of a man? Well, if she had, he probably would have to give in, but *poor child*! Wasn't there some way to save her from a future like that? And so he went on thinking, and trying to dictate with the other half of his brain. It was well he had a smart secretary who knew his ways and framed her sentences with a view to his usual habits of diction.

But as the morning went on, he grew more and more opposed to the plans that Dan Seavers had outlined to him, and less and less able to concentrate on his business. And at last about lunchtime he called up his wife and asked her what time she was going to be at the house, saying he had something important he wanted to talk over with her. But when he found that she was not to be back from a committee meeting until late in the afternoon, he settled back grimly to work again, getting a lot of important trifles out of the way and giving definite orders about matters of business to his efficient secretary, planning the morrow's work pretty fully for her, with the idea in mind that he simply couldn't do any real work down here at the office himself until this matter of Dan's proposition was settled one way or the other.

As the day wore on he felt much as if there were a sudden and calamitous illness in the house, the outcome of which could not yet be foretold.

He tried to tell himself that this was ridiculous. That he simply must not get so upset at the idea of Blythe's belonging to anybody else but her parents. He tried to tell himself that probably all loving parents felt the same way when called upon to give up a beloved daughter and let her go away to make a new home of her own. And of course it was right that she should. He wasn't a fool, and he had always counted on such a possibility. But somehow it seemed too soon. Why, she was just home from college, and they had so counted on her coming back to them! And then to have her marrying this unsatisfactory playmate of her childhood, this Seavers fellow he had never quite liked. It was unthinkable! It was unbearable! He couldn't *stand* it!

Over and over these thoughts ran through his mind, winding in and out of the business he was forcing upon himself. He would resolutely put all thoughts of this fantastic proposition of Dan's out of his mind, and then the next moment it would come blasting back into the depths of his soul again, threatening to disarm him utterly.

And then that phrase of having a wedding almost immediately! Why, it was preposterous! A war wedding! *His* daughter. A wedding was a sacred thing that should be approached deliberately and with solemnity, and consideration. Not rushed into with a frenzy of enthusiasm to keep up with the times. It certainly was not going to help the war to be won to have a host of young people mating off in droves, merely because everybody else was doing it. Even if a man were going out to die, it would not help him any better to die to have gone through a hasty ceremony. But this young man was not even going off to die. He was taking over a comfortable berth in an office, and there was no rush about it. There was plenty of time for Blythe to be sure what she was doing. No marrying in haste to repent at leisure for *his* daughter. She must be *sure* she had the right man, and be sure there was mutual love. Not just fondness!

Again and again he would come back to that unfortunate word "nuts," and his lip would curl with distaste at the thought of the way Dan had said it, with a casual tolerance in his attitude. Oh, he couldn't stand it to have Blythe go off with that young man! He would never be able to trust her with him.

Then he would get up and pace across his office, back and forth, and dictate with all the feverishness that a most momentous business proposition might have caused, out of all proportion to the importance of the letter he happened to be dictating.

He sent his secretary out to her lunch early and had a cup of coffee sent up from the restaurant for himself, but still his unhappy musings continued. The situation seemed to grow more and more impossible as the day went by.

When the late afternoon drew on he began to wonder about his wife. Did Alice know about this? Had Dan talked to her? Had she talked with Blythe about it? Did Blythe have any inkling of Dan Seavers's feeling for her?

Fondness, indeed! You needn't tell him that even the modern young people had got to the place where they were contemplating an immediate and hasty marriage without some preliminary courtship? The world couldn't have changed that much since he and Alice were courting. But then the thought of courtship between his daughter and a man who merely professed a "fondness" for her became so obnoxious to him that he could scarcely contain himself, and though it was a full half hour before the time he had promised himself he might with self-respect go home and go into this matter most thoroughly, he finally told his secretary that she had done well and might go home and finish the last few letters that he had dictated in the morning. She had worked hard and must be tired.

The secretary gave him a puzzled, half-worried look but thanked him and departed, and eagerly he got into his overcoat, took his hat and briefcase, and started on his way, the same old thoughts thrashing themselves out in the weary brain.

When he reached home he found that neither his wife nor daughter had as yet arrived, and in despair he put on his dressing gown and slippers and went and lay down on his couch and went to sleep!

Chapter 12

When Mrs. Bonniwell came in half an hour later, she saw her husband asleep and tiptoed around, not to waken him. Poor Father! He was working so hard these days, he must be all worn out, or perhaps he was sick. She found a light shawl and softly spread it over him, drew the shades down so that the light would be dim, preparing to get quietly out of the room and keep the house still. But Bonniwell wasn't so sound asleep but that he heard her and felt her ministrations, and his spirit underneath the light sleep was still so troubled that he came sharply awake and sat up.

"Alice!" he said, blinking at his wife. "Is that you? I thought you would never get here. What's kept you so long?"

"Why, I came as soon as I could after you called," she said. "There were some matters in the committee that I had to settle first, and then I had to wait for a bus. But I'm here now. What is the matter? Are you sick? I never saw you lie down in the daytime. Have you a fever?"

"No, I haven't any fever, except inside. I'm just worried. Alice, has our little girl been falling in love with that nincompoop, Dan Seavers? Because if she has, I won't have it! I tell you I *won't have it*! He has a weak chin and shifty eyes. I know you women think he's handsome, but if you like that sissified beauty in a man, I *don't*. I tell you, he's no man for our girl. But if she thinks she's in love, we've got to deal with it carefully, for I won't have her hurt. But I want to know the *truth*, the *whole* truth about it, and *right away*! It's important, I tell you."

"The truth about what, Daddy?" chirped Blythe, suddenly arriving from the side door and coming into the room, rosy and radiant.

Mr. Bonniwell gasped and then faced the issue.

"The truth about you, child. Are you in love with anybody? I want to know the whole truth. Are you planning to run off and get married without our knowledge? Tell me at once!"

For answer Blythe laughed merrily.

"Why, Daddy! Where did you get that idea? Of course not. You didn't think I'd ever *elope*, did you?"

"Well, I didn't *think* you would, but you haven't answered my question. Are you in love with anybody?"

Then the mother put in:

"Now, Daddy, aren't you being awfully abrupt with your only child?"

The father glared at his wife.

"You keep out of this, Alice. I want my question answered."

Blythe flushed and then looked up with a wheedling glance,

perceiving in her heart that the time for confession might be near at hand.

"Daddy! And suppose I was, do you think I would like to have the fact drawn out of me like a sore tooth?"

"You haven't answered me! *Are* you in love?"

Blythe's cheeks got rosier, and she gave one swift glance at her mother then lifted her eyes bravely to her father's face.

"Well, Daddy, I might be," she said sweetly. "What of it?"

Her father came up, standing.

"With that nincompoop, Dan Seavers?" he thundered.

Then Blythe laughed out merrily again.

"*Daddy! Where* did you get that idea? Whoever could have told you that?"

Mr. Bonniwell watched his daughter sharply, grimly, his jaw set, his brows drawn, his gaze steady.

At last he spoke.

"Blythe, I *insist* on being answered. Are you in love with someone?"

"Well, Daddy, I've always been in love with *you*—and *Mother*," she added mischievously. She gave a whimsical little giggle. Was this the time for her to tell about Charlie?

"Blythe! I *mean* it! I am asking you seriously. I want an answer at once and no more nonsense!"

Blythe grew serious at once.

"Well, Daddy, yes, I am in love with somebody, and I have just been waiting from day to day to have a good opportunity to tell you and Mother about it. I guess this is as good a time as any. Let's go into the library where we won't be interrupted and sit down. And don't look so blank over it, it's nothing to feel bad about. Dad, you look as white as if you were going to fall over in a faint. Shall I help you to a chair?"

"Child, it can't be *possible* that you are wanting to marry that lazy good-for-nothing Dan Seavers?"

But Blythe only laughed.

"No, Daddy, certainly *not!*" she said with a happy little lilt to her voice. "It is somebody a great deal finer than Dan. Dan's just an old childhood friend, but I *never* was in love with him."

"Oh, my child!" said her father with a relieved sigh, sinking down in a nearby chair.

"But my dear," spoke up Blythe's mother, "what is this you are saying? Somebody *else?* Oh, my dear! You've never said anything about somebody else to me."

"No, Mother, I haven't. There hasn't been any chance since it happened. You were always going somewhere, or things were sort of strenuous, and I was waiting until I could tell you calmly."

Mrs. Bonniwell's face was white now and her eyes full of anguish. It might be bad enough to have Blythe fall in love with somebody who wasn't perfection, whom they had known from childhood; but this person that Blythe was talking about was as yet an unknown quantity, and the very thought of it made Mrs. Bonniwell weak. She sank down in another chair and looked wildly at her child who suddenly seemed to have grown up away beyond her.

"Who is it, Blythe?" she asked in almost a whisper, unable to speak clearly with her shaken voice.

"Why, Mother, you wouldn't know him. At least, I may have spoken of him sometimes, but you wouldn't remember, I'm afraid."

"But, my dear! You wouldn't certainly engage yourself to a

stranger we didn't know without at least telling us of it."

"Wait, Mother. Let me begin at the beginning and explain. Father asked me if I *love* anybody and I have answered him truly, yes, I love somebody. Now, let me tell you all about it. Do you remember, Mother, I used to tell you about one of the boys in our high school who was very bright, and always at the head of the class?"

"Why, yes, I do recall something like that, Blythe, but that was a long time ago, and he was only a young boy. Surely you wouldn't mean that you have stuck to an ideal of your high school days and fancy yourself in love with him! Why, child, you haven't had any opportunity to really get acquainted with him. It seems to me you never spoke of meeting him socially. Who is he? Who are his people? Are they all right? You know we couldn't ever consent to letting you marry into a questionable family."

"Let her tell, Mother," interrupted the father. "Let her tell it in her own way."

"All right, Blythe, but tell quickly. I feel as if I could scarcely breathe."

"Don't feel that way, Mother. I'll tell it as quickly as I can. Please calm down and don't take it for granted that it is bad. I think it is very beautiful."

"Oh, *Blythe!*" cried her mother, almost in tears. "To *think* it should have gone *so far*, and we didn't know anything about it."

"Keep still, Alice. Reserve your judgment till you hear the whole story," said Mr. Bonniwell. "Go on, Blythe. What is his name?"

"His name is Charlie Montgomery," said Blythe calmly, lifting her head proudly. "They're not important people, not *now*, if that's what you mean. Charlie's father died about the time he entered high school. His mother is gone, too, now. But he's a wonderful person, and if you could know him, I'm sure you would say so."

"But, Blythe, when did this all happen? How is it that we have not heard anything about it before?" asked her mother in a trembling voice. "It isn't like you to make a mystery of anything you are doing."

"Nothing has *happened*, Mother," said Blythe cheerfully. "Charlie and I were in classes together four years. I knew that he was a boy with a lot of courage and principle, honest and fine, and a good student. He hadn't much time to get acquainted with anybody in high school, for he was working after school, and sometimes evenings. He took care of his mother, and I guess he had a rather wonderful mother from little things he has told me. But that doesn't matter now anyway, except that she has been a great influence for good in his life, I am sure."

"But how do you *know* all this, Blythe, if you didn't have much to do with him in school?"

Blythe gave her mother a clear straight glance, and smiled.

"I'm not sure *how* I know it, Mother," she said thoughtfully. "I just *know* it. I think I have sort of grown into the knowledge of all that during our years of school together, not so much from anything he said about it, for he never said much to me about anything except our studies, until a few days ago."

"*A few days ago!*" exclaimed her father. "Do you mean that this is something *new*, Blythe? I don't understand it. Where has the young man been that we haven't seen him about at all?"

"He's been away to college, as I was, of course," answered Blythe.

"Well, but—have you been corresponding?" This from her mother.

"No, Mother. Never. But one day—just a few days ago—you were busy with your War Bond drive you know, and I couldn't interrupt you. But Charlie came one morning to see me, and told me that he was being sent on a special mission by the government into enemy territory, under circumstances that made it very unlikely that he would ever return alive."

She hesitated an instant and her voice trembled, her eyes cast down. Then she caught her breath and went on:

"He said he wasn't even sure whether I would remember who he was, but he had felt he wanted to let me know before he went away that he loved me; that he had been loving me all the years through high school, and afterward when we didn't even see each other; and he wanted me to have the knowledge of his love before he went away. He wanted to say good-bye. His mother is gone now, and he hasn't any other near relatives. He thought, since he was not expecting to return, I wouldn't mind if he laid his love at my feet as a sort of tribute to what he felt I had meant to him all these years." Blythe paused an instant and her mother saw that her eyes were full of happy tears, and a smile, like a rainbow was over her face.

"Well, that is certainly the strangest love story I ever heard," said her father. "Is that all? Wasn't there more? And when are we to see him? Surely he is coming to see me, isn't he?"

"No, that's about all, Father. He had only a very short time. He said that he had waited till the last minute so that he would not embarrass me. He was very humble. He considered it a tribute to what I had meant to him during the years. He said he would not presume to think I cared for him. He had no wealth, nor social prominence."

She paused again.

"Well, what happened then?" asked her father impatiently. "Is that all?"

"No. I suddenly knew that I loved him, that I, too, had been admiring him for a long time, and I told him so. And then"—Blythe lowered her voice gently as if she were speaking of what was very sacred to herself—"then he put his arms very gently around me and held me close, and kissed me most reverently. It seems rather awful to tell it all out this way to you in words, something that has come to be a very precious experience to me, but I thought you had a right to know. And since Father has asked me, I *want* you to know what he is. He is really *very wonderful*, Mother dear!" And Blythe lifted a face glowing with a great, deep joy.

"But—why isn't he here?" said her father. "Can't he come over this evening and let us talk with him? I certainly would like to have some idea what he is like. Go to the telephone and call him, Blythe!"

Blythe's eyes grew sorrowful.

"He has gone, Daddy. By this time he is far away. And he couldn't tell me where he was going. I'm not sure that he knew where the army was sending him. It's a military secret. A very special one. And it was really a good-bye, I am afraid. He seemed to be very sure of that. It was something he volunteered to do, *knowing* there was probably death in it." Suddenly Blythe's face went down into her lifted hands and the tears flowed.

"I think that was a terrible thing to do. It was *cruel!*" said

Blythe's mother. "To come here and make you suffer this way! It was *cowardly*—it was—"

Blythe's head came up with a flash, and more rainbow-shining in her eyes.

"No, no! Mother don't say that! You don't understand! It was the most lovely thing that ever came into my life! I would not be without the memory of it, not for everything that life can offer! Even if he never comes back—and he was very sure it would not be possible—it will be my joy all my life to know he loved me that way. I am glad, *glad*, that he came and told me of his love! But I'm sorry if you don't understand. I was afraid perhaps you wouldn't, and that's another reason why I didn't tell you right away, although there really wasn't any time when it seemed we wouldn't be interrupted."

"Yes, I see," said Mrs. Bonniwell thoughtfully. "But, my dear, you surely must realize that this thing is all very much out of order, quite unique, and even interesting perhaps, but surely you wouldn't think of taking it seriously? You certainly did not go so far as to engage yourself to this young man on the spur of the moment as it were!"

"No, of course not, Mother," said Blythe with an anguished voice. "Does one get engaged to a man who is on his way to death?"

Her mother gave her a startled look.

"Oh, of course, I didn't realize. But, my dear, that was most wise of you. I am sure you can always be counted on to do the wise, right thing. I have always felt that you could be trusted with anybody, and you would not go beyond convention, no matter who urged you to do so."

A flash of almost anger, and then despair went over Blythe's face.

"But Mother, there never was any question of an engagement. He wouldn't have thought of suggesting it. He felt that he was on his way to his death, and we were not considering life on this earth. We were facing separation. It was enough for us that we loved one another. We had no right to consider— afterward—!"

There was a distinct silence, and the father and mother were evidently impressed. It was a unique situation, and they marveled that their daughter, whom they had until this time considered barely out of little-girlhood, had so far matured as to be able to utter such thoughts as she had just voiced, with such sweet poise and assurance. There was something almost ideal about her attitude, they felt. Was it possible that a girl could love as she had asserted she loved, and yet talk so coolly about the likelihood of her lover's death?

The mother shivered at the thought and said in her heart, *She can't possibly understand what it means. She couldn't really care, and yet take it this way!*

And yet when she looked into her child's eyes and saw that exalted look, as if she had somehow had a vision from heaven and was still under its spell, she knew that her conclusion was wrong.

"But, Blythe," began her mother with a troubled hesitancy, "you have left us without anything to go on, just your word that you admired this young person when he was a mere boy in school. We haven't even an idea how he looks. If we only had something tangible by which we could judge him."

A swift look of decision passed over the girl's face.

"I have, Mother! Just wait a minute and I'll get it."

Blythe jumped up and hurried out of the room and lightly

up the stairs. Now was the time to show them Charlie's letter!

While she was gone the mother looked hopelessly across the room into her husband's eyes.

"Isn't it *terrible*, Father? It seems to have taken such hold on her. Do you think she'll ever get over it?"

"Of course," said the troubled man. "Such things don't last, and she's young, you know. They get over it. Unless—"

"Unless what, dear?"

"Unless it's *real*," said her husband thoughtfully. "And it certainly looks as if she thinks she has something there."

But now they could hear Blythe coming down, breathlessly, a soft flush on her cheeks, a couple of small photographs and a folded letter in her hands.

"This is the way he looked in high school," she said excitedly, handing out a photograph. Her father got up, came over to stand behind his wife's chair and look over her shoulder at the picture.

"Why, yes, he is very good-looking for a young boy," said her mother leniently, studying the picture. "I'm not surprised that you admired him. He looks like a smart boy, too. You say he was a scholar. The head of the class, you said?"

"Yes," said Blythe. "At least he doesn't have a weak chin."

"He must have been a handsome lad, dear. Of course I can see how you admired him, but young boys often lose their good looks as they grow older, and coarsen up. And you are apt to idealize people and stick to what they appeared to be at first. Of course you must take that into account."

There was gentleness and indulgence in Mrs. Bonniwell's voice.

For answer Blythe handed out the other picture, Charlie in

his officer's uniform, handsome and manly and assured.

"This is the way he looks now, Mother," said Blythe quietly.

"Oh!" said Mrs. Bonniwell. "*Indeed!* Well he certainly has fulfilled the promise of his youth. He is *very* good-looking. I don't wonder you fell for him, Blythe. But you know, appearances are sometimes deceitful. You cannot always be sure just by the looks of a person. And a uniform certainly does a lot for anybody."

But Mr. Bonniwell reached for the second picture and studied it carefully, and then, holding it off, he looked again.

"Well, Daughter," he said. "I am bound to say you have chosen well, if one may judge from appearance. That young man looks as if he had character, and a lot of it. So far as I am concerned, I think you are to be congratulated, child. At least he hasn't a weak chin, and that's a great relief to me. I never could endure having a son-in-law with a weak chin!"

"Son-in-law!" exclaimed Blythe's mother in horror. "But John, as I understand it, they have no idea of that. They are merely admiring friends."

"No, Mother," said Blythe decidedly, "we are courting. It may never be anything else, because Charlie is going out to meet death, but please don't speak as if it would be such a dreadful thing if it could ever be a closer relationship."

"But Blythe, dear, after all, while he makes a very good appearance, and as your father suggests he does look as if he had some character, still you must remember that you know him very little, and we, your parents, do not know him at all. I think you should not expect us to judge him and rejoice in your new pleasure, until we know him better. Remember, we have never talked with him, we have never heard him talk, and we shall certainly have to reserve our judgment until such a time, if there ever be such a time, when we can meet him and get really acquainted—find out if he be suited to our beloved child."

"Yes, I know, Mother. I knew that you would feel that way, and so I have brought down a couple of his letters that you may read his own words and know just what he felt. At first I thought they were too sacred to show to even you, but after I had thought it over, I felt that it was only fair that you might know how he looks on this thing that has come to us. And I am sure he would be entirely willing that I should show you his letters. You have a right as my parents to judge him from his own lips. Here, Daddy, read this one first. This was his first letter after he went away. It came a few hours after he had gone."

Mrs. Bonniwell was still studying the picture, taking in little details that even Blythe had not had time yet to analyze.

"I like the way he holds his head," she commented pleasantly, as if it was going to be her policy not to antagonize her daughter.

Blythe's anxious eyes watched her mother. She was going to be fair, that was plain, but she was not so overwhelmingly carried away with the young man as Blythe had hoped. Though it was a hope against hope, for Blythe had rightly judged that it would take a great deal to carry her mother away at first sight, with any unknown quantity.

But it was her father's attitude that was giving Blythe her great hope. For Mr. Bonniwell was carefully, earnestly reading the letter she had given him and did not try to hide the fact that he was greatly pleased with it.

At last he folded the letter carefully and handed it back to her.

"Well," he said heartily, "that's a fine letter. I can see no fault in that at all. I think it shows unusual character, and you certainly are to be congratulated on having such a friend, even if he were only a friend. As for the beloved part, I cannot conceive of more delicacy of feeling, discerning appreciation, and restrained tenderness. I think you would be most fortunate indeed to be loved by such a man, and I for one can give my hearty endorsement to *that* young man. I certainly hope he comes back. I wouldn't mind having him for a son-in-law."

"John!" reproved his wife in a startled voice. "But it seems so cruel in him to have forced himself upon her this way, and *compelled* her to recognize his love when he says he has no hope of returning. I cannot see anything fine and delicate in such actions."

"Read it, Alice, read it! You can't help seeing how really superior that letter is."

"But John, you can't mean that you think a man who was expecting to die in a few days had any right to dare to offer his love to a decent girl."

"Why not, Alice? It seems to me that that very fact shows a fineness of soul, and an unselfishness that is exceptional. It sets his love in a class all by itself. It puts love on a higher plane than merely fleshly pleasure and worldly advantage. And I cannot see that even a jealous mother can object to a lover who puts his hopes on a plane that only looks for consummation in heaven."

"John! How can you talk so? I can't see any reference to heaven in this letter. In fact, it doesn't seem to be in the least *religious*. And that's it. What do we know about him? What church did his people attend? You can't be sure that he even believes there is a God."

"Oh, but Mother, there is another letter I want you to see. It just came this morning."

"Well, I haven't finished this one yet. Wait. But I will say this in favor of the young man, he certainly writes a handsome hand, very clear and readable. You seldom see such penmanship."

But Blythe, light-footed, was already on her way upstairs for the letter that had been written that early morning after Charlie had given himself to Christ in Lincoln Silverthorn's meeting. In a moment she was down again and put the letter in her father's hand that was held out for it.

Then Blythe went and sat down in a shadowed corner where the window draperies half hid her face, and watched her father's expression. She had been loath to show this almost sacred letter to anyone, dreading sneers and misunderstanding, but the look on her father's face fully justified her having shown it. She felt sure in her heart Charlie would be glad to have that letter, especially, shown to anyone.

Chapter 13

As she watched her father read the letter, her mind was going over it sentence by sentence, as it seemed to be graven on her heart.

Dearly beloved:

I have risen early that I may talk a little while with you alone, before the rest of the camp is astir. For I want to tell you of something extraordinary that happened to me last evening. It seems to me that my eyes have been opened to the greatest thing in the world, or in the whole universe, and I want you to see it, too, my dearest.

I have told of a man I have heard of, a chaplain,

going about from camp to camp, bringing cheer and salvation and hope to the men who are going out presently to die. I had heard that his preaching was wonderful, and when I found myself dropped here for a brief stay on my way, and saw his name in shining letters over the hall where he was to speak, I was glad, for I knew that I needed something more before my life went out.

A boy from our hometown, Walter Blake, hailed me when I arrived, and went with me to the meeting. The name of the speaker was Silverthorn.

At first, when we entered, they were singing. All the men in the place singing with mighty power, and we presently began to sing, and the prayer that followed stirred my heart to its depths.

But when this Silverthorn began to speak, it was not as if a man was talking. It was as if something was being enacted there before us on the platform. For I presently saw Jesus Christ standing there alone being tried for my sins. Sins He had never committed.

I have never considered myself much of a sinner, but as Christ stood there alone, with the shadow of a great cross beginning to appear in the dim background, I began to realize that He was a sinless One, and as I looked at Him, I saw myself in contrast, as most sinful. I learned a great truth right then and there, as I looked at the Jesus who was ready to die, for me, and that was that one does not fully recognize sin in one's self until one has looked into the face of Jesus.

So, as I sat there and watched Him, looked into His eyes, He turned and looked into mine, and I realized that He had been loving me all the blank years of my life. I had been trying to cultivate the brains He had given me and get a great education, and He had been loving me and had died in my place, and I hadn't been thinking at all about Him! Then I was made to see that that was sin, the greatest sin of all sin, unbelief and indifference.

It does not sound as great as it really was when it is merely written down, but I want you to know that before the evening was finished I went down on my knees with Silverthorn and gave myself to my Lord who died for me. Or, as they say it here, I accepted Christ as my personal Savior.

Perhaps you did this long ago, but if you did not, then I hope you will right away.

And now I am sure that whatever comes, I shall be safe in the hands of my Lord, and life or death, I shall be sure of heaven. I wanted you to know this.

You will perhaps be interested to know that the lad, Walter, belongs to the Lord also. We knelt together with the same prayer.

There used to be an old hymn my mother sang, something about Christians meeting around the mercy seat. It went something like this:

"There is a place where spirits blend,
Where friend holds fellowship with friend,
Though sundered far, by faith they meet,
Around one common mercy seat."

*And it has come to me that so you and I may
hope to meet, at the feet of our Lord Jesus, and
talk to Him about one another, and of our love
for Him. Will you meet me in prayer at the mercy
seat, my precious friend?*

Now the camp is astir and I must close.

*But I want you to know that I am very glad
in the knowledge of the Lord Jesus, and filled with
a great peace.*

May He be with you.

I love you.
Charlie

As Mr. Bonniwell read this letter a mist stole out on his lashes, and tears rolled unnoticed down his cheeks. As he finished and handed the letter to his wife he commented, "A beautiful letter! A most extraordinary setting forth of sacred things. My dear daughter, I congratulate you."

"It seems to me it must be a very gloomy letter," commented Mrs. Bonniwell as she took it from him. "You are both crying!"

"Oh, no, not gloomy!" said her husband. "It is full of peace."

Blythe and her father were very quiet while the mother read that letter, and she held it thoughtfully in her hand for a full minute after finishing before she spoke in a reserved, husky voice: "Very—commendable—I'm sure."

Then she handed the letter to Blythe, and the three, without further talk, went quietly up to their rooms.

When the father and mother had silently prepared for sleep, and all sounds had ceased from behind Blythe's closed door, her parents, now lying in their beds, staring wide awake in the dark room, stirred uneasily. At last the mother began in a fearsome whisper:

"John, she'll soon forget him, don't you think so? She's so young! You think so, don't you?"

There was another silence for a moment and then the father replied:

"I trust not! No, certainly not! If I thought that Blythe was vapid enough to forget a man like that, I should be in despair about her."

"But John! You certainly don't want your little girl to go mourning all her days for a dream-man; a person she doesn't really know, and never has. You can't possibly think she won't forget him after a little while!"

"Suppose an angel from heaven should come down and talk with you for an hour? Would you forget that in a little while?" asked her husband.

"Oh—well, an angel—of course. I wouldn't *forget* it, exactly. It would be a kind of a pleasant memory, but it wouldn't hinder my going right on living a normal life, John, clubs and war work and things like that."

"No, I suppose not," said the man thoughtfully. "Bridge clubs and dinners and the latest fashions of course."

"Now, John, you're being sarcastic. I know you don't care for bridge, but is that any reason why I shouldn't play once in a while? I don't really spend much time at it, especially now that there is so much war work to be done."

"Yes, I suppose so," said the disinterested voice of the man.

"John, you're not listening to me."

"Oh yes, I am."

"John, what are you thinking about? You act so absorbed, just as you do when you've brought business home with you. John, are you worried about Blythe and that strange boy who dared to upset her before he went away to war?"

"No," said John thoughtfully. "I'm less worried about Blythe than I have been for a long time. I'm delighted that she's interested in such a young man. A fellow with real thoughts in his head, and a sane way of expressing them, I tell you, that young man has got hold of something we all need, in these times especially, a real hold on God, a knowledge of God. And he's got the kind of courage that won't fail at anything he has to do. I wish I felt as sure of heaven as he does."

"Why, *John*! How ridiculous! *You* to talk that way! Why, you've been a Christian man for years. You've been a trustee of the Presbyterian Church. Of *course* you're sure of heaven."

"No, Alice, I don't think being a trustee of any church makes you sure of heaven. It takes more than that, and I never thought about it before. If you want to know what I'm thinking about, that's it. I was wondering, if I had to go to war, in some job from which I was pretty sure I wouldn't ever return, I was wondering if I had enough faith in God to take along with me and protect me in danger. Alice, I don't believe I have."

"Nonsense, John! You're all unstrung by this odd thing that has happened to Blythe. You always did take things that happened to Blythe so terribly to heart. You'll snap out of it and be your normal self in the morning. I believe you ought to have some vitamins. I'll get you some in the morning, and see that you take them, too! And now, for pity's sake, let's get some sleep. I have an early committee meeting in the morning. Don't worry about Blythe. She'll be all right when she wakes up. She's just excited over this unusual happening, and I don't blame her a bit. I think it was a perfectly awful thing for that fellow to do, when he had never paid any attention to her before. Don't you think so, John?"

"*No!*" said John shortly. "I think it was a beautiful thing to do, and I wish I might have had a little chance to know a fellow like that. I admire him greatly. I'd like him for a son-in-law, and I hope somehow his God keeps him alive and brings him back to our little girl."

"*John!* How perfectly terrible! I never heard you talk like this before. It seems to me you've taken leave of your senses."

"On the contrary I've been wondering if I've ever had any before. You see, Alice, we've been walking by the pattern of all our neighbors, and I think the time has come to stop and get a pattern of our own. I'd like to know God better. I think perhaps that's why war came, to teach us that it was God we needed. Come now, Alice, don't you honestly feel that it is reassuring for Blythe to have a friend who is religiously inclined instead of wanting to go to nightclubs all the time?"

"Well, I'm not so sure," sighed Mrs. Bonniwell. "It's easy to go too far religiously, of course. I shouldn't like Blythe to get tied up with a fanatic, would you? And when people talk like that last letter she showed us, they are apt to go too far and become fanatics."

"Yes? And just what is a fanatic? Would you define it as

being one who knows God too well?"

"*John!* Why, you actually sound irreverent, speaking of God in that light, familiar way. I never heard you talk so before."

"Well, I'm not sure that I've ever been stirred so deeply before as I was by that letter. A young man who is consciously going out to die, with very little hope of returning, to surrender his whole self to the God who made him, and who is really his only hope of eternal life! And he not only has done that, but he has been able to put the thing he has done into clear logical words that have come back to his girl's father and convinced him that he, too, needs such a Savior."

"But John, I don't like you to talk as if you didn't have all you need in a Christian way."

"Nevertheless, it's true, Alice, and I'm not going to drop it at this. I'm going to make it my business to find out what that young man says he has found."

"Well, all right, John, only please do drop the subject now. I'm very weary. This has been a long, hard day, and the evening was most exciting. I really must get some sleep if I am to run that committee meeting in the morning, and it's going to take some maneuvering to get everything through and keep every woman satisfied and not at swords' points with all the rest."

"Yes, go to sleep, Alice. We'll talk of this another time. Good night."

There was silence in the room after that, but it was a long time before the master of the house slept.

And over across the hall, Blythe was down upon her knees beside her bed, praying a real prayer, perhaps her first real prayer since her little childhood's believing days. For she, too, was seeking the Christ that her beloved had found.

"Dear God," she prayed, "won't You show me the way to see Your Son, Jesus Christ, the way my Charlie has found Him?"

But the sweet loving mother slept the sleep of the just to get ready for her strenuous committee on the morrow, serene in the knowledge that she was a good Christian woman and did not need to have keen insight into spiritual things, resting in the firm belief that her precious daughter would soon recover from this imagined obsession that she was in love with an unknown stranger who couldn't possibly be the type of boy that would be suited to a girl as cultured as her daughter.

And all the while, out in the night world, Daniel Seavers and Anne Houghton, with whom he had happened to be thrown that evening, were seeing life together.

Anne hadn't been at all the companion Dan would have chosen to help him forget his annoyance at Mr. Bonniwell's reception of his gracious propositions. But he had to get through the evening somehow, since his plans were being held in abeyance for a brief space, and perhaps it would be as well to let his future father-in-law see that his daughter wasn't the only pebble on the beach, the only girl in the city. Just give him a day to himself and he would come around. If he didn't, then Dan would wait no longer. He would collect Blythe and they would carry out the threat of an elopement. Of course, that would be one way to get the high hand with a father-in-law. Let him see that Dan meant what he said and would take no orders from anybody from now on. He had obeyed the conventions and asked permission to address Blythe, but if it didn't bring prompt action, then Dan would just forget the conventions and do as he pleased. He was very sure he could bring Blythe to his way of thinking, if he went about it in the right way, for he had had plenty of years in which to study her and know the best ways to get around her, to bend her to his will. Of course, he wasn't taking into account the years in which they had been separated by college life, and the explosive power of a new affection that had come into this girl's life. He was a young bully who had always been accustomed to having his own way, and he intended to have it now without delay.

So he took the first girl that came along, and it happened to be Anne Houghton. He didn't particularly admire her, but he knew her to be a good sport on occasion, and she was handy to his need, so he asked her to have dinner with him and take in some nightclubs afterward. Daring and reckless, Anne was, and she fitted in with his disgruntled mood, so they went from one bright spot to another, till they had reached a place where their jaded sensibilities were ready for anything.

Driving home in the small hours, their way led over Wolverton Drive, and Anne indulged in a few sharp pleasantries about Dan's erstwhile playmate, Blythe Bonniwell.

The Bonniwell house, sitting quietly back among its beautiful trees, sheltering its sleeping family with strong comforting walls of stone, looked impregnable under the shadowed waning moon, and it somehow angered both young people.

"Poor Blythe," babbled the spiteful Anne, with a tongue let loose by the many drinks she had taken. "She thinks she owns the earth with a gold fence around it, doesn't she? I'm glad you took a night off from letting her wind you around her pretty little finger and are showing her that you can have a good time with some other girl now and then. It will do her good. She really is getting insufferable."

"Oh, I don't know," drawled Dan lazily. "I never have any

trouble bringing her to terms if I want to bad enough. The trouble is, she's too much under the dominance of a puritanical father and has prudish ideas of what she wants to do. Of course, if I chose, I could take that out of her, if I thought it were worth the trouble. But it's been good sport to go out with a girl who knows her way about in the world. I don't know when I've had such a good time. We'll have to try it again sometime. How about it, Anne?"

"That will be all right with me," said Anne, with a triumphant ring to her voice. "I like to step out with you, and anytime you want to show that demure little mouse where to get off, you can count on me to help you out. But frankly, I should think you'd be terribly bored with her. I tried to talk with her in the Red Cross class the other day, but we really haven't two ideas in common. I finally gave it up. And she has such common tastes. She's always taking up with some poor little scrap of humanity who doesn't really belong in our crowd. I think it's a pose, showing how kind and benevolent she can be, you know. But of course, she's very young."

"Yes, quite," said the young man drowsily. "I think she'll grow out of it. I've known Blythe since we were children, you know. I guess she'd be all right if she could get away from her family. They dominate her entirely too much."

They were driving past the Bonniwell place now, and Anne cast baleful glances at the peaceful house in the moonlight. She would show that Bonniwell girl just how much hold she had on Dan Seavers! Just give her two or three more nights like this one, and she would soon have him where she wanted him, and then Blythe might smile her prettiest, but she would have lost her Dan.

They drew up in front of the Houghton residence, and Dan took care to find the deepest shade, not directly in front of the house, where thick shrubbery hid the car completely.

"Now," he said, "we've had a good evening. Suppose we rest a bit just to say good night." He reached his arm and drew Anne close within his clasp. He put her head down on his shoulder, and looking into her face, he slowly stooped and brought his lips to hers, in a hard, passionate kiss, to which Anne responded fervently, her warm soft lips lingering tenderly on his own.

"That was good," said Dan, settling down beside her and drawing her closer. "This is cozy, isn't it? Why didn't we ever do this before? Boy, I believe I'm tired. It feels good to rest, and you're a pleasant little body to have around." Then he laid his lips on hers again.

Yes, Anne was pretty and responsive, but she hadn't any money, though she did have "family." But she lived with a stingy married brother who had a number of children to get his money.

And down the drive a few blocks away, in a quiet house where dawn was beginning to bring out its protective lines, slept the girl whom Dan had decided to marry because she had plenty of money. The girl of whom he had said he was "fond." The girl who had a wonderful boyfriend gone to war, and who had just been dedicating her life to finding his Christ.

On his way home at last, with the streaks of dawn more distinct in the sky now, Dan's thoughts reverted to Blythe. She had always been shy of any suggestion of love making. She held herself aloof. But what would Blythe be like if she were married to him, and felt it the conventional thing to let herself go? Or would she ever be demonstrative? Boy! Anne Houghton certainly had it over Blythe when it came to showing a man how she felt about him. The touch of her lips was still upon his, and he certainly had had one night to remember. But tomorrow morning he must go to Mr. Bonniwell and deliver an ultimatum. Now or never. Permission for his whole plan, wedding and all, with a hint of a big settlement; or an elopement! Let him have his choice.

Chapter 14

$\mathcal{D}$an presented himself at Mr. Bonniwell's office very soon after the work of the day had begun, and Mr. Bonniwell was deep into the morning mail.

When the young man went blustering into the outer office, he told the assistant who met him that he wanted to see Mr. Bonniwell at once. It was very important, and he hadn't any time to spare.

Word came back over the telephone to the clerk at the desk that Mr. Bonniwell was very much engaged at present, but though he had not yet sent for Mr. Seavers, it would be all right. He would see him as soon as he could finish his present interview, if he cared to wait. Or if not, Dan might return that afternoon any time after two o'clock.

Dan frowned.

"I'll *wait!*" he said shortly. "But tell him to make it snappy!" he added.

The young man at the desk did not, however, transfer this latter sentence over the telephone, and Dan sat down and glowered at the young official. Well, perhaps it was as well to bide his time and get these preliminaries over, but when he was finally married, he certainly would pay his father-in-law back in full for all he had cost him.

It was almost an hour before a man and a secretary emerged from the inner office and Dan was told that Mr. Bonniwell would see him now. During this time Dan had sighed and writhed and wriggled, and drummed on the table with his fingers, and in every way manifested his impatience. So he was on his feet at once and pranced into the audience chamber with an arrogant manner.

"Well, you certainly took your time," he announced impudently to the man he expected to make his father-in-law.

"Yes?" said Mr. Bonniwell, with an amused lifting of his eyebrows. "And now you are taking mine. Well, sit down."

Dan dropped into the most comfortable chair in view and frowned again.

"Well?" he said sharply. "Let's get this over with. I've waited too long already."

"Yes," said the businessman, with a twinkle, "perhaps you have. So, what I have to say is that you have my permission to talk this matter of marriage over with my daughter. Is that what you want?"

"Why, yes, of course," snapped Dan, utterly flabbergasted. He had been much wrought up by the night's delay he had endured, and had fully expected some kind of a long argument before he got any satisfaction out of the man. He was actually embarrassed to get what he had asked without question.

"Oh—why, yes," he began awkwardly. "Well, now, that's very kind of you, and I appreciate it of course, though I do wish you could have said yes at the beginning without all this forethought. However, what's done's done, and I'll get to work and carry out my plans as fast as possible. I hope you told your wife what is going to happen so she'll be ready to cooperate with us without holding up the affair any longer. But then, women, I will say, are usually all in favor of anything like a wedding."

"But aren't you forgetting a little matter?" asked the father, watching the young man still amusedly.

"Forgetting?" said Dan. "Why, no, I'm not forgetting anything. What is it you refer to?"

"Why, I only gave you permission to talk this matter of a marriage over with my daughter, and you are assuming that the arrangements are as good as settled."

"Oh," said Dan, with a sudden, sharp look at the older man. "Have you then laid your commands upon your daughter? Is that your way of answering me?"

"No," said the father. "I haven't even talked it over with her. Blythe is fully able to settle her own affairs, I feel. I think she will tell you what she wants. You merely have my permission to address her. There is, however, one question I would like to ask you before you leave."

"Yes?" said the young man, alert at once.

"I would like to know, just as a matter of personal interest, what you think of God? How well do you know Him?"

"God!" exclaimed Dan, a kind of shiver of horror going over him. "What in heck has God got to do with anything?"

"Well, when you have lived as long as I have lived, young man, you will find that God has to do with almost everything, more or less. You can't get away from that. I was just interested to know what you thought of Him."

"Well, if you want to know, I never thought anything about Him. It wasn't in my line, and what's more, I never saw any indication that it was in yours either."

"That is quite possible," said Mr. Bonniwell. "I'll have to own that it hasn't been. But I've come to see that it should make a difference in a man's life and in his relations with his family and friends. That is all, young man. I'll have to go back to my work now, but I certainly hope that you may learn a great deal about the best things of life before you are done. Good morning!" Mr. Bonniwell buzzed for his secretary. She appeared promptly and held the door open for the exit of the somewhat bewildered caller.

As Dan went his way he was saying to himself, "Now what in heck did he mean by all that gaff? I wonder, has he got something up his sleeve? I just can't figure that he would give up as easily as this after all that baloney about taking time to think, unless he talked it over with Blythe and told her where to get off. But maybe after all he is really pleased at the arrangement, or perhaps his wife has taken a hand at the argument. I can't help feeling she rather likes me. At least, she's a good friend of my mother's, of course."

So Dan went on his way and tried at once to call up Blythe to make a date for a good talk to get things settled.

But Blythe was off to her day nursery, and he had to wait again. However, he was fairly comfortable in his mind about her, for he felt sure he could handle Blythe and get her to see eye to eye with him about their marriage.

And in the meantime he called up a few friends whom he would like to have figure in the wedding party, not telling too much about his plans, but enough to give them an idea of what to expect. And while he was about it, perhaps it would also be a good idea to find out if the church the Bonniwells attended, and the pastor who officiated there, were available on the day he had fixed his mind upon as the suitable time for this hasty marriage. And so the hours marched on with a fair amount of interest and excitement for the would-be bridegroom, and Anne Houghton never once entered his thoughts, except as a pleasant background for a dull evening that hadn't turned out so badly after all.

But when the day drew toward evening, and, having failed twice at her home to locate her, he called up again at dinnertime.

"Hi, beautiful!" he said when he heard her voice answering. "I've been hunting you all day and couldn't get a trace. What's been doing that has kept you so busy?"

"Oh, Dan! Good evening! Sorry I have been so elusive, but you see, I went to one of the centers for soldiers and got so interested I stayed all the afternoon."

"For sweet pity's sake! What could you possibly find interesting in a lot of half-baked boys in uniform? I should think you'd be good and sick of that war stuff by this time. Why don't you cut it out and give a little attention to your friends? What's the idea? Do you think you can fight the whole war alone? I don't like women doing war work. I think you ought to let the men fight the war and the women ought to stay at home and be feminine."

"Oh!" said Blythe with a catch in her breath. "Is that the way you feel about it? But, Dan, *you're* a man. What are *you* doing about the war?"

"Me? Oh, I'm right in it with both feet. Haven't you heard? I've got my commission now," said Dan, with a satisfied smirk that almost could be heard over the wire. "You haven't been in evidence yet to be told about it, but it's come, and I've some interesting things to tell you about what is going to happen. I'll be over this evening to tell you all about it."

"Oh, I'm sorry Dan, but I guess your news will have to wait. I have an engagement this evening."

There was a displeased silence on the wire, and then a question snapped out:

"Beginning when?"

"Beginning now," said Blythe firmly. "I am leaving in half an hour."

"Break it!" ordered the young man, with a voice equally firm.

"Oh, but I couldn't possibly," said Blythe. 'It's something I couldn't miss. It means a great deal to me."

"Oh, is that so? And I and my wishes don't many anything. Is that the way you feel?"

"Why no, Dan, if there was something I could do for you at a time when I am free, I'd be glad to do it. But this is something that I cannot cancel."

Another instant's silence and then the spoiled arrogant voice of Dan came sternly over the telephone:

"Well, I'm coming over there right away, and I think you'll change your mind after you hear what I have to say! Goodbye!" And the telephone was slammed down.

Blythe hung up quietly and turned away with a sinking of her heart. Oh dear! Was she going to have trouble getting rid of Dan? If only she could get away before he arrived. Would it be possible? She glanced at the clock. No, there was no time. She knew too well how quickly Dan could get to their house when he was anxious to get there in a hurry. He had so often done it in his childhood. He knew every inch of the way, every stick and stone and pebble to cross, every flower bed to circle. No, she could never get away before he arrived, and she must not stay, for she would miss the meeting that she was so anxious to attend, a meeting that the Silverthorn that Charlie had written about was to address. She was taking Mrs. Blake. She was meeting her at a certain spot at the city train station, and it was but a short ride to the camp where he was to be. She would not disappoint Mrs. Blake for all the Dan Seavers in the world.

Rapidly she finished the hasty toilet: hat, coat, gloves. She was ready and on her way downstairs when Dan walked in the back door and met her at the foot of the stairs.

"Yes, I thought I'd find you running away from me," he declared, offended, "but you're not getting away this time, lady. I got here just in time. Come into the living room and sit down. I've something important to tell you, and something important to give you also."

"But I can't, Dan. It's impossible! I'm meeting somebody at the station and taking her to a meeting."

"Listen, beautiful! I'm sure what I have to tell you will stop all that. You see, it's very important. You and I are going to be married one week from today, and going on our honeymoon right away. And does that make you open your eyes and take notice?"

For answer, Blythe suddenly broke into peals of merry laughter.

"Oh, Dan!" she said, and dropped down into a chair and put her laughing face down in her hands. "You certainly are a scream. Am I to understand that this is the most modern form of a proposal, or is it just a joke?"

Dan stood gazing sternly down at her, displeased, indignant, puzzled.

"Well, I like that!" he said, a furious note in his voice. "Here I'm offering you the greatest honor a man can give a woman, and you ask if it's a joke! Really, Blythe, this is serious business, and I haven't a whole lot of time to waste. I've got my list of ushers made out. I've inquired tentatively if your church will be free at the hour I've selected for the ceremony and did a little feeling out to see if your pastor will be at liberty. I've got as many things in line as I could before I got your word that the time suited you, and now I've come for that. If you're so busy as you claim, all you've got to do is say the arrangements suit you and I'll go ahead, so that you won't have a whole lot to do and can concentrate on your trousseau. Any little details you care to add to my arrangements we can talk over, but in the meantime, I want your formal consent. And I might add, in case you are still a stickler for conventions, I have your father's permission to address you formally. Now, will you stop that silly giggling and sit up and take notice? I don't see what's funny about this, anyway. Come, I want *action*, I tell you."

Blythe suddenly straightened up, wiped the laughter tears from her eyes, and drawing a deep breath, looked straight at her angry would-be lover.

"Excuse me, Dan," she said, her voice growing steadier as

she spoke. "I'm sorry I misunderstood you. I didn't, of course, realize that you had any such serious intention in mind. I didn't know what you meant. But no, Dan, I couldn't marry you, either now or next week or *anytime*. I don't think we have enough in common for marriage. I don't love you, and I don't think you love me. We've been good friends for a long time, but that was all, and I have never thought of marriage with you, nor wanted it. I wouldn't want to be unpleasant about it, of course, but I certainly can't marry you, and we might as well settle it now as later. Perhaps I should thank you for the honor you have done me, and of course I hope you'll understand that it is nothing against you that I do not want to marry you. You have been a longtime friend, and I certainly wish you well, and I hope in good time that you will find somebody a great deal better for you than I could possibly be, but definitely it could never be me."

Dan regarded her with disgust.

"Yes, I thought so. Your father said he hadn't talked it over with you, but I can see quite plainly that he laid his commands upon you all right, and it is up to me to overcome those commands, so we better get at it at once, for I haven't much time to spare, and I want the invitations to get into the hands of the engraver at once. I've already arranged that he will attend to them very swiftly, but he wants the wording at once, so we'll have to work fast. Come, we're going to take dinner in a quiet place where we will have opportunity to talk and a place to write our lists. My car is outside. Are you ready? Is this the handbag you are taking? Come, don't keep me waiting."

Blythe took the handbag from him and tucked it under her arm, looking up at him with her pleasant lips firmly set.

"You are mistaken, Dan. My father has laid no commands upon me on this subject or any other. And I am sorry to disappoint you, but I cannot possibly take dinner with you tonight. But even if I did have another engagement, I would not want to go anywhere with you to discuss this matter, either now or at any other time. Definitely, Dan. I will not marry you, and you will have to reconsider and cancel your plans without further discussion. It is utterly out of the question. Now, I must go at once. I have a definite appointment with someone, and a train to catch, so good-bye, and I'm sure you'll soon get over this nothing and find the right person to marry. Good-bye!" Blythe smiled and turned and suddenly flashed out of the room and the house and hurried down the walk to the taxi that was waiting at the side door for her. She vanished out of his sight while Dan stood astonished and indignant, unable to believe his senses.

Chapter 15

$\mathcal{D}$an Seavers seldom wasted much time even in being angry. He could almost always think up something else to do that would be more interesting and yet be in a fair way to help carry his point, and it wasn't long before he reflected he could still make progress in some other line to further his determined plans. So he cast about him for some other line to follow and presently thought of Blythe's mother. She was a good friend of his. A pretty good sport at times. He would go and talk to her. She would lay down the law to Blythe and then he would have smooth sailing.

So he went back to the Bonniwell house and discovered that Mrs. Bonniwell had just come in from a full day among her committees and was very tired. She welcomed Dan pleasantly, though her manner was a bit abstracted. She had always liked the handsome Dan. Moreover, there was still hovering in the back of her mind a wistfulness about her daughter's old playmate. He had seemed so altogether desirable to her.

"Mother Bonniwell," he said with a smoothly flattering tone, "I think I need your help and counsel."

Now, Mrs. Bonniwell always liked to give counsel to anyone, particularly to a pleasing young man, and she beamed on him and settled down to hear what he had to say.

"You see," he said, "Blythe and I want to be married next week, and I've come to you to help me get things straight. I've got this thing beautifully planned out, thought of simply everything, I'm sure, and even got reservations in some things, and priorities. And now, Blythe is trying to hold things up. And I thought you would know how to go about this thing with more finesse than I evidently have, smooth down Blythe's ruffled feathers, and set her ideas straight. Will you understand and help us out?"

Mrs. Bonniwell gave the young man a startled look, lifted her well-groomed eyebrows, and said, "*Married!* You say you are planning to be *married?* Since when did this happen? Blythe has said nothing to me about it, and she always tells me everything. How long has this been going on?"

"Why, surely, you've understood we've had that in mind for several years past. Everybody else has, I know. I find it has been sort of taken for granted for a long time. And now that I have my commission and am very likely to be sent to a location very soon, I thought it would be best for us to get married at once, and be ready to go together. So I've set the day, and I want your help in bringing Blythe to see that it is the wisest and best thing for us to do."

"But I don't understand, Dan. What does Blythe say about it?"

"Well, she doesn't say much, only that she doesn't want to get married now. She's too busy with war work and the like, and she thinks it's too soon to get her trousseau ready and all that, but good night, the stores will still be here after we are married, and she can pick out her togs at her leisure. I thought you could make her see that. And lots of girls are hurrying their marriages now before their men go overseas. It's quite the swagger thing to do. And I thought if you would just advise her about this, Mother Bonniwell, and get her to see the thing straight, it would be a great convenience to me. You see, I don't want to be rushed at the last minute, and if Blythe would only cooperate, everything would go smoothly. You'll help me, won't you?"

"But Dan, this is utterly new to me. I didn't dream you had any such move in mind. In fact, well, I would have to talk with Blythe before I made any promises."

"Now look here, Bonny! You might as well own up at the start. You and Papa Bonny have been hashing this thing over and agreed on what you'll say, haven't you? That's the same kind of hooey stuff he gave me last night. Now own up."

Mrs. Bonniwell raised an offended chin and looked the young man in the eye.

"Certainly not, Dan! I don't know what you mean. I don't consider that is a very respectful way to speak to me."

"There, there, Bonny, now don't get your ire up! I just thought it was funny you and your man had the identical same reply ready."

"There is nothing strange about wanting to think over as serious a thing as marriage," said Mrs. Bonniwell, "and I couldn't possibly agree to further your plans without being sure that my family were agreed. However, why don't you tell me your plan in detail, and then I can think advisedly."

So Dan adroitly painted the picture of his proposed marriage, wedding ceremony, invitations, trousseau, and honeymoon, as fully as he had done it for Mr. Bonniwell, except that he went still further into details. Gradually, as he named prominent people who were to have part, the good lady was half intrigued and sat nodding acquiescence, as she in her mind's eye saw the wedding procession marching down the aisle of the most aristocratic church in the community and envisioned the number of full dress uniforms that would be a part of the picture.

"It sounds all very lovely, Dan, and you seem to have planned a beautiful order of things, though I'm afraid perhaps it sounds a trifle too elaborate for wartimes. However, Dan, I would have to talk with Blythe and find out just what her objections are before I could promise anything. Just what objections has she given you?"

"Well, you see, she won't really settle down and talk it over. She says she has engagements, and I haven't been able to get her to discuss it with me. She hasn't comprehended that haste is a necessary factor in the whole arrangement, and there's where I thought you would be able to help me. You know Blythe, and you know how to make her listen. So, will you talk it over with her and call me up either early this evening or tomorrow morning at the latest? It really ought to be tonight to make things work smoothly. Will you do that, Bonny?"

"Well, I'll see what I can do, Dan, but I'm not at all sure that I can make Blythe see things as you do. However, I will endeavor to get her to give you an immediate opportunity to talk with her, and you will have to do the rest. Blythe won't be home till late this evening. And if she's not too tired, perhaps I can say a few words to her then, and phone you at once. Will you be home all the evening? Or at the latest, the first thing in the morning? I'll let you know what to expect. But remember, Dan, I'm not promising anything. It's all got to depend on Blythe."

Dan rose with a bitter, dissatisfied look on his face, almost a sneer.

"Same old bunk!" he muttered. "You needn't tell me that you and the old man haven't talked it over. But I can tell you, Mamma Bonniwell, if you go against me, Blythe and I are going to elope and make a pretty scandal in the town for you and Papa Bonniwell to swallow, so keep that in the back of your mind while you think it over!"

"Well, really, Dan! I'm not accustomed to such talk. If you feel that way, I certainly don't think you are a fit man to marry my daughter."

"Oh, now Bonny, don't get excited. You know I'm all right. I just want to get things going in a hurry. These are wartimes, you know, and you can't afford to loiter, it's so hard to get anybody to do anything these days."

"Very well, Daniel, I'll see what can be done and let you know, but I'm not promising anything. I feel that Blythe's life is her own, and she must plan it the way she wants it, but I'll endeavor to put before her what you are suggesting and then I will let you know, or ask her to let you know, when you can see her. And now, Dan, I'm afraid I'll have to ask you to excuse me. I have to meet a delegation of women at quarter to eight, and I simply must snatch a few minutes of rest before they come, for I am all but worn out."

So Dan, inwardly cursing his ill luck, yet priding himself that he had got Mamma Bonny pretty well on his side, took his way home, to await the message.

Mrs. Bonniwell went to her room and composed herself to rest, hoping still to snatch a few minutes of actual sleep, but her mind was in a turmoil, and though she closed her eyes and lay very still, she could not keep her mind off the problems that were thickening around her.

To begin with, there was Blythe and that alarming absurd obsession she had that she was in love with an absolute stranger.

Of course, it was quite possible that this proposition of Dan's might be a very good thing to come just now and help Blythe to forget the abrupt and fanatically inclined unknown. On the other hand, might it not be too soon to hope to have that romantic happening offset by a sensible marriage into her own set? It would be comfortable, too, to think of Blythe with a husband who was wealthy in his own right, and not dependent upon her fortune. Also, Mrs. Seavers was her friend, and she certainly would like to use her influence to help with what Dan's mother wanted, the assurance that Dan could be saved from questionable girls, girls who were beautiful perhaps, but absolutely nothing else, just gold diggers—wasn't that what they called such girls, always out to lure some rich young man?

On the other hand, Blythe was happy and bright just now, and they certainly were enjoying her presence in the home after her long absence at college. And it would be truly beautiful to have her with them now, with that almost unnatural glow of joy in her eyes, a real lovelight, and it was utterly useless to hope that it could change into such a glow for Dan. He wasn't the kind that could bring romance in such an enchanted form to a girl. He was solid and cheerful and good, maybe even dependable, but not one who could easily turn Blythe's fancied romance into love for himself. It really would be wiser in him to lay this marriage business aside until Blythe had forgotten the boy Charlie, or perhaps till word had come that Charlie was "missing in action," or something, as it likely would pretty soon, unless he had gotten up a cock-and-bull story to storm his girl's heart. Though somehow the letters hadn't seemed to make him that kind of a lad either. Rather too solemn, perhaps. Strange that her girl would be interested in a staid young man like that. Stranger still that she had never said much about him before, even when she was a child in school. Well, she must talk with Blythe as soon as she returned, and she must prepare her approach and not antagonize her. She simply must find out just how her daughter felt about this marriage. It wouldn't do for her girl to miss the chance of a happy marriage with a finely set-up young man like Dan, just because of some silly romance between herself and a young man who was confessedly going out to die.

So Mrs. Bonniwell thrashed the matter over carefully and did not get her much-needed nap. She studied over what she would say to Blythe as carefully as if it were one of her popular addresses to women's clubs, or a speech to mold the pliable opinions of her committee. And when the duties yet before her called her from the couch, she went with half her mind occupied still with what she was going to say to Blythe that evening when they got together. All through the rest of the hours as she went from one appointment to another, the arguments were growing stronger by which she intended to lead Blythe on to see that she had no right to fill her mind with a stranger when her lifelong playmate was needing her. And then, when the late evening hour came, and Blythe arrived, her face shining with a wonderful light and real joy in her eyes, the mother began hastily to consider whether she had any argument on her whole list that could combat a joy like this. At least while it lasted it was going to be hard to turn her girl aside from the ideas that seemed to possess her.

"Oh Mother," she said as she came in, "it was really wonderful! It was just as Charlie said in his letter. That Mr. Silverthorn spoke right to the men's souls. They sat and listened as if they were spellbound, and I listened, too, and found more wonderful hope than I have ever heard in any sermon I listened to in church."

"Well, now, dear, that is going pretty far. I am glad you enjoyed your evening instead of being bored as I was afraid you would be, but when you go to discounting the orthodox churches, I really can't agree with you."

"Oh Mother, I wasn't discounting churches, not the real kind, but this talk tonight was something that seemed to help me so much. It made God and Christ so real that you felt as if you never could doubt Him again. And you got that feeling, just as Charlie said, that Jesus Christ was right up there on the platform beside him. You saw Him being tried, you saw His eyes, so full of love and pity and suffering for a world that was sinning against Him, and *enjoying* the sinning, while He was getting ready to die for that sin as if it had been His own."

"He must be a very magnetic speaker," said Mrs. Bonniwell, trying to explain to herself the effect of the speaker on her daughter, forgetting for the moment the subject that had filled her mind the last half of the day. "There are not many speakers who have that dramatic power to make their audience see those about whom they are speaking. It is a wonderful gift, and would be just the way to influence young men who were hungry for something different."

"Oh Mother, it wasn't just that," said Blythe, struggling eagerly for words to convey the wonderful message that had reached her own heart that night. "It was like a real message sent from heaven, just as Charlie said. He made you see yourself and how sinful you were to have ignored a love like His."

All unseen, Mr. Bonniwell had come softly in the front door and now was standing in the hall, listening as his daughter went on, but Mrs. Bonniwell had reverted to her promise of the afternoon for which she had been preparing for several hours, and smoothly she assented to what her daughter was saying, and then skillfully slid into a different note.

"Well, that sounds very beautiful, dear," she said graciously. "Perhaps sometime we can all go somewhere and hear this wonderful man. Such orators are always worth studying, no matter what subjects they specialize in. I'd really like to hear him myself. But in the meantime, dear, I have been staying awake to tell you something that is quite as important, and must have an immediate decision."

"Oh! Yes?" Blythe said, with a quick flash of anxiety. What was coming now? Her mother's voice was definitely antagonistic, somehow not in sympathy with the wonderful things she had been telling about the meeting she had been attending. She dropped into a chair, yet alert, and fixed her eyes on her mother's.

"Dan Seavers has been over here—" began her mother, floundering around in her mind for the careful approach she had planned to this interview. But Blythe put a sudden end to the subject by the finality of the tone in which she answered:

"Oh! He *has*! I thought he wouldn't be suppressed very easily. So he has appealed to you also, has he, as well as to Dad? Well, Mother, you can just tell him nothing doing. I do not intend to marry him—*ever*—I told him so decidedly. I will not be enticed into talking it over anymore. If worse comes to worst you can tell him I love someone else. Although I don't really think it is any of his business until I get ready to tell it myself."

"No! Of course not," the mother hastened to say. The thing she really wanted least was to have anybody else know anything about this absurd obsession of her daughter's. Let it rest in quietness until it died away of its own accord. Have no publicity about it, not even to save Dan's feelings. That was much the best policy.

"But really, Blythe, I think you owe it to Dan as an old friend, to listen to what he has to say, the plans he has made. You gain nothing by running away from anything. It is always better to face a matter clearly, politely, and in a way that you won't regret later when you think it over."

Blythe looked at her mother thoughtfully an instant, and then said, "All right, Mother dear. When and where do you want me to see him? Was there any special time stipulated?"

"Why no, dear, only that he wants to see you at the first possible moment because he has several plans he is trying to arrange that depend upon your answer. I think just in courtesy you owe him that."

"Very well, Mother, I'll go to the telephone and arrange to see him at once. It's best to get this thing over. Best for us both!" She turned to go out the door.

"Wait a minute, daughter," said Mrs. Bonniwell.

Blythe paused and looked at her mother inquiringly.

"I want to suggest that you be very sure of yourself before you go into this interview. You should consider just what you would be giving up if you turn this offer down. And you can't tell just what reaction you may bring about in Dan. He is very impulsive, you know."

"Yes, Mother, I'll remember. But I can't marry a man just to keep him from marrying a chorus girl or jumping in the river. You wouldn't have me do that, would you, Mother?"

There was a merry twinkle in Blythe's eyes as she said it, the kind of twinkle that always brought an answering smile from her mother, no matter how much she frustrated her motherly plans, and Mrs. Bonniwell gave the smile, and said, "Why no, of course not, dear," and Blythe turned with a laughing "thank you," and went to the telephone.

It was not until she was gone that the mother discovered her husband standing in the shadow out in the hall by the door, and smiled at him.

"What a child she is!" said the mother, half worried, half pleased. "She doesn't grow up very fast, does she?"

"Well, I'm not sure but she's more grown up than her parents," said Mr. Bonniwell, coming in and sitting down. "Personally, I think she has more sense than either of us, in more ways than one. I certainly am glad she is turning that Seavers kid down. I never liked him. He isn't even intellectually on a par with our girl."

"Now, John, don't be too sure of what she is going to do. Dan had some very pleasant plans for their wedding, and you can't tell what he may persuade her to do when she once gives him a chance to talk it over."

"I'll bank on our girl every time," said her father. "If she lets that ninny wheedle her into marrying him in a hurry to repent at her leisure, I shall be dreadfully disappointed in her. Especially since she has somebody real in her heart."

"Oh *John*! I think you are foolish to put so much faith in a couple of snapshots and a letter or two. You might not like this old schoolmate of hers any better than you like Dan."

"Well, we'll just let it rest at that and see what Blythe does," said her father.

And then Blythe came back, smiling, as if from an unpleasant duty well done.

"When is he coming?" asked her mother.

"Right away," said Blythe.

"Well, don't worry about how long he stays. I'll have your dinner saved for you if he is very long."

"He won't be," said Blythe cheerfully. "I told him I could spare him only ten minutes and he had to make it snappy."

"Blythe!" reproached her mother. "Don't you think that was a bit rude?"

"No, Mother. It's the language all young people are using today, and I've already told him once before today that I didn't want to talk about this subject anymore."

"Oh, my dear! But look here. Don't you think you should get into a fresher dress? You look a bit dreary and shopworn in that dark one. At least you can do Dan the courtesy of looking fresh and neat."

"No, Mother, I'm not holding this matter up to make myself charming. I want to get it over with. There he is now," as the bell sounded through the house, and Blythe jumped up and ran down to the door herself instead of waiting for the servant to admit her caller.

The father, sitting in a shadowed corner of the room, smiled to himself at the summary way in which his daughter was handling this matter.

"She's a great girl!" he said aloud, with satisfaction in his face.

The mother cast a troubled glance at him.

"Yes, but I'm afraid she is acting in haste and will do something that she will regret all her life," she said, with a deep sigh.

"She won't!" said her father, with confidence. "You'll see."

They sat in silence, listening, as they heard low voices murmuring in the room. Then suddenly they heard the man's voice rise. They heard his footsteps tramping back and forth in the library, and the mother cast an anxious glance toward her husband, but he sat quietly amused and waiting.

Low voices again, quiet, gentle murmur. That would be Blythe. Then a deep, angry growl, then loud angry words, and suddenly the tramping of an angry young man's feet as he went out of the house and slammed the door furiously behind him. "There! John! I was afraid she would offend him, and she must have done it. I just knew she ought not to have gone at this thing in such a hurry."

"Alice, look here, don't you know enough about that young man yet after all these years to understand that he would be offended at anybody who refused to fall in with his plans? He wants to be *it*, and he won't stand for anybody who hinders him."

"It's very strange, John, that you should so easily be won over to someone you don't know at all."

"No, it's not strange, Alice, Blythe's Charlie is *real*, and this Dan isn't. And someday you'll see it yourself and be glad you had a daughter with a lot of common sense."

Then they heard Blythe's light step coming up the stairs, and Blythe's voice singing softly a hymn she had heard at the meeting.

> *"Keep me in the shadow of the cross,*
> *Purge my weary soul of its dross,*
> *Fill me with Thy spirit till the whole wide*
> *   world may see*
> *The light that shone from Calvary,*
> *Shining out through me."*

A soft light came into her father's eyes as he caught the words.

"She seems to be pretty happy, whatever it is," he said gently.

"Oh, John, do you think so?" said the mother. "Such gloomy, pathetic words. She's just the type that can be made into a fanatic so easily. Talking about purging her soul of dross! As if that child ever had a grain of dross in her. You know yourself she's always been the sweetest, most reasonable child. I almost never had to punish her, even when she was very little. Talk about dross in her, it's ridiculous! I tell you, that boy she thinks she's in love with is the wrong type for her. He'll just lead her into being a whining old woman before her time."

"Perhaps he won't," said the father, with a twinkle in his eyes. "Perhaps he'll die, as he told her he was likely to. I suppose you'd be glad if he would."

"Now, John, you know I never was so awful as that I would want anyone to die before his time. But I certainly don't see that he's good for Blythe."

"No," sighed the father, "you'd rather see her tied to that weak-chinned Dan, who will go on all his life getting drunk whenever he wants to, and going wild over one nightclub dancer or singer and then another after he's taken his wife safely home and got her to bed out of the way. That's the way you want it, isn't it?"

"John! You know Dan isn't that kind of fellow! You know he's fine and clean and self-respecting."

"*Self*-respecting, yes, but I'm afraid not fine nor clean. My dear, you have lived a fairly sheltered life, and you don't know all I know about the ways of the world today. But I can vouch for it that Dan Seavers is well started on the way to such a life as I just described, and I should never be willing to consent to his marrying my daughter, no, not even if he professed a thousand times to reform."

Then Blythe came into the room and her father looked up. "Well, you did that in fairly good time. How did you come off?"

"Why, Daddy, I just told him I didn't want to marry him, now or ever, and that was all. Of course he was pretty haughty and pretty mad, but he went away."

"But didn't you let him tell you all his lovely plans for the wedding?"

"Oh yes, Mother, he began before I was fairly seated, and he told everything, even to how the wedding invitations were to be worded and what kind of trousseau he wanted me to have. The next applicant won't have very much to do to prepare," and she gave a funny little wry smile. "That's Dan all over. He always planned out everything for the whole crowd and *made* them do it, whether they wanted to or not. However, he's good at that sort of thing, and if I had been in for a big show-off, he might have tempted me. But it all seems so vapid and utterly out of keeping with the times to get up a big showy wedding when a lot of the boys, our good friends, are across the seas somewhere, dying for our country. However, when he had finished and asked me if I didn't think it was a lovely plan I said, yes, it would make a beautiful wedding. But that I did not want to be the bride, that he would always be my old friend and playmate, but marriage on those terms was impossible for me. I wished him well, said I was glad he had his commission and such fine prospects, and I hoped he would soon find the right girl to share it with him. And that made him *very* angry. So he said he had no doubt but that he would, and he made quick work of getting away."

"Well, that's good!" said her father. "And now, Blythe, I wish you'd go on and finish telling about that meeting you attended. I was interested to hear just what that Silverthorn speaker said."

"Oh yes, Dad, I'd love to tell you."

Then the mother rose.

"I do hope you'll excuse me," she said wearily. "This isn't anything really important, and I feel I must get some rest if I am to go on with those convention plans tomorrow. Good night."

Chapter 16

On the high seas, Charlie Montgomery found himself at last, on his way to an enemy-infested land, going on a mission of extreme danger, every step of which was fraught with peril, and knowing that one false move would bring forfeit of his life, or worse.

Charlie himself did not know how his going had been arranged, nor by what various routes he was to travel, save that the final stage of his journey would be by plane. He would receive his last order before he set out for his final goal, and he did not yet know the exact location of that goal. But his real business, when located, would be to discover what was going on among the enemy, what was planned; and to send out alarms by well-planned and efficient means: by underground, by hidden radio in code, by trusted messenger, by any way that could get the information back to Allied lines in time to frustrate what the enemy had planned. Sooner or later, of course, he knew he would likely be discovered, and shot or imprisoned or buried in an internment camp to waste away, or maybe even be beheaded or tortured. But he had come, knowing all this, and ready to lay down his life for the great cause of freedom and righteousness, for putting down the tyrants, and setting oppressed peoples free. And he was going *now* in the strength of the Lord. For he firmly believed that God had called him to this work, and he was ready to sacrifice his life.

Two great joys he carried with him in his heart that gave him strength to go forward, unswerving, that gave him calmness, even peace in the midst of conflict and alien surroundings. One was the love of God and the nearness of Christ, his newfound Savior. The other was the knowledge that the sweet girl whom he had watched and loved from afar had given him her love and trust, and that if he were never able to come back to her in this life, they would surely meet in heaven, and she would understand through it all. On those two facts his soul rested hard and took comfort.

For it was not an easy task he had set himself, to go among men who did not believe as he did, whose sympathies, if they had any at all, were in opposition to all his opinions; yet he must act and be as one of them, in order to accomplish the purpose for which he had come.

Sometimes he stood on deck and looked off to sea, wondering if he would ever sail back again alive, and he thought of the girl he loved and what it would be like if he were free to go back to her and take her on a wonderful trip, seeing strange lands, exploring beautiful and wonderful places that both of them had studied about. Then something would grip his heart with an almost unbearable longing to take her in his arms again and set his lips upon hers.

And at other times he would stand on deck looking up at God's stars. They were *God's* stars even if he should happen to be looking at them from the deck of an enemy's ship, and God was able to care for him there as if he were at home. God did love him. He believed it with all his heart, and he felt he could trust and not be afraid of anything that might come.

He spent much time studying his Bible, the Bible that Silverthorn had been delighted to give him before he left him. Much of it he could remember repeated by his mother's gentle voice. But it had never meant anything personal to him before. Now, however, it was everything. It seemed to be the very air he breathed that made him live, the hope of life forever.

"What is it you find to read that seems to be so interesting?" asked a uniformed man pausing beside his deck chair as he sat reading one day.

Charlie looked up with a smile.

"Orders!" he said tersely.

"Orders?" asked the surprised officer. "Do you mean Naval Aviation orders? I never saw any bound that way before. May I see them?"

"No," Charlie said. "Not Naval Aviation orders, Captain. It deals with still higher orders than Naval Aviation. These orders come straight from God."

"From *God*?" asked the wondering captain, looking down at the small pliable book in his hands, admiring the feel of its binding, and turning the pages perplexedly. "But—isn't this a Bible? Just where do you get orders from that? What does it order you to do? Do you mean you really find orders here? And are they at variance with Naval Aviation orders?"

"Yes, I find orders here. And no, so far they have not been at variance with my service orders."

"But I don't understand. What, for instance, do you find yourself ordered to do? I mean, your God's orders? Is there a definite order?"

"Oh yes," said Charlie. "I find myself ordered to witness. That really is the gist of all orders. Witnessing. I find that's really why I am on this earth."

"But—I don't understand! What are you witnessing of? Is it in the nature of a testimony?"

"Yes," said Charlie, "that's the idea. And I have to testify to what the Lord Jesus Christ has done for me since I took Him for my personal Savior."

The officer looked at him steadily, studying him, still holding the little soft book in his hand, as if the very feel of it held charm for him.

"Well, go on," said the officer. "Testify! What has He done for you?"

Charlie's face lighted. He answered quickly, eagerly.

"He took all my sins away and bore the punishment that was my due. And He's made me happy in Him. Even in the face of war! And He'll do the *same for you!*"

"How do you know that?"

"Because He says so in His word. He says, 'He that heareth my word, and believeth on him that sent me, hath everlasting life, and shall not come into condemnation; but is passed from death unto life.'"

There was silence for a moment while the officer looked

thoughtfully out to sea, and then Charlie spoke again:

"Are you saved, Captain?"

There was another silence while the older man seemed to study the question, and at last he lifted his eyes to Charlie's, slowly. "I don't suppose I am. It has never seemed important to me."

"But, you'll find it is," said Charlie. "You can't be saved just on the glory of bravery in winning a battle. It takes believing in what Christ did for you, and making it *yours*."

The other man studied Charlie's face again. At last he said, "Perhaps I'll think about it. Do you mind if I borrow your book a little while? I'd like to look it over."

"Yes, take it," said Charlie, with an eager smile. "You'll find it's all I said, for *I* did."

The officer walked away with the little book in his hand, and Charlie sat for a long time with his eyes closed and prayed for that man who was reading his Testament. And later he went to his quarters and wrote a few brief words to Blythe to tell her how he had had an opportunity to witness for his Lord. Just a few lines, out of the depths of his heart, because he was longing to speak to her. And yet, he was not at all sure that he would ever be able to send them to her, not till the war was over, for he had been told that where he was going there would be no opportunity for him to communicate with the outside world, except in so far as was arranged for his duty in his special war service.

It came to Charlie as a surprise that "witnessing" was a thing that brought returns of great joy, instead of being a task.

But Charlie was not reading his Bible all the free time. He was in demand for sports. Somebody recognized him as a former football hero and broadcast it, and the other fellows flocked around him, always wanting him to join in anything they had on hand in their leisure time. So Charlie was popular, and had ample opportunity to use his commission to "witness."

He did not go around preaching. He seldom talked of his newfound joy. He simply lived it. Hs face radiated peace. The men talked about him now and then.

"Didn't some of you say that guy was going out on a special mission without much chance of returning?" asked one.

"They sure did. I heard his captain telling another man. They say there isn't a chance in a thousand he'll ever come back. And they say he *volunteered*. He wasn't just asked to do it, he volunteered."

"But say, I don't understand," said another fellow. "Hasn't he a girl back home?"

"Yes, Jack, I asked him the other day if he had one and he said he had. I judge she's a pretty swell one, too, from the way he spoke."

"Well, say, I don't get it. How comes it he always looks so happy? He's as cocky every day as if he was on his way home to get married or something, instead of going as fast as he can to his death. I don't see how he can look that way."

"I'll tell you what it is," said another quiet fellow, who didn't often take part in their discussions. "It's his faith."

"His *faith*?" exclaimed another. "So what? What's faith got to do with it? Faith in *what*? Do you mean he's superstitious?"

"Not on your life," said the quiet fellow. "It's his faith in God. He thinks God knows all about this war and is using it for the good of the world, or something of that sort, and he thinks God is guiding everybody that believes in Him, and takes care of them or something like that. And he believes that things will come out for us the way God wants them to, for our best good, or something of that sort. He just *trusts*, and that's what gives him that sort of look of glory on his face."

"Well, I should say that might be a good thing to have, a faith like that, only how would one go about to get it?" asked another man.

"Oh, he'll tell you how to get it," said the quiet one. "That guy has it all down fine. He knows all the whys and wherefores, and he likes to tell you if you really want to hear, only he'll never force it on you."

And it was so that during that long voyage Charlie carried out his new "orders," and became a daily testimony to his companions, so that in the fearful months that were before them all, his testimony came back to many in their hour of need, when grasping for any help in the dark was all that they could do.

But there came quiet times when he could be by himself for a little while, and in these he wrote precious messages to Blythe, told her of the loveliness of sky and sea and stars, told bits of anecdotes about his companions.

But there came a day when he was to be parted from all these companions who had grown so near to him, and was to go out on his own, into that vast unknown that was to be his destiny.

And before he left he was told that if he had letters to write before he went into that great necessary silence he might write them now, and they would be sent in due time back to the loved ones, yet there was to be no mark about them to show where they were written, nor from what post sent; they were to be brief and simple personalities, like a message from the dead.

Charlie was one of seven who were to go on like missions, though they were not going together, nor to the same destinations.

And so he wrote that night:

> *My darling:*
>
> *My orders have come, and I am to go in an hour. This may be the last letter I can send to you on earth, but if so, there is always heaven, and I shall be waiting for you there. Keep on praying for me till you get word I am gone, and after that look up and think of me with my Savior.*
>
> *But if God in His goodness shall will that I can come back, then there are such things as miracles, and God can bring one for us. But I can truly say that I am willing He shall do His will with me.*
>
> *Beloved, I pray much joy for you, even though it may have to be mingled with sorrow. But He knows best.*
>
> *Yours,*
> *Charlie*

And then, into a starless night, he set sail toward a battlefield, his instructions written in his heart, his instruments of service well hidden, his plans well laid. And if he came not back, so be it! He was satisfied. He was going in the strength of the Lord, though his sponsors were not aware of that. They only knew that he was an unusual young man, and it was a pity that such a man had to die. Yet no other man they knew could do the work he was going over to do, as well as he could. That was why he had been chosen for the job.

So at last Charlie Montgomery was on his way to his meeting with death.

Meantime, back in his own land, Charlie's first good-bye message entrusted to Walter Blake had just reached Blythe.

It came about in this way. Walter, when he found that he was not to have the hoped-for few days' furlough before he went overseas, had kept he little message wrapped, still in his Testament, with the faint hope that somehow there might happen to be a brief stop at his hometown, even if only for a few hours, and he could still have time to take it around to the Bonniwell house himself and present it, perhaps to the lady herself, for he much craved to see how she looked, this ladylove of his beloved hero.

But at the last minute Walter's orders were changed, and he was slipped into the place of another fellow who had been taken ill and had to go to the hospital. So Walter Blake did not get home as he had hoped, and the tiny scribbled message was carried overseas with him. It often troubled Walter, but things had been so hurried at the end. What else could he have done?

In due time Walter arrived in a semi-stationary place overseas, and one day in going over his effects he came on the little wrapped message and decided that he ought to do something about it.

So he sat down to write home to his mother and put the note in her care. If she thought it wasn't too late she would be able to give it to Miss Bonniwell.

So he wrote this letter:

Dear Mom:

By this time you know I didn't get home when I thought I would, and now I've come across the great water, and I'm safe across and ready to pitch in and do my part. But somehow it doesn't seem real, being over here. Of course I can't tell you where I am, but anyhow, I'm HERE.

The last few days up in camp were kind of slow, after my pal, Montgomery, left. You see, we got pretty close even in those few days we had, and so it went hard having him get his orders so quick. For he is real, Mom, and no mistake about it. He's the kind you like, Mom, and so when he got his orders I was just all worked up, almost as bad as when I left home, for you see, he was from our hometown, and it sort of seemed as if we belonged to each other. The worst of it is, too, Mom, he was going out on a very dangerous as-signment, and they didn't give him any hope he would ever come back, so it was really good-bye when he went.

I went with him to his train, and while we waited for the train to leave he was talking. He knew I was expecting to get leave home for a few days before I went over, and he asked me would I deliver a good-bye word to his girl. Of course

*I said sure, so he stood on the bottom step of the
car when the train began to move and wrote this
scrawl, and swung out holding to the rail as the
train got under way, and put it in my hand. So
I did it up carefully, Mom, and now I'm located for a few days, and they tell me I can send a
letter back, too, so I'm putting the message in for
you, Mom, to deliver, and will you please look
up Miss Blythe Bonniwell, and tell her how this
was written. If she's the right kind, same as he
thinks she is, she'll be glad to get it. And maybe
you can send me word what she says, so if I ever
see him again I can tell him I delivered it anyway. Will you, Mom?*

*So now, Mom, don't you worry about me. I'm
in God's hands, and I'm not afraid anymore, even
if I have to die. I learned that from Charlie, and
from his Mr. Silverthorn. So, good-bye Mom, and
keep on praying for your boy.*

Walter

The next day after Mrs. Blake received this was Red Cross
class day, and Blythe Bonniwell would likely be there. She
hunted out a clean envelope and put the soiled worn little
cellophane packet in it, put the envelope in her handbag, and
started happily on her way.

Blythe was a bit late that morning. There was a dressmaker
at the house doing a little altering, shortening skirts, and the
like, and she had been in demand for trying on and being

measured. So she came in a little late and went to her usual seat beside Mrs. Blake, which was always carefully left for her now, and was greeted by a radiant smile from the grateful woman who basked quietly in her lovely presence.

"I've a bit of a letter for you," she said in a low tone, after they were seated and the work of the day mapped out.

"A letter for me," said Blythe happily. "Why, how lovely!"

"Yes," said the other woman shyly. "It's my boy Walter has sent it. Maybe he was a bit presuming, but he asked me to pass it on to you, and I guess it'll be all right."

"But—a letter for me—from your son?" asked Blythe interestedly. "That is nice. But how did he come to write to me?"

"Why, you see, it isn't from Walter, strictly speaking, but he's sending it on to you from a young man who says he is a friend of yours. He's someone Walter met at the camp on the way, and he's a young man Walter always admired. You see, he was a football hero, and Walter was just that crazy about him during his school days. I could scarcely get him home in time to do his evening work. He was always going to those games. And when he got out to this camp, here comes this young man walking off the train and smiling at Walter, like home folks, and he was that glad to see him that he stuck by him whenever he had the chance. His name is Charlie Montgomery. Will you be remembering anybody by that name?" Mrs. Blake studied the girl's face anxiously to see how she reacted to the name, and when the rosy color flew into her cheeks, she had no more fear.

"Charlie Montgomery! I should say I do! Do you say your boy has sent me a message from Charlie?"

"Yes, that'll be it," said Mrs. Blake, and she opened her purse and took out the small envelope that contained the battered note Walter had sent.

Blythe took it in eager trembling fingers, unwrapped it carefully, and read with a radiant glow on her face. Mrs. Blake watched until she was satisfied that the girl was pleased, and then she fumbled in her bag and got out Walter's letter and presented it.

"That's my boy's letter, telling about how he met Mr. Montgomery," she said shyly. "I brought it along. I thought perhaps you'd like to read it. Of course, it's not much of a letter. He's only a little over seventeen, you know, and not yet through his school, but I had to sign up for him, he felt so left out when his brothers went to war and left him behind."

"Oh, yes, I'd love to read it," said Blythe, accepting the young soldier's letter as if it was a privilege to see it, and the look in her face as she read it made more than one woman in the class look at the girl enviously and admiringly.

"What in the world is that woman showing Blythe Bonniwell that she's making such a fuss over?" asked Anne Houghton contemptuously. "Probably some petition she wants signed or some contribution for her church or something. Blythe doesn't seem to realize she's just simply spoiling that woman. She'll be after us all probably, and get to be unbearable. I declare I think somebody ought to warn Blythe not to be so horribly chummy with a woman like that. It just reacts on the rest of us."

"How you must hate that girl," said Mrs. Felton, who happened to be sitting next to Anne. "What's the idea? Are you jealous of her, or something?"

A great smoldering anger burned up into Anne's face as she flashed her eyes at Mrs. Felton. "I, *jealous*? What an idea!

What has she got for me to be jealous of, I'd like to know?" she asked with contempt.

"I'm sure I wouldn't know," said Mrs. Felton amusedly. "But it looks as if there must be something, for you never lose an opportunity to say something mean about her, and I wonder why?"

Anne tossed her head and shrugged her shoulders indifferently.

"Oh, you don't understand," said Anne. "I don't think she's of enough importance for that, but it amuses me the airs she takes on with people she must see the rest of us haven't taken up yet. I suppose she's trying to reprove us, she thinks she's so superior and so righteous. She makes me tired. Well, it doesn't matter." And Anne yawned daintily, behind a jeweled hand. "I suppose there will always be all kinds of people in the world, and we just have to put up with them."

"We certainly *do*," said Mrs. Felton pointedly.

But Blythe was reading Walter's letter and seeing Charlie as he stood on the step of the car and wrote that precious tiny message to her. Her face was radiant, and her eyes bright.

"Just look at her," said Anne, with a sneer. "You know she's not that interested in any papers that woman can bring. Not *that* interested anyway."

And then Mrs. Felton was prompted to put this to a test. She turned quickly toward Blythe.

"What is it, Blythe, that interests you so? Read it out and let us all enjoy it."

Then Blythe looked up and smiled, her eyes alight. She wasn't embarrassed, not even a little bit, for Blythe had poise, lovely poise.

"Oh," she said pleasantly, just as if she thought they were

all dear friends. "Why, you see, it's a letter from Mrs. Blake's boy, Walter, and he's been meeting an old friend of mine who sent me a message. Wasn't that great? They're somewhere on the other side. Of course we don't know just where, but it's wonderful to get word from people who have been gone so long, after the great silence that envelops them once they are doing anything important."

"Oh," said Mrs. Felton interestedly, "have you a son in the service, Mrs. Blake? I didn't know that before."

"Yes," said little Mrs. Blake quietly, a soft flush spreading over her shy cheeks, "I have three sons in service."

"Why, Mrs. Blake! How wonderful!" burst forth several women in chorus. "How was it we never knew that before? We certainly ought to honor you. You're one of our war mothers."

Mrs. Blake looked uncomfortable. She did not desire this publicity.

"I'll tell you what we ought to do," said one of the younger married women. "We'll give her a tea. I'll make the cookies and maybe some darling little sandwiches. I suggest we have it Thursday afternoon. Will that be a good day for you all? Can you come then, Mrs. Blake?"

"I'm sorry, no. I couldn't come any afternoon. I work in a war plant afternoons. And please, don't give me any tea. I couldn't take time to come at any time, and it really wouldn't be right in these wartimes. Send the cookies to your own boys at the front, and forget about me, please. And now, if you'll excuse me, I must go or I shall be late at my job. Good-bye." And Ms. Blake picked up her coat and hat from the hook on the wall nearby and slipped quietly out of the room. But Mrs. Felton gave an amused withering look toward Anne Houghton before she folded her work and went to get her own wraps. Anne was wearing an inscrutable look, with her haughty chin in the air, and Blythe was stepping out the door like one who walked on wings. There must have been something in that Blake boy's letter beyond a mere hello from a soldier boy to make Blythe's eyes shine like that. Mrs. Felton was a wise woman, and a good reader of faces. Moreover, she liked Blythe, and she did not like Anne Houghton.

But it turned out after that that everybody in the class became kind and gracious toward Mrs. Blake. All but Anne Houghton. They smiled at her when she came in, and asked after her boys at the front, and made little pleasant remarks to her just as they did to the other women, and Mrs. Blake began presently to feel like one of the crowd. Not that she had minded their distant attitude so very much. She was very humble-minded, but it was nice not to have that chilly feeling around her heart whenever she entered the Red Cross room. So she was grateful.

But she was glad most of all about the look in that sweet Blythe's eyes when she gave her the bit of paper her Walter had sent. To think that it should be Walter's adored friend who was *her* friend!

Chapter 17

Walter Blake was really only a kid when he went into the army, but he went with his whole heart, determined to give his all if need be to help win the war.

But when Walter met his old admiration, Charlie Montgomery, and went through those three days with him in that training camp on the way "somewhere," and what is still more, after Walter had gone with Charlie to those three wonderful meetings under the leadership of Lieutenant Silverthorn, there was a great difference. He would never forget those meetings nor the truths he learned there. He had that feeling of constant companionship now with God, that gave him strength and courage and had taken away the fear he used to have sometimes when he thought about going out to face the fire of the enemy.

So Walter began to grow in spirit as he grew in stature, and others began to notice it and to take account of him. His officers began to see, and now and again to favor him.

One day he was on duty near his captain's quarters, and the captain, as he had been doing lately, fell into casual conversation with him, asking a few questions about his home—just a friendly gesture with a soldier to whom he had taken a great liking.

Then suddenly Walter asked a question.

"Captain, there's something I would like to ask you, if it's all right with you. If it's something you oughtn't to answer, why that's all right by me. I'll understand. But it's something I'd like very much to know."

The captain looked up, surprised.

"Why, of course, son, go ahead." The captain spoke like a man and a father, rather than a captain, with a gleam of sympathy in his eye.

"Well, sir, how would one go to work to get transferred to another line of service? Is that possible when one has got so far?"

"What's the matter, son? Don't you like your outfit? Don't you like your officers?"

"Oh, yes sir! Sure I like 'em all right. But you see, sir, I always wanted to get right into the thick of things. Real fighting, you know. Real danger. You see, I've got two brothers in this thing, and I want to do my share."

"Oh, you needn't worry about that, kid," said the captain. "You'll get all the fighting and danger you'll want to see pretty soon. I mean it for a fact, soldier boy. Doesn't that make you feel any better?"

"Yes, sorta." But Walter's face did not brighten to suit his professed zeal.

"What is it, kid? What's on your mind? It won't do any harm to own up. I may be able to straighten it out for you."

Walter was still for a minute and then he said, lifting a grave face, "Well, you see, Captain, I got a buddy. Or maybe he was more of a pal, though he was older than I. But he comes from our hometown, and he's a swell fellow. He was tops in football when he was in college, and I've followed him around and watched his games for years, even when I was just a little kid in grammar school. And now he's gone out on one of those special assignments where they never expect to come back, you know. I don't know where he's gone. He didn't know himself the last I saw him before we left the States, and I'd have given a good deal if I could have gone with him. But of course that wasn't possible. His was a solo assignment. But I've been thinking a lot about him lately. If I could just get exchanged to be somewhere near him, I'd like it a lot. You see, I feel he might need someone to help him out, help him mebbe to get back home to his girl, if he was to get wounded or be taken prisoner or something. I'd like to get near where he was so I'd be there to help if he needed me. Of course, I know everyone can't be near the ones they think the most of, but since he's gone to a post of great danger, if there was any way to get near him, I'd like to try for it."

"I see," said the captain thoughtfully. "And you've carried this on your mind for some time, haven't you?"

"Yes sir."

"Well, what makes you so anxious about it just now? Got any idea where he might be?"

"No sir, only I was hearing the radio telling about the enemy offensive, and if he should be one of the men to go into danger after information about what's going to happen, I should think that would be perhaps about where he would be. I just thought he might not be so far off."

"Well, that sounds like reasonable thinking," said the captain, looking thoughtful. "Do you care to tell me the soldier's name? Or is that a military secret also?"

The boy lifted troubled eyes.

"His name's Charlie Montgomery," he said, lifting his head proudly, "and he's a swell guy. But of course, he may be killed by this time. He fully expected that. Only I can't rest easy till I'm sure he wouldn't need me."

"I see," said the officer. "Well, lad, I'll look into this, and make the inquiries about transfers and so forth, but I'm pretty sure that the place where you belong is the place where you are. If you're needed elsewhere that might come later. Just do your duty day by day, and if greater tasks are ahead, wait till they catch up with you. Still, I might be able to look up some records and find out if your friend is still alive. Give me his rating, and I'll try and find out. Would that help any?"

"It sure would help a lot," said Walter.

"Only, how about it? If he isn't living, would that upset you so you couldn't be as good a soldier?"

"No sir, I'd want to be a better soldier, to sort of make up for his going, for he's an all-right guy, and no mistake. I know I couldn't ever make up for him, but I'd do the best I could."

The captain winked back a mist that came to his eyes as he watched Walter march tall and straight and proudly away when he was relieved from guard, and he marveled again at the mere boys who were showing such mature degrees of bravery. He would do his best to find out about Montgomery now, he told himself, and he sincerely hoped that he was still alive.

That was the beginning of a closer relationship between Walter and his captain, and many a brief talk they had on one subject or another, till the captain came to respect the lad who seemed to have such a firm faith in God even in the midst of war, and to wonder over the influence that the other young man seemed to have acquired over him even though he was older and had not been closely associated with him during the years, and then only a few days at the end. But the captain took the pains to have the records looked up, and after a time he took the trouble to hunt Walter up and tell him that so far there had been no report of Charlie's being killed, or even that he was missing in action, so that he must still be "somewhere" on his important and secret mission.

That was a comfort to Walter, although it did not prevent him from constant watching for word from his friend. And when there had been a battle nearby, and it was at all possible for him to get permission to help with the group who went out to rescue and bring back their wounded and dead, Walter was always a volunteer.

From one huddled still form to another he would go, give a keen glance into the dead face, and pass on, or offer a drink of water from his canteen to the parched lips of a dying man, or a kindly word. And sometimes he would kneel and pray for a soul that was going out into darkness alone and wanted a prayer. There were many such opportunities. And although Walter wasn't a chaplain, and made no pretensions religiously before the men, he came to be known as one who was good to send to a dying man, a "guy who knew just the right thing to say," and his own heart-life grew richer as he was able to help others. So with days of drill and nights of grave searching among the dead, the lines of Walter's young face, which had been almost childlike when he first joined the army, became more deeply graven, and a great gentleness and peace came into his eyes that made his superiors wonder as they observed him from day to day.

It was about this time that he wrote a letter to his mother.

Dear Mom:

It beats all how these fellows came out here to fight, and never seemed to think to get ready themselves to die. I guess they thought it was such a great thing they were doing, killing enemies, that their own lives would be spared, and when they find themselves wounded, or just about to die, or even starting into a battle, they get scared. They're afraid to die. They train 'em to shoot and to obey orders, and to keep their uniforms clean and their buttons bright, but they don't seem to think about training 'em to die. Oh, they talk about being brave and all that, but a lot of them don't know anything about Christ, and that He died for them, and that they can take hold of that when they get to the end and just trust. Why, Mom, it seems they don't really know anything about God or the Bible. I don't see why their mothers didn't teach them that. You taught me. Maybe you think

I didn't pay any attention to it at home, and I don't know as I did then, much, but I'm sure you taught me enough, even if I was indifferent, so that I would have cried out to God for help. Even if I hadn't met Charlie Montgomery and heard Lieutenant Silverthorn preach and got to know the Lord sort of personally, I would have known He was a Savior, and the only One to help me die, just from what you taught me. But I guess mostly their mothers didn't know those things, or else they would have taught their boys and not let them come out here as dumb and scared as they are. My! But I'm grateful to you that you weren't that kind. And I'm glad I know the Lord and can tell some of these scared, dying fellows how to be saved. Say, Mom, you better be praying a lot. There are so many people going out without God, and then they need Him a lot. They certainly do.

Now I got to go on duty, so good night, dear Mom.

Your boy,
Walter

That was one of the letters that Mrs. Blake passed on to Blythe to read, one of the letters that Anne Houghton wondered about as she enviously noticed the happy look on the faces of the woman and the young girl.

Anne Houghton studied Blythe's face and tried to figure her out. Blythe wasn't in evidence at the parties anymore, and she didn't seem to go with Dan Seavers—at least they were never together anymore. Yet Dan was not coming to ask Anne to go places with him. Had he found another girl? She must do something about this herself, she decided. It must be that Blythe had found another soldier boy and had turned Dan down, but she had fully hoped and expected that such a move on Blythe's part would send Dan to find her. Something must have happened. And yet Blythe seemed perfectly content.

And then the next thing that happened was they heard that Blythe was taking a nurse's course, and perhaps going into the army herself. Anne wasn't interested in taking up a gesture like that on her own part, so she put on her war paint and began to call up Dan Seavers.

But Dan was sulky. He had been out for several wild nights on his own and was not in a mood to take on Anne at present. He was still angry at Blythe and determined not to give in to her refusal. She must marry him, of course, he had always intended that. So he went on indulging his lower nature with the idea of getting it back on Blythe to show her she couldn't treat him that way.

But Blythe did not even know of his drinking and carousing, for she was engaged in more serious matters and went out socially not at all. She had entered an entirely new world, that centered around human woes, and the old social group was not even in her thoughts anymore.

But Anne got in touch with Dan at last and proposed another "evening," said she was about fed up on war work and wanted to get out and have a good time again, and she couldn't think of anybody that could show it to her better than Dan.

But Dan had other ideas in mind for that evening. He had been intending to call up Blythe and have it out with her, take another line of reasoning with her and see what he could do. So he hesitated. He felt he would rather get Blythe in line than to go dancing with Anne. If he failed with Blythe, there would be time enough for Anne. He felt that there would always be Anne, and Anne didn't have any money in her own right. So he hesitated.

"Well, I'm sorry, Anne, I'm not sure I can make it tonight. There's something else I ought to do. But wait, suppose I call you up in an hour and let you know if I can make it or not? Will that upset your plans very much?"

Anne wasn't altogether pleased, and she let it be known as she hesitated and said, "Well, no, I guess not. But let me know as soon as you can, Dannie dear. If you can't go, there's a soldier in town tonight I might be able to get, although of course I'd rather have you."

That was Anne's method. Show that he wasn't the only chance of a good time she had. And it usually worked pretty well with this lad.

He paused thoughtfully, waited a moment, half resolved to call her back and say he would go with her, but then he realized that the time was getting short to carry out his original plans, and so he called up the Bonniwell house and asked for Blythe.

"Why, Miss Blythe isn't here now. She's in training," said Susan importantly.

"In *training*?" exclaimed Dan indignantly. "What do you mean?"

"Why, didn't you know she's begun training in the hospital? This is her first week, and she won't be home tonight at all."

"My *word*!" said Dan furiously. "Let me speak to Mrs. Bonniwell."

"I'm sorry, but Mrs. Bonniwell is lying down. She came in tonight and didn't feel able to eat her dinner. She's been over-doing on that war chest drive. You know she always will work so hard."

"Well, I'm sorry, but I've absolutely got to talk to her at once, Susan. You tell her I said it was important, important for both hers and Blythe's sake."

At last he convinced Susan that his business was important enough to wake Mrs. Bonniwell, and presently Blythe's mother's voice sounded faintly at the other end of the wire. "Yes?"

"That you, Bonny? This is Dan. I'm sorry you're sick, and I wouldn't have disturbed you, but I simply *had* to find out what is all this about Blythe and the hospital. You don't mean she's taking on more hospital work?"

"Why, yes, Dan. She's gone into training, regularly. She's quite enthusiastic about it."

"But now, Bonny, you know that's absurd! How can she keep that up if we're going to be married soon? You know she'll have to give it up. It's much too far to commute for a morning's work, even if this is war, where I'm going, and besides, I won't have my wife looking after other people, doing loathsome services for them, and being at the beck and call of every doctor in the place. I should have thought you would have known that. Gone in training as a nurse and going to be married very soon! What's she trying to be? Sensational? She'll make the front page of the paper all right if she keeps this up."

"But Dan," said the quiet voice of Blythe's mother, "I understood my daughter to say that she had told you quite definitely that she was not going to marry you either next week or any other time."

"Oh, but Bonny, you know she didn't mean that!"

"I'm sure she did, Dan, and you might as well accept it and get used to it at once, and not carry on this way."

"Now look here, Bonny. I want you to call Blythe up and tell her to come home at once, and then I'll come over and get this thing amicably settled between us, Mamma Bonny. Now please do that for Dannie boy, won't you?"

But Mrs. Bonniwell was not to be wheedled.

"No, Dan, I can't do that. It's against the rules of the hospital to call a nurse out from duty, and it would be quite impossible for me to do it. And even if we could do it, Dan, I'm quite sure what Blythe's answer would be. She does not want to marry you, she does not want to marry anyone at present; and no amount of wheedling, even by you, will change her mind. Now, you'll have to excuse me, Dan. I'm not feeling well, and I've got to go and lie down. Good night." The lady hung up, and blank silence was all that answered Dan's continued insistent ringing.

So at last he called Anne Houghton back and told her he would be around after her in a few minutes and to be sure to wear her prettiest outfit. And that was the way that Anne won out.

Quite triumphantly she put on her most ravishing garments and went down to meet Dan at the door, holding her head high and resolved to get away with something very definite before this night was over, for she felt it would not be good to dally too long and give Blythe a chance to change her mind. If Dan was in a mood to marry before he left for his war job, whatever that was, she hadn't as yet heard, she was ready to marry him at a moment's notice. She would show Blythe

Bonniwell that she couldn't dally too long with a soldier's feelings. She must take him when he wanted to be taken, or he wouldn't hang around and wait. So Anne was blithe and bright and eager for the evening, and it wasn't long before she had definitely banished the gloom that Dan brought on his face when he arrived.

Pretty? Why, yes, he hadn't noticed before how very pretty she was. Twice as vivid and dashing as Blythe could ever be. Perhaps this was going to be the solution to all his difficulties after all. And maybe it would be a good thing not to have any bothersome father-in-law to deal with, always asking annoying questions and insisting on conventionalities, and demanding deference to himself and his family.

So quite happily Dan went out with Anne, resolved at least to make the most of the evening.

Chapter 18

Dan Seavers and Anne Houghton were married two weeks later in a great rush of furbelows and uniforms. It was only a little later than the date that Dan had originally set for his wedding with Blythe, for Anne said she simply could not get ready a suitable trousseau any sooner. Besides, her favorite cousin was on furlough at the later date, and that would make another uniform. Anne was keen on uniforms.

Mrs. Seavers shed a great many tears, for she didn't like Anne, and neither did Anne like her, and she sent for Mrs. Bonniwell and stayed in bed to talk with her, and complained about Blythe not marrying Dan as if it were Mrs. Bonniwell's fault.

Mrs. Bonniwell was not feeling well herself that morning, and she stood it as long as she could and then she said, "But my dear! I couldn't possibly help it that my child did not want to marry your son. Of course I've always been fond of him, the way he has run in and out of my house and been a good friend to Blythe, but young people have their own ideas today whom they wish to marry, or whether they wish to marry at all, and I don't really think it makes for happiness to try and bend them to your wishes, do you?"

"But my dear Mrs. Bonniwell," said the aggrieved Mrs. Seavers, "surely you can't contemplate with any sort of comfort having your child become an *old maid*?"

"Why, I don't think it is absolutely necessary that she become an old maid because she doesn't choose to marry your son, do you? After all, you married the man you wanted to, and she has the same right. But even if she should become an old maid, what's so bad about that? I know a lot of elderly women who have never married, who have lived very happy, contented lives, don't you? Could anybody be happier than Sylvia Comfort, or the Gracewell sisters, or Mary Hamilton? Yet they have never married, and I never heard anybody call them old maids, either."

"But you certainly wouldn't want that fate for your daughter!" declared the mother of the unwanted son. "Come now, be honest. Would you?"

"Well, I certainly would rather have my daughter have a fate like that than to marry somebody she doesn't love and doesn't want to marry."

"Well, I don't think you're stating that in the right way. I don't think you have any right to say that your daughter doesn't want to marry my son, or doesn't love him either. You know perfectly well that you and John influenced Blythe, put the screws on her, and made her think she didn't want him. Blythe wasn't acting from her own free will. In fact, you've always influenced her about everything, until she has no will of her own." Then the handkerchief came into play, with more tears. Suddenly Mrs. Bonniwell began to feel inexpressibly weary, as if she couldn't stand another bit of such talk. She looked at her onetime friend with a kind of desperate determination.

"Matilda," she said, "I won't stand another word like that. Neither John nor I had anything to do with Blythe's decision. In fact, we didn't talk the matter over with her at all. She made her own decision, and insisted upon it. And now, if you persist in saying such things, I really am done with our friendship. I'm sorry you are disappointed, but I could not think of influencing Blythe on a matter like this. And after all, Dan seems to be fairly well satisfied. He's marrying a nice girl, and will have a very pretty wedding."

"But I don't *like* her," sobbed the mother-in-law-to-be. "I never did like her, she isn't pretty like Blythe, and she's awfully modern. I just won't stand it, that's all."

"But what can you do about it, my dear?" said Mrs. Bonniwell. "It's your son's life, not yours."

"Yes, that's it! I can't do a thing about it. Dan has practically told me it's none of my business, after I've loved him and slaved for him. And now he brings a girl I don't like and practically forces me to accept her."

"Listen, my friend. You oughtn't to talk that way. You won't want to remember some of these things you are saying to me. She's a nice girl well brought up, has been in our social set all her life. It won't be like some of those dance-hall girls you were afraid of. Anne will know how to do the proper thing, and you won't have to be ashamed of her. If I were you, I would just make up my mind from the start to accept her and make the best of it. Then there won't be anything on your part to repent."

"Oh, yes, it sounds well for you to talk that way, but it isn't *your* child! If your girl had accepted my son, everything would have been all right. He had the plans made for a lovely wedding, and he wouldn't have stopped at giving her anything she wanted. Oh, why did she have to be so stubborn? I believe it's your fault! I believe you influenced her! Yes! Yes, I *do*! *You* influenced!" And then the poor lady burst into another flood of weeping.

"But my dear," Mrs. Bonniwell began in an attempt to stop this tirade, "I tell you I had nothing whatever to do with this."

"Oh, yes, you did! No matter what you say. You *did*! It was all your fault. Your fault and that nosy fanatical husband of yours. You thought your girl was too good for any man that ever walked the earth. Too good for my angel child who had been her playmate practically all her life. You stopped it, and I shall *never* forgive you!"

Broken and weary at last, Mrs. Bonniwell abandoned her old friend to her tears and laments and went home, too worn out to think of going anywhere else that day. Even Red Cross and war drives had to be abandoned while the good lady took a real rest and went to bed.

It was so that Blythe found her mother, when, an hour later, she ran home to get a few of her belongings that she found she needed.

"But Mother, this isn't like you, going to bed in the daytime. Lying there by yourself and *crying*! Mother, what *is* the matter? Are you sick?"

"No, I'm not sick," protested her mother. "I'm just worn out with Mrs. Seavers's whinings and crying. An hour and a half, Blythe, and she blames *you* for all her trouble. And then she blames *me*, says your father and I influenced you, and she'll never forgive us!"

"Oh well, Mother, don't worry about her. She always was dramatic! She'll get over it. And anyway, why should you care? I certainly am glad I don't ever have to call her mother. She is a pain in the neck, and what do you worry about her for anyway? She never was worthy of being your friend. She's a selfish woman who doesn't care what she does to her friends if she can only manage to get what she wants for herself."

"There, there, Blythe! Don't be hard on her. I really feel sorry for her, and it must be pretty hard on her to have to give you up and get Anne Houghton in your place."

"Oh Mother, you're the limit!" laughed Blythe. "First you take to your bed because your neighbor has worn you out weeping and wailing, and then you begin to weep for her because she can't have the daughter-in-law she wants. Well, you'll have to excuse me. I can't find any cure for your ailment but to go to sleep and wake up in the morning to find something more interesting to think about. Now, I'm tucking you up the way I do my patients, and I want you to go to sleep at once. I'll be telephoning Susan after a while to find out if you are better, and if you're not I'm telephoning Dad. Understand?"

But Blythe went back to the hospital with a worry on her mind. After all, there had been dark circles under her mother's eyes, and surely they were not here because she, too, was troubled that her daughter was not going to be married to Dan Seavers. Well, so that was that, but definitely Blythe felt that her mother had been overworking. For Blythe had been in the hospital long enough now to recognize that look of pallor, that tiredness in the face she loved, and tonight she must call up and talk to Dad about it. Dad would do something. He would perhaps take Mother away for a rest or something, and let her have a good time, although there weren't so many good times to be had in these wartimes. Also, a woman who was used to organizing committees and carrying on successful drives could not easily switch to just good times either. Dinner parties and clubs and such things would be a letdown after the hard work her mother had been doing.

That evening the invitations to Dan's wedding arrived, and there was another complication. Mother would say that of course they must all go to that wedding. It would be just too conspicuous if they stayed away, and everybody would say that Blythe was jealous if she wasn't there. Blythe had been so much with Dan.

Not that Blythe minded going to the wedding, but she knew her mother would mind it keenly if they did not go, and she and Dan's mother would sit glumly and let their eyes say to one another what they could not let their lips say. It certainly would be good if her mother could be away at the time of that wedding. But she didn't see how it could possibly be managed. The wedding was so soon. Of course her mother would overrule them all and they would go, with satisfied smiles on their faces, and well-bred gestures. And there would be at least two of those smiles that would be *real*, hers and her father's. For she was sure Dad hadn't ever wanted her to marry Dan, and certainly, she never had desired it.

So Blythe called up her father and urged him to get Mother to rest, and then the next day when she had time off she went to the store and bought the most expensive, most exquisite piece of table decoration for a wedding present that she had seen in these wartimes. It was a centerpiece of crystal in the form of a beautiful ship, delicate in its workmanship as a crystal cobweb, yet perfect in all its details, standing on a mirrored sea, and arranged for lighting. There could not have been anything more lovely, and Blythe was pleased that she could find something that was so beautiful and so seasonable and yet had no possible connection with anything that she and Dan had ever done together. He couldn't possibly torture his mind into a sentimental meaning that she might have had in mind in sending it. She arranged for it to be sent at once, and then with a great sigh of relief put Dan and his bride out of her mind. If her mother decided later that they should go to the wedding, why, that was all right with her, of course, if her duties at the hospital didn't prevent it, but that would be to be discussed the next time she went home.

So instead of bringing depression to Blythe by marrying Dan Seavers, as Anne had hoped it would, the wedding was settling into a normal, pleasant event that didn't make the least bit of difference to her.

Blythe didn't get home again to talk with her mother for several days, but when she did she found that her mother was most determined that they would all go to the wedding, and that Blythe should have a new dress, if possible. But Blythe declared that she had no time at all to go and select a dress. If her mother wanted to do it, all right, but she simply couldn't get away, not if she was to ask for leave for the wedding. It was simply impossible.

Then the question of the wedding present came up, and Blythe described the crystal ship elaborately and saw that it entirely pleased her mother.

But she saw also that her mother did not look at all well, and she resolved that as soon as this wedding was over she simply must manage to get her away somewhere to rest. She would talk to her father the very next day.

So Blythe went to her night work in the hospital and put the wedding and everything concerning it out of her mind. She didn't want to go to it, but she was going of course, and it was silly for her to care. She had a strange, uneasy feeling that in some way Anne would try to be disagreeable, and she wasn't altogether sure but Dan might still be angry enough to mortify her in some way. However, whatever came would come and would pass, and what did it matter? She didn't love Dan, she couldn't have loved him ever, and she was glad he was going to be married and go away.

Then there came a warm, happy feeling to her heart that there was someone she did love, someone she had a right to love, and who loved her. While she couldn't think of being married to him because he might never return to claim her, still she felt her life belonged to Charlie, and she was happy in the thought of him.

But quite early on that wedding morning everything changed. There came a telephone message for Blythe at the hospital from her father. Her mother was very sick and it would be necessary for her to come home at once. There followed days of anxiety when it was not sure whether the mother would pull through or not, and because nurses were so exceedingly scarce, and because the hospitals were so overcrowded, it seemed best for Blythe to give up her course of training and come home to take care of her mother in this terrible emergency. Of course that would have been Blythe's wish anyway, and she was proud and pleased to be able to take over her mother's case, with the assistance of a part-time nurse after the first few trying days, when they were able to get two skilled nurses, a few hours at a time.

Wedding? Why, they had no thought nor memory of the wedding, and at the hour when, if she had followed the dictates of Dan Seavers, she would have been marching down a church aisle to be married to him, Blythe was standing at the bedside of her darling mother, counting her pulse, watching the quiet breaths that came so intermittently, trying to look brave when she saw the anguish in her dear father's eyes. No, Blythe did not go to the Seavers's wedding, and neither did any of her family, and the best thing about it was that her dear mother didn't have to know anything about it at all, not at least until it was far over and no one could blame them for not being there. Everybody knew how very low poor Mrs. Bonniwell was, and no one would think of expecting any of them to leave their home.

So Anne Houghton had no opportunity to gloat over Blythe or give one single triumphant toss of her head or glint of her eye. Anne had chosen her path and would walk down it in pride, but not with any envious eyes turned in her direction.

So the organ rolled and the flowers drooped and the young men and maidens in uniforms or colorful chiffons went carefully, measuredly up the aisle; but Blythe was not there to see.

"Why, where is Blythe Bonniwell?" asked someone of the bride as the guests went down the line. "Surely she is here somewhere, isn't she? I wanted to ask her a question about the work in the hospital. Has she gone down the line yet?"

Anne shrugged.

"I really wouldn't remember," she said haughtily. "With all this mob here how could I tell if one certain girl went by?"

"Why, certainly she's here," spoke up the bridegroom. It wasn't believable that she hadn't come when all this show had been started just to impress her and make her understand what she had lost. "She accepted the invitation, didn't she, Anne?"

"I believe she did," said Anne, with utmost indifference.

"Well, then, of course she's here," said Dan.

"*Why* 'of course'?" said Anne amusedly. "Personally, I'd be surprised if she came."

"I guess you don't realize she's one of my very oldest friends. Of course she's here," said the bridegroom fiercely.

"It may be so," said Anne with another shrug. "I don't recall having seen her. But then, she isn't one of *my* very oldest friends." And Anne gave a little disagreeable laugh.

Dan motioned to a servant.

"Find Miss Bonniwell and bring her here," he demanded arrogantly.

"Aren't you making her rather conspicuous?" said the bride of the hour. "But then she probably likes that sort of thing. That's likely why she does it."

Mrs. Felton turned sharply from talking with Mrs. Seavers and answered Anne:

"Why, is it possible you hadn't heard?" she asked mildly as from superior knowledge. "Didn't you know that Mrs. Bonniwell was taken very ill this morning? Blythe was called home from the hospital to nurse her mother till another nurse could be found."

"Oh! Really?" said Anne affectedly, with that haughty air of discounting the news. "But I suppose that's nothing but an alibi, isn't it? It might have been embarrassing for her to come, you know."

Mrs. Felton eyed the bride thoughtfully, like a cat contemplating homicide, and then she bared her nice little teeth and pounced:

"No," she said gravely, "it's not an alibi. I just met the doctor coming out as I was coming in here, and I stopped to ask how she was. He says she is very low. They are not sure she will live through the night."

Dan turned with a whirl on her.

"What's that? Who are you talking about? Who is not expected to live through the night, Mrs. Felton?"

Mrs. Felton looked the bridegroom over sharply.

"I was speaking of Mrs. Bonniwell," she said coldly. "You knew she was taken very ill this morning, didn't you? The doctor told me just now that she may not live through the night. 'She's a very sick woman, Mrs. Felton,' he said. 'You see, she has been going too hard with her war work and all, and not stopping for proper rest.'"

"You mean that was *Bonny* they were talking about? Do you mean that was Bonny the doctor said might not live through the night? If that's so, why didn't somebody tell me? Why, she's one of my best friends. I ought to run right over there and see her."

"Oh for heaven's sake!" said the bride. "Can't you shut up? You've had too many drinks. Don't make a spectacle of yourself, whatever you do."

"But Bonny is sick, Anne, and she's one of my best friends!"

"Keep still, I tell you," said the bride in a low tone. "It's probably just an act. Can't you see? She would choose a time like this to get sick when she could take the attention away from us. This is some of that Blythe's doings, and I don't mean mebbe. I certainly will get even with her one of these days."

But Anne had her hands full that night to keep her tipsy husband within bounds, for constantly he kept returning to the subject, and it was plainly evident that it had greatly upset him to know that the Bonniwell family were permanently out of the picture, with a reason that everybody but himself seemed to have known all about.

"This is *awful*!" he said, more than once, as he mopped his forehead and cast his eyes about to be sure that Blythe wasn't there somewhere.

But at last the festivities drew to a close, the bride retired to change to traveling garments, the guests assembled and made ready to catch the bride's bouquet and pelt the newlyweds with rice and rose petals, and Dan's mother, still searching angrily to find a Bonniwell in the crowd, gave a hopeful glance at her husband and thought that it was almost time to go home and weep some more. It was done. This great awful farce was over, and she could never again lift up her head proudly, for there would always be that terrible daughter-in-law!

Then the going away was over, and the guests who did not remain to dance went out into the cool moonlight to pass that quiet Bonniwell house among its trees, with its night lights burning and the doctor's car standing ominously outside the door. And then some of those guests looked at one another said, "Why, it must have been true. I thought they were telling it about as a joke, didn't you? Anne didn't seem to make much of it."

And then they walked by with more reverent tread. In the morning, with shocked voices, they called up the doctor, whose only response was, "She is still living, that is all."

Chapter 19

Then began days of tense anxiety for Blythe and her father, day after day the beloved one hanging between life and death, and death seemingly waiting impatiently at the door to take her.

Mr. Bonniwell spent much of the time in his home, even after the doctor gave a hope of recovery, for the hope was so slight that death was still hovering near, and the tide might turn at any hour. The business could practically carry itself now if they only had their full number of trained workers. But of course, like all other businesses, their workers were few, so many having gone into the war, or war work. But business or no business, Blythe's father hovered very near the wife of his youth while any danger threatened. So Blythe was not alone in her anxiety, and during that time of anxious waiting the father and daughter grew very close to one another and often opened their shy hearts to speak of the things of eternity, which had up until now been a closed topic so far as the family conversation was concerned. And often, when one or the other had been absent from the sickroom for a little while and would return, it was not unusual for the one who had stayed there to be found sitting with bowed head and closed eyes. They came to understand that this meant an attitude of prayer, and that the prayer was an earnest petition for the life of the dear one. This prayer was gradually modified to include a clause, that at least the mother might live to know the Lord as they were beginning to know Him.

The two did not talk much about these things, but now and again a word would pass between them that showed the trend of their thoughts, and a beautiful bond of sympathy grew sweet and strong between father and daughter.

There were several changes in the Red Cross class. Of course, Anne Houghton was no longer there, and Blythe Bonniwell had been gone even longer from her place beside the window where Mrs. Blake usually sat.

Mrs. Blake was still there, as quiet as ever, but very friendly with all the ladies. She was counted an old member now, and a certain halo shone above her from her friendship with the departed Blythe. Everybody respected the Bonniwells, especially now that there was no Anne Houghton to disparage her and sneer at the woman with whom she had been friendly.

For Anne Houghton was no longer a poor relative in a stingy household. She was young Mrs. Dan Seavers, the wife of the handsome new officer at the camp, and she was engaged in arrogantly feeling her way into a new group and making an impression that would serve her as long as she stayed in the place. But neither was she mourned in the Red Cross class she had left behind her, and the place seemed far more friendly since she had left. People suddenly began to know that the quiet, despised Mrs. Blake was a most useful and helpful member of the class, for she could not only do well almost everything that had to be done, but she was quite willing to show them the best and swiftest ways to do it. Mrs. Felton was one of the first women to recognize this. Moreover, it turned out that it was through Mrs. Blake that the latest and most accurate news of how Mrs. Bonniwell was progressing could be learned, for she was in daily contact with Blythe, and that added to their respect for Mrs. Blake. She seemed to be one who was a regular friend at the Bonniwell house, and so it was through Mrs. Blake that the Red Cross finally sent gorgeous flowers to Blythe when it was learned that her mother was decidedly on the mend, although it might be months before she could hope to be around again, as in the past.

But in the meantime, most amazing things were going forward on the "home front," as Blythe called heir home life. The Bonniwell family were living as a family in a simple, home-life way, as they had not done since the years when Blythe was a little girl and they used to gather at night around her little crib to hear her say her nightly prayer. But that was years ago, Blythe would have told you, and she scarcely remembered it herself. There hadn't been any gatherings for prayer in that household since.

But one night, the night that Mrs. Bonniwell was first allowed to sit up against her pillows for five minutes before she went to her night's sleep, the most unexpected change came about in that home.

The five minutes were up, and Blythe had rearranged the

pillows for the night. The father was sitting in the big chair near the bed, as he usually sat while the mother was dropping off to sleep. And now Blythe was putting away a few things. Then suddenly the father's voice broke the quiet:

"I'm going to read a few words, Alice. Listen. I think they will help you to sleep. Call them a pillow for your head."

And then his voice dropped pleasantly into words they all knew well, but hadn't been thinking about of late years.

> *"He that dwelleth in the secret place of the most High shall abide under the shadow of the Almighty. I will say of the LORD, he is my refuge and my fortress: my God; in him will I trust. Surely he shall deliver thee from the snare of the fowler, and from the noisome pestilence. He shall cover thee with his feathers, and under his wings shalt thou trust: his truth shall be thy shield and buckler. Thou shalt not be afraid for the terror by night; nor for the arrow that flieth by day; nor for the pestilence that walketh in darkness; nor for the destruction that wasteth at noonday. . . . There shall be no evil befall thee, neither shall any plague come nigh thy dwelling. For he shall give his angels charge over thee, to keep thee in all thy ways."*

Blythe had softly settled down in a chair near the door as soon as she recognized what her father was reading, and she watched the quiet face of her mother and wondered how she would take this. But then, she knew, of course, she would accept it in her sweet gracious manner just as she took her orange juice or glass of milk, something beautiful done for her because they loved her, something in perfect harmony with a lovely life.

And then suddenly, even Blythe was surprised, for her father bowed his head, and in the same gentle tone that he would have spoken to her mother or herself he said, "Oh Lord, we do feel to thank Thee tonight that we have passed a blessed milestone on the way toward the recovery of our dear mother, and we know that it has been in answer to our prayers that Thou art bringing health and strength back to our beloved one. We thank Thee for the verses we have read, precious promises that Thou hast made good to us. We ask Thee to help us henceforth to live a life that is pleasing to Thee, and that shall give glory to Thy name. Thank You, dear Lord. Amen."

There was an instant of silence, and then Blythe softly slipped from her chair and turned out all but the small night-light as usual. But before she left the room she glanced at her mother to see if she was entirely comfortable, and she caught the vision of her mother's eyes opening, looking full at her husband, and her wan face was wreathed in a lovely smile. Blythe's heart leaped up with joy. Mother not only had not minded, she had thought it beautiful! Could any joy be more desired just now than this?

And then she saw her father's hand reach out and take his wife's frail hand in a close warm clasp, and Blythe slipped away, wishing there were some way she might tell Charlie about it all, it was so wonderful. Her mother and father's love story! Charlie would understand and love it, too. Would it be too late in heaven to find pleasure in talking over the beautiful things of the earth that had been left behind?

That night before she slept Blythe wrote another letter to Charlie, to add to the little pile in a lovely leather box that she kept locked and hidden away in a locked drawer of her desk. She liked to pretend to herself as she wrote, that these letters were going to Charlie on the next mail, although she knew that these were no letters for the eye of a censor. They were about intimate family affairs and must be held with a number of other precious confidences to talk over with Charlie in case he ever came back to claim them. These letters in the box were pieces of her own heart that she was putting in permanent form to read over perhaps in the years to come, when the mystery of death had been solved, or when she no longer could even hope that Charlie would come back to her on this earth.

So tonight she wrote a tender letter that was like painting a masterly portrait of her parents, with all the soft lights and shadows of the years in their faces, culminating in that few moments with the blessed words on the air, and the bowed heads, and that wonderful humble grateful prayer, like a golden atmosphere of praise sifting into the quiet evening silence. She painted it with pigments taken from her heart life, showing even the divine reflection that had come into her father's face and glowed like a light in the darkened room while he was reading and praying. Charlie hadn't known that father and mother through the years, and she wanted him to know them and understand them.

So she wrote her letter and locked it in the secret box, and then she knelt to thank God for that little holy time before her mother slept.

And in the room where Mr. Bonniwell sat long beside the bed with his wife's frail hand lying softly in his, it may be that God was there speaking to hearts that were tender and were thinking of Him.

Chapter 20

All day the thunder of battle had been raging. There had been no letup from sickly gray dawning to the terrifying set of sun. A bright brass sun, trying to set in the normal way through putrid black and green and purple snarls of clouds, the sky heavily frowning to a black night and shaking a warning head at a cool slice of silver moon that occasionally gave a fearsome glance between the tattered clouds, just long enough to suggest what a night might be if peace were once restored. Was this sunset accomplished at the instigation of the enemy?

The enemy had brought fresh troops across that little winding river. Where did they get so many? Word had come from time to time through their intrepid informer that there was to be no rest that night. More troops were coming all the time. The darkness was making it possible for them to come in droves. There appeared to be endless numbers. The enemy had determined to hold this location, and the road to which it was the key, at all costs. And the costs would be plenty on both sides.

Hour after hour the intelligence continued to come, warnings of the next enemy move.

"That fellow's a wiz," Walter heard his captain say in a low tone to a fellow officer in a momentary lull of fighting. "I don't see how he stands it. He's been on alert since midnight last night. By all the rules of health he should have been dead long ago."

"Who is it? Some fellow you know?"

"I think they call him Charlie, though we're not sure. He never comes out for us to see."

"But how does he manage to get his intelligence across the enemy line to you?"

"He has three points of contact. Two are up in tall trees, and when he can't give information from one treetop or the other, he gives a flash from that far mountain over beyond, or speaks it over a telephone contraption down in his foxhole, some contrivance of his own. No one knows exactly but himself, perhaps. Mostly I guess he stays in that foxhole all day, possibly altering its location from day to day, sometimes almost under the feet of the enemy."

"But what does he live on? Surely the enemy does not feed him?"

"No, I think he took a lot of those pill-foods, vitamins and the like, with him. Now and then they say he gets across to our own camp in the night when things are quiet probably, but always on the double quick to get back before he can be discovered. But he's been going a long stretch of hours this time, and scarcely a minute when there wasn't some news of some sort. After all, he's human, and man can't stand everything. But I understand he volunteered for this and expected to die when he came in. A pity a man like that has to be lost to the world because of these dirty dogs of enemies. But he's clever all right. Nearly all his means of service are his own device, and if he can't get us word by one method he'll find another. But he'll get to the end pretty soon. If all the hints he's given us today come true, this night will almost see the finish, of this engagement at least. He says the enemy is determined to hold this point at all risks, and *we'll* have to have reinforcements ourselves if the enemy continues to bring new troops. We *must win* this location! And Charlie can't continue to stand up in a tree getting news if a moon like that looks over a cloud for even only a second at a time, without getting caught by some sniper. Sometime soon the intelligence will cease, and we'll have to go on our own, and that will be good-bye for Charlie! But there's no doubt about it, we wouldn't have won all we have in this sector if it hadn't been for Charlie's magnificent work."

Walter moved quietly on in the darkness, his heart swelling with pride at what his captain had said of Charlie. Walter had been convinced for some days that the work that was being done out there somewhere between the enemy and their own men was Charlie's work, but this was the first time that he had heard the fact openly acknowledged. So, his captain had looked up the old friend from the hometown, after all, but he hadn't told him. Probably wasn't sure but he, Walter, might lose his head and go out after Charlie and give him away, perhaps. But there was a warm feeling around Walter's heart as he thought that his captain was acknowledging the worth of his hero, too. And now, if anything happened to Charlie, and the intelligence should suddenly cease, he, Walter, would search among the dead most carefully for his beloved idol.

That night as the firing began again and the young soldier listened to the orders given, he knew that the worst was on its way, and if Charlie would ever need his help, it would likely be tonight.

The fighting was bitter indeed, and grew worse as the darkness drew on. Company after company of enemy troopers poured into the enemy ranks. There came planes, and other instruments of warfare, and now and again as Walter's duties led him back to the captain's tent he found that everything was happening as had been told them by Charlie that it would happen. Charlie was doing great work.

"God, be with him," he prayed in his heart continually. "If he is in peril, protect him; if he is weary with the long battle, give him strength; and if he needs a helper, send me, please, Father God."

On into the night they went, till it seemed the morning would never come. Black night everywhere, for the moon had gone its way now, and the clouds were folded across till scarcely a star dared glisten through the murky darkness of smoke and fire and death. It must be that the angels mourned as they looked down upon that night of carnage.

The firing had been incessant, the fight fierce on every hand. The dead were everywhere, and no man had time for rest. This was a battle to the death.

Walter had been everywhere, doing his duty without a thought of self or fear, and his heart was filled with prayer. "Oh God, keep Charlie."

Perhaps the captain understood how he felt and kept him busy. Now and again came messages, signals from treetops or the underground. Walter was waiting for a message from the captain to be passed on to his major when the word came, "Impossible to hold outlooks longer. Tanks are uprooting trees. Look out for 246. Coming down."

Walter's heart began to tremble.

"Oh, God, aren't You going to let him get through? Aren't You going to keep Your promise?"

He was praying so hard that unconsciously he had closed his eyes and bowed his head. His captain looked at him curiously, almost reverently, and a shade of pity went over his face. Then Walter looked up and caught his captain's glance.

"Captain, that's Charlie!" he said. And the captain bowed his head in assent.

"Yes, son, that's Charlie," he said, and there was infinite sadness in his glance. "Now, get this to the major as quick as possible. We must put in some men and stop that flank movement." Then he saw the alert look come back into Walter's eyes as he took the message with a quick "Yes sir" and sprang forward. The captain had rightly judged that the boy who loved Charlie so would be quickest reached by duty, a message to be carried forward.

It was two hours later and still blackest night when Walter heard a voice almost beneath his feet. Charlie's voice. He must have moved his underground radio. A hurried emergency station, trusting it would be heard. There! That was the voice again! "Keep it up till morning and we'll be more than conquerors. The enemy is on the run. Sorry I can't go on. They got me as I came down the tree. I'm getting out now. I'm done.

Somebody take over. This is Charlie signing off."

Walter crept closer and called in that cautious tone they had all acquired when the enemy might be near, "Charlie! Charlie! This is Walter! Wait! I'll come and get you."

There was no sound but a kind of grating noise from underground like a heavy body pulling out, and Walter realized it was his business to report this to his superior officer at once. Reluctantly he turned away, marked the location by treetops overhead as well as he could, and sped back to headquarters with his report.

The captain listened understandingly and gave swift orders for the next move in following the enemy. Then he turned to Walter.

"Can you find that place where you heard Charlie's voice, son?" he asked.

"Yes sir, I'm sure I can. I looked up and got the location."

"Ah!" said the captain. "Perhaps we don't look up enough."

"Sir?" asked Walter.

"It's all right, son, you did the right thing," he said. "Lead these men to the place. This man knows how to take over if Charlie left his machine still there."

"May I stay till I find Charlie?"

There was such pleading in the boy's eyes that the captain could not tell him no.

"Not too long, boy. We can't afford to lose you, too. Charlie wouldn't want that."

"I'll be careful, Captain," said the boy, overjoyed to have the permission at last he had craved so long. And Walter went away into the blackness. Looking up, he found his skyline, pointed out the place, and silently in darkness they went to work, meantime keeping keen watch for stray snipers. And at last they found the machine that had brought so many of Charlie's messages to headquarters and saved so many lives, but they did not find a man inside the foxhole. Charlie had got out and crept away. Where? How far? Into more enemy fire?

The man who took over Charlie's work crept inside the foxhole, sending his guards here and there to watch. But Walter stole away into the darkness, searching for Charlie.

The rest of the night he searched, coming to body after body lying dead on the ground, now and then finding one that he wasn't sure of, turning on his small flashlight to study the face, but none of them was the right one. How far had Charlie been able to go after he crept from that hole?

The morning was beginning to break, but the fighting had died away. Was it true that the enemy was on the run? Still he crept on. Mindful of his promise to his captain, he crept low, over the piles of slain, looking sharply at them one by one, telling himself that he must be sure. Charlie would have changed some perhaps, all these months of strenuous work! Oh, he must make no mistakes. Even the dead body of that beloved one would be better than nothing. He had a trust to keep for that girl that Charlie loved. She would ask him someday if he did everything that could have been done to find her beloved.

On he crept, praying, "Oh God, guide me to him!"

Over the ridge he crept, where the fighting had been the thickest all the day before and last night. The slain were piled high, with no one to care except those at home who would never know just how their dear ones went. Some of these dead were lads he knew, but most of them were enemies, fallen as they fought, together. Would God gather them and separate them according to His judgment? Walter was thankful it was not his task to judge any of them. Some of them were likely saved ones, and more of them had never known their God at all, or else rejected Him. But there they lay together, awaiting the Judgment Day and a just and righteous Judge.

Solemn thoughts were these to come to this young Christian as he crept among the slain, seeing only now and then one who stirred or moaned. And once or twice he lifted a dying head and gave parched lips a drink of water from his canteen. Till all the water at last was spent.

Then as the pale dawn crept into the east, he saw below him a gleam of water. A narrow winding river. He would go down quickly and fill his canteen. It might be desperately needed before long.

So cautiously he crept on, careful to look above to the treetops for his bearings and keeping a watch out for any stirring enemy or sniper. But all was quiet. He must get out of here quickly. If there should be an enemy nearby, now as the dawn was lightening, he would be an easy mark, here with the reflection of the bright water on his tired face.

Below him on a shelving piece of flat rock at the very brink of the river, he saw a still form, prostrate, as if trying to drink from the river. The back of the man's shirt was soaked with blood, a wide crimson gash, and there was crimson on the water where he had drunk. Poor soul, he had likely been shot as he lay slaking his thirst after a terrible night of fighting. The thought hastened Walter's own movements. He must go on with his search. It was important that he find Charlie before he lost too much blood. He must fill his canteen full and get on quickly.

He found a clear place in the water, filled his canteen, and started to go back up over the ridge, but something in the attitude of that quiet form lying at the water's edge startled him, something familiar. He could not get away from it, and in spite of his promised caution, he had to turn back to look again at that man. Was he really dead?

Softly he knelt down and crept close; closer down to the river's brink where he could look into the man's face. He did not know why he felt he must do this, but there was something that compelled him, and so, bending low, he flashed for an instant the tiny light he carried into the soldier's face, and suddenly he saw that it was Charlie! Thin, emaciated, ungroomed, his hair heavy over the weary brow, but still it was Charlie. Charlie, who had been out there meeting death day by day, all alone with God and death! Charlie, whom he loved, and whom the girl back in the hometown loved. Charlie!

Then suddenly the necessity was upon him to get Charlie out and away from this place, where if there was an enemy about he could so easily be seen. He must get Charlie, dead or alive.

Walter did not stop to question whether Charlie was still alive—just unconscious but alive—or whether he was dead. It made no difference now until he had him safely away from further danger.

So with strong young arms he went to work, lifting and drawing the thin body away from the bright water, turning him over, and trying to get the right grip to bear him away. No time now to make the usual tests to see if life was still there. He must get that precious body safely away first.

And so, slowly, working with all his strength, his heart calling upon his God for help, Walter at last succeeded in getting the man in his arms and up across his shoulder, so that he could climb the ridge and get him back to friendly territory, back where there was a doctor and nurses, and a hospital not so far away. Panting, deliberately he climbed, knowing he could not complete the task if he used his own energy too quickly. Climbing till he reached the top of the ridge, where he paused and looked around him—still the same as when he came that way before, a field of dead men. He looked above and took his bearings again from the treetops, then turned and made his way laboriously until he came to the place where he had heard the voice coming from the ground. There he found the guards, two of whom came at once to his assistance.

"Oh, that's bad!" said one. "Is he dead?"

"I don't know," said Walter. "Don't wait to find out. Let's get him quick to the doctor. I don't believe he's dead. God wouldn't let him die."

They gave him a strange look. The guards did not know Walter, nor Charlie either. They were tired and hungry and had had a long, hard night. They wanted it to end and get some rest. But they went silently, helping to carry that gallant, tattered soldier, and they marched to headquarters like a funeral procession, bearing him as one would bear the body of a great hero, and laid him down tenderly on the cot that had been hastily prepared. Then the doctors and the nurses came quickly and worked, listened, made tests. Was the hero-conqueror still living?

Walter Blake stood apart in the shadow of the dawning morning, and watched and prayed.

And over on the other side of the world a girl knelt by her bedside and prayed.

Chapter 21

"We certainly miss Blythe Bonniwell," said Mrs. Felton, as she looked over the enormous pile of partly finished garments left from the last meeting. "Look at all these little nighties, all finished but the buttonholes! We certainly can't find anybody to take Blythe's place on buttonholes. Look at that one, will you? Somebody has just simply tried to *whip* over the buttonholes. Imagine it. Just about five stitches to a hole, too. They would never stay buttoned half a minute, and they would tear right out by the second day. Now, every one of those buttonholes has got to be ripped out and done over."

"But I thought that whole pile was finished," complained Mrs. Frazee, a worried, frivolous little trifle of a woman who didn't do anything very well anyway, and simply *couldn't* make buttonholes.

Mrs. Felton looked up and immediately knew who had over-and-overed those buttonholes.

Then Mrs. Butler came in from the back room where she had been going over a box that was supposed to be packed and ready to go to headquarters in the city. Her arms were filled with a sizeable pile of unfinished garments. Obviously unfinished!

"Well, of all things!" said Mrs. Felton, looking at the unfinished ones. "Where did you get those?"

"Out in the back room, all nicely packed in with the finished things. I caught a glimpse of a stain on the top one, and when I looked at it, I found the whole lot was unfinished. Why, look, only the side seams are basted up. Just *one shoulder* finished!"

"Hm!" said Mrs. Felton significantly. "Those are the last ones that Anne Houghton worked on before she went out and got married. Don't you remember, she pricked her finger? That's the blood stain. She certainly was the laziest and the most petty gal I ever came across. I'm certainly glad she's married and out of the way for a while."

"For a *while*?" said Mrs. Frazee. "What do you mean, 'for a while'?"

"Oh, that kind seldom stays married very long. They always carry a divorce up their sleeves. That is, unless they have a subnormal husband with a wide patience, and if I know my onions, I wouldn't judge Dan Seavers to be one of those," said Mrs. Felton.

"Well, I've seen some pretty dirty tricks from people who ought to know better and were brought up to have good manners," said Mrs. Butler, "but this beats them all. Sliding out of the work and pretending it was all done, and then leaving all that stuff undone to go off and count against our group. But what gets me is, how are we going to get all this back work caught up in time to make our report?"

Mrs. Blake had come in while they were talking, and now she spoke.

"Why," she said smiling, "I believe I know. We'll get Blythe to take these extra buttonholes home and do them. She has a lot of time on her hands when her mother is resting, and yet she had to be there lest she should waken. She was saying yesterday that she missed her war work and wished there was something she could do at home in her extra time."

"Why, that's wonderful!" said Mrs. Felton. "Do you really think she would?"

"Surely I do," said Mrs. Blake happily. "I'll go to the telephone right away and ask her. I don't mind asking her in the least, because she said to me she wanted something."

So Mrs. Blake telephoned Blythe and explained how far behind they were, especially on buttonholes, and that they had no one who could make good ones, and Blythe accepted with enthusiasm. Mrs. Blake came back smiling.

"She says she'd love to do it," she said, picking up her work and dropping briskly onto her chair. "I told her I'd bring the garments over with me when I got home this noon. Mrs. Felton, you get it all together. And put in *every*thing! 'The more, the better' she said."

"Well, that's a great relief," said Mrs. Felton. "I think we can begin to take a new heart of hope about our report now."

The class became a busy, happy place for the next two hours. They talked of war and how it would be when peace would come. They spoke of the boys coming home sometime. They spoke softly, guardedly, of some who would not come back.

"They say there's two or three from our town who are reported this morning as missing in action," lisped Mrs. Frazee. "I don't know who they are. At least, I heard the names, but I didn't know any of them. It won't be a very merry Christmas for their families. That 'missing in action' is such a horrible thing, you know. That might mean almost anything dreadful in this war. Prisoners of war, internment camps! They say they simply starve them there. And then, so many seem to be taken out and shot or something. It really doesn't seem very Christmasy, does it? It doesn't seem a very good background for our Christmas party. Oh, dear me! And the favors are so very lovely and the invitations *hand painted*, and quite modern."

It doesn't seem to me it's very patriotic to have such fool things as parties when this terrible war is going on," said Mrs. Butler grimly. "I, for one, would much rather see them get up a prayer meeting, though goodness knows I'm not much for praying and hardly ever go to a prayer meeting myself. But somehow I can't see how people can be so frivolous when their relatives are being tortured and killed by the thousand, and we're all going without proper meat and butter and working our heads off to win the war. And then somebody gets up a big party and they have a supper that would feed all the refugees in the nation. And they buy a lot of fool dresses that don't half cover them, and go around flirting and smirking and eating and drinking just as if there was nothing the matter with the world and some of their best friends weren't dying every day, just as if they were doing it all to be patriotic. Personally I don't think it's *right!*"

"*Right!*" said little Mrs. Frazee in alarm. "You don't think we ought to sit around and weep all the time till the boys come back, do you?"

"Mercy no, what good would that do?" said Mrs. Butler. "But I don't think we should get up big blowouts and spend a lot of money and eat up a lot of unnecessary food, when there are folks who are starving."

"But if we make plenty of money having parties and buy a lot of war bonds with it, that would make it all right, wouldn't it?" Mrs. Frazee's big baby-blue eyes were lifted pitifully.

"You can't make a wrong thing right by doing good with it," said Mrs. Butler grimly.

"But, Mrs. Butler, you can't think it is *wrong* to have parties can you?"

"Well, there are times that are more suitable for parties than the present," said Mrs. Butler fiercely. "Personally, if my son was out there fighting, I wouldn't feel like going to a merry-making." Mrs. Butler's face had a self-righteous glow. "It certainly isn't good taste to be giddy when the nation is in sorrow."

"Do you mean the government is against parties?" asked Mrs. Frazee, "I thought they were saying we must keep cheerful."

"They do," said Mrs. Felton. "Don't be silly. You've got to go ahead with your party now it's started. Mrs. Butler just means we've got so much really necessary work to do in more practical lines that it seems a pity to waste time hand-painting invitations, but maybe there are some people who couldn't do anything else, so why worry? Mrs. Butler, will you pass me those scissors? I seem to have left my own at home."

There was quiet in the room for a little while as the women thought over and sifted out the ideas that had been brought forth. Very few of those women in that room had stopped to think that this war wasn't just a game, just another function in which they could be delightfully active. Somehow life seemed to be taking on a more serious attitude, and they were not sure it was going to be quite so interesting.

Then at last with a little glad escape of a sigh Mrs. Frazee said, "Well, anyhow, it's too late to give up this party, isn't it? The invitations are all sent and the tickets are paid for. It wouldn't be honest not to have the party now, would it?"

Then they all laughed. Mrs. Frazee was so delightfully childlike, so full of the little frilly things of life, and so empty where anything real was concerned. She couldn't even baste up a baby's nightie without getting the shoulders all hindside-before. And today, no matter how many of them had to be ripped out and done over again, she promptly put the next day's shoulders all at loggerheads, and she finally cast them down in despair, saying:

"Well, I don't see what earthly difference it makes anyhow. Why won't they be all right when you get the sleeves sewed in?" And then she dropped down on her chair and burst into childish tears. So they finally decided that Mrs. Frazee would be invaluable pulling out bastings. And strangely, she was pleased. Why, pulling out bastings was something she could really understand, and her heart thrilled as she worked away at it, feeling that with every basting that came out she was pulling down a whole battalion of enemy soldiers.

So Mrs. Frazee worked happily away at her bastings, jubilant over the fact that at least this party had to go on, this party on which she had spent so much time and thought, and for which she had developed so many original ideas. She smiled to herself to think that what she used for a conscience was released from obligation to these women, at least, and she could go on and enjoy herself and her plans.

But the other women sat thinking, planning what the world should be when the war was over and Utopia perhaps would arrive, which was a development of their part-pagan religion they had developed from within, communing with self and their own desires. It was so much easier for them to explain life and religion in terms of their own wishes than to try and understand a book called the Bible. They felt, as they put away their work and got ready to go back to their world again, that they had been thinking some great thoughts, and that it was practically up to them as women to make the postwar world what it should be.

That afternoon Blythe, with her big bundle of babies' nighties by her side and her gold thimble on her flying fingers, sat in her mother's room, not far from the big chair where the invalid rested, and made buttonholes, with a lovely smile on her lips and a happy light in her eyes. She was so glad to have her mother getting well, and to be able to do some real work again. The days of anxiety had been long and trying, and it was good to have sunshine in the home and mother beginning to look as she used to look when Blythe was a little girl. Mother with that rested look on her face again, and no longer a strained, anxious expression.

Her mother watched her silently for a while, smiling to think how lovely her girl was, and then thinking about her thoughts over the last few weeks before she was taken sick. At last she spoke:

"It's so dear to see you sitting there, Blythe, working on those little garments."

Blythe gave a happy smile.

"Oh, but Mother, it is I who should be saying that. It is so nice to see *you* sitting there so rested and happy-looking and really getting well after your long illness. It was so dreadful when you lay so still and didn't know us at all. But don't let's think about that. I'm just glad, glad, you are *really* better, and will be well pretty soon. The doctor says it won't be long now. He told Daddy so this morning. I heard him."

"That's nice," said the mother, "but somehow I'm not in a hurry. I'm quite content to rest here and not to have to hurry at present."

"I only blame myself that I didn't see how worn out you were getting," said the daughter. "You know, I thought you liked all that planning and worry and hustling from one thing to another."

"Why, I guess I did," said Mrs. Bonniwell reminiscently, "but I'm glad I don't have to do it now. I just like to lie and watch you sew those cute little nighties."

The mother was still for a few minutes and then she spoke again:

"Blythe, what about that wedding? Did Dan Seavers get married? I don't seem to have heard anything about it. Did it finally come off?"

Blythe laughed.

"Don't ask me," she said amusedly. "I wasn't there. I was getting hot water bags, and hunting more blankets and trying to get you warm. You know, Mother, if I hadn't been so frightened about you that I couldn't think straight, I believe I would have been grateful to you for creating a really good reason that nobody could question why I didn't have to go to that wedding.

But of course at the time, I was too troubled to even think about the wedding."

"So it did come off! Well, to think of that! And you didn't feel badly about it, dear, having your old friend go off with another girl?"

"Feel *badly*, Mother! What do you mean? Did you ever think I wanted to marry Dan? Why Mother, I thought I told you—"

"Oh, yes, I know you did. But I was afraid you might find out afterward that you had made a mistake."

"No," said Blythe definitely, "I did *not* find I had made a mistake. I did not *ever* want to marry Dan. He was a playmate in childhood, that was all. He never meant a thing to me. And I strongly suspect he has just the right kind of a wife to suit his plans and ambitions. She'll climb as far up the social ladder as he wants her to, and she'll egg him on to get in everywhere and get ahead. And I, why Mother, you don't know how glad I am that he and his wife are married and gone away from here. It seems somehow as if the atmosphere was clearer for right living."

The mother's face was thoughtful as she watched her daughter and listened to her decided pronouncement. After a moment Blythe went on.

"But you know, Mother, you ought to have understood all that after I told you about Charlie. You *couldn't* think that I could ever want to marry anyone else when I loved Charlie, and since he loved me. Didn't you understand that, Mother?"

The mother hesitated before she answered.

"Well, dear, I wasn't sure about that. I thought it might be only a passing fancy, and that it would fade away."

"Oh *no*, Mother! It can never fade away. It is the real thing,

Mother. Love, the kind you and Daddy have for each other. Could you have married anyone else, Mother?"

"Oh no, of course not, dear. But he was—well, I'd known him a long time, and I love him a great deal."

"Yes, Mother, that's the way I feel. Of course, we haven't had the fun together we might have had, because Charlie was too busy, and too humble, but perhaps we've loved all the better for that."

The mother was still again, and then she said slowly, half pitifully: "But, my darling, this lover of yours was going out to war with the avowed expectation of dying, and I couldn't bear to think of my bright, lovely daughter starting out her life in the shadow of death. Don't you see? Don't you understand how I felt, dear?"

"Yes," said Blythe, trying to speak gently. "I see how you looked at it, from an earthly point of view, but you didn't understand how great our love was, how great it *is*, I mean. Our love is a thing of our spirits, not entirely of our bodies and souls. Of course, body and soul count some in any loving, but so many loves don't have anything to do with the spirit. Ours is deeply of the spirit, Mother, I love Charlie even more today than I did the day he went away, and I'm just as glad that he came to tell me of his love as I was then. Even a great deal gladder."

"But—even if he never comes back?"

"Yes, Mother, even if he never comes back—to this earth."

"My dear! That's very beautiful! I dreaded sorrow for you, but I'm glad that you have found joy in these very hard times. I had hoped you might have forgotten him, but now, well perhaps I understand."

Blythe suddenly laid down her sewing and went and knelt beside her mother's chair; then stooping, kissed her forehead and her lips.

"Thank you, Mother dear. That's the sweetest thing you could have said to me. Now I can be really happy in loving Charlie."

For some time the girl knelt there by her mother with their hands tenderly clasped. At last the mother said, "You dear, dear child!" Then after a moment, "And have you heard nothing more from—Charlie?" She hesitated over the unaccustomed name, yet spoke it as if giving her sanction to the relationship, and that brought great joy to Blythe's heart.

"Yes Mother, I've had a few more letters. Would you like to see them? Dad has read some of them."

"Yes," said the mother interestedly. 'Yes, I would like to see them, that is, if you don't mind, dear. If you think Charlie wouldn't mind."

"No, he wouldn't mind, I'm sure, and I'm glad to have you know him. I want you to know him as well as I do. I'll get them."

She hurried away to her room and brought the few letters that had come before the great silence enveloped him, and together the mother and daughter read them. And when the reading was over and Blythe had told about the different ones, how and when they came, the mother handed them back.

"I'm glad you let me see them, dear. I do not wonder now how you love him. He must be a remarkable young man. I surely feel that God has greatly blessed you to give you a love like that, even if it was but for a little while. Some women never have such great love. I am glad my girl knows what love is."

After Blythe had put the letters away and come back to take up her sewing again, they spoke about the different letters.

"But I don't understand about that little message that came wrapped in cellophane. Who did you say sent it?"

"Mrs. Blake's youngest son, Mother. He used to admire and love Charlie when he was just a kid and follow him around when Charlie played football in the big college games, and when it happened that they met at a camp before Charlie went over, and were together for two or three days going to those meetings, Charlie knew that Walter was hoping to get home on furlough for a few days before he went overseas, and he asked Walter Blake to bring this to me, his last good-bye. Wasn't that dear? But Walter didn't get his furlough after all, and was sent overseas unexpectedly soon, so after he got over there he sent the message to his mother and asked her to give it to me."

"His mother? Blake? Walter *Blake* did you say? Do you mean it is the son of that sweet little Mrs. Blake who comes in to rub my back for me sometimes when I am very tired? Why how dear of her! I shall like her all the better, now that I know this. I hope she comes soon again. I like the feeling of her strong, warm hands. They are such little, gentle hands, yet they seem to have a power behind them. She was from your Red Cross class, wasn't she? Is that how you got acquainted?"

"Yes, Mother. I felt she was the most interesting person in the whole class. I felt she was a real friend."

"She is," agreed Mrs. Bonniwell. "I like her very much. My dear, I wonder if this war isn't going to do a lot of things to the world, like getting people to know other people of like tastes and beliefs and making them love one another, where formerly these same people were separated by social lines and things like education and money? Things good in themselves, perhaps, if taken in the right proportion, but deadly when they are exalted beyond their place. When I get well, Blythe, I want to try and straighten out some of these differences between me and my neighbors, both rich and poor. And I would like to begin by getting very well acquainted with Mrs. Blake."

"Oh Mother! You're making me so happy!" said Blythe.

"What's all this?" asked Mr. Bonniwell, suddenly appearing in the doorway. "Let me in on it, won't you? 'Mrs. Blake' I heard you say. Is that the mother of the Walter-lad I know about, Blythe?"

"The same, Daddy," said happy Blythe, pushing forward her father's chair and running to get his slippers. "Come sit down, Daddy, and let me tell you what a wonderful mother I have, and what a sweet wife she's been all these years."

And so amid laughter, and sometimes a bright tear, they told the father all their talk, and the three of them were happy together.

"And now," said Mr. Bonniwell, "wouldn't it be nice, Mother, if Charlie should walk in someday?"

"Indeed it would!" said the mother in a fervent sincere tone. "Someday *very soon*."

"Oh Daddy! Mother!" said Blythe, and suddenly sat down on a low stool between her father and her mother, and broke into happy tears. Then lifting a rainbow smile she said, "That's the sweetest, dearest thing you could have said."

Chapter 22

The men were very tenderly lifting Charlie, though most of them believed he was already beyond help. But there was something about Walter's almost reverent handling of him, the way he looked at him, that caused them to walk cautiously. And when they learned who he was, that he was the guy who had given his life to make sure they would have the right information about the enemy; when they knew he had been living for weeks, hustling from one treetop to another and back down to his marvelous contrivance underground; that he had brought the right intelligence and made possible the several victories, one after another, through which they had been working; the guy that hadn't stopped for sleep, nor had much to eat, and had just gone on making it possible for them to win as they had done, there was no man there but would have done much for Charlie. They knew there were heroes among them, they had seen some of them, dying for the cause for which they were fighting, but this one in endurance and terrible persistence of self-sacrifice had outdone them all. His name, they knew, would go down in history as a great one. He had all but accomplished the impossible.

They came solemnly and brought Charlie to their captain, and he gave one look.

"Is he still living?"

One nodded.

Then the doctor:

"This man might have a chance if we could get him to the hospital, but here, there isn't a chance."

"Would he live to get there?"

"I doubt it. He *might*."

The captain's glance rested on Walter, and his eyes kindled.

"Get him there!" said the captain quickly. "Where's Graham?"

"Took his truck down to the base with a load of wounded men."

"*I'll* get him there, Captain, if I have to carry him myself." said Walter, looking at the captain eagerly, determinedly.

A tender smile played over the captain's face.

"*You couldn't*, son."

"Yes sir, I could, if there wasn't any other way. He's *got* to be saved! There's a girl, Captain, and she *cares*."

"I understand," said the captain. "*We all* care. He must be saved, but it will be easier for him another way. Call Michelli. You couldn't stand carrying anyone that far."

"I *could*—" said Walter with deep earnestness.

"Do you know, Captain," spoke up one of the guards who

had been with them when Walter brought the wounded man to the top of the ridge, "I believe he *could*. If it hadn't been for Walt, he wouldn't be here now. He carried him all the way up the ridge on his shoulder."

"Yes," nodded the others. "He was *swell*. Just as careful!"

The captain's eyes glowed warmly.

"He *would*," he said in a soft voice. And then as Michelli came up and saluted, he turned and gave quick orders then turned back to Walter.

"You go with him," he said. "Stay by him as long as he needs you. And Michelli, see that the doctor looks Blake over, too. He has blood on his sleeve. Has he been hurt?"

"Just a sniper's bullet grazed me. It's nothing," said Walter.

"Have it attended to at once. We can't take chances with our best men!" The captain's voice was warm as he said it. "Now, *go!*"

The little interlude in the day's battle was over, the brief time when the captain had time to show his own human heart. The men talked out of his presence thoughtfully, saluting the man as well as the officer. A moment more and Charlie was on his way to any hope there might be for recovery, his head and shoulders resting in Walter's arms. Walter felt that the privilege of a lifetime was his now, and tenderly he performed any little service that was to be done. His heart was swelling with thankfulness that the captain had let him go.

Oh, God, he kept praying in his heart, *it's up to You now. Please remember Your promises!* And then he looked down at the white face and the closed eyes of Charlie, his hero. It certainly looked hopeless, but there was God. God could do *anything*.

The days that followed were solemn days. The fighting was still going on in the distance. The enemy had returned with reinforcements and renewed the battle, and wounded men were being brought in constantly. They gave an account of what had happened. They said the man who had taken Charlie's place was not as good, not as thorough, did not always get his information across in time to save the situation. They spoke in high terms of Charlie's exceptional work in the intelligence line, told what the captain had said about him. But Charlie was still lying unconscious in the curtained alcove that was as near to privacy as the primitive hospital afforded, and did not hear, nor care. Charlie was still hovering on the border, and there was sharp doubt as to whether he would not yet slip away from them. The wound had been a deep one, and complicated, and the hospital supplies were scant. There were so many things against his recovery. It was pitiful.

Walter listened to all the veiled talk about it and sharply understood. It meant so much to him that Charlie should get well. It would mean so much to the girl—that is, it ought to. Oh, was she good enough for him? Charlie was so wonderful!

Although Walter's own less serious wound proved an unpleasant experience, he was not interested in himself. He desired to make little of his part in this affair. Yet the doctor persisted in dressing the wound carefully and asking questions.

"You know, you may still be wanted for something important, boy," he said, "and you don't want this thing to get infected."

So Walter submitted, though he felt that he would rather the doctor would tell him more about the possibilities in Charlie's case than to waste time on him.

But there came a day at last when the frown on the doctor's brow smoothed out as he came to look at Charlie, and Charlie's "valet," as the soldiers now called Walter, felt hope springing very faintly in his heart.

"This wound is in better shape than I ever hoped it could be," said the doctor. "Now we can really begin to work on other things."

And Walter smiled, a broad beam, just like sunshine.

But it was a slow process, that recovery. For Charlie was really very, very weary. He had gone without food so often, either because he hadn't time to replenish his pellets or he felt what did it matter whether he ate when there was urgent work to do that might make all the difference in the world which way the battle went. You see, Charlie was fighting his part of the war as if he were the *only* soldier, and he *had* to make it to victory. He simply had to, whether he died or not, just so he lasted as long as he should be needed.

That idea had been so thoroughly ingrained into his mind that Charlie hadn't looked forward to anything after he was once in action, except to die when the time came. And he knew he was ready to die, so there was nothing to worry about. But as good a soldier as that setup made him, it did not conduce to build up a fine physique, though Charlie really used to have a very fine physique. The only trouble was he thought it could last forever, at least as long as it was needed.

Intensive feeding was the order of the day now, and little by little this was having its effect on the weary man who lay there with closed eyes and no apparent interest in what went on about him. So there did come a morning when Charlie opened his eyes and looked up at the young soldier who was feeding him, and smiled. Vaguely at first. Then, as he looked still harder and began to get the lines of the face and figure of the soldier standing beside him, he smiled again. More definitely. Then he spoke, in the old quizzical tone:

"That's you, Walt, old pal! How'd you get here?"

Walter grinned and winked.

"Same way you did, Charlie. Eat your breakfast and don't talk. Them's orders, see?"

Charlie swallowed another mouthful, studied his young friend, and then spoke again:

"You in my outfit?"

"Something like that, buddy."

"I see. Well, how'd *I* get here? What happened?"

"Nothing to fret about. Captain just gave you a new location for a time."

Charlie looked thoughtful.

"Yes, I'm beginning to remember. They got me while I was taking a drink of water. Right?"

"Right."

"Had to climb the ridge. Couldn't make it without a drink. But how did I get up? Did I make it after getting hit?"

"Yep. You made it."

Charlie studied his face a minute.

"But I didn't make it alone, you old rascal. How did I get up?"

"Oh, I happened along, and we made it together. You see, I'd been hit, too. Some sniper got me. Now, finish this soup and don't talk anymore or the doc will put me off duty."

That was the beginning of sanity again for Charlie, and the doctor was greatly pleased at the way the patient was responding to the treatment. But there was still a long way ahead, and Walter, to his delight, found himself detailed especially to look after Lieutenant Montgomery, and keep him quiet enough to really recover.

Of course the first question Charlie wanted to ask as soon

as he began to get his bearings was, "How was the battle going when you left?" And Walter had his instructions on that subject, too.

"You are not to discuss the war. Tell Charlie, *when* he *asks*—no sooner—that *he* saved the day for us, and left the enemy in full retreat. Tell him Wheatly took over his work, what there was to do. Say it just that way, and you don't know any other details, see?"

That was really very well at first, but Charlie had too bright a mind, and was himself too vitally concerned, to be satisfied with no further details, and soon he was asking on every hand. It had, however, been made a rule of the hospital that the details of war were not to be discussed among the patients, so that helped. The patients were told that it would help in their recovery to keep their minds entirely off the harrowing details of what they had been through. So Walter was able to keep a pleasant countenance and be as indefinite as the doctor wanted him to be. In due time Charlie began to relax and to think of something else besides climbing trees and discovering enemy's secrets and crawling into holes in the ground to broadcast them to his officers who were waiting to know what they ought to do next.

And then one day Walter got a letter from his mother that greatly cheered the way. How it had found him he didn't know, for of course he hadn't been allowed to tell in his own letters where he was at the time, but it was wonderful to have a letter come wandering across the world and find him, even when he wasn't with his own unit. It was as if God had sent it—God, the only One who really knew where he was, and how he needed it.

"They can call it the army if they like," he said as he sidled up to the chair near Charlie's bed, "or they can name it the government if they want, but *I* say it's God that saw to it that I got this letter. Would you like to hear a little of it?"

"Swell, buddy! Anything from the hometown would be good to me."

"Okay. Mom's letters are always interesting I think. And I know she wouldn't mind you hearing them. She knows you, you know, so you can call it part your letter. Okay, here it is.

> *"Dear Son:*
>
> *It seems a long time since your last letter, but I suppose you are far away somewhere and maybe not allowed to write at present. Your last letter spoke as if you were going into action soon. I suppose that word 'action' means battle, but I try not to think about it. Just leave it with God to take care of you. You can't ever know what a comfort it is to me, now that I know you know God, too, and are trusting yourself to Him.*
>
> *I suppose you'd like to hear some news from the hometown, but there doesn't seem to be so much anymore. Nearly all the boys you used to know are either in camp or overseas, except Ray Donohue and Orville Casey. Ray has a bad eye, and Orville's limp is against him, so they are both working in defense plants. The girls you knew are working, too, some taking hospital training, some WACs and WAVES, and some of those other letters they have. Nellie Casey is a secretary in*

the Warner Company, the three Brown sisters are working in the big grocery, have good positions. It's hard to get anybody to work anywhere now. Annie Holmes's kid brother Tom is delivering mail.

Dan Seavers was married a short time ago. I guess you knew him, his father is one of the rich men. Dan married a Miss Anne Houghton, a girl who used to be sewing in the Red Cross class. I guess you didn't know her. They had a big wedding in the church, and a fashionable reception, for all the world just as if there wasn't any war going on. Dan is an officer now and has an office somewhere out west, I think. They went off in style.

You remember the Bonniwells? Blythe Bonniwell's mother has been very sick. They didn't think she would live for a while, but she is better now. Blythe had to give up her nurse's training course at the hospital and come home to care for her mother. Nurses are almost impossible to get anymore.

You'll be surprised that I'm getting to be a frequent visitor at the Bonniwell house. First I went to take some buttonhole work to Blythe from the Red Cross, and then I found out I could help out a little giving Mrs. Bonniwell a massage now and then. But now we seem to be real good friends. She likes me to come in and see her, and I like to go. She's almost as sweet as her daughter. And they are Christian people, real Christians I mean, the mother and father as well as the daughter.

My, I wish you could have seen Blythe's face

the day I gave her that message from Charlie Montgomery! It shone like sunshine, and her eyes were so bright and happy. I just hope that boy Charlie is half as good as you say. He'd have to be wonderful to be good enough for her.

I suppose you don't know where he is anymore. She told me the other day that it was long time since she had heard from him. If you hear anything let me know, for I know she has her heart on him with all there is in it. And she's so gentle and sweet, waiting on her mother, sewing for the Red Cross, never seeming to care to go out anymore the way the other young folks do. Just stays with her mother, and yet she seems content to have it that way. She has the happiest face I know, and yet it is a kind of still happiness, as if the source of it was far away. Almost perhaps not till heaven.

There is very little other news to tell you. Your sister is doing well in school. She has joined the Junior Red Cross and is interested in all their war activities, and very proud of her three wonderful brothers.

And your mother is praying for you, Walter, yes, and for your wonderful Charlie-friend, and hoping you will both, if it be God's will, come back to bring us joy and to work for your Lord.

Your loving mother"

There were tears in Charlie's eyes when the reading of that

letter was completed, and he said in a husky voice, "You have a wonderful mother, buddy. I wish mine could have known her. But they will someday know each other in heaven. And mine will be glad that your mother is praying for me. But I cannot thank her enough that she has given me news of my lovely girl. Somehow that makes me almost sure she has not forgotten me. That she still loves me."

It was more as if Charlie were talking to himself, but Walter answered him, his voice half indignant.

"Of course she loves you, you poor simp! Could anybody forget you, Charlie?"

Charlie grinned.

"Not everybody is as foolish as you, kid," he said in the old teasing way.

"Well, I'll be willing to wager your girl is, anyway, if I'm foolish."

But Charlie's definite interest in getting well dated from the reading of that letter.

Before that, Charlie had talked only of the time he would be able to go back into service, always with that solemn keen look of going into death once more. Not that he seemed to mind the death part. It was the job he had undertaken. But when he had spoken of it there was always that weary look around his eyes, as if he were too tired yet to be eager for it, though more because of being too tired to do the job right, rather than with the dread of making death his daily companion once more. Charlie wasn't really afraid of death anymore. His intrepid spirit had taken firm hold of the One who had conquered death. But his wearied body wasn't yet up to the alertness he needed to go back.

And one day he asked the doctor, "Doc, when do I go back and help get this enemy licked? Seems to me I'm getting pretty lazy lying around here admiring myself."

The doctor gave him a keen, admiring, amused look.

"Not for a while yet, Lieutenant. You see, you have to give the other fellow a chance to get some of the stars and hearts and medals of honor. You can't just think you alone can do the whole job of conquering the world. No, fella, your duty is to stay here awhile yet. And when I'm through with you, and can give you a clean bill of health, I think you're due for a furlough. You ought to go home and rest up awhile, get built up, before you talk about going back and trying any more of your special kind of treetop antics."

That talk came just the day before Mrs. Blake's letter. And that letter brought Blythe so clearly before him, made him think that Blythe just *might* still be loving him, and made him sick with longing to see her again. From that time forth he began to ponder on what it would be like to go home again.

Somehow it had been as if he had closed the door definitely on the thought of any life for them together on this earth when he came away expecting to die. But now, was there still such a possibility for them?

With the thought of going back home, questions came crowding that he had never permitted himself to think of before. As long as his future was held by death, he had a definite feeling that Blythe was his. But if he went back, alive and fairly well, everything would be changed. Or would it? There would be the question of what attitude her parents would take. Even of what attitude she herself would take when she saw him again. There would, of course, be the question of marriage, the natural, normal outcome of loving; the usual, honorable matter of asking a girl to marry when you had told her of your love. It was one thing to admit love for a poor fellow who was going out to die, but it might be quite another thing to marry him if he came back. Was her love great enough for that? What had he to offer her? A broken, weakened body, and a life that was all disorganized. Could he take care of her like such a girl ought to be cared for? He hadn't contemplated his own possible return to normal life again, although she had said she was praying for it, and his mind had been so thoroughly filled with the idea that he must die that he had kept the thought of such joy for himself out of his mind. He knew if he dwelt on such a possibility it would unnerve him for the work he had to do, and he had vowed to be a conqueror. He must not let anything stand in the way of putting his very best into his job of helping to make the world free from tyranny.

For a couple of days after Walter read him his mother's letter, Charlie was very quiet and thoughtful, and at last one day Walter, who had an uncanny way of reading his idol's mind, asked a question right out of the blue. He asked it quite casually, as if it were not very important, but he waited breathlessly for the answer.

"You two going to get married when you go back home?"

Charlie gave him a startled look, and then in a minute answered quietly:

"We hadn't talked about marriage," he said. "I was going out to die, not to come back. All that has passed between us was on that basis."

"Sure," said Walter, as if he thoroughly understood. "But

that doesn't count now. God's letting you go back. And my mom always told me that the right kind of a guy asked a girl to marry him when he told her he thought a lot of her. It sort of implies that, doesn't it, when you tell a girl you love her?"

Charlie was still for a long time. Then he said, "But I've got to be sure she still cares. The situation is changed, you know."

"Oh sure," said Walter like a connoisseur in marriage, "but you know she does. You've got to take all that for granted. You've got to trust she's got the same kind of love you have for her. Why wouldn't she care, I'd like to know? You're the same guy that went away, only you're ten times grander. You've got citations and things, and you're a lot wiser, I suppose. 'Course, she cares just the same, only more perhaps."

Walter was embarrassed, but he felt it was something that ought to be said. But the silence this time was longer still as Charlie considered his future.

At last Walter burst forth with another question.

"Aren't you going to write to her? You can, now, you know. They send mail out from here every day. I think you ought to think of her and how she must long to hear from you. Mom seems to think she cares an awful lot. You could at least let her know you're still alive."

At last Charlie said thoughtfully, "I suppose I could. I hadn't realized. I've looked on myself as dead so long. Well, bring on your implements. Got a pencil and paper? I don't know what kind of a stab I'll make at writing, with this arm still bandaged, but I can try."

So Walter brought the writing materials, and noted a lighting of Charlie's eyes as he set about writing.

It wasn't a long letter, for the right hand was pretty well

hampered yet by bandages to help support the wounded shoulder, but he finished it, and lay back with his eyes shut while Walter hastened to mail it. Charlie lay there thinking over what he had written, wondering if it was the right thing. He still had a feeling that perhaps he was presuming to come back from the dead this way. They had planned on meeting in heaven, yes, but what of this earth? Would that change the situation for her? He still was greatly conscious of her wealthy parents, for whom he had much reverence of her social position, and delicate rearing. Somehow those things had seemed to fade away when he held her in his arms, when he wrote her those letters, but now, after his long-enforced silence, they had returned. And so he had written briefly, out of his own heart-hunger, yet still protecting her from even his love.

My darling:

It seems that I am getting well of my wounds and am being invalided home in the near future. Do you still want me back, or would it be a relief if I didn't come?

Forgive the question, but I have to know. When you gave me your love it was with the knowledge that I would not likely return. My love is still the same. The greatest joy that earth could give me would be if you would marry me and we might spend the rest of our lives together. I could not ask you this before, because I did not expect to return. With this in mind, do you still want me to come?

I shall be letting you know later of my orders,

> *and I am sending you all my love.*
> *May the peace of God abide with you, my love.*

> *Yours,*
> *Charlie*

After the letter was gone, Charlie got to worrying about it. Just the act of writing it had given him the touch with Blythe that he needed to bring him back to normal again. Perhaps his letter had been unworthy of a real trust in the love she had given him. And yet he had to give her the chance to speak plainly. Perhaps he ought to have waited until he could ask her face-to-face. It had been a weakness in himself to write that letter. He should have waited till he got back, but somehow he shrank from bearing the uncertainty all that time on the way home. Well, he had evidently grown soft. It hadn't been fair to the great love she had promised him that he should have written, so he would write her again at once, taking it for granted that she loved him as he loved her.

And so he wrote another letter and filled it with his great love and told her of the joy that the thought of her was bringing him, and that he might hope to see her at some time not too far off.

When Walter came back from mailing the other letter he had the second one ready, and Walter rushed out to see if it could still be gotten into that day's mail. When he returned he found Charlie with his face wreathed in smiles.

"God is good, isn't He, Walt?" he asked in his old cheery way. "I hadn't thought there was anything yet ahead on this earth for me, but now I see God is handing it out to me, and

I've been too self-centered to hold up my hands and take it. Thank you for your part in showing me what I was doing. Bless you!"

And so the joy light came back into Charlie's eyes, and his recovery became more marked day by day.

"Boy!" You really are going some!" said the doctor when he came in to see him one afternoon. "I think I can soon give you a clean bill of health. I'm writing your captain today, and I'll tell him. Maybe your orders will be coming along soon. Do you still want to get back to your job?"

A sudden blank look came over Charlie's face for a minute, but then the brightness surged back.

"Why, yes, if I can go back, I want to go. I want to be a conqueror. Of course, you had got me all steamed up to get home for a while first, but if I'm needed back in action I'm ready to go."

"Good boy!" said the doctor happily. "I knew you were a conqueror. You certainly have the victory over yourself more than anybody I know. Ready to go back, even when you were all set to get home. Well, don't worry, we're not sending you back at present. You're to go home. I got the orders this morning, and you can begin to get ready. Your plane reservations are all secured. You start day after tomorrow, and your buddy goes with you. So there you are. And I understand your citation for a purple heart is on the way. Now, are you satisfied?"

"Me? A purple heart?" said Charlie, grinning. "What have I done? I came out here to conquer the enemy, and I haven't done that yet."

"Well, you did a good deal toward it, I understand, and your time has come to rest a bit now, so get ready to go. We'll all miss you here. You've kept the place cheery, both of you, and by the way, Walter gets a silver star." And the doctor's smile included Walter.

So then, as soon as Walter knew definitely, he went out and sent a cable to his mother. And his mother, dear soul, hurried over to tell Blythe.

The cable reached the hometown even before the two letters, and the entire Bonniwell household was filled with a great joy. Blythe beamed like a ray of sunshine, her mother seemed happy and content, and her father made quaint jokes and looked up ships and times of plane landings. They would telephone when they reached New York, Walter had said.

So Father Bonniwell arranged to take the family and Mrs. Blake to New York to meet the conquering heroes and take them home. There hadn't been so much joy in the Bonniwell home for years, for all of them were looking forward to knowing and loving the new son whom they had never seen.

And Mrs. Blake was overjoyed at the pleasure of going with them to meet Walter. It was greater happiness than she had ever counted on having on this earth.

As the great ship of the air started on its final lap toward home, Charlie grew very silent. All his "inferiority complex" as Walter called it, returned upon him, and he began to think what a terrible thing it would be if Blythe had lost her love for him during the long absence. How was he going to bear it? His solemnity grew with each hour they flew across the great, wide sky.

At last Walter came over to him as he sat staring out at the sky, and said, "Hey, Lieutenant! Seems to me you've lost your faith!"

"Lost my faith? What do you mean, Walt? I still have my

faith, thank the Lord."

"Oh no," said the younger soldier. "You haven't! You don't think God is able to carry this thing through to the winning. You think God would take all this trouble to get you well and bring you back, and then let you lose in the final inning? That isn't like you, Lieutenant."

Charlie looked at him, astonished. Then he smiled.

"I guess you're right, kid. I didn't trust, did I? I'm not much of a conqueror, after all. I set out to win, but I lost faith. Well, from now on, there's to be no more of that. I'm trusting to the end. I'm putting myself into God's hands to do with as He wills. I guess He who began it is able to carry it through, and I'm ready to leave it with Him."

A smile of satisfaction rested on the younger soldier's lips as he repeated, smiling, "More than conqueror, through Him that loved us."

A little while later they got out at the airport, and there were the dear ones waiting for them, and Charlie hadn't any more doubt about whether he was wanted.

There stood Blythe, watching for him to come, and she went straight to his arms like a homing bird, and was folded close, regardless of interested watchers. In fact, the whole family had a beautiful glimpse of the lovelight on those two faces, and all their hearts were rejoicing that it was so.

Walter was folded in his happy mother's arms, too, and presently Charlie and Blythe came out of their spell long enough to introduce the new son to his new father and mother, and the Bonniwells felt that their cup was full. This young soldier was as good, if not better-looking than the pictures of him they had seen, and his whole attitude was just what they had been led from his letters to expect.

There were outsiders at the airport, waiting for the plane to Miami Beach, Florida, among them Mr. and Mrs. Dan Seavers.

"My word, Dan! Look at that perfectly stunning soldier kissing that girl. My, but he's good-looking! Find out who he is, Dan. I want to meet him. See! He's wearing a purple heart, and the other one has a silver star. They must be some heroes!"

Dan looked and frowned. Where had he seen that good-looking face before? And who was the girl he was kissing?

"My word, Dan. The girl is Blythe Bonniwell! Can you imagine it? Somehow she always did have good luck getting all the good lookers."

Dan looked again in blank amazement, and a wave of envy went over his narrow little soul. Blythe was looking very beautiful, and she was definitely not for him and never had been.

"Come, Dan, let's go up and speak to Blythe, and she'll have to introduce us," said Anne, taking Dan's arm firmly in her white glove. "I'm dying to find out who that good-looking lieutenant is."

"Well, I'm not," said Dan in a gruff, ugly tone. "And I guess if that's the case, you'll have to die, for I don't want to meet that lieutenant, nor the girl, and what's more I *won't*. If you want to meet them, you'll have to go alone." And Dan jerked his arm from her grasp and walked away.

But then the Bonniwells got into their car and drove away, and the Miami plane arrived and took the others away, but Dan was ugly all the way, as he thought it out, and finally realized that the handsome lieutenant was none other than the boy who used to star in his marks in high school and became a great football player later in college. Charlie Montgomery, the boy who worked for his living and starred through college! Dan had never liked him, because he was entirely too conscientious to get along with, and wouldn't be bossed!

But on the road to the hometown the Bonniwells were having a wonderful time, and no longer did Charlie doubt his girl's love. He was filled with a great wonder and delight, and the things that had troubled him seemed all to have melted away. Was it always so when one trusted it all to God?

GRACE LIVINGSTON HILL (1865–1947) is known as the pioneer of Christian romance. Grace wrote over one hundred faith-inspired books during her lifetime. When her first husband died, leaving her with two daughters to raise, writing became a way to make a living, but she always recognized storytelling as a way to share her faith in God. She has touched countless lives through the years and continues to touch lives today. Her books feature moving stories, delightful characters, and love in its purest form.

If you enjoyed
GI *Brides*
look for. . .

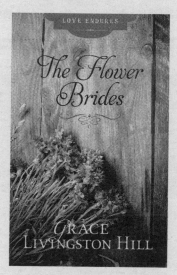

The Flower
Brides